MELODY/
HEART SONG

V.C. Andrews® Books

THE NEW

VIRGINIA ANDREWS®

MELODY/
HEART SONG

LONDON NEW YORK SYDNEY TORONTO

This omnibus edition published 1997
by BCA
by arrangement with Simon & Schuster Ltd,
A Viacom Company

CN 8126

Printed in England by
Clays Ltd, St Ives plc

CONTENTS

MELODY

Prologue

I think as soon as I was old enough to understand that Mommy and Daddy were having serious arguments, I felt like an outsider, for if I appeared while they were having one, both of them would stop immediately. It made me feel as if I lived in a house with secrets woven into the walls.

One day, I imagined, I would unravel one of those secrets and the whole house would come down around me.

Just a thought.

But that is exactly what happened.

One day.

1
&

The Love Trap

When I was a little girl, I believed that people could get what they wished for if they wished hard enough and long enough and were good enough, and although I'm fifteen now and long ago stopped believing in things like the Tooth Fairy, Santa Claus, and the Easter Bunny, I never completely stopped believing there was something magical in the world around us. Somewhere, there were angels watching over us, considering our wishes and dreams and occasionally, when the time was right and we were deserving, they granted us a wish.

Daddy taught me this. When I was still small enough to sit comfortably on his muscular right forearm and be carried around like a little princess, he would tell me to close my eyes really tight and wish until I saw my angel nearby, her wings fluttering like a bumble bee.

Daddy said everyone had an angel assigned to him or her at birth, and the angels did all they could to get humans to believe. He told me that when we are very little it's much easier to believe in things that grown-ups would call imagination. That's why, when we're little, angels will appear before us sometimes. I think some of us hold on a little longer or a little harder to that world of

3

make believe. Some of us are not afraid to admit we dream even though we're older. We really do make a wish when we break a chicken bone or blow out our birthday candles or see a shooting star, and we wait and hope, even expect that it will come true.

I did so much wishing as I grew up, I was sure my angel was overworked. I couldn't help it. I always wished my daddy didn't have to go down into the coal mines miles under the earth, away from the sun in damp, dark caverns of dust. Just like every other coal miner's child, I had played in the openings of the deserted old mines, and I couldn't begin to understand what it would be like going down deep and spending a whole day below the fresh air. But poor Daddy had to do it.

As long as I could remember, I wished we lived in a real house instead of a trailer, even though right next to us, living in their trailer, were Papa George and Mama Arlene, both of whom I loved dearly. When I wished for a house, I just added a little more and wished they would live in the house next to ours. We would both have real backyards and lawns and there would be big maple and oak trees. Papa George would help me with my fiddling. And when it rained hard, I wouldn't feel as if I were living in a tin drum. When the wind blew, I wouldn't fear being turned over and over while asleep in my bed.

My wish list went on and on. I imagined that if I ever took the time and wrote all the wishes down, the paper would stretch from one end of our trailer to the other.

I wished hard that Mommy wasn't so unhappy all the time. She complained about having to work in Francine's Salon, washing other women's hair and doing perms, even though everyone said she was an excellent hairdresser. She did enjoy the gossip and loved to listen to the wealthy women talk about their trips and the things they had bought. But she was like a little girl who could only look in the window at beautiful things, one who never got to buy any of them herself.

Even when she was sad, Mommy was beautiful. One of

4

my most frequent wishes was that I would be as pretty as she was when I grew up. When I was younger, I would perch in her bedroom and watch her at her dressing table meticulously applying her makeup and brushing her hair. As she did so, she preached about the importance of beauty care and told me about all the women she knew who were attractive but neglected themselves and looked simply awful. She told me if you were born pretty, you had an obligation to look pretty whenever you were in public.

"That's why I spend so much time on my hair and my nails, and that's why I have to spend so much money on these special skin creams," she explained. She was always bringing home samples of shampoo and hair conditioners for me to use as well.

She brought home perfumed bath oils and would soak in our small tub for over an hour. I would wash her back or, when I was old enough to be trusted, polish her toenails while she manicured her fingernails. Occasionally, she did my toenails and styled my hair.

People said we looked more like sisters than mother and daughter. I had inherited her small facial features, especially her button nose, but my hair was a lighter shade of brown, hair the color of hay. Once, I asked her to dye my hair the same shade as hers, but she shook her head and told me to leave it be, that it was a pretty color. But I wasn't as confident about my looks as she was about hers, even though Daddy told me he rushed home from work because now he had two beautiful women at home waiting for him.

My daddy stood six foot three and weighed nearly one hundred and ninety pounds, all muscle from working in the mines so many years. Although there were times when he returned home after a very long day in the mines aching, and moving slowly, he didn't complain. When he set eyes on me, his face always burst out with happiness. No matter how tired those strong arms of his were, I could run into them and he'd lift me with ease into the air.

5

When I was little, I would anxiously wait for the sight of him lumbering up the chipped and cracked macadam that led from the mines to our home in Mineral Acres trailer park. Suddenly, his six feet three inches of height would lift that shock of light brown hair over the ridge and I would see him taking strides with those long legs. His face and hands would be streaked with coal dust. He looked like a soldier home from battle. Under his right arm, clutched like a football, was his lunch basket. He made his own sandwiches early in the morning because Mommy was always still asleep when he woke and got ready for work.

Sometimes, even before he reached the Mineral Acres gate after work, Daddy would lift his head and see me waving. Our trailer was close to the entrance and our front yard faced the road from Sewell. If he saw me, Daddy would speed up, swinging his coal miner's helmet like a flag. Until I was about twelve, I had to wait close to Papa George and Mama Arlene's trailer, because Mommy was usually not home from work yet herself. Many times, she would go someplace and not make it home in time for dinner. Usually, she went to Frankie's Bar and Grill with her co-workers and friends and listened to the juke box music. But Daddy was a very good cook and I got so I could do a lot of the cooking myself, too. He and I ended up eating alone more times than not.

Daddy didn't complain about Mommy's not being there. If I did, he urged me to be more understanding. "Your mother and I got married too young, Melody," he told me.

"But weren't you terribly in love, Daddy?" I had read *Romeo and Juliet* and knew that if you were desperately in love, age didn't make a difference.

I told my best friend Alice Morgan that I would never marry anyone until I was so head-over-heels in love I couldn't breathe. She thought that was an exaggeration and I would probably fall in love many times before I was married.

6

Daddy's voice was wistful. "We were, but we didn't listen to older, wiser heads. We just ran off and eloped without thinking about the consequences. We were both very excited about it and didn't think hard about the future. It was easier for me. I was always more settled, but your mother soon felt she had missed out on things. She works in that beauty parlor and hears the rich ladies talking about their trips and their homes and she gets frustrated. We got to let her have some freedom so she doesn't feel trapped by all our love for her."

"How can love trap someone, Daddy?" I asked.

He smiled his wide, soft smile. When he did that, his green eyes always got a hazy, faraway glint. He'd lift his gaze from my face to a window or sometimes just a wall as if he were seeing images from the mysterious past float by. "Well . . . if you love someone as much as we love Mommy, you want her around you all the time. It's like having a beautiful bird in a cage. You're afraid to let the bird free and yet you know, it would sing a sweeter song if it were."

"Why doesn't she love us that much, too?" I demanded.

"She does, in her own way." He smiled. "Your mother's the prettiest woman in this town—for miles and miles around it too—and I know she feels wasted sometimes. That's a hard thing to live with, Melody. People are always coming up to her and telling her she should be in the movies or on television or a model. She thinks time's flying by and soon it will be too late for her to be anything else but my wife and your mother."

"I don't want her to be anything else, Daddy."

"I know. She's enough for us. We're grateful, but she's always been restless and impulsive. She still has big dreams and one thing you never want to do to someone you love is kill her dreams.

"Of course," he continued, smiling, "I have every reason to believe you're going to be the celebrity in this family. Look how well Papa George has taught you to play the fiddle! And you can sing, too. You're growing

7

into a beautiful young woman. Some talent scout's going to snap you up."

"Oh Daddy, that's silly. No talent scouts come to the mining towns looking for stars."

"So you'll go to college in New York City or in California," he predicted. "That's my dream. So don't go dumping dirt on top of it, Melody."

I laughed. I was too afraid to have such dreams for myself yet; I was too afraid of being frustrated and trapped like Mommy thought she now was.

I wondered why Daddy didn't feel trapped. No matter how hard things were, he would grin and bear it, and he never joined the other miners to drown his sorrows at the bar. He walked to and from work alone because the other miners lived in the shanties in town.

We lived in Sewell, which was a village born from the mine and built by the mining company in the lap of a small valley. Its main street had a church, a post office, a half dozen stores, two restaurants, a mortuary, and a movie theater open only on the weekends. The shanty homes were all the same pale brown color, built with board-and-batten siding and tar-paper roofs, but at least there were children my age there.

There were no other children near my age living in Mineral Acres trailer park. How I wished I had a brother or a sister to keep me company! When I told Mommy about that wish once, she grimaced and moaned that she was only a child herself when she had me.

"Barely nineteen! And it's not easy to bring children into the world. It's hard on your body and you have to worry about them getting sick and having enough to eat and having proper clothing, not to mention getting them an education. I rushed into motherhood. I should have waited."

"Then I would never have been born!" I complained.

"Of course you would have been born, but you would have been born when things were better and not so hard for us. We were right in the middle of a major change in our lives. It was very difficult."

8

Sometimes, she sounded as if she blamed me just for being born. It was as if she thought babies just floated around waiting to be conceived, and occasionally they got impatient and encouraged their parents to create them. That's what I had done.

I knew we had moved from Provincetown, Cape Cod, to Sewell in Monongalia County, West Virginia, before I was born, and we didn't have much at the time. Mommy did tell me that when they first arrived in Sewell as poor as they were, she was determined not to live in a shanty, so she and Daddy rented a mobile home in Mineral Acres, even though it was mostly populated by retired people like Papa George.

Papa George wasn't really my grandfather and Mama Arlene wasn't my real grandmother, but they were still like grandparents to me. Mama Arlene had often looked after me when I was a little girl. Papa George had been a coal miner and had retired on disability. He was suffering from black lung, which Daddy said was aggravated by his refusal to give up smoking. His illness made him look much older than his sixty-two years. His shoulders slumped, the lines in his pale, tired face were cut deep, and he was so thin Mama Arlene claimed she could weigh him down with a cable-knit sweater. Still, Papa George and I had the greatest of times when he helped teach me the fiddle.

He complained that it was Mama Arlene's nagging that wore him down. They always seemed to be bickering, but I didn't know any other two people as dedicated to each other as they were. Their arguments were never really mean either. They always ended up laughing.

Daddy loved talking with Papa George. On weekends especially, the two could often be found sitting in the rocking chairs on the cement patio under the metal awning, quietly discussing politics and the mining industry. Papa George was in Sewell during the violent times when the mining unions were being formed and he had lots of stories, which, according to Mama Arlene, were not fit for my ears.

9

"Why not?" he would protest. "She oughta know the truth about this place and the people who run it."

"She got plenty of time to learn about the ugly things in this world, George O'Neil, without you rushing her into it. Hush up!"

He did, mumbling under his breath until she turned her fiery blue eyes on him, making him swallow the rest of his angry words.

But Daddy agreed with Papa George: the miners were being exploited. This was no life for anyone.

I never understood why Daddy, who was brought up on Cape Cod in a fisherman's family, ended up working in a place where he was shut away from the sun and the sky all day. I knew he missed the ocean, yet we never returned to the Cape and we had nothing to do with Daddy's family. I didn't even know how many cousins I had, or their names, and I had never met or spoken to my grandparents. All I had ever seen was a faded black and white photograph of them with Daddy's father seated and his mother standing beside his father, both looking unhappy about being photographed. His father had a beard and looked as big as Daddy is now. His mother was wispy looking, but with hard, cold eyes.

The family in Provincetown was something Daddy didn't discuss. He would always change the subject, just saying, "We just had differences. It's better we're apart. It's easier this way."

I couldn't imagine why it was easier, but I saw it was painful for him to talk about it. Mommy never wanted to talk about it either. Just bringing up the family caused her to start crying and complaining to me that Daddy's family always thought little of her because she'd been an orphan. She told me she had been adopted by people who she said were too old to raise a child. They were both in their sixties when she was a teenager and they were very strict. She said she couldn't wait to get away from them.

I wanted to know more about them and about Daddy's family, too, but I was afraid it would start an argument between her and Daddy, so after a while, I just stopped asking questions. But that didn't stop their arguments.

One night soon after I had gone to bed, I heard their voices rising against each other. They were in their bedroom, too. The trailer home had a small kitchen to the right of the main entrance, a little dinette and a living room. Down a narrow hallway was the bathroom. My bedroom was the first on the right and Daddy and Mommy's was at the end of the trailer.

"Don't tell me I'm imagining things," Daddy warned, his voice cross. "The people dropping hints ain't liars, Haille," he said. I sat up in bed and listened. It wasn't hard to hear normal conversation through those paper-thin trailer walls as it was, but with them yelling at each other, it was as if I were right in the room with them.

"They're not liars. They're busybodies with nothing else to do with their boring, worthless lives than manu-facture tales about other people."

"If you don't give them the chance . . ."

"What am I supposed to do, Chester? The man's the bartender at Frankie's. He talks to everyone, not just me," she whined.

I knew they were arguing about Archie Marlin. I never mentioned it to Daddy, but twice that I knew of, Archie drove Mommy home. Archie had short orange-red hair and skin the shade of milkweed with freckles on his chin and forehead. Everyone said he looked ten years younger than he really was, although no one knew his exact age. No one knew very much about Archie Marlin. He never gave anyone a straight answer to questions about him-self. He joked or shrugged and said something silly. Supposedly, he had been brought up in Michigan or Ohio, and had spent six months in jail for forging checks. I never understood why Mommy liked him. She said he was full of good stories and had been to lots of exciting places, like Las Vegas.

She said it again now during the argument in the bedroom.

11

"At least he's been places. I can learn about them from him," she asserted.

"It's just talk. He hasn't been anywhere," Daddy charged.

"How would you know it's just talk, Chester? You're the one who hasn't been anywhere but the Cape and this trap called Sewell. And you brought me to it!"

"You brought yourself, Haille," he retorted, and suddenly she stopped arguing and started crying. Moments later, he was comforting her so softly I couldn't hear what he was saying and then they grew quiet.

I didn't understand what it all meant. How did Mommy bring herself here? Why would she bring herself to a place she didn't like?

I lay awake, thinking. There were always those deep silences between Mommy and Daddy, gaps they were both afraid to fill. Then the arguments would pass, just as this one did, and it would be as if nothing ever happened, nothing was ever said. It was as if they declared a truce over and over because both knew if they didn't, something terrible might happen, something terrible might be said.

Nothing was as mysterious to me as love between a man and a woman. I had crushes on boys at school and was now sort of seeing Bobby Lockwood more than any other boy. Since my best friend Alice was the smartest girl in school, I thought she might know something about love, even though she had never had a boyfriend. She was nice, but unpopular because she was about twenty-five pounds overweight and her mother made her keep her hair in pigtails. She wasn't allowed to wear any makeup, not even lipstick. Alice read more than anyone I knew, so I thought that maybe she had come across some book that explained love.

She thought a moment after I asked her. She replied it was something scientific. "That's the only way to explain it," she claimed in her usual pedantic manner.

12

"Don't you think it's something magical?" I asked her. On Wednesday afternoons she would come to our trailer after school and study with me for the weekly Thursday geometry test. It was more for my benefit than hers, for she ended up tutoring me.

"I don't believe in magic," she said dryly. She was not very good at pretending. I was actually her only real friend, maybe partly because she was too brutally honest with her opinions when it came to the other girls at school.

"Well then why is it," I demanded, "that a man will look at one woman specially and a woman will do the same, look at one man specially? Something's got to happen between them, doesn't it?" I insisted.

Alice pressed down on her thick lower lip. Her big, brown round eyes moved from side to side as if she were reading words printed in the air. She had a habit of chewing on the inside of her left check, too, when she was deep in thought. The girls in school would giggle and say, "Alice is eating herself again."

"Well," she said after a long pause, "we know we're all made of protoplasm."

"Ugh."

"And chemical things happen between cells," she continued, nodding.

"Stop it."

"So maybe a certain man's protoplasm has a chemical reaction to a certain woman's protoplasm. Something magnetic. It's just positive and negative atoms reacting, but people make it seem like more," she concluded.

"It *is* more," I insisted. "It has to be! Don't your parents think it's more?"

Alice shrugged. "They never forget each other's birthdays or their anniversary," she said, making it sound as if that was all there was to being in love and married.

Alice's father, William, was Sewell's dentist. Her mother was his receptionist, so they did spend a great deal of time together. But whenever I went to have my

13

teeth checked, I noticed she called her husband Doctor Morgan, as if she weren't his wife, but merely his employee.

Alice had two brothers, both older. Her brother Neal had already graduated and gone off to college and her brother Tommy was a senior and sure to be the class valedictorian.

"Do they ever have arguments?" I asked her. "Bad arguments?" I wondered if it was just something my mommy and daddy did.

"Not terribly bad and very rarely in front of anyone," she said. "Usually, it's about politics."

"Politics?" I couldn't imagine Mommy caring about politics. She always walked away when Daddy and Papa George got into one of their discussions.

"Yes."

"I hope when I get married," I said, "I never have an argument with my husband."

"That's an unrealistic hope. People who live together must have some conflicts. It's natural."

"But if they do, and they're in love, they always make up and feel terrible about hurting each other."

"I suppose," Alice relented. "But that might be just to keep the peace. Once, my parents didn't talk to each other for nearly a week. I think it was when they argued about the last presidential election."

"A week!" I thought for a moment. Even though Mommy and Daddy had their arguments, they always spoke to each other soon afterward and acted as if nothing had happened. "Didn't they kiss each other good night?"

"I don't know. I don't think they do that."

"They don't ever kiss good night?"

Alice shrugged. "Maybe. Of course, they kissed and they must have had sex because my brothers and I were born," she said matter-of-factly.

"Well that means they are in love."

"Why?" Alice asked, her brown eyes narrowing into skeptical slits.

14

I told her why. "You can't have sex without being in love."

"Sex doesn't have anything to do with love per se," she lectured. "Sexual reproduction is a natural process performed by all living things. It's built into the species."

"Ugh."

"Stop saying *ugh* after everything I say. You sound like Thelma Cross," she said and then she smiled. "Ask her about sex."

"Why?"

"I was in the bathroom yesterday and overheard her talking to Paula Temple about—"

"What?"

"You know."

I widened my eyes.

"Who was she with?"

"Tommy Getz. I can't repeat the things she said," Alice added, blushing.

"Sometimes I wonder," I said sitting back on my pillow, "if you and I aren't the only virgins left in our class."

"So? I'm not ashamed of it if it's true."

"I'm not ashamed. I'm just . . ."

"What?"

"Curious."

"And curiosity killed the cat," Alice warned. She narrowed her round eyes. "How far have you gone with Bobby Lockwood?"

"Not far," I said. She was suddenly staring at me so hard I had to look away.

"Remember Beverly Marks," she warned.

Beverly Marks was infamous, the girl in our eighth-grade class who had gotten pregnant and was sent away. To this day no one knew where she went.

"Don't worry about me," I said. "I will not have sex with anyone I don't love."

Alice shrugged skeptically. She was annoying me. I sometimes wondered why I stayed friends with her.

"Let's get back to work." She opened the textbook and

15

ran her forefinger down the page. "Okay, the main part of tomorrow's test will probably be—"

Suddenly, we both looked up and listened. Car doors were being slammed and someone was crying hard and loudly.

"What's that?" I went to the window in my bedroom. It looked out to the entrance of Mineral Acres. A few of Mommy's co-workers got out of Lois Norton's car. Lois was the manager of the beauty parlor. The rear door was opened and Lois helped Mommy out. Mommy was crying uncontrollably and being supported by two other women as they helped her toward the front door of our trailer. Another car pulled up behind Lois Norton's with two other women in it.

Mommy suddenly let out a piercing scream. My heart raced. I felt my legs turn to stone; my feet seemed nailed to the floor. Mama Arlene and Papa George came out of their trailer to see what was happening. I recognized Martha Supple talking to them. Papa George and Mama Arlene suddenly embraced each other tightly, Mama Arlene's hand going to her mouth. Then Mama Arlene rushed toward Mommy, who was now nearly up to our steps. Tears streamed down my cheeks, mostly from fear.

Alice stood like stone herself, anticipating. "What happened?" she whispered.

I shook my head. I somehow managed to walk out of my room just as the front door opened.

Mommy took a deep breath when she saw me. "Oh Melody," she cried.

"Mommy!" I started to cry. "What's the matter?" I asked through my sobs.

"There's been a terrible accident. Daddy and two other miners . . . are dead."

A long sigh escaped from Mommy's choked throat. She swayed and would have fallen if Mama Arlene hadn't been holding on to her. However, her eyes went bleak, dark, haunted. Despair had drained her face of its radiance.

I shook my head. It couldn't be true. Yet there was

16

Mommy clutching Mama Arlene, her friends beside and around her, all with horribly tragic faces.

"Nooo!" I screamed and plowed through everyone, down the stairs, outside and away, with my hands over my ears. I was running, unaware of which direction I had taken or that I had left the house without a coat and it was in the middle of one of our coldest Februaries.

I had run all the way to the Monongalia River bend before Alice caught up with me. I was standing there on the hill, embracing myself, gasping and crying at the same time, just gazing dumbly at the beach and the hickory and white oak trees on the other side of the river. A white-tailed deer appeared and gazed curiously at the sound of my sobs.

I shook my head until I felt it might snap off my neck, but I somehow already knew all the *No*'s in the world wouldn't change things. I felt the world horribly altered. I cried until my insides ached. I heard Alice calling and turned to see her gasping for breath as she chugged her way up the hill to where I was standing. She tried to hug and comfort me. I pulled away.

"They're lying," I screamed hysterically. "They're lying. Tell me they're lying."

Alice shook her head. "They said the walls caved in and by the time they got to your father and the others—"

"Daddy," I moaned. "Poor Daddy."

Alice bit her lower lip and waited for me to stop sobbing. "Aren't you cold?" she asked.

"What difference does it make?" I snapped angrily. "What difference does anything make?"

She nodded. Her eyes were red, too, and she shivered, more from her sadness than the wintry day.

"Let's go back," I said, speaking with the voice of the dead myself.

She walked beside me silently. I don't know how I got my legs to take those steps, but we returned to the trailer park. The women who had brought Mommy home were gone. Alice followed me into the trailer.

Mommy was on the sofa with a wet washcloth on her forehead, and Mama Arlene beside her. Mommy reached up to take my hand and I fell to the floor beside the sofa, my head on her stomach. I thought I was going to heave up everything I had eaten that day. A few moments later, when I looked up, Mommy was asleep. Somewhere deep inside herself she was still crying, I thought, crying and screaming.

"Let me make you a cup of tea," Mama Arlene said quietly. "Your nose is beet red."

I didn't reply. I just sat there on the floor beside the sofa, still holding on to Mommy's hand. Alice stood by the doorway awkwardly.

"I'd better go home," she said, "and tell my parents."

I think I nodded, but I wasn't sure. Everything around me seemed distant. Alice got her books and paused at the doorway.

"I'll come back later," she said. "Okay?"

After she left, I lowered my head and cried softly until I heard Mama Arlene call to me and then touch my arm.

"Come sit with me, child. Let your mother sleep."

I rose and joined her at the table. She poured two cups of tea and sat. "Go on. Drink it."

I blew on the hot water and took a sip.

"When Papa George was down in the mines, I always worried about something like this happening. There were always accidents of one sort or another. We oughta leave that coal alone, find another source of energy," she said bitterly.

"He can't really be dead, Mama Arlene. Not Daddy." I smiled at her and tilted my head. "He'll be coming home soon, won't he? It's a mistake. Soon he'll be coming over the hill, swinging his lunch basket."

"Child—"

"No, Mama Arlene. You don't understand. Daddy has an angel looking over him. His angel wouldn't let such a terrible thing happen. It's all a mistake. They'll dig out the mine and find Daddy."

"They already found him and the other poor souls,

18

honey." She reached across the table to take my hand. "You've got to be strong for your mother, Melody. She's not a very strong person, you know. There's a lot of hardship to endure these next few days. The whole town is in mourning."

I gazed at Mommy, her eyes shut, her mouth slightly open. She's so pretty, I thought. Even now, she's so pretty. She's too young to be a widow.

I drank some more tea and then I got up and put on my coat. I went out to stand near the front entrance and gaze down the road. As I stood there, I closed my eyes and wished and wished as hard as I could that this wasn't true, that Daddy would soon call out to me.

Please, I begged my angel, I don't care if you don't grant me another wish but this one. I took a deep breath and then opened my eyes.

The road was empty. It was twilight. Long shadows crept over the macadam. The sky had turned an angry gray and tiny particles of snow began to appear. The wind picked up. I heard a door slam and turned to see Papa George emerge from their trailer. He looked over at me and then he sat in his rocker and lit his cigarette. He rocked and stared at the ground.

I gazed once more at the hill.

Daddy wasn't there.

He was gone forever.

2

A Coal Miner's Grave

It was snowing the day we buried Daddy, but I didn't feel the cold flakes on my face or the wind blowing my hair when we walked to the church or afterward, when we walked behind the hearses to the cemetery.

Daddy's and the two other miners' caskets were side by side at the front of the church, one casket really indistinguishable from another, even though I knew Daddy was the tallest of the three and the youngest. The church was filled with miners and their families, store owners and Mommy's friends and co-workers at Francine's Salon, as well as some of my school friends. Bobby Lockwood looked very uncomfortable. He didn't know whether or not to smile at me or just look sad. He shifted in his seat as if sitting on an ant hill. I gave him a tiny smile, for which he looked grateful.

I heard lots of sobbing and noses being blown. Way in the rear of the church, someone's baby cried. She cried throughout the service. It seemed fitting.

Papa George said there should have been more representatives from the mining company there and that the

20

mine should have been shut down for a few days in honor of the dead. He and Mama Arlene walked beside Mommy and me when we followed the hearses to the cemetery. Except for the crunchy sound of everyone's footsteps on the snow and the far-off wail of a train carrying away the coal, it was terribly quiet. I actually welcomed Papa George's stream of complaints.

He said that if there hadn't been an oil embargo to put pressure on the coal miners, my daddy wouldn't have been killed.

"Company saw the dollar signs," he charged, "and pushed them miners too far. But it ain't the first time, and I'm sure it ain't gonna be the last." We passed under the granite archway to the cemetery. Angels were carved in the stone.

Mommy kept her hood over her head, her eyes down. Every once in a while she released a deep sigh and intoned, "I wish this was over. What am I going to do? Where do we go now? What am I going to say to all these people?"

Mama Arlene had her arm through Mommy's and patted her hand gently and muttered back, "There, there, be strong, Haille. Be strong."

Papa George remained close to me when we reached the grave site. His flecked brown eyes filled with tears before he lowered his head, still thick with hair and as white as the flakes that flew into our faces. The other two miners who had been with Daddy when the walls caved in were being buried on the north end of the same cemetery in Sewell. We could hear the mourners singing hymns, their voices carried by the same cold February wind that tossed the flakes over the West Virginia hills and the shanties under the gray sky.

We raised our heads when the minister finished his prayer. He hurried off to say another prayer over the other two miners. Although Mommy wore black and no

21

makeup, she still looked pretty. Sadness simply lit a different candle in her eyes. Her rich maple-brown hair was pinned back. She had bought the plain black dress just for the funeral and wore a hooded cape. The hem of the dress reached only a few inches below her knees, but she didn't appear cold, even though the wind whipped her skirt around her legs. She was in a daze even deeper than mine. I grasped her hand much more tightly than she held mine.

I imagined that if Mama Arlene and I were to let go of Mommy's arms she would just float away in the wind, like a kite whose string had snapped. I knew how much Mommy would rather be anywhere but here. She hated sadness. If anything happened to make her unhappy, she would pour herself a gin and tonic and play her music louder, drowning out the melancholy.

I gazed at Daddy's coffin a final time, still finding it hard to believe he was really shut up inside. Soon, any moment, the lid would pop open and Daddy would sit up laughing, telling us this was all his little joke. I almost laughed imagining it, hoping for it. But the lid remained shut tight, the snowflakes dancing over its shiny surface, some sticking and melting into tears.

The mourners filed past, some hugging Mommy and me, some just pausing to touch our hands and shake their heads. Everyone said the same thing, "Sorry for your trouble." Mommy kept her head down most of the time, so I had to greet people and thank them. When Bobby took my hand, I gave him a small hug. He looked embarrassed, mumbled something, and hurried off with his friends. I couldn't blame him, but it made me feel like a leper. I noticed that most people were awkward and distant around us, as if tragedy was something you could catch like a cold.

Afterward, we all walked back from the cemetery more quickly than we had walked to it, especially Mommy. The snow fell faster and harder, and now that the funeral was over, I felt the cold cut right through to my bones.

The other two miners' families and friends were getting together to eat and comfort each other. Mama Arlene had made a pot roast thinking we would all be there, but as we left the cemetery, Mommy told her she wasn't going. She couldn't get away from the sadness fast enough.

"I can't stand any more sad faces around me," she wailed and shook her head.

"Folks need each other at times like this," Mama Arlene explained.

Mommy just shook her head again and quickened her pace. Suddenly, Archie Marlin caught up with us in his imitation patent leather shoes and his shiny gray suit, with his glossy red hair parted in the middle.

"Be glad to drive you home, Haille," he offered.

Mommy's eyes brightened and more color returned to her face. Nothing could cheer her up as quickly as a man's attention. "Why thank you, Archie. That's very kind."

"Ain't much. I wish I could do more," he remarked, flashing me a smile.

Behind us I saw Alice widen her round eyes even more.

"Come on, honey." Mommy reached for my hand, but I stepped back.

"I'll walk home with Alice," I told her.

"That's silly, Melody. It's cold."

"I'm not cold," I said, even though my teeth wanted to chatter.

"Suit yourself," Mommy said and got into Archie's car. Two large cotton dice hung from the rearview mirror and his seats were upholstered with an imitation white wool that shed on your clothes. The wiry threads were sure to get all over Mommy's black dress, but she didn't care. Before we had left for church, she told me she expected to throw the dress in the garbage the moment she took it off anyway.

23

"I don't intend to spend weeks mourning and wearing black," she declared. "Sadness ages you and it doesn't bring back the dead. Besides, I can't wear this black thing to work, can I?"

"When are you going back to work, Mommy?" I asked, surprised. With Daddy's death, I thought the world would stop turning. How could our lives go on?

"Tomorrow," she said. "I don't have much choice. We don't have anyone supporting us anymore, do we? Not that it was much support anyway," she mumbled.

"Should I go right back to school?" I asked more out of anger than a desire to return.

"Of course. What are you going to do around here all day? You'll go crazy looking at these four walls."

She wasn't wrong, but somehow it didn't seem right to simply go on with our lives as if Daddy hadn't died. I would never hear his laughter or see him smile again. How could the sky ever be blue or anything taste sweet or feel good? I would never again care about getting hundreds on tests or parading my newfound knowledge. Daddy was the only one who cared, who was proud of me anyway. Mommy gave me the feeling she felt education was frivolous for a girl. She believed once a girl was old enough to catch a man, nothing else mattered.

Walking home from the cemetery with Alice, I felt my heart had turned into one of those large chunks of coal Daddy used to hack out of the walls hundreds of feet below the earth: the coal that had killed him. Alice and I barely spoke while we hurried toward the trailer park. We had to keep our heads bowed because the snowflakes were streaming down from the gray sky and into our eyes.

"Are you all right?" Alice asked. I nodded. "Maybe we should have gone in Archie Marlin's car, too," she added mournfully. The wind howled. It screamed.

"I'd rather walk in a storm ten times worse than get in his car," I said vehemently.

When we entered Mineral Acres, we saw Archie

Marlin's car parked at our trailer. And then, as we drew closer, we heard the sound of my mother's laughter.

Alice looked embarrassed. "Maybe I should go home."

"I wish you wouldn't," I said. "We'll go into my room and close the door."

"Okay."

When I opened the door, we found Mommy sitting at the dinette with Archie. A bottle of gin sat on the table with some mixers and ice.

"Happy now that you froze your feet walking?" Mommy asked. She had already taken off the black dress and wore a blue silk robe. Her hair was down around her shoulders. She had put on more lipstick.

"I needed the walk," I said. Archie looked at Alice and me with a grin.

"There's water on the stove if you want some tea or hot chocolate," Mommy said.

"I don't want anything right now, thank you."

"Maybe Alice wants something."

"No thanks, Mrs. Logan."

"You can tell your mother everything's clean in my house," Mommy snapped. Alice was nonplussed.

"She didn't say it wasn't, Mommy."

"No, really, Mrs. Logan, I—"

"It's okay," Mommy said with a tiny ripple of nervous laughter. Archie smiled and poured two more drinks.

"We're going to my room," I said.

"Maybe you should have gone to the wake, Melody. I don't have anything for dinner, you know."

"I'm not hungry," I said. I marched down the short corridor to my room, Alice trailing behind. After I closed the door, I threw myself on the bed and buried my face in the pillow to smother the anger building in my chest as much as my sobs.

Alice sat on the bed, too frightened and amazed to speak. A moment later we heard Mommy turn on the radio and find a station with lively music.

"She's just doing that because she can't stand crying

anymore," I explained. Alice nodded, but I saw she was uncomfortable. "She says I should go right back to school."

"Are you? You should," she added, nodding.

"It's easy for you to say. Your daddy's not dead." I regretted saying it immediately. "I'm sorry. I didn't mean that."

"It's all right."

"I know if I live like nothing happened, I won't feel so sick inside. Only, what will I do when it's time for Daddy to be coming home from the mine? I know I'll just stand out there watching the road every day, expecting him to come walking over the hill as usual."

Alice's eyes filled with tears.

"I keep thinking if I stand there long enough and concentrate and hope hard enough, all this will never have happened. It will just seem to be a bad dream."

"Nothing will bring him back, Melody," Alice said sadly. "His soul has gone to heaven."

"Why did God put him in heaven?" I demanded, pounding my small fists on my thighs. "Why was I even born if I can't have a Daddy when I need him the most? I'm never going back to that church!" I vowed.

"It's silly to think you can hurt God back," Alice said.

"I don't care."

The look on her face said she didn't think I meant what I was saying.

But I did mean it, as much as I could mean anything. I took a deep breath, the futility of my outbursts and anger washing over me. "I don't know how we will go on without him. I'll have to quit school maybe and go to work."

"You can't do that!"

"I might have to. Mommy doesn't make very much money working in the beauty parlor."

Alice thought a moment.

"There's the miner's pension and social security, too."

"Mommy said it won't be enough."

26

We heard a loud outburst of laughter come from both Mommy and Archie Marlin.

Alice grimaced. "My father doesn't know how Archie Marlin keeps out of jail. Daddy says he waters the whiskey in the bar."

"Mommy's just trying not to be sad," I said. "She'd entertain anyone right now. He just happens to be around."

Alice nodded, unconvinced.

I picked up my fiddle and plucked at the strings.

"Daddy loved to hear me play," I said smiling, remembering.

"You play better than anyone I know," Alice declared.

"Well I'll never play again." I threw the fiddle on the bed.

"Of course you will. Your daddy wouldn't want you to give it up, would he?"

I thought about it. She was right, but I wasn't in the mood to agree with anything anyone said right now.

Another peal of laughter from Archie Marlin reached our ears.

"The walls of this trailer are made of cardboard," I said. I put my hands over my ears.

"You're welcome to come to my house," Alice said. "My brother's the only one home."

Alice lived in one of the nicest homes in Sewell. Ordinarily, I loved going there, but right now I felt it was a sin to do anything enjoyable.

Suddenly we heard Mommy and Archie singing along with a song on the radio, followed by their laughter again.

I stood up and reached for my coat. "Okay. Let's get out of here."

Alice nodded and followed me out of my room and down the short corridor. Mommy was sprawled on the sofa now and Archie was standing at her feet, holding his drink in his hand. They didn't speak, then Archie reached to turn down the volume on the radio.

27

"I'm going to Alice's house."

"Good idea, honey. Daddy wouldn't want you moping around the trailer."

I wanted to say he wouldn't want you laughing and singing and drinking with Archie Marlin either, but I swallowed my words and pounded my feet over the thin rug to the front door.

"Don't be late," Mommy called after me.

I didn't reply. Alice and I walked away from the trailer, the radio music turned up behind us again. Neither of us spoke until we rounded the turn toward Hickory Hill. The Morgans lived at the top and from their living room and dining room windows could look down on the valley and Sewell proper.

Alice's mother was very proud of their home, which she told me on more than one occasion was a colonial revival, a house with historical architecture. It had two stories and a front porch. They had an attached garage. The house had twelve rooms. The living room looked as big as our entire trailer. Alice's room was certainly twice the size of mine, and her brother Tommy's room was even bigger. The one time I looked in at the master bedroom with its own bathroom, I thought I had entered a palace.

Tommy was in the kitchen when we entered the house. He sat on a stool, smearing peanut butter on a piece of bread and holding the phone receiver between his ear and shoulder. The moment he saw me, his eyes widened and his eyebrows lifted.

"I'll call you back, Tina," he said and cradled the receiver. "I'm sorry about what happened to your father. He was a really nice guy."

"Thank you."

He looked at Alice for an explanation of what we were doing, why she had brought me to their house. Everyone was making me feel as though I carried a disease. No one wanted to be directly confronted with sorrow as deep as mine.

"We're going up to my room," Alice told him.

28

He nodded. "Would you like something to eat? I'm just having a snack."

I hadn't really had anything substantial to eat for days and my stomach bubbled at the suggestion.

"Maybe I should eat something."

"I'll make us some sandwiches and bring them up to my room," Alice said.

"Mother doesn't like you to have food in your room, Alice," Tommy reminded her.

"She'll make an exception this time," Alice retorted. Her older brother retreated from the fury of her eyes and her stern expression.

"I don't want to make any trouble," I said softly.

"I guess it will be all right as long as you don't make a mess," Tommy relented. "How's your mother doing?"

"She's doing fine," I said hesitantly. He nodded, gazed at Alice who continued to glare at him defiantly, and then he took a bite of his sandwich.

"Let's go up to my room, first," Alice suggested, pivoting and taking my hand. I followed.

We went quickly up the carpeted, winding stairway to her room.

"Sorry my brother is such a dork," she said. "We're always fighting because he's so bossy. You can lie down if you want," she said nodding at her fluffy pillows and comforter on her queen size bed. It had pink posts and a frilly light pink canopy. The headboard was shaped like a Valentine heart. I dreamed of having a bed like this instead of the simple mattress and box springs I had now.

I took off my coat and sat on the bed.

"I thought Bobby Lockwood was going to come to your house," Alice said.

"I knew he wouldn't. He looked terrified at church and at the cemetery," I said.

"I know you like him, but I don't think he's that mature," Alice remarked.

"No one's very mature when it comes to this sort of thing. I don't blame him for running away from me."

29

"If he really liked you, he would want to be with you, to help you."

I knew Alice hated whenever I had a boyfriend because it took me away from her.

"Right now, I don't care very much about boys," I said.

She nodded, pleased.

"I'll run down and make us some sandwiches and bring them up with milk, okay?"

"Don't get in trouble on my account."

"I won't. Just rest or read something or turn on the television set, if you want. Do anything you want," she offered.

"Thanks."

After she left, I did lie back and close my eyes. I should be with Mommy now and she should want to be with me, not Archie Marlin. She'll be sorry when he leaves and she's all alone in the trailer, I thought, and then I decided I wouldn't stay away that long. I kept hearing Daddy explaining her actions, cajoling me to understand her weaknesses. He always felt more sorry for her than he felt for himself. I was sure he was doing the same thing right now, even though it was he and not she who was shut up in a coffin.

I wondered how long it would be before my friends would stop looking at me strangely. It would be so hard to return to school, I thought: all those pitying eyes aimed at me. I imagined even my teachers would gaze at me sorrowfully and speak to me in softer, sadder tones.

Maybe Mommy was right: maybe it was better to pretend nothing had happened. That way other people weren't so uncomfortable in your presence. But wasn't that like slapping Daddy's memory in the face? Somehow, I had to find a way to keep my sorrow private and go on with my life, as empty as it now seemed to be.

If I had a brother like Alice had, I wouldn't be fighting with him all the time, I thought. Right now, a brother would come in pretty handy. He would help with

30

Mommy and we would have each other to comfort. If he were older than I was, I was sure he would be like Daddy. I resented Mommy for being too weak and too selfish to have another baby. She didn't have to have a litter, but she might have considered my need for a companion.

I must have been a lot more tired than I realized, for I didn't hear Alice return. She placed the sandwiches and the milk on the night table beside the bed and sat reading our history assignment while she waited for me to open my eyes. It was twilight by the time I did. The lamp was on.

"What happened?" I asked, scrubbing my cheeks with my palms and sitting up.

"You fell asleep and I didn't want to wake you. The milk's a little warm, but the sandwich is all right."

"Oh. I'm sorry."

"Go ahead. Eat something. You need it, Melody."

I saw from the empty plate beside her and the empty glass, she had already eaten her snack. I took a deep breath and bit into the sandwich. I was afraid what my stomach might do once solid food dropped into it again. It bubbled and churned, but the sandwich tasted good, and I finished quickly.

"You were hungry."

"I guess so. Thanks. What time is it?" I gazed at the small grandfather clock on her dresser. "Oh. I better get home."

"You don't have to go. If you want, you could even sleep here tonight."

"No. I should go home," I insisted. "My mother needs me. I'm sorry I wasn't much company."

"That's okay. Are you going to school tomorrow?"

"No. I'm not. I'm staying home at least one day," I said firmly.

"I'll bring you all the homework and tell you what we did."

"Thanks." I paused and smiled at her. "Thanks for being my best friend, Alice."

31

It brought tears to her eyes and she flashed a smile back at me. Then she followed me down the stairs. Her house was so quiet.

"My parents are showering and getting dressed for dinner," she explained. "They always do that after they come home from work. Dinner is very formal in my house."

"That's nice," I said pausing at the front door to gaze back at her beautiful home. "It's nice to sit at the table like a family and all be together. You're lucky."

"No, I'm not," she said sharply and I opened my eyes wide. "We're rich, maybe, and I get the best marks in school, but you're the lucky one."

"What?" I almost laughed. Of all days, to say such a thing, I thought.

"You're the prettiest girl in school and everyone likes you and someday, you'll be happier than anyone."

I shook my head as if she had just said the dumbest thing, but she didn't soften her determined expression. "You will."

"Alice," we heard coming from upstairs. It was her mother. "Did you bring food upstairs?"

"I'd better go," I said quickly. "Thanks."

"See you tomorrow," she mumbled, and closed the door. Somehow, I don't know how, I left feeling more sorry for her than I did for myself.

When I returned to the trailer, Archie Marlin's car was gone. It was dark inside with only a small lamp on in the living room. The glasses and nearly empty bottle of gin were still on the coffee table. I gazed around, listened, and then walked softly down the corridor to Mommy's bedroom. The door was slightly ajar so I peeked through the opening and saw her sprawled on her stomach. Her robe was up around the backs of her knees and her arm dangled over the side of the bed.

I walked in and gazed at her face. She was breathing heavily through her mouth and was in a deep sleep. I covered her with the blanket and then left to clean up the trailer. Just before I was about to go to bed myself, there was a gentle knock on the door. It was Mama Arlene.

"How are you, honey?" she asked, coming in.

"I'm all right," I said. "Mommy's asleep."

"Good. I brought some of the food back from the wake for you to have." She put the covered plates in our refrigerator. "No sense letting this go to waste."

"Thank you."

She came over to me and took both my hands in hers. Mama Arlene was a small woman, an inch shorter than I, but according to Papa George, she had a backbone tempered with steel. Although diminutive, she still seemed able to hold everyone else's troubles on her shoulders.

"Times will be hard for a while, but just remember, we're right next door anytime you need us, Melody."

"Thank you," I said, my voice cracking, the tears burning under my eyelids.

"Get some sleep, sweetheart." She hugged me and I hugged her right back. It broke the dam of tears and I started to sob again.

"Sleep," she said softly. "That's the cure. That, and time."

I took a deep breath and went to my room. I heard her leave and then all was quiet. Off in the distance, the wail of a train whistle echoed through the valley. Some of the coal in those cars, I thought, might have been dug out by Daddy before he . . . before he . . .

Some place up north, someone would shovel the coal into a stove and for a while, be warm. I shivered and wondered if I would ever be warm again.

I wondered if Mama Arlene was right about the power of time. In the days and weeks that passed, the ache in my heart became a numbness. But that ache was always resurrected when my mind went to Daddy or when I heard someone who sounded like him. Once, I even

33

thought I saw him walking along the road. I hated going by the mine or looking at the other miners. The sight of them made my stomach tighten and sent pins into my heart.

Mommy never returned to the cemetery, but I did—almost every day for the first few weeks and then every other day or so after that. Everyone treated me differently at school for the first few days after I returned, but soon, my teachers spoke to me just the way they spoke to everyone else, and my friends began to stay at my side longer, talking to me more, and laughing around me.

Bobby Lockwood drifted away, however, and seemed interested in Helen Christopher, a ninth grader who looked more like an eleventh grader. Alice, who somehow managed to eavesdrop on conversations all day long, told me Helen was even more promiscuous than the infamous Beverly Marks. Alice predicted it was only a matter of time before she would be pregnant, too.

None of this mattered. I didn't shed a tear over Bobby's betrayal. Things that used to mean a lot now seemed small and petty. Daddy's death had jerked me headlong into maturity. On the other hand, with Daddy gone, Mommy became flightier than ever. The biggest effect Daddy's death seemed to have on her was to make her even more terrified of becoming old. She spent a great deal more time primping at her vanity table, fixing her hair, debating over her makeup. She continually reviewed her wardrobe, complaining about how old and out of style all her clothes were. Her talk was always about herself: the length and shade of her hair, a puffiness in her cheeks or eyes, the firmness leaving her legs, what this bra did for her figure as opposed to what another could do.

She never asked about my school work, and between what I made for dinner and what Mama Arlene did for us, she never cooked a meal. In fact, she seldom even came home for dinner with me, claiming she'd get fat.

"I can't eat as much fatty food as you can, Melody," she told me. "Don't wait for me. If I'm not home by six, start eating without me," she ordered. It got so she was only home for dinner once or twice a week. Mostly, I ate with Mama Arlene and Papa George.

Even though Mommy was worried about her complexion and her figure, she continued to drink gin and smoke. When I asked her about that, she got very angry and told me it was her only vice and everyone need a little vice.

"Perfect people end up in monasteries or nunneries and eventually go mad," she explained. "I have a lot of tension now with your father gone. I need to relax, so don't make any new problems for me," she ordered. Which I knew simply meant, "Leave me alone."

I did.

I wanted to complain too: about how often she saw Archie Marlin and how often he was at our house. But I buttoned my lips and swallowed my words. It took so little to set Mommy off these days, and after she went on a rampage—shouting and flailing about—she would break down and cry and make me feel just terrible. It got so I began to feel as if I was her mother and she was my daughter.

Our bills piled up, some simply because she just never got to them. Twice, the phone company threatened to shut off our service and once the electric company came by and put a warning on our door. Mommy was always making mistakes with our checking account. I had to take over the bookkeeping, do our grocery shopping, and look after the trailer. Papa George helped me with that, but Daddy's death had had a big impact on him, too. He looked older, sicker, and much more tired these days. Mama Arlene was always after him to take better care of himself, however he wouldn't stop smoking and he even began drinking a little whiskey in the late afternoon.

There were nights when I was wakened by the sound of Mommy's laughter and then heard Archie Marlin's voice. Soon, that laughter was coming from Mommy's bedroom. I pressed my hands over my ears, but I couldn't shut out the sounds that I knew were sounds of lovemaking.

The first time I heard that, I got so sick to my stomach and I had to run to the bathroom to vomit. Mommy didn't even hear me and never asked what had happened. Usually, Archie was gone before I rose in the morning, and if I heard him moving about in the kitchen or living room, I'd wait as long as I could before rising.

All of this had happened too quickly—far too quickly for most people in Sewell. I knew there was a lot of gossip about us. One night Mommy returned from work enraged. She had gotten into an argument with Mrs. Sampler, who had always been one of her best customers. They fought because Mrs. Sampler had made a remark about Mommy's not spending enough time in respectful mourning. From what I heard afterward, Mommy had become so shrill and wild, Francine had asked her to leave.

She was fuming, and started to drink as she recited the argument. "Who is she to tell me how to act? Does she know how hard my life is? How much I suffered? She lives in her fine house and looks down on me, judging me. Who told her she could be judge and jury?"

Mommy paused now and then to make sure I was on her side. I knew it was better not to get her any more furious than she already was, so every time she looked at me with her narrowed eyes I nodded enthusiastically and acted as outraged as I could about someone openly criticizing her.

"I hate these people. They think just because they have money, they can lord it over us. They're so small-minded. They're so—" She struggled for the right word and looked to me for a suggestion.

"Provincial?"

"Yes. What's that mean?" she asked.

"They just haven't been to enough other places to get a wider point of view," I said. She liked that.

"You are smart. Good. And you're right, too. Archie's always saying the same thing. He hates this town as much as I do. And you do," she added.

"I don't hate it, Mommy."

"Of course you hate it. What's here for you?" She gulped her cocktail and then went to the phone to call Archie and tell him what had happened.

I didn't realize how serious the incident at the beauty salon had been until days later when I came home early from school and found Mommy lying on the sofa watching a soap opera. She had obviously not even gotten dressed that day. I didn't even have to ask. She saw the look on my face and told me before I could utter a question.

"I'm not working for Francine anymore," she said.

"What! Why?"

"We had an argument. After all these years, you'd think she would be more loyal to me. I broke my back for her, did her all sorts of favors. The ingrate. That's what she is. That's what they all are."

"What are you going to do?"

"I'm not thinking about it right now. I'm too angry," she said, pouting. "What are we going to have for dinner?"

"There's the chicken from yesterday to warm up and I can make some potatoes and some green beans."

She smirked.

"If that's all we have, I guess that's what it will be," she said and closed her eyes.

My hands shook as I prepared our dinner. What would we do now? Who was going to give Mommy a job? What sort of a job could she manage? There was only one beauty salon in Sewell. Maybe, what I had told Alice would come true: I would have to quit school and find a job myself.

Daddy hadn't had enough life insurance and what we were getting from social security wasn't enough. Besides, Mommy had spent a lot of that money on new clothes.

But she didn't appear worried. After I had the meal prepared, she changed her mind about not liking it. She ate and drank and talked a blue streak about this new outfit she was getting, with matching shoes. After dinner, she went to her bedroom while I cleaned up, and she suddenly appeared in a new skirt and blouse with new earrings. She modeled it all for me and I had to admit, she looked beautiful. Maybe she could become a professional model, I thought, and made the mistake of saying so. Unfortunately, it started her on one of her favorite rampages.

"That's what I should have been. Only I didn't have the right advice or someone who was sophisticated enough to take me to the right places. And what did I know? You have to have someone who has been places, who knows things and will help you, who will guide you. That's why the choice of a man to marry and love is so important. You can't just let your heart tell you what to do. But it still might not be too late for me," she added, happily gazing in the mirror.

The possibility cheered her.

"I just have to go to the right places and see the right people," she told me. She clapped her hands together and nodded. "Yes, that's what I have to do." Her face beamed. She rushed back to her bedroom as if the right person were waiting there.

I felt my heart flutter. A feather of fear tickled the inside of my chest. It was one thing to dream and to wish for things once in a while. Daddy had taught me to hope for things and look forward to another tomorrow, but it was different if you lived in a world of wishes and never saw the reality of today and never cared about responsibilities. Mommy was getting more and more like that.

After I did the dishes, I went to do my homework. A short time later, I heard a knock on my door and Mommy peeked in, still dressed in her new skirt and blouse.

"I'm going to town," she said. "Leave the door unlocked."

A car horn honked and she was off. I didn't need to take two guesses whom she was with.

What will become of us? I wondered.

Two days later, I got my answer. It was more shocking than anything I expected.

3
&

Sad, Beautiful Dreamer

I returned from school that afternoon with an emptiness
that made my chest feel hollow. One foot followed the
other mechanically, the soles of my shoes barely leaving
the road. A group of grade school children ran past.
Their laughter had the tinkling sound of china, crisp and
musical in the clear, sharp air. Children, I realized, don't
really have to contend with deep sadness. They are
wooed out of it with the presentation of a toy or a
promise. But being mature means realizing life is filled
with dark days, too. Tragedy had sent me headlong into
reality. All the things I had seen before now looked
different, even nature.

The snow had melted. The white oaks, with their
powerful broad branches, the beech trees and poplar
trees, all had leaves turning a rich shade of green. I was
vaguely aware of the birds flitting from branch to branch
around me. Above me, the lazy, milk-white clouds
seemed pasted against the soft blue sky, but they looked
like nothing more than blobs of white. Their shapes no
longer resembled camels or whales. My imagination was
imprisoned in some dark closet.

Usually, the first warm kiss of sunshine filled me with excitement. Things that normally made me depressed or unhappy looked small and insignificant against the promise of budding flowers or the laughter of young children rippling through the air.

But all the spring glory in the world wouldn't bring my daddy back. I missed his voice and his laughter more every passing day. Mama Arlene was wrong: time wasn't healing the wound. It made the emptiness wider, longer, deeper.

As I plodded along, I carried my school books in the dark blue cloth bag Daddy had bought me long ago. I had two tests to study for and lots of homework, so the bag was full and heavy. Alice had remained after school for Current Events Club. There was also a rehearsal for the school talent show, and I was supposed to play my fiddle in it. I had volunteered months ago, but since Daddy's death, I hadn't picked up my fiddle once. I no longer had the desire or the confidence.

Everyone else seemed to have something to do, friends to be with, activities to join. Once or twice I tried to muster some enthusiasm about something I had done before Daddy's death, but an important part of me had died with Daddy. I knew my friends at school, even Alice, were losing patience with me. After a while, they stopped pleading, begging, and encouraging me to do things with them, and I began to feel like a shadow of myself. Even my teachers had begun to treat me like a window pane, gazing through me at someone else, hardly calling on me in class, whether I raised my hand or not.

My smiles were few and far between. I couldn't recall the sound of my own laughter. Even before she had lost her job, Mommy had been complaining about my moods. Now, it was a constant grievance.

"If I can let go, you can," she lectured. Then she declared, "Maybe, he's happier where he is. At least he doesn't have to fight getting old. You won't remember him as anything but young. And where he is, he doesn't have to worry about money."

41

I told her that was a horrible thing to say, but she just laughed. "Suit yourself. If you want to walk around with a sad-sack face all the time, do it. You won't have any friends and you certainly won't attract any handsome boys."

"I don't care!" I shouted back. Boys and parties, long conversations on the telephone, scribbling some boy's name in my notebook—none of that mattered to me anymore. Why couldn't Mommy realize that?

I didn't want to have an argument with her today, but since she had lost her job at Francine's and not found another yet, I expected she would be home when I arrived. She said I was so depressing to be around, I made her lose her appetite. It always sounded like just another excuse to go off with Archie Marlin. Today would be no different. I braced myself for another lecture.

But when I opened the trailer's front door, I wasn't greeted with her criticisms. Instead, I saw suitcases spread open on the floor. Mommy rushed about, folding clothes and dropping them into the luggage.

"Good!" she said when she saw me. "You're home early. I was afraid the one time I wanted you here, you'd find something silly to do."

"What are you doing, Mommy? Why are you packing these suitcases?"

"We're leaving," she said smiling. "Now, these two suitcases are yours," she instructed, pointing to the smaller ones near the sofa. "I'm sorry that's all you can take, but that's all that we'll have room for in the car right now. Pick out your most important things and pack them."

My mouth dropped open. "Leaving? Where are we going? I don't understand."

"I don't have a lot of time to explain, Melody." She put her hands together and looked up at the ceiling as if giving thanks. "The opportunity has come and we're taking it," she declared. "Hurry! Get your best things

42

packed, and remember, we don't have room for anything else right now."

"I don't understand." I stood in the doorway and shook my head.

"What's to understand? We're leaving," she cried. "Finally leaving Mineral Acres! Be thankful. Be gloriously thankful, sweetheart," she pleaded.

"But why are we leaving?"

She held out her arms, turning her eyes from her right hand to her left, as if the answer were right before us. "Why?" She laughed thinly. "Why would I want to leave this Godforsaken place, this town of busybodies, of people who have no imagination, no dreams? Why would I want to leave a two-by-four trailer in a retirement park filled with people inches away from their own graves? Why?" She laughed again, then lost her smile.

"You're supposed to be a smart student. You get all those hundreds on your school tests and you ask why?"

"But Mommy, where will we go?"

"Any place else," she said. She stared at me for a moment and then her eyes grew small. "We're going to explore, look for a nice place to live where I can have an opportunity to do something more with my life and not be smothered and stifled. Now that your father is dead, we have no reason to continue living in a coal mining town, do we?"

She smiled again, but something about that smile seemed false.

"We've always lived in Mineral Acres." I said weakly.

"Because your father was working in the mines! Really, Melody. Besides," she went on, "I've spent more money than we have in the bank trying to cheer myself up after your father's death. The life insurance is gone and you know what our bills are, how close we are to not paying them every month. You're always warning me. I can't even pay for this trailer without a job and I'm not going to beg for my job back at Francine's. There just aren't any other jobs here for me. I'm not going to

43

become a waitress. Look at me!" she said throwing wide her arms. "Do I look like I can make a living for us in this town? I can't type and if I could, I would hate to be caged in some mine company office. We have no choice. I have to get to where there are opportunities before it's too late!"

"But how are we going?"

"Archie will be here in twenty minutes," she replied. "So we don't have much time to jabber about it."

"Archie?"

"He's leaving, too. Actually, it was his idea," she added with a happy smile. "We'll go off in his car and—"

"Archie? We're going away with Archie Marlin?" I asked, incredulously.

"It's more like he's going away with us," she said and followed it with her nervous little laugh. "But he's going to be a big help. He has friends in the entertainment business. He says I can be a model."

"Oh Mommy, he's lying! He's telling you these things just so you'll stay with him."

"What? How dare you." She wagged her forefinger at me. "Archie is a sensitive person. He cares about us. As it turns out, he has no one either. It makes sense for us to all go off together. Please," she pleaded, rolling her eyes. "Get busy packing."

"But what about my school and—"

"You'll make up the work in a different school—a better school! Oh honey," she said, clapping her hands together, "isn't this exciting? What could possibly be wrong with our trying to find a new place to live? I know you're not happy here anymore, right?"

"That's because of what happened to Daddy."

"Exactly. And nothing is going to change that, so why stay? A new beginning—a fresh start—is what we all need. But we have to do it before it's too late, Melody. Do you want me to wait until I'm too old to have another chance? That's what happened to a lot of the people who

44

are stuck here. Well, it's not going to happen to me," she said with determination.

She smiled again. "I have another surprise. I was going to save it until we actually left, until we were on the road with nothing ahead of us but a better future," she said.

I stared at her dumbly, wondering what additional surprise she could possibly have.

"Don't you even want to know what it is?" she asked when I didn't speak.

I shook my head and gazed around. It was overwhelming. The suitcases on the floor, the house in a mess, clothes thrown everywhere . . .

"What?" I finally asked.

"Our first stop is going to be Provincetown, Cape Cod. You're going to see your father's family, finally. Well?" she said when I didn't reply. "Aren't you excited? You were always asking about them. Now, you'll get all the answers."

"Provincetown? Daddy's family?"

"Yes. Isn't it a good idea?"

"I don't know," I said. She was right: she had surprised me, something wasn't ringing true. I took a deep breath. My heart pounded. With everything happening so fast, I couldn't think straight.

"Shouldn't we plan this better, Mommy? Can't we sit and talk about it first and get organized?"

"No, because that usually means we won't do it," she whined. "As Archie says, if you don't do something when you have the urge, you probably never will."

"Why do we have to go with him?" I pursued.

She tightened her face and narrowed her eyes. "I like Archie, Melody. He makes me laugh and I'm tired of crying and complaining. I'm tired of people looking at me as if I were some sort of freak because my husband was killed in a mining accident.

"But not Archie." She sat down on the sofa and motioned for me to join her. I sat down next to her, but I was cautious. Then she pulled me into her arms for the

45

first time since Daddy had died. She held me tightly and began to stroke my hair and slowly I began to relax. It felt so good to have my Mommy back. I'd missed her so much. "You'll like Archie once you get to know him. He's just the medicine I need and you need, honey." She paused, but kept caressing my hair. I hoped she would never stop. "The only thing," she added softly, "is after we leave Sewell, I don't want you to call him Archie anymore."

"Why not?"

"His real name is Richard. Archie is just a nickname."

"How come he can leave so quickly? He has a job," I said, hoping she wouldn't get mad and stop holding me. Perhaps he had been caught watering the whiskey as Alice's father thought.

"It's not the sort of a job a man like Arch . . . Richard wants for the rest of his life. So we made a decision. Now, Pumpkin, I want you to go pack, and remember, only two suitcases."

"But I'll have to leave so much behind," I protested.

"George and Arlene will look after it," she said. "And after we're settled somewhere nice, we'll have everything shipped to us."

"Mama Arlene," I muttered, realizing this meant I wouldn't see her anymore. "Did you tell her about this?"

"I was just going to do that," Mommy said, "but forcing me to stand here and talk, talk, talk, has cut down on my time. I have things to pack, too."

"But don't I have to tell the school and don't—"

"Will you stop all this chatter, Melody, and get packed! Everything will be just fine. We're not the first people to move, you know. Although, I bet you can count on one hand how many escaped this rat-trap."

She smiled again and rushed off to her bedroom.

I just stood there, gazing around, still finding it hard to believe we were going to leave Sewell for good! What about going to Daddy's grave to say good-bye? And what about Alice and my other friends? I had to turn in my library books! What about our mail? And the bills we

46

still owed—surely, we had to go to the bank. There was so much to do.

I put down my book bag and walked slowly down the short corridor. Mommy had her closet open and her clothes thrown on the bed. She stood in the center of the room, pondering.

"I hate to leave so much behind, but I'll get new things, won't I?" she decided.

"Mommy, *please*. Let's wait and do this right."

"Aren't you packing?" She turned to me angrily. "I'm warning you, Melody. When Archie arrives, we're going out that door," she threatened. "What you have packed, goes. What you haven't, stays. Understand?"

I swallowed down the lump in my throat and thought a moment. A suggestion born of desperation came to my mind.

"Maybe I should stay and live with Mama Arlene and Papa George until you find a new home for us, Mommy."

She shook her head. "I thought of that, but Papa George is sicker than ever and Mama Arlene has her hands full with him as it is. Besides, they are not really your family and can't be your legal guardians. It's too much responsibility for old, decrepit people to bear."

"They're not old and decrepit," I insisted.

"Melody, get your things into those suitcases!" Then her voice softened. "Don't make things harder than they have to be, honey. I'm depending on you to be a big girl. I'm a little frightened, too. Everyone's afraid when they start a new life. I need your support, Melody." She paused when I didn't move. "Besides, you know Daddy would want you to do what I ask," she said. "Wouldn't he?" She smiled. "Wouldn't he?"

"Yes," I reluctantly admitted.

I lowered my head and turned away. When I stepped into my small room and gazed about, I found myself confronted with an impossibility. There were so many precious mementos, especially things Daddy had bought me, like my first doll, and all the pictures. Those

47

suitcases Mommy had set out for me were barely big enough to hold a tenth of my clothes, much less stuffed animals. And what about my fiddle?

"Ten minutes!" Mommy cried from her room.

I had ten minutes to decide what I would leave behind, maybe forever. I couldn't do it. I started to cry.

"Melody! I don't hear you putting things into your suitcases," she called.

Slowly, I opened the dresser drawers and took out what I knew were necessities, my underthings, socks, some shoes and sneakers. Then I went to the closet and chose my skirts and blouses, two pairs of jeans, and some sweaters.

The suitcases filled up quickly, but I gathered as many of my photographs as I could and stuffed them under the clothes. Then I tried to squeeze in my first doll, my stuffed cat and Teddy bear, and some gifts from Daddy. Mommy came out and saw how full my suitcases were and how it was impossible to close them properly.

"You can't take all that," she said.

"Can't I have another suitcase?"

"No. Arch . . . Richard has his things, too, and I have to take four suitcases myself. I need my good clothes so I can look nice when I go for job interviews and auditions," she claimed. "I told you, we'll send for the rest."

"But I don't need much more. Maybe a small carton and—"

"Melody, if you can't decide what to leave here, I'll decide for you," she said and reached down to pluck the stuffed cat out of the suitcase.

"No!," I cried. "That was the last thing Daddy gave me!"

"Well, it's obviously either this or that Teddy bear or some of your clothes. Decide. You're a big girl now. You don't need toys," she snapped and threw the cat back onto the clothes in the suitcase.

I pressed the stuffed animals down and then I sat on the suitcase so it would close and managed to get the snaps to hold. The sides of the suitcases bulged and they

48

were heavy, but I had gotten in the things I would positively not leave behind.

"You only need the one coat," Mommy instructed, "and the boots you're wearing. Don't forget your gloves."

"I'm taking my fiddle," I said.

"Your fiddle? Melody, please. That's a backwoods, mountain person's instrument."

"Daddy loved to hear me play."

"Well, he can't hear you now. You're not going to play it much where you'll be going, I'm sure. Maybe you'll learn how to play the guitar or—"

"I won't go if I have to leave the fiddle, Mommy." I folded my arms under my breasts and planted my back firmly against the wall. "I won't. I swear."

She sighed.

"I guess it will take time to get the shanty town out of you. Suit yourself." She marched down the corridor to finish packing up her cosmetics. I had forgotten my own toiletries and had to open one of the suitcases to get them in. I was still struggling to close it when Archie Marlin arrived.

He wore a brown sports jacket, a shirt and tie, and brown slacks. He looked a little better dressed than usual.

"Hi," he said, entering my room without knocking. "Almost ready?"

"No," I said mournfully.

It only made him smile. "I bet you're excited, huh?"

"No," I said, firmly this time.

"Scared, huh? Well, there's no need to be scared. I've been down this road before and there's nothing to fear." His voice was full of bravado.

"I'm not scared. I'm upset we're leaving so quickly."

"Best way to go is to just get up and go." He snapped his fingers. "Either you're a man of action or you're just a talker." He straightened his shoulders and pumped out his chest. I turned away so he wouldn't see the tears glistening in my eyes. "Haille!" he called.

49

"Oh, you're here, good." Mommy came into my room. "I'm just about packed. You can start loading the car, Richard."

He widened his eyes.

"She knows it's your real name and Archie's just a nickname," Mommy explained.

"Oh? Good. Never liked that nickname." Archie-Richard winked at me and went to get Mommy's bags.

"Are you packed?" she asked me.

"The bags are full. I just have to get this one closed."

"No problem." Archie paused as he dragged Mommy's two largest bags over the floor. He left them a moment to sit on my suitcase, pressing the fasteners in and snapping them shut. "You need anything, Melody, you just ask," he told me. I snorted, hating the idea of asking him for anything.

"While we pack the car, why don't you go say good-bye to Mama Arlene?" Mommy said.

I lowered my head and put on my coat. Then I took my fiddle in its case and started for the door. Archie complained about how heavy Mommy's bags were. He struggled to get them down the steps behind me.

"Careful!" Mommy screamed. "Some of my nicest things are in those bags."

Daddy could have picked them up with just a couple of fingers, I thought.

I knocked on Mama Arlene's trailer door.

"Melody, honey, what's wrong?" She knew there was something the moment she looked at my face.

"Oh, Mama Arlene. We're going away. We're leaving Mineral Acres for good!" I rushed into her arms.

I told her everything quickly, including my suggestion I remain behind and live with her and Papa George. We hadn't even moved from the doorway before I had it all said.

"Oh," she said nodding. "So that's why she was asking me about George's condition. Well, come in a moment," she said.

"Where is Papa George?" I asked, not seeing him in

50

his favorite oversized chair watching television and smoking. Before she could reply, I heard his heavy cough from their bedroom.

"He's a bit under the weather tonight," she said. "The doctor wanted him in the hospital, but you know Papa George. He wouldn't go. When did you say you were going?"

"Today! Right now!"

"Right now? But she never said . . . Right now?" The realization shocked her almost as much as it had me. Her small hands fluttered up to her throat like two little song birds. She shook her head in disbelief.

"She wants you to keep our things until we send for them," I explained.

"Of course. I'll take good care of everything. Oh Melody," she said, actual tears flowing from her eyes now. "We'll miss you. You're the grandchild we never had, the child we never had."

"I don't want to go," I wailed.

"You got to go with your mother, honey. She needs you."

"She doesn't need me," I said defiantly. "She has Archie Marlin."

"Archie Marlin? Oh." She took on a look of disapproval and sadness, her eyes darkening.

"What's going on out there?" Papa George called from his bedroom.

"You better go say good-bye to him." The way Mama Arlene said it put an icicle in my chest, chilling my heart. I walked slowly to the bedroom doorway and gazed in.

Papa George looked tiny under his comforter. Only his head, crowned with that stark white hair, showed. He coughed violently for a few moments and spit into a metal tray at the side of the bed. Then, he took a deep breath and turned to me. "What are you women jabbering about?"

"We're going away, Papa George," I said.

"Who's going away?"

"Mommy and me . . . and for good," I said.

51

He stared, took another breath, coughed a bit and then pushed hard to get himself into a sitting position.

"Where she taking you?"

"We're going to see my daddy's family. They live in Cape Cod."

The old man nodded. "Well, maybe that's best. Leaving on quick notice, though, ain't you?"

"Yes. I haven't said good-bye to any of my friends and I haven't been to the cemetery yet."

He thought a moment and then reached over to his night table drawer. He took something out and beckoned for me to come closer.

"I want you to have this," he said and handed me a gold-plated pocket watch. I had seen it once or twice before and knew that on the inside was the inscription, To George O'Neil, Ten tons of coal! "It still keeps good time," he said. When the watch was opened, it played one of Papa George's favorite tunes: "Beautiful Dreamer."

"I can't take that, Papa George. I know what it means to you."

"It will mean more to me to know Chester Logan's little girl has it now and forever," he said, urging me to take it. I reached out and clutched it in my hand. "This way, you won't be able to forget me."

"Oh Papa George, I can't ever forget you," I moaned and threw my arms around him. He felt so small, all skin and bones, and his hug was barely anything. I was shocked. It was as if he were wilting, disappearing right before my eyes.

He started to cough again and pushed me back so he could lower himself under the blanket. I waited for him to catch his breath.

"Send us postcards," he said.

"I will. I'll write every day."

He laughed. "A postcard now and then is all we need, Melody. And don't forget to play that fiddle. I didn't spend all that time teaching you for nothing."

"I won't."

52

"Good," he said. He closed his eyes. "Good."

Hot tears streamed down my cheeks. I felt as if my lungs would burst, the ache was that deep. I turned and saw Mama Arlene standing in the bedroom doorway, her tears falling just as hard and fast. She held out her arms and we hugged. Then she followed me out.

Mommy and Archie had finished loading his Chevy. He slammed the trunk closed and got behind the wheel. Mommy came over to Mama Arlene.

"I didn't know you meant you would be leaving this soon, Haille."

"It's just worked out that way, Arlene. I guess Melody already asked you to look after our remaining things, if you can."

"I'll keep an eye on the place, sure."

"Once we're settled, I'll see about getting what else we want. Where's George?"

"He's lying down," she said.

"Oh."

They exchanged a knowing glance that made me weak in the knees.

"Well, I'll call and I'll drop you a line now and then," Mommy promised.

My mind was racing. There was too much to think about. "Mama Arlene. I'm going to leave my school books on the kitchen table. I'll call my friend Alice and she'll come by to get them and my library books, okay?" I asked.

"Of course, dear."

"Here's the keys to the trailer." Mommy handed them to Mama Arlene. She took them reluctantly. Her gaze went to me and her lips trembled.

"I better go put the books on the table, Mommy," I said.

"Hurry. We want to be on the road. We've a lot of distance to cover," she said. "Go on. I'll wait here with Arlene."

I ran back to the trailer and entered. For a moment I just stood there gazing around. Yes, it was a tiny place to

53

live and our furniture was very ordinary. Yes, the rugs were worn, the curtains thin, the wallpaper faded. The faucets dripped and the sinks were stained with rust at the drains. The heat never worked right and in summer, the place was an oven. I had wished and wished to have a real house instead, but this had been home to me, and now I felt as if I were deserting a poor old friend.

Daddy and I had eaten thousands of meals at that small dinette. I had curled up in his arms a thousand times on that worn sofa while we watched television. I blew out candles on many birthday cakes here. In that corner we had decorated our small Christmas tree. Although the pile of gifts under it was never impressive, it was always exciting for me.

Good-bye trailer home, I thought. Good-bye to the sound of the rain's drum beat on the roof while I slept or studied or ate my meals. Good-bye to every creak and groan in the wind; to the funny moaning sound in the plumbing that brought laughter to Daddy and me dozens of times.

And how do I say good-bye to my small room, my small private world? Once, this was my special place and now I was looking in at it for the final time.

I bit down on my lower lip and pressed my palm against my heart, holding in the ache, and then I scooped up my school books and the library books and put them on the kitchen table.

Archie Marlin honked the car's horn. I glanced at everything one last time, pressing it forever into my memory. Archie honked again.

"Good-bye," I whispered to the only home I had ever known. I rushed out the front door, afraid that if I paused or looked back, I would never be able to leave.

"What took you so long?" Mommy complained, her head out the window.

I got into the back seat. It was half covered with some of Mommy's clothes. I put my fiddle on the car floor.

"Be careful of my things," she said.

"Here we go." Archie pulled out of our lot. I pressed

my face to the window. Mama Arlene stood in her doorway, small and sad, her hand frozen in good-bye. The tears blurred my vision and some of them ran down the glass. I sat back to catch my breath as Archie spun around the entrance to Mineral Acres and shot onto the road.

"We're stopping at the cemetery, aren't we, Mommy?" I asked.

"What? What for?"

"To say good-bye to Daddy," I replied, my voice filled with desperation.

"Oh, Melody. Can't we start this trip on a happy note?"

"I've got to say good-bye to Daddy!" I exclaimed. "I've got to!" My voice was full of desperation.

Archie looked at Mommy and she shook her head.

"It's on the way out," he said.

"Well, I'm not going in with you," Mommy said. "I can't bear it."

Archie stopped at the entrance to the cemetery. Mommy said it would break her heart again to drive in. It reminded her too much of the funeral.

"We're only waiting five minutes, Melody," she told me.

"Are you sure you don't want to come, Mommy?"

She stared at me a moment, her eyes looking genuinely sad. She gently shook her head.

"I said my good-bye some time ago, Melody. I had to or I couldn't go on with my life."

I opened the door and jumped out, running up the pathway past the monuments until I reached Daddy's stone. I walked up to it and threw my arms around it the way I used to throw them around him. I pressed my cheek to the hard granite and closed my eyes.

"Oh Daddy, we're going, but I'll come back as often as I can. Mommy has to get away. She can't live here anymore.

"I know you would forgive her. You forgave her for everything," I said a little bitterly. "And I know you

55

would tell me to be a help to her, but I can't help how I feel."

I fell to my knees in front of the stone and bowed my head to say a little prayer and then I plucked a blade of grass growing on the grave and put it inside Papa George's pocket watch. It would always be with me, I thought. I kept the watch open so some of "Beautiful Dreamer" would play. Daddy loved that song, too.

Mommy and Archie were honking the Chevy's horn again.

I closed the watch, stood up, and gazed at the mountains in the distance, drinking in the trees and the bushes. I wanted to press the memory of this place into my mind as firmly as I had pressed the blade of grass into the pocket watch.

Then I kissed Daddy's gravestone, leaving some of my tears on top of it before I turned to walk away. I got back into the car without a word. Archie and Mommy both glanced at me and then he turned the car around and we started down the road that would lead us north, first to Richmond.

Mommy squealed with delight as we passed through the town and beyond the sign that read, Now Entering Sewell, West Virginia.

"I'm leaving!" she cried. "I'm really getting out of here. My prison sentence is over!"

I gazed at her and squinted. What had she meant by that? I would have asked, but my chest ached so, I knew my voice would crack as soon as I tried to speak.

Archie sped up. They turned on the radio and began to sing along with the music. Mommy swung around to look at me.

"Oh, be happy, Melody. Please. Be happy, if not for yourself, then for me."

"I'll try, Mommy," I said in a voice barely above a whisper.

"Good."

The scenery whipped by. I barely paid attention, but I saw enough familiar territory fall back to fill my heart

56

with sadness. I gazed through the rear window, watching Sewell disappear behind a hill, and with it, the cemetery in which Daddy rested.

Then I turned around and looked ahead. Trembling, I felt no less frightened and confused than a newborn baby pulled kicking and screaming into the future, terrified at the unknown.

4
∞

The Girl out of the Country

I closed my eyes and lay back in the seat. Before Daddy was killed, he, Mommy, and I had gone to the beaches in Virginia a few times, but other than those trips, we hadn't traveled many places. I had never been north, and had only read about and seen pictures of cities like New York, Washington, D.C., and Boston. Mommy tried to get me excited about the trip by telling me we would see Washington and Boston on the way to the Cape. Someday, she said, we'll go to New York City. She said she had been there once herself, but she went with her elderly adoptive parents who weren't much fun. She could barely remember it.

"But we'll have wonderful times going to museums and shows and eating in the famous restaurants. Right, Richard?"

"Absolutely," Archie replied. "Your life is really just beginning, Melody."

"See?" Mommy said.

As we rode on, I listened to their conversation. Archie talked about the cities he had been to, comparing them, complaining about this one or that one, raving about the others. He claimed to know the best restaurants in New York and Chicago. He had been to Las Vegas many times and Los Angeles at least three times. He bragged about the people in the entertainment industry he had met and gotten to know at the various bars and restaurants where he had worked. He said he was sure he could call any of them on the phone and get them to consider Mommy. Mommy squealed and laughed with delight at all his promises. I couldn't believe she was so gullible, but then I remembered Daddy once telling me that if you want something to be true hard enough, you'll ignore all the proof that it's not so. Mostly, you won't ask questions that give you answers you don't want to hear.

Mommy should be asking Archie Marlin if he was so friendly with all these important people, why didn't he have a better job himself? How did he end up in Sewell? I was tempted to lean forward and fire these questions at him myself, but I didn't want to anger Mommy so I tried to sleep instead.

We stopped for gas, got some snacks and drove until we reached Richmond. Archie bragged about knowing a little Italian restaurant, the owners of which he claimed would surely remember him and give us special treatment. He promised Mommy he would take us someplace special every step of the way. However, when we turned down the street where the Italian restaurant was supposed to be, it wasn't there anymore.

"That's the trouble with these little restaurants," he remarked. "They go in and out of business so quickly. Let's just stop at that roadside diner," he decided and pulled into the parking lot.

I wasn't hungry, but Mommy insisted I eat something. While we waited for our food, I took a closer look at Archie Marlin, trying to understand what Mommy liked about him, especially after she had been married to a man as handsome and strong as Daddy.

Besides having patches of freckles on his face, Archie had them on the backs of his hands as well. His pink skin

59

was interrupted here and there by white blotches. It looked as if he had been splattered with permanently staining milk. I thought his wrists were not much wider than mine or Mommy's, and I laughed to myself at the thought of him lifting a pick axe or a shovel. No wonder the heaviest thing he ever hoisted was a glass of beer.

Archie Marlin was full of nervous energy. He lacked Daddy's strong, quiet, calm manner. Archie's gaze was forever wandering. When he answered questions, he rarely looked at you. He looked down or up at the ceiling or fiddled with a spoon while he replied. While we waited for our food he described how he had once been a Blackjack dealer in a Las Vegas casino. He demonstrated how he would flip cards and hide aces in the palm of his hand. He'd been one of the best Blackjack dealers in the whole city, he said.

"So why did you leave that job?" I blurted, finally filled to the brim with his stories.

"I was underage," he said. "And," he added with a wink, "I was throwing my pay back into the casino looking for the big win all the time, just like the rest of the poor fools. But it was fun for a while."

"It must have been exciting," Mommy said. "The lights, the glamour, all those rich people, the entertainers you must have met."

"Yeah, sure," he said, as if he had been doing that all his life. "I've had some pretty good times in Vegas, but I have a pretty good time wherever I am."

"Then why did you end up in Sewell?" I asked as sharply as I had intended. Mommy threw me a reprimanding look, but I kept my eyes fixed on Archie. He hinged his lips at the corners and smiled like a cat.

"It looked like a nice little town at the time," he replied. "I thought I'd settle down, take it easy. I thought I was ready for the simple life, but I was wrong." He laughed, then Mommy laughed too. "Boy, was I wrong about that."

"There's nothing wrong with a simple life," I snapped. They both stopped laughing. "What's wrong with having

60

a decent job and friends you can count on and a nice house?"

Archie shrugged. "Nothing, if you're seventy-five or eighty."

"That's stupid," I said.

Mommy scowled. "Melody. You apologize. Go on."

"It's all right," Archie said. "She's confused. Remember what they say, you can take the girl out of the country, but you can't take the country out of the girl." He winked at me.

"I don't care if the country stays in me," I muttered.

"That's because you really haven't been anywhere yet. Just wait," he promised. "You'll come around to my way of thinking."

Hardly, I thought. I'd rather be buried forever in a coal mine.

Our food came. I ate sullenly while they jabbered on about the things they were going to see and do. Every time Archie mentioned a new place, Mommy squealed. He had been to Niagara Falls, of course, and he had traveled through Yellowstone and he had seen the Grand Canyon, had ridden over the Golden Gate Bridge and had been to the Grand Ole Opry in Nashville. He had even seen the Alamo, and claimed he had gone riverrafting and skiing in Utah.

"You must be a lot older than you look," I remarked in a casual tone.

"What? Why?" He held his forkful of food at his mouth and waited for my reply, his thin lips stretching into another plastic smile.

"Because if we believe all the places you've been to, you're about a hundred."

The smile finally left his face. "Well, I don't lie, missy," he said. "I can't help it if you've been shut up in a small town all your life." He realized how angry he sounded, glanced quickly at Mommy, and replaced his angry expression with a syrupy smile. "But, thankfully, that's all going to change. Right, Haille?"

"Yes." She shot a fiery look at me. "It definitely is."

61

I shut up after that. They wanted to have coffee and dessert, but I didn't. I asked to be excused and was permitted to wait in the car. Neither seemed unhappy about getting rid of me. Archie gave me the keys and I left the diner and flopped in the rear seat, fuming and frustrated. They took their time. It was nearly a half hour before they came out, arm in arm, giggling like children.

"How's the country princess doing?" Archie asked as he started the engine.

"Wonderful," I said.

"Good, because we don't want any unhappy country princesses in our chariot, do we Queen Haille?"

"No," she said. "It's against the law to be unhappy, isn't it?"

"Exactly. I, King Archie—I mean, King Richard—do hereby declare all tears and sadness prohibited from our lives from this day forward. Anyone who complains about anything gets a demerit. Anyone who has two demerits becomes the gopher."

"Gopher?" Mommy asked.

"Yeah, you know: go for this, go for that."

Mommy got hysterical with laughter and we were off.

"Where were you born?" I asked Archie after a few minutes on the road.

"Me? Detroit."

"Don't you have any family?"

"Not that I care to remember," he said.

"Why not?"

"Melody," Mommy chastised, "I taught you better than that. You know better than to pry into someone else's personal affairs," she said.

"I wasn't prying. I was just making conversation, Mommy. You complained about my being too quiet before, didn't you?"

"Yes, but you don't have to cross-examine Richard, do you?"

"I just wondered if it wasn't the other way around," I said with a shrug.

62

"What do you mean?" Archie asked.

"I just wondered if it wasn't your relatives that would rather not remember you."

"Melody!"

Archie wagged his head. "She's a card. You're going to do just fine, Melody." In the rearview mirror, I saw his smile fade and his eyes suddenly turn glassy cold.

"She's not usually like this," Mommy explained. "It's all the excitement, I'm sure."

Archie said nothing. He turned on the radio. Darkness grew thicker and we drove into a shower that turned into a downpour. The windshield wipers couldn't keep up and they were apparently worn out anyway. The window became lined with streaks.

"Looks like we won't make as much time and distance as I had hoped," Archie remarked. "Best thing would be to find a motel and pull in for the night."

"Whatever you think, Richard," Mommy said. "You're the seasoned traveler. We're in your capable hands." It was enough to make me want to puke. I stared angrily out the front window into the darkness, interrupted now and then by oncoming car headlights. They made the drops of rain look like slivers of ice that sent shivers down my spine.

About ten minutes later, Archie turned the car into the parking lot of a motel. Rain was falling in sheets by now, so hard we could barely see the motel's neon sign. Archie pulled his jacket over his head and ran through the raindrops to the office door.

The moment he left the car, Mommy turned on me. "Melody, I wish you would treat Richard with respect. He is an adult, you know."

"What did I do?"

"You talked to him as if he was one of your schoolfriends, and I don't want you asking lots of personal questions. It's impolite. If he wants to tell us about himself, he will. Okay?"

"I really don't care."

"Well, start caring. We're going to be together for a

63

long time. We have to get along. We should be grateful Richard is doing all the driving." She leaned toward me, her eyes full of pleading.

"Oh, honey, try to be happy. Soon you're going to see wonderful new things. Think of that," she cajoled. "You should be happy that you're getting this opportunity. It's one I never had. I was forced to live with people I didn't like and endure terrible things."

"Like what?" I asked, my interest piqued.

"Someday I'll tell you," she replied, a distant look in her eyes, the look of someone lost in her memories.

"When will you tell me?"

"When you're old enough to understand."

"I'm old enough, Mommy. I'm fifteen. You should take a good look at me once in a while. I'm not a child anymore."

"I look at you plenty. You're still growing and at a sensitive stage. I remember how it was when I was your age. Trust me." She reached over the seat and put her hand on mine. "I want only what's best for you. You believe that, don't you, Melody?"

"Yes, Mommy," I said, wanting so much to believe her.

The door was pulled open and Archie hopped in, slamming it shut behind him. He brushed the rain off his face.

"Man, what a storm! But we're in luck. This place was almost filled. They had one room left."

"Good," Mommy said.

One room? I thought. All of us in one little room? Archie drove ahead and parked in front of Room C.

"Okay, we're going to have to move quickly. I'll get the door open first and then you girls decide what you need for overnight and we'll just bring that in, okay?"

"A-ok," Mommy said.

He jumped into the rain again.

Mommy turned to me. "What do you need, Melody?"

"Mommy, how can we all sleep in the same room?" I asked, mournfully.

64

"I'm sure there's two beds, silly."

"But . . ."

"Now start acting like the grown-up you want me to think you are. Concentrate. What do you need?"

"The small suitcase," I replied petulantly.

"All right. Why don't you run inside? Richard and I will bring in all the things we need. Go on, honey."

I opened the door. It raged like a hurricane outside. With my hands over my head, I rushed toward Room C. Its door was wide open and I lunged through it.

I looked around the room. It had dull brown walls, stained near the baseboard. There were two double beds with a dark brown night table between them, on which sat an old fashioned telephone. Behind me were a dresser and a standing lamp with a faded yellow shade. The closet, open, some hangers dangling, was next to the bathroom doorway.

I went to the bathroom and tried to close the door, but it was out of alignment. There was no shower curtain around the tub and there was a long rust stain down its middle, from the back to the drain. Water dripped in the sink, above which was a cabinet with a cracked mirror.

Mommy and Archie came charging in from the rain, laughing. Was everything going to be funny, even this horrible room?

"The bathroom door won't close," I declared. They both stopped laughing and looked at me.

Archie raised his right forefinger.

"That's one," he said.

"One what?" I asked.

"Complaint. One more and you're our gopher for the whole trip."

"Very funny," I said with my hands on my hips. "But what about the door?"

His laugh wound down like a dying lawn mower as he approached to inspect it. "When you close it," he said after a moment, "just lift up on the handle."

"Thank you."

I took hold of the door handle and stepped back into

65

the bathroom, closing the door as he had instructed. It still didn't close tightly, but it would have to do. I heard them both giggling again.

When I stepped out, I saw Archie had a bottle of gin and he was pouring some into two glasses. "This oughta take the chill out," he said.

They tapped glasses and swallowed.

"I just noticed there's no television set in the room," Mommy said. "Did you bring something to read, Melody?"

"No. We left home too quickly, remember? I had to leave my books behind anyway because there was no room in the suitcases," I complained. Archie leapt to his feet.

"That's two! Two complaints! You're the gopher."

Mommy laughed. They clinked glasses again.

"We really need something to mix this with, don't you think, Haille?"

"It would help," she said.

Archie dug into his pocket and produced two dollars.

"Why don't you run down to the motel office and get us a can of tonic water or some ginger ale." Archie thrust the money my way. "Stay under the overhang and you won't get wet."

I looked at Mommy. She sat on the bed, a wide grin on her face. "Be a good sport, honey."

I plucked the bills from Archie's hand and grabbed my coat on the way out the door, thinking I needed to get away from them for a while anyway. Their laughter followed as I slammed the door behind me.

Looking around, I saw how dreary the motel was. The parking lot was torn up in many spots, and the neon sign had some letters burnt out. Closing my coat tightly around myself, I hurried under the overhang, noticing as I went that there apparently *were* other empty rooms.

The office was small. Inside was a red imitation leather settee with slits and cracks in it, a worn cushioned chair, a coffee table, and the counter, behind which sat a short,

66

bald man. He had long, bushy eyebrows and thick lips that looked as pale as day-old dead worms.

When he smiled, I saw he was missing a lot of teeth.

"How can I help you?" he asked.

"I need a can of tonic, please."

"The machine's broke, but I got some in the fridge back here," he said, indicating a room behind his office. "Just tonic water?"

"Yes, please."

"One minute."

He brought it out and I paid him a dollar. I noticed the pay phone on the wall behind the settee.

"Can I have change for the phone, please?"

"Sure thing."

He gave it to me and I went to the phone. He sat again and picked up his magazine, but his attention was fixed on me.

I dialed Alice's phone number, put in the required change, and waited for her to answer. She did so on the second ring.

"Alice, it's Melody."

"Where are you? I tried to call you four different times after school."

"Oh, Alice, I don't know where I am. Some place near Richmond, Virginia."

"Richmond, Virginia?"

I gazed at the man behind the counter. He wasn't pretending to be interested in anything but me now.

I turned so that my back was to him and spoke as softly as I could. "We left, Alice. Mommy had it all planned. When I got home, she was packing. We're with Archie Marlin," I moaned.

"What? Where are you going?"

"Provincetown, on Cape Cod, at least at first. Then I don't know. Mommy wants to find a new place to live."

"You're gone for good?" Alice asked incredulously.

"Yes." My tears blinded me. "Could you say good-bye to everyone for me, and especially Mr. Kile?" He was my favorite teacher.

67

"But how will I know where you are?"

"I'll write as soon as it's decided. Oh, before I forget, I left my school and library books on the kitchen table in the trailer. Mama Arlene knows. Would you go by and get them and return them for me, please?"

"Sure. I can't believe this."

"Imagine how I feel. You know I hate Archie Marlin," I said. The operator interrupted to say I needed to put in more change, but all I had left was a nickel. "Good-bye, Alice. Thanks for being my best friend."

"Melody!" she called as if I were drifting away like a ghost.

The connection went dead. I stood there holding the mute receiver, afraid to turn and show the motel manager my tears. I took a deep breath, wiped my face with the back of my hand, and cradled the receiver.

"Really raining out there," the manager commented.

"Yes."

"You folks come far?"

"Sewell."

"Not that far."

I started away.

"You forgot your can of tonic," he said nodding toward the can I had left on the shelf by the telephone.

"Oh, thanks." I went back for it and then paused on the way to the door again. "Are you all booked up here tonight?"

"Booked up?" He laughed silently, his shoulders shaking. "Hardly."

"I thought so," I muttered to myself and left.

When I returned to the room, I found Mommy and Archie dancing to music on the radio. Mommy looked embarrassed for a moment, then smiled. "Richard can make even the dreariest situations happy."

"Here's your tonic water." I thrust the can at him.

"Thanks, princess," Archie said. "Any change?"

I handed him the nickel.

"I needed to call Alice to tell her to get my books," I said. "We owe you ninety-five cents."

68

"Plus interest," he said winking at Mommy. Then he snapped open the can and poured some into his glass and Mommy's.

"There are other empty rooms," I declared.

Archie paused with a surprised look painted on his crimson face. "There are? That's not what baldy in the office told me. Well, how do you like that? He just wanted to get us into a more expensive room, I bet."

"Wouldn't he be better off renting two?" I asked, snorting.

"Naw. This room is more expensive than two," he asserted.

"What difference does it make now?" Mommy said.

"The difference is I'm tired."

"So go to sleep. We'll put down the lights for you," she said and did so. Then she turned the radio low.

Seeing that I had no other choice, I unbuttoned my blouse with my back to them and took it off. Then I kicked off my shoes, slipped out of my skirt and quickly slid under the blanket. It smelled as if it had been stored in a box of mothballs. I kept my back to them, but I knew they continued to dance, drink their gin, and whisper. I prayed to fall asleep quickly, and miraculously, maybe because I was so exhausted, I did.

But later in the night, my eyelids snapped open. I heard a soft moan and a subdued giggle, followed by the sound of bed springs squeaking. They thought I was asleep, so I didn't turn around. I had heard similar sounds before through the thin walls of our trailer. I knew what they meant then and I knew what they meant now.

How could Mommy let another man put his hands on her and be so intimate with her so soon after Daddy's death? I wondered. Didn't she still see Daddy in her mind, hear his voice, remember his lips on hers? Archie Marlin was so different from Daddy, too. He was a weakling. Couldn't Mommy wait until she met someone with whom she was really in love?

She was just confused, frustrated, afraid to be alone, I

69

told myself. Maybe it would all change when we found another place to live and she was happier with herself. Surely she wouldn't want to spend the rest of her life with a man like Archie Marlin.

I squeezed my eyelids tighter and pressed my ear to the pillow. I tried to think of something else, but their heavy breathing grew louder. Mommy moaned and then they grew silent. Moments later, Mommy slipped into bed beside me.

For now, at least, we were all supposed to pretend I heard and knew nothing. In the morning she would be here in bed with me and Archie Marlin would be in his.

It was a sad way to start a new life . . . lying to each other.

We left the motel as soon as we were all washed and dressed the next morning. In the daylight, the motel looked seedier. Even Mommy commented. Archie laughed it off, saying, "Any port in a storm. I've slept in lots worse."

"I believe that," I muttered. If either of them heard it, they didn't react. We stopped for breakfast off Route 95 north of Richmond and then continued. I saw the Capitol building in the distance from the highway, but we didn't stop in Washington, D.C., to do any of the sightseeing Mommy had promised. Nor did we go to Baltimore or any city along the way. It was apparent that Mommy and Archie Marlin wanted to get us to Provincetown as soon as possible. I began to think about the family I was about to meet.

I knew very little, of course, but I did know that Daddy had a younger brother who lived on the Cape with his family and that Daddy's family had been in the lobster business for a long time. Daddy's father was retired and he and my grandmother lived in a house too big for just the two of them. That was all I knew. When I asked Mommy how many children Daddy's younger brother had, Mommy said she remembered he had twins, a boy and a girl. Another child had been born after

70

she and Daddy left Provincetown. She couldn't remember if the third child was a boy or a girl, but she did say that she thought the twins were about my age, maybe a year older.

"Daddy's brother got married before you and Daddy?" I asked.

"I think so. Maybe. I don't remember. Please, Melody, don't flood me with questions I can't answer. You'll get all your answers when you get to Provincetown."

"But . . . well, how much younger than Daddy is his brother?"

"A year or so," she said. "He's different," she added.

"What do you mean?"

"You'll see," she said and refused to do anything but leave it at that.

With all this family mystery looming ahead me, I couldn't help being nervous. Mommy had obviously told them about Daddy's death. Was his parents' grudge over? How come, after all these years, we were finally going to see them?

When I pushed Mommy about why we were finally going to see Daddy's family, she sighed deeply and said, "It's what your father would want now, I'm sure."

I told myself that must be true and I must be strong and do what I could to make things right again among all of us.

"You know," Archie Marlin said as we headed into Massachusetts, "I just realized I've never been to the Cape."

"How is that possible?" I asked dryly.

Mommy flashed her eyes at me, but Archie widened his smile. "I'm not one for sailing or fishing," he said.

"But I thought you went riverrafting," I followed quickly.

"That's not sailing or fishing. That's just a thrill," he replied.

"Cape Cod has its charms," Mommy said, "but the people can be hard. The ocean makes them that way."

"It didn't make you hard," Archie said lustily.

71

I turned my attention back to the scenery flying by. That night we slept in a much nicer motel. We stayed in a suite and I had the sofa bed all to myself. I was able to wash my hair and shower, too. We ate dinner at the motel and I returned to the room while Mommy and Archie remained in the lounge listening to music and drinking. They stumbled in hours later, giggling and whispering. I pretended to be asleep as they clumsily made their way into the bedroom and shut the door.

Even though the conditions were better, I had a harder time falling asleep. Now that we would be in Provincetown the very next day, and meeting Daddy's family, I had a small trembling inside. Where was my new home to be? I felt like a balloon, floating, bouncing, carried this way and that by the winds of Mommy's and Archie Marlin's fancy. Maybe we didn't have all that much back in Sewell, but now I had nothing: not a friend, not a familiar sight, no one in whom to confide. I had never felt so alone. I could squeeze my eyelids shut until they ached, but I couldn't close out the fears that kept me tossing and turning, fretting in and out of nightmares until the first light of morning streaked through the motel room curtains.

Mommy and Archie slept very late. I washed and dressed and sat reading a visitor's guide, wondering if at least we could do some sightseeing. Finally, tired of being shut up in the stuffy room, I went for a walk around the motel. By the time I returned, Mommy and Archie were awake. We went for breakfast. They were both very subdued, they hardly talked and their eyelids drooped.

"Are we going to do some sightseeing before we go on to Provincetown?"

Archie groaned.

"On the way back," Mommy said quickly. "We want to get to the Cape as early as possible today."

"I thought we were exploring new places," I muttered.

"Oh Melody, please. No complaints today. I'm afraid I had a little too much to drink last night," she said.

72

I said nothing. After breakfast, we moved mutely, repacking the car and getting in for the drive. I saw many good views of the ocean, especially when we crossed the Cape Cod Canal. It was a beautiful warm day. The sailboats and fishing trollers looked painted on the blue water. As I smelled the salty air, I had the funniest feeling, as if I were truly returning home. Perhaps I was experiencing what Daddy would have felt if he were alive and with me on this journey. I would learn more about him by going to this place. I began to overcome my nervousness and fear. In a way, Daddy would be with me.

Mommy fell asleep as we continued our journey up Route 6. The miles slid by like a long ribbon with no end. When the road signs indicated we were getting closer to Provincetown, a tiny charge of excitement passed through my heart. How could Mommy sleep through this? After all, she was going home, too. Finally, Archie, who had been quiet himself, announced we were close to the tip of the Cape, Provincetown. Mommy stirred, opening her eyes and stretching.

I caught sight of the dunes. "It looks like the desert."

Then Pilgrim's Monument came into view and Mommy told me what it was.

"The pilgrims supposedly landed here first," Mommy said. "The blue bloods make a big deal of that."

"Blue bloods?" I asked.

"People who trace their family history back to the Mayflower. Your father's family," she added disdainfully. "They think that makes them better than the rest of us."

"Is that why you and Daddy left?"

"That among other things," Mommy said and sewed her lips shut.

"Where do we go?" Archie asked.

"Turn left," Mommy ordered.

"Are they expecting us today, Mommy?"

"Yes," she said. "Jacob should be home. I see the tide is in."

"How can you tell?" I asked.

"The waves are breaking on the beach up at the beach grass. See?"

I nodded.

"Fishing boats go out and come back at high tide," Mommy explained. "I remember that much, but don't ask me too much more," she said quickly. It was as if it were painful for her to remember.

Archie followed her directions. We moved slowly through the narrow street, on both sides of which were small souvenir shops, boutiques, restaurants advertising fresh lobster dinners, and taverns with names like The Buccaneer and Mast Head. Here and there were signs advertising bed and breakfast accommodations. The buildings, some of which looked very old, were made from gray cedar shingles. All had Vacancy signs dangling in the breeze.

Mommy explained that it wasn't the season yet, so the tourists really weren't here. "These small streets get so crowded in the summer, it's wall-to-wall people."

"Yeah, just like the Vegas strip," Archie commented.

"Turn here," Mommy directed. We went east on an even narrower street that had small Cape Cod houses on both sides, none with much more than a couple of a hundred feet of rough-looking grass in front. But some had flowers. I saw one with a lilac bush towering as high as its roof. As we rolled along, I heard Mommy mumble, "It seems like a hundred years ago, but not much has changed."

Suddenly, there were no more houses, just a stretch of dunes. I thought we would stop, but Mommy told Archie to continue following the road. It turned north, and then, on the right, just a few hundred yards or so farther, a house appeared. I could see the beach and the ocean not too far away. A flock of terns circled over something on the sand.

"There it is," Mommy said, nodding at the house. There was a light brown pickup truck parked in the gravel driveway, and in front of that a dark blue, four-

74

door automobile with its right rear end jacked up. A tall, lean man with hair Daddy's color was bending over a tire. He didn't turn to look at us, even when we stopped near the driveway.

"That is your uncle Jacob," Mommy said softly.

He finally glanced up. I saw the resemblances in his face, especially in his chin and cheekbones, but he was much leaner in build and he looked older than Daddy, not younger. Even from this distance I could see the deep lines at the corners of his eyes. He had a much darker complexion than Daddy's had been. He stared a moment and then went back to his tire as if he had no interest in who we were or why we were here.

"Should I pull in?" Archie asked.

"Yes," Mommy replied with a deep sigh. "Well, Melody, it's time to meet your family."

5
❦

The Only Mother I Had

Archie slowly pulled into the driveway. Uncle Jacob didn't turn around again until we came to a full stop. Then he stood up and gestured emphatically for Archie to back up.

"I need the room to work here," he explained.

"Sorry," Archie said. He backed up a good ten feet and we all got out of the car. Uncle Jacob, his back to us, continued to work on removing the flat tire.

"Hello Jacob," Mommy said. He nodded without turning around.

"I'll be a while with this," he finally replied, still not looking our way. "Go on inside. Sara's been waiting on you all morning. Thought you were supposed to be here last night." He groaned as he turned the nut on the flat tire. The muscles in his long arms tightened and the muscles in his neck bulged with the effort. The nut loosened and he relaxed again.

"It took longer than we expected," Mommy said.

Uncle Jacob grunted.

Mommy looked at me and then at Archie, who had his lips twisted in disgust. She put her hand on my shoulder and guided me toward the front door. The house was a Cape Codder with a widow's walk that faced the ocean. The trim on the railings and shutters was a Wedgwood blue, but like the cedar siding, it was faded by the salt air. There was a short, narrow cobblestone walkway to the front door.

On the windows were dainty eggshell white curtains, and on the sills were flower boxes full of tulips and daffodils. A bird feeder dangled from the roof of the small porch and a tiny sparrow fluttered its wings nearby, cautiously waiting for us to pass.

Mommy tapped gently on the door. Then, after a moment, she tapped again, a bit harder.

"Just go on in," Uncle Jacob called from the driveway. "She won't hear you. She's in the kitchen, I'm sure."

Mommy turned the knob and we entered. A small entryway led us to the living room on our right. A massive brick fire place consumed most of the far wall. There was a bluish-gray throw rug on the tongue-and-groove floor. A deep-cushioned sofa and the overstuffed chair beside it were the only things that matched. The rest of the furnishings were antiques, which included a well worn rocker, two small pine tables at the ends of the sofa, an old sewing table in the corner, and lamps made of cranberry glass and milk glass. On the mantle were framed photos. Mounted on a dark blue board and hanging over the fireplace, was a swordfish that looked at least seven feet long. Its glass eye seemed to turn toward us as we entered.

"Sara?" Mommy called. "We're here."

We heard a pan being dropped into a metal sink and a moment later, my Aunt Sara appeared in the doorway to the kitchen.

A tall woman, maybe an inch or so taller than Mommy, she wore a long, flowing light blue skirt that made her look all legs. Over her skirt she had a plain white apron, on which she wiped her hands. Her

77

blouse had frilled sleeves and pearl buttons closed almost to the top. The collar parted just enough to reveal her very pronounced collarbone and a thin gold chain that held a gold locket. Her chestnut brown hair hung down over her shoulders. Through it were delicate streaks of gray. Aunt Sara wore no makeup to brighten her pale complexion, and she wore no jewelry but the locket.

She might once have been pretty, but the silvery webs at her temples were deep and her eyes looked a dull, dark brown. The darkness spread to the puffiness beneath her eyes, too. She had a small nose and high cheekbones with gracefully full lips, but her face was thin, almost gaunt.

"Hello, Sara," Mommy said.

"Hello, Haille," Aunt Sara replied without changing her expression. The way Mommy and Aunt Sara gazed at each other made my stomach turn. It was as if they were not only looking at each other across this room, but across time and great distance. Neither made an attempt to hug or even shake hands. A deep silence lingered for a confusing moment, making me feel as if I were floundering in the world of adult quicksand.

What sort of welcome was this? I stood there, full of a thousand anxieties, butterflies panicking in my chest.

"This is my friend, Richard," Mommy said feeling she had to explain Archie's presence first, I suppose. "He was kind enough to drive us here from West Virginia."

Aunt Sara nodded but her eyes quickly went to me with greater interest, her face brightening in anticipation.

"And this is Melody," Mommy added, putting her hands on my shoulders. Aunt Sara's gaze was so penetrating I thought she could look right through me. A small smile, almost impossible to notice, formed at the corners of her mouth.

"Yes," she said nodding as if I were exactly the way she imagined I would be. "She's about Laura's size and height, only Laura's hair was darker and she never kept it that long," she said, sadness making her face long and hollow eyed.

"I'm so sorry about all that," Mommy said softly.

"Yes," Aunt Sara said, still staring at me. I looked to Mommy. What was she sorry about? Who was Laura? Apparently, she knew more than she had admitted about Daddy's family.

"I bet you're hungry," Aunt Sara said to me, a smile returning to her lips. I smiled back, but my stomach was tied in so many knots I didn't think I could ever put food in it. "I've got a chicken roasting. Cary will be home from school soon with May. They're both very excited about your coming here." She turned to Mommy and Archie. "In the meantime, I have some clams steamed for you."

"Oh good. In the years since I've been here, I've never had any good as yours, Sara."

"I don't do anything more with clams than anyone else around here does," she said modestly. "You scrub them and drop them into a clam kettle with just enough water to cover them. No mystery about it," Aunt Sara said, her voice suddenly harder, sterner.

"Maybe it's just the clams here," Mommy said. She seemed awkward and uncomfortable under Aunt Sara's icy glare.

"That's it for sure," Archie said. Aunt Sara raised her eyebrows and looked at him as if she had just noticed his presence.

"Well now, come into the dining room and make yourselves to home," she said.

An antique trestle table stretched nearly the whole length of the dining room. It had a captain's chair at each end and four straight chairs in a perfect line on each side. Lying at the head of the table was a leather-bound Bible. There was a small pine table in a corner of the room with a vase of yellow roses on it. On the wall was an oil painting: a seascape with a lone sailboat moving toward

79

the horizon. I looked closer and saw what looked like a ray of bright sunshine pouring through an opening in the overcast sky with a godlike finger in the center of the ray of light. The finger pointed at the lone sailboat.

"Please take a seat," Aunt Sara said. "That's Jacob's chair," she added and nodded toward the captain's chair at the end of the table where the Bible lay. Obviously, no one else was permitted to sit in it. "Everyone like cranberry juice?"

"It makes for a great mix with vodka," Archie quipped.

"Pardon?" Aunt Sara said. Mommy gave him a reprimanding look.

"What?" He recovered quickly. "Oh, sure we like it. Thank you." Aunt Sara hurried back to the kitchen.

"Who's Laura, Mommy?" I asked. "Why didn't you tell me about her?"

"It's too sad," Mommy whispered and brought her finger to her lips. "Not now, honey."

Aunt Sara reappeared carrying a pitcher filled with cranberry juice on a tray with three tall glasses, each with two ice cubes. She gave us each a glass and started to reach for the pitcher.

"Let me pour that," Archie volunteered. Aunt Sara nodded to him. She gazed at me again, drinking me in for a long moment, her eyes twinkling with pleasure and approval. It made me feel uncomfortable to be scrutinized so closely. I looked away.

"Do you like clams, dear?" she asked.

"I guess so," I said. "I don't remember eating them."

"She loves them," Mommy said quickly.

"Laura loved them so," Aunt Sara said. She sighed. "I'll go get them."

She returned to the kitchen.

"Mommy?" I said, pleading for information.

"Just wait, Melody. Let everyone get to know everyone before you start asking all your questions." She looked at Archie. "She's always full of questions."

"You don't have to tell me." He gulped down some cranberry juice. "Hey, this is good."

"Cranberries are a big thing here," Mommy said. "I'd like a penny for every one I harvested. I'd be rich."

"You're gonna be rich," Archie promised. Mommy's smile warmed and she turned to me. "Isn't this a nice house, honey? There's a beach right behind it and a dock, too." She took a deep breath and closed her eyes. "I forgot how refreshing the ocean air could be," she said, which I thought was funny. She had never enjoyed our trips to the ocean as much as Daddy had.

"Yeah, it sure cleans the coal dust out of your lungs," Archie said.

Aunt Sara brought in pretty blue-and-white china soup bowls and set them in front of us. Then she brought in the kettle of clams and a bowl of melted butter.

"Please help yourselves," she said. Archie dipped his hand into the kettle quickly and brought out a clam. He plucked the meat with his thumb and forefinger and dipped it in the butter and sucked it down quickly.

"Great," he said.

"Use your fork," Mommy instructed as quietly as she could.

"What? Oh. Sure." He took a handful of clams out of the kettle and dropped them into his bowl, this time digging into the clams with his fork.

Aunt Sara smiled quickly and then looked as if she were at a loss as to what to do next.

"Aren't you having any, Sara?" Mommy asked.

"No. I'm fine. Go on. You eat, Haille." She looked at me again, stabbing me with her penetrating gaze. I nervously reached into the kettle and scooped up a few clams. I put them into my bowl and picked out the meat of one with my fork. Aunt Sara watched my every move, approving with a little nod every gesture I made. I felt like a specimen under a microscope. I looked at Mommy.

She didn't seem to notice or care about the way Aunt

81

Sara was looking at me. "These clams are as wonderful as I remember them. It's been a long time."

"Yes," Aunt Sara said. After a deep sigh, she finally sat in her chair. "Was it a hard trip?"

"Naw," Archie said. "Some rain along the way is all."

"We had an unusually cold winter this year," Aunt Sara said. She looked around. "This house never seemed to warm up."

"How do you heat it?" Archie asked.

"Fireplace, and kerosene stoves. It's an old house, but we've been here ever since."

"Ever since what?" Archie asked.

"Ever since Jacob and I got married," she said. She looked at Mommy a moment. "You haven't changed all that much, Haille. You're still so pretty."

"Thank you, Sara."

"Melody has inherited your best features," Aunt Sara added, gazing at me again. I couldn't help blushing.

"Yes," Mommy said. "Everyone says so."

"Cary, he takes after Jacob, but May looks more like my side of the family. Laura . . . Laura was special," Aunt Sara added softly. Her eyes grew glassy and her gaze grew faraway. Then, suddenly, as if realizing we were there, she turned to me again and smiled. "Are you a good student?"

"Yes, ma'am."

"She's a *very* good student," Mommy said. "All A's."

"Just like Laura," Aunt Sara said. She shook her head. "Cary isn't like his twin sister was. He gets by, but he's not much for being shut up in a classroom. He's more like Jacob," she said. "Give him something to do outside and he'll be happy, no matter how cold it is or how much it's raining. When the Logan men get busy, the world could come to an end around them and they wouldn't know it."

"I know," Mommy said.

Aunt Sara sighed again, so deeply I thought she might shatter like thin china right before our eyes. "I'm sorry about Chester. Might as well tell you that before Jacob comes in. He won't want me speaking about him."

I looked at Mommy. Why wouldn't Daddy's brother permit anyone to speak about him even now, after he was dead? Mommy nodded, as if she had no trouble understanding.

"So how old's Cary now?" she asked, deliberately changing the topic.

"He's sixteen. May was ten last month."

"I bet she's a good student," Mommy said, struggling for conversation. Aunt Sara raised her eyebrows.

"Yes, but she goes to the special school, you know. Cary sees she gets there all right and home all right. He's devoted to her. I think more so since Laura . . . since Laura's been gone," she said.

Again, I looked at Mommy. She shifted her eyes away.

"You don't like the clams, dear?" Aunt Sara asked me, poised to be disappointed.

"What? Oh, yes," I said and dug my fork into another.

"How are Samuel and Olivia?" Mommy asked Aunt Sara. I knew those were my grandparents so I stopped eating again to listen.

"They both suffer from arthritis now and then, but otherwise they're well. I told them you were coming," she said, almost as an afterthought.

"Oh?"

Aunt Sara said nothing more about them. The topic disappeared as quickly as a popped soap bubble, but neither Mommy nor Aunt Sara seemed unhappy about that. I wanted to know more. They had never seen me. Were they curious about me as I was about them?

The door opened and closed. Uncle Jacob appeared, a rag in his hands. The shape of his chin and mouth resembled Daddy's, but he had a longer, sharper nose and larger ears. His eyes were more hazel than green.

"Clams are sweeter this year," he said.

"They're great," Archie said. Uncle Jacob finally considered him.

"This is my friend Richard, Jacob. He drove us here."

83

Uncle Jacob just nodded and then looked at me.

"She's not as tall as I thought she'd be," he said. The way he said it made me feel as if I had failed at growing properly.

"Melody, this is your Uncle Jacob," Mommy said, her eyes on him.

"Hello," I said, my voice cracking.

He didn't smile. He wiped his hands and stared at me. "Plenty of time for us all to meet later," he declared. "I got to do some work on the boat right now. Sara, send Cary down as soon as he's home." He left through the rear of the house.

"It's very important to look after the boat," Aunt Sara explained, with another quick smile. "Well," she continued, "I imagine you plan on staying the night, Haille."

"No," Mommy said quickly. "We have a tight schedule."

"Oh."

Why had we come so far if we were going to leave so quickly? I wondered. Mommy had talked about showing me Provincetown. Before I could ask, we heard the front door again.

"That should be Cary and May," Aunt Sara said. A few moments later, my cousins appeared in the dining room doorway.

Cary was tall and did indeed take after his father. He had the same dark complexion as Uncle Jacob only he had a more sensitive face with much softer features. He had green eyes like Daddy, but because his hair was darker, almost coal black, his emerald eyes seemed brighter. He wore his hair rather long, almost to his shoulders. He was dressed in jeans and a dark blue shirt with the sleeves rolled up to his elbows.

Beside him, still clinging to his hand, was my cousin May. She was small, birdlike for ten, diminutive except for her round, very bright hazel eyes. Her hair, the same chestnut shade as Aunt Sara's, was cut short in a pixie style. She wore a light blue dress with an embroidered

84

bodice and saddle shoes. Her feet were so small, they made her look like a doll. She smiled, but Cary kept a very serious expression on his face, his gaze quickly moving from Archie to Mommy to me. When he fixed his eyes on me, I thought his look softened.

"Well, now, say hello to everyone," Aunt Sara said. "This is your aunt Haille, her friend Richard, and your cousin Melody."

Cary immediately turned to May and began to move his hands. She watched him and nodded when he stopped. Then she turned to us and said, "Hello." She stretched the syllables so that it sounded mechanical.

I couldn't help my look of surprise, but I saw it displeased Cary.

"Yes, she's deaf," my cousin said sharply to me.

"Well, ain't that a shame," Archie muttered. Cary threw him an angry look that, were it a knife, would have cut off Archie's head.

"How was school today, May?" Aunt Sara asked her, signing as she spoke.

May proudly held up a paper with a bright gold star at the top.

"She got a hundred on the spelling test," Cary boasted.

"That's nice, dear," Aunt Sara said. She seemed a bit more uncomfortable with the hand movements than her son was. "Your father wants you to go right down to the dock, Cary," she said. He nodded. "You can visit with everyone at dinner."

Cary turned immediately and signed something to May. She nodded and then looked at me. He glanced at me once more before heading out back.

"Go up and change your clothes, dear," Aunt Sara signed to May. The young girl nodded and signed something back before hurrying off. "Cary takes such good care of her," Aunt Sara remarked with a sigh.

"I didn't know she was deaf," Mommy said softly. "I don't think Chester knew either."

85

"Yes, she was born deaf. Seems like that should have been enough of a burden for us, but then . . . there was Laura."

A heavy pall fell over the table.

Archie couldn't stand it. "Why don't we go into the town and see the sights before dinner, Haille?"

Mommy nodded.

"Can we take May along?" I asked Aunt Sara.

"Oh, I don't think we should," Mommy said quickly. "We're still strangers to her."

"Your mother is right, dear. It's a little soon," Aunt Sara said. She got up and started to clear off the table.

"Let me help you, Aunt Sara," I said. She turned with surprise.

"Why, thank you, dear, but I can manage fine. Why don't you go and get your things and I'll show you your room now."

"My room?"

Aunt Sara smiled and went into the kitchen. I turned to Mommy.

"My room? What's wrong with her, Mommy? Didn't you say we weren't staying overnight?"

"Let's go outside, Melody," Mommy said in a whisper.

I followed her and Archie out. He headed for the trunk of the car.

"Let me talk to her first, Richard," Mommy told him.

He paused and shrugged. Then he dug a cigarette from his pocket and leaned against the car.

"What's going on, Mommy?"

"Nothing terrible," she replied quickly. "Isn't it pretty here? Look at the view of the ocean you get from the house, and it's not too far from the town, is it?"

"Mommy, what is happening?" I demanded.

"Now just listen carefully, Melody, and don't go into a tantrum." She glanced over at Archie. He looked at his watch. "Let's take a little walk by ourselves," Mommy suggested. She started away. I followed, but I was

86

stretched like a tight wire inside, so taut I thought I might snap in two.

"It really wasn't right for the family to be separated for so long," Mommy began. "It wasn't right that you never met your cousins until now, and it certainly wasn't right for you never to have met your grandparents," she recited. It sounded like something she had memorized.

"So? I thought that was why you wanted us to come here first," I said.

"It was. It is. I mean, yes." She took a deep breath and pressed her lips together. Tears came to her eyes.

"What's wrong, Mommy? What is it?"

"Oh Melody, you know that I love you, that I will always love you."

"I know that, Mommy."

"You know that even though I love you, I always thought it was a mistake for me to have had a child so early in my life. I want to warn you about that," she said sternly. "Don't have children until you're at least thirty-five."

"Thirty-five!"

"Yes. If you're smart, you'll remember that. Anyway, you know that I've tried to be a good mother. I know I'm not the best mother."

"I'm not complaining, Mommy," I said. There were burning tears coming to my eyes now, too. "We'll be all right."

"Oh, I know we will, honey, but first I have to do things. I have to try, don't I? You wouldn't want me to feel I never tried when I had the chance. You wouldn't want me frustrated and shut up in another place like Sewell, would you? Because if I'm not happy, Melody, I can't make you happy, can I? Can I?" she repeated.

"No," I said. I tried to take a deep breath, but my lungs felt as if ice had entered them and shriveled them with constricting pain.

"Good. So you understand why I've got to go places and meet people and do auditions and learn things," she said.

87

"You already told me all this, Mommy."

"I know, but . . . well, it's not the kind of life I can put you through right now. You're still in school and you need stability. You need friends and boyfriends and to go to parties and—"

"So, why can't I do that wherever we are, Mommy?"

"Because I'm not going to be anyplace for a while, maybe a long while. I'll have to travel around. If I get an opportunity, I have to pick right up and go. You can't turn down good opportunities, not at my age," she emphasized. "And what would life be like for you under such circumstances, huh?"

"But Mommy—"

"Listen, honey. Imagine just having made some new friends or starting out with a new boyfriend, and me coming home and saying, we're leaving tomorrow. You know now how hard that was this time, how terrible you felt? How would it be feeling that all the time? And then having to sleep in cheap motels and eat on the road and . . . everything. After a while you're just going to hate me, and then I would hate myself, and then I wouldn't try to be someone," she explained. "We would both be unhappy."

She smiled. "I don't want you to be unhappy, honey."

"What are we going to do, Mommy?" I asked and held my breath.

"Well, now here's where everything worked out for us. After your daddy died, I called Uncle Jacob and Aunt Sara and told them, of course, and then I explained what I was going to do with my life now. It was Aunt Sara who suggested it."

"Suggested what, Mommy?"

"Suggested you stay here while I'm off making a career change," she said. "She's very happy to have you and this is a wonderful place to live. You'll make so many new and interesting friends, I'm sure."

"You can't leave me here." I shook my head.

"Just for a while, honey. I'll call constantly and I'll

come back for you as soon as I'm established some place. But for now I've got to go off with Archie and I know you're not crazy about traveling with us."

"You mean Richard," I said dryly. "And I know he's not happy about having me travel with you."

"It's not because of Richard."

"Are you going to marry him, Mommy?"

"Of course not," she said, but not with a great deal of firmness. "Anyway," she said, gesturing toward the house, "this will be fine for a while. You'll be staying with family."

"I don't want to stay here, Mommy. I don't want to be away from you," I moaned.

"Oh, you won't be, not for long anyway. I promise." She stroked my hair and smiled and then kissed my forehead. "I just need this chance, honey, and I can't go off and get it worrying about you, too. It wouldn't be fair to you. I'd neglect you even worse than I have in the past. And you're so very smart. You understand, don't you? I have no fear that you'll do well here, too. Everyone likes you, Melody."

I lowered my head slowly like a flag of defeat and stared at my feet. A southern breeze blew, caressing my cheek, making strands of my hair dance around my face. I heard the cry of nearby terns and the roar of the ocean.

Daddy was the glue that had held our little family together. Now that he was gone, we were coming apart.

"I'd rather have stayed home with Papa George and Mama Arlene, Mommy."

"I know. I thought of that, but Papa George is a very sick man. Mama Arlene can't be responsible for a young girl, too. It wouldn't be fair to dump you on her, honey."

I looked up sharply.

"So instead you want to dump me here?"

"No, Melody. Living with your own family for a while isn't the same thing as dumping you some place, is it?"

89

"These people . . . I don't know them, Mommy, and they don't know me."

"An even better reason to stay with them, Melody. You should get to know them, right? Aren't I right about that?" She waited for the answer she wanted.

"I don't know, maybe. But why didn't we ever speak to them before? Why was Daddy so upset with them?"

"Because they didn't want him to marry me, Melody. I told you. They looked down on me because I was an orphan, adopted. I wasn't one of their bluebloods and your grandparents—your father's parents—wanted him to marry someone else, someone they had chosen. He refused. Chester Logan fell in love with *me* and we got married. Then they wouldn't talk to him and he wouldn't talk to them. Now everyone realizes how foolish they were, I'm sure. They want to make it up to your father, but it's too late for that. The only way they could make up for their bitterness and unpleasantness is to care for you. That's why they were so anxious to do it and why I agreed. I only wish you'd see the logic in it and let me leave with a happy heart.

"Because if I feel happy about you, I will be able to concentrate on my new career and I'll be able to do things for us faster, Melody," she added.

"What are you going to do, Mommy? You don't even have a specific plan."

"Sure I do. I'm going to be a model and an actress," she said firmly. Then she laughed and spun on her heels. "Did you ever see anyone who is more qualified, anyone prettier?"

"No, Mommy."

"Won't it be wonderful seeing me in magazines or in the movies? Can you imagine telling your friends that's your mother?" She laughed and twirled her hair. She was beautiful. Maybe she would become a model and be in magazines. If I went into a tantrum and stopped her from going without me, she would blame me for failing, I thought. I didn't want Mommy to hate me.

90

I looked back at the house. Archie paced behind the car impatiently. At least I wouldn't have to be with him any longer. I was the eternal cockeyed optimist, always looking for a rainbow after any sorrowful storm.

"Well?" Mommy said. "Will you stay with the family a while? Will you, Melody?"

"If that's what you want me to do, Mommy," I said in a tired, defeated voice. She clapped her hands together.

"Oh, thank you, honey. Thank you. Thank you for giving me my chance. I won't let you down. I promise, honey."

I nodded and took a deep breath. When I looked at the house again, I saw May come out and look our way. She had a ball and paddle and began to play with them, her eyes trained on me and Mommy.

"What happened to Laura, Mommy?"

"She went sailing one day with a boy and they got caught in a storm."

"She drowned in the ocean?"

Mommy nodded.

"We didn't find out about it until months afterward. Daddy decided to call your uncle then, but he still wouldn't speak to Chester. This house has seen a lot of sadness, just like ours. But they'll be lucky for a while," Mommy added. I looked up at her.

"Why?"

"They'll have you," she said. She put her arm around me and we started back toward the driveway. Archie looked up expectantly and Mommy nodded. Then he hurried to the trunk to unload my bags.

"What about the rest of my things, Mommy? I don't have much."

"I'll get in touch with Arlene and see about having them shipped up here. Don't worry," she said. May was still watching us with great curiosity.

Mommy noticed the girl. "Hello, honey."

May smiled at her but turned quickly to me. Then she

thrust her hand at mine and seized my fingers tightly, tugging me to go someplace with her.

"Go on, honey," Mommy said. "Richard and I will see to your things."

"But . . ." May pulled again. I let her lead me away. She quickened her pace when we reached the sand and soon I was running alongside her.

"Where are we going?" I cried, for a moment forgetting her deafness. We were heading toward the dock and the ocean. First, we had to climb to the top of a dune covered with scrub pine. The sand gave way beneath my feet. It was hard to run on the dunes, and before long, I felt my calf muscles ache. Little May didn't seem to have the least bit of difficulty. She was as light as air, remaining ahead of me all the way to the crest of the small sandy hill.

When we reached it, I paused to look at the vast ocean. In the distance two fishing boats trolled toward shore and farther out, a sailboat gracefully glided over the waves, its white sail fluttering. Off to my right there were shacks along the dunes. Above us, a flock of Canadian geese flew north in formation against a deep blue sky dappled with smoke-blue puffs of clouds. The sight was invigorating and the fresh sea air seemed to wash the sadness from my heart. This, I thought, was once my father's playground. And now, for a while at least, it would be mine.

May tugged on my hand and pointed toward the dock.

"Car . . . ry," she said. "Come on."

I laughed and followed her down the dune. We continued to run, my chest heaving. Finally we slowed to a walk as we reached the dock.

My uncle's lobster boat bobbed gently in the water. It was a white and gray boat, and although it looked old, it looked very clean and well kept. The boat was named *Laura* and the name had been recently repainted on its side. At first we saw no one, but then Cary came out of the cabin with a pail and a brush in his hands. He had his shirt off and didn't see us immediately. May called up to him.

"Car-ry."

When he saw us standing on the dock, he immediately put down his pail and brush so he could sign to May. Whatever he was telling her, he was telling her emphatically. He looked angry, too.

"Is anything wrong?" I asked. The falling sun gleamed off his shiny brown skin. He looked muscular and hard and wore a silver necklace I hadn't noticed before.

"She knows she can't come down here by herself," he said.

"She's not by herself. She's with me," I replied.

"You're a landlubber," he snapped. "It's the same as if she were by herself." He signed again and May turned and started back toward the house. I stared up at Cary.

"She only wanted to show me," I said.

"She knows better. Take her home," he ordered and picked up his pail and brush. Turning his back on me, he returned to what he had been doing. I fumed for a moment and then hurried to catch up to May, who was walking much more slowly with her head down. I grabbed her hand when I caught up with her and she smiled.

"It's all right," I said. She tilted her head. She had beautiful hazel eyes, bejeweled with flecks of blue, green, and gold on the soft brown. "Your brother shouldn't have gotten so nasty," I added, but she looked confused and I felt frustrated. I was speaking loud, as if that mattered. It made me feel stupid. I glanced back once and saw Cary looking after us. Behind him, the sky was turning a dusky lavender.

"If it's so dangerous around here," I muttered, "why live here?"

I pounded my feet into the sand and clung to May's hand as we returned to the house. When we arrived, I found Mommy and Archie waiting by the car. May released my hand and ran into the house.

"Where did you go, honey?" Mommy asked.

"Just for a walk to the dock to see the lobster boat, but that was apparently off limits for May," I said. "Cary isn't very nice."

"Oh, I'm sure it's just because you two don't know each other yet," Mommy said.

"Haille," Archie said raising his eyebrows.

"Honey," Mommy said stepping closer so she could take my hand. "Archie and I think we should start out now so we can get back down to Boston. He has someone for me to meet there tonight."

"You're leaving now? But what about dinner?"

"We're just going to grab something on the highway," she said.

"Didn't you want to look at the town and—"

"Oh I know this town," she said laughing. "Don't forget how long I lived here."

"But . . ." I looked at the house and then back toward the ocean. "Don't you want to talk with Uncle Jacob?"

"I think he'll be happy to avoid it right now," she said. "We put your things in your room. It's a very nice room, honey, nicer than what you had in the trailer. The window looks out on the ocean. Aunt Sara is going to see to it you get enrolled in the school and the school will get all your records from West Virginia easily enough. I've already signed the papers I needed to sign to give Aunt Sara the authority," Mommy added.

"When?" I asked, astounded at how much had really been done already.

"Um, just now. Aunt Sara found out what had to be done. She's very excited about having you."

Archie got into the car and started the engine. My heart began to beat wildly like a jungle drum.

"Mommy?"

"Now don't make this any harder than it has to be, honey. I'll be calling you in a few days to tell you where I am and what I've been doing, and before you know it, I'll be coming back for you."

94

"Time ticks," Archie called.

"Can't you stay a little longer?" I pleaded. My heart was doing flip-flops.

"A little longer isn't going to make any difference to you, but it will make a lot of difference to us because we have to drive so far, honey. Please."

She hugged me, but I kept my arms at my sides. Then she kissed me quickly on the forehead.

"I don't have to tell you to be a good girl. I know you will be. See you soon," she added and turned toward the car.

"Mommy!"

I ran to her and hugged her tightly, clinging to her, clinging to the only life I had known, clinging to the memories of our laughter and tears. Maybe she wasn't the best of all mothers, but she was the only mother I had, and there were nice times, too. There were the picnics and the dinners, the Christmases and birthdays. All I could remember now was being a little girl and clinging to her hand as we walked through the streets of Sewell. Everyone looked at us; Mommy was so beautiful and I was so proud.

"Melody," she whispered. *"Please,* honey."

I let her go and backed away.

She smiled. "I'll call you soon." She walked quickly around the car to get in.

Archie smiled at me. "Don't do anything I wouldn't do, kid," he said and winked.

"There's not much you wouldn't do," I replied. He laughed.

"Going to miss you, princess. I got no one to be my gopher." He laughed and backed the car out of the driveway. I took a step forward.

Mommy turned as they pulled away, waving.

Another picture to press down into my memory. I watched as the car disappeared down the street. I stood there, still in disbelief.

Then I heard the door open behind me and I turned to

see Aunt Sara nervously wiping her hands on her apron. "Laura always liked to help set the table. Would you like to help?"

I nodded and she smiled.

"I thought so."

She went back inside. I lowered my head and followed. I felt like someone who'd been cast off a boat. I was searching desperately for a lifesaving raft.

6
&

Laura's Things

Aunt Sara had the dinner dishes on the kitchen counter and the silverware piled next to them. She folded linen napkins. The kitchen was as long as it was wide, with pots and pans hanging on the wall, two metal sinks side by side, a large cast-iron stove, and a refrigerator. There was a pantry off to the left. The late-afternoon sunlight poured through the large window on the west end, providing the only light.

"I'm putting out my better china tonight," she said smiling as she meticulously folded the napkins. "Your arrival is a special occasion. Set out five places," she told me. "You'll sit directly across from May and next to me. That's where Laura used to sit."

"Where is May?" I asked.

"May went up to her room, probably to start on her homework. She's a diligent student. Laura taught her that."

"She took me to the dock and Cary yelled at her," I said.

Aunt Sara nodded. "He won't permit anyone else to take her near the water. He's afraid." She took a deep

97

breath and held her right palm against her heart. "We're all just a little more afraid," she muttered.

I gathered the dishes and brought them to the dining room. I felt I was sleepwalking. Was this really happening? Had Mommy truly gone and left me here?

When I returned to the kitchen to get the silverware and folded napkins, Aunt Sara was checking the chicken. Something simmered on the stove. Potatoes baked while pies cooled on the windowsill. The hustle and bustle in Aunt Sara's kitchen gave me a warm feeling. Everything smelled wonderful. I had been too nervous this morning to eat much of a breakfast, and except for the few clams I had nibbled when we first arrived, I had eaten very little all day.

"Laura loved to cook with me," Aunt Sara said as she worked. "While other girls her age were off giggling over boys, she was home, helping. She was always like that, even as a little girl. You never saw a more selfless person, worrying about everyone else before she worried about herself.

"You know what Jacob says?" She turned to me. "He says the angels must have been so jealous of her, God granted them their wish and took her to heaven sooner than planned."

She smiled, her face softened, her chin quivering. Tears glittered in her eyes.

"I'm sorry," I said. "I'm sorry I never got to meet her."

"Oh, yes. Wouldn't that have been wonderful?" She thought a moment and then sternly added, "You should have met."

I wanted to ask her why we hadn't, why this family had been so bitter and mean to each other, but I thought it might be the wrong time to bring up such questions.

She took a deep breath. "You better put out the silverware, dear."

After the table was set, Aunt Sara said she'd take me to

my room. "Your things are already there. I want to show you where to put them away and all that you can use, too."

"Use?" I wondered what she meant as I followed her up the short stairway leading to the second floor. The steps creaked and the railing shook as we ascended. At the top was a small landing.

"May's room and Cary's room are down that way," she said pointing right. Without windows, the hallway was dark. "Jacob's and my room is the last room on the left and your room, which was Laura's room, is right there." She pointed to the first door on the left. "That's the bathroom, of course," she added, curtly nodding at the doorway across from what was to be my room.

"Here you are." She stood back after opening the door. I gazed in slowly, shocked at what I found. The room was cluttered with things that had once belonged to my dead cousin. It looked as if she had just died yesterday. The walls were covered with her posters of rock and movie stars, the shelves crowded with stuffed animals and ceramic dolls. There was a collection of ceramic and pewter cats on one shelf. Below the shelves was a small table with a miniature tea set and a big doll in a chair.

It was a very pretty, cozy room, with pink wallpaper spotted white. There was a canopy bed, just like the bed Alice Morgan had, only the headboard didn't have a heart design. The bedding, comforter, and pillows all matched the mauve shade of the canopy, and at the center of the two fluffy pillows was a large, stuffed cat that looked almost real and very much like the one I had brought.

There was a vanity table with a large mirror and a matching dresser. In one corner was a desk and chair. An open notebook lay on the desk and beside it was a pile of school textbooks and what looked like library books.

Why weren't they ever returned? I wondered.

The sliding doors on the closet were open, so I could

99

see the garments hanging inside. On a hook next to the closet doorjamb was a pink terrycloth robe. The slippers were at the foot of the bed.

Two open windows, one on each side of the bed, faced the ocean. The breeze made the curtains flutter and wave. The scent of the sea air overpowered the vague, sweet perfume I smelled when first looking into the room.

"Isn't it beautiful?" Aunt Sara said.

"Yes."

"I want you to be comfortable here," she said. "Use anything you want and need. It would be a great joy to me to see you wearing one of those pretty dresses. Try one on," she said anxiously. "They look just your size."

I shook my head gently.

"I don't know if I should, Aunt Sara." Despite its recently lived-in appearance, the room felt more like a shrine to a dead girl.

"Of course you should," she said, her eyes full of panic because I had suggested otherwise. "That's why I wanted you to stay here. There's so much going to waste and now it won't. If Laura were standing right here beside us, she would say, 'Cousin Melody, use anything you want. Go on.' I can almost hear her saying that." She tilted her head as if to catch someone's voice in the breeze. "Can't you?" She wore a strange, soft smile.

I walked into the room and looked more closely at everything. On the desk was a pile of letters wrapped in a rubber band. The brushes and combs on the vanity table still had strands of dark brown hair twirled through them. On the top of the dresser was a framed picture of my cousin Laura standing at the front of the house holding a bouquet of yellow roses.

"That was her sweet sixteen picture," Aunt Sara explained. "Taken almost a year ago now. Laura and Cary's birthday is next month, you know."

Cary would be seventeen. "Is Cary a senior?"

"Yes. Laura would have been the class valedictorian

100

and have made the speech on graduation day. Everyone says so."

I looked more closely at the girl in the photograph. Aunt Sara was right. Laura had been very pretty. She had Cary's eyes and they had similar noses and mouths, with the exact same shade of dark brown hair. Laura's features were smaller, feminine, dainty. She looked about my height and weight, but not as full as I in the bosom. Staring at the photograph, I understood why Uncle Jacob told Aunt Sara the angels were jealous, however. Laura had a glow in her face, a soft, spiritual quality that made her look as if any moment she might sprout angel wings and fly away.

"She was very pretty," I said.

"Yes."

"And who is this?" I picked up a wallet-size photograph of a brown-haired boy that was wedged in the frame of Laura's sweet sixteen photograph. He was handsome.

"That was Robert Royce," Aunt Sara said. She sighed yet again. "He was taken along with Laura that terrible day."

"Oh. How horrible!"

"How horrible," Aunt Sara parroted. She gazed around the room. "I haven't touched anything in here except to dust and clean. It's just as it was the day she died. Please try to keep everything where it is, Melody dear. Put everything back exactly where you found it. But as I said, use whatever you want.

"I suppose you could use a little rest after traveling so long and so far. Dinner is in an hour. Jacob likes us all to look nice come the evening meal. I left this drawer for you to put your own things in," she said showing me the third drawer in the dresser, "and you can find enough space in the closet for what you have brought, I'm sure."

"Mommy said she was going to have my other things sent," I said.

"Until she does, use these things," Aunt Sara said

101

gesturing at everything. "Tomorrow morning," she continued, "I will take you to the school to get you enrolled. It's not far. You can walk home with Cary and May every day, just as Laura did."

Aunt Sara turned, paused in the doorway, and then marched back to the closet.

"I might suggest something for you to wear to dinner." She sifted through Laura's garments. "Now this, yes, this would be perfect." She held out a blue dress with a white collar and white cuffs on the three-quarter sleeves.

"It looks as if it might be tight here," I said holding my hands on my ribs.

"Oh no, it won't be. This material gives a bit, but even if it is, I'll let it out for you. I'm a talented seamstress," she added with a laugh. "I used to adjust all of Laura's clothes. I made her this dress." She pulled a pink taffeta off its hanger to show me. "She wore this to a school dance."

"It's nice."

"Perhaps you'll wear it to a school dance, too." She gazed at it a moment before returning it to the closet. She hung it between the exact same two dresses, right where it had hung before she retrieved it to show me.

She lay the blue dress on the bed and stepped back.

"What size is your foot?"

I told her. She looked disappointed.

"Laura had smaller feet. It's a shame for you not to be able to use any of her shoes."

"Maybe May will get to wear them," I suggested.

"Yes," she whispered, looking heartbroken. "Anyway," she said, "I'm sure the dress will fit. Welcome to our home, dear."

Before leaving, she again paused in the doorway.

"It's so wonderful knowing all these things will be used and loved again. It's almost as if . . . as if Laura sent you to us." She smiled at me and left.

A chill passed through my breast. I felt like an intruder in this bedroom. It was still Laura's room. My small

102

suitcases were stacked beside each other against the wall and my fiddle in its case was resting on top of them. There was so little of me here, so much of Laura.

I unpacked, putting my own stuffed cat next to the one already on the bed. They looked as if they'd come from the same litter. I put my teddy bear above them on the pillow, too. Then I hung up what clothes I had brought and used the drawer Aunt Sara had cleared for me.

When I was finished, I went to the window and stared out at the ocean and the beach. Cary and Uncle Jacob walked back from the dock. Cary still had his shirt off and had tossed it over his shoulder. His shoulder gleamed in the sunlight as he plodded along with his head down. Uncle Jacob appeared to be lecturing him about something.

Suddenly, as if he knew my eyes were upon him, Cary gazed up at the window and for a strange moment, it was as if Laura herself were gazing up at me through his emerald eyes.

I jumped when I heard someone behind me. May stood in the doorway.

"Hi," I said and waved. She came into the room with a book. She plopped on the bed and opened the book, pointing to a page. I sat and gazed at her math text. "You want help?" I asked. I pointed to the page and to myself and then to her. She nodded, signing what I assumed meant, "Yes, please help me."

"This is just figuring percentages," I muttered. "It's easy."

She stared at me. I kept forgetting she couldn't hear a single word. What would it be like, I wondered, to live in the world and never hear a bird sing or music, never know the comforting sound of a loved one's voice. It seemed unfair, especially for a little girl as nice as May.

"Okay," I said nodding. I gestured at the desk and she followed. I sat with her standing beside me and began to do the problems, struggling to explain what I was doing. Despite my difficulty to communicate, she appeared to

103

understand my guidance, carefully reading my lips. When she did a problem, she quickly followed my lead. She was clearly a bright girl.

We did another problem and again she picked up my suggestions quickly.

"What's going on?" I heard and turned to see Cary in the doorway.

"I was just helping May with her math homework."

"I help her with her math," he said. "She can't hear you. It makes it too difficult for her," he said.

"She's doing just fine with me."

He signed something to May and she looked upset. He signed again and she shook her head.

"If she doesn't do well, it will be your fault," Cary snapped and walked away.

"He's not very friendly," I muttered.

May didn't see my lips move, but she was apparently not bothered by Cary's attitude. She smiled at me and went to my suitcases, inquisitively tapping on the fiddle case. She looked at me curiously.

"It's a fiddle," I said. I opened the case and took out the bow. Her eyes widened with surprise. How horrible, it occurred to me: she won't be able to hear me play.

But she urged me to do so anyway. I smiled and shook my head, but she seemed to plead with those big eyes.

"But how can you . . .?" I was confused.

She nodded at my fiddle.

I shrugged, picked up the bow, and played.

May stepped closer. I ran the bow over the strings and played a jaunty mountain ditty. Slowly, she raised her hand and put her fingers on the fiddle. She closed her eyes.

She's feeling the vibrations, I realized, and sure enough, her head moved slightly up and down with the undulations in the rhythms. I laughed happily and continued.

Suddenly, Cary was at my door again, buttoning a clean white shirt. "What are you doing with her now?" he demanded.

I stopped, lowering the fiddle. May opened her eyes with disappointment and then turned to see what I was looking at.

"She wanted to know what this was and then she wanted me to play it for her."

"That's a pretty sick joke," he said.

"She was listening through her fingers," I began to explain, but he shook his head and walked away again.

I fumed.

"Your brother," I told May, "is a . . . a monster." I exaggerated my eyes and twisted my mouth when I pointed to the doorway. She looked at me, shocked for a moment, then when she realized what I meant she laughed.

May's sweet laughter calmed my temper.

"I better get ready for dinner," I told her and pointed to Laura's dress. I pantomimed bringing food to my mouth. She nodded and scooped up her math book and papers to go off and get dressed herself.

I put my fiddle away, thinking about Daddy, recalling him, Papa George, and Mama Arlene sitting on their patio and listening to me practice. How I missed them all!

Aunt Sara had made it sound as if dressing for dinner was very important in this house. I went to the bathroom and washed up, then returned to my room's vanity mirror to fix my hair. I wanted to clear away all of Laura's things and make room for my own, but I remembered Aunt Sara asking me not to move anything. I found small places for my own stuff and crowded everything in together.

Laura's blue dress was snug, especially around my bosom. I had to leave the top two buttons undone, but it was somehow important to Aunt Sara that I wear it.

Maybe it was because I was wearing this clinging dress, but when I gazed at myself in the mirror, I had a new sense of myself, a feeling that I had reached a level of femininity. Despite the way Mommy always talked

105

about herself, I felt guilty being proud of my looks, my figure. In church the preacher called it a sin of pride.

But as I ran my hands over my bosom and down the sides of my body to my hips, turning and inspecting myself, I thought that I just might look pretty. Perhaps I, too, would turn men's heads the way Mommy did. Was it sinful to think like this?

A loud rapping on the door shattered my moment of introspection, making me feel as if I had been caught doing something naughty.

"It's time to come down," Cary growled. "My father doesn't like us to be late."

"I'm coming." I fixed a loose strand of hair. I opened the door. Cary and May stood outside in the hallway, waiting.

I saw his look of surprise. The mask of sternness and fury shattered. He looked handsome with his hair brushed back. He wore a tie and a nice pair of slacks.

"That's one of Laura's dresses," he whispered.

Panicky butterflies were on the wing again, battering my brain with doubts, buffeting my heart with indecision. Perhaps I shouldn't have put on her dress. Maybe I was violating another unwritten code in this confusing house.

"Your mother picked it out for me to wear to dinner," I replied.

The answer satisfied him and his face softened. May took my hand. Cary glanced at her and then pivoted and strutted to the stairway, leading us down. May signed to me and I imagined she said, "You look very nice."

Uncle Jacob was seated at the table. His hair was wet and brushed back, parted in the middle. He was cleanly shaven and wearing a white shirt, a tie, and slacks. Cary glanced at me before sitting. May followed. I hesitated.

"I'll see if Aunt Sara needs help," I said. Uncle Jacob nodded and I went into the kitchen. "Can I help you bring the food to the table, Aunt Sara?"

She turned from the stove.

"Of course, dear. That's what Laura always did." She

106

nodded at the bowls of vegetables and the potatoes, the bread and the cranberry sauce.

I started to bring out the food. Uncle Jacob had his Bible open and was silently reading. Cary and May sat ramrod straight, waiting, but Cary's eyes lifted to follow my movements around the table. The last thing I brought in was a pitcher of ice water. I poured some in everyone's glass and then sat as Aunt Sara brought out the roast chicken. She smiled at me and took her seat.

"Let us give thanks," Uncle Jacob said. Everyone lowered his head. "Lord, we thank you for the food we are about to enjoy."

I thought that was it when everyone looked up, but Uncle Jacob handed Cary the Bible.

"It's your turn, son."

Cary shot a look at me and then gazed at the pages Uncle Jacob had opened for him.

"What man of you having a hundred sheep, if he lose one of them, doth not leave the ninety and nine in the wilderness and go after that which is lost, until he find it?" Cary read in a voice so hard and deep, I had to look twice to be sure he was reading.

He continued. "And when he hath found it, he layeth it on his shoulders, rejoicing.

"And when he cometh home, he calleth together his friends and neighbors, saying unto them, Rejoice with me; for I have found my sheep which was lost."

"Good." Uncle Jacob took the Bible. He nodded to Aunt Sara and she rose to serve the vegetables, beginning with Uncle Jacob.

As he cut the roast chicken, he finally looked at me. "I see that you're settled in," he began. "Your aunt will give you a list of your daily chores. Everyone pulls his weight here. This ain't a Cape Cod rooming house." He paused to see if I was listening closely.

"I did most of the chores in our house in West Virginia," I said firmly.

"You lived in a trailer, I understand," he said, putting the chicken on May's plate.

107

"There was still lots to do, cleaning, washing, cooking."

"I bet there was." He shook his head. "Haille was never one for doing home chores." He paused and turned to me. "What was that music I heard before?"

"I was playing my fiddle for May."

Uncle Jacob raised his eyebrows as if I had said the most astonishing thing. "Who taught you how to do that? Chester wasn't musical." He paused and then added, "Although Dad says his Pa was."

"Papa George taught me," I replied, quickly explaining who he and Mama Arlene were.

"So he was a coal miner, too?" He shook his head. "I don't know how anyone could shut himself inside a mountain for his daily bread," Uncle Jacob said. "Especially someone who was brought up on the ocean, breathing God's freshest, cleanest air. It's what we were meant to do. We weren't meant to live like moles."

"It wasn't something Daddy wanted to do," I replied.

Uncle Jacob grunted. "You make your bed and then you lie in it."

I was afraid to ask what he meant. We all started eating.

My uncle paused after a few moments and looked at me again. "This year, we're going to have our best cranberry crop. If you're still here in the fall, you can help harvest."

"Cranberry crop?"

"We got a bog just over the hill here." He nodded toward the north end. "Helps supplement what I make lobstering. That ain't what it was when my father had his fleet of boats working."

He nodded at Cary. "Cary can tell you all about the cranberry harvesting. We're not millionaires, but it's easier than clawing black rocks from the earth's gut," he muttered.

My eyes went to Cary. His eyes were on me. He shifted them quickly away and I looked at May. She smiled. The one bright spot at the table, I thought.

108

Then I looked at Aunt Sara. She hadn't yet eaten a bite of supper. She had been staring at me the whole time, smiling.

I helped Aunt Sara with the dinner dishes and silverware, then decided to take a walk. The entire time I was in the kitchen, Aunt Sara went on and on about Laura, describing how much of a help she had been and how good she was at making cranberry muffins and jams. Aunt Sara wanted me to learn how to do everything Laura had been able to do. I didn't mind, I suppose, but it was strange being constantly compared to my dead cousin. If I voiced any hesitation, however, Aunt Sara would stop whatever she was doing and smile at me.

"But you have to try, dear. Laura would want you to try." She said it with such certainty. It was as if she could still speak to her drowned daughter. It gave me the willies.

Leaving the kitchen, I felt drained, but I had more tension ahead of me. I had to walk through the living room to the front door. Uncle Jacob sat in the rocker reading a newspaper. He looked up sharply when I appeared.

"Dishes done?" he demanded.

"Yes, Uncle Jacob."

"Well, then take a seat there and we'll have our talk now." He folded his paper and nodded at the settee across from him.

"Our talk?" I slowly entered the room and sat. He put his newspaper on the sea chest table, tapped the ashes from his pipe into a seashell ashtray, and sat back in his rocker, gazing more at the ceiling than at me.

"When Sara told me Haille wanted to bring you here to live a while, I was against it," he admitted frankly. "It didn't surprise me none to hear that she was trying to avoid her responsibilities. That was the only Haille I ever knew. But Sara had her heart set on this, and Sara has suffered far more than a decent, hardworking wom-

109

an like her should. We can't question the burdens God gives us. We've just got to bear them and go on.

"Sara," he continued, fixing his cold, steely gaze at me, "thinks God sent you here to help fill the hole in our hearts we got from Laura's passing. You ain't never going to fill that hole. No one can fill that hole. But Sara's got a right to hope, a right to put her tears to bed. Can you understand that?"

"Yes," I said meekly. I held my breath.

"Good. I want you to promise never to disappoint Sara. You got off to a good start here helping out with dinner like you did without anyone having to tell you to do it. It's the way Laura would have behaved.

"Laura was a good girl. She read her Bible, said her prayers, did well in school, and never gave us none of the grief some of the young people today are giving their folks. I never caught her smoking . . . anything," he added. His eyes burned with warning. "And she never drank beer or whiskey outside of this house. If she went on a date, she was always home the proper time and did nothing about which we would be ashamed to hear."

I let out the breath I was holding. Surely, Laura wasn't a total saint, I thought. I dared not suggest it.

"This is a small town. Everyone knows everyone else's itches and scratches. What you do reflects on us and we'll hear about it, you can be sure of that."

"I didn't get in trouble back in West Virginia, and I won't get in trouble here. I won't be in Cape Cod very long," I promised confidently.

He grunted. "Good. I'll hold you to that. Do your chores, do well in school and mind Sara, then we'll all be fine." He reached for his pipe and stuffed new tobacco into it.

"I didn't even know until today I was going to be staying here," I said.

His eyes widened. "That so?"

"Yes. I thought we were coming here only to visit."

He nodded, thoughtful. "Haille always had a lot of

problems with the truth. It was like hot coals in her hands."

"Why don't you like my mother? Is it only because she didn't have ancestors that went back to the Pilgrims?"

"We're all sinners," he said. "Our first parents, Adam and Eve, caused us to be cast from Paradise and wander the earth struggling with pain until we're granted mercy. No one's better than anyone else."

"She said you treated her poorly because she was an orphan," I threw back at him.

"That's a no-account lie," he snapped.

"Then why didn't you and my daddy talk all these years?"

"That was his doing, not mine," Uncle Jacob said. He lit his pipe.

"What did he do?"

"He defied his mother and father," he replied, a hard edge in his voice. "It says in the Bible to honor thy mother and father, not defy them."

"How did he defy them?"

"Your mother never told you?"

"No."

"And my brother, he never said nothing about it either?"

"Nothing about what?" I asked.

He tightened his lips and pulled himself back in the chair. "This ain't a proper conversation for me to have with a young woman. The sins of the father weigh heavily on the shoulders of his sons and daughters, too. That's all I'll say about it."

"But . . ."

"No buts. I've taken you in and asked you to behave while you stay. Let's leave it at that."

I held back my tears.

He lit his pipe again, took a few puffs, and looked at me. "Sunday you'll meet my parents. We're going to their house for dinner. You be on your best behavior. They ain't happy I took you in."

111

It was as if an electric shock had passed through me. What sort of grandparents were these? How could they hold a grudge so deeply?

"Maybe I shouldn't go," I said.

He pulled the pipe from his mouth sharply. "Of course you'll go. You'll go anywhere this family goes as long as you're living under this roof, hear?" His eyes seemed to sizzle as they glared at me.

"Yes, sir," I said.

"That's better." He rocked gently but continued staring at me.

I started to rise from the chair.

"It ain't proper to leave without first asking permission."

I sat again.

"May I please go?" I asked in a brittle voice. I felt like bone china myself and feared I would shatter any moment.

"This place you lived in West Virginia—"

"Sewell."

"Yeah, Sewell. It's in the back hills, ain't it?"

"Hills. Yes, I suppose."

"Where those families have those rotgut whiskey stills and feud and marry their cousins."

"What?" I started to smile, but saw he was deadly serious. "No, it was just a coal mining town," I said.

He snorted with skepticism. Then he leaned forward, pointing at me with the stem of his pipe. "There are places in this country, havens for the devil where his own do his work. The fiend's at home there as much as he is in Hell itself," he added. "It don't surprise me Chester went to such a place directly after leaving here with Haille." He sat back again and took a puff on his pipe, rocking and thinking a moment. "Maybe Sara is right. Maybe God did send you here to be saved."

"My daddy was a good man. He worked hard for us," I said. "He was no sinner."

Uncle Jacob continued to rock and stare. Then he

112

stopped. "You might not even know what a sinner is. You've been brought up a Godfearing girl?"

"I went to church with Daddy."

"That so? Well, maybe Chester made his peace with the Lord before he was taken. I hope so for his soul's sake."

"My daddy was a good man. Everyone in Sewell liked him. More than his own family," I added, but Uncle Jacob was lost in his own thoughts. He didn't hear me.

He blinked and looked at me again. "Who was this man brought your mother here?" he asked.

"A friend of hers who knows people who can help her," I offered weakly. He heard the doubt in my voice and shook his head.

"She know him before or after your daddy's death?" he asked, his eyes small and suspicious.

"She knew him before, too," I reluctantly admitted.

"Thought so." A wry smile was smeared over his lips.

I looked away so he couldn't see how thick my tears were getting. It stung my eyelids to keep them from flooding my cheeks. "May I please go now? I want to take a walk," I pleaded.

"Don't go far or be out there long. Sara has to take you to school tomorrow and get you started."

I rose. I wanted to turn and shout at him. I wanted to scream back and say "Who do you think you are? I thought you said no one is better than anyone else. What makes you so perfect and how dare you judge my daddy and mommy and say such things?" But my tongue stayed glued to the roof of my mouth. Instead, I fled the room and hurried out the front door. I felt like a coiled fuse attached to a time bomb. Sooner or later I was bound to explode. However, right now I wished I could run into my father's steel arms.

But there was only the strange darkness to greet me. Except for the light from the windows of the house, there was nothing to illuminate the street. Behind the house, the dunes were draped in thick darkness. A sea of clouds

113

had closed away the stars. The wind twirled the sand. Beyond the hill, the ocean roared.

This world was completely different from the world I had lived in all my life. I felt cold and alone, without the trees and songbirds and flowers of my past. Instead, I heard the scream of terns. Something ghostly white flapped its wings against the wall of night. Someone could have easily pluck my nerve endings and hear them twang like my fiddle's strings.

Embracing myself, tears streaking down my cheeks, I walked over the cobblestones to the driveway and then went a little way out toward the dunes and the sea. I stared up at the sky, hoping for sight of a star, just one star of hope and promise. But the ceiling of clouds was too thick. Nothing but darkness greeted me everywhere.

I wondered where Mommy was tonight. Was she thinking about me? Surely her heart was as heavy as mine was at this moment.

Or was she drinking and dancing and laughing with Archie someplace? Was he introducing her to so many exciting people that I never came to mind?

I wanted desperately for her to call me on the telephone.

I started to turn to go back into the house, when Cary appeared out of the darkness like some night creature. I gasped when his silhouette first took shape and then gazed with astonishment when he drew close enough to be caught in the dim light from the house windows.

He looked just as surprised to see me.

"What are you doing out here?" he demanded.

"I'm just taking a walk. Where were you?" I asked.

"I had to check something on the boat and didn't want to have to do it in the morning," he said, walking toward me.

"But it's so dark out there."

"Not for me. I've been back and forth over that piece of beach in storms and in darkness more times than I care to remember," he said. "You get to know it as well as the back of your hand and your eyes get used to the

114

darkness." He stared at me for a moment. "You look cold."

"I am cold," I said. I was shivering more from emotional ice than from the weather.

"So why don't you go inside?"

"I am going."

"Fine," he said curtly before continuing toward the house.

"Why don't you like me?" I asked. He stopped and turned back to me.

"Who said I didn't like you?"

"I did."

"I don't know you enough to not like you," he said. "Wait until I get to know you and then ask me again," he added.

"Very funny." I started back to the house. "How do I learn sign language?"

"You want to learn sign language?" he asked with surprise.

"Of course. How else will I communicate with May?"

He considered a moment.

"There's a book I'll give you," he said.

"Could you give it to me now?" I followed quickly. He glanced at me again.

"Yes," he said and continued toward the house. I was right behind him, but he walked quickly to stay ahead. When we entered, he went to speak to Uncle Jacob and I went up to my room where I found Aunt Sara waiting for me at the closet.

"Oh hi, dear. I thought I would choose a dress for you to wear to school tomorrow. This one is the one Laura wore the last day she attended school," she said holding out a dark blue, ankle-length dress. It had a matching belt. "It should fit you perfectly."

"I brought some of my own things to wear, Aunt Sara, things I wear to school."

"But this is such a nice school dress. Laura often wore it," she insisted.

"All right," I relented. It really was a nice dress.

"That's good, dear. Well, do you feel a little more at home now?"

"It's very different here," I said. "But you've been very kind," I quickly added before she took on a look of disappointment.

She smiled and put her hand on my cheek. "You're a very pretty young lady, a sweet girl. It is like having Laura back." She drew me to her to hug me and kiss my hair. "Have a restful sleep, dear, so you can be fresh and ready in the morning. Good night." She kissed me again.

Aunt Sara was fragile, but she was a nice lady. I wanted to make her happy, but I was frightened by the look in her eyes, too. She expected too much of me. I could never be the daughter she had lost.

How ironic, I thought sadly. My mother gave me away so nonchalantly and Aunt Sara would cut off her right arm to have her daughter back for an hour.

I threw myself down on the bed and buried my face in the comforter. I was lying there, forgetting the door was still open, when I heard a knock and looked up quickly.

"Here," Cary said. He tossed the book onto the bed. "Don't lose it or spill anything on the pages," he instructed. His eyes lingered on me for a moment and then he turned away quickly, as if in pain, and marched down the hallway to his room.

I gazed at the sign language book and then I sat up, took a deep breath to help swallow back the tears, and opened the cover.

May would never hear the sound of my voice, but right now I thought I was as small and as vulnerable as she was. It seemed she would be the only one in this house who would understand how deep my well of tears went.

I sat at the vanity mirror and practiced the hand movements until my eyelids drooped. It had, after all, been one of the longest days of my life, second only to the day Daddy died. After I put on my own nightgown, I realized it was too sheer for me to walk around in, so I put on Laura's terrycloth robe and went to the bathroom.

116

When I came out, Cary was waiting to go in. He had the strangest expression on his face, a pleasant look of surprise.

"Is May asleep?" I asked.

"I put out her light and say good night first," he replied.

"I learned how to sign good night. Can I try?"

"Don't keep her up," he said, returning to the bathroom.

I went down the hall to May's room and looked in. She was in bed, reading a young adult novel. I had to move up to the bed for her to see me. She lowered the book and smiled. Then I signed good night.

Her face beamed and she signed back. Then she held out her arms. I embraced her and kissed her cheek, signed good night again, and left her room. Cary glanced at me and as we passed in the corridor I said, "Good night."

"Good night," he mumbled, sounding as if I had forced him to say it.

It brought a smile to my face.

I returned to my room, closed the door, and slipped under the comforter. The windows were still open, but I didn't mind the breeze. It was a comfortable bed, the sort I could snuggle in.

I gazed at Papa George's pocket watch, running my fingers over its outside. Then I opened it carefully and touched the blade of grass I had taken from Daddy's grave. The watch tinkled its tune. It gave me comfort.

I didn't want to think of anything sad. I didn't want to remember Mommy driving off. I didn't want to hear Uncle Jacob's harsh words, yet they rang in my ears. "The sins of the father weigh on the shoulders of his sons and daughters?" What sins?

Outside the window, the sound of the ocean's waves stroking the shore resembled a lullaby. In the darkness of the room, I wondered about Laura falling asleep to the same rhythmic ocean song. I wondered about her hopes and dreams, and her fears, too.

Then suddenly, I couldn't help crying for my mother. I closed Papa George's watch and put it back on the night table.

I took a deep breath and then I signed good night to myself. I closed my eyes and hoped for the magic of sleep.

7

"Grandpa" Cary

Sunlight filtered through the wall of morning fog. First it trickled, then it poured through my bedroom windows: lifting darkness and sleep from my eyes. I blinked and stared at my new surroundings, feeling still embroiled in an elaborate dream. This entire journey, Mommy's leaving me in the home of my estranged relatives, my waking in my dead cousin's room, had to be part of some nightmare I had suffered after Daddy's death. Surely, if I blink again, I thought, I will be back in Sewell. Any moment I might wake up, get dressed, have breakfast, see Mama Arlene and Papa George, and then be on my way to school. I'll just close my eyes, take a deep breath, make a wish, and when I open them again, all will be as it was.

But the door of the room opened before I could make my wish. Aunt Sara stood there, her lips formed in an O, her eyes wide. Her palms rested on her chest. Then she blinked rapidly and smiled down at me.

"Good morning, dear," she said. "I'm sorry if I frightened you, but when I opened the door and looked in and saw you there in Laura's bed . . . just for a moment it was as if Laura hadn't . . . Laura was still here. Did you sleep well? But of course you did," she said, answering her own question. "Laura's bed is so comfortable, isn't it?"

I rose on my elbows and then sat against the headboard and ground the traces of sleep from my eyes.

"What time is it?"

"Oh, it's early. We rise early. Jacob wanted me to wake you with everyone else, but I told him you had such a trying day yesterday you needed a little extra sleep. Cary and your uncle Jacob have been up for more than an hour preparing the boat. I've already made them and Roy breakfast."

"Roy?"

"Jacob's assistant."

"Oh. Then May is up, too?"

"Yes, she's eating breakfast." Aunt Sara spotted something and entered the room. "She and Cary will be off to school soon. But that's all right." Aunt Sara went to the dresser and moved a picture of Laura back to the exact place it had been. She turned to me. "You and I will have a little time together and then we'll walk to school, stopping at Laura's grave in the cemetery. I visit her every morning." She returned to the doorway. "Come down as soon as you're ready." She took a deep breath and closed her eyes. "It's going to be a glorious day. I can feel it."

She left and closed the door. I gazed at the picture on the dresser. I had obviously not put it back exactly where I had found it.

The room was brightening with the strengthening morning light. More than ever I felt that I was invading a shrine. I felt guilty enjoying the things my cousin Laura should be enjoying—her bed, her clothes, her beautiful vanity table.

Nevertheless, after I showered, I put on the dress Aunt Sara had chosen for me to wear on my first day in a new school. I had seen how important it was to her that I do so and I didn't have the heart to refuse. I gazed at myself

120

in the mirror. Were there any resemblances between me and my dead cousin? There were none I could see beyond the general things: both of us being about this height and weight when she was my age. Our hair color wasn't the same, nor our eyes, nor the shapes of our faces.

Cary and May were already gone by the time I went downstairs.

"I knew that dress would fit. I just knew it!" Aunt Sara flitted around the kitchen excitedly. She had prepared something she called flippers, fried dough that accompanied my eggs. It was good. She sat and sipped coffee, watching me eat, describing the town, the school, the places Laura enjoyed, the things Laura liked to do.

"She was always in the school plays. Were you ever in a school play?"

"No, but I was in the school's talent show, playing my fiddle."

"Oh. Laura wasn't musically inclined. She sang in the chorus, but she didn't play an instrument." She thought a moment and then smiled. "I imagine she could have though. Laura could do just about anything she put her mind to.

"I was so different," Aunt Sara continued. "I only went as far as high school. My father didn't believe a young girl needed much formal education. My mother wanted me to go to college, but I didn't know for what. I was never the best student. It was finally decided I would marry Jacob and be a homemaker."

"What do you mean it was decided?" I asked.

"Jacob's father and my father were close. They were matchmaking Jacob and me before we went to high school." She followed that with a light laugh that reminded me of tinkling glasses.

"But weren't you in love with Uncle Jacob?"

"I liked him, and my mother always said love was something you grow into rather than something that explodes in your heart the way romance novels and movies portray it. Real, lasting love, that is." She nod-

121

ded, her face firm. "It makes sense. That's why there are so many divorces nowadays. People claim to fall in love rather than grow into love. Growing into love takes time, commitment, dedication. It's as Jacob says, marriage and love are just other kinds of investment."

"Investment? Love?" I nearly laughed at the idea.

"Yes, dear. It's not as silly as you think it sounds."

"My father fell in love with my mother," I insisted. "He told me so many times."

"Yes, I know," she muttered sadly and looked away.

"Isn't it true that everyone in the family was upset about it only because my mother was an orphan?"

"Who told you that?" A curious, tight smile appeared on Aunt Sara's face.

"My mommy."

"No one disliked your mother for being an orphan. That's silly. Everyone was always kind to her, especially Samuel and Olivia."

"I don't understand. Why else did this family stop talking to my daddy? Wasn't it just because he married her?" I continued.

Aunt Sara bit down on her lower lip and then rose and began clearing the dishes.

"Uncle Jacob told me my daddy didn't honor his father and mother. Wasn't that what he meant?" I pursued.

"I don't like to talk about Chester and Haille." Aunt Sara was near tears. "Jacob forbids it." She took a deep breath, as if the subject stole the air from her lungs.

"I'm sorry. I don't mean to upset you," I told her. She took another breath and nodded.

"It's over and done. As Jacob always says, we've got to go with the tide. You can't fight the tide. Now you're here and I would like you to be happy with us." She turned, smiling again. She could flip emotions like someone surfing television channels. "Okay, dear?"

I pouted for a moment. Why was it all such a great secret? What more could there be?

122

"Let's get ready to go to school, dear."

I nodded, rose from the table, and went upstairs to take one last look at myself. I had my hair brushed down and tied loosely with a light pink ribbon I had found in Laura's vanity drawer. I dabbed some of her cologne behind my ears, but decided not to wear lipstick. I noticed that the tiny freckles that were under my eyes looked more prominent. There was nothing I could do about that. Cake makeup only seemed to emphasize the freckles.

Going to a new school and making new friends was terrifying. I had seen how other girls who had moved to Sewell were sometimes treated the first few days and how nervous and timid most of them were. I always felt sorry for them and tried to help them get oriented quickly, but some of my friends felt threatened by new faces. Boys were always more interested in fresh faces, at least for a while, and every girl who had a steady boyfriend was paranoid.

Aunt Sara was waiting at the foot of the stairs. Just as I started to descend, she stopped me. "You're going to need a pen, a pencil, and a notebook. They're on Laura's desk, honey," she instructed.

I hesitated, then returned to the room. Taking the pen and the pencil was fine, but the notebooks all had Laura Logan written on their front covers in big, black letters. Many of the pages were written on, too. I'll take one for now, I thought, and get a new notebook later.

Aunt Sara was pleased. "Laura usually made her own lunch for school, but since you had so little time this morning, I decided to give you the money to buy your lunch." Aunt Sara put two dollars into my hand.

"Thank you, Aunt Sara."

"I want you to be happy." She kissed me on the cheek. "You look so pretty, so perfect. Like Laura."

We started toward town. The fog had burned away and left a turquoise sky dabbed with puffy clouds moving quickly with the wind. There were many fishing boats and sailboats in the bay, and off in the distance, gliding against the horizon, was a large cargo vessel. To my left, junipers on a hill swayed in a melancholy rhythm. Aunt Sara explained that just beyond the bend in the road was the cemetery.

"We won't be long," Aunt Sara said as we turned in the direction of the cemetery. There were two rectangular granite columns at the entryway. Atop each column was a sculptured bird that looked like a raven. The cemetery road was gravel and forked just after the entrance. We went left and then again left, stopping at the Logans' plots. Laura's headstone was a soft shade of gray. Under her name, Laura Ann Logan, and her dates was inscribed, Let the saints be joyful in glory: let them sing aloud upon their beds.

Aunt Sara knelt at the grave site and placed a deep red wild rose against the monument. She closed her eyes and prayed and then she turned to me and smiled.

"Laura loved the red rose most. As soon as they bloom, I bring them to her."

"I like them, too," I said.

"I knew you would," she replied, her eyes bright.

She stood up and wiped off her skirt. Before we left, I noticed two fresh stones with the names, Samuel Logan and Olivia Logan engraved on them. Beneath the names were the dates of birth but no dates of death.

"Aren't those my grandparents?" I asked, astounded.

"Yes, dear. Samuel put the stones in this year to be sure it would be done the way he wanted it done." She laughed. "The Logans don't trust anyone, even their own. Samuel wanted to be sure he was facing the east so the rising sun would warm his plot every morning."

She took my hand as we left the cemetery. She was quiet for a while, but when the school came in view, she began to talk excitedly again, describing how much Laura had liked school and her teachers and how much they had liked her.

"They almost called school off the day of her and

Robert's funerals. So many students wanted to be there, and teachers, too."

We marched up the walkway to the main entrance and entered. A sign directed us to the principal's office. Aunt Sara had made an appointment, so we were expected. The principal's secretary, Mrs. Hemmet, greeted us with a warm smile and gave me papers to fill out while we waited to see the principal, Mr. Webster.

"So this is your niece?" Mrs. Hemmet said to Aunt Sara.

"Yes. Isn't she pretty?"

Mrs. Hemmet nodded. She was a thin, spidery woman with long, skinny arms and salt-and-pepper hair cut into short curls that hung on her scalp like tiny springs. While I filled in information on some forms, Aunt Sara and Mrs. Hemmet discussed the town, the upcoming tourist season, and the fall's cranberry harvest. Aunt Sara gave Mrs. Hemmet the letter Mommy had written authorizing Aunt Sara to act as my guardian.

"All right," Mrs. Hemmet said, perusing my paperwork, "I'll send for your school records right away."

"You'll find she's been an excellent student," Aunt Sara assured her. She had accepted that on faith, but I was confident everyone would be pleased with my grades.

"Unless something has to be changed," Mrs. Hemmet continued, "this will be your schedule."

She handed me a card listing my classes, rooms, and teachers. Then she knocked on the principal's door and announced our arrival.

Mr. Webster was a short, stout man, with light, thinning brown hair, a firm mouth, and thick bulbous nose, red at the bridge where his thick-framed glasses rested. His cheeks had a crimson tint and his dark brown eyes were roofed with bushy eyebrows. He greeted Aunt Sara warmly and scrutinized me for a moment before offering his hand and a smile.

"Please sit," he said gesturing at the chair in front of

125

his desk. Aunt Sara sat in the one beside it. "West Virginia, eh?" he said, gazing at my file. "Coal mining country. Tell me a little about your school there."

I described it simply. He wanted to know more about my extracurricular interests than my schoolwork, it seemed, and when I told him I played the fiddle, he raised those bushy eyebrows, gazed at Aunt Sara, and then nodded at me.

"That will be different," he said. "We have an annual talent show to raise money for scholarships at the end of the school year. I hope you'll participate."

"I'm sure she will," Aunt Sara offered.

"Well then, your being Sara and Jacob Logan's niece, I don't think I have to tell you to behave yourself, Melody, but here's our school code and our rules to follow." He handed me a pamphlet. "Look it over and if you have any questions, don't hesitate to come knocking on my door. Good luck and welcome."

I thanked him. When I came out of the office there was a diminutive girl with a caramel complexion and shoulder-length ebony hair waiting in the outer office. She had eyes as black as her hair. She wore a necklace made of tiny seashells and a light blue blouse, matching skirt, and sandals with no socks. Her toenails were polished in bright pearl.

"This is Theresa Patterson," Mrs. Hemmet said. "Theresa's one of our honor students. She'll show you around today."

"Oh Theresa, how nice that you're going to help Melody," Aunt Sara said. "I remember how Laura used to help you with your work sometimes."

"Hello, Mrs. Logan," Theresa replied. She didn't crack a smile. She was a very serious looking girl, pretty but dour to the point of seeming angry. She turned to me. "You have a schedule card?"

"Yes." I showed her. She gazed at it, then nodded. "All my classes. Let's go. We're missing the American history lecture and Mr. K. doesn't like to repeat himself," she said. She started away. I looked at Aunt Sara.

126

"Have a nice day, dear."

I nodded and hurried to catch up with my obviously reluctant guide.

"Why did you get here so late?" she asked, her face forward as she marched down the corridor.

"I had to visit with my aunt this morning. She wanted to bring me to school herself and she always stops at the cemetery first to spend a moment at my cousin Laura's grave. She drowned almost a year ago."

Theresa glanced at me, her right eyebrow raised.

"Don't you think I know that?" She paused and turned. "Don't you know who I am? Why they picked me to show you around?"

I shook my head.

"No."

"I'm Theresa Patterson. My father is Roy Patterson. He slave-works for your uncle Jacob, so naturally they just assumed I should slave for you," she added and walked on.

Welcome to your new school, I thought and hurried to catch up with Theresa.

School was not much different here from what it had been in Sewell, I decided. The desks were the same type and we had even been using the same history textbook, so I wasn't behind the other students. In fact, I had read enough ahead to actually raise my hand and answer a question the first day, even though I was full of a thousand anxieties. The teacher, Mr. Kattlin, whom the students called Mr. K., was obviously impressed. Theresa simply offered me a smaller smirk.

"Did you take algebra, too?" she asked as soon as the bell rang to end the period.

"Yes."

"Good. Then I won't have to do much," she commented. "Let's go. Math is all the way at the end of the corridor and we often get surprise quizzes. I like to look over last night's work before class starts," she added.

It turned out I was actually a chapter ahead of the class

127

in algebra, but I didn't volunteer any answers this period. The teacher did spring a quiz on the class, and I surprised him by offering to take it, too. Some of the other girls who had been in my history class looked annoyed with me. I was afraid that if I did better than they did, the teacher would use me to mock and chastise them. I had seen my teachers back in Sewell do that.

After math we had our lunch break and Theresa showed me to the cafeteria.

"I've got my own lunch," she told me and showed me her brown bag. "Buying lunch is too expensive for all of us."

"All? How many brothers and sisters do you have?"

"I have two sisters and a brother, all in elementary school, and my father doesn't make enough money."

"Oh. Your mother doesn't work too?" I asked.

"My mother's dead," she said sharply. "I'm going to get a seat over there," she said nodding toward a table in the rear where other students with dark complexions sat. "But you probably don't want to sit with the bravas."

"Bravas?"

"Half black, half Portuguese," she explained and walked away, leaving me in line.

I looked for Cary and saw him way on the other end sitting with two boys. He was a senior so I knew he wouldn't be in any of my classes, but I was hoping we would at least see each other at lunch. He looked my way, but made no gesture for me to join him. Instead, he continued to talk to his friends.

Alone in a large room full of strangers, most of whom were staring at me, made me feel like the proverbial fish out of water. What better place to feel like that, I thought, than Cape Cod? The idea brought a smile to my face and I turned toward the food counter.

"Hi." A tall, slim, brown-haired girl appeared beside me. She had the brightest blue eyes I had ever seen and a pretty smile. "I'm Lorraine Randolph."

She offered me her hand and we shook.

"Melody Logan," I said.

"I know. This is Janet Parker." Lorraine nodded at a dark brunette who had harder features and dull hazel eyes. She had two prominent pock marks on her forehead, too, and, being large breasted, was quite a contrast to Lorraine Randolph.

"Hi," she said.

"I'm Betty Hargate." The shortest of the three pushed herself between Janet and Lorraine. She had her dark blond hair cut in a page boy and wore a cap to match her designer blouse and skirt. There was a puffiness under her eyes and a twist in her mouth that made her look as if she were smirking. Her small nose looked as if it had been planted at the last minute of birth between her bloated cheeks. She was the only one of the three who wore earrings. She had a gold necklace and a ring on every other finger, too.

"Hi," I said.

"So you're Grandpa's cousin, huh?" Betty asked.

"Grandpa?" I smiled, confused.

"Cary Logan. We call him Grandpa," Lorraine explained.

We moved down the food line.

"Cary? Why?"

"Because he acts like it," Betty explained. "Don't you know your own cousin?"

"We just met, actually," I replied, and chose my lunch. I moved quickly, not comfortable with Betty's tone of voice. They followed and Lorraine asked me to sit at their table. I wanted to walk over to Cary's table even though he hadn't invited me, but I didn't want to turn down any prospective new friends, either.

"How come you just met Cary?" Janet asked before putting half her hot dog into her mouth.

"We lived too far away from each other for our families to see each other." That seemed to satisfy them.

"So you never knew what he was like then," Betty concluded.

129

"What do you mean: what he's like?" I asked. "I don't understand."

"All he cares about is working with his father and saying his prayers. He doesn't smoke or drink, never goes to any of our parties. He talks to us as if we're all . . ."

"What?" I asked.

"Jezebels," she said. They all laughed.

"What?"

"Didn't he tell you about Jezebel?" Janet asked.

I shook my head.

Betty leaned toward me. "Jezebel was the wife of Ahab and worshiped pagan gods."

"It means wicked woman," Lorraine explained.

"If you don't know your Bible, you're in for hell and damnation living with Grandpa," Betty said.

"I know my Bible," I said defensively. "I just didn't understand why Cary would call you that."

"You will, once you get to know him better and he starts calling you that," Betty told me.

I gazed at Cary. He was looking at us with some interest. He didn't smile, but when our eyes met, he seemed to soften and nod slightly.

I continued eating my lunch, answering questions about life in Sewell, West Virginia, the music I liked, movies and TV shows I watched. The girls acted as if I had come from a foreign country.

"You can forget about television as long as you're living with the Logans," Janet said.

"Why?"

"They don't have a television set, right?"

I thought about it for a moment and then was amazed that I hadn't noticed myself. "No, they don't. I wonder why."

"Television is full of sinful acts," Betty quipped.

"Grandpa doesn't even know what the Beatles sang. He still thinks we're talking about insects," Lorraine said. Their laughter attracted the attention of everyone around us. I felt guilty sitting here listening to them mock Cary.

130

"You shouldn't make fun of him," I said. "He and his family have suffered a great loss."

They all stopped smiling and laughing.

"You mean Laura," Betty said.

"Yes. Did you know her well?"

"Of course we knew her," Lorraine said. They exchanged glances as they continued to eat. Silence fell over our table and those who had been looking at us, listening and smiling along with them, turned back to their own conversations.

"My aunt is still very upset," I continued, angry at how cruel and insensitive they seemed to be. "It was a terribly tragic accident, wasn't it?"

The three glanced at each other. Janet wiped her lips with her napkin and gulped down her apple juice. Lorraine's eyes shifted quickly from mine, but Betty sat back, stretching.

"Better ask Grandpa about it," she said. The other two looked shocked that she had said it.

"What do you mean?"

She shrugged.

"Just ask him about Laura and Robert. They were using Grandpa's sunfish when they got caught in the sou'wester," she replied as if that explained it.

"Sunfish?"

"It's a shell with one sail on it," Lorraine said.

"Not the sort of boat to be in when bad weather hits," Betty continued. "Grandpa knew that better than anyone. He was born on a wave and came in with the tide."

They laughed again.

"I don't understand. What are you trying to say?"

"We're not saying anything," Betty replied quickly, her smile evaporating. "And don't tell anyone we did."

The bell rang. I stared at the three of them for a moment and then stood up.

"Where do we dump our trays?" I asked.

"Just follow Theresa. She knows how to clean off tables," Janet told me.

I rushed from their annoying laughter. It was making

131

my blood boil. I followed the others to an opening in the wall where trays and dishes were placed. Theresa waited for me there.

"Making new friends?" she asked dryly.

"More like new enemies," I responded. Her eyebrows lifted. I thought I even detected a small, tight smile on her lips.

"English is next," she said. "We're reading *Huckleberry Finn.*"

"I read it."

Theresa paused and turned to me. "You did? Good. Then maybe you can help me for a change."

"I'd love to," I shot back, my voice as tight and firm as hers.

She stared a moment and then she smiled warmly for the first time. Her pearl black eyes brightened and she laughed. I laughed, too.

Betty, Janet, and Lorraine stared at us with amazement as they walked past and down the corridor.

"Do the witches from *Macbeth* have English now, too?" I asked Theresa.

"Witches?" She gazed after Lorraine, Janet, and Betty. "Oh. Yes."

"Good," I said firmly.

We walked on, Theresa talking more freely now about our teachers, our classes, and the way things were.

Cary waited outside the school building at the end of the day. He looked up sharply when I appeared.

"My mother wants you to walk home with May and me," he explained. "But you don't have to if you don't want to."

"I do," I said. He started walking quickly.

"Are we walking or running?" I asked, keeping up with him.

He glanced at me.

"I don't like to be late for May," he said.

"She doesn't know how to get home by herself?" I asked innocently. He stopped and spun on me.

"She's deaf. She might not hear a car when she crosses the street."

"I bet she would look carefully first," I said. "She's a bright girl."

"Why take chances?" he said.

"She needs to feel she can be on her own," I told him.

"She's only ten. There's plenty of time for that. Besides, we're wasting time standing here and arguing."

"We're not arguing," I said keeping up with his pace. "We're only having a conversation."

He grunted like Uncle Jacob and kept his face forward as he took long strides.

"I see you made friends with the most popular girls at school already," he commented.

"I'd rather be friends with Theresa Patterson," I replied. He shot a glance at me, a look of surprise on his face.

"She's a brava."

"So?"

"If you hang out with them, the others won't be as friendly. You won't be included in their gossiping and you'll never get invited to their wonderful parties."

"I'll risk it," I said. Although he didn't turn back to me, I saw a smile form.

May was waiting patiently for us at her school. She broke into a wide, happy smile when she saw I had come for her, too, and I signed hello. She ran to us, but Cary began to sign quickly. Whatever he told her calmed her down and she walked along holding tightly to his hand. I was at a great disadvantage not knowing the language of the deaf. I made up my mind to learn as much as I could as quickly as I could.

Aunt Sara stood at the front of the house when we arrived. She rushed to us, her face full of expectation. I could tell that the way she was gazing at us as we all came walking up the street made Cary uncomfortable. I heard him mumble something under his breath, and then he quickened his pace, tugging May along.

133

"How was your day, children?"

"The same as always," Cary muttered and walked through the gate and past her quickly. May paused to tell Aunt Sara her school news. Her fingers and hands moved so quickly, I wondered how Aunt Sara could keep up. She didn't seem to be paying much attention either, because as she nodded and smiled, her eyes were focused on me.

"It's so good to see three of you come down the street instead of only two. Was school okay? Did you make new friends, dear?"

"It's hard to make friends the first day," I replied, without revealing anything in my tone of voice.

"Of course," she said. "Would you like something cold to drink? Laura and I would enjoy a glass of iced tea about this time of the day."

"That sounds nice. Did my mother call?" I asked hopefully.

Her smile wilted like a flower without sunshine and water. "No, dear, not yet."

I tried not to look disappointed. "I'll just go and change into something else. I'd like to see the cranberry bog."

"Oh, yes. It's right over the hill. Maybe Cary will take you," she suggested. May tried to get Aunt Sara's attention and interest again. Her hands resembled small fluttering birds, but Aunt Sara babbled on about her quiet afternoons with Laura. By the time I got to my room, Cary was emerging, dressed in a worn pair of pants, dirty sneakers, and an old shirt.

"I've got to go help my father with today's catch," he said as he passed. I was standing in the doorway. "I don't have time to take someone sightseeing."

"Can I help?" I called after him, but he was bouncing down the stairs and didn't reply.

Why did he avoid me? Coming home from school, he had looked embarrassed walking with me at his side, and whenever he spoke to me, he always looked at something else. Was I that detestable? I was sure it had something to do with his resenting my being in Laura's room, using Laura's things. I couldn't wait for Mommy to call so I could at least get the shipment of my other things.

I changed into my own jeans and blouse, loosened my hair, and put on my older pair of sneakers. May had already changed out of her school clothes and was waiting for me. She signed something I didn't understand.

"Wait," I told her and scooped up the book on sign language. "You and I will practice, okay?" I said holding up the book.

She nodded and I took her hand. As we descended the stairs, Aunt Sara called from the kitchen.

"Is that you, dear?"

"It's May and me," I replied. She appeared with only one glass of iced tea in her hand. "Come, sit with me a minute on the porch," she said, handing me the glass.

"Thank you, but doesn't May want any?" I held up the glass. May started to nod.

"May has something to do," Aunt Sara said harshly. She gestured at her and May's smile faded. She looked at me a moment and then ran to the rear of the house.

"Where's she going?"

"May helps with the laundry, folding towels and putting away the linens. It's her chore. Everyone has a list of chores," Aunt Sara said.

"Where's mine?"

"Oh, there's time enough for yours, dear. I want you to get settled in first."

"It's not fair," I said looking after poor May. "Maybe I can help May."

"No, dear. She'll be fine. Come." Aunt Sara led me to the porch. "Tell me all about your day at school. Laura used to describe everything so well that I felt I had been right there beside her," she said with a short, thin laugh. She sat in a rocker and I sat on the small bench.

A tiny song sparrow perched itself on the red maple tree and paraded as if to show off its plumage. The afternoon sun had fallen behind a thin layer of clouds,

135

and a cool breeze passed through my clothes, giving me a sudden chill. I looked toward the beach where the sunshine was still strong.

I told her how I felt about my teachers and how I thought I really wasn't behind in my schoolwork, how I was even a little ahead in some classes. She listened attentively, but she looked disappointed, as if I wasn't telling her what she really wanted to hear.

"You didn't make friends with anyone yet?"

"Theresa Patterson's nice," I said and she grimaced.

"You should make friends with the daughters of the better families in town, dear. That way you'll get to meet nice, respectable young men." She smiled. "I'm sure you will. You're too pretty not to succeed. It's what I always told Laura, and sure enough . . . sure enough . . ." She hesitated as if she had forgotten what next to say and then she turned abruptly toward the ocean. "We're going to have a neap tide tonight, Jacob says."

"What's a neap tide?"

"It's when the moon's at its first or third quarter. It's at its third quarter. The breakers could be as high as seven feet. Stay away from the water tonight," she added. She sighed deeply. "Laura went out on the neap tide and never came back. I never laid eyes on her face again." She shook her head slowly. "Only Robert's body was recovered."

"But Laura has a grave," I said.

"Yes. I had to have a monument for her, a place for her spirit." She smiled. "Only a clamshell's toss away as you saw. I can go there whenever I want and talk to her. I told her all about you last night, so I'm sure her spirit's looking over you. That's why I know she'd want me to give you this." She dug in her dress pocket. "Hold out your left hand, dear," she ordered. I did so slowly and she put a gold charm bracelet around my wrist and locked it on before I could resist. "Oh, it looks perfect on you."

"I can't take this," I said. "It isn't right."

136

"Laura wouldn't want you to have it if it weren't right. It will bring good luck. You know why, don't you?"

I shook my head, afraid to even guess.

"You were born June twelfth, right?"

"Yes," I said, holding my breath.

She widened her smile.

"Don't you know, dear?"

"Know what?"

"Laura was born June twentieth. You're both Gemini. Don't you see?"

I shook my head, still holding my breath.

"Gemini, the twins. That was Laura's sign, that's Cary's sign, and it's your sign," she said. "Isn't that wonderful?"

"I don't know anything about astrology," I said.

"One night when it's clear, I'll show you your constellation. Laura and I loved to see it in the night sky." She gazed up as if it were already night and the sky were blazing with stars. May timidly appeared in the doorway. Aunt Sara asked her if she had completed her chore and she signed back that she had.

"Maybe May can show me the cranberry bog?" I suggested. Aunt Sara nodded, disappointed that I didn't want to sit and talk some more. She reluctantly told May my request. May beamed, took my hand, and urged me to follow her.

"Come right back!" Aunt Sara called from the porch.

"We will," I promised.

"I've got nice flounder for tonight's dinner. It was one of Laura's favorite meals," she cried.

May pulled harder. I laughed as we broke into a run around the rear of the house and over the pinky-mauve and pearly pebbles toward the hill. Toward the ocean I could see Cary on the boat working with his father and Roy Patterson. It looked as if he was gazing our way, but he didn't wave.

May lead me to the top of the hill. We paused and I looked down at the cranberry bog. It was all in blossom.

137

It looked like a second sea of pale pink. May gestured wildly with her hands. I was sure she was explaining the planting, the flooding, the draining, and the harvesting of the berries. It was frustrating not to understand.

I sat her down beside me on the top of the hill and opened the book about sign language. If we worked together, I thought, I would make faster progress. We were still practicing gestures when Cary and Uncle Jacob returned from the dock.

"Hey!" Cary barked. "Get her back to the house." He made some gestures and May stood up.

Using my new skills, I thanked her. She hugged me.

When I looked back, I saw Cary glaring at us. He lowered his head and then plodded after Uncle Jacob. I took May's hand and we followed.

"May showed me the cranberry bog," I told him when we entered the house. He was in the living room with Uncle Jacob. "It's beautiful."

He snorted. "See if you still think it's beautiful when it comes harvest time." He cut past me quickly to go upstairs.

"If I'm still here," I called after him. Couldn't I say anything that would please him?

"Go see if Sara needs any help with dinner," Uncle Jacob commanded. He didn't even say hello and he had no questions for me about my first day at school. He snapped his newspaper and sat back to read.

May looked at me, wondering, I was sure, what all the dark faces meant. I smiled at her reassuringly. Then I heard the phone ringing.

Oh let that be Mommy, I prayed. I had never longed to hear her voice so much. No matter what her faults were, how much she had annoyed or disappointed me before, I would be grateful for the sound of her voice.

Uncle Jacob lifted the receiver reluctantly and said hello. His eyes were on me.

"I said go help Sara," he ordered. I took a step past the doorway, but paused to hear him talk.

"Yeah," he said, "She's here. She's looks a lot like

138

Haille. Guess you'll see for yourself soon enough," he added. "It's bound to bring back memories."

Suddenly, I felt eyes on me and turned to look up the stairs. Cary was standing there glaring.

"Eavesdropping isn't very ladylike." He went back upstairs, leaving me feeling cold.

I choked back my tears and went into the kitchen, where I was sure Aunt Sara waited to tell me how she was preparing Laura's favorite meal.

8
A Stormy Warning

As we had at dinner the night before, we began with a prayer and a Bible reading. Uncle Jacob gazed at Cary, glanced at May, and then turned to me. "You might as well start right off," he said. "It's your turn."

"My turn?" I looked at Aunt Sara.

"He wants you to read an excerpt from the Good Book, dear. Laura always followed Cary."

"I could read again if she doesn't want to," Cary volunteered with a smirk.

"It's all right," I said quickly. "I'd like to read. What do I read?"

Uncle Jacob handed me the Bible with his thumb on the section he wanted read.

I began. "Who can find a virtuous woman? For her price is far above rubies.

"The heart of her husband doth safely trust in her, so that he shall have no need of spoil.

"She will do him good and not evil all the days of her life."

I gazed quickly at Cary because I felt the heat of his eyes on me as I read.

"She seeketh wool, and flax, and worketh willingly with her hands."

"Yes," Uncle Jacob said nodding, obviously pleased with how I read.

Cary glanced down as I continued until the chapter was completed.

"Good," Uncle Jacob said. "Words to remember. Amen." His eyes fixed on me. I knew what he thought of my mother. Did he choose this chapter because he thought I would be just like her? I was afraid to ask.

As soon as we began to eat, Uncle Jacob and Cary got into a conversation about the lobster catch and the construction of more traps. While they talked, I tried to converse with May. I saw Cary watching us out of the corner of his eye, and something I did brought a smile to his face. But Uncle Jacob suddenly looked furious.

"Will you tell your daughter to eat and not talk at dinner," he commanded Aunt Sara. "It's distracting."

"Yes, Jacob." Aunt Sara signed his orders to May, who immediately dropped her gaze to her food and stopped trying to communicate with me.

It occurred to me that I had yet to see Uncle Jacob use sign language with May. Up until now, it had been only Cary, Aunt Sara, and I.

"I'm sorry," I said. "It was my fault. I am trying to learn sign language."

"Well do it after dinner," Uncle Jacob snapped and turned back to Cary to talk about the new traps.

After dinner I helped Aunt Sara clear away the dishes and put away the food. She went on and on about the wonderful things Laura had learned to do with fish.

"Got so her filleted bass was good enough to be in a contest. You should have tasted her fish pie, too. The crust always came out so light. That girl had magic in her fingers."

"I cooked for my daddy often," I said.

"Oh, did you, dear? Yes, I bet you did. I don't remember Haille being much of a cook. She had other things on her mind."

141

"Like what?" I pursued.

"Not fit to discuss." Aunt Sara sewed her lips shut.

"What's that mean?" I demanded.

She shook her head and then gazed at the doorway before lowering her voice to a whisper. "Truth is, Jacob don't even like me mentioning her and those days."

"Well, I'd like to hear more about her," I said.

"No you wouldn't dear. I must show you some of Laura's needlework," she said to change the subject. "Did I tell you she used to do that? I have it all in my bedroom on the walls, but there is one she never got to finish. It's in my closet. Have you ever done needle-work?"

"No," I said, sulking.

"Oh you should try needlework, dear. I bet you would be good at it, too."

"I don't think so," I said. "Is there anything else I can help you with, Aunt Sara?"

"What? Oh. No dear, thank you," she said. "That's right. You have to do homework now, don't you?"

"Yes," I said.

"Then go on, dear. I'll see you before I go to sleep," she said.

I hurried upstairs. When I ascended the stairway, I noticed a ladder had been lowered from the roof above the second floor landing. It led up to a door in the ceiling. I approached slowly and gazed up at the lighted attic. Curious, I started up the rungs and stopped at the top to peer into the room. Two oil lamps illuminated a table and a chair, chests, boxes, all sorts of antiques and old paintings. But the most interesting thing to me were the model boats constructed of balsa wood. One was partially completed on the table. The others were lined up on shelves, all painted, too, and some with tiny sailors manning the sails.

There was a very worn–looking couch on the right and a telescope pointing at the sole window.

"What are you doing?" I turned to see Cary staring up at me from the bottom of the ladder.

"I was just wondering what was up here. Do you do the boats?"

"First, they're not boats, they're ships. And second, the attic is a private place, if you don't mind."

"I'm sorry." I started down the rungs, but slipped on the next to last one and fell into his arms. For a moment our faces were inches apart. The moment he realized he was holding me in his arms, he released me and I landed hard on my feet on the floor.

"That's why I don't like anyone going up there," he said moving past me quickly. "It's dangerous." His cheeks were crimson.

"I'm sorry. Is that your hobby?" I asked before he reached the top.

He dropped a "Yes" back at me before pulling the ladder up after him.

"I don't have the measles or anything you know!" I cried.

He hesitated a moment before closing the door.

"Good riddance!" I marched to my room, and lost myself in my homework. Once in a while, I heard the sounds of Cary moving above me. I gazed up at the ceiling and listened until he grew quiet again.

The telephone rang below in the living room. I waited, holding my breath and then, I heard Aunt Sara call my name.

"Telephone, dear."

"Mommy!" I cried. "Finally!" I hurried down the stairs.

"It's Haille," Aunt Sara said. "Hurry, it's long distance."

I rushed to the living room. Uncle Jacob sat in his chair, smoking his pipe and thumbing through a mail-order catalogue. He glanced at me and then back at his pages, but he didn't get up. Aunt Sara stood in the doorway, watching. I would have no privacy for this phone call. Nevertheless, I seized the receiver. "Mommy?"

"Hi Honey. See, I told you I would call you first

143

chance I got. Aunt Sara says you've already started school there and you said you were right up with the work."

"Yes, Mommy. Where are you?"

"We're on our way to New York City," she said excitedly. Her voice dropped. "The people in Boston weren't available when they told Richard they would be so we never met them, but he has people for me to meet in New York and then in Chicago. After that we'll head for Los Angeles."

"Los Angeles? But Mommy, when will I . . . when will we be together again?" I asked my question as quietly as I could.

"Soon, honey. Real soon, I promise."

"I could still meet you someplace, Mommy. I could take a bus and—"

"Now don't make things harder than they are for me, honey. I've already suffered a serious disappointment. Please, cooperate."

"But I need my things," I said. "You didn't leave me any money, Mommy. I can't call my friends. I can't call Alice or Mama Arlene. It's long distance."

"I'm calling Mama Arlene as soon as I get to New York," she promised. I heard a horn blaring and someone shouting.

"Coming!" Mommy shouted back. "I've got to go, honey. I've already held us up longer than I should have. I'll call you as soon as I can. Be good, honey. Bye."

"But Mommy—"

The phone went dead. I held it tightly. Silent screams stuck in my throat and tears froze behind my eyes.

"Hang it up properly," Uncle Jacob instructed. "I'm waitin' on an important call."

I cradled the receiver with my back to him and walked out of the living room quickly, not glancing at Aunt Sara either.

"Just a minute, there," Uncle Jacob growled. "Get yourself right back in here, young lady."

I sucked in my breath, turned, and marched back. My

heart thudded madly, drumming out a tune of fright in my ribcage.

"Yes sir?"

"It's proper to thank people when you use their things. Sara ain't your secretary."

"I'm sorry. Thank you, Aunt Sara."

"You're welcome, dear. Is everything all right with Haille?"

"Yes," I replied.

"Good."

"Humph," Uncle Jacob grunted.

"I'll bring you a glass of hot milk tonight," she offered.

"You don't have to do that, Aunt Sara."

"I always brought Laura a glass of warm milk. I bring one to May as well." Her huge scared eyes stared woefully at me. I glanced at Uncle Jacob. He looked ready to pounce.

"Oh, then thank you, Aunt Sara."

Her face brightened, the darkness evaporating from her eyes. I forced a smile and hurried up the stairway. When I reached my room, I closed the door behind me and threw myself on the bed, burying my face in the pillow to smother my sobs.

I didn't want to be here! I hated it! No wonder my father stopped speaking to his family. He was nothing like Uncle Jacob. I would be happier if Mommy had dumped me in an orphanage, I thought. My shoulders shook with my muted crying. Suddenly, I felt something touch my shoulder and I turned quickly to see little May staring at me, her face full of fear and sympathy. She had come in so quietly that I had not heard her. Her hands moved rapidly, wondering why I was so unhappy. What made me cry?

"I miss my mother," I said. She tilted her head. I let out a deep breath and located the book on sign language. I found the gestures and produced them. May nodded and signed how sorry she felt for me. Then she offered me a hug.

How sweet, I thought, and how sad that the only one

145

in this house who made me feel at home was the only one who couldn't hear the sound of my voice.

Nor could she hear the sounds of scuffling and footsteps above, but she saw where my gaze had gone and understood.

"Car . . . ry," she said and demonstrated the construction of a model ship.

"Yes. Do you go up there?" I signed. "Or doesn't he even let you up there?"

She thought a moment and then shook her head.

"No?"

She shook her head and gestured "only . . ." She pointed to Laura's photograph.

"Only Laura?" May nodded. "Only Laura," I thought aloud and gazed at the ceiling. May grunted and then gestured about his great sorrow.

I gazed at the ceiling again. Cary was in pain, I thought, and for a moment at least, I stopped feeling sorry for myself.

May returned to her room to complete her school work. After I finished mine, we practiced sign language until it was time for her to go to bed. I washed and dressed for bed myself and then Aunt Sara brought my glass of warm milk. There was something rolled under her arm. She took it out and showed me Laura's unfinished canvas of needlework. It was a picture of a woman on a widow's walk gazing at the sea.

"Laura drew the picture herself," Aunt Sara explained. "Isn't it beautiful?"

"Yes," I said.

"Don't you want to finish it for her, dear? I can't get myself to do it," she said with a deep sigh.

"I'd be afraid I would mess it up, Aunt Sara."

"Oh, you won't, I'm sure. I'll just leave it here and bring up the threads tomorrow and show you the stitch."

"I never did something like that before," I said, but she didn't seem to hear or care.

"My goodness," she said, her gaze falling on the two

146

nearly identical stuffed cats. "Where did this one come from?"

"It was mine, a present from my daddy. I brought it with me in my suitcase."

"Isn't that remarkable. Cary won the other one for Laura at a fair one summer. And this Teddy bear you brought along, too?"

"Yes."

"Geminis," she said. "All of you."

She gazed around the room sadly, looked at me, smiled and then left, after wishing me a good night's rest.

I was tired. It had been an exhausting day, my emotions on a rollercoaster. I had gone through the tunnel of fear, been angry, sad, and curious. I enjoyed being with little May and appreciated that she sincerely welcomed me. That was the only ray of sunshine in this gloomy world of sadness.

Impulsively, I picked up my fiddle and played a mournful tune. It was the mood I felt and the music came from deep within me. I closed my eyes and pictured Daddy sitting on the sofa in our trailer living room, a small smile on his face, his eyes full of pride as I played. Afterward, he would pull me to him and give me one of his bear hugs, smothering my cheek and forehead with kisses.

Suddenly, there was a loud rapping on the wall.

"Stop that noise!" Uncle Jacob ordered. "It's time for everyone to sleep!"

My memories of Daddy popped like soap bubbles. I put away the fiddle and crawled under the comforter. Then I turned down the oil lamp, closed my eyes, and listened to the roar of the ocean. The house was very quiet for a few moments, and then I heard what I recognized as the distinct sound of someone sobbing.

"Just go to sleep!" Uncle Jacob commanded gruffly, his voice seemingly coming out of the walls.

The sobbing stopped.

The ocean came roaring through my window again,

the same ocean that had taken Laura from this house and the melancholy world in which I now found myself.

Following Aunt Sara's instructions the next morning, I made lunches for both Cary and myself. It was something Laura always had done and I assumed it was to be one of my chores. We were to have a sandwich and an apple, and we were given fifty cents to buy a drink. May's lunch was provided for her at the special school.

When we left the house, May took my hand instead of Cary's. He paused for a moment, visibly annoyed, but said nothing about it.

"Let's go. We don't want to be late," he muttered and plodded along ahead of us, moving so quickly, May practically had to run to keep up. We dropped her off first and then started for our school. I tried to make conversation.

"How long have you been constructing model ships?" I asked. He glanced at me as if I had asked a stupid question.

"A long time and they're not toys," he added.

"I didn't say they were. I know grown-ups can have hobbies, too. Papa George used to carve out flutes from hickory branches. He even made my fiddle."

"Why do you call this person Papa George?" he said disdainfully. "He's not your grandfather. This Sunday you'll meet your grandfather."

"Papa George is the only grandfather I've known. He and Mama Arlene are my real grandparents as far as I'm concerned," I replied firmly.

"Don't they have any children of their own?"

"No."

"So why didn't Haille leave you with them while she went rushing off to become a movie star?" he asked, his eyes sparkling wickedly.

"Papa George is very sick. He suffers from black lung," I replied.

He grunted. "That's a convenient excuse," he said.

Furious, I seized him at the elbow and pulled him to a

148

stop, spinning him around. He was genuinely shocked at my outburst of physical strength. I shocked myself.

"It's not an excuse. He's very sick. I don't know why you don't like me, Cary Logan, and the truth is, I don't care to know. If that's the way it has to be, that's the way it has to be, but don't think I'll let you ridicule me or say bad things about the people I love."

He went from astonishment and shock to what looked like appreciation and pleasure, before returning to his stoic self.

"I can't be late for school," he said. "I already have two demerits."

He walked on and I hurried to catch up.

"*You* have two demerits? What for?"

He was silent.

"What did you do?" I pursued, keeping pace with him. I was curious what possible infraction of the rules Mr. Perfect could have committed.

"Fighting," he finally replied.

"I wonder why that comes as no surprise?" I said. I couldn't resist.

He glared at me and I thought if looks could kill, I'd be long dead and buried. Then he pumped his legs harder, remaining a foot or two ahead of me the rest of the way to school.

Theresa Patterson was friendly and spoke to me between classes, but since she didn't have to be my guide any longer, she stayed with her own friends. She didn't have to say it, but I knew if she brought me along, her friends might resent it. Just as in my school, and probably in most schools, clumps of girls and boys clung to each other in cliques, feeling safer and more comfortable hanging around with those whom they perceived to be their own kind.

At lunch I sat at a table alone until Lorraine, Janet, and Betty brought themselves and two other girls over to join me. I saw by the mischievous twinkle in Betty's eyes that they had been plotting something.

149

"So after nearly two days here, how do you like our school?" Lorraine asked innocently.

"It's okay. The teachers are nice," I said.

"Are the boys better looking than the boys in West Virginia?" Janet asked.

"I haven't had a chance to look," I said. When they all looked skeptical, I added, "It's hard starting someplace new during the last quarter of the year. I've got to take the same finals you will take."

One of the new girls looked sympathetic, but Betty tucked in the corner of her mouth and said, "You don't look like you're going to have a problem with school-work."

"Grandpa might have a problem, though," Janet said. "He's barely passing. He might not graduate, I hear."

"Billy Wilkins told me Grandpa is going to fail English," Lorraine said nodding.

"Maybe you can tutor him," Betty suggested.

"That's right, like show him how to do it," Janet said. They all laughed.

"What's that supposed to mean?" I asked. The girls glanced at each other and ate.

"Do you sleep in the same room?" Betty asked me.

"Same room?"

"With Grandpa? We heard Laura and Cary slept in the same room ever since they were born."

"Of course not," I said. "And they didn't."

"I wouldn't be so sure about that," Lorraine said.

"Laura had a very nice room. That's the room I use. None of you have ever been in my aunt and uncle's house?"

"No," Betty said.

"Laura was a very strange girl," Janet offered. "That whole family's strange."

"She didn't want to do anything with girls her age," Lorraine said. "She was like an old lady—cooking, cleaning, canning fruit with her mother."

"I hardly saw her at any of our dances," Janet complained.

150

"Robert Royce was the only boyfriend she ever had," Lorraine said.

"Unfortunate for him," Betty added.

"Whereas, Grandpa has never been with anyone we know," Janet said.

"Now we have someone who will tell us,"Lorraine said, eyeing me. "Tell us, Melody."

"Tell you what?"

"Does Grandpa spend a lot of time in the bathroom, maybe sneaking in with girlie magazines?"

More laughter. The blood rushed to my neck and face.

"When he goes to sleep, do you hear the bedsprings squeaking?" Betty continued. The girls giggled.

"You're all disgusting," I said. Their laughter stopped.

"Oh come on, Melody. I'm sure you're curious about him, too," Janet said.

"He's not bad looking," Lorraine offered gazing across the cafeteria at Cary. He stared back at us. "Maybe you can get him to loosen up, relax. We could help you."

"What do you mean?" I asked.

The girls were quiet a moment, all eyes on the teacher monitor. Betty nodded at Lorraine. She opened her school bag, which she had set between me and her, and took something out quickly. Then she pressed it into my hand. I gazed down at what looked like one of Papa George's self-rolled cigarettes.

"I don't smoke," I said.

"That's not a cigarette, stupid," Betty said. "And keep it below the table so Mr. Rotter doesn't see."

"What is it?"

"It's a joint," Lorraine whispered loudly.

"I don't want it," I said and tried to give it back, but she pushed my hand away.

"Just keep it in case you get a chance to offer it to Grandpa. It'll loosen him up."

"Just tell us what happens, that's all," Betty said.

"Put it away, quick," Lorraine said as Mr. Rotter started down the aisle between the tables.

Little butterflies of panic fluttered in my head. Gazing

around, it seemed as if everyone were looking at me, waiting to see what I would do.

"Hello, girls," Mr. Rotter said smiling down at us. "Are you making our new student feel at home?"

"Yes, Mr. Rotter," Lorraine fluttered her eyelids.

"Is that true, Melody?" he asked me.

I was afraid my voice would crack. "Yes sir," I said.

"Good. Good." He continued through the cafeteria. I let out my breath.

"Very nice. You did well," Betty said. The other girls apparently agreed.

"We're having a beach party Saturday night. We'll meet about eight at Janet's house. You want to come? It will be a chance for you to meet some normal boys," Betty said.

"I don't know if I can. I'll ask my aunt."

"Don't tell her where you're going," Janet said, "or she won't let you come. Just say you're coming over to my house to study for a test. That always works."

"I don't like to lie," I said.

She smirked. "You haven't been living with the Logans long. After a while, you'll get to like it."

The bell signalled the end of lunch period. Everyone rose to leave. I was the last to get up, not realizing until that moment, that I still had the joint of marijuana clutched in my hand. I dropped it into my sandwich bag and then dropped the bag in the garbage can on the way out of the cafeteria.

At the doorway, someone bumped into me hard, and I turned to look into the most perfect face I had ever seen. His blue eyes were positively dazzling and his smile was the warmest and sweetest I'd ever seen. Strong, full lips were turned up gently at the corners, revealing teeth as white as piano keys. A wave of dark brown hair floated over his forehead. He was tall and broad in the shoulders with a narrow waist. His face wasn't as tanned as Cary's, but he had a creamy rich complexion and looked like a male model or a movie star.

"Excuse me," he said. "Did I hurt you?"

152

"No. It's all right."

"I'm afraid I had my mind on my upcoming European history exam. I'm not usually this clumsy."

"It's okay. I'm fine."

"You're the new girl, right?"

"Yes," I said smiling.

"I'm Adam Jackson."

"Melody Logan," I returned.

"Welcome to Provincetown," he said. "I see you've already made friends with some of the girls. Are you going to their beach party Saturday night?"

"I don't know. I . . . I'll see."

"I hope to see you there," he said. His face glittered with a handsome smile as he moved away to join his friends, who, I saw, included a very pretty brunette. She glared at me as she threaded her arm through his and moved him down the hall and away. I stared after him until Lorraine nudged me. The girls had been standing nearby, watching.

"Be careful," Lorraine said. "That's Adam Jackson."

"I know. He told me."

"Did he tell you he puts a nick in the bow of his sailboat for every girl he takes to bed?"

"What?"

"One more nick and that boat might sink," Betty added. We continued toward class before I could catch my breath.

"But maybe she won't mind becoming one of Adam's nicks," Janet quipped. "Would you, Melody?"

"What?"

Everyone laughed again. I was beginning to feel as light and helpless as a balloon caught in a crosswind, blown one way, then another. And I had been here only a couple of days!

Mr. Malamud, my chemistry teacher, spent some time with me after class to be sure I was up-to-date with the class. It was my last period of the day. Cary wasn't waiting for me when I finally emerged from the building.

153

I gazed around for a few moments and then hurried along. I assumed he had picked up May from her school already, so I just took the shortest route back.

"Oh Melody, dear, I was worried about you," Aunt Sara said when I entered the house. "Cary and May have been home a while."

"I had to stay after school for a few minutes to get some extra help from my science teacher," I explained.

"You should have let Cary know," she told me.

"I don't see or speak to Cary much after we arrive at school, Aunt Sara, and that's not all my fault either," I added. I went upstairs to change into a pair of jeans. I found the needlework picture spread out on the bed with a box of colored thread beside it. Moments later, Aunt Sara was in the doorway.

"I'll show you how to make the stitch," she said.

"I'm really not good at this, Aunt Sara."

"Once you start, you will be, I'm sure," she insisted. I was about to continue my protest when Cary appeared in the hallway behind her.

"If she doesn't want to do it, don't keep forcing it on her, Mother," he snapped. Aunt Sara's mouth fell open and her hand fluttered up to the base of her throat.

"I didn't mean to . . . I—"

"It's okay, Aunt Sara," I said, shooting my own sparks of anger from my eyes, "I'd be happy to learn."

Cary took on a look of amusement that added fuel to the fire before he hurried down the stairs and out of the house. Aunt Sara smiled and came into the room to demonstrate the needlework. I picked it up quickly and did enjoy it.

"As soon as this is finished, I'll get a frame for it and put it up with the others," Aunt Sara promised. "But you don't have to work on it now. You've been cooped up in school all day. Go get some fresh air. Laura liked to walk on the beach and hunt for seashells."

May was still completing her chores so I went out by myself. The sky still had patches of deep blue, but most of it had become covered with what looked like storm

154

clouds, bruised and sooty puffs that rolled angrily from the horizon. The ocean looked more tempestuous, too. I could see Cary and Roy Patterson on the lobster boat bobbing beside the dock. I walked out a little way. Cary left the boat and started back toward me and the house.

"There's going to be a storm," he said as he approached. "It's a nor'easter," he added, continuing past. I said nothing and continued to walk toward the ocean. "Didn't you hear what I said?" he called.

I turned.

"Look at the sky. Even a landlubber like you should be able to see rain comin'."

"Don't call me a landlubber."

He smiled. "Well what are you?"

"I'm a person, just like you, only I was brought up in a different place. I'm sure you wouldn't know your way around a coal mine, but I wouldn't call you silly names just to pump myself up."

"I'm not doing it to pump myself up."

I turned away. To my surprise, he was at my side in moments. "Keep walking in this direction and you'll get caught in a downpour. Look at the breakers. The ocean is talking to us, telling us what to expect. See how the terns are heading for safer ground, too."

"Where's Uncle Jacob?" I asked, gazing toward the dock.

"He took today's catch into town. It wasn't good. Only four good-size lobsters in the traps."

"How do lobsters get trapped?" I asked.

"We bait them with stinky dead fish and set them on the ocean bottom. The lobster crawls into the living room and gets caught."

"Living room?"

"That's what we call that part of the trap. Later, we pull up the traps and if the lobsters meet the measurement, we prepare them to take to market."

"How do you prepare them?"

"Well, you got to put rubber bands on the claws so

155

they can't pinch. One claw is a cruncher claw, strong, dull; the other is like a scissor, sharp and quick."

"I didn't know they were so dangerous."

"It's not really so dangerous if you're careful. I've been pinched a bit, but only once had blood drawn." He showed me his right hand. I could see a faint scar along his forefinger.

"Did Laura go lobstering with you?" I asked. He blinked rapidly and turned toward the ocean.

"No, not much," he replied.

"She didn't know the ocean as well as you did?"

"We should go back to the house. There goes Roy." Cary nodded at the tall, broad black man who hurried away from the dock.

"Where do the Pattersons live?"

"In the saltbox houses on the other side of town."

"What happened to Theresa's mother?" I asked.

"You're stuffed full of questions, aren't you?"

"Wouldn't you be if the shoe was on the other foot and you just arrived?"

His lips made that tiny turn up again and he permitted his eyes to stay on me for a few moments longer.

"I guess," he finally admitted. "Theresa's mother died in a car crash coming home from work. She was a chambermaid in a hotel in North Truro. Terrible accident. Man driving a tractor trailer lost control in the rain and crossed the road. Smacked her clear into the other world. Dad says it was meant to be."

"How can something so terrible be meant to be?"

"It's what my father believes," he said.

"Is that why he doesn't seem one bit sad about my father's death, even though my father was his brother? It was meant to be?"

Cary was silent. He kept his head down and kicked some sand. A particularly loud tern cried at the approaching storm.

"And your sister's death," I pursued. "Was that also meant to be?"

He looked at me, his eyes glistening with tears.

156

"I don't like talking about Laura's . . . Laura's disappearance."

"If you keep sadness and pain bottled up, it swells and swells inside you until you burst," I said. "Mama Arlene told me that."

"Yeah, well I never had the pleasure of meeting Mama Arlene," he replied. "I'm going back to the house. Do what you want."

"Why did your father stop talking to my father?" I demanded, my hands on my hips. He hesitated and then turned. "He told me my daddy defied his parents. What did he mean by that? What did my daddy do to them?"

"I don't know."

"But Aunt Sara and Uncle Jacob must have talked about it often."

"I don't listen in on their private talks," he said. "Besides, it's over and done, why talk about it now?"

"I know. You've got to go with the tide."

He widened his eyes and lifted his eyebrows.

"Well," I continued, "sometimes you have to swim against the tide and just be strong enough to get past it, too. Sometimes, you don't give up and give in."

"Really?" he said, amused by my defiance.

"Yes, really."

"Well, first chance I get, I'm going to take you out in my sailboat and let you buck the tide."

"Good."

He shook his head, his smile widening.

"The girls in school told me Laura and her boyfriend went out in your sailboat. Was that so?"

The smile quickly faded. "I have a different sailboat now. And I told you," he said, turning away, "I don't talk about Laura's disappearance with anyone. Especially strangers."

I watched him walk away, shoulders sagging, his head bent, his hands clenched in fists.

The wind grew stronger and whipped past me, catching my hair. Sand began to fly from the beach into my face. The small patches of blue had disappeared from the

157

sky, now completely overcast with dark, brooding clouds. I could feel the ocean spray even this far from the beach. It all began to terrify me. How could weather change so rapidly?

I started for the house, bucking the wind, every step harder than the one before it. My feet slipped on the sand that gave way beneath them. It was harder than walking on ice. The wind was so strong, my eyes began to tear. I had to keep them closed and pump my legs hard. I tried to run. My blouse flapped over my breasts and ribs.

Just before I reached the house, the first sheet of rain tore down, washing over me. I screamed and ran harder for the front door. When I burst in, Cary stood in the hallway, a look of glee in his eyes, an "I told you so" written on his lips.

"I hate it here!" I screamed at him and charged up the stairway.

The wind howled around the house and whistled through it. I thought it might take the roof off, but at the moment I didn't care. Let the sky fall, let the rain swell the ocean and wash over this place, I thought. I embraced myself at the window, watching the trees bend to the point of breaking. The rain came down like bullets fired by God. The street was being pounded. I shuddered and stripped off my blouse. Then I rushed to the bathroom to get a towel for my hair.

Moments later, when I emerged, Cary was in the hallway. He glanced at me before I realized I was standing there in my bra. I draped the towel around myself.

"I'm sorry," he said. He looked repentant. "I shouldn't have left you out there."

"It was my own fault. I didn't listen," I admitted. "Where's May?"

"She's in her room. Sometimes, it's a blessing to be deaf," he said. "She can't hear how hard it's raining and blowing."

"How do you say it's raining?" I asked.

He demonstrated. "This means it's raining hard," he

added and showed me. Then he smiled. "Not the same thing as being out there, huh?"

I relented and smiled. "No."

"Maybe you ain't such a landlubber after all," he allowed. He blushed before going to his room. It was the closest he had come to giving me anything akin to a compliment.

Daddy would say, "Be grateful for the little things."

I went into my room to work on the needlepoint until it was time to help Aunt Sara with dinner. Before it was time to go down, I heard a knock on my door.

"Yes?"

Cary poked his head in.

"I just thought I'd let you know what we do in case it's still raining in the morning."

"What do we do?"

"We walk faster," he said. For the first time since I had come to Provincetown, I heard the sound of my own laughter.

159

9

Something Special

It rained most of the night. Twice, the loud drumming of the drops on the windowpanes woke me. I heard Aunt Sara come to my door after the second time. She stood there gazing in at me, her face in shadow, her head silhouetted against the dim hallway light. I said nothing and she finally closed the door softly.

The rain stopped just before morning. After I dressed and went downstairs, I was surprised to find most of the windows crusted with salt. It reminded me of ice and I remarked about it at breakfast. Aunt Sara said it wasn't unusual after a storm.

"The salt even peels the paint from our window casings. The weather is hard on us, but we endure it."

"The weather's hard on people everywhere," Uncle Jacob declared. "But it's good to us too, and we should be grateful for our blessings. Mark that," he said sharply, waving his long right forefinger at us like some Biblical prophet.

"I can help you clean the windows after school today," I told Aunt Sara.

"Why thank you, dear. It's kind of you to offer."

"Kind? She should do nothing less," Uncle Jacob fixed his eyes on me. "Most young people today don't know what it is to have regular chores and responsibilities. They think everything is owed to them just because they were born."

I wanted to snap back at him and tell him I hadn't been brought up to be spoiled and selfish. I did plenty of work around our home in Sewell, and I often helped Mama Arlene and Papa George with their housework, too. I never asked them anything for it and I never expected anything. It was enough that they gave me their love.

I glared back at Uncle Jacob, the crests of my cheeks burning. He didn't know me. He had hardly spoken ten minutes to me my whole life. What right did he have sitting there on his high and mighty throne and lumping me in with all the spoiled young people he saw in town?

Cary must have sensed those words were at the tip of my tongue, for he shot me a look of warning before I had a chance to part my lips. I stared at him a moment and saw a gentle, but definite shake of his head. I looked down at my hot cereal and swallowed back my anger, even though it threatened to get stuck in my throat and choke me all day.

"Your father is an ogre," I told Cary as we left for school that morning.

Cary didn't reply for a few moments and then said, "He's just afraid, that's all."

"Afraid?" I nearly laughed. "Your father? Afraid of what?"

"Of losing another one of us." Cary marched on, his lips tight, his eyes so focused on the street ahead he barely glanced at me the remainder of the way to school. Despite what Cary said, I think he was ashamed at how his father sometimes behaved.

Since it was Friday, at the end of the school day, Betty, Lorraine, and Janet reminded me about their beach party Saturday night. I said I would try to go, but I reminded them I couldn't go without permission.

161

"Then you won't be there," Betty predicted. "You'll miss a great time."

"I can't help it. I have to ask my uncle and aunt first. My mother left them in charge of me."

"Just do what Janet told you to do: tell them you're going over to her house to study," Lorraine instructed. "A little white lie is no big deal. We all do it."

"It sounds like more than a little white lie. If my uncle found out I lied—"

"He won't find out," Betty assured me. "We don't tell on each other."

"Of course, if you tell Grandpa, he'll turn you in," Janet said.

"Stop calling him Grandpa," I snapped. "He's not anything like an old man."

"Oh? Why do you say that? Do you know something we don't?" she asked quickly. The girls all smiled, waiting with expectation for my reply.

"No," I said.

"Did you get him to smoke the joint?"

"No."

"He didn't see it and tell your uncle, did he?" Lorraine asked quickly.

"If my uncle even thought I had something like that—"

"He'd turn you over to the police," she suggested.

"He'd turn his own mother over to the police," Betty added. "Do you still have it or did you smoke it yourself last night?" Betty asked.

"No, I didn't smoke it." I didn't want to tell them I had simply thrown it out.

"You can smoke it at the beach party," Janet said.

"Let's go, girls," Betty said.

"Be at Janet's house at eight. You won't be sorry. Adam Jackson will be at the beach party," Lorraine sang back at me as they all walked off.

I watched them go down the hallway and then I hurried out to meet Cary and walk home. I wanted to tell him about the party and ask his opinion, but I was afraid even to mention it. I knew how much he didn't like these girls, but I wanted to go. I had never been to a beach party and I had to admit, Adam Jackson's eyes had been in my dreams last night.

I decided to wait until after dinner when I was helping Aunt Sara with the dishes. She had done all the windows herself, even the upstairs ones. "I would have helped you," I told her.

"I know, dear, but don't fret about it. Work gets me through the day. Jacob always says idle hands make for mischief."

I shook my head. What sort of mischief could she ever commit? And why did she permit her husband to treat her as if she were another one of his children and not his wife, his equal in this house? She did everything he asked her to do and as far as I could see, she never uttered a single complaint. He should worship the ground she trod upon and he should have been the one to have done the hard manual labor. My daddy would have done it for my mother, I thought. The more I learned about this family, the more it was a mystery to me.

"Aunt Sara, I was invited to a party Saturday night."

"Oh? A party? Already? What sort of party? Birthday? School party?"

"No. Some of the girls in my class are having a hot dog roast on the beach," I said. "It starts about eight o'clock."

"What girls?"

I gave her the names. She thought a moment.

"Those are girls from good families, but you'll have to ask your uncle," she said.

"Why can't you give me permission?"

"You'll have to ask your uncle for something like that," she replied. I could see that the very idea of her solely giving me permission terrified her. She busied herself with the dishware. If I wanted to go to the beach party, I would have to talk to Uncle Jacob about it. There was no avoiding it.

He was in the living room reading his paper after

dinner as usual. I approached him with my request. "Excuse me, Uncle Jacob," I said from the doorway.

He slowly lowered the paper, his eyebrows tilting and the skin folding along his forehead. I couldn't recall speaking to Daddy without seeing a smile in his eyes or on his lips.

"Yes?"

"Some of the girls in my class at school are having a party on the beach tomorrow night and they have invited me. Aunt Sara said I should ask your permission. I would like to go. It's the fastest way to get to know people," I offered as a practical reason.

He nodded.

"It don't surprise me you'd like to go to a party where they'll be no adults supervising."

"What do you mean?"

He leaned forward with a wry smile. "Don't you think I know what goes on at those beach parties: how they drink and smoke dope and debauch themselves?"

"De . . . what?"

"Perversions," he declared, that irritating forefinger raised like a flag of righteousness again. "Young girls parade around with their revealing clothing and then roll around on blankets with young men to lose their innocence. It's pagan. While you are under my roof, you will *live* decent, *look* decent, and *act* decent, even if it flies in the face of your instincts." He snapped his paper like a whip. "Now, I don't want to hear another word on it."

"What instincts?" I asked. He ignored me. "I am decent. I've never done anything to shame my parents."

He peered over the paper at me.

"It would take something to shame them, I suppose, but I know what's in the blood, what's raging. If you give it free rein, it will take you straight to hell and damnation."

"I don't understand. What's raging in my blood?"

"No more talk!" he screamed. I flinched and stepped back as if slapped. My heart began to pound. A white line had etched itself about his tightened lips as the rest

164

of him flamed with bright red fury. I had never seen rage inflamed by so small a spark. All I had asked was to go to a party.

I turned away and marched up the stairs. The girls were right, I fumed. I should have just lied and said I was going to Janet's to study. Lying to such a man wasn't wrong. He didn't deserve honesty.

Cary was at the foot of the attic stairway, waiting for me to reach the landing.

"What was all the yelling about?"

I told him and he snorted.

"You should have asked me. I would have spared you his reaction to such a request."

"Why is he so mean?"

"I told you. He's not mean, he's just . . . afraid."

"I don't understand. Why should he be so afraid?"

Cary stared at me a moment and then blurted, "Because he believes it was his fault and that he was being punished." He turned away to go up his ladder.

"What was his fault?" I drew closer as he moved up the rungs. "Laura's death? I don't understand. How could that have been his fault? Was it because he gave her permission to go sailing that day?"

"No," Cary said, not turning, still climbing.

"Then I don't understand. Explain it!" I demanded. My tone of voice turned him around. He gazed down at me with a mixture of anger and pain in his face.

"My father doesn't believe in accidents. He believes we are punished on earth for the evil we do on earth, and we are rewarded here for the good we do as well. It's what he was brought up to believe and it's what he has taught us."

"Do you believe that, too?"

"Yes," he said, but not convincingly.

"My daddy was a good man, a kind man. Why was he killed in an accident?"

"You don't know what his sins were," he said and turned away to continue up the stairs.

"He had no sins, nothing so great that he should have

165

died for it! Did you hear me, Cary Logan?" I rushed to the ladder and seized it, shaking it. "Cary!"

He paused at the top and gazed down at me before pulling up his ladder.

"None of us knows the darkness that lingers in another's heart." He sounded just like his father.

"That's stupid. That's another stupid, religious idea," I retorted, but he ignored me and continued to lift the ladder. I seized the bottom rung and held it down. He looked down, surprised at my surge of strength.

"Let go."

"I'll let go, but don't think I don't know what you're doing up there every night," I said. His face turned so red I could see the crimson in his cheeks even in the dim hallway light. "You're running away from tragedy, only you can't run away from something that's part of you."

He tugged with all his strength, nearly lifting me from the floor with the ladder. I had to let go and the ladder went up. He slammed the trapdoor shut.

"Good riddance!" I screamed.

May, locked in her world of silence, emerged from her room with a smile on her face. In my mind, she was the luckiest one in this damnable home.

She signed to me, asking if I would let her come into my room. I told her yes. She followed me in and watched me angrily poke the needle and thread into the picture her sister Laura had drawn just before she died. As I worked I glared up at the ceiling and then down at the floor, below which my coldhearted uncle sat reading his paper. After a while the mechanical work was calming and meditating. I began to understand why Laura might have been entranced with doing so much of it. Everyone in this house was searching for a doorway.

May remained with me until her bedtime, practicing communicative skills, asking me questions about myself, my family, and our lives back in West Virginia. She was full of curiosity and sweetness, somehow unscathed by the turmoil that raged in every family member's heart.

166

Perhaps her world wasn't so silent after all. Perhaps she heard different music, different sounds, all of it from her free and innocent imagination. When her eyelids began drifting downward, I told her she should go to bed. I was tired myself. I felt as if I had been spun around in an emotional washing machine, then left in a dryer until my last tear evaporated.

Cary lingered in his attic hideaway almost all night. I was woken just before morning to the sound of his footsteps on the ladder. He paused at my doorway for a moment before going to his own room.

He was up with the sunlight a little over an hour later and had gone out with Uncle Jacob by the time I went down for breakfast. Aunt Sara said they were going to be out lobstering all day. I walked to town with May and we spent most of the afternoon looking at the quaint shops on Commercial Street, then we watched the fishermen down at the wharf. It wasn't quite tourist season yet, but the warm spring weather still brought a crowd up from Boston and the outlying areas. There was a lot of traffic.

Aunt Sara had given us some spending money so we could buy hamburgers for lunch. She didn't mind my taking May along with me. She saw how much May wanted to be with me, and I was growing more confident with sign language.

Aunt Sara remarked at how quickly and how well I had been learning it. "Laura was the best at it," she told me. "Even better than Cary."

"What about Uncle Jacob?" I asked her. "Doesn't he know it?"

"A little. He's always too busy to practice," she said, but I thought it was a weak excuse. If my daddy had to learn sign language to communicate with me, nothing would be more important, I thought.

About midday, I counted the change I had left and went to a pay phone. It wasn't enough for a call to Sewell, but I took a chance and made it collect to Alice. Luckily, she was home and accepted the charges.

"I'm sorry," I told her. "I don't have enough money."

167

"That's okay. Where are you?"

"I'm in Provincetown, on Cape Cod, living with my uncle and my aunt."

"Living with them? Why?"

"Mommy's gone to New York to get an opportunity as a model or an actress," I said. "If she doesn't get a job there, she's going on to Chicago or Los Angeles, so I had to stay here and enroll in the school."

"You did? What's it like?"

I told her about the school and about my life at my uncle's house, Laura's disappearance and death, and May's handicap.

"It sounds sad."

"It's hard to live with them, especially with my cousin Cary. He's so bitter about everything, but I keep telling myself I won't be here long."

"What are the girls like at school?"

"They're different," I told her. "They seem to know more about things and do more things."

"Like what?"

I told her how they had given me a joint of marijuana in the school cafeteria.

"What did you do? You haven't smoked it, have you?"

"No. I was scared. Actually, I was terrified when a teacher came to our table. Afterward, when the girls weren't looking, I threw it in the garbage."

"That's what I would have done," Alice said. "Maybe you should stay away from them."

"They invited me to their beach party tonight, but my uncle won't let me go."

"A beach party!" She hesitated and with some envy said, "Sounds like fun. Maybe you're going to like living there after all."

"I don't think so," I said. "I wish I were back home."

"I was passing the cemetery yesterday and I thought about you so I went in and said a little prayer at your father's grave for you."

"Did you? Thank you, Alice. I miss you."

"Maybe, if you're still there, I can come up to visit you this summer."

"That would be great, but I expect to be gone from here by then. Mommy's coming to get me as soon as she gets settled. Which reminds me, have you seen Mama Arlene? Mommy was supposed to contact her to send me my things."

"I saw her, but George is real sickly."

"I know."

"I think he may be in the hospital."

"Oh no! Would you please tell Mama Arlene I called?"

"I'll go right over to see her," Alice promised.

I gave her my uncle's name and telephone number and she promised to call me the next weekend.

"I really have no friends since you left," she admitted at our conversation's end. It brought tears to my eyes. After I hung up, May wanted to know why I was crying. I tried to explain, but I really didn't know enough sign language to reveal all the pain in my heart. It was easier just to go home.

When we arrived, Aunt Sara explained that dinner was going to be different this night. Uncle Jacob had invited another lobster man and his wife, the Dimarcos. May, Cary, and I were to eat first and be gone by the time the adults sat at the table. I thought that was a blessing and was grateful for a meal without Uncle Jacob glaring at me as if I were one of the Jezebels he saw on every corner.

However, late in the afternoon, Cary and Uncle Jacob returned home in a very happy mood. Apparently, they had one of their best days at sea, a catch of fifteen lobsters as well a dozen good-size striped bass.

To celebrate, Cary declared that he, May, and I were going to enjoy a real New England feast: clam chowder, steamed muscles, grilled striped bass, potatoes, and vegetables. Cary said he would prepare the fish himself outside on the barbecue grill. "Mother's busy with her own dinner. We can have our own picnic," he said.

169

"Fine," I told him.

"It won't be as exciting as the beach party, I'm afraid."

"I said, fine."

He nodded and told May, who was very pleased with the idea.

"You two can set the picnic table, if you like."

I nodded without smiling, even though I was happy with the idea.

Cary went about preparing the meal meticulously. He was much better at it than I had expected. None of the boys I had known in West Virginia knew the first thing about preparing fish and vegetables. He thanked me when May and I finished setting the table. I decided to make civil conversation.

"I still don't understand how you fish for lobster," I said standing nearby and watching him grill the fish. "You don't need a pole?"

He laughed.

"We don't fish for them exactly. We set traps at the bottom of the ocean floor and attach buoys that float above."

"How do the other fishermen know which trap is theirs and which is yours?"

"Each lobster fisherman has his own colors on his buoys. We're using the same colors my great grandfather used. They sort of belong to our family, like a coat of arms or something. Understand?"

I nodded.

"After we bring up a trap, if there is a lobster in it, we measure it with a gauge from its eye socket to the end of its back. An average lobster runs anywhere from two to five pounds. My father once brought up a trap with a lobster in it that weighed over thirty."

"Thirty!"

"Yeah, but someone else trapped one closer to forty last year. Lobsters with eggs on their tails have to be thrown back in immediately. We have to do all we can to keep up the supply. It takes about seven and a half years for a lobster to grow to decent size."

"Seven and a half years?"

"Uh huh," he said smiling. "Now you know why we grow and harvest cranberries, too."

"Is this what you want to do for the rest of your life?" I asked him.

He nodded.

"You don't want to go to college?"

"My college is out there," he said pointing toward the ocean with the fork.

"There's more to life than just fishing and sailing, and there are wonderful places to visit on land, wonderful things to see."

"I see enough here."

"I never saw someone so young act so—"

"What?" he asked quickly. I swallowed back the words and chose less painful ones. "Grown up."

He nodded.

"Go on," he said. "If you want to call me Grandpa, too, you can. I don't care."

"You're nothing like a grandpa."

He looked at me curiously for a moment. I felt, since he was being honest, I should be. "But you're too fixed in your thinking for someone your age. You should have a more open mind about things."

"Sure," he said. "And be willing to smoke dope and drink and waste my time just like those other jerks in school."

"They're not all jerks, are they?"

"Most are."

"You can be pretty infuriating," I told him.

He shrugged and began serving the fish. "I don't bother anyone and just ask they don't bother me," he said. "Let's eat."

He made sure May had her meal first. The way he took care of her, saw to her needs and happiness, softened my frustration and anger toward him.

"How hard was it for May when Laura died?" I asked him as we sat at the picnic table and began our meal.

"Real hard," he said.

"Poor thing. To have such a tragedy on top of her handicap."

"She does fine," he said angrily.

"No one is saying she doesn't, Cary. You don't have to jump down my throat. There is such a thing as being too protective, you know."

"You can never be too protective," he replied. "Once you go out there, you'll understand." He nodded toward the ocean.

"When am I going out there?" He was silent. "I've never been on a sailboat. Daddy used to take us to the beach, but Mommy hated boats so we just went swimming and got suntans."

"What a bunch of tourists," he quipped.

"You shouldn't make fun of the tourists. They buy your lobsters, don't they?"

"And ruin everything, litter the beach, poison the water, make fun of us."

"I think you'd be happy just being a hermit," I concluded. It didn't faze him. He shrugged.

"This is good," I told him after I ate some of the fish, but it sounded like a complaint.

"Thanks," he said without any feeling.

"You're welcome," I growled.

We ate silently, shooting darts at each other with our eyes, but when we turned to May we saw her staring at us and smiling a wide smile of amusement. Cary's eyes shifted to mine. We gazed at each other a moment and then we had to laugh.

It was as if a sheet of ice had cracked and let in some warm air. Our conversation lightened up and I talked about the scenery. I was taken with the apricot glow of the sunset as we looked out over the ocean. I hadn't realized how beautiful the ocean could be. That pleased him and he revealed that when he was a little boy he and Laura would lie on their backs in their father's rowboat at dusk and watch the sky change colors.

"It seemed magical," he said.

"It is."

172

There was real warmth in his eyes and I thought the girls were right: he was good looking when he wanted to be. Suddenly, though, he became self-conscious and quickly reverted to his serious, hard look. However, after dinner when I helped him clean up, he surprised me by suggesting we walk into town with May for some frozen custard.

"And see what damage the outsiders are doing," he added.

"And what money they're leaving with the local merchants," I added. He hid his smile, but I caught it.

For the first time, when we walked with May, he allowed her to hold both our hands. Cary led us a different way that took us past high grass, bushes, and scrub oak trees. I heard the peepers in the marsh.

"Theresa and her brother and sisters and her father live down there," he pointed when we turned a corner.

I gazed at a street that wound east. The houses were small and the grass in their yards was spotty and rough. Closer to the town, the houses were nicer, with real lawns and flowers, like yellow tea roses in a bed of Queen Anne's lace, dark purple iris, and hydrangeas.

The Cape was truly amazing. Toward the ocean, there were rolls and rolls of sand that looked as dry and sparse as any desert, but a short distance away were oak trees, blueberry bushes, red maple trees, and houses with lawns full of crocus clusters, emperor tulips, and sprawling lilac bushes. It seemed like two different worlds. Cary said there was often two kinds of weather. It could be stormy on the east with the sun shining brightly on the west.

Perhaps the differences in the land explained the differences in the people, I thought, some hard, frugal, with religious ideas carved in stone; other carefree, impulsive, jolly, and hungry for fun and excitement. Some lived to work and some worked just enough to live.

At night the little town was exciting, especially with all the people, the music from the bars and restaurants, the carloads of tourists yelling to each other, the crowds

173

down at the dock. My eyes went everywhere. He bought May her frozen custard and asked me if I wanted one, too. I did. He got himself one as well.

May wanted to go to the dock and watch the deep-sea fishermen try to entice the tourists to hire them. I had never been in a real tourist town at night before, and was taken with all the lights, and the way store owners and desert tour operators barked at the people, tempting, cajoling, practically begging for their business.

"I hate those desert tours," Cary remarked when a jeep load rolled by. "Once, a couple of jeeps pulled up behind our house and the guide pointed to my mother and Laura, describing them as native fishermen's women."

"So, that's what your mother is, right?"

"She's not a freak for tourists to gape at, no," he said, "and Laura certainly was not. How would they like a sightseeing bus coming around to their backyards and having people gape at them while they did their housework?"

I nodded, understanding some of his anger.

"You're right. That isn't nice." He looked appreciative, but quickly checked his smile and gazed at May.

"Better get back," he said. "May's sleepy."

When we returned to the house, Uncle Jacob was entertaining his fisherman friend in the living room while their wives chatted in the kitchen. We went directly upstairs. May went to sleep quickly.

"Thanks for the custard and the walk," I told Cary in the hallway.

He stared at me a moment.

"Are you very tired?"

"No, not very," I said.

"Want to see something special?"

"Sure."

"Come on," he said, leading the way down the stairs. We stepped quietly through the house, but Uncle Jacob heard us and came to the living room doorway.

174

"Where you going now, son?" he asked.

"Just going to check the bog," Cary replied.

Uncle Jacob looked at me, his eyes growing smaller before he nodded softly and returned to his company.

Cary said nothing. He hurried out of the house and led me over the grounds to the hill. When we reached the top, he paused and we gazed at the bog. The moonlight played tricks with the blossoms. They dazzled like jewels in the night.

"What do you think?" he asked.

"It's beautiful."

"I thought you might like it."

To our right the ocean roared in the darkness. I embraced myself.

"Cold?"

"A little," I admitted.

"I bet you really wanted to go to that beach party," he said.

"I've never been to one."

"All they do is smoke dope or drink around the fire. Some of them go off into the darkness, of course."

"Don't you want a girlfriend some day?" I asked him.

"When I find someone sensible, I'll speak to her," he replied.

"No one's sensible?"

"And pretty, too," he admitted. He stood there with his hands in his pockets, kicking the sand and occasionally glancing at me and then at the ocean. "What about you?"

"What?"

"Did you have a boyfriend back in West Virginia?"

"For a while I was going steady, but after Daddy died . . . I stopped going to school dances and things."

"Yeah, I didn't want to do anything after Laura died. I didn't want to work or ever go back to school."

"That was the only good thing about us leaving Sewell," I told him. "Not having to go to the places Daddy and I used to go to anymore, not having to look at the coal miners and wait for him to come home."

175

He thought a moment. "I couldn't leave here ever."

"Most of the young people I knew were always talking about getting away from home someday."

"Not me. This is where I belong, where I was meant to be. I got saltwater in my blood."

I laughed.

"I probably won't graduate anyway," he added.

"Why not?"

"Doing pretty bad in English."

"Badly."

"What?"

"You're doing badly, not bad."

"See what I mean?"

"Maybe I can help you. I'm a very good English student."

"It's probably too late. If I don't pass the final—"

"Then you'll pass it," I told him. "I'll help you every night. Okay?"

"I don't know. I don't know if I even care."

"You've got to care! Besides, I'm sure you'll do well if you try."

He smiled.

"I understand Laura was a very good student. Did she help you?"

He looked away instead of answering and then he turned back and started down the hill. "Let's go back to the house."

I followed him. When we entered the house again, Uncle Jacob asked Cary in to talk about the lobster business with them. I told them good night and went to my room to read. A little while later I heard Cary go up to his attic hideaway. I listened to him scuffle about and then all grew quiet, but for the muffled voices of Uncle Jacob, Aunt Sara, and their friends below.

My eyelids felt heavy. I dozed off, woke up, went to the bathroom, returned, and dressed for bed. After I put the lights out, I gazed out the window and saw the moon walk on the ocean. How beautiful. Had Laura looked out this window and been thrilled by it? What was she really like? I had Aunt Sara's constant descriptions, comparisons, and remarks, but somehow I thought there was more to her daughter than she knew.

Cary knew, I thought. She had been his twin, but he was afraid or unwilling to talk about her. It would take time, but more importantly, it would take trust. I wondered if I could ever get him to trust me with the secrets of his heart. I knew he had secrets buried deeply.

I closed my eyes and lay back on my pillow and thought about Mommy. Where was she tonight? I swallowed back my tears and pressed for sleep to keep myself from thinking sad thoughts.

Was that what Cary did every night?

10
&

A Cocoon of Lies

*T*he next morning, Sunday, we went to church then
came home and prepared for our visit to my grandparents as if we were going to visit royalty. Aunt Sara
explained that everyone had to wear his and her best
clothes and be prim and proper.

She paraded through the room explaining what I was
to wear and how I was to wear my hair and carry myself.
"Olivia doesn't like women to have their hair loose and
down. She says it makes them look like witches. Use the
bobby pins and combs to wrap your hair neatly. And no
makeup, not even lipstick. You can wear the charm
bracelet, of course, but rings and necklaces, and especially earrings don't belong on young ladies, she says."

"Is that what you think, too, Aunt Sara?"

"What I think doesn't matter when we go to Samuel
and Olivia's home," she replied. "Jacob's pleased when
they're pleased."

"And you? When are you pleased?"

Aunt Sara paused and gazed at me as if I had asked the
most ridiculous question. "I'm pleased when Jacob's
pleased, as any wife would be."

"I hope that my husband will want me to be happy, too, and care about my feelings as much or more than he cares about his own. My daddy was like that."

"Oh dear, don't say things like that in front of Jacob. Especially not today," she warned.

"Maybe I shouldn't go along," I said. Alarm sprang to her eyes.

"You have to go! It's Sunday. We always go to Samuel and Olivia's for Sunday brunch," she said. "Why, Laura used to look forward to going. Olivia always has wonderful things to eat. Laura loved the tiny cakes with frosting and jelly in the center, and Samuel always gave her a crisp five-dollar bill when we left. She was the apple of his eye. She was . . ." She paused to take a deep breath.

For a moment she seemed locked in a daze. Then her eyes snapped closed and open and she spun around. "Try to keep your shoulders back and your head up when you walk. Olivia hates the way young people slouch today. She's always saying posture shows character and embellishes good health."

"No one's ever said I slouch."

"No, you don't, but just be more attentive to it. Well, I must see about May."

I took a deep breath and rose, feeling even more nervous this morning than the day I had first arrived. When I finally thought myself dressed well enough and looking somewhat the way Aunt Sara wanted me to, I descended the stairs to find the family waiting in the living room. Everyone was still dressed in their church clothes.

Uncle Jacob wore a dark blue suit and tie and Cary wore a light blue sports jacket, tie, and slacks. His shoes were spit shined. May looked sweet in her pink cotton dress with her hair tied in a pink ribbon. She wore black patent leather mary janes. Aunt Sara had on a dark blue, high-necked dress with a belt at the waist. As usual she wore no makeup and only the locket for jewelry. Her hair was pulled back in a severe bun and held there with a bone-white comb.

They all stared at me when I entered. I was being inspected. I waited for approval. Cary's eyes widened and then went darker before he looked away. I was sure it was because I was wearing another one of Laura's dresses—this time a pretty cream-colored one. I couldn't wait for my own things to arrive.

"Well, she looks very nice, doesn't she, Jacob?" Aunt Sara asked meekly.

"Aye," he said reluctantly. "Did you talk to her about her behavior?"

"Not yet," she said.

"What have I done now?" I asked.

"It's not what you've done. It's what you might do," Uncle Jacob remarked. Then he turned to Sara. "Well, do it and then come out," he said rising. He nodded at Cary, who got up quickly, took May's hand, and left.

"Just sit a moment, dear," Aunt Sara said. "There are a few other things you must remember."

"What other things?" I sat on the settee.

"Olivia, your grandmother, is very particular about how children behave in her home."

"I'm not a child," I said. "I'm nearly sixteen."

"Oh, I know, but until you're married yourself, she thinks of you as a child." Aunt Sara obviously spoke from her own experience.

She stood before me like a teacher in school. "Most important, speak only when you are spoken to. Olivia thinks it's rude for a young person to demand answers from adults or give an opinion without being asked to do so. And especially, never, never interrupt when someone else is speaking."

"I don't," I said.

"Good. Remember to say please and thank you and never sit with your legs apart. Put your hands in your lap. At the table be sure to bring the spoon and the fork to your mouth and not vice versa, and remember to keep only one elbow at a time on the table. Always dab your lips with your napkin after you put something in your mouth. Sit with your back straight and don't stare at people," she recited as if she had memorized some etiquette book. "Do you understand everything?"

I nodded.

"It doesn't sound as if I'm going to enjoy myself very much," I muttered. She went white.

"Oh dear, never say such a thing. Please! Keep such thoughts under lock and key."

"Don't worry, Aunt Sara, I've never embarrassed my parents. I won't embarrass you." I rose, my legs very reluctant, and left the house. Cary and May waited in the rear of the car. I got in beside May.

"How far away is it?" I asked Cary softly.

"About twenty minutes."

My teeth were actually chattering in anticipation of Grandma Olivia's disapproval and rejection. But why? I was finally going to meet my father's parents, my real grandparents. I should have been excited. All the grandparents I ever heard of loved their grandchildren dearly.

But, I reminded myself, our family is different.

From the outside, my grandparents' house did not look cold and impersonal. It was a large, wooden clapboard house.

Aunt Sara said that the house was very old and prestigious, the original portion having been built around 1780. Cary shook his head and raised his eyes toward the car ceiling when Aunt Sara went into her lecture about the house, a lecture I guessed Grandma Olivia had given her so many times it was stored forever in her memory.

The grounds were certainly the prettiest I had seen on the Cape. The beautifully cared for green lawn was uncommon, and the flower garden was the most elaborate with its baskets of gold, purple pansies, roses, and geraniums. There was a small duck pond to the right with about a dozen or so ducks in it. Most impressive were the large, blooming red maple trees. Between two on the far right was a bench swing with a canopy over it.

We stopped in the driveway and got out. Aunt Sara

181

immediately brushed a loose strand of my hair back and straightened the shoulders of my dress.

"Leave her be," Cary muttered.

She stood next to Uncle Jacob as he rang the bell, the three of us standing behind them. A moment later the door opened.

I set eyes on my grandfather for the first time in real life. Up until now, all I had seen was that old photograph of my daddy.

Grandpa Samuel was still a tall, straight-standing man with a proud, strong demeanor. I saw my daddy's resemblance in his face immediately. Daddy, as did Cary, shared his green eyes. Grandpa Samuel's hair was mostly gray, but he still had a full head of it. It was trimmed neatly at the ears and sides, with the top brushed back. There was a trace of a wave running through it.

Daddy had had the same straight, firm nose, but Grandpa Samuel's lips were thinner and his chin more carved. He had Daddy's large hands and long arms, and for a man his age, I thought he had very firm, full shoulders.

"Hello, Jacob, Sara," he said. He gazed past them quickly to focus on me. I thought I saw a small smile at the corners of his mouth, the same light and gentle twist that Daddy often had. He looked quickly at Cary and May. "Children."

"Hello, Papa," Cary said.

"Hello . . . Pa pa," May said.

"This is Melody," Aunt Sara said stepping to the side to bring me forward.

"Pretty girl. Lot of Haille in her, eh Jacob?"

"Aye," Uncle Jacob replied glancing at me.

"Hello, Melody," my grandfather said.

I didn't know whether I was to shake his hand or curtsey or just nod.

"Hello," I replied. "I'm pleased to meet you." I almost added, "finally." He nodded, holding that small smile on his lips.

"Well, come on in," he told us and stepped back. "Olivia's seeing to the brunch, of course."

We entered a short, marble-floored entryway with paintings on both sides: pictures of the Cape and boats, pictures of sailors. The house was full of the perfume of flowers.

Grandpa Samuel showed us to the room on the right, the sitting room. It looked like a showcase in a furniture store window. The oak floor was so polished I was sure I would be able to see my face in it if I looked down. On every table, on every shelf, there were expensive-looking glass pieces, vases, and occasionally, photos in silver and gold frames. I just glanced at them, but they looked like pictures of my grandfather and grandmother when they were younger, and some pictures of Uncle Jacob, Aunt Sara, Laura, Cary, and May. There were no pictures of Daddy.

"Sit with Cary and May over there," Aunt Sara instructed. We took the settee on the right. Grandpa Samuel sat in the chair and Aunt Sara and Uncle Jacob sat on the settee across from us. Although he kept his eyes on me, Grandpa Samuel spoke to Uncle Jacob.

"So how was your week, Jacob?"

"Fair to middling," he replied. "We had a good day yesterday, eh Cary?"

"Yes sir," Cary said. He shot a glance at me.

Grandpa Samuel nodded. Then he turned toward me. "So you're Melody. How old are you?"

"Fifteen, almost sixteen."

"Aye, that would be right." He thought a moment and then smiled. "I hear you can play the fiddle. My grandfather played the accordion. I ever tell you that, Sara?"

"No," she said, her eyes wide.

"I've told you the same before," Uncle Jacob snapped at her.

"Did you? I don't remember your speaking about your grandfather playing the accordion, Jacob."

"Aye, he was good at it," Grandpa Samuel said,

183

directing himself to me. "I can still remember hearing his jolly tunes."

"There are better things to remember than a lazy fisherman," I heard a sharp, small voice say. We turned to the doorway to see Grandma Olivia. She stood a little over five feet tall, and wore a pale yellow dress. Her snow-white hair was pulled back in a bun as severely as Aunt Sara's, which only made her eyes look bigger and her forehead look wider. There were tiny age spots clustered at the foot of her hairline and on her cheeks. Without lipstick, her lips were a dull pink. Below her jaw, her skin hung loosely like a hen's.

There was no bend in her back, and because she had such a regal posture, she looked taller, sturdier than I was sure she was.

"You're early," she accused, gazing at us, her eyes fixing tightly on me.

"We were ready, so we came," Uncle Jacob remarked.

"Early's better than late," Grandpa Samuel said. She shot a look at him and his smile faded quickly.

"Well, then," she said, nodding at Sara, "make the proper introductions."

"Yes, Olivia." Aunt Sara turned to me. "This is Melody, Haille's Melody."

Haille's, I thought. Why not Haille and Chester's? Was even my father's name forbidden in this house?

Aunt Sara nodded at me to tell me to stand. I rose and Grandma Olivia came closer. She drank me in, gazing at me from head to foot quickly, and nodded to herself to confirm some previous notion.

"Looks healthy. Tall, too, with good posture."

Tall? I wasn't so tall, I thought, but then I realized almost anyone would be tall to her.

"Well then, what do you say?" she asked.

I glanced at Aunt Sara who nodded and smiled.

"Hello, Grandma Olivia," I replied. The words appeared to sting her. She tightened her body and lifted her shoulders.

"We'll eat even though we're a bit early," she said,

184

"and you'll tell me all about yourself, Samuel," she ordered and he rose. Cary and May stood and Aunt Sara got up quickly with Uncle Jacob.

For a moment I felt as if we were all in some army and Grandma Olivia was the general. She started out and we followed. We crossed the hallway to the dining room.

It was a beautiful room, with dark, oak-paneled walls and a glossy, long cherry-wood table. All the chairs were upholstered with high backs. The china looked very expensive and the candle holders looked as if they were made of real gold. The silverware was heavy. Everyone had a linen placemat and linen napkins.

Cary, May, and I were put on one side, Aunt Sara and Uncle Jacob on the other. Grandma Olivia sat at the far end of the table and Grandpa Samuel on the other end. A maid brought out the brunch.

It began with a tossed salad, glittering with plum tomatoes and the greenest peppers and lettuce I had ever seen. Long loaves of bread were sliced and placed on silver serving plates. Everyone was given tall glasses of ice water. Following that, a large dish of perfectly arranged jumbo shrimp on a bed of lettuce was presented. There were small, cold potatoes, asparagus spears, and then two beautifully roasted ducks, all sliced.

Grandma Olivia took tiny portions of everything, but Grandpa Samuel ate as much as Uncle Jacob and Cary. I felt Grandma Olivia's eyes on my every move and recited Aunt Sara's instructions for etiquette at the dinner table to myself as I chewed, sipped, and reached for things.

"So then," Grandma Olivia said suddenly, as if we were all still in the midst of a conversation that had previously begun. "Haille called?"

"Yes," Aunt Sara said. "The other night she spoke with Melody."

Grandma Olivia turned her cold, steely eyes on me. "Where is your mother?"

"She called from someplace between Boston and New York," I replied.

"And how long does she intend to carry on like this?" she asked.

I shook my head. "Carry on?"

"Pretending she's doing something with her wretched life," she explained.

I felt the heat rise into my neck and face. "She has auditions, meetings, appointments," I said. "She's trying to become—"

"A what? A model, an actress?" she interrupted with a small, thin laugh. Then she looked at Grandpa Samuel. "An actress she's always been," she said. He looked away and she turned back to me.

"Your father left you and your mother no money after all these years of so-called honest labor?"

"We had something, but expenses were high for us and Mommy needed things and—"

"Wasteful. Never changed a bit," she muttered. "What did she look like?" she asked Aunt Sara.

"Oh, she's still very pretty, Olivia. Maybe she can be a model."

"Ridiculous. With her posture? Cary," she snapped, deciding to move on to someone else at the table, "how is your schoolwork now?"

"Not much better than it was, Grandma, I'm afraid," he said.

"Well, what do you plan on doing about it, Cary? You don't have all that much more time left, do you?" she asked.

"I'm thinking of being tutored," he said, shifting his gaze to me. I saw the small smile on his lips and smiled, too. Grandma Olivia caught the look between us and turned to me again.

"You are a good student, I understand?"

"Yes, Grandma. I've always been on the honor roll."

"Hmph," she said and shook her head. "Your mother didn't even graduate from high school, you know."

I looked up quickly.

"Yes, she did," I said.

Aunt Sara made a tiny gasp and brought her napkin to

186

her lips. She shook her head slightly at me. Was I supposed to just sit by and let Grandma Olivia say untruths?

"She told you that, did she?"

"Yes," I said.

She smiled that cold smile again, twisting her thin lips until they looked as if they would snap. "That girl never could distinguish between reality and illusion. No wonder she's gallivanting around the country trying to be an actress or a model," Grandma Olivia continued.

How do you know so much about my mother? I wanted to ask. You who disowned my father after he married her. But I lowered my eyes and nibbled on my food instead. Then I gazed at May, who sat eating and staring ahead with a soft smile on her face. I wondered if either Grandma Olivia or Grandpa Samuel knew how to communicate with her. All I had seen so far were smiles and nods from Grandpa Samuel. Grandma Olivia barely acknowledged her, from what I had seen.

We ate in silence, with everyone but Grandma Olivia keeping his eyes on the food before him. Finally, Grandpa Samuel looked up.

"The word I been getting," Grandpa Samuel said to Uncle Jacob, "is there'll be a good tourist season this year with the price of travel overseas going up and all."

Uncle Jacob nodded. "Aye. I heard that the hotels were looking good. There'll be lots of garbage to clean off the beach come this fall," he added. I knew where Cary got his attitude about the outsiders.

"How are the cranberries coming along?" Grandpa Samuel asked.

"They look good. We're anticipating a decent crop."

"Does she expect to leave you here over the summer?" Grandma Olivia suddenly asked me.

"I don't know," I said. "I hope not."

She raised her eyebrows.

"And why is that? Aren't you being treated well at my son's home? They gave you Laura's room, I understand, and you're even wearing her things, aren't you?"

"Yes, I'm being treated well," I said quickly. "I just meant I would like to be with my mother. I miss her."

She smirked. "A girl your age should have a home and not be living out of a car running on someone's pipe dreams," she muttered.

"We had a home and we'll have another one," I said, my voice full of defiance.

"What kind of home did you have in West Virginia?" she asked, not intimidated by my tone of voice.

"We lived in the trailer park. Daddy worked very hard in the coal mine. I never went hungry."

"And your mother, what did she do?"

"She worked in a beauty parlor."

"That figures," Grandma Olivia said. "That woman could wear out a mirror."

Before I could respond, Grandma turned quickly to call the maid. "The adults will have coffee in the sitting room, Loretta."

"Yes, ma'am."

"Bring out some ice cream and some of the petit fours for the children," she ordered.

Children? I looked at Cary to see how he liked being referred to that way. He tucked the corner of his mouth in and gazed at the wall.

"Lucky for you that your Aunt Sara saved all of Laura's clothing," Grandma Olivia told me. "She always had such nice things."

"Mommy's sent for my things," I replied. I glanced at Aunt Sara and saw the hurt look on her face. "Although I am grateful for what Aunt Sara has given me to use. I'm just sorry about the circumstances."

Grandpa Samuel nodded, his look softening.

Grandma Olivia raised her eyebrows. "And what do you know about the circumstances?" she demanded.

"What? Well, I was told—"

"Olivia, must we go through this again?" Grandpa Samuel asked softly.

Grandma Olivia snorted. "Jacob says you can play the fiddle well," she said. I was shocked. Uncle Jacob had

188

said something nice about me? "Maybe one day you'll come over and give us a concert," she added. My jaw nearly dropped. Was she serious?

She stood up. "Let's go into the sitting room for coffee, Samuel," she commanded.

"Right, dear," he said rising.

The maid brought out three dishes of ice cream for Cary, May, and me and served them with a plate of small cakes, the ones Aunt Sara told me Laura had loved.

"Sorry, we only have vanilla ice cream," Grandma Olivia remarked. "Cary, you can show Melody the grounds when you're finished, and entertain yourselves outside. But don't track in any dirt. Make sure May understands," she concluded.

"Okay, Grandma," he said and signed instructions to May.

"How is she?" Grandma asked, remaining at the table and looking at her with pity.

"She's doing very well, Grandma," Cary said, before his parents could reply. Grandma Olivia nodded, shook her head as if to drive the thoughts away, and led the adults out of the dining room.

I felt a ceiling of oppressive gray clouds and heavy air, too thick to breathe, go out with her.

"You should call this place the Ice House," I remarked.

Cary smiled. "She's not as tough as she makes out."

We ate the dessert and, I had to admit, I did like the small cakes. "This house itself is very nice, nicer even than Alice Morgan's."

"Who's she?"

"My best friend back in Sewell." I gazed at the pretty things, the antique hutch filled with expensive crystal, the beautiful chandelier above us, and the rich, large paintings on the walls.

"How did Grandpa make so much money?" I asked Cary.

"A great deal was left to Grandma Olivia when her

189

parents passed away. Grandpa had a fleet of fishing vessels, including five lobster boats. But, he lost most of them during bad times. Luckily, my father had his own by then. Come on. I'll show you around."

He signed to May and she gulped down one more spoonful of ice cream. I took her hand when she came around the table. Cary led us through the house, down the corridor, past the door to the kitchen, past a den-office on the right, finally to a rear door. It opened on a small porch.

Behind the house was a large gazebo, some benches and a rock garden with a small fountain. The rear of the property was on the beach and there was a dock with a large sailboat and a small motorboat tied to it.

"This is a beautiful place," I declared.

"Aye. They actually have a small cove here so it's not as rough as it is up and down the beach."

We walked down to the dock and looked at the ocean. The waves were gentle. Milk-white streaks of clouds lay against the blue sky. To the right against the shoreline were large rocks.

"See the mussels clinging to those rocks," Cary said pointing. They were dark purple against the stone. On the sand, seagulls strutted about searching for clams. I saw one circle the rocks and then drop something from its beak. The moment what it had dropped hit the rock, it swooped to retrieve it.

"What is that bird doing?"

"Seagulls drop the clams on the rocks to break the shells and then drop to eat them as soon as they hit the stone. Smart, eh?"

I shook my head in amazement, not only at what I saw, but at how much Cary knew about nature.

I looked down the beach to our left. A large sailboat bounced over the waves, its sail flapping in the breeze. "I can understand why my daddy wanted to go to the seashore so much. He missed this."

Cary nodded, glanced at me, and then checked the

knot on the rope that held the motorboat to the dock. May signed to us she was going to look for seashells.

"Not too far," Cary signed. She nodded and directed her attention to the beach.

"Our grandmother sure hates my mother, doesn't she?" I said.

Cary kept his watchful eyes on May. "Looks that way," he admitted.

"Do they often talk about her and my daddy?"

"Hardly ever," he said. He started for the beach and I followed.

"I can't understand what my daddy could possibly have done to make them so angry. Why shouldn't a man have a right to chose the woman he loves to marry? Why did they have to disown him? She's very cruel, or are you going to tell me it's simply because she's afraid, too?"

He spun around, his eyes filled more with pain than anger. "Grandma's bark has always been worse than her bite," he said. "After you're here a while, you'll see that, too. It takes her a little time to warm up to strangers."

"I'm not a stranger. I'm her granddaughter, whether she likes it or not."

He looked away. May was close enough to the water for the tide to just touch her feet. "Damn!" He rushed to her and pulled her farther back. I thought he was unnecessarily rough with her and said so. Then I took her hand and we walked away. I told her I would help her find seashells. Cary followed.

"She can't swim, you know," he said in his defense.

"She can't swim?"

"No. Even if she could, the undertow can sometimes pull the strongest swimmer out to drown."

I kept us a good distance from the water.

"I understand why you are so protective of her, Cary, and it's a good thing, a loving thing, but you've got to let her breathe."

He stared at me. The wind made the strands of his hair dance around his face. I felt the sea spray on my own. Above us, the terns circled and cried.

191

"I know why the family had nothing to do with your father and why he and your mother ran off," he confessed.

"You do?"

"Yes." He knelt down and plucked a shell out of the sand and handed it to May. "It wasn't something anyone told me," he continued. "I learned about it all in bits and pieces over the years just being nearby when they would discuss it.

"When my father realized what I had learned and knew, he pulled me aside one day and forbade me to ever mention anything, especially in my grandparents' presence."

"Tell me." I asked softly.

"Your mother should have been the one to tell you, or your father, but I'm sure they were too ashamed and afraid," he added.

My heart seemed to stop and then start, and accompanying that came a thumping that made my blood rush to my head.

"Ashamed of what? What had they done?"

"Married," he said.

"So? Are your parents and our grandparents so conceited, so arrogant, that they can look down on someone who wasn't from what they call the best families? Someone who was an orphan? Just who do they think they—"

"Your mother was an orphan, yes. But she never told you the truth about who her adopted parents were."

I held my breath.

"What do you mean? Who were they?"

"Grandma and Grandpa," he said. "Your mother and your father grew up like brother and sister, and when they found out she had become pregnant with you, it was even more of a disgrace."

I shook my head and nearly laughed aloud.

"That's stupid. That's some ridiculous lie your father told you to cover up for the disgraceful and disgusting way they treated my daddy."

"It's the truth," he insisted.

"No!" I put my hands over my ears. "I won't listen to another horrible word."

May stared at me, her face in a grimace. She started to sign quickly, asking what was wrong. I shook my head at her.

"I thought you should know so you would understand why everyone has these feelings about your mother and father. Maybe you won't blame Grandma and Grandpa and my father and mother so much."

"I blame them more!" I screamed at him. "More for lying."

"They're not lying," he said softly. "I'm surprised those gossipmongers in school haven't said anything to you. It's an old story, so maybe they don't know, or maybe they just don't realize who you are."

I shook my head and backed away from him. "You're just getting back at me for what I said about May. You're cruel. I hate you," I said. "I hate you!"

I ran down the beach, tears streaming down my cheeks. I ran as hard and as fast as I could, my feet slipping and sliding in the sand. I even splashed through some water without caring, and then I fell forward on the sand, exhausted, my chest feeling as if it would explode. I took deep, hard breaths.

He had to be lying, or passing on their lies. Why wouldn't Mommy or Daddy ever have told me?

Moments later, Cary stood at my side. "I knew I shouldn't have said anything."

"You shouldn't have said anything so stupid," I retorted, looking up at him. He stood holding May's hand. She looked frightened, as if she might start to cry herself. I got to my feet and brushed off my clothing.

"When we get back to the house, I'll show you something," he said. He turned and started away. I took May's hand and we followed.

At the rear door, Cary paused. "This way." He took us around to the north side of the house where there was a

193

metal cellar door. He reached down and pulled it open. There was a short, cement stairway that led to another door. "It's the basement."

I hesitated. He went down the stairs and opened the next door, stepping in to pull a cord that turned on a swinging, naked bulb. When I walked down the stairs, I saw the basement had just the ground for a floor, but there were metal shelves against the old fieldstone foundation. I passed through cobwebs. There was a dank and musty odor.

"This is under the oldest section of the house," Cary explained. "I think it was once the fruit and vegetable cellar. Something like that. Laura and I used to think of this as our clubhouse. We didn't mind the dampness or the spiderwebs and mice."

"Mice?"

"They've scurried into their hiding places by now." He smiled, then stepped across the small room to one of the metal shelves and pulled a carton off the second shelf, lowering it to the basement's dirt floor. The cardboard, left in this clamminess, was soft and nearly ripped under his touch as he opened the box slowly.

"Here," he said, waiting for me to approach. I took slow steps, my chest feeling as if I had swallowed lumps of coal that now lay stuck against my heart. May remained at my side, clinging to my hand. I gazed into the box. It was filled with photo albums. He took out the first one and opened it.

"Your parents were gone by the time Laura and I had discovered all this, of course. When we asked Grandma Olivia about these pictures, she forbade us ever to come in here again. We didn't for a long time," he said.

I looked at the pictures. They were old photos taken of children, two boys and a girl.

"This is your father and your mother and this is my father," Cary pointed out. He turned the pages, which contained pictures of Daddy, Mommy, and Uncle Jacob as they grew older. The resemblances became sharper and clearer with every turn of the page. "Your father was

194

always a big guy, huh? And your mother, she was pretty from the start," he said.

Tears streamed down my cheeks as he slowly turned the pages, revealing pictures taken at lawn parties, on the swing bench, near the flower gardens, pictures on sailboats and fishing boats. There were school pictures, as well as group family pictures.

I shook my head in disbelief.

"I'm sorry," he said. "I'm sorry you never knew the whole truth."

I bit down on my lower lip and sucked in air through my nose, ignoring my hot tears. He put the albums back in the carton, neatly closed it, and placed it back on the shelf.

"There's a lot more here, but maybe some other time," he said.

I turned away, releasing May's hand. It felt as if I had let go of a lifeline and I was now drifting in space. Dazed, I went back to the cement steps and up into the daylight, vaguely hearing Cary put out the light and close the basement door behind us. I stared out at the glittering sea, the ocean looking like a floating mirror, mesmerizing.

A cocoon of lies had been spun around me. Cary had sliced it open and I was looking out at the world with different eyes.

But more was yet to come. I sensed it, and that ominous dread put thunder in my heart. I would know it all, I vowed, no matter how damning the truth might be.

11
❧

He Says I'm Pretty

Cary stepped up beside me and stood there for a few moments without speaking. Two terns flew by. Their cries sounded like screams to me. Maybe that was because I felt I was screaming inside myself. In moments my world had gone topsy-turvy. The blue sky now looked gray. The soft blue water had turned to ice.

"I'm sure my parents were unaware that you didn't know about Haille, Melody. At least, I never heard my father say anything. I'd appreciate it if you didn't let them know I was the one who told you," Cary said.

I spun on him so sharply, he winced as if he expected to be slapped. "I guess I could lie and tell them Mommy had told me all this. Or I could pretend someone at school told me. Maybe I just figured it all out myself, right? I mean, everyone here grows lies as abundantly as the cranberries. I have lots to choose from, don't I?"

He nodded. "I understand how you feel."

"Do you?" I snapped, the skin on my face feeling hot and sunburnt.

"Yes," he replied firmly. His green eyes grew dark, but

held me with their sincerity. "I do, Melody. When I first realized you didn't know the whole truth about your parents, I was shocked. Even before today, I thought about telling you because I was tired of hearing you complain about how my father treated your mother and your father, but—"

"But what, Cary Logan?"

He looked away, swallowed, and then turned back.

"I didn't want to happen just what is happening now," he blurted.

"And what's that?" I demanded, hands on my hips. Out of the corner of my eye, I saw May watching us, confusion on her face. "Well?" I demanded.

"I didn't want you hating me," he confessed.

My heart continued to thump, but the steel in my shoulders and back softened. I relaxed and looked back at the ocean.

"I don't know what you mean," I muttered.

"I don't remember the story, but I remember the lesson the teacher taught," he continued. "It was something about how we always hate the messenger who brings us bad news. That's why we hate to deliver it."

"I don't hate you for telling me the truth," I said. "But I *am* angry, mostly at my mother. She should have told me everything before she brought me here and dumped me on the family that hates the sight of me."

"No one hates the sight of you. How could anyone blame you? But you're right: your parents should have told you," he said, nodding. "They should have trusted you with the truth about their past and all that had happened. I guess my father hit the nail on the head: they were ashamed of themselves. That's why they ran from here to live in West Virginia after they had gotten secretly married."

"But . . . I just don't understand it all." I shook my head. "Why did Grandpa Samuel and Grandma Olivia take my mother into their home and adopt her if they considered her inferior? And even though my parents lived like brother and sister, they weren't brother and sister. Why was it so terrible, terrible enough to disown my father, to hate him so much that none of you even mourns his death?"

"Look, I don't know details. As I said, no one likes to talk about it. Maybe now your mother will tell you everything," he concluded. "You can ask her."

"Yes, I will ask her," I moaned, "if she ever calls me or comes for me."

"I'm sorry, Melody," he said. "It all stinks like a rotten fish."

I gazed into his now softened emerald eyes and saw how deeply he felt my pain.

"Thank you for caring," I said. His eyes brightened and a small smile formed on his lips.

May stared up at me, waiting for an explanation. My outbursts and anger had frightened her. Why should someone so innocent and sweet be hurt by my miserable mood? I thought.

"Everything's all right," I signed and reached for her hand. She grinned from ear to ear.

"We better go back inside now," Cary said. "They'll be looking for us." He told May to be sure her shoes were clean before we all re-entered the house.

"There are the children," Aunt Sara said as we appeared in the living room doorway. "I was just going to call you. Where did you go, Cary?"

"We took a walk on the beach."

"Find any interesting seashells?" she asked me. "Laura always found the most unusual ones, didn't she, Jacob?"

He grunted.

It was so hard looking at them all, now that I knew more of the truth. Grandma Olivia sat in the oversized high-back chair, her arms on the arms of the chair, her back straight. She looked furious when she gazed at me. I felt her eyes burning through me. I don't care what Cary says, I thought. She hates me. She hates the sight of me because she can't look at me without seeing my mother. I couldn't wait to leave.

On the other hand, Grandpa Samuel's face was softer, a small smile on his lips. "You take your cousin sailing yet, Cary?" he asked.

"No sir."

"There's no hurry," Aunt Sara said, her voice fluttering with fear.

"I can't think of anyone I would trust more in a sailboat than Cary," Grandpa Samuel said, his eyes still fixed on me. Cary blushed. "He's the best sailor the family's ever had, eh Jacob?"

"Aye," Uncle Jacob said. "That he is." He slapped his hands on his knees and stood. "Well, I guess we had better be moving on." He glanced at Aunt Sara and she rose quickly. Then he looked at Cary.

"Thank you for the brunch, Grandma," Cary said quickly, prodded by his father's look of expectation. Uncle Jacob's gaze moved to me.

"Thank you," I said, my lungs so hot I didn't think I could make sounds. I wanted to add sarcastically, "Thank you for keeping my mother and father's pictures buried in a carton in the basement. Thank you for hating your own son so much that you won't even mention his name, much less mourn his death. Thank you for blaming me for anything and everything they did." But I swallowed back the thoughts and turned to watch May signing her thank you. They barely acknowledged her. Maybe that was their way of pretending she didn't have a handicap, I thought. Another lie was being added to the piles buried in the Logans's sea chests and dark closets.

"I'll call you during the week, Sara," Grandma Olivia said, barely turning her head, "and tell you when the dinner will be."

"Fine, Olivia. Thank you," Aunt Sara said. She looked at Uncle Jacob for direction. When he started out, she followed. I noticed no one kissed anyone good-bye, just as no one had kissed anyone hello. Only Grandpa Samuel followed us to the door.

"Have a good week, Jacob," he said.

"Thanks, Dad," Uncle Jacob replied. He shook his father's hand and started for the car, all of us following.

"I'm looking forward to hearing you play your fiddle," Grandpa Samuel called to me. "Bring it with you when you come to dinner."

I gazed back at him. He was smiling warmly, his eyes twinkling. We had barely exchanged any words or spent any time in each other's presence, but I thought he seemed too nice to have disowned my father, too nice to carry anger in his heart so long and so firmly.

"Did you have a good time, Melody?" Aunt Sara asked me after we had all gotten into the car. Cary glanced at me nervously.

"Yes, Aunt Sara. The food was wonderful and this is a beautiful place," I recited dryly.

"Isn't it though? I love coming here. Laura used to visit Grandpa and Grandma Logan often. In time you will, too, I'm sure."

"I'm not so sure," I muttered under my breath. Cary was the only one who heard me, but he didn't say anything.

"We've all been invited to dinner this week. Isn't that nice?" Aunt Sara said. No one, not even Uncle Jacob, replied. We drove home in silence, with May the only one comfortable in such a muted world, I thought.

It was a relief to change out of formal clothes and put on dungarees, sneakers, and a sloppy blouse. I had felt so constrained in Laura's clothes. Aunt Sara treated them like holy garments. I buttoned my own blouse half-way down and tied the front ends in a knot at my waist, just the way Mommy often tied her own. My mind still reeled from the discoveries and revelations about my parents.

When did they first realize they were in love with each

200

other? Was it really like falling in love with your brother or your sister, even though they weren't blood relatives? How did they tell Grandpa and Grandma Logan? There was so much I didn't know about my family. I felt like someone who had been living with strangers.

Everyone else was still changing when I stepped out of my room. I knew May was looking forward to spending time with me, but I craved solitude. I hurried down the stairs and out of the house. Confused, angry, and frightened, I dug my feet into the sand and furiously marched toward the ocean. The breeze whipped through my hair. Large, puffy clouds blocked the sun. I felt a bit chilled and realized I should have worn more than a cotton blouse. But I didn't want to turn back.

On the hard-packed sand of the beach, the tide rushed up so fast I had to leap out of the way to dry ground. It was as if the ocean itself were snapping at me. I took off my sneakers and socks and waded through the water, oblivious to the cold. If I came down with pneumonia, it would be Mommy's fault. No one would care anyway. I fumed so hard I imagined smoke pouring out of my ears.

How could Mommy not tell the truth? Didn't she think the day would come when she would have to admit to all the lies?

Surely Daddy would have eventually told me everything. He was just waiting for me to be old enough. Daddy wouldn't have wanted to see me hurt this way. But Mommy must have realized I would hear the whole story while I was here. All she worried about was getting away and doing her thing, becoming famous.

"It's not fair!" I shouted at the ocean. My words were drowned by the roar of the waves.

I didn't realize how far I had walked until I turned to look back at the house. I folded my arms across my breasts and sat on a dry mound of sand, staring across the ocean waves. There was a constant breeze, but the sky wasn't as cloudy as it had first seemed. The weather here changed so quickly it was as if a Cape Cod magician

201

controlled it. I sensed the sun was stronger down by the water, reflecting off the sand. Like a Ping-Pong ball, I was bouncing from warm moments to cool ones. The breeze brushed the tears from my cheeks. I sighed so deeply I thought I might snap like a brittle piece of china. I even envisioned my face shattered in pieces like some alabaster puzzle. All the king's horses and all the king's men . . . couldn't put poor Melody together again.

Suddenly, I saw and heard a motorboat skipping over the waves, the spray flying up around it. Whoever was driving it turned it sharply toward the shore and sped up, heading directly toward me. I watched with curiosity as it drew closer until it was near enough for me to realize who was driving. Adam Jackson waved. He shut off the motor and the boat drifted in with the tide.

"Hey!" he called, his hands cupping his mouth. "What are you doing out here all by yourself?"

The boat lifted and fell until he was nearly to shore.

"Just taking a walk," I shouted back.

"I thought it was you. I have great eyesight, huh?" He laughed and then held up a pair of binoculars. "Come on. I'll take you for a spin."

I shook my head. "No, thank you."

"Come on," he urged. "You'll have fun."

"How will I get to the boat? I'll get soaked to the bone and shrink to death."

He laughed and hopped out. He was wearing a tight black bathing suit and a light blue polo shirt, which was getting wet, but he didn't mind. He pulled the boat closer until the bow hit the sand. Then he took off his shirt and threw it into the boat before he beckoned.

"Come on. I'll make sure you don't get too wet."

"I don't think so."

"You don't look too happy," he said. "A ride in this thing will drive your gloom away. You have the Adam Jackson one hundred percent guarantee."

I looked toward the house. Aunt Sara and Uncle Jacob would have a fit if they saw me get into the boat, but

Adam's shoulders gleamed invitingly in the afternoon sunlight. I stood up, my heart thumping.

Why not? I thought. I'm not a prisoner here. "Okay," I said impulsively.

"Good," he cried. "Hurry up. The Atlantic Ocean isn't exactly a bathtub yet," he said laughing and pretending to be shivering in the water.

I rolled up my dungarees as high as I could, cradled my sneakers and socks in my arms, and then stepped into the water. The tide kept rising, however, and I screamed and retreated. He laughed and rushed forward, scooping me into his arms before I could protest. Then he carried me to the boat as if I weighed nothing and gently lifted me over the edge. Once I was in, he pushed the boat out, pulled himself up and swung over.

"See. Barely a drop on you."

"I can't believe I'm doing this."

"What's the big deal?" he said shrugging. "Boats, water, fishing . . . they're as common as breathing to us Cape Codders, and now that you're becoming one, too, you have to get used to it all or risk forever being known as an outsider. And you know how we treat outsiders," he said. He widened his eyes as though that would be a fate worse than death. He laughed and started the motor.

The boat lifted and fell with the waves so sharply, I had trouble standing.

"Isn't it too rough today? I feel as if I'm in an egg beater."

"Call this rough? Hardly." He started the engine. Then he patted the seat beside him. "Sit up here so you get a good view. I'll even let you steer if you want."

"Really?"

"Sure. Come on, sit," he urged and I did so. "I haven't been out much myself this year," he said. "I'm glad I had the desire to do so today." He turned to me with a twinkle in his soft blue eyes. "It wasn't just an accident finding you on the beach, you know."

"Oh?"

"It's fate, what's meant to be," he said with a wink.

And then he gunned the engine so fast and hard, the front of the boat lifted and we hit the water with a hard bounce.

I screamed. I had to cling to him, but he didn't seem to mind.

"Do you have to go so fast?" I cried. The spray was hitting us and the wind made my blouse flap so much, I thought it would tear off. My eyes were tearing, too.

"Of course," he said. "You want to get a thrill, don't you? Going slow is not for people like us."

People like us? I thought. Who did he think I was?

The boat bounced so hard each time it hit the water, I was afraid it might fall apart. My heart was pounding. Finally, he slowed down and told me to try steering myself. He slid over and I took the wheel. Then he pulled himself around, straddling me, and reached over my shoulders with both his arms to put his hands over mine.

"I'll show you how to do it first," he said, his cheek against my cheek. He was wearing some wonderful-smelling aftershave lotion. The water, the breeze, the scent of the ocean and his lotion made me dizzy. I felt myself spinning, but it was wonderful and exciting. For a while anyway, I could forget the secrets and the lies.

He accelerated slowly and I turned the wheel, impressed and fascinated with my power to direct the boat. I was so entranced with it that I didn't pay much attention to his lips moving over my ears and down my cheek.

"You're delicious," he suddenly said.

"What?" I pulled to the side to look at him. He was staring at me, those remarkable eyes drinking me in, then swallowing me down. I quickly fastened one of the buttons of my blouse that had opened, but my garments felt flimsy and transparent under his piercing gaze. It took my breath away. Without warning, the boat bounced sharply, tossing him into my lap. We both screamed and he recovered quickly enough to drop the speed and straighten the bow. We caught our breaths and the boat bobbed gently. This far away from shore, the water was calmer and more inviting.

"You have to keep your eyes on what you're doing," he said.

"And you have to keep yours in your head. I have pupil prints in places I'd rather keep unblemished."

He laughed and leaned back. "You sure talk funny sometimes, but it's refreshing. All the girls here sound the same. Everything's groovy, know what I mean?"

I nodded.

"Why didn't you come to the party last night?" he asked. "I kept looking for you."

"I couldn't," I said. "I wanted to, but—"

"Your uncle and aunt wouldn't let you?"

"Something like that."

"I figured." He shook his head. "Must be hard for you. I bet you feel as if you're in some kind of a prison or a nunnery, huh?"

I didn't say anything.

"All the girls are jealous of you, you know."

"What? Why?"

"I heard them talking about you last night, saying how pretty you are."

"They did not."

"Swear," he said raising his hand. "It's true. You're about the prettiest girl I've seen and I've seen quite a few." He leaned toward me. "I've even gone out with college girls, but you've got that one-in-a-million look about you, the magic that makes for movie stars and models. I heard from the grapevine that your mother is a model. Now I understand."

I sat there with my mouth gaping open. I had never heard a boy in our school talk like this and certainly never about me.

"Wait a minute," he said before I could respond. He got up and went to a cabinet to take out a camera. "I'd

205

like to get a few shots of you just the way you are, natural, the wind in your hair."

"What do you want me to do?"

"Just sit there. Steer the boat and be yourself." He aimed his camera and snapped pictures. "These will be worth something someday after you're famous."

I laughed and shook my head. "I am not so pretty. I have freckles and my ears are too big. I'll never become famous."

"Adam Jackson knows pretty women and I'm telling you, Melody, you're one of 'em. Don't argue with an expert." He kept on looking at me with that gleeful smile in his eyes. He was making me very nervous.

"Can I make it go faster again?" I asked.

"I knew you would want to. Just move the lever ahead slowly."

I did so, getting better at controlling the boat. He even gave me a compliment about it.

"You've got your sea legs," he said and ran his palm down the side of my right leg. "And they're really nice." He laughed at the look on my face. "You better get used to compliments, Melody. They're going to rain down on you like a hurricane as you get older and prettier."

The blood rushed to my face. Was he just saying these things or did he really mean them? He put his arm around my shoulder and helped steer with his other hand. He held me tighter, drawing me against him until I felt his breath on my cheek again and then the soft touch of his lips.

"I think you better take me back," I told him, my voice close to cracking. "My aunt will be turning over rocks looking for me." He laughed.

"Okay, but only if you promise to meet me tomorrow night about eight o'clock."

"Meet you? Where?"

He thought a moment.

"Meet me right there where I found you sitting, or are you afraid to walk the beach at night?"

206

"I'm not afraid," I said quickly. "It's just that—"

"You might not be able to get out? Don't let them treat you like a child," he said, his eyes narrowed.

"I don't," I protested, but in my heart, I knew he was right.

"Then it's settled. I'll bring a radio and a blanket and something to drink."

"Something to drink?"

"Something to keep us warm. You've done that before, haven't you?" he asked.

"Sure," I said, not even positive what he meant. Was he going to bring a thermos of hot chocolate, coffee, tea, or did he mean whiskey?

"I thought so. You have a more sophisticated look about you. I'd like to hear what it was like growing up in West Virginia. My college friends tell me that girls from the coal mining towns know the score. The girls here like to think they're so sophisticated. They talk a good game, but when it comes right down to playing it, they're not home. You know what I mean?"

"No," I said.

"Sure you do."

"I'd better get back."

"Aye, aye, Captain," he replied sitting up quickly and saluting. I laughed as he hurriedly took the controls and turned the boat around. "You want me to put you back where you were or closer to the house?"

"Better put me back where I was," I said. "My aunt would turn inside out if she saw me riding in a motorboat, and my uncle would put a ball and chain on my ankle."

"The Logans are strange, and not because of what happened to Laura. They were strange long before that."

I wanted to see just how much he knew and how much the people here gossiped. "You mean about my mother and father?" I asked.

"No." He shook his head. "I don't know much about them, except what I was told in school. I'm sorry about

207

your father. That must have been a terrible accident, too."

"It was."

"You've got a lot of good reason to be sad, Melody, but you're too beautiful to remain melancholy long." He brought the boat as close to the shore as he had brought it before. My heart skipped beats when he smiled at me again. Then he hopped out. "Sit on the side," he ordered. "Don't worry. I won't drop you."

I clutched my sneakers and socks and did as he said. He scooped under my legs again, this time holding me tighter around the waist. Our faces were inches apart. I thought I would drown in his eyes. He leaned in and kissed me softly on the lips.

"No fair," I said. "I'm trapped like a cat up a tree."

He laughed. "That's right. And if you don't kiss me back, I'll drop you in the ocean." He pretended to let go and I screamed. "Well?"

"All right, but just once," I said. This time, our kiss was long and his tongue moved between my lips, grazing mine. It sent a chill down my spine, but it wasn't unpleasant.

"I've got to get back," I said, practically whispering. My heart pounded so hard, I thought I wouldn't be able to get out the words.

"No problem," He gracefully moved through the water and set me down on dry land. "Until tomorrow night." His face turned serious. "I'll see you in school tomorrow, but I'd rather we kept this our little secret. If we don't we'll have company. I know these kids here. They can be pains in the rear end. Besides, I like secrets, don't you?"

"No," I said quickly and so firmly, he raised his eyebrows.

"Not even secrets of the heart?"

I didn't want to tell him that I had never really had any, so I just shrugged. He laughed. "Bet you just got a sea chest full of love secrets," he teased.

"You'd lose." I started backing away. "I have to go. Thanks for the ride."

He stood there, watching me walk quickly over the sand. Then he turned and waded through the water to his boat. I stopped to watch him accelerate and spin through the waves. I felt as if I had stepped in and out of a movie. He had been right about the boat ride. The dreariness that had washed over me had dried up with my tears. I had a new bounce in my step as I hurried over the beach toward my uncle and aunt's house, wondering if I would have the nerve to meet Adam Jackson tomorrow night.

"Where were you, honey?" Aunt Sara asked as soon as I entered the house. She was in the doorway of the living room. She looked at my sneakers and socks in my hand. I had simply forgotten to put them on or roll down my dungarees.

"I just took a walk on the beach," I said quickly.

"You shouldn't go anywhere without telling your aunt or me," I heard my uncle Jacob cry from behind her in the living room. "Your aunt shouldn't have to go looking for you, hear?"

"Yes," I said. "Sorry," I told Aunt Sara and ran up the stairs before she could ask or say anything else. Cary heard me pound the steps and came out of his room.

"You all right?" he asked as I turned down the hallway.

"Yes."

His eyes grew smaller with interest and he stepped closer, a textbook in his hand.

"I heard you run out, but by the time I put on my sneakers, you were over the hill. I figured you wanted to be alone, maybe to sort things out," he said.

"Sort things out?" I started to laugh. "It would be easier to unravel a bee hive."

He nodded and then his eyes widened with interest. "You look like you got some sun."

209

I couldn't keep my eyes from shifting guiltily away. Did he notice the flush on my face, the excitement in my eyes? Daddy used to say they were like little windowpanes, with my thoughts as clear as newsprint.

"You were walking in the water?" Cary continued nodding at my sneakers in my hand and my rolled up dungarees. Tiny grains of sand were in between my toes.

"I'm tired," I said moving to my room. "I'm going to rest before dinner."

"Melody?"

I turned.

He held up the book.

"I was wondering if after dinner you might—"

"That's your English textbook?"

"Yes. We have a test tomorrow on clauses. The only clause I know is Santa Claus," he said glumly.

"It's not really hard. I'll show you some tricks my teacher in West Virginia showed me."

"Thanks."

"Where's May?"

"She's doing her homework, too," he said. I nodded and went into my room, softly closing the door behind me. For a few moments I stood there, reining in my emotions. I had gone from anger and sadness to excitement and thrills. I couldn't be more confused about this place, I thought. My family was hard and unpleasant, but May was sweet and hungry for love, and Cary . . . Cary was more sensitive and caring than he let on. The ocean could be cold and gray, and no thunderstorm in West Virginia was as frightening as the storm we had had the other night—the nor'easter Cary called it. Yet today, the ocean was delightful, exciting and the beach was warm and inviting.

Didn't I hate it here? Didn't I want to just run away?

And yet, Adam Jackson's handsome face lingered before my eyes and his compliments echoed in my ears. Was I really as pretty as he said I was? I gazed at myself in the mirror. Was there as much potential beauty as he claimed he saw? Was he making up what he had told me the other girls thought of me? I didn't want to become conceited, and yet, I didn't want to underestimate myself and become some mousy creature with no self-confidence, terrified of life like . . . like Aunt Sara hovering in Uncle Jacob's dark shadow.

I sat at the vanity table and thought and then I gazed down at the pile of letters bound with a rubber band. They were Laura's letters from her boyfriend. I had no right to look at them, and yet, I couldn't help wondering what sort of a relationship they had had before their tragic end.

I took off the rubber band and opened the first envelope. The handwriting was pretty, an almost artistic script. The letter had been written on blue stationery.

Dearest Laura,

I had a wonderful time yesterday. I don't know how many times I've walked on that beach, but yesterday, with you, it suddenly seemed more beautiful than ever. I didn't mean to take you away from your work. I know Cary was upset with me for just appearing unexpectedly. When I get a chance, I'll apologize to him for stealing you away and leaving him with all the lobsters and fish.

But I'll never apologize for taking you anywhere. I'm glad you feel the same way about me that I feel about you. I've felt this for a long time, but I didn't have the courage to tell you. Don't ask me why I have it now. I think it's because of the way you smiled at me in the cafeteria that day. It gave me all the nerve I needed.

I'm not used to writing letters to girls or anyone. Actually, you're the first girl I've ever written a letter to, not counting my cousin Susie. I know it's hard for you to talk long on the telephone. Besides, it's kind of exciting receiving letters from you, too. I'm just nervous about mailing the letters and maybe having someone else read them. You know who. He never seems to be happy to see me around, even when I'm not taking you away from helping your father.

Maybe, when he feels about a girl the way I feel about you, he'll be more understanding. I know what you meant when you said you were afraid of how you felt about me sometimes. It's a bit overwhelming, but I'm not ashamed of it and never will be. I hope you feel that, too. I promise, I'll try to control myself more, but you know what they say about promises lovers make. Just kidding, only, please don't hate me for loving you more than I should.

I like writing to you, Laura. I see your face in front of me as I think of the words. It makes me want to write to you all night. Until I see you, hold me in your heart.

Love,
Robert

Tears filled my eyes. Would I ever have anyone love me as much as Robert Royce loved Laura? If they had something so beautiful, why did they have to die so tragically and so young? I sighed and thought about reading another letter, but there was a sharp knock on my door. I guiltily stuffed the letter back into the envelope.

"Yes?"

Cary entered. His gaze moved from me to the pile of letters and then back to me.

"My mother says you have a phone call. A girl friend from Sewell."

"Alice!" I jumped up. "Thanks."

I went downstairs quickly, forgetting that I still hadn't put on my sneakers and socks. This time, Uncle Jacob wasn't sitting near the phone, ready to listen. Aunt Sara held the receiver away from her as if it were a forbidden object that might contaminate her.

212

"Jacob doesn't approve of young people gossiping on the telephone," she whispered. "Don't be long."

"Thank you," I said and took the receiver. "Alice?"

"Hi. Was it all right for me to call now? Your aunt sounded upset."

"It's all right. I'm happy to hear from you so soon."

Aunt Sara gave me a look of warning and stepped gingerly out of the room.

"I miss you and I miss Sewell," I added as soon as she was gone. "More than I ever expected."

"Oh? Well, I don't have good news. Papa George is in the hospital and when I asked Mama Arlene about your mother and your things, she told me she hasn't heard a word from your mother since you all left."

"Mommy never called her?"

"Not yet. I thought I had better tell you."

"How is Papa George doing?"

"He's in intensive care. He's very sick, Melody. I'm sorry."

"I should be there," I moaned. "I don't know what to do."

"What can you do?" Alice asked in her habitual blunt manner.

"Nothing until Mommy calls me."

"You really hate it there?"

"There's a lot happinging, Alice."

"Tell me," she pleaded.

"I can't. Not on the phone. I'll write you a letter."

"Don't wait. Write it tonight."

"Melody, dear, not too long," I heard Aunt Sara say through the wall. She was probably just on the other side of the door all the while, I thought.

"I've got to hang up, Alice. Thanks for calling."

"Write me and I'll call you the moment I hear that your mother called Mama Arlene," she said quickly.

"Thanks. Bye."

I cradled the receiver just as Uncle Jacob came

213

through the front door. He saw Aunt Sara standing in the hallway and me by the phone.

"Was that your mother?" he asked me.

"No. A friend from Sewell."

He glared at Aunt Sara.

"She wasn't on the phone long, Jacob."

He grunted. Then he noticed my bare feet.

"We don't walk through the house half dressed here," he said. For a moment I didn't understand. "Your feet," he said nodding at them.

"Oh. I just came down quickly. It was a long-distance phone call and—"

"A decent girl always thinks about those things first," he chastised.

"I am a decent girl," I fired back.

"We'll see," he said, undaunted, and started up the stairs. "Getting dressed for dinner," he muttered toward Aunt Sara.

"Okay, Jacob. We'll have a good Sunday dinner," she promised. "Don't worry," she whispered to me. "He'll soon see that you're as sweet as Laura was, and then everything . . . everything will be wonderful again," she added. Her eyes glittered with hope. "Hurry and get cleaned up and dressed so you can set the table, dear."

I watched her walk away with that fragile smile on her face. Aunt Sara had wrapped herself snugly in her illusions, but illusions, I thought, were just dressed up lies. Someday the weight of the truth would come down on her glass house and shatter her dreams even more.

I didn't want to be here when all that happened. I wanted to be far away. I wanted to be in a place where people didn't have to lie to each other to live with each other.

Was there such a place? And even if there were such a place, could I, a daughter born in a world of deceit, ever hope to find it?

With Daddy dead and gone and Mommy off searching for her own private dreams, I felt like an orphan, a hobo

214

begging for a handout of love. No wonder my eyes saw Adam Jackson's eyes and my ears were so receptive to his words.

I'll meet him tomorrow night, I thought defiantly. Not even one of Cape Cod's treacherous nor'easters could keep me away.

12
&

An English Lesson

At dinner everyone appeared to be in a subdued mood, even May. After Uncle Jacob read his selection from the Bible, we ate in near silence. I thought the heavy atmosphere in the house might be a result of the weather. Although it wasn't raining, a thick fog had rolled in on great billowing waves. It shrouded the landscape, turning everything cold and dreary. Once again, the weather on the Cape surprised me with its fickleness and its ability to change so abruptly. I wondered if there was any way to tell right now what it would be like tomorrow night. Would it rain and thus put off my rendezvous with Adam Jackson?

"Does it often get foggy like this at night?" I asked as innocently as I could. Uncle Jacob raised his eyebrows. Aunt Sara smiled as if I had asked the silliest little question, and Cary looked amused. "This time of year it often does."

"Weathermen might as well toss the dice, as good as they predict these days," Uncle Jacob muttered. "Better off just listening to the creak in your bones."

"Aye," Aunt Sara said. "More potatoes, dear?"

"No thank you, Aunt Sara," I answered.

"I won't be having coffee tonight," Uncle Jacob announced as if the whole country were awaiting his decision. "Got a big day tomorrow. Getting up early to bring the boat to Stormfield's in North Truro for an engine tuneup."

"I could skip school tomorrow," Cary offered immediately. He glanced quickly at me because he knew I understood why he would like to cut classes. He hoped I wouldn't say anything. There was no reason to worry. It was none of my business and I certainly wouldn't want to be responsible for getting him in trouble with Uncle Jacob. I wouldn't do that to my worst enemy.

"No need," Uncle Jacob said, rising. Cary's face folded in disappointment. "Roy and I can handle it. Well," he said stretching, "I'll just have a pipeful in the den and go up to bed. I'd like a peaceful night," he added glaring at me as if I were a noisy teenager who played rock music late into the evening.

I rose to help Aunt Sara with the dishes. May wanted me to go to her room and help with her homework, but I explained I was helping Cary study for a test tomorrow. She looked disappointed, so Aunt Sara offered to help her. She still looked disappointed, but I could see she was too considerate to hurt her mother's feelings.

After we had put away the dishes, I went up to my room and waited for Cary. I had just a little of my own schoolwork left and finished it quickly.

He knocked on my door and peeked in timidly. "Got time now?" he asked.

"Yes." I pulled a chair up alongside my own at the desk. "Sit here."

"I hate this stuff," he complained as he entered. He tried to narrow his vision just to me and the desk, but his eyes flitted from one side of the room to the other, the look on his face sad and as painful as a raw wound that refused to heal. He caught me scrutinizing him. "I don't come in here often," he confessed. "Anymore."

"I understand," I said.

217

Skepticism clouded his face and gave birth to a small frown. Did he think that because I had no brother or sister, I couldn't appreciate what it was like to lose someone I loved?

"It was really hard for me to look at things in our trailer that reminded me of my father after his terrible accident," I explained. Cary's skepticism faded as I went on. "I was closer to him that I am to my mother. And when he died, I thought the world had come to an end. It still doesn't seem the same. Nothing does."

He nodded, his eyes softening. "I wish I could have gotten to know him."

"I wish you had too. I wish this family wasn't so vindictive."

He tilted his head.

"Vin-what?"

"Cruel," I continued. "When you love someone, you don't hate them to death for mistakes they make. You try to understand them, help them, and if that doesn't work, you feel sorry for them. But you don't disown them forever and pretend they never lived."

He stared at me a moment and then he smiled and shook his head gently. "That's something Laura would say. She always looked for the good in everyone. The girls at school mocked her, ostracized her, were jealous of her, but she was always nice to them. We had lots of arguments about it," he said. "It was practically the only thing we argued about. We agreed about most everything else."

"Even Robert Royce?" I asked quickly. When he looked at me this time, there were shadows in the emerald depths of his eyes.

"That was something entirely different. She was blinded by—"

"By what?" I asked, intrigued.

"Blinded by his lies, his phony charm, his handsome face," he replied bitterly.

"How did you know he was a phony?" I asked. His letter to Laura seemed sincere.

218

"I just knew," he insisted. "She always listened to me. We were close and not just because we were twins. We really did like the same things and feel the same things. We didn't have to speak to each other lots of times either. We just looked at each other and understood. She would smile at me or I would smile at her and that was enough.

"But after Robert . . ." His gaze drifted, his eyes growing smaller—darker—when he looked at Laura's picture on the dresser.

"What happened after Robert came into her life?"

He turned to me, his watery eyes hard. "She changed. I tried to help her see, but she wouldn't listen."

"Maybe what she saw she liked," I offered softly.

He grimaced. "Why is it that girls who are normally smarter than boys are so dumb when it comes to boys?" he asked me.

I stared at him. He blinked his eyelids rapidly. He had long, perfect eyelashes, which most girls I knew would die to have.

"That's a matter of—"

"What?" he interrupted.

"I was going to say opinion, but it's really more a matter of the heart."

He blew air through the side of his mouth. "Matters of the heart," he said disdainfully. "An excuse for stupidity."

"Cary Logan, are you going to sit there and tell me you don't believe in love? You don't believe two people can fall in love?"

"I didn't say that exactly," he retreated. "But it's silly to think you can fall in and out of love the way you . . . you catch a cold."

"From what I understand, that doesn't sound like a good description of Laura. She didn't have lots of boyfriends, did she?"

"That's not the point. She thought she was in love and that he loved her, but . . . Let's just say I know it was a mistake, okay, and leave it at that." He glared down at

219

his textbook. "I hate this stuff. What does it have to do with what's important?"

"It's important to understand our language so we can express ourselves," I said, my voice hard and firm. Like a splinter, Cary had a way of getting under my skin.

He grimaced again and raised his eyebrows.

I wasn't intimidated by him.

"You're not just going to spend all your life talking to lobsters, Cary Logan. You're going to have to talk to your customers, too, and if you sound as if you don't know what you're doing, they won't believe in you, no matter how good a fisherman you are."

He broke into a smile. "Don't get so mad."

"I'm not mad. I'm—"

"What?" he teased.

"Mad," I said. "Why should you have to be talked into educating yourself? We don't live in the Dark Ages. Even up here in Cape Cod heaven where everyone is supposedly so perfect, people still need to be educated," I snapped.

He laughed. "Okay, help me talk to my customers."

I gazed at the page.

"Clauses are easy to recognize. Just test them. If they don't have a subject and a verb, throw them back in like a lobster that's too small."

His smile widened. "I like that. That, I can understand."

I went over what a subject does in the clause and then what the verb does.

He listened, tried some examples, and then widened his eyes. "I understand what you're saying. I just don't understand how you know whether it's an adverb or an adjective."

"Test it again," I told him. "Here's one way: if you can move it around in the sentence, it's an adverb. Look at this one: Because I got sick, I had to go home. I had to go home because I got sick. See?"

His eyes lit up.

220

"Yeah."

"Your teacher never showed you that?" I asked.

"I don't remember. I guess I wasn't paying as much attention to her as I paid to you. Maybe you should be a teacher."

"Maybe I will. Do those exercises at the end of the chapter. I'll correct them when you're finished."

"Yes ma'am."

I went to the closet to sift through the clothing. Tomorrow, I would wear one of my own things, I thought, not that I had much from which to choose. How could Mommy not have called Mama Arlene yet? She knew I needed my clothes.

"Laura always looked really good in that," Cary said. I hadn't known he was watching me. I held a light yellow cotton dress in my hands. "You thinking of wearing that to school?"

"I might just wear a pair of jeans and a blouse I brought with me," I said.

"Laura never wore jeans to school. My father didn't think it was proper."

"Well he's not my father," I replied. "And I'm not Laura."

He shrugged. "I'm just telling you."

"Are you finished with the exercises?"

"No, I—"

"Then finish," I commanded.

"Right," he said turning back.

I smiled to myself and considered the yellow dress again. It had a square collar with frilled sleeves and a gently billowing skirt. I imagined it might look nice on me. I *did* want to look nice for Adam, I thought.

"Finished," Cary declared.

I put the dress back and went to the desk. He had one mistake, but even I might have made it, I thought. "Not too bad," I said.

"I hope I can do it tomorrow."

"You will. Just remember the tricks," I told him.

221

"Thanks," he said standing. "I owe you one." He thought a moment. "Maybe I'll do what Grandpa suggested this weekend."

"What's that?"

"Take you sailing. Would you like that?"

I thought about Adam. What if he invited me to go motorboating again?

"I . . ."

My hesitation jarred him. "Don't if you have better things to do." He turned for the door.

"No, it's just that I've never really gone sailing."

He looked back at me. "Whatever. If you want to, we'll do it."

"We'll go over the material again on the way to school," I told him.

He rolled his eyes. "Can't wait," he said and left.

A little while later I heard him go up to his attic hideaway. I didn't know for certain, of course, but I was willing to bet that he spent more time up there alone since Laura's death than he had when she was alive.

We all retreat to different attics when we're unhappy, I thought. I was still looking for mine.

Uncle Jacob had eaten his breakfast and left by the time May, Cary, and I went downstairs the next morning. I decided to wear Laura's yellow dress, and when Cary saw me in the hallway, he said I looked very nice.

"It's not going to rain, is it?" I asked him.

"No. It's going to be a nice day and a pretty nice night," he told me. I breathed relief and felt a tingle of the excitement of anticipation.

Downstairs, Aunt Sara was frenzied. Grandma Olivia had called last night and told her the dinner would be tomorrow night. Apparently, from the way she spoke, I understood that dinner at my grandparents' house wasn't merely dinner, it was an elaborate affair. There would be someone else there, some highly respected member of the community. We would all have to be on

222

our very best behavior, be well dressed, and be more polite than the Queen of England.

"Don't forget Grandpa wants to hear Melody play her fiddle," Cary teased. Aunt Sara gasped and gazed at me with abject terror in her eyes.

"Oh, I don't think he meant this particular dinner," she said in a voice just above a whisper.

"Sure he did," Cary continued, deliberately raising his own voice. "We all heard him, Ma."

Aunt Sara shook her head. "But Olivia didn't . . ."

"It's all right. I don't want to bring my fiddle anyway," I said.

"Grandpa's going to be disappointed," Cary warned. "He might just send you back for it. Why don't you bring it along and leave it in the car, just in case," he pursued.

Aunt Sara shook her head again, this time more emphatically. "Jacob might be upset. I don't know if—"

"I'm not bringing it along, Aunt Sara. Stop worrying," I declared firmly. I gazed at Cary, whose green eyes sparkled with mischief.

May wanted to know what we were all talking about so intensely. Cary signed and explained, mimicking my playing the fiddle. Her eyes lit up with encouragement.

"See, Ma, even May wants her to bring it along, and she can't even hear."

"Oh dear," Aunt Sara said, wringing her hands.

"Stop it," I told him sharply. "You're going to get me into trouble."

With a tiny smile on his face, he finished eating his breakfast quietly. On the way to school, I chastised him. "You shouldn't tease your mother that way, Cary Logan."

"I wasn't teasing. I'd like you to play your fiddle, too. It will spice up the dinner party. I've been to enough of them at Grandma's to know what to expect. They could use some excitement."

"Well under the circumstances, I'm not feeling much like fiddling. It only reminds me of my daddy and

223

Grandma Olivia's house is no place to be thinking about him," I said bitterly.

Cary's impish grin faded. "Maybe if they heard you play and learned more about your father after he and Haille left here, they'd be more inclined to feel sorry about things, too," he offered.

"They should feel sorry! My daddy's gone and the damage that was done is done forever and ever."

Cary was silent. The subject sank deeply in the pool of our thoughts. We dropped May at her school and continued to our own, reviewing the material Cary would have on his English test. As soon as Cary and I arrived at school, we split up. Fortunately, he didn't hear the girls heckle me when I went to my locker. I'm sure he would have become very angry.

"We missed you Saturday night," Janet said. "Too busy darning socks or something?"

"Or did you have to make cranberry muffins?" Lorraine asked.

"I tried to come," I told her. Betty closed in beside her and Janet to listen to my explanation. "But my uncle wouldn't let me go."

"We told you he wouldn't. We told you to lie," Betty said. "But you're just like Laura, aren't you? You're too goody-goody to have any real fun. It must run in the family or something—Grandpa, Laura and now you. I bet the mute is the same."

"She's not a mute," I snapped, my face filling with blood so fast I thought I would blow the top of my head off. "She's deaf, but she can talk."

"I've heard her talk. Who could understand that?" Betty said. The others agreed.

"If you take the time, you can understand her. She's a bright, sweet little girl."

"Right. Anyway, we all had a good time. A certain boy was heartbroken that you weren't there," Lorraine said, a twisted smile on her lips.

As if on cue, Adam sauntered down the corridor and paused when he reached us. All three of the witches from

Macbeth fluttered their eyelashes and beamed their most seductive smiles, but his eyes were on me.

"Good morning, girls. Exchanging feminine secrets or can I listen in?" he asked with that beguiling smile. Even early in the morning, he looked perfect enough to have just walked out of an aftershave advertisement in a men's magazine.

"We were just telling Melody about what a great beach party she missed," Janet said.

"That's right. It was a great party," he agreed, his eyes still fixed on me.

"Debbie McKay certainly had a good time," Betty said. "Didn't she, Adam?"

"You'll have to ask her," he replied with a nonchalance that made the three giggle.

"I'm sure we'll find out," Lorraine said. "Debbie's the kind who kisses and tells. See you later, Melody," she sang.

"Yeah, see you later," Betty echoed. The three walked off, leaving me with Adam.

"Now you know why I want you to keep the things between us secret," he said looking after them. "The gossipmongers around here work overtime. I'll walk you to homeroom," he offered when I closed my locker. "Everything else all right? You didn't get into trouble after our ride yesterday, did you?"

"No," I said.

"Good."

I noticed everyone's interest as we continued down the corridor. Even Mrs. Cranshaw, the librarian, peered at us over her thick lenses.

"I really had a good time with you," Adam said softly. "Did you like it, too?"

"Yes, I did."

"Good. Until eight o'clock," he whispered at the homeroom door. "Don't disappoint me." He squeezed my hand and walked away.

My heart pounded. Was I really going to meet him? Did I have the courage? His lips had the lure of forbidden fruit, but oh, how luscious, ripe, and delicious was the promise they had left on my own when he held me in his arms and kissed me! I sighed.

When I turned to go into the classroom, I saw each and every girl was looking my way. All looked curious, many looked envious.

"That didn't take long," Theresa Patterson said coming up behind me as I walked to my desk.

"Pardon?"

"For Adam Jackson to find a new fish," she muttered, walking by.

The girls in this school, I thought, gave the word catty a new meaning. Adam wasn't wrong about that. Cary had told me much the same thing.

I didn't see my cousin until lunch time in the cafeteria. When I did, he looked very excited and happy. He had taken his English test and for the first time, he felt confident of the results afterward.

"Every time I considered an answer, I could hear your voice, your advice. It didn't seem as hard as I thought it would be."

"Good," I said. I looked past him toward the cafeteria's entrance, hoping to spot Adam. I expected he would want to sit with me, but when he came in, he was with some boys and they all went to a table on the right. He gazed my way and smiled. He looked as if he were holding court. Cary saw the direction of my interest and my expression of disappointment.

"Thanks for your help," he said dryly and started away.

"Cary," I called. He turned. "Mind if I sit with you? I'd rather skip my new girl friends for the moment."

I could see they had a place open for me at their table, but it would have been like delivering myself to the Spanish Inquisition, torture chamber and all.

Cary shrugged and looked in Adam's direction. "Suit yourself," he said. "It won't be the most exciting table, though." I followed anyway and he introduced me to two of his friends, Billy Beedsly and John Taylor. Their

226

families were also in the lobster and fish business. They asked me a lot of questions about coal mines, but they were frustrated by my limited knowledge of the industry.

"My father was stuck down in the shafts, locked away from sunlight and air, and I hated thinking about it. He didn't like talking about it much either."

"Why did he do it then?" Billy asked. Cary and I exchanged knowing looks.

"It was the best work for the money at the time," I offered and then Cary managed to change the subject.

At the end of the day, Cary eagerly waited for me, a wide, satisfied grin on his face.

"I wasn't sure you were going straight home," he said, obviously pleased that I was alone.

"I am. You look as if you have a secret."

"Oh, I do," he said starting away quickly. I had to walk fast to catch up.

"Well, what is it?"

"Nothing much."

"Cary Logan." I seized him by the elbow and spun him around. "Tell me this moment."

"Mr. Madeo stopped me in the hall as I was on my way out of the building to tell me he corrected the English tests already. I got a ninety-eight! He wanted to congratulate me and ask me how I had done it. I told him I had a great tutor and he said, 'Don't stop working with her.'"

"Oh Cary. Ninety-eight!"

"It's the best test grade I ever got!" he exclaimed.

"See. You can do it if you want to."

He shrugged. "Thanks to you. Anyway, I decided you were right. I have to learn how to talk properly and be educated if I'm going to be a businessman." He was grinning from ear to ear.

"Congratulations. I'm so happy for you."

"Let's celebrate," he said. "Let's do something special tonight after dinner. I'll take you to town for custard."

My heart sank into my stomach. He saw the expression plain as day on my face.

"What?" he asked.

"I already made a promise to someone," I said.

He nodded. "Okay," he said and walked ahead.

"Maybe tomorrow night," I offered, running to catch up.

"Sure," he said. "But let's wait and see. You might have made another promise by then." He shut up like a turtle, his shoulders rising, his neck sinking. It made me feel sick inside. I realized how much it must have taken for him to reveal his feelings to me. Since Laura's death, he was all clammed up.

I felt pinched by contradictory emotions. They were like scissors cutting me in half. One part of me was full of excitement—counting the minutes to my rendezvous with Adam—while another part of me longed to share Cary's elation and be part of his return to trust, to hope, to a world where there were sunshine and stars and not the gloom of his tragic memories. Just for tonight, I thought, I wished I could duplicate myself and be in two places at once.

But I couldn't, and there just wasn't anything to do about it but feel sorry.

Cary walked ahead of me all the way to May's school. When he saw her run to me, he just kept walking. "See that she gets home all right," he called behind himself.

"We're coming. Wait up!" I cried.

But he didn't slow down and May was full of questions and stories. I had to watch him round the bend and disappear, his shoulders still scrunched up, making him look like an old man. It brought tears to my eyes, but I held them back and put on my best smile for May, who chatted away with her hands all the way home.

Cary remained down at the dock with Uncle Jacob until just before dinner. As usual, I helped Aunt Sara prepare the meal, but right before Uncle Jacob and Cary returned, the phone rang. Aunt Sara answered it and called out to me excitedly.

"It's your mother, dear!"

My heart stopped and then started again, pitter-pattering so quickly, I thought I wouldn't have the voice with which to speak. I walked slowly into the living room and took the receiver from Aunt Sara, wondering if the wires could hold the heat of the words I wanted to scream over them.

"Hello," I began.

"Hi, honey. I just have a couple of minutes, but—"

"Don't you dare rush off again, Mommy. Don't you dare."

"Oh Melody, we're in Los Angeles and I'm—"

"How could you lie to me so much?" My throat started to tighten almost immediately. I thought I would choke before I got out my words. "How could you have kept your real adoptive parents a secret? Why didn't you ever tell me you and Daddy grew up together?"

After a short pause, she replied, "Your father didn't want to tell you all that, Melody. He wanted to protect you from all that was unpleasant."

"Don't put it all on him, Mommy. He's dead. He can't answer."

"Well, it wasn't just me! He wanted it that way, too," she proclaimed.

"Why?" I cried. "Why not tell me the truth about how you really met and fell in love? Why not tell me why the family was angry?" I demanded. The tears were burning under my lids.

"Chester thought you were too young to understand."

"But I'm not too young now! Why did you leave me here without telling me the truth, the whole truth about you and Daddy? How could you do that?"

She was quiet a moment and then she admitted, "I didn't think you would stay if I told you all that, Melody, and I didn't have much choice at the time. If you are as old as you claim you are, you'll understand."

"Mommy, these people hate you and they hate Daddy for what you two did. How can I stay here?"

"Uncle Jacob will never throw you out, Melody," she

229

said. "And he has no right to be so high and mighty, believe me. Don't let him talk down to you. Don't be a troublemaker, but don't take his . . . garbage,"

"I can't stay here, Mommy, and I want to know more. I want to know everything."

"You will. I promise. You're obviously old enough now to know our side of the story. Who told you anyway, Jacob, Sara, or Olivia?"

"I saw your pictures. Grandma Olivia put all the pictures of you and Daddy in cartons," I told her. "They don't mention Daddy's name, they don't talk about his accident. It's horrible."

"Olivia's doing, I'm sure. The whole time I lived there, I could never call her anything but Olivia, you know. I could never call her mother," she said with bitterness.

"But why did they take you into their home? Why did they adopt you?"

"It's a very involved story, honey. That's another reason why I couldn't get into it before I left Province-town. Just hold out a little longer. Put up with their snobbery a little longer," she pleaded.

"Mommy, you never called Mama Arlene to get my things sent up here."

"I'll do it right after I hang up," she promised.

"And Alice called and told me Papa George was in the hospital, very sick."

"It was expected, honey."

"Mommy, I can't stay here. Please come back for me or send for me. I'll meet you anywhere and put up with anything, travel, running about from city to city. I'll never complain about anything. I promise. I swear."

"Melody, I'm in Los Angeles! I'm in Hollywood! I have appointments, auditions. Can you imagine? Some-thing wonderful is going to happen and soon, just as I told you. Give me a little longer. Finish school there, at least. Then, during the summer months—"

"Mommy." Tears streamed down my face. "Why did they hate you for marrying Daddy? Why didn't they accept it? You weren't blood relatives."

"We disobeyed Queen Olivia," she quipped. "Just stay out of her way. She'll die soon and put everyone out of their misery. *Ooo,*" she said, "I just hate talking about them. They made us suffer. Get everything you can out of them. They owe you. That family owes us more than it can ever repay. Do your own thing and ignore them. Uncle Jacob won't throw you out."

"Mommy—"

"I have to go, honey. I have an appointment. I'll call Arlene. I promise."

"But where are you? How can I reach you?"

"We haven't settled into one place yet. I'll let you know," she said. "When we're together again, we'll have a long talk, a grown-up talk, and I'll tell you everything, every last crummy detail. Be good, honey."

"Mommy!"

The click sounded like thunder.

I shouted louder. *"Mommy!"* I squeezed the neck of the receiver with all my might and screamed into it again.

Aunt Sara came running.

The front door opened and Uncle Jacob stopped in the corridor with Cary right behind him.

I was crying hysterically now, bawling without control.

"What's going on here? What's the meaning of this outburst?" Uncle Jacob demanded.

"She was talking to Haille," Aunt Sara explained.

"Well I won't have this sort of emotional display. Stop it!" he commanded.

I cradled the receiver slowly and then wiped my cheeks with the back of my hand, glaring at him. The fury in my eyes took him aback and he blinked.

"Go clean yourself up," he ordered, "or you won't have any dinner."

"I don't want any dinner. I don't want anything from you," I said through clenched teeth.

Uncle Jacob reddened. Cary's mouth fell open and Aunt Sara gasped.

231

"I don't want anything from this . . . this horrible family." I ran from the living room.

"See!" Uncle Jacob cried after me as I started up the stairs. "And you thought she was like Laura. That's Haille's daughter."

I stopped abruptly and turned, glaring down at him.

"What's wrong with being Haille's daughter? Why do you always say that? What did she ever do to you?" I demanded.

He looked at Aunt Sara and then at me. "She didn't do anything to me. What she did, she did to herself and to Chester."

"What? *What?*" I screamed.

"Go up to your room until you calm down," he said, visibly shaken. I didn't move. What was it Mommy kept saying: he would never throw me out? How did she know? What made her so sure? Every time I uncovered one secret, there were ten more bundled beneath it, I thought. "Go on," he ordered.

"I'll go where I like when I like," I said defiantly. My boldness surprised us both and left him stuttering for the right words. I trembled, but tried to look calm so I could continue to face him.

"Ah, suit yourself," he finally said. "I'll have none of it. You wanted her here, you put up with her," he told Aunt Sara. Then he waved his hand as if chasing flies and marched through the house. Cary stared up at me, a stunned look on his face.

"Oh dear. Oh dear, dear," Aunt Sara mumbled.

"I'm sorry, Aunt Sara," I said. I took a deep breath. "I have to rest for a little while."

She looked up at me sadly and shook her head. "It was all going so well, wasn't it, Cary?"

"Let her be," he said and followed after Uncle Jacob.

I turned and continued up the stairs to my room. Behind the closed door, I let my tears of sorrow, tears of fear, and tears of loneliness flow freely.

I was on my stomach on the bed so I didn't hear May knock and then come in to see me. I felt her little hand

232

on my shoulder and turned sharply. She looked as if she was about to cry because I was crying.

"What's wrong?" she signed.

I smiled through my tears. "I'm all right," I told her. "I'll be all right."

Then I sat up and hugged her, clung to her as tightly as I would cling to a life raft in a sea storming with turmoil.

13
✷

Angry at Them All

*M*ainly because I didn't want May to be upset any more than she was, I went down to dinner. I had no appetite. The heavy atmosphere of the night before was nothing compared to the cemetery stillness that pervaded the dining room tonight. It was so quiet I could hear Uncle Jacob crunching his food between his back teeth, and Aunt Sara's little whimpers between her bites and swallows. The tapping of silverware, clanking of dishes, and pouring of water created the most noise. Everyone spoke in monosyllables or short sentences whenever he or she spoke.

"Bread, Jacob?"

He grunted yes.

"Would you like more chicken, Cary?"

"No, Ma."

Cary watched my every move. I ate like a bird, pecking at my food, keeping my eyes down. I didn't know whom I was more angry at: Mommy, Uncle Jacob, my grandparents. Maybe I was equally angry at all of them. I was even angry at myself for agreeing to remain here. How could I have believed Mommy's promises? One lie spun

234

another when it came to the Logans, and Mommy had caught their lying disease.

Aunt Sara tried to cheer me up by talking about the Blessing of the Fleet, a June festival that took place yearly in Provincetown. She said there would be lots of boats, people in costumes, great food and games. Whenever she asked Uncle Jacob about something, he would simply grunt a yes or a no, his eyes mostly on me. I sensed that I had scratched a scab on his memory when I had screamed my questions at him in the hallway. He didn't look irritated as much as stunned.

Aunt Sara made a final attempt to inject some joviality into our dinner by mentioning Cary's English test result. Uncle Jacob expressed surprise and approval, but when Cary explained that it was all because of my tutoring, Uncle Jacob grew dark again.

"Laura used to help Cary like that, too. Remember, Jacob?" Aunt Sara said smiling.

"I remember," he said. "I have something to do at the dock." He pushed himself away from the table and stood. "Don't make me any coffee."

"I'll have some hot water steaming for tea for you when you return, Jacob," Aunt Sara promised. He glanced at me once more, then left the room.

"If you have homework, you don't have to help me with the dishes tonight, Melody," Aunt Sara said. She was trying her best to make things right again. I felt sorry for her, but even sorrier for myself.

Cary's eyes were fixed on me. They were strangely haunted. Was he still angry at me or did he feel sorry for me? From the day I arrived, I had felt Cary carried deep secrets in his heart, secrets that resembled chunks of lead weighing him down, making him grow older faster. It was why he seemed so bitter all the time and why the girls at school saw him as Grandpa.

"I do have something to do tonight, Aunt Sara," I said. "I'm going to study for a test with a friend."

Cary looked down, his head lowering as if in prayer.

"Oh? Well . . . yes, Laura did that once in a while. Who was it she studied with, Cary? Sandra Turnick?"

"Yeah," he said quickly, but he didn't look up.

"She has a sister in your class, doesn't she, Melody? Is that who you're studying with tonight?"

"No," I said. Cary lifted his eyes and gazed at me. "It's someone else. Janet Parker," I said. Cary looked disappointed and once again dropped his gaze to his plate. "But first, I promised May I would do some homework with her," I added.

Aunt Sara smiled. "That's nice of you, dear. I'm sure May appreciates it."

She signed to her and May signed back, expressing her enthusiasm. I went upstairs with her and worked with her on her reading and speaking exercises. At a quarter to eight, though, I had to leave. I explained that she would probably be asleep when I returned, so I kissed her goodnight.

Cary had gone up to the attic. I heard him moving about while I worked with May, but now he was quiet, still. I found a blue cardigan sweater to wear over Laura's yellow dress. It was a little over sixty degrees outside, but the sky was clear with a three-quarter moon that put a bone-white glow over the sand.

"Don't be too late, dear," Aunt Sara called from the living room when I headed for the front door.

"I won't," I promised. My heart was pounding, both from the excitement and from guilt. I hated lying to her, but there was no doubt in my mind what her and Uncle Jacob's reactions would have been if they had known I was planning to meet a boy on the beach.

They have no right to restrict me, I told myself. This family, especially, has no right to tell me what I should and shouldn't do. Never before did I feel as much on my own, as much in control of my own destiny. Mommy had deserted me, lied to me, ignored my feelings and my needs. She knowingly left me with people who looked down on us. She had left me to fend for myself. And that's just what I would do, I told myself.

All my life I had believed in being honest. I believed in the ultimate goodness of people, only to find out that my own parents had deceived me. Who did I have but myself? I thought. Driven by my rage as much as I was drawn by Adam Jackson's magical eyes, I bounced quickly down the steps and walked away from the house. I looked back once. I thought a curtain in an upstairs window moved, but other than that, there was no sign of anyone watching, so I veered left onto the beach and plodded through the sand. I quickly discovered it was easier to walk with my shoes off. The sand, still holding on to the day's sunlight, felt warmer than the air.

As I drew closer to the ocean, I saw the moon walk on the water and heard the roar of the surf. The water looked inky, mysterious and the stars on the horizon blazed with a brightness that filled my heart with even more excitement. In moments I was far enough out on the beach to sense the solitude. The Logans' house was lit up, but looked toy-like and distant after another few minutes of my walking away from it.

I went up and down the hilly terrain. At the top of the dune, I gazed toward the place on the beach I had been when Adam had first found me. I saw the glittering flames of a small bonfire and my heart thumped. Would he be surprised to see that I'd actually come, I wondered. I was surprised, myself.

When I drew closer, I saw his motorboat anchored on the beach and heard music from his radio. He was sprawled on the blanket, his hands behind his head, and he was gazing up at the sky. He wore a white polo shirt and a pair of white shorts. He was barefoot. If he heard me approach, he didn't show it. I stood beside him for a moment before he slowly turned, his face glimmering in the moonlight with that polished smile. He sat up.

"I'm glad you came," he said. "It's a great night. It

237

would have been a shame for you to miss it." He patted the space beside him on the blanket. "Did you have any trouble getting out?"

"No," I said. "I dug a tunnel."

He laughed. "Great. So?" he said after a moment, "Are you just going to stand there? You didn't come all this way to watch me lie on a beach blanket, did you?" he asked.

"Maybe. Don't forget my uncle and aunt don't allow television in their house."

He threw back his head and roared with laughter. Then he grew serious and gestured for me to come to him. "It's very cozy on this blanket."

I lowered myself to my knees and put my shoes down before sitting on the blanket, close to the edge.

He stared with a quizzical look on his face and then he shook his head, still smiling. "Aren't you the tease?" he said. "All right, I'll play hard to get, too." He lay back on his hands to look up at the sky.

"I'm not a tease."

"Of course you are. All girls are."

"Well, it's not true about me."

He turned over and braced his chin on his hand to gaze at me. "Really? Well, why do you work so hard at being beautiful if not to have boys look at you longingly?"

"I don't work so hard at being beautiful."

"I imagine you don't," he said nodding. "You are what I would call a natural beauty. That's why all the cats in school are clawing at you. So," he said, sitting up again, "tell me about your life in coalmineville. Leave a boyfriend crying in his beer when you came to the Cape?"

"No."

"I'll bet. Well, his loss is my gain." He snickered. "Come a little closer. I won't bite," he said. "You want me to beg? Is that it?" he asked when I didn't move.

"I don't want you to beg, no."

238

"So?"

I shifted on the blanket until I was beside him.

"Now that's better. At least I can smell your hair." He put his nose to my head and then kissed my forehead. "And I can look into those terrific eyes. You know you turn me into jelly, don't you?"

This time, I had to laugh. "Don't you mean cranberry sauce?" I asked.

That brought a wide smile to his face. His blue eyes seemed to sizzle as they blazed down at me. "You're smart as well as beautiful. A rare jewel." He kissed me on the lips, but I was so tense I thought he would hear my nerves twang.

He gazed at me with a curious smile, then he leaned over to his right where he had a cloth bag. He produced a bottle of vodka and two glasses. Then he dipped his hand into the bag and came up with a jar of cranberry juice. "How'd you know I had cranberry juice? Some little bird at school whisper in your ear?"

"I didn't know."

"It's a great drink with vodka. My father's favorite. Let me fix us a couple."

"I don't like drinking whiskey," I said quickly.

"This isn't whiskey. It's vodka. Doesn't stink on your breath as much, and when you cut it with the cranberry juice, you hardly notice it. But it sure makes you feel good. I'm sure you've had it, right?"

"Of course," I said, even though I never had. All I had ever tasted was Mommy's gin and I never could understand how or why she liked it so much.

After he made the drinks and handed me my glass, he tuned the radio to a station that played softer music.

"Let's make a toast," he said tapping his glass against mine. "To us. To good times and good weather forever."

I took a sip. He was right. It didn't taste as bad as Mommy's gin.

"So where did you used to go at night with your boyfriends in West Virginia: old coal mines?"

"Sometimes," I said, even though the very thought of going into a coal mine at night was terrifying. I didn't want him to think I wasn't as experienced or as sophisticated as the girls here.

He brought his glass to his lips and urged me to bring mine to my lips. "Keeps you warm inside," he promised. I drank some more. "Was the sky as beautiful at night in West Virginia?"

"Yes."

"But you didn't have the ocean. The ocean makes the sky look better, doesn't it?" He moved closer, putting his arm around my waist. I looked at the sky where it merged with the horizon. The water was glimmering and the stars did seem brighter than ever, some actually twinkling on the water. He nudged my cheek with his nose and kissed me softly on the neck.

A flow of warmth rushed down over my shoulders to my breasts. Nervous, I drank some more. Then I pulled a little away from him.

"I like this song," I said. "Don't you?"

"What? Oh, yeah." He reached for the bottle of vodka and refilled my glass. "Feels good, right?"

"Yes."

"Let's see, this time we'll toast to . . . the end of school. May it come quickly and put me out of pain." He clinked my glass again. "Quick, drink or we won't get our wish," he urged. I took a long sip and thought this time the vodka was a lot stronger.

"I thought you were a good studious—I mean student," I said.

He laughed. "I do all right. Adam Jackson does just enough to make his father happy with his grades," he bragged.

"Isn't your father a lawyer?" I asked him.

"Yeah, but don't worry. I won't sue you if we don't have a good time tonight."

"Do you want to be a lawyer?" I asked quickly as he leaned over to kiss me.

240

"Maybe. I don't know. My father wants me to be." He brushed his lips against mine and then turned abruptly and lowered his head to my lap so he could look up at me. "You look great from down here," he said. He reached up and fingered the buttons on my cardigan sweater. I put my hand over his. "You're not cold, are you?"

"A little," I said.

"Take another drink. Go on," he urged. "You won't be cold long."

I did and he smiled. His finger undid one button and then another.

"You looked great in this dress today," he said. "Like a fresh flower. I was jealous at the way some of my friends were looking at you."

His finger traced the valley between my breasts. Then he lifted himself slowly, reached behind my neck, and gently brought me down to meet his lips. It was like a kiss in the movies, his lips pressing against mine, his tongue moving between my lips, the music around us, the stars above us. I felt warm all over. My mind reeled. He took my glass of vodka and cranberry juice from me, urged me down to the blanket, and then turned so he was lying face down over me.

"I just knew you and I would click," he said.

"How did you know?"

"Adam Jackson knows women."

"You talk about yourself as if you were someone else." I giggled. "I never heard anyone do that."

"Simple explanation," he said, shrugging, "I'm bigger than one person."

He lowered his lips to mine and kissed me long and hard, his right hand moving over my ribs to my breasts.

"You are delicious," he said. My pulse was racing. I looked past him at the stars and they seemed to blur and merge. He kissed my neck, then lowered himself so he could move his tongue under my collar, toward my breasts. I felt him lift me gently and find the zipper

241

behind my dress. I started to resist, but the zipper flew down and he quickly nudged my dress over my shoulders, driving his mouth to my breasts.

It was as if I were on a magic carpet and not just a beach blanket. It seemed to lift both of us off the sand and begin to turn in a counter-clockwise circle. He had the straps of my bra down and was manipulating the hook with surgical expertise. It popped and his hand moved up under the garment instantly, lifting it away. Before the air could touch my naked bosom, his lips were there, nudging, strumming my nipples.

I felt a weakness in my legs as his legs moved in between and forced mine to separate. It was happening so fast—the blinking, out-of-focus stars were falling like a downpour of diamonds around us, the blanket was spinning, his hand was under the skirt of my dress and his fingers were toying with my panties. The roar of the ocean covered my small protests and he was saying, "You're perfect. I knew we would be great together."

But this wasn't romantic and lovely. This frenzy of passion frightened me more than it excited me. Too fast, I thought. It's happening too fast.

I pushed at his chest and shook my head, but he smothered my exclamation with his lips, jabbing his tongue harder into my mouth. I nearly gagged, and when he pulled back I screamed. "Stop it!"

"What?" he cried. "You wanted this, didn't you? Otherwise, why would you come here? Just relax. Lie back and enjoy Adam Jackson."

My arms were too small and weak to hold back the weight of his upper body. I started to cry as he lifted me easily and began to slip my panties down my thighs. I was shaking my head and pleading. I could hear his heavy, hard breathing and I tried to turn my mouth from his, but he seemed to have grown in size. I saw him in the same distorted way I saw the stars. He resembled a great jellyfish spreading over me, encompassing me.

"Please . . . stop!" I pleaded.

He pulled his head up to look down at me disdainfully.

"You are a tease," he said, "and Adam Jackson is not to be teased."

I thought I would pass out beneath him. My eyes rolled, my mind went dark for a moment, and then, suddenly I felt him rise off me, his head going back first and then his lower body lifting. I opened my eyes to see Cary pulling him away, clutching his hair, and grasping his right arm. He jerked him so hard he fell back on the sand.

"Get off her!" he cried.

Adam turned over on the beach quickly and got to his feet. I sat up, my stomach gurgling. The two boys faced each other. Cary's hands were clenched into small mallets. With his shoulders hoisted like a hawk, he stepped toward Adam.

"Come on," he said. "Let's see how you protect that precious handsome face of yours."

"Get out of here!" Adam whined. "She wanted it," he said pointing at me. "She came here, didn't she?"

Cary gazed at the bottle of vodka on the blanket.

"You got her drunk, you bastard. You took advantage of her."

Cary lunged at him and Adam jumped back.

"You're crazy!" he cried. "Your whole family's crazy, including her!" He backed away. "I'm not going to fight over her." He continued to back toward his boat. Cary stood glaring at him. Then he turned, reached down for the bottle of vodka, and heaved it in Adam's direction. The bottle smashed against the side of the boat and splattered.

"You're out of your mind! You'll be sorry," Adam threatened, but he pushed his boat away from the shore and quickly jumped into it when Cary threatened to come after him. "This isn't the end of this. You'll hear from me!" he screamed.

"Sue me!" Cary retorted, his hands on his hips.

Adam started his engine and turned the boat away. A moment later he was bouncing over the water, fleeing.

I turned over on my left side and buried my face in the blanket. I felt Cary kneel down and touch my shoulder.

"You all right, Melody?" he asked softly.

"No," I said. I felt sick and embarrassed and suddenly very, very tired.

"Come on. I'll help you home," he said.

"I don't want to go home. That's not my home!" I cried. "I don't have a home!"

"Sure you do. You're with us until your mother comes back."

"I don't care if she ever comes back."

"Sure you do."

"Stop saying sure I do. You don't know what I want. None of you know or care."

"I care," he insisted. "Come on," he urged. He started to zip up the back of my dress. "You'll feel better after you walk a while."

"I'll never feel better. I don't want to feel better. Just leave me here on the beach and let the water come in and pull me out to sea. I'd rather drown."

He laughed. "Come on. You're just a little drunk."

"I am not drunk," I said and spun around, only when I did, the whole world spun with me and kept spinning. I moaned and fell into his arms. The gurgling in my stomach turned into a volcano and it began to erupt. He held me as I heaved. All the vodka I had drunk on top of a relatively empty stomach came up like molten lava. It burned its way up my throat and poured out of my mouth. The pain of heaving doubled me over. If it had not been for Cary holding me, I was sure I would have fallen face forward into the sand.

Finally, it stopped. I took deep breaths, gasping for clean air.

"You all right now?"

I was feeling better after getting rid of the vodka. I nodded and he lowered me to the blanket.

244

"Just rest a moment," he said.

I took shorter breaths, the heaviness in my chest lessening, but there was an ache in my eyes and my stomach felt as if I had been punched a dozen times. The good thing was that the spinning had stopped.

"How did you find us?" I asked, starting to realize all that had happened.

"I followed you. I had a suspicion you were going to meet that creep," he said. "He has trouble keeping his bragging tied at the dock. He was telling some of his friends that he was going to have a good time tonight on the beach and he would have a big story for them tomorrow. He didn't mention your name, but I was afraid it was you, and then, when you told me you couldn't go to town with me because you had made other promises, I was even more suspicious. That lie you told at dinner clinched it. I knew you wouldn't go to Janet Parker's house to study."

"I'm sorry," I said. "I'm sorry I made trouble for you."

"No trouble for me," he said with a laugh. "Trouble for Mr. Perfect."

"He threatened you."

"He'll be too embarrassed to tell anyone what really happened. Don't worry."

I tried to sit up.

"Think you can walk?" Cary asked.

"Yes," I said. He had pulled the zipper of my dress up, but my bra was still undone. For the moment it didn't matter. I started to stand. He came around behind me and lifted me at the elbows until I was on my feet, but I wobbled and fell against him.

"Whoa," he said. "Steady as she goes. Seas are a bit rough tonight."

"Maybe I should be wearing a life jacket," I said and he laughed. We started away. "What about the blanket and the radio and all?"

"Leave them to the ocean. She has a way of cleaning

245

up the messes left on her beaches," he said. He held my right arm as we continued walking.

"I must look like a mess," I said. "My stomach feels as if I swallowed a beehive."

"We'll get you home and to bed, but you'll probably feel crummy in the morning."

"Your mother will be very upset with me, and if your father sees me—"

"He won't," Cary promised.

"It's too soon. Your mother will wonder why I'm back from studying already."

"We'll smuggle you in," he promised.

I walked with my eyes shut, my head against his shoulder, feeling heavy with the burden of shame I carried. He held me as if I were made of spun glass and any second I'd break. When I stumbled, he held me even tighter and more firmly. It seemed to take forever to go back over the hill, and then when we started to descend the second one, he abruptly stopped. "Wait."

I opened my eyes.

"What?"

He squinted at the darkness.

"My father," he whispered. "He's coming back from the dock."

"Great. Now all I'll hear is how this proves I'm my mother's daughter. He'll have me reading the Bible all night."

"Shh! Just don't move for a moment." Cary was quiet a long moment. "All right, he's just about to the house. Let's go to the boat for a little while," he said. "You'll clean up and straighten up and then we'll go in. Come on. You'll be all right," he promised. His words spread a magic shawl of comfort about my shoulders. I relaxed and followed his direction.

He turned me right and we moved down the hill toward the ocean again. Moments later, we were at the dock. He helped me onto the lobster boat. It bobbed gently in the water, but I was still too unsure of myself to walk without Cary's support.

246

"Easy." He guided me into the cabin, leading me to a cushioned bench. He turned on a small oil lamp. "How are you doing?"

"I feel as if I'm stuck on a runaway roller coaster. My ribs ache, my head feels like a hunk of coal, my stomach wants to resign from my body . . . I've never been drunk before. Lucky you were there for me," I said. "Thanks."

He stared at me. "I hate guys like Adam Jackson. They think everything's coming to them because they were born with silver spoons in their mouths. They all oughta be harpooned, or taken out to sea and left there floating on their egos."

I laughed. but it hurt and I moaned.

Instinctively, he reached for my hand. "You want a drink of water?"

"Yes, please," I said and he rose to get it. That was when I looked down and saw the mess I had made on the front of my dress. "Oh, Cary, look. Aunt Sara will be devastated. One of Laura's dresses. It will be stained."

He turned and gazed at me. He thought a moment. "I got a tub on deck, and some soap. We'll scrub it clean and then I'll put it on the kerosene heater for a half hour and that'll dry it enough." He poured me a glass of water and handed it to me. "In the meantime," he took a rubber raincoat off a hook, "you can wear this."

I drank the water.

"I'll go fill the tub and get a brush."

"I'll wash it," I said. "You don't have to do that."

"It's all right. If I can wash smelly fish guts off the deck, I can wash off some used vodka."

"Ugh," I said, laughing.

He left, and I took off the dress, fastened my bra and put on the raincoat.

"All set," he called out.

"I'll do it," I insisted.

"You sure?"

"Yes."

He took me to the tub and I scrubbed the dress clean

247

while he lit the kerosene heater in the cabin. When I thought the dress was clean enough, I brought it in and he draped it carefully over the heater.

"Shouldn't take too long," he said. I sat on the bench. He went to a closet and took out a pillow. "Here," he said placing it on the corner of the bench. "Lie back, close your eyes, and rest."

"Thank you. You're a regular rescue service," I told him.

He sat at the base of the bench, his back against it, his arms around his legs. The small flame in the oil lamp flickered, making the shadows dance on the walls of the cabin. I could hear the water licking at the sides of the boat. The pungent odor of seaweed and salt water was as refreshing as mint at the moment. I took a deep breath and sighed.

"I'm a mess," I said.

"You're not. You're bright and pretty. Everything is going to be all right." He said it with such assurance, I wondered if everyone else could see my future clearer than I could. "Don't feel bad about what happened. Guys like that fool girls every day," he added bitterly.

I thought about Laura and Robert Royce and imagined that was what Cary meant.

"I read a letter Robert Royce wrote to Laura," I confessed.

"That garbage?" Even in the dim light, I could see his frown.

"It didn't seem like garbage, Cary. I read only one, but I thought he was sincere."

"He knew how to use sincerity to get what he wanted," Cary said sharply. "He was a conniving, sneaky—"

"How can you be so sure?"

"I can," he said firmly.

"I'm not even confident about people I've known all my life, people I've seen on a daily basis. You can't possibly know what things Laura and Robert said to each other, what they told and promised each other, and

248

from what I've learned about her, she must have been a very bright person, Cary. Maybe you were just—"

"Just what?"

"Overly worried. It's only natural, I suppose. Tell me about the accident."

"There's nothing to tell. They went sailing, a storm came, and they got caught in it."

"They had no warning?"

"They were out there too long. He was probably . . ."

"Probably what?" He didn't answer. "Cary?"

"Probably trying to do to her what Adam Jackson tried to do to you tonight. She resisted and he kept her out there and they got caught in the storm. He's responsible for what happened. He's lucky he died too, otherwise, I would have killed him with my bare hands. In fact I wish he hadn't died. I wish I could have been the one to kill him."

I was quiet for a moment. His shoulders, hunched up with rage, relaxed a bit.

"Don't you think that if Robert Royce were that sort of a boy, Laura wouldn't have continued seeing him, Cary?" I asked softly. "I certainly don't want to be alone with Adam Jackson again."

He didn't reply for a while. Then he sighed, lowered his head and shook it. "She was confused, is all. She was in a rush to have a boyfriend."

"Why?"

"Because of those . . . busybodies in school always teasing her about not having one, saying nasty things to her about . . ."

"About what?" I held my breath.

"About us. They spread dirty stories about us and she thought it was because she didn't have a boyfriend. So you see, she didn't really like Robert that much. She was just trying to please everyone and get them to stop. She thought it was bothering me and she blamed herself."

"That's terrible," I said. He nodded. "Why did they make up those stories about you two?"

"Why? Because they're dirty, mean, selfish. They couldn't understand why Laura and I were so close, why we did so much together and for each other. They were jealous so they made up stories. They're as responsible for her death as Robert was," he concluded.

"I'm sorry, Cary." I touched his shoulder.

He nodded. "Don't bother reading any more of those phony letters. They're full of lies. He wrote and said whatever he thought would get him what he wanted," Cary assured me.

"Why doesn't your mother throw them out, then?"

"She wouldn't touch anything in that room. For a long time afterward, she refused to believe Laura wasn't coming back. They've never found her body, so she refused to accept her death. And then, my father had the gravestone put in and forced her to go there with him. Finally, she accepted that much, but she still clings to the room, to her things, her clothes. I was surprised she wanted to take you in and let you stay in Laura's room, but it's almost as if she thinks . . ."

"What?"

"Laura's come back through you. That's another reason why my father hasn't been the most hospitable person. It's not that he dislikes you for any reason."

"There's a reason," I said prophetically. "Something happened that has made him so bitter about my mother, and I want to know what it was. Do you know anything else?" I asked.

"No," he said quickly. Too quickly, I thought.

"Then, I'll just have to ask our grandparents to tell me everything."

He turned, a look of disbelief on his face.

"You wouldn't just come out and ask them?"

"Why not?"

"Grandma Olivia can be . . . tough."

"So can I," I said firmly. "When I have to be."

He laughed.

"Maybe you shouldn't, Melody," he said after a moment, his smile gone. "Maybe some things are better left below deck."

"Secrets fester like infections. After a while they make you deathly sick, Cary. That's the way I feel. It's the way you felt when people were making up stories about you and Laura," I said searching for a way to make him understand how important it was to me.

"I tell you what," he said, reaching for my hand. "I'll make you a promise. I promise to try to find out as much as I can about your parents, too."

"Will you? Oh thank you, Cary."

He held on to my hand. "It's okay," he said. "You're probably right. You probably should know everything there is to know about the Logan family."

I smiled at him. "When I first came here, I thought you hated me."

"I did," he confessed. "I knew why my mother wanted you here and I felt bad about it, but . . ."

"But?"

"You're very nice," he said. "And the only cousin I have, so I have to put up with you."

"Thanks a lot."

"Let's check the dress," he said and got up. "It's not completely dry, but it's dry enough. You'll get by with it."

"Thanks," I said rising. He handed me the dress and I started to take off the raincoat.

"I'll wait outside," he said.

I changed, hung up the raincoat, and joined him on the deck.

"How do you feel?" he asked.

"Tired and wobbly, but a hundred percent better than I did, thanks to you."

"Let's go home," he said taking my hand. He didn't let go until we were at the house.

"How do I look?" I asked him, brushing back my hair.

"Fine," he said gazing at me in the glow of the porch light.

251

Uncle Jacob was in the hallway when we entered. He was heading for the living room with a mug of tea in his hand. He paused and looked at us, his eyes growing small and dark.

"Where were you two?" he asked.

"I met Melody coming back from studying with her friend," Cary said quickly.

Uncle Jacob's gaze shifted from Cary to me and then back to Cary before he continued toward the living room.

"Get home as soon as you can tomorrow," he said. "Lots to do."

"Okay," Cary said.

Aunt Sara appeared in the kitchen doorway.

"Oh, hi. Is everything all right?"

"Yes, Aunt Sara," I said. "I'm tired and going to sleep."

"Good night, dear," she said.

Cary followed me up the stairs.

"I'm sorry you had to tell your father a lie, Cary," I told him at my door.

"It was only half a lie," he said. "You were on the way home." He smiled.

"Good night and thanks again," I said. I leaned over and kissed him on the cheek. He blushed. I flashed the best smile I could and retreated to my room. He was still standing in the hallway when I closed the door. I heard him pull down his attic steps and go upstairs.

I changed and dressed for bed. I hated the sight of myself in the mirror and wondered if those shadows under my eyes would be gone by morning. Nothing felt as good as the mattress and covers. My eyelids were like two steel doors slamming shut. The last thing I remembered was wishing Cary hadn't lied for me. It all starts with little half lies and then it grows until, until . . . you become like Mommy and lose track of the difference.

It won't happen to me, I vowed.

It won't.

The chant worked like a lullaby. The next thing I knew, I was fluttering my eyelids at the flood of sunlight penetrating the window curtains and nudging me to start another day.

14

&

A Helpless Creature

*U*nfortunately, Cary wasn't right about Adam Jackson. It was true that his ego had been bruised, but his embarrassment over my rejecting him turned into something uglier. By the time Cary and I had arrived at school, Adam's lies had spread like a brush fire in a drought. The moment I saw the expressions on the faces of girls like Lorraine, Janet, and Betty, I knew something mean and vicious had been poured into their ears and would soon be poured into mine.

As soon as we entered the building, Cary sensed the negative electricity in the air. He hovered about me like a nervous grizzly bear. Usually, when we arrived at school, he would scamper away to join his few friends, but today Cary lingered at my side while I organized my things at my locker. Nearby, the girls watched us, giggling. Other boys walking by held smirks on their faces and twisted their lips as they whispered. I marveled at how completely Cary could ignore everyone when he wanted to. For him, they didn't exist at the moment. He heard no evil and saw no evil. If he looked in their direction, he gazed right through them.

"Good morning, Cary," Betty said as she passed us with Lorraine and Janet.

"Good morning, Cary," Lorraine echoed.

"Good morning, Cary," Janet mimicked.

Something slippery and ugly obviously was hidden beneath their wide smiles. Cary didn't respond. He escorted me to my homeroom and was there at the sound of the bell to walk with me to my next class.

"You don't have to be worried about me," I told Cary after I found him waiting in the hallway outside my first period classroom.

"Oh, I'm . . . not," he fumbled. "I was just nearby and thought I might as well walk along with you as with anyone."

"Thanks a lot," I said, smiling at his clumsy effort to explain his presence.

"I mean, I like walking with you, it's just that—"

"You're usually too busy?"

"Yes," he said, grateful for my suggestion.

Although he wasn't there after my next period ended, he wasn't far behind in the corridor. It was nice having him look after me. For the moment at least, I felt as if I had a brother.

In my classes and in the hallway when I passed from room to room, I noticed how the girls kept their distance, and in class, I saw them looking at me and passing notes. But no one said anything. When I entered the cafeteria at lunch time, however, I found Janet, Lorraine, and Betty waiting anxiously, their eyes sparkling with glee.

"You're kind of cozy with Grandpa today," Betty teased immediately. "Any special reason?" She swung her eyes toward her friends.

"Cozy? I don't know what you mean," I replied. I stepped toward the counter to get a container of milk, but I caught the way they traded smiles and glances as they moved behind me in the lunch line.

"We heard you've taken Laura's place in more ways

255

than one," Janet whispered in my ear. It made the hairs on my neck stick up.

"What?" I turned to confront them.

"You're still carrying her notebook," Lorraine pointed out, "and you wear her clothes."

"You sleep in her room, use her things," Betty recited.

"And whatever she did with Cary, you're doing," Janet concluded.

I felt the blood rush so quickly to my face, my cheeks burned.

"Whatever she did with Cary? What's that supposed to mean?" I demanded.

"You know." Betty rolled her eyes.

"I don't know because my mind isn't in the gutter. What are you saying? Who told you these things?"

"Who else, but the eyewitness?" Betty said with the firmness of a prosecutor. She nodded toward Adam Jackson who had come in with his crowd of buddies. He strutted across the cafeteria, his shoulders back, his face full of himself when he glanced my way. I saw a wicked, twisted smile take shape on those perfect lips.

"Eyewitness?"

"No sense pretending with us anymore," Lorraine said stepping closer to me. "Adam told us what he found you two doing on the beach last night."

"He did what?"

"He said he was riding in his motorboat, saw the bonfire and pulled up before you two had a chance to make it look innocent," Betty detailed.

"He told you that?"

"Surprised he told?" Janet asked.

"He described how you begged him not to, and promised him something good if he didn't," Betty added.

"Is that what you did back in coal country, bribed boys with your body?" Lorraine asked.

I tried to speak, but the words choked in my throat. I shook my head instead. Out of the corner of my eye, I saw Cary watching with concern. He looked as if he was about to get up. Panic nailed my feet to the floor, but I knew I had to do something and fast, otherwise there would be a terrible scene in front of the whole student body.

"Those are lies," I finally said. "The real truth is he's just angry at me for not doing what he wanted me to do on the beach last night. Really!"

"Really?" Betty quipped. "Is that why you and Grandpa are like two peas in a pod today? Practically holding hands? If he were any closer to you, he'd be under your dress."

"It's disgusting," Janet followed. "You're first cousins, aren't you?"

"The Logans give the Cape a bad name," Lorraine declared. The other two nodded.

"What are you waiting for?" Betty said, shifting her eyes toward Cary. "He's waiting for you. The two of you can hold hands under the table. Or do whatever else you do."

The three laughed and moved ahead to get their food. The moment they did, other girls gathered around them to feed on the gossip like chickens in a pen.

I felt my heart pounding. Everyone was looking at me, waiting to see what I was going to do. Cary was still watching from the table where he sat with his two friends, an expression of deep concern on his face. I hesitated. If I went to him, all these tongues would surely cluck, but sitting with the girls today was like putting myself in a Roman Coliseum. They would eat me alive.

"Aren't you going to sit with him?" Janet asked nodding in Cary's direction as she carried her tray past me.

Theresa was walking by with her friends.

"I promised Theresa I would sit with her today," I said loud enough for her to hear. She turned with a look of surprise, but lost it quickly when she saw the expression on my face and the three witches from *Macbeth* closing in. She waited for me to join her.

"Thanks," I whispered. "I especially don't want to sit

257

with them today. All they want to do is make fun of Cary and me," I explained.

"Oh." She wore a knowing look.

When we were at the table and had taken our sandwiches from our bags, I leaned closer to her. "Why did you say 'oh,' like that?" I asked. "Did you hear dirty gossip, too?"

"There's never a bad day's catch when it comes to dirty gossip around here," she said, "especially when it's about Cary Logan. He and Laura were often the hot topic around here."

"Why?"

"There are other brothers and sisters here, dozens," she continued gesturing at the students in the cafeteria, "but none of them behaved as if they had invisible handcuffs tying them together. Anyone will tell you, so it's not like I'm letting a two-pound lobster out of the trap. If Cary could have followed her into the girls' room, I think he would have."

"Wasn't that all just an exaggeration?"

"No. They came to school together, they sat next to each other in every class, they sat with each other at lunch time, they sat with each other in the library, they left school together. The first time I saw Laura at a school party, she came with Cary," Theresa added, "and even danced with him. She danced with a couple of other boys. but she danced with her brother first."

"Maybe he thought she was too shy and just wanted to make her comfortable, or maybe he was too shy," I said. There had to be a hundred other reasons besides the one she was suggesting.

Theresa snorted.

"Well, she did have a boyfriend, didn't she?" I pointed out.

She bit into her sandwich and then shook her head.

"You really are like a stranger to your own family, aren't you?"

"Yes," I admitted.

258

"When Laura started to see Robert Royce, it was a comedy show for these gossips. Cary would sit by himself or with those nerdy friends across the cafeteria and glare at Laura and Robert. He plodded through the hallways with a chin down to his ankles. The other boys started teasing him and he got into a few fights."

I looked across the cafeteria at him and saw he was still staring at me with deep concern. My heart beat in triple time. Had he heard the stories about us?

"So now that Laura's gone, they just picked up on you," Theresa said.

"With someone else's help," I added glaring across the cafeteria at Adam. He was obviously elaborating on his lies, gesturing emphatically and nodding in Cary's direction.

"They don't ever stop. They'd eat each other to the bone if they could. But Cary and Laura," Theresa said, "they gave them something to chew on." She shook her head again. "It was as if they didn't care, as if they thought no one could touch them with nasty words and looks. I couldn't understand it."

"Your father works with my uncle and with Cary, what does he think?"

She pulled back a moment and gazed at me indignantly. Then she calmed and sat forward again. "He doesn't talk about the Logans except to say they are hardworking people," she remarked with an and-that's-that tone.

"I don't know which one of them first suggested it," I said, nodding at Janet, Lorraine, and Betty, "but they implied that Cary had something to do with Laura and Robert's accident. They made it sound as if he deliberately put them in harm's way."

"Some people think that," Theresa said.

"Do you?"

She ate for a while and then she sighed. "Look, I didn't exactly hang out with Laura Logan or Robert Royce. Laura was always polite and nice to me and I liked her,

259

but she sat on one side of the world and I sat on another one. Cary . . . he sat somewhere in outer space. I'm not swearing for anyone, but I'm not spreading any gossip, so stop asking all these questions."

She paused and turned completely to me so her back was to her friends. Then, in a low voice, she added, "Just like the rest of the bravas here, I mind my own business. What happens in the homes of the rich and famous isn't my concern. My daddy taught me that was the best way to stay out of trouble. Now don't you go telling anyone I said anything else, either," she warned with cold ebony eyes.

"I wouldn't do that."

"Good." Theresa turned back to her food.

I had barely touched mine. Was no one on our side? I gazed at Cary again. He looked so lost and lonely. In my put-away heart, I thought it wasn't fair. It wasn't fair what they were saying about him and me and what had happened to him.

I nibbled my sandwich, my stomach feeling like a tight drum. Theresa talked to her friends for a while and then gazed at me. The hard shell she had formed over herself cracked a bit.

"Look, it doesn't make sense that Cary would do something that would hurt Laura just to get at Robert Royce, does it?" she asked me.

"No."

"So? Don't let them drive you nuts about it. The trouble with them," she said, nodding at Janet, Lorraine, and Betty and their friends, "is they have nothing real in their lives so they make up soap operas. Maybe I'm not as rich as they are and I don't live in as nice a house, but I'm not anxious to trade places."

I smiled. "I don't blame you," I said.

Her smile widened. "Just ignore them and maybe they'll get bored or start on someone else," she suggested.

But it wasn't going to be that way for a while, and they

260

were just getting started building their fire of pain. While Theresa and I spoke, neither of us had noticed that notes were being passed from table to table in the cafeteria. At each table they reached, everyone quickly stopped talking and leaned in to read the slander. Soon, the girls at Theresa's table grew curious and one of them got hold of one of the notes. She read it and passed it down to Theresa.

Printed on the slip of paper was: Incest is best. Just ask Cary and Melody.

I felt as if my lower body had evaporated. I had no legs. I would never be able to get up from the table. The cafeteria was buzzing with loud chatter and laughter. My heart was pounding so hard, I thought I could hear it drumming over the noise.

"Bitches," Theresa muttered. Her friends nodded. Again, everyone's eyes were on me. I shifted my gaze slowly toward Cary. Someone had tossed one of the notes over to his table. After he read it, he crumbled it in his fist and turned to me. I shook my head to say, "Don't pay it any mind. Ignore it," but I could see he was fuming.

"Cary!" I called when he stood up. His gaze was fixed on Adam Jackson across the cafeteria. "Oh no," I muttered.

"Don't get in his way," Theresa warned me. "I've seen him pull up a net full of ten-pounders as if it were a net full of nothing more than balloons."

"This is just what they want," I wailed. Cary's determined strut across the room silenced the cafeteria. The lines in his face were taut and his shoulders were raised. One of the teacher monitors, Mr. Pepper, looked up from his newspaper curiously as Cary marched past him.

I got up as Cary rounded the table beside Adam Jackson's. Adam sat there, smirking, his arms folded over his chest.

"Careful," Theresa said touching my arm as I started after him.

261

"You spread a bunch of filthy lies about us today, didn't you?" Cary accused, loud enough for everyone to hear.

"Hey, if you're embarrassed by the truth, don't blame me," Adam said.

"What's going on there?" Mr. Pepper called. If he moved any slower, I thought, he'd make a turtle look like a cheetah.

Cary didn't waste words. His whole body had turned into a fist—it was that tight. He reached across the table and grabbed Adam at his collar and literally lifted him from his seat and pulled him over the table, knocking trays of food everywhere.

Adam struggled to break free of Cary's grip, but it was as firm and rigid as lockjaw. Adam looked like a fish out of water, twisting and turning, flailing about, kicking up his feet and swinging his arms wildly.

Cary turned him over and pinned his arms to the table. Everyone drew back. Mr. Pepper finally put on some steam and reached the table, shouting. "Stop that this instant! Cary Logan . . . Stop!"

Cary ignored him. He gazed down into Adam's terrified face.

"Tell them the truth! Tell them!" he screamed. "Was there anything between me and Melody? Was there?"

"Cary Logan, let him go," Mr. Pepper cried, but he didn't touch Cary. It was as if Cary were on fire and Mr. Pepper knew he would burn his hands. "Go get the principal," he shouted at one of the nearby students, who reluctantly turned, disappointed he would miss the action.

"The truth!" Cary screamed down at Adam and raised his fist over his face. To Adam, it must have looked as if a sledgehammer were about to fall on his precious handsome visage.

"All right. Nothing happened. Nothing happened! I made it all up. Satisfied?"

Cary relaxed and Adam sat up quickly, now indignant

262

and embarrassed. He started to say something, but when Cary turned back to him, he shrank quickly.

"Mr. Logan, you march yourself right down to the principal's office this instant, you hear?" Mr. Pepper said.

Cary didn't acknowledge him. He looked at me. "You all right?" he asked.

I wasn't sure I had any breath in my lungs. I nodded, reserving my words.

"If anyone else bothers you, tell me later," he said loudly. Then, moving like a prisoner condemned to the gallows, he marched ahead of Mr. Pepper toward the door.

The moment he left, the cafeteria burst into a storm of chatter.

"Satisfied with yourselves now?" I asked Janet, Lorraine, and Betty as I reached their table on the way back to Theresa's. They were too frightened to reply. "Adam Jackson invited me to meet him on the beach last night. I made the mistake of doing so and he tried to rape me," I told them. Their eyes bulged. "He talked me into drinking vodka and cranberry juice and got me drunk."

I saw from Janet's expression that she believed me. Maybe she had had a similar experience.

"Cary arrived just in time and drove Adam away. He literally tore him off me," I told them. "This is his revenge and you and your mean gossip helped him. Now Cary's in bad trouble. Thanks a lot." I turned on my heel and went back to Theresa.

"That Adam Jackson better watch his step or Cary's going to make him fish bait," she said.

"He'll only get himself into more trouble and it's all my fault," I wailed. I plopped into my seat just as the bell rang. The sea of chatter flowed out of the cafeteria with the students. The teachers in the afternoon classes would have a hard time keeping their attention today, I thought. I waited until most everyone was out before getting up to follow. Theresa lingered behind with me.

263

"What will they do to him?"

"Probably suspend him again," she said.

I felt just dreadful. I sat half dead in my seat in all my classes, barely listening, never answering a question. I couldn't wait for the day to end, and when it did, I found Cary waiting for me outside, his hands in his pockets, his head down, pacing back and forth like a caged animal. The moment he saw me, he perked up.

"You all right?" he asked quickly.

"Yes, but what happened?"

"I got two days vacation," he said.

"Oh Cary, near the end of the year when you need the review for your tests? This is horrible."

"It doesn't matter," he said.

"Yes it does. I'm not going to let the principal do this to you. It's not fair. He should see the nasty notes that were passed around."

"He saw them. It didn't make any difference. He told me I didn't have a right to lose my temper and take things into my own hands."

"He's right," I said.

"I told him it hadn't happened to his family so he could say that."

"What did he say?" I asked, shocked at his courage.

"He stuttered a bit and then said that wasn't the point. But don't worry. I'll walk you to school anyway and be here for you afterward and if Adam Jackson or anyone bothers you—"

"I won't tell you," I said. "You'd . . . you'd turn them into fish bait," I declared, using Theresa's language. He nodded, pleased with the description.

"Exactly, and they know it."

We started away.

"I appreciate your protecting me, Cary, but I hate to see you get into trouble."

I saw a smile take form on his lips.

"How can you be happy?" I asked him.

"This is the way it used to be between me and Laura,"

he said softly. Then he lost his smile. "Until Robert stepped into her life."

I said nothing. We walked on, each chased by troubled thoughts.

Cary didn't have to tell Aunt Sara and Uncle Jacob what had happened at school. The principal had called and told Aunt Sara before we returned home. Uncle Jacob was still down at the dock and didn't know yet, however, and Aunt Sara was visibly shaken just with the thought of what would happen once he found out. She wrung her hands and shook her head in despair.

"Don't worry, Ma. I'll tell him myself. I'll go down to the dock now," Cary said.

"How did this happen, Cary? You haven't been in any trouble for a long time, and it's so close to graduation."

I was about to take the blame, but Cary spoke first. "This boy was saying ugly, disgusting things about us and our family around the school, Ma. I did what I had to do."

"Why was he doing that?"

"Because he's a shark who needs to be harpooned, and that's all there is to say." Cary glared at me with eyes of warning.

"Oh Melody, was it dreadful for you, too?"

"Yes, Aunt Sara. I'm sorry Cary's in trouble, but the other boy was at fault."

She sighed.

"What are we going to do? All this happens on the day we're going to your grandparents for dinner. Don't mention anything about this to them," she told us fearfully.

"I won't if you won't," Cary promised. He winked at me and went up to change his clothes.

May, who had learned only bits and pieces about everything, was desperate to know what had caused all the commotion. Neither Cary nor I had told her much on the way home since neither of us was in the mood to talk. I explained it to her as best I could, leaving out the nasty details of the rumors.

She signed back that she was sorry Cary was in trouble again. It had always made Laura sad and it made her sadder still, she said. In her large, shadowed brown eyes lingered more dark secrets and sufferings than a child her age should know, I thought. And with her handicap, most of them remained trapped in her heart.

"Go up and try on your dress for tonight," Aunt Sara told me in a tired, defeated voice. "We have to do our best under the circumstances."

"Yes, Aunt Sara."

She followed me upstairs. The dress hung with a slip on the closet door. On the floor beneath them was a brand new pair of shoes she had bought to match the dress, since Laura's shoes wouldn't fit me.

"Aunt Sara, you shouldn't have done that. I could have worn something that would match my own shoes."

"No, this was the last dress I made for Laura," she explained. "She never got a chance to wear it."

"Oh."

I looked at the dress with different eyes. It took on a strangely spiritual feel, like the dress of a ghost. It was an ankle-length, straight beige silk dress with a Victorian collar that had a lace neck.

"Besides," Aunt Sara said, "we're all going to dress with extra care tonight. Olivia and Samuel are having Judge Childs as their guest. She called especially to tell me so we would all look our best. He was a state supreme court judge, you know. He's retired now, but maybe you've heard of his son, the artist Kenneth Childs."

"No." I shook my head and stared at the dress. I could almost see Laura in it.

"I just thought you might have, because you've been here a while and he's one of our most prominent sculptors. His work is in the Provincetown Artists museum and it's in all the good galleries."

I shook my head.

"The Childs have always been good friends with

266

Olivia and Samuel. Kenneth practically grew up with Chester and Jacob, he was at their house so much. Judge Childs's wife died two years ago. His other sons and daughter all live in Boston. Kenneth's brothers and sister don't have much to do with him, but Kenneth was the judge's favorite even though he didn't do anything with his law degree. The judge and his wife gave him enough money to do his art. They supported him for a quite a while and there are some hard feelings in the family because of it. Jealousy, I imagine."

She sighed deeply.

"Every family has its hardships. I wanted you to know a little about it so you don't say anything out of place, if the judge asks you a question."

"Why are we always on pins and needles when we go to my grandparents', Aunt Sara?" I asked. It seemed to me that time spent with family should be the most relaxing time of all.

"Oh, we're not on pins and needles. We're just trying to do the right thing, say the right thing, look the right way. It's what—"

"What Grandma Olivia wants," I provided. "I'm surprised she has any friends at all."

"But she does! She has many friends and they all come from the best society."

"That doesn't always mean they're the best friends to have, Aunt Sara."

She smiled as if I had said something only the most inexperienced young person might utter.

"Go on, dear, try on your dress. I want to be sure it fits and there's no need for alterations," she urged.

Betty, Lorraine, and Janet's words haunted me as I took the dress down and began to take off my clothes. "We heard you're taking Laura's place in more ways than one." But what else could I do? I had nothing nicer than this to wear. Of course, none of my other things had arrived.

The dress fit a little snugly in the bosom, but other than that, it was perfect.

"I think we can get by with it as it is," Aunt Sara said, scrutinizing me. "How does it feel?"

"It's fine, Aunt Sara."

"Good, and the shoes?"

"They're fine," I said.

"Then you're all set. I'll see to May. We'll be going about five," she told me.

After she left, I stood there gazing at myself in the mirror. It was a nice dress—beautiful in fact—and at any other time, under any other circumstances, I would be happy to wear it, but right now it seemed as if I were wearing a shroud. I couldn't shake an eerie feeling.

The more I learned about Laura, the more I touched her things, read her letters, wore her clothes, the more I felt I was disturbing her peace and stirring up things better left uncovered, buried at the bottom of the sea along with her and her lover.

I was dressed, my hair brushed, and ready. Cary and Uncle Jacob had yet to return from the dock. May looked very pretty in her pink taffeta dress with matching shoes. She and I sat in the living room waiting while Aunt Sara paced nervously in the hallway. "Where are they? They have to get ready and we're going to be late."

I couldn't help wondering if something terrible had happened after Cary told his father about his being suspended. Finally, the door opened and the two entered. Cary gazed into the living room and then ran up the stairs without a word.

Uncle Jacob paused and peered in at us. He fixed his eyes on me and nodded. "I knew it wouldn't take you long to get him in trouble," he said.

"It wasn't her fault, Jacob," Aunt Sara responded. "It was that nasty Adam Jackson's fault."

"I warned you," he told her. "I warned you what it would be like having Haille's daughter."

I shot up as if I were sitting on an ant hill.

"Why do you keep saying that? What's that supposed to mean?" I demanded.

"Ask your mother next time she calls," he said. He

looked at Aunt Sara. "I got to clean up and get dressed. No time for this nonsense now." He started up the stairs.

"Why does he keep saying that, Aunt Sara? I have to know what he means."

She shook her head, pressing her lips together as if she were afraid the words would escape.

"I'm not going anywhere until I get some answers," I insisted.

"Oh dear, oh dear. Why does all this have to happen before we go to Olivia and Samuel's?" She sat on the sofa and started to cry. May ran to her to hug her. I felt just terrible as she sobbed and May stroked her hair lovingly, concerned. "You look so beautiful in that dress, too," she wailed. "What have we done to deserve this? What have we done?"

May looked up, confused, hurt, tears building in her soft eyes. All I seemed capable of doing was hurting everyone.

"All right, Aunt Sara. I'm sorry. I'll go."

She sucked back her tears and dabbed her cheeks with her handkerchief. Then she smiled.

"It's going to be all right," she said. "Once everyone gets to know you better, it will be fine. Look how nice Laura's dress looks on you. That's no coincidence. It's an omen, a good omen. Jacob will realize it, too. Fishermen are very aware of good and bad omens. You'll see."

I just stared. She sighed and patted May's hair.

"My pretty little seashell," she said, kissing her daughter. She held her to herself and rocked for a moment. "We all deserve some happiness now, dear. Don't we?"

"Yes, Aunt Sara," I answered.

"Then it's settled. We'll all be happy," she said. It was as if she believed words themselves could change the world around us.

She left to wash her face and straighten her hair. May sat beside me and we looked at one of her books together. Cary came down the stairs and stood in the doorway. He was dressed in a blue suit and tie and looked very handsome.

"You look nice," I said.

"I feel as if I'm in a strait jacket." He tugged on his shirt collar. "I hate wearing a tie. I feel like . . ."

"A fish out of water," I suggested.

"Aye. I'm going outside to wait," he said. "It's my favorite time of day."

"Okay, we'll come along." I signed to May and she closed her book and followed, taking my hand. We strolled in front of the house.

Just over the western horizon, the sun was a rich saffron color, almost orange. The wispy clouds resembled veils of light cotton being pulled across the azure sky. Terns called over the ocean. The breeze was constant, but warmer than usual.

I had to admit Cape Cod was a beautiful place. How it must have broken my father's heart to leave.

Cary glanced at me, and his glimmering eyes met mine.

"Your father's right, you know," I said. "It was my fault."

"Don't start that again," he warned.

"After school ends, I'm not staying here," I told him. "No matter what, I'm leaving. If my mother doesn't want me, I'll go live with Mama Arlene back in Sewell. I'll get a part-time job and help out, but I can't stay where I'm not wanted, where I can only make trouble for people I like," I said.

A tiny smile took form on his lips. "Summer's the best time of the year up here. You can't leave. Besides, I'm depending on your help come cranberry season."

I shook my head.

Everyone refused to face reality here, I thought.

May suddenly began to tug my hand hard and gesture toward the beach.

"What is it, May?" I put my hand over my eyes and gazed. "Cary? Why are those people gathering down there?"

"Where?" He looked. "Oh no, not again," he said, and started over the sand.

270

"What is it?" We hurried to keep up with him. A thousand yards or so away, a number of people circled something big and dark on the beach. "Cary?"

"It's a beached sperm whale," he called back. He broke into a trot. May and I tried to keep up.

Nearly two dozen people had already reached the pathetic creature. It was at least fifty feet long. It lay on its side, its one visible eye open, bulging. It was gigantic and powerful looking, but right now it was helpless, dying. Most of the people, tourists, who had come to see it were timid and remained a dozen feet or so away, but some young teenagers demonstrated their bravado by rushing to it and slapping their hands on its body. Cary drew closer, keeping far enough back to prevent his shiny good shoes from getting wet. I drew closer with May.

"What happened?"

"It beached itself," he said.

"Why?"

"Lots of theories about that. Some think they become ill and seem to know that coming to shore or beaching will help them die."

"Does it look sick?"

"I don't know."

"What other reason might the whale have for doing this?" I asked.

"Whales have a built-in sonar system with which they navigate deep water. Sometimes, when they're in water only one hundred or two hundred feet deep, it disturbs the sonar and the whales get echoes and become confused, so they end up beached."

"What's going to happen? Can't it swim away with the tide?" I asked.

"The problem is when they reach land like this, the weight of their bodies is so great it crushes their lungs or hampers their breathing so much they become overheated and die. It looks as if that's what's happened here."

"Oh Cary, isn't there anything we can do?"

"You think you can push that back out to sea?" he

271

said. "And even if you get him back into the water, he'd probably wash up again down shore. Anybody send for the Coast Guard?" he asked the crowd.

"Somebody said something about that," a tall man replied.

"If they come, they might try to do something. If they don't show up soon . . ."

"What?"

He gazed around. The kids were still tormenting the whale, slapping it, going up and gazing into its eye, one threatening to poke the eye out with a stick he had found on the sand.

"Stop it!" I screamed.

They paused for a moment, saw it was only me, and continued their pranks.

"That's not so bad," Cary said. "People sometimes come down at night and start to cut off pieces while the whales are still alive," he explained angrily.

"Oh no, Cary."

We heard a car horn and looked back. Uncle Jacob and Aunt Sara had pulled down the road and were gesturing.

"We've got to go," he said.

"This is horrible, Cary."

He sighed. "I know." he said, turning away.

"Cary?"

"We'll come back later, after we return from Grandma's," he promised. He stared at the whale for a moment more and shook his head. "Not that we can do anything. Come on," he urged.

I followed, but after a few steps, I looked back at the helpless giant creature that had somehow found itself trapped on this beach. It was probably too confused and stunned to realize what had happened and what was soon to come.

Just like me, I thought walking slowly behind Cary and gazing back every few moments: beached.

15

&

Cary's Attic Room

*P*erhaps it was because of the family secrets that had begun to unravel around my heart: something frail within me cracked and ached as we turned up the driveway to my grandparents' house. I was on the verge of hysterical crying. Tears blinded my eyes. I turned away and stared out the car window so May wouldn't see how close I was to sobbing.

From what I now knew, I envisioned my parents, not much older than Cary and I, secretly holding hands and secretly pledging their love for each other in the shadowy corners of Grandma Olivia's house. Had Uncle Jacob always known? Was that one of the reasons he was so angry at my father?

Uncle Jacob shut off the engine.

"Now remember, best behavior," Aunt Sara instructed, signing the same to May.

"If we behaved any better, Ma, we'd be in heaven," Cary quipped.

Uncle Jacob glared at him and Cary quickly looked away.

The car beside Uncle Jacob's in the driveway

273

was much older, but so clean and shiny, it looked newer.

"The judge is already here," Uncle Jacob muttered. "He keeps this car better than most people keep themselves. There's a man knows the value of quality craftsmanship." He looked at Cary to drive home his lesson.

Grandma Olivia hired special servants for her formal dinners. A butler came to the door. He was a tall, slim man with a narrow, pointed nose and round, dark brown eyes. His hair was curly but so thin, I could see his scalp and the brown spots beneath the piano-wire strands when he bowed.

"Good evening, sir. Madam," he said with a smile that looked smeared across his face with a butter knife. He held the door open, gazing at all of us to see if any of us had a coat or a hat for him to take. We didn't. "Everyone is in the sitting room, sir," he said. He led us to it as if Uncle Jacob didn't know where it was. Aunt Sara thanked him and smiled back, but Uncle Jacob acted as if the servant weren't even there.

Grandma Olivia was in her high-back chair looking like a queen granting an audience. She wore an elegant black velvet dress and a rope of pearls with pearl earrings. Her hair was held back in a severe bun by a pearl comb decorated with small diamonds. Grandpa Samuel was more casual. He sat with his legs crossed, a tall glass of whiskey and soda in his hand. He wore a diamond pinky ring in a gold setting that glittered in the early twilight that poured through the open curtains on the window. His dark suit looked rather dapper, I thought. As before, he had a wide, warm smile when he looked at me.

On Grandma Olivia's right side sat a distinguished looking elderly man. His gray hair still showed traces of light brown. It was neatly trimmed and parted on the right. He wore a tuxedo and a bow tie. When Judge Childs turned to us, I saw he was still a handsome man. His face was full and his complexion robust with wrinkles only in his forehead. He had light brown eyes that dazzled with a glow more like those of a man half his age.

"You're late," Grandma said before anyone else could utter a word.

"We had a problem with the boat that kept us busy," Uncle Jacob said.

Grandma Olivia didn't consider that a valid excuse. "Boats can wait, people can't," she replied.

"Now, now, Olivia, don't be too harsh on those who still do an honest day's labor these days," the judge chided. "How are you, Jacob?"

"Fair to middling, I suppose," Uncle Jacob said. He nodded at his father, who still had his pleasant smile. "And you, Judge?"

"At my age, you don't dare complain," Judge Childs replied.

"Oh, come now, Nelson," Grandpa Samuel said, "you're only a year and a half older than I am."

"And you're no spring chicken, Samuel," the judge retorted. They both laughed. Then the judge turned with interest toward me. "Well now, Sara, you've got another chick under your wing, I see. And a pretty one at that."

"Yes, Judge." Aunt Sara put her hands on my shoulders and pulled me forward. "This is Melody. Haille's Melody."

"Looks just like her," the judge said, nodding. "Just as I remember her at that age. Hello, Melody," he said.

"Hello."

"How old are you now?" he asked.

"I'll be sixteen in a few weeks."

"Oh, that's nice. Another June birthday celebration."

"Kenneth's a Gemini, too, isn't he?" Aunt Sara asked the judge.

"Oh Sara, not that astrology again," Grandma Olivia warned. Aunt Sara shrank back.

"Well, he was born June eighteenth. Does that mean anything?" the judge asked.

"Geminis are May twenty-first to June twentieth,"

275

Aunt Sara said in a small voice, her eyes full of fear as she glanced quickly at Grandma Olivia.

"I see," Judge Childs said. "I'm afraid I don't keep up with that star business." He shook his head at Grandpa Samuel and Grandma Olivia. "My maid Toby won't start her day without first checking those predictions in the newspaper."

"Nonsense and stupidity, ramblings of the idiotic," Grandma Olivia said.

"I don't know," Judge Childs said shrugging. "Sometimes, I wonder what's better. Most of the fishermen I know are quite superstitious. Speaking of that, how's the lobstering been so far this year, Jacob?"

"Erratic," Uncle Jacob said. "With all the pollution, the oil spills, I doubt if my grandchildren will be doing much lobstering."

The judge nodded sadly. Aunt Sara directed Cary, May, and me toward the settee as the butler approached to see what sort of cocktail Uncle Jacob wanted.

"I don't drink," he said sharply.

"You oughta ease up on that, Jacob," Judge Childs said. "Doctors are now saying a drink a day is good for the heart. I know I followed that prescription even before it was the fad."

"My son's afraid to cloud his judgment," Grandpa Samuel said.

"And he's always had good judgment," said Grandma Olivia. "Especially moral judgment," she added, sending sharp arrows his way with her eyes.

Grandpa nodded. "That he has, that he has."

I noticed that throughout most of the conversation Judge Childs kept his attention fixed on me and held that soft, small smile on his lips. Finally, as though no one else were in the room talking about anything else, he asked me how my mother was doing.

"How would she know?" Grandma Olivia snapped. "Haille's off to be a movie star."

"Is that right?" the judge asked, still directing himself to me.

"Many people have told my mother that she was pretty enough to be a model or a movie star," I said. "She has auditions and meetings in Hollywood."

"Is that so?"

"Likely story." Grandma Olivia looked at Uncle Jacob, who nodded and sneered with a face that was nearly a replica of his mother's. My daddy had taken after his father much more than his mother, whereas it was the exact opposite for Uncle Jacob.

"She was one of the prettiest girls in Provincetown," the judge said. "Don't forget that beauty contest. I was one of the judges."

"What beauty contest?" I blurted out. Aunt Sara brought her hand to her mouth to cover a gasp. I was breaking a rule: I was speaking before being spoken to.

"Your mother never told you?" Judge Childs asked.

"Apparently, her mother told her very little," Grandma Olivia said with a twist in her thin lips.

"Oh, some company or another—I forget which one now—sponsored a Miss Teenage Cape Cod contest and it ended up here, with your mother one of the five finalists. They paraded around in their bathing suits and pretty dresses and answered questions with their eyelids batting." He laughed. "None of the other four had a chance, did they, Samuel?"

"Not a chance," he said nodding.

"Hardly an accomplishment to talk about now," Grandma Olivia said.

"Oh, we all thought it was a lot of fun back then, Olivia. You had a celebration here, didn't you?" he reminded her. She glanced quickly at Grandpa Samuel.

"That wasn't my idea. I went along with it, but I never thought it was anything to brag about."

"Why, as I recall, Provincetown folks were proud that one of their own took the prize. You know how people get competitive, especially with those Plymouth Rock folk," Judge Childs added winking at me. "Didn't she get a trophy or something? You never saw it, Melody?" the judge asked me.

"No, sir."

"Maybe she pawned it," Grandma Olivia mumbled just loud enough for us all to hear.

"There wasn't a boy in town who wasn't in love with Haille in those days," the judge continued. Grandma squirmed in her chair. "That's when Kenneth started camping out on your front lawn." He laughed.

"How's he doing these days?" Grandpa Samuel asked. "I can't recall the last time I saw him."

"Same as always," the judge said shaking his head. "If I didn't go to his studio, I wouldn't see him either. He's married to his work, worse than a monk. I hear that those small clay sculptures of the terns are going for ten thousand dollars. Imagine that, Jacob?"

"I can't," Uncle Jacob said. "Just a lot of foolish rich folk, I guess."

"Kenneth's not complaining." The judge gazed long and hard at me again. "What are your interests, Melody?"

"I'm not sure yet," I said. "Maybe teaching," I added, glancing at Cary. He blushed.

"Good idea," the judge said nodding.

"She plays the fiddle," Grandpa Samuel said. "You bring it tonight?"

I looked at Aunt Sara quickly and then back at him.

"No, Grandpa," I said.

"Oh, that's a shame. I was looking forward to a concert."

"I can go back and fetch it for her," Cary volunteered, that impish smile on his face again.

"There's no time for that," Grandma said, rising quickly. "It's time for dinner. Jerome," she called and the butler popped into the doorway as if he had been dangling just above it.

"Madam?"

"Tell the kitchen we are ready to sit at the table," she commanded.

He nodded. "Very well, madam."

278

The judge rose and held out his arm.

"Olivia, allow me to escort you," he offered, while throwing me a coy smile.

Holding her head high and her shoulders back, Grandma took his arm. Grandpa Samuel followed behind them and we walked behind him into the dining room.

The table was as elegant and as rich a table as I had ever seen, even in movies. The dishes were on silver platters and there were crystal goblets for the wine. There were three tall candles in each of two silver candelabra as well. Between candelabra was a spray of white roses. For this dinner the judge sat at Grandma's right side and Uncle Jacob sat on her left. Grandpa sat where he had sat before, as did Aunt Sara, May, Cary, and I.

Uncle Jacob said grace, which seemed to go on twice as long as usual, and the meal finally began. It was orchestrated like a theatrical performance with as many people serving the meal as were eating it, each person seemingly assigned the serving of one course. We began with a caviar appetizer. I was ashamed to say I didn't know what it was, but the judge's eyes twinkled with laughter when Uncle Jacob said, "I always feel guilty eating fish eggs."

"I swear, Olivia," the judge said, "you've raised a saint here."

"Jacob is a good man," she bragged. "We've been blessed."

Uncle Jacob didn't blush at the compliment. He merely looked satisfied. But the judge threw me a smile and a wink. He was the main reason I was feeling relaxed at all.

Jerome poured wine for the adults and the judge offered a toast to everyone's good health and continued happiness. I was impressed with the way he could imbue his voice with senatorial power. There was an immediate sense of authority and strength. He could bring seriousness to a gathering in seconds, I thought.

The appetizer was followed with delicious cream of asparagus soup. While we ate, the judge discussed the local political scene and the fall elections. The adults listened attentively, as if they were party to classified information.

After the soup came a mixed salad of baby field greens and walnuts sprinkled with feta cheese in a raspberry vinaigrette dressing. That started everyone talking about the price of fresh produce, but to me it seemed that money problems were the smallest of worries for this family.

I was surprised when we were served a small ball of orange sorbet. Was the meal over and was this dessert? I wondered. The judge saw the confusion in my face and laughed.

"I don't think your granddaughter is familiar with this culinary custom, Olivia," he said.

"How could she be, growing up in the back hills of West Virginia. The sorbet's meant to cleanse your palette. You know what your palette is?"

"Yes," I said sharply. I glanced at Cary who was scowling at Grandma Olivia. She caught the look on his face and turned back to the judge to talk about the race for governor.

All the kitchen staff and the butler served the entrée, which consisted of roasted quails with wild rice and baby vegetables. There were servants all around us, replacing silverware, fixing napkins, pouring wine and water. One of the servants appeared to be assigned to Grandma Olivia only. The moment she started to reach for something, the maid was there to get it for her. It was truly an overwhelming feast, capped with a dessert that brought an exclamation of delight from the judge.

"Your favorite," Grandma Olivia announced.

It was crème brûlée—something I had never seen nor tasted before. The moment I did, I knew why the judge loved it so.

"Good, isn't it?" he asked me.

"Yes, sir," I said.

"Nothing wrong with enjoying rich things occasionally," he said. "Is there, Jacob?" he asked, enjoying teasing my uncle. I had to admit, I enjoyed seeing him do it.

"As long as you know whom to thank for them," Uncle Jacob said.

"Oh, I do. Thank you, Olivia, Samuel," he said and laughed. My grandpa joined him, but Grandma Olivia shook her head as if he were behaving like a naughty little boy.

"Really, Nelson," she said chidingly.

"I'm just kidding, of course. No one is more thankful than I for my good fortune. I only regret Louise couldn't be with me longer," he added, losing his smile for a moment.

"We all miss her," Grandma Olivia said.

"Thank you, Olivia."

Coffee was served. Cary and I were permitted some. I had never tasted French vanilla coffee, either, but I didn't want to appear as unsophisticated as Grandma Olivia was making me out to be, so I sipped it as if I drank it every day.

When the meal ended, Grandpa suggested brandy and cigars in the parlor.

"This is when we could have heard that fiddle concert," the judge remarked, his eyes glittering at me.

"I could still go fetch it," Cary offered.

"By the time you returned, it would be too late," Grandma said. "Another time."

Cary looked disappointed, but I was relieved. I would have hated to perform before such a critical audience.

"You children amuse yourselves, but do not go out and then track in mud, Cary," she warned.

As the judge passed me, he leaned over to say, "I'll hear that fiddle yet." He winked and followed my grandparents and Uncle Jacob and Aunt Sara out of the dining room. The staff began to clear the table.

"You want to walk on the beach or just sit on the porch in the back?" Cary asked me.

I thought a moment.

"I'd like you to take me downstairs again and show me more of the pictures," I said. He smiled.

"I had a feeling you were going to ask me to do that." He signed to May, who looked excited about the idea. Cary fetched Grandpa Samuel's flashlight. We went out the rear of the house.

We didn't need the flashlight to walk around the outside of the house. The moon was fuller and brighter than ever, turning the ocean into silvery glass and making the sand glimmer like tiny pearls. I could see the horizon clearly delineated against the inky night sky in the distance.

"No wonder ancient people thought they would fall off the earth if they sailed out too far," I said. "It looks so flat." Cary nodded. I took May's hand as he led us around the corner of the house to the basement door.

"Don't let her get her dress dirty," he warned, "or there'll be hell to pay."

I signed the same to May as Cary opened the basement door. He turned on the flashlight, found the light switch for the single dangling bulb, and then beckoned us to follow. Because the shadows were so deep, we still needed the flashlight to find the cartons and sift through them.

"Easy," Cary said when he brought one off the shelf. "The dust is thick. You'll get it all over yourself."

I didn't care about that when I started to dig into the pile of pictures.

"You really do look a lot like your mother did when she was your age, Melody," Cary said. "And you're just as pretty."

I glanced at him and saw how intently he stared at me. May stood by my side as I squatted beside him. We were inches apart and the glow of the flashlight made his eyes glimmer.

282

"No I'm not," I said. "I could never win a beauty contest."

He laughed. "Sure you could, and I'm sure you will."

"You're beginning to sound like Adam Jackson," I said.

His warm smile evaporated. "I didn't mean to," he snapped.

"I just meant that was the kind of thing he was telling me."

Cary nodded and gazed down at the pictures. "Well," he said softly, "the difference is he didn't mean it. I do."

I kept a smile to myself as I sifted through the photographs. Under the ones I had seen before, were earlier pictures of Mommy and Daddy in boats, on the beach, on swings behind the house. Uncle Jacob was in most of the pictures, too, but he always seemed to be off to the side or even a little behind Daddy and Mommy. I found their high-school graduation pictures and could see how Mommy had developed into the beautiful woman she now was.

She was photogenic: the pictures all caught her in funny, happy poses. I imagined it was Daddy who had taken the pictures, but when I turned one of them over, a picture of Mommy in a bikini posing on the beach, I saw the initials K.C. and the date.

"What does this mean?" I asked Cary. He gazed at it a moment and then smiled.

"Oh, I bet that's Kenneth Childs. Here." He pulled another album from the stack and searched through its pages. He pointed to a picture of a good-looking young man, his arms folded across his chest, leaning against an apple tree. His light brown hair fell loosely over his forehead and lay in long strands down the sides and back of his head. He wasn't smiling. He looked serious, almost angry. "That's him. He doesn't look all that different now. He still has long hair, only he keeps it in a ponytail."

"He does?"

"Uh-huh. Sometimes he wears an earring."

"I don't believe it," I said. "Judge Childs's son?"

"Kenneth is an artist," Cary said. "He can do whatever he wants and get away with it."

I nodded, wide eyed. Cary flipped the pages until he found another picture of Kenneth Childs. In this one, he was at least sixteen or seventeen. He was taller, but his face hadn't changed all that much. He still had long hair and I thought I saw an earring in his left earlobe. He was dressed in a pair of jeans and just a vest with no shirt underneath it.

"Any more pictures of him?"

Cary shook his head.

"He was the one who used to take the pictures. My father told Laura and me that once."

I stared at Kenneth's photo a moment longer. Then I gazed at the other pictures in the album. There was a really nice one of my daddy and mommy when they were in high school. They sat on a bench in a gazebo, Daddy's arm around her. She had her knees pulled up, her arms around them, and her head was back against his. There was a rose in her hair. Her face was radiant. Daddy looked as happy as I had ever seen him.

"I like this one," I said.

"Do you?" He gazed at the photograph. "They were good looking. Why don't you just take the picture?" Cary suggested.

"Really?"

"Who's going to know?" He shrugged. I looked at May and then ripped the picture from the page.

We looked for a while longer. There were pictures of relatives I had never heard of. Finally, we came to a set of pictures of a mousy-looking woman who continually looked as if she were going to burst into tears.

"And who's this?" I asked.

"That's Grandma Olivia's younger sister," Cary said.

"Really? I didn't see any pictures of her in the house. Does Grandma Olivia have any brothers?"

"No."

"Where does her sister live?" I asked.

He paused as if to decide whether or not to tell me. "She's in some sort of hospital."

"Hospital?"

"She's not—" He pointed to his temple and shook his head.

"She's in a mental hospital?"

"Yeah, I guess. She had a drinking problem and other problems. We don't talk about her much. Grandma Olivia doesn't even like anyone asking about her."

"How terrible."

"I guess so," Cary said. "She was brought here for a little while years and years ago, but she couldn't handle life on the outside. I really don't know much about her," he added.

"What's her name?" I stared at the small-featured woman holding herself as if she thought she might fall apart.

"Belinda," Cary said.

"What a nice name. What's wrong with her?" I looked closer at the photographs. In one she looked more comfortable, even pretty. "I mean, why did she have a drinking problem and other problems? Did anyone ever mention that?" I asked.

"No, not really. I once heard my father say she laughed after everything she said and looked at every man as if he were her long-awaited prince, no matter how old or what he looked like."

"How sad," I said. I studied her face a moment longer and then turned the pages. I hated having to admit it, even to myself, but Grandma Olivia had been pretty when she was younger. Grandpa Samuel was always a good-looking man. As I perused these family pictures that captured moments like birthdays, parties, afternoon outings on boats and on the beach, I wondered about Mommy's childhood. There must have been happy times living in these rich, comfortable surroundings. How I wished she had told me more about them. How I wished there had been an earlier end to the lies.

May was getting fidgety and Cary was afraid she would get dirty moving around the basement so much, so we put the pictures back. I held on to the photo of Mommy and Daddy and we left the basement. We were surprised to find the butler on the back porch, searching for us.

"Oh, there you are. Good," he cried when he saw us coming. "I was sent to fetch you. It appears Mrs. Logan is somewhat under the weather and your father wants to take you all home."

"Ma's sick?" Cary said. He hurried on ahead of May and me.

Aunt Sara had apparently been struck with an upset stomach, and while we were down in the basement, she had spent most of the time in the bathroom throwing up her rich, delicious supper. Uncle Jacob looked distraught and angry.

"Where have you been?" he snapped. "We're going home. Your mother's got the heaves."

"What happened?"

"I don't know."

A maid helped Aunt Sara from the bathroom.

"I'm sorry," Aunt Sara wailed. "I've ruined everyone's good time. I'm sorry, Olivia," she said from the doorway. Grandma Olivia was sitting on the settee, alone in the sitting room. The judge and Grandpa Samuel had been banished outside to smoke their cigars. Grandma Olivia had accused them and their smoke of turning Aunt Sara's stomach.

"Men and their filthy habits," she remarked. "Get her some fresh air, Jacob."

"Right, Ma. Say good night and thank you," he muttered at us. Cary paused in the doorway first and did so. Then May followed, signed, and smiled. Grandma Olivia closed and opened her eyes as a response. They followed Uncle Jacob and I paused.

286

"What's that in your hand?" she demanded before I could utter a word. Apparently, she had eyes like an eagle.

"An old picture of my mother and father," I replied.

"So Cary's taken you into the basement," she said nodding. I thought she was going to become furious. That, on top of everything else, would turn Uncle Jacob into a volcano. However, Grandma Olivia just sighed deeply and shook her head. "I don't know why, but he and Laura used to love spending the most beautiful afternoons in that hole under the house." She caught herself and grew stiff again. "You better hurry along. Sara needs to go to bed."

"Yes, Grandma." My heart was pounding. Cary, May, and Uncle Jacob were at the door following the maid and Aunt Sara out of the house. "I was wondering," I said quickly, so I could hold on to my courage, "if I could come by to see you by myself."

"See me?" She pulled her head back. "When?"

"As soon as possible. Tomorrow after school?"

She looked amused by the idea and then stiffened her lips. I was sure she was going to brush me off, but she turned toward the wall and said, "I'll be in my garden tomorrow afternoon."

"Thank you, Grandma Olivia," I said. "I'm sorry about Aunt Sara." She turned back to me and I forced a smile and hurried after everyone.

Grandpa Samuel and the judge were standing off to the side watching the maid escort Aunt Sara to the car. The smoke from their cigars spiraled into the night.

"Just give her some bicarbonate, Jacob," Grandpa Samuel said.

"That's what comes of a steady diet of plain and simple food, Jacob. Take your wife out for a restaurant meal once in a while." the judge suggested with a grin.

"Feed her poison so she gets used to it? No thank you," Uncle Jacob said.

The judge roared. He looked at me. "Good night,

Little Haille," he said. "Don't forget to practice that fiddle."

We got into the car. Aunt Sara had her head back. The maid had given her a wet cloth to put over her forehead.

"I'm sorry, Jacob," she said. "It just all started bubbling in my stomach."

"Let's not talk about it, Sara. It will only make it worse." He drove home as quickly as he could.

For the whole ride back, May sat forward holding Aunt Sara's hand and looking concerned. Cary tried signing that she would be all right, but May remained near tears until we got Aunt Sara into the house and into bed.

Finally, my aunt's color returned and she told us she was more comfortable. She kept apologizing to Uncle Jacob, who finally said it was all right. He thought the food was too rich and admitted he had a hard time holding it down himself.

"Get some sleep now," he declared. May kissed her mother good night and we left the bedroom.

"I'm just going to listen to some news on the radio," Uncle Jacob told Cary. "See that your sister gets to bed."

"Aye," Cary said. He turned to me and I helped him get May into her room and calmed enough to go to sleep. Afterward, we paused awkwardly in the hall.

"I wonder what happened to the whale on the beach," I said.

"Let's change and go see," he suggested.

About ten minutes later, both of us were in jeans and sneakers.

"Where are you going?" Uncle Jacob called from the living room.

"To see about that beached whale," Cary said. "Be right back."

"Make sure you are," Uncle Jacob warned.

We hurried out of the house and over the beach. The absence of a crowd of people indicated something had occurred. When we drew nearer, we saw the whale was gone.

288

"Coast guard must have come and dragged her out to sea," Cary said.

"Think it's all right?" I gazed over the dark water.

"Either she swam off or sank where they unhitched her," he commented with characteristic Cape Cod bluntness.

"At least she won't be victimized by cruel people."

"Yeah," he said. Even in the darkness, I could feel his eyes on me. "You sure look a lot like your mother in those pictures."

"Thank you," I muttered, looking down at the sand. Then I took a deep breath of the fresh salt air. "I guess I'll catch up on my reading for social studies," I said.

"Catch up? I bet you mean go ahead."

"Something like that," I confessed, and he laughed. "I'll try to see all your teachers and get them to give me your work so you don't fall behind."

"Whatever," he said.

We started back to the house. I walked with my arms folded over my breasts, my head down. Above us, the night sky burst with stars, but I felt afraid to look up, afraid I would be hypnotized and spend all night standing on the beach.

"Say," Cary said, "would you . . . would you like to see my model ships?"

"Up in the attic?"

He nodded.

"Sure."

When we entered the house, we heard a voice on the radio droning about sin and damnation. Both of us peeked into the living room and saw Uncle Jacob slouched down in his chair, asleep, and snoring almost as loudly as the radio. Cary put his finger on his lips and smiled. We walked up the stairway quietly and he pulled down the ladder to the attic.

"Careful," he said as I started up after him. He reached down to help me make the last few steps.

It was smaller than I had thought. On my earlier quick

289

look, I hadn't seen how the roof slanted on both sides of the room. He had a table on which he worked on his model ships. The completed ships were lined up on a half dozen shelves. It looked as if he had done a hundred or so different models. To the right was a cot and on the left were boxes and sea chests.

"Careful," he said when I stood up, "Watch your head." The roof slanted sharply, so I had to move forward to stand up straight. "This," he said, going to the shelves, "is my historical section. They go left to right chronologically. This is an Egyptian ship." He lifted it gingerly and held it in front of me. "About three thousand B.C. It has a double mast, joined at the top, from which the sails are hung."

He put it back and lifted another.

"This is Phoenician. They were better shipbuilders. It's called the round boat, one of the first to depend mostly on sails rather than oars, and as you can see, it has a larger cargo space."

I saw how serious he was when he talked about his ships. His face filled with enthusiasm and brightened. His voice was full of energy and he talked so fast and so much, I was overwhelmed, but I tried to keep up.

He went through the Greek and Roman models, showed me a Norse vessel that he said was used to invade England. He had even constructed a Chinese junk. He said that although it was still used, it lacked three components regarded as fundamental to ships: a keel and stem and stern posts. He lectured and illustrated everything on his models, but I saw that he was most proud of his sailing ships.

"This," he said in a low, breathy voice, "is a replica of the H.M.S. *Victory,* the flagship of the British admiral Horatio Nelson."

"It's beautiful, Cary."

"Isn't it?" He beamed. He put it back carefully and lifted another. "This was Laura's favorite," he said, "the American clipper. This is a replica of the *Great Republic,* built in 1853. These ships set records for transatlantic crossings."

"The parts are so tiny. How do you do it?"

"With great patience," he said laughing. "I renamed this *Laura,"* he said and showed me where he had carefully engraved her name on the side. He held it a moment longer and then put it back lovingly on the shelf.

"I've got a lot more here: steamships, container ships, tankers, and of course, luxury liners. Know what this one is?" he asked, holding it up.

"I'm not sure," I said.

"It's the *Titanic."*

I shook my head in amazement.

"You know so much about ships, Cary. You should do better in history."

He grimaced. "One thing has nothing to do with another."

"Did you ever make a report on ships?"

"Yes," he said. "I got an A but I had so many spelling and writing errors, the teacher reduced it to a C."

He put the model back and went to the small window where he had a pair of binoculars.

"Laura and I used to spend a lot of time right here gazing out at the ocean," he said. He handed the binoculars to me when I stepped up behind him and I looked out at the ocean. Way in the distance, I saw a small light.

"What is that?"

"A tanker, maybe heading for England or Ireland. We used to love to imagine where they were going or imagine ourselves on them." He smiled to himself. Then he sat on the cot. "Laura and I spent a lot of time up here. She would lie on this cot and read or study while I worked on my models." He grimaced. "Then she stopped spending time up here after she started going with Robert Royce." His face grew angry.

"She just got interested in boys, Cary. It wasn't weird for that to happen," I said softly.

"Yeah, well, he wasn't the right one."

"How can you be certain?"

"I just am," he said. He had his eyes squinted shut as if trying to drive out some scene scorched on his brain.

I turned to look out the window again. "Then why did you let them use your boat?" I asked with my back to him.

"Laura was a good sailor, almost as good as I am," he said. "She wanted it."

I turned around and looked at him.

"I never said no to Laura," Cary said sadly. "If only I had . . . just that once." He looked at the floor so I wouldn't see the tear escape from his eye.

"I'm sorry." I was close to tears myself. I gazed at the ocean again. It could be beautiful and so deadly. "To lose her like that. It's as if she just disappeared."

"No," he said, so softly at first I thought I imagined it. But when I turned back, he repeated it. "No. It wasn't really that way."

"What do you mean, Cary?"

He stared at me a moment. "I've shared this with no one, not even my parents."

I held my breath.

"After Laura and Robert failed to return, I borrowed a friend's boat and went looking for them. I looked every day for nearly a week, combing the beach, getting so close to the rocks at times, I nearly crashed into them myself. Then one day something caught my eye."

"What?" I asked, my heart pounding.

He rose and went to one of the chests. He opened it, dipped his hand into it, and came up with a pink silk scarf. "She liked wearing this around her neck when she sailed. I found it floating in the water."

"Why didn't you show your mother?"

"I wanted to keep the hope alive, and then I felt so guilty about not showing it, I never told. It doesn't matter any more. She's accepted the grave. Laura's gone."

I felt the hot tears streaming down my cheeks.

"You're the first person who I thought would understand," he said. He gazed at the scarf and then brought it to me. "I want you to have this."

"Oh no, I couldn't."

"Please, take it and wear it," he said. He pushed it into my hands.

"Thank you," I said softly. "I'll take good care of it."

"I know." He raised his head and our eyes locked. The depths of his pain made me forget my own.

We heard Uncle Jacob coming up the stairs below. He paused at the attic stairway and then he plodded on to his bedroom and closed the door.

"I'd better go down," I said.

He nodded.

"I'm going to see Grandma tomorrow," I told him. If he could trust me with his deepest secrets, I could trust him, I thought.

"Why?"

"To get her to tell me everything. I'm going after school."

"Do you want me to be there too?"

"No. I've got to speak to her myself. But thanks."

"Remember, her bark's worse than her bite."

"Good night, Cary. Thanks for showing me your models."

He smiled and then abruptly, awkwardly, he planted a kiss on my cheek.

"Careful going down," he said as I lowered myself on the ladder. After I reached the bottom, I looked up at him.

"Good night," I said.

"Good night."

He lifted the ladder as if he wanted to lose all contact with the world below and then he closed his attic door and shut himself up with his memories and his own voices.

Clutching Laura's silk scarf in my hand, I went into her room and prepared for my own dreams, filled with my own memories and voices.

We were alike, Cary and I, haunted by lies and sadness, two sailboats drifting, looking for a friendly wind.

16

Daddy Who?

Although Cary had been suspended from school, he was up and ready to escort May and me the next morning. He carried my books since he didn't have to carry any of his own. It was gray and overcast when we started out. The mist was so thick, we couldn't see very far ahead of us. It was like walking through clouds.

"It will burn off by early afternoon," Cary promised. Despite his being punished for attacking Adam Jackson in the cafeteria and Uncle Jacob and Aunt Sara's disappointment with him, Cary was uncharacteristically animated. He talked continuously, permitting only a few seconds of silence to linger between us. It was as if he thought that silence would make us think and thought would make us sad.

He was especially excited about his plans to build his own sailboat this summer. For now he had to use his father's.

"I've had enough practice building the models, eh?" he said. He was thinking he might even get into the leisure boat–building business someday.

"I can't depend on the lobster and fishing industry,"

he explained. "Someday I'm going to be responsible for more than just myself," he added.

I held May's hand and listened, a small smile on my face, as I looked down and walked. Cary continued to voice his plans. He wanted a home just outside the village and he wanted a garden and, of course, his own dock. He would raise a family with at least four or five children and he would take trips to Boston and maybe even New York.

"Provincetown is a good place to raise a family," he assured me. "It really is. I mean, it takes a lot longer for the bad stuff to get up here, and when it does, it can't hide as well as it can other places. Know what I mean?"

I nodded, but before I could speak, he added, "I knew you would. You're so much smarter than the girls around here, and I don't mean just book smart. You have common sense."

"Thank you," I said.

He smiled, sucked in his breath, and looked at the fog.

"It will clear but rain's coming later tonight. I can smell it."

After we brought May to her school, he insisted on continuing on with me.

"Just to be sure you're okay," he explained.

When we arrived at school, he glared back furiously at any of the students who gazed at us with gleeful smiles on their faces. They turned away immediately and hurried into the building as if to escape freezing cold temperatures.

"You just tell me if anyone bothers you, Melody. Don't let them torment you in any way, hear?"

"I won't."

"I'll be here after school to check on you."

"But I told you I was going to see Grandma Olivia," I reminded him. His eyes grew small with worry and disappointment.

"I know, but I'll just check anyway before you go," he insisted. He gave me my books.

296

"What are you going to do?"

"I'll work on the plans for my boat," he said. "My father won't let me help him with anything when I'm in trouble, as if I might contaminate him." He sounded critical of his father for the first time. "People who've done wrong bring bad luck. Well . . ." He hesitated, looking at the front entrance to the school.

"I'll be fine, Cary. Stop your worrying." I squeezed his hand and rushed into the building. When I turned at the door, he was still standing there, looking after me.

Most of the students kept their distance in the hallway, all gazing at me with some interest. Theresa met me at my locker.

"How did it go for Cary at home?" she asked.

"Not well. My uncle Jacob was very angry. Actually, he's just as angry at me."

"It wasn't his fault or yours. You tell them that?"

"Yes."

"I like Cary," she said. "At least he doesn't put on a phony face," she added, loud enough for some of the girls to hear. Janet, Lorraine, and Betty walked by quickly, just giving me a passing glance.

This day I concentrated only on schoolwork, even though I sensed there was a good deal of whispering and note passing going on behind me. There was just one critical moment in the cafeteria after I entered. The jabber lowered and all eyes were on me for a few seconds. Theresa came up and began talking to me. Then the din in the cafeteria rose again and everyone appeared to go back to his or her business. It left me feeling I had swallowed a spoonful of nails.

Theresa told me that Adam Jackson had tried to recoup his reputation by telling everyone Cary's actions just proved him right. But he stayed away from me, not even glancing in my direction. Toward the end of the school day, I had the distinct sense that everyone had grown tired and bored with this scandal. Some of the students in my classes who had often talked to me about

297

the work did so again. I felt more relaxed and at ease moving through the corridors.

All of Cary's teachers were glad to give me assignments for him, and every one of them said he or she felt Cary could do better if he only tried or cared. Mr. Madeo winked at me and said he was sure Cary would pass his English final if his tutor would stand by him.

"I'll see to it she does," I told him.

True to his word, Cary was waiting after school, his hands in his pockets, his hair over his forehead, his face drawn in a scowl, right at the entrance to the school when the bell rang ending the day.

"Everything's fine," I told him immediately. "It's over, forgotten."

"Sure."

"It is. Here." I thrust the pages of assignments in his hands. "This is your schoolwork, Cary Logan, and I expect you will do it even though you're not attending classes."

He gazed at the papers and then looked up at me and smiled. "You'll make me an A student yet, eh?"

"You'll do it yourself."

We started away and at the end of the street, we paused because I was going to walk to Grandma Olivia's.

"It's not a short walk," he warned. "If I hadn't gotten suspended, my father would have let me use the pickup and I could have taken you, but—"

"I know how far it is. I'll be all right. I want to do it. I have to do it," I said. He nodded and kicked a stone across the macadam.

"You sure you don't want me along?"

"Cary, you have to see to May," I told him.

"She can make her way home alone if she must."

"I once said that and you nearly bit my head off."

He smiled. "I did. I remember. All right, go on, but don't get upset and—"

"Mr. Worry Wart, stop it!" I ordered.

"All right."

I started away.

"Her bark's worse than her bite!" he shouted after me.

"So's mine," I shouted back. He watched me walk off for a while and then he went to fetch May.

It was a long walk, and when I broke out to the main highway, it was harder, because the cars were whizzing by, some so close I felt the breeze in their wake lift my hair. Suddenly, an elderly man driving a rather beaten up light orange pickup truck stopped.

"You shouldn't be walking on this highway," he chastised.

"I have no other way to go," I said.

"Well, get in and I'll drop you off. Come on. My wife would give me hell if she heard I let a young girl walk along here."

I smiled and got into the truck. The seat was torn and there was a basket of what looked like seashells on the floor of the cab, along with all sorts of tools.

"Don't worry about any of that stuff. My granddaughter likes to make things with seashells," he explained.

He had gray stubble over his chin and the sides of his jaw, and his thin gray hair ran untrimmed down the sides of his temples and the back of his head, but he had kind blue eyes and a gentle smile. He reminded me of Papa George. Papa George, I thought, how I missed him.

"So where are you heading with your sails up like that?" he asked.

"My grandparents' house, the Logans," I told him, and his eyes widened.

"Olivia and Samuel Logan?"

"Yes," I said.

"I heard their granddaughter was deaf."

"I'm a different granddaughter."

"Oh. Didn't know. Course, I don't keep company with your folks. I worked for your grandfather once a long time ago. Built a tool shed for him. Paid me on time, too," he added. His truck rumbled along about half the speed of the cars that flew by us, but he didn't care.

"Everyone's in a mad rush," he muttered. "Chasing the almighty dollar, but they miss the good stuff along the way."

He smiled at me and then he grew serious as though the thought just crossed his mind.

"You're Chester's little girl?"

"Yes, sir."

"What ever happened to him? No one seemed to know much about him after he left here with your mother."

"He was killed in a coal mine accident," I said, my throat choking up immediately.

"Coal mine? Is that what he left here to do? I never could understand . . ." He gazed at me a moment and saw the sad look on my face. "Sorry to bring it up. Didn't know," he muttered awkwardly. Then he turned into a concerned grandparent again. "I'm surprised to see Samuel Logan lets his granddaughter walk along this crazy highway."

"I just decided to do it on my own," I said quickly.

He nodded, but his eyes remained suspicious. "That's it ahead," he said.

"I know. Thank you."

He stopped and I got out and thanked him again.

"Now you don't walk that highway no more, hear?"

"Yes sir," I said.

"I'm sorry about your father. I just knew him when he was younger, but he seemed to be a fine young man."

"Thank you."

"Bye," he said, and drove off.

I sucked in my breath, straightened my shoulders, reaffirmed my determination, and walked up the driveway to my grandmother's home. Before I reached the front door, a dark-skinned man of about fifty or so came around the corner of the house, pushing a wheelbarrow.

"You looking for Mrs. Logan?" he asked.

"Yes."

"She's around back in the vegetable garden," he said.

I thanked him and went to the rear of the house, where Grandma Olivia was on her knees in her fenced-in

300

garden. She was dressed in a pair of old jeans and she wore a flannel shirt and work gloves. She had a wide-brimmed hat with a few fake carnations sticking up in the rear of it. I was so shocked to see her looking so casual, I paused to watch her dig out weeds. The contrast between the woman who reigned like a queen in the elegant house and this woman with her hands in dirt, wearing old and tattered clothing, was so great, I thought I was looking at a stranger.

She sensed me behind her and turned. "Hand me that iron claw there," she ordered, pointing to a pile of tools nearby. I hurried to do so. "Careful where you step," she said. "I don't want to lose any of those carrots." She took the tool from me and scratched the earth around a tomato plant. "You walk all the way?" she asked as she worked.

"No, Grandma. Some kind old man in a pickup truck stopped to give me a lift."

"You were hitchhiking?"

"Not exactly."

"You always get into trucks with strangers?"

"No."

She paused and wiped her forehead.

"It's going to rain tonight," she said with the same tone of voice Cary had used when he made his weather prediction. "We need it. I had a better garden last year."

"It looks nice."

She shook her head and stood up. Then she pointed to a small table. There were a mauve ceramic pitcher and some glasses on it.

"You want some lemonade?" she asked.

"Yes, thank you."

She poured me a glass and a glass for herself. Then she sat and looked up at me as I drank.

"All right, you've come to see me. Why?" she demanded.

My lemonade caught in my throat for a moment. I took a deep breath and sat across from her.

"I want to know the truth about my parents," I said.

"I'm tired of not knowing the truth and knowing only lies."

"That's good. I can't countenance a liar, and goodness knows, this family's had more than its share of them. All right," she said sitting back. "What is it you want to know?"

"Why do you hate my father so? He was your son."

"He was my son until she stole him from me," Grandma Olivia said.

"But I don't understand that. You adopted my mother, right? You wanted her in your home."

She looked away for a moment.

"That was something I couldn't help. I never wanted her in my home, but I had to have her."

"Why?" I pursued.

She turned back to me.

"Haille was my sister's illegitimate daughter," she said. "My sister was a spoiled, silly girl from the start. My father spoiled her and she grew up thinking anything she wanted, she could have. She couldn't tolerate waiting or disappointment. Her solution was to turn to alcohol and drugs. I always did my best to protect and shelter her from herself, and maybe I'm to blame as much as my father, but I made him a foolish promise on his deathbed: I promised to look after Belinda and see to her happiness."

Her sister was my grandmother? My mind spun. I tried not to look overwhelmed for fear she would stop talking.

"What happened to your mother?" I asked.

"My mother was a weak woman herself. She couldn't face unpleasantness and always pretended it wasn't there. The truth was my father had three daughters, not two. My mother died of breast cancer. She ignored the diagnosis, just as she had ignored all bad news.

"Anyway, my sister became pregnant with your mother and I made the stupid mistake of having her here during the birth. I made the second mistake of not giving

302

the baby away. My husband," she said bitterly, "thought that would be a horrible thing to do, and he reminded me of my oath to my father on his deathbed. So," she said with a deep sigh, "I took Haille into my home and raised her with my sons, something I'll regret until my dying day."

"Then Belinda is my grandmother?"

"Yes," she said with a nod and a twisted smile. "That wretch living in a home is your grandmother. Go claim her," she said. She looked as if she were going to end our conversation, so I repeated my original question.

"But why do you hate your own son, my father? Because he married his cousin and had me?" I ventured.

She regarded me with a cold, hard stare. "You think you're old enough for the truth?" she challenged.

"Yes," I said, my heart pounding, my breath so thin I could barely utter the word.

"Your mother grew up here, had the best of everything. My husband spoiled her just the way my father had spoiled my sister. All Haille had to do was bat her eyelashes at Samuel and he'd do her bidding: buy her the dress and jewelry, permit her to go out when I had already said no and on and on. I warned him about her, but he wouldn't listen. She was the little girl I had never given him. Just like all men, he thought he was supposed to spoil his little girl. They confuse flooding them with gifts and their kisses of thanks and hugs as love.

"She had boyfriends. Dozens of boys marched through this house, followed her everywhere, came at her beck and call, groveled for her kisses. Every time I forbade something or punished her for something, Samuel overruled me, and what was the final result? The hand that fed her was bitten."

She paused. The telling of the story was exhausting her emotionally and physically. She sipped some lemonade and shook her head.

"What do you mean, the hand that fed her was bitten?" I asked after she had rested.

303

"Just like her mother before her, she slept around, and what do you think? She got pregnant, too. With you! Then she did the unforgivable thing." Grandma paused as if to get up enough breath and strength. "She blamed Samuel. She stood before me in this very house and claimed my husband, her stepfather, had slept with her and made her pregnant. Samuel was devastated, but I told him he deserved it for what he had done all those years."

I shook my head.

"I don't understand," I said, the tears filling my eyelids.

She laughed a wicked, short laugh.

"What's there to understand? She thought if she blamed Samuel, she could escape blame herself."

"But my daddy—"

"Your father, my son, turned on his own father. Chester turned on me," she said. "He took her side, believed her, actually believed his own father could have done such a thing. Can you imagine the heartbreak I endured, sitting there in that house and hearing my son tell me he believed that—that whore and not his own father? Can you? I told them both to get out, and as long as he took her side, to stay away. I told him I would have nothing more to do with a son who turned on his own parents that way. He knew Haille's background, but he . . . She beguiled him, too, just as she beguiles everyone she touches.

"Jacob was heartbroken as well. He couldn't believe his brother would do such a thing. They had a terrible fistfight on the beach behind this house and never spoke again."

I shook my head.

"None of this can be true. Why did my mother bring me back here?" I cried through my tears. Grandma smiled and nodded.

"Why? She wanted to get rid of you, dear, and she knew about Sara's loss. Sara's always been a kind person.

304

She was willing to take you in, and Jacob, God bless him for his kindness, too, wants to do nothing but what will make Sara happy again. Haille took advantage of someone in this family once more. It's that simple.

"I kept quiet about it," she continued. "After all, you are my sister's granddaughter, and, remembering the promise I made to my father on his deathbed, I didn't oppose it as long as I didn't have to set eyes on your mother."

I sat there, shaking my head. It had to be more lies, lies built on lies.

"My daddy never treated me as anything but his own daughter," I said. "He loved me."

"I'm sure he did. If he only had remembered his love for his mother and father as well," she said.

I stared at her, trying to make sense of it, slowly realizing what it meant if what she was saying was true.

"If my daddy thought that Grandpa Samuel was my father then . . . he knew he wasn't my daddy," I concluded.

"Precisely," Grandma Olivia said with some renewed energy. "And yet he still ran off with her, he still took her side and turned his back on his own mother and father."

"But . . . who is my father?"

"Take your pick. It could be anyone," she said dryly. "Maybe someday your mother will tell you, only the truth leaves a bitter taste in her mouth. She can't stomach it."

I continued to shake my head.

"I don't believe my daddy wasn't my daddy," I insisted.

"Suit yourself." Grandma Olivia sipped the rest of the lemonade in her glass. "You demanded I tell you the truth and I have. You said you were old enough and I believed you. If you want to continue living in a world of illusions and lies along with your mother, be my guest, only don't come around here accusing anyone of anything.

305

"What you should do," she said, standing, "is get your mother to come back for you and bear up to her own responsibilities. But I wouldn't get my hopes up." She gazed down at me. "As long as you behave, do as your told, pull your share, Jacob won't throw you out of his house. They tell me you really are a good student, so if you deserve it, I'll see that you get an education. I'll do it for my father, because of the promises I made."

"I don't want anything from you," I said bitterly.

She laughed a laugh that reminded me of glass shattering.

"In time, I'm sure you'll change your mind about that. Just make sure you don't do anything to change my mind about being generous," she warned, pointing her small, crooked little forefinger at me. "That includes making my son and his family unhappy. I'm going in now to wash up. If you want, I'll have Ralph, my handyman, take you home."

I sat there, my shoulders shaking, the sobs rattling my rib cage and throwing a terrific chill over me. I embraced myself.

"I don't have the time to stand here and watch you become hysterical," she said. "When you're finished, come into the house and I'll see to it you're taken home."

She started away. I looked out at the ocean. The heavier cloud cover was making its way toward shore and the wind had grown in intensity, lifting the white-caps. For a few moments the monotonous way in which the ocean waves slapped the rocks hypnotized me. Terns screamed. I tried to shrink into that small hiding place in my brain where I could feel safe and unafraid, but that place felt like a cage.

I hate Cape Cod, I thought. I hate being here another moment. I rose quickly, but I walked slowly, pensively toward the front of the house. When I looked back, I thought I saw a curtain part and Grandma Olivia gaze out, but the sun dipped behind one of those heavy oncoming clouds, and the shadows that fell over the house darkened the window and, like black magic, changed it into a mirror.

When I reached the highway, I didn't turn toward town. For a long time, I just walked, feeling mesmerized. Cars and trucks whizzed by, but this time their closeness, the breeze in their wake, the loud horns that blared—none of them bothered me.

My daddy wasn't really my daddy. He could be anyone. Is that what Grandma Olivia had said, with spite? How could Mommy have left me drifting in such a hellish place? She really was selfish. I didn't want to believe the terrible things Grandma Olivia had said about her, but in my deepest soul I knew it all made sense. If I honestly faced up to what and who Mommy was now, I would have no trouble believing who and what she was back then. But to make such a disgusting claim, to blame my grandfather for my existence . . . I almost sided with Grandma Olivia and Uncle Jacob.

I don't know how long I walked or how far I actually had gone before I heard a continuous horn blaring and turned to see Cary in his father's pickup. He pulled to the side of the road behind me and hopped out.

"Where are you going? I've been crazy with worry. Everyone has, even Grandma Olivia."

"She told me the truth, Cary," I said.

The sky had become almost completely overcast. The wind was even stronger and the temperature felt as if it had dropped a dozen degrees. I had been shivering without even realizing it. Cary quickly peeled off his jacket and put it around my shoulders.

"Come home," he said.

I shook my head and backed away from him.

"That's not my home, Cary. Your father is not my uncle and your mother is not my aunt."

"What are you saying?" he asked, a confused, half-silly grin on his face.

"Just that. My daddy was . . . my daddy—"

"What?"

307

"He wasn't my daddy. Mommy was pregnant with me by someone else and she accused—" I had to swallow first before I could continue. "She accused Grandpa Samuel. Daddy believed her and that's why they stopped talking to him. Your father and—my—" It suddenly occurred to me who he was. "My stepfather had a fistfight on the beach and never spoke to each other again. You didn't know that?"

I saw from the expression on his face that he knew something.

"I knew that they'd had a fight, but I never knew why," he admitted.

"Why didn't you tell me that?"

"I didn't want you to hate us and leave," he confessed.

"Well, that's what I'm doing. I'm leaving this place." I turned and started away. He caught up and took me by the elbow.

"Stop. You can't just walk down this highway."

"And why not? I've got to go home," I said. "I've got to see Mama Arlene and Papa George."

"You're going to walk back to West Virginia?"

"I'll hitchhike," I said. "I'll beg rides. I'll do chores to get people to give me lifts or money for bus tickets. But I'll get home. Somehow, I'll get there," I said, my eyes seeing him, but looking beyond and seeing the old trailer house, Mama Arlene waving goodbye, Papa George smiling at me from his bed, and Daddy's grave, the tombstone I had hugged with all my heart before I was forced to leave. "Somehow," I muttered.

"Won't you come home and get your things first? Have a good meal?"

"I don't want to eat and I don't care about those things," I said. "Tell Aunt Sara I'll send this dress back first chance I get," I added and started walking again.

"Wait a minute, Melody. You can't do this."

I kept walking.

"Melody!"

"I'm going, Cary. Not you, not anyone can stop me," I

said, full of defiance and anger. I walked and he was silent for a few moments. Then he caught up and walked alongside me. "Why are you doing this, Cary? You can't stop me."

"I know. I'm just thinking about it."

I stopped and turned to him.

"What do you mean?"

He thought and then nodded his head. "All right." He dug into his pocket and came up with a money clip stuffed with bills. "I'll drive you to Boston and give you the money you need for your bus ticket."

"You will?"

"Of course, I will. I'm not going to let you walk down Route Six and hitchhike, and I can see you are determined. Wait here. I'll go back and get the truck."

"But your father will be furious, Cary."

"It won't be the first time or the last, I imagine. He's already going to be mad about my taking the truck," he added and shrugged. "Don't worry about me."

He ran back to the truck and drove up to me. I got in and we started down the highway.

"It's a long trip back to Sewell, West Virginia, Melody."

"I know, but it's the only real home I've ever known where there are people who love me."

"There are people who love you here," he said. He turned and smiled. "May and me for starters."

"I know. I'm sorry about May. You'll explain it to her. Please."

"Sure. But who will explain it to me?"

"Cary, it was horrible, sitting there and hearing the story and seeing Grandma Olivia's anger. I never felt more like an unwanted orphan," I explained.

He accelerated.

"She shouldn't have done that. She should have made something up, something more sensible, something that wouldn't have upset you this way."

"More lies? No thank you. I've been brought up with

309

lies. I've eaten them for breakfast, lunch, and dinner. It's time for the truth. It's time to get back with people who don't know what lying is."

"Everyone lies, Melody, to someone else or to himself," Cary said.

Raindrops splattered on the windshield. I thought about him having to drive back alone.

"I feel terrible about you doing this, Cary."

"Don't. I would feel terrible not doing it," he said. "Tell me more about what Grandma Olivia said."

I recounted our conversation and he listened attentively, his green eyes growing darker and smaller.

"It makes some sense now, the whispers, the words I picked up here and there."

"It's terrible. I feel as if my insides will be tied into knots forever. I feel betrayed, fooled, Cary. The man who loved me and called me his princess wasn't really my daddy."

"Well, being a father doesn't have to be dependent on blood, does it? He was good to you, wasn't he? You never doubted he loved you. You told me."

I nodded, swallowing back my tears. "Still," I said softly, "it leaves me feeling . . . incomplete. You've got your family name, your heritage. It's so important to you and your family. I see that, even more than I saw it in West Virginia. I'm nobody. I'm Melody Nobody," I said laughing. He looked at me. I laughed harder. "Meet Melody Nobody." My laughter started to hurt and soon turned into tears, sobs that shook my shoulders so hard I thought I would come apart.

He pulled the truck to the side and stopped. Then he slid over and embraced me, kissing the tears off my cheeks and holding me tightly.

"Don't do this to yourself," he said.

I caught my breath and sucked in some air with deep gasps. Then I nodded.

"I'm all right. It's okay. I won't do that again. I promise."

"It's okay to do it as long as I can be next to you," he

310

said, "but I hate to think of you alone out there, crying your eyes out with no one to comfort you, Melody."

"There'll be Mama Arlene," I said.

He stared at me a moment and then slid behind the wheel again. We drove on. Car headlights blinded us in the rain, but he drove relentlessly, firmly.

Cary talked me into stopping for something to eat. I did it for his sake more than my own, although the hot coffee helped and something warm in my stomach gave me needed energy. I lost track of time afterward and fell asleep with my head on his shoulder. When I opened my eyes again, he told me we were pulling into Boston and heading for the bus depot. I sat up and scrubbed the sleep from my cheeks with my dry palms.

Cary went into the bus station with me. We spoke with the ticket seller who, after we explained where I wanted to go, said the best ticket was one to Richmond. There was a shuttle service to Sewell, but he couldn't guarantee the schedule after I had arrived in Richmond.

"Once I get to Richmond, I'll be fine," I said. Cary paid for the ticket and then insisted I take another fifty dollars.

"Somehow, I'll pay you back," I promised.

"You don't have to as long as you promise to call me from Sewell and then write letters."

"I'll promise you that if you promise me you'll pass all your tests and graduate."

"Big promise, but okay," he said. "You've convinced me to work harder." He smiled.

"That's the bus to Richmond now," the ticket seller announced.

Cary gazed into my eyes, his eyes full of sadness and fear for me.

"I'll be all right once I get home," I said. "Don't worry." He nodded.

"I wish that somehow you had come to think of Provincetown as your home."

"When you have no real family, home has to be where you find love," I said.

311

"You found it in Provincetown," he said indicating himself.

"I know," I whispered. I leaned toward him and kissed him softly on the cheek. "Oh," I said. "Your jacket." I started to take it off.

"No, please keep it."

"Thanks," I said.

He followed me out to the bus and watched me get on. After I sat at the window, he held up his hand.

"Good-bye," I mouthed through the glass. The bus driver started the engine. Cary's face seemed to crumple, his lips trembling. There were tears on his cheeks, and his tears put tears in my heart. I put my hand against the glass as if I could stop his crying by doing so. He raised his hand. The bus started away. He walked alongside it for a few feet and then the bus turned. He was gone.

I knew where he would go when he got home. He would go to his attic and he would curl up on his cot and he would think of Laura and me and wonder why all that was good and soft in his world seemed to slip through his fingers.

I closed my eyes and thought about Mama Arlene's smile and Papa George and Alice and the warm living room in my old trailer home.

Like a beacon in a storm, the light from those memories held out a tiny spark of hope.

17
∞

There's No Place Like Home

I rode the bus all night. People got on and off at various stops, but I didn't take notice. I was vaguely aware that someone sat down next to me after one stop, but I curled up and fell back asleep. When I opened my eyes again, whoever it had been was gone. It wasn't until an hour or so later, when I was fully awake and moving around in my seat that I realized so was my purse. The shock of it put electric sparks in the air. I screamed so loud, the bus driver hit the brakes and pulled off for a moment.

"What is it? What's wrong back there?" he called. Everyone on the bus was looking my way.

"I can't find my purse with all my money in it," I wailed. It had been right at my feet and I had Cary's fifty dollars in it, the money that was supposed to get me home.

Someone laughed. Most people shook their heads. The bus driver snorted as if to say, "Is that all?" and started away. A small black woman with kind eyes sitting two rows down smiled at me. "You ain't much of a traveler, are you, honey?"

"No ma'am."

"You can't take your eyes off valuable things when you travel, honey. I wear my purse under my dress," she said. She shook her head in pity and turned away.

I sat there stunned and angry. How could someone be so cruel? Another voice inside me asked, "How could you be so stupid?" By now I should have known to trust no one, to depend on no one, to believe in no one. "Expect nothing and you'll never be disappointed," the little voice continued.

It was morning when we reached Richmond. I stepped off the bus, still dazed from the trip and from being robbed. I found my way through the depot and could only look longingly back at the ticket counter where I might have been able to purchase a ticket to Sewell. Now, I had to find my way to the right highway and hitchhike.

I was hungry, and even more so when I passed counters where people sat enjoying their breakfast. My stomach churned as the aromas of fresh rolls, bacon and eggs, coffee, and Danish pastries visited my nostrils. I was tempted to finish a chunk of discarded white bread I spotted on a bus depot bench, but the birds got there before me.

I hurried on, getting directions from a gentleman in a gray suit who looked as if he were on the way to work. He was in such a rush he continued to walk as he shouted back the route I should take. I followed him like a fish on a hook. I listened to his directions and then shouted my thanks.

I walked along the street, my head down, my limbs still aching from the cramped position I had been in most of the night. At least it wasn't raining. In fact it looked as if it was going to be a nice day. Some time later I reached a turn in the road and a sign indicating the direction to Sewell. Cars flew by with the drivers glancing at me and my stuck-out thumb, but none so much as slowed down. Discouraged, I walked rather than just stand there and wait for another vehicle. Standing and

314

waiting only reminded me how hungry and tired I was. Every time I heard a car, I spun around and jerked my thumb in the air, again with no success. One woman driving by glared at me with such disapproval I thought she might stop her car and get out and lecture me.

There was a lull, then another stream of vehicles. This time a light brown van with dents all over it slowed and pulled up just a few feet ahead of me. I hurried to catch up. When I looked into the van, I saw a man with a rainbow-colored headband. He had a straggly brown beard and wore dark sunglasses. An earring dangled from his right ear and he had a necklace made of what looked like bullet shells. His hair was dirty brown and long, but it looked as if he had either chopped it away from his ears himself or had an amateur do it. He wore a faded gray sweat suit.

"Where you headed?" he asked.

"Sewell."

"I'm not going there, but I'm going nearby," he said.

I thought for a second. The closer I got, the better it would be, I concluded.

"Thank you," I said and opened the door, but to my chagrin, there was no passenger seat.

"You'll have to crawl in back. Someone stole the seat last night," he explained.

"Stole your seat?"

"These seats are in demand and they're expensive. They sell them to chop shops," he said. "If you're coming along, get in. I got to make Jacksonville before nightfall."

I hesitated. No one else had stopped for me and I was tired. I decided to go so I stepped into the van and then crouched to go into the rear. There was a mattress with a ragged sheet placed sloppily over it, a pillow with no pillow case, and a thin, tattered wool blanket. Beside that was a small Sterno stove, some cans of food, packages of bread, cookies, jars of peanut butter, jelly, and jam. There was a pile of clothes to the right and two cartons filled with magazines.

He leaned over to close the door of the van.

"Just find a spot," he said. "You can sit on the bed."

He pulled away quickly and I nearly fell. I lowered myself gently to the mattress. There was the odor of stale food and general mustiness that came from someone living and sleeping in here for some time.

"What's your name?" he called back.

"Melody."

"Great name. You sing?"

"No."

"How come you're hitchhiking?"

"I had my purse stolen while I was on a bus."

"Boy, if I have heard that story once, I've heard it five hundred times. If you're hungry, nibble on anything you want," he said.

I gazed at the food, trying to decide what, if anything, looked clean enough to eat. I thought maybe a piece of bread and a little peanut butter might be all right.

"Thank you."

I dug deep into the package and came up with a slice of bread. It felt a few days old, but wasn't moldy. I wiped off a butter knife and dug out some peanut butter.

"How far you come?" he asked.

"I rode the bus from Boston, but I started out on Cape Cod."

"No kidding." He turned to look at me. "How old are you?"

"Almost seventeen," I said.

"What are you, a runaway?"

"No." I chewed and swallowed. "In fact, I'm going home," I said. He nodded with a skeptical smile.

"Ain't we all," he muttered, and put on some music. I saw him reach over and take something from the glove compartment. When he lit it, I recognized the sweet aroma. "Want a joint?"

"No thank you."

"Gotta stay cool in this world," he said. "Don't let the stress get to you. That's the secret." Then he began to sing it to the tune of "London Bridge is Falling Down":

316

"That's the secret of my life, of my life, of my life, that's the secret of my life, my fair lady." He laughed.

I stopped eating and looked more closely at one of the cartons of magazines. The flap of one was open just enough for me to see what was on the magazine cover. It looked like a picture of a naked little boy.

"Are you in the magazine business?" I asked, realizing he had never told me his name.

"You might say I'm a distributor." He laughed. "But if you're only seventeen, you can't look at those." He turned and smiled. "Now you really want to look at them, right? That's the way to get someone to buy into your concept—forbid them to do it. Stupid politicians," he mumbled.

His dark eyes were slick as oil, scary. My heart stopped and then started to thump. A clump of ice formed at the base of my stomach and telegraphed chills up and down my bones, making my hands and feet feel numb. I felt as if I couldn't move and the terror that had begun to take form, like some ugly beast in my brain, grew bigger and bigger with every passing second he stared back at me.

"I've been riding for hours myself," he said. "And I forgot to eat. I'll just pull over here and get something."

He slowed the van and turned off the road onto what felt like a gravel drive. I couldn't see the ground because I was so low down, but I did see some trees.

"Here we are, a safe spot," he said. He shut off the engine.

I couldn't swallow. I couldn't breathe. He got up slowly and turned into the rear of the van.

"How's the bread?" he asked sliding beside me.

"Fine," I managed. "If we're stopping, I'll just go out and get some air," I said.

He laughed.

"What's the matter, my house smells?"

I didn't reply.

"You look older than seventeen. I bet you can pass for nineteen, huh? I bet you've done that, gotten into places where you could drink, see X-rated movies."

317

I shook my head.

"Hey, I've been there," he said jabbing his thumb into his chest. "I understand. Don't worry." He puffed on his joint and then again offered it.

I shook my head. "No thank you."

"It's good stuff."

"No, thanks," I said. He shrugged.

"More for me." He puffed again.

"Can I get out?" I asked.

"Sure." He leaned back so I could get by him, but as I started past him, he flipped his joint into the front of the van and seized me at the waist.

I started to scream as he turned me around hard and slapped me back on the mattress.

"Come on," he said. "Stay inside. It'll be nicer." He laughed thinly.

"Let me go!" I tried to sit up, but he kept his weight on my shoulders and looked me over. The stink of his marijuana, mingled with the sour smell of his body and clothes, reeked down at me, churning my stomach.

"I can get you into a magazine," he said. "I know lots of photographers real well. You can make serious money."

"No thank you. Now let me up."

"Sure, only first you got to pay the fare."

"What fare?"

"I forgot to tell you. This is like a bus. You get on, you pay the fare."

"I have no money. I told you I was robbed."

"There's other ways to pay." He smiled, revealing uneven teeth streaked with green and brown stains.

He slid his hands over my breasts and then moved down to straddle my legs. Desperate and terrified, I found the glass peanut-butter jar and clutched it like a rock. While he explored under my skirt, I swung the jar with all my strength and struck him on the side of the head. The jar shattered, but it stunned him enough to drive him off me and I jumped up. He howled as I dove for the door. My hand found the handle just as his found the hem of my skirt. He tugged, but I flew forward and he lost his grip.

I stumbled from the van, quickly realizing we were a dozen or so yards from the road. When he appeared in the doorway, a streak of blood ran down the side of his face. I got to my feet and ran for the road, screaming for help.

He didn't follow. At the highway, I practically ran in front of an oncoming tractor trailer. The driver hit his horn as hard as he hit his brakes. I got across the road just in time, but his truck came to a stop.

The van backed out of the driveway and spun around, kicking up gravel. It headed in the direction from which we had come.

The truck driver got out of his cab and strutted angrily toward me. He was a tall, stout man about fifty. "What do you think you're doing? Do you know you could have caused an accident and been killed? Who—"

"That man tried to rape me!" I cried, pointing to the disappearing van.

He stopped and looked after it.

"I got out and ran just as you were coming. I'm sorry." I gasped, trying to regain my breath.

"Who was he?" he asked.

"I don't know. I was hitchhiking."

"Hitchhiking?" He shook his head. "Where are all the parents in this country?"

I started to cry, the realization of what I had just escaped finally hitting me.

"All right, take it easy. Where are you going?" he asked.

"Sewell," I moaned through my tears.

"Is that where your parents live?"

"Yes," I lied.

"All right. Get in my truck. I'm going through Sewell. I'll drop you off. Even though I'm not supposed to take riders," he emphasized. My hesitation infuriated him. "Get moving if you want to get home," he ordered. I walked back with him and got in the truck. He checked

319

the road, shifted, and started away, glancing at me with disapproval. "Don't you kids know how dangerous it is hitchhiking? Especially for a girl!"

"No, sir. I don't do it much, so I didn't know."

"Well, in a way I'm glad you got a good lesson," he said. After a few minutes, his anger subsided. "I've got a ten-year-old girl of my own and it's a battle today raising kids."

"Yes," I said. He glanced at me.

"How come you're so far from home all by yourself?"

"I—"

"You should be in school, right? You ran away, didn't you? And then you realized how good you had it back home and couldn't wait to get back, right?" he said with confidence.

I smiled to myself.

"Yes."

"Thought so. Well, at least you're okay now."

"Thank you," I said. I told him how I had been robbed on the bus and he felt sorry for me.

"There's some cold orange juice in that jug there if you'd like to pour yourself a cup."

"Thank you."

I did. As we bounced over the highway, I lay back. My heart began to beat normally and my body suddenly felt as if I had sunk into a warm bath. I closed my eyes. I heard him talking about his family, his daughter, his younger son, the crazy people on the highways. I must have fallen asleep out of emotional exhaustion, for the next thing I knew, he was poking me gently on the shoulder.

"We're coming into Sewell," he said, and I sat up. I never thought the sight of those hills and trees would be as wonderful as it was at that moment.

We passed the cemetery and rolled into the center of town. All the familiar stores, Francine's beauty parlor where Mommy had worked, the garage, the restaurants, filled my heart with warm joy. The truck driver noticed my happiness.

320

"You've been away a while, huh?"

"Yes, sir, I have. But I'm back."

"Well," he said, bringing the truck to a stop at a corner, "I got to continue, so I'll let you out. You think twice before you leave home again, young lady. No matter how bad things might seem to be, they're often worse someplace else, especially when you're alone."

"Yes, sir. Thank you," I got out of the truck. He nodded and I watched him drive away. Then I turned and looked at the village as if I couldn't drink it in enough. Some familiar faces turned my way and I waved, even to people who had never said hello to me before. Some waved back, some shook their heads in disapproval. I realized why. It was the middle of the day: I should be in school.

I started for the trailer home development, my heart pounding in anticipation. I couldn't wait to set eyes on Mama Arlene and have her set eyes on me. As I walked past the street that led to Daddy's mine, I felt a wave of sadness wash over my renewed jubilation. Going away and coming back didn't change the tragic facts. I climbed the hill that he took every day after work and I thought about how I would wait for him, anticipating, waving, calling him. I almost saw myself ahead, a little girl, excited because her daddy was returning home to sweep her up in his arms and flood her face with his kisses. How she longed for his laughter.

The entranceway to Mineral Acres looked no different, but when I turned up the street to Mama Arlene's, I paused. Her and Papa George's trailer was dark. Its small front patio was covered with fallen twigs, grass, and gravel, something Mama Arlene would never tolerate. I broke into a run and reached the trailer door quickly. It was silent inside. I rapped hard and called, "Mama Arlene! Mama Arlene, it's me, Melody!"

Silence greeted me. I pounded harder.

"Hey," I heard someone say. I turned and saw Mrs. Edwards, one of Mama Arlene's gin rummy partners. She was a woman of the same age. "What are you doing

321

over there?" She came walking from her home. "Oh, Melody. I didn't know it was you."

"Hello, Mrs. Edwards. I was looking for Mama Arlene."

"You've been away," she said as if just remembering. "That's right. Well, dear, Arlene isn't here. She's gone, honey."

"Gone?"

"Gone to live with her sister in Raleigh. She left soon after George passed away."

"Papa George . . . died?"

"Didn't you know? Yes, I'm afraid so. He suffered so. It was for the best," she said, nodding. "Where's your mother, honey? She back, too?" she asked gazing past me.

"What?" I shook my head. I couldn't talk. Dead? Mama Arlene gone?

"Here comes that service man to fix my washing machine," she said, as a truck pulled into the development. "Only two hours late. I got to go see to him. Nice to see you back, honey. Say hello to your mother. Hey there! I'm here!" she called to the driver, who poked his head out of the truck window. She marched away and I turned back to the door of Mama Arlene and Papa George's trailer.

It can't be, I thought. They can't be gone. I peered through a front window and saw the furniture covered and the trailer dark. Disappointment weighed me down. My legs felt as if they were lead. I gazed at my old trailer house. It looked just as deserted.

Where would I go now? Who would I go to? I wondered, but I was too tired and to overwhelmed to care. I went to our old home and tried the front door. There was a For Rent sign on it. Of course it was locked, but all that had happened to me on the trip and the shock of this news put me into a frenzy. I searched the yard until I found a short metal rod, which I brought back to the door. I jabbed it into the small space between the door and the trailer and I pulled and tugged, shaking

322

it and putting all my weight behind it until the door snapped open and I went flying back on the patio. I got up, threw the rod away, and went inside. One way or another I was home again, I thought.

Everything had been turned off in the trailer home: electric and gas, and even water. The cupboards were empty, the refrigerator door left open with nothing on its shelves. Someone, probably the bank, had come into the trailer and removed everything else.

After I had wandered through the trailer, I curled up on the ragged living room rug just about where the sofa had been. I didn't know the time. There were shadows in the corners and whispers in the walls. Time was as irrelevant as honesty, I thought. I lay there sobbing until I fell asleep again. The sound of someone calling my name woke me. I sat up, grinding the sleep from my eyes. The late-afternoon sun was blocked by some high clouds, so the trailer was dark and I could see only a shadowy silhouette in the doorway.

"Melody?"

"Alice!" I cried, so happy finally to hear a friendly, familiar voice. "How did you know I was here?"

"Your cousin Cary called me very late last night. He found my phone number in your notebook and remembered you had mentioned me as your best friend in Sewell."

"Cary?"

"Yes. He told me he put you on a bus and he was very worried that you would arrive safely," she said.

"I almost didn't," I replied and described my nearly disastrous adventure.

"Wow!" she said when I had finished. "You're lucky you got here, but . . ." She gazed around. "Is your mother supposed to meet you here?"

"No. I don't know where Mommy is, Alice," I wailed. I sat on the floor again and she sat beside me just the way we used to sit together on the floor of her warm room in her beautiful house.

323

"What do you mean, you don't know where she is? Didn't she call you? Didn't she tell you to meet her here? I don't understand," she said.

Finally, I told her my story.

With her eyes widening as I spoke, she absorbed it and then dropped her jaw in amazement and shock. "Chester Logan was not your father? And you don't even know who your real father is?" I shook my head. "What are you going to do?"

"I don't know. I ran away because I was hoping to live with Mama Arlene," I said. "I never heard about Papa George."

"I went to the funeral," she said. "Papa George is buried close to your . . ."

"I know. I don't know what to call him either." I sighed deeply. "I'll just keep calling him Daddy until I find out the truth about my real father."

"You must be starving. Come home with me and get something to eat," Alice urged.

"I am starving, but I know what your parents will say. No thanks, Alice."

"You can't stay here. This place doesn't belong to you anymore. It belongs to the bank."

"I'll stay until they throw me out, I guess. In the meantime, can you loan me some money? I'll buy some food."

She thought. "I know what I'll do. I'll go home and get some food for both of us. I'll tell my parents I'm studying chemistry with Beverly Murden and I'll come back here. I'll bring us some candles, too. It'll be like a picnic. Like the old days, okay?" she said with enthusiasm.

I laughed. How ironic. My predicament provided Alice with the most excitement she'd had in months.

"Okay," I said.

"Your cousin left me a telephone number so I could call to tell him whether you arrived safely. You want me to tell him anything else?"

"Just say thanks, but don't tell him about the other

324

things. I don't want him to know how terrible my trip was, okay?"

She nodded.

"It will take me a little while to get everything together and get back."

"That's all right. I want to go to the cemetery to pay my respects to Papa George and visit my daddy's grave."

"You mean the man you thought was your daddy," she corrected.

"Yes."

"Okay. I'll meet you back here. I'll bring a radio that works on batteries so we can have music. I've got a lot to tell you about the kids at school. Bobby Lockwood's going with Mary Hartman."

"Okay," I said, trying to sound interested, even though it sounded very insignificant to me at the moment.

"I'm glad you're back, even if it's not for long," Alice said, squeezing my hand. "See you in about an hour."

She hurried from the trailer. I followed soon afterward. The sky became more and more overcast, making everything gray and dreary by the time I arrived at the cemetery. It didn't take me long to find Papa George's fresh grave. Under his name were the dates of his birth and death.

"I'm sorry I wasn't here to see you one more time, Papa George. You were my real grandfather and will always be in my heart."

I kissed the top of his tombstone and then walked down the path to Daddy's. For a long moment I stood there, just looking at the familiar carving. Then I shook my head, the tears running down my cheeks.

"Why, Daddy? Why didn't you tell me the truth?" I glared at the grave. I wanted to be angry, to hate him, but all I could see was his smiling face, his warm eyes, his happiness at the sight of me.

"I'm all alone now, Daddy. I'm really all alone."

I knelt at his grave and said a prayer. I asked that he

and Mommy be forgiven for anything terrible they might have done and I asked for mercy. Then I stood up and stared at the tombstone for a long moment until a funny thought came to mind.

"If Papa George is with you, he's bawling you out for sure, Daddy. I can almost hear him."

I sighed deeply and then walked back to Mineral Acres. Soon afterward, Alice arrived bearing bags of food and news.

"Your cousin answered the phone. He said he was waiting for my call all day. He sounds nice, Melody."

"He is. You didn't tell him any of the bad things, did you, Alice?"

"No," she said, but the way she lowered her eyes quickly told me otherwise. "He said he hopes you'll come back."

"You told him about Mama Arlene and Papa George then?"

"He asked me. You didn't tell me not to tell him that," she protested.

"It doesn't matter, I suppose."

She smiled and began to unpack. She had brought two candles and candle holders and we had to light them right away because the twilight—blocked by the heavy clouds—made it very dark in the dingy trailer.

"I didn't know what to bring," she said, "so I brought whatever I could."

Her leftovers included chicken, some cold pasta, fruit, cookies, bread, a jar of honey, tuna fish, and two bars of chocolate. The sight of food reminded me how very hungry I was. Alice, still quite overweight, didn't need any reminders or excuses. Whatever I ate, she ate. As we gobbled away, she related all the stories about the kids at school. She described Bobby Lockwood's new love affair as if it were the hottest relationship in America. Finally exhausted, she begged me to tell her about the students in Provincetown. I was reluctant to stir up the raw memories, but she pleaded and pleaded, telling me how unfair it was for me to have listened to her and not tell her anything. Finally, I gave in and described the last few weeks. She was glued to my every word.

The candles burned down. Darkness closed in around us and with it, the cool air.

"You should at least come to my house to sleep," she said. "You can come back here in the morning if you want. What are you going to do?" She fired her questions at me before I could think of a single idea.

Finally, something occurred to me. "How much money can you lend me, Alice?"

"I could manage to scrape up about a hundred and fifty dollars, maybe a little bit more. I know where my brother keeps some money in a drawer. He won't miss it."

"Good."

"What are you going to do?"

"I'm going to go to Los Angeles and find Mommy," I said.

"Wow." She thought a moment. "A hundred and fifty dollars won't be enough to get across the country, Melody."

"I'll get there. I got here, didn't I?"

She nodded.

"Okay. I'll give you the money."

"Thank you, Alice. You are my one true friend."

"Are you coming to my house to sleep?"

I gazed around the trailer. Even without furniture, it seemed like home again. I could easily imagine where everything had been and I could remember conversations and moments at practically every spot.

"No, I'll just curl up here. You'll get into trouble if your parents find me. I've made enough trouble for enough people."

"But," she gazed around, "can you sleep here?"

"Yes," I said. "I can. Cary's coat is pretty warm."

"All right," she said. "I'll get up a little earlier in the morning and come here with the money before school. I'll leave the radio with you for company."

"Thanks, Alice."

327

"I'm going to miss you all over again," she said.

"As soon as I get to Los Angeles and find Mommy, I'll write. Maybe you can come visit."

"Yes, maybe," she said, excited with the idea. "Okay. Good night, Melody."

"Good night."

She left, and the candles burned out, leaving me in the darkness, surrounded by memories of Daddy's voice and laughter, Mommy's voice and laughter. I softly wept for a while and then curled up and fell asleep.

I woke in the middle of the night when I thought I heard footsteps. My heart pounded as I gazed into the pitch blackness of Mineral Acres, half expecting to see Mommy emerge from the dark. Something scurried over the floor and I realized it was either a squirrel or a rat trying to work up enough nerve to get to the remnants of our picnic.

That thought made me uneasy and for the remainder of the night I woke up continually, listening and then falling asleep, only to wake up again. By the time the first light of morning came through the dirty, smudged windows, I was almost as tired as I had been when I first tried to sleep. Nevertheless, I rose and used the bathroom, even though the toilet didn't work. I had no choice.

I heard voices around the trailer, other people going to work or to town, so I remained hidden inside, quiet, waiting for Alice. She was true to her word and arrived before going to school.

"You don't look as if you slept too well, Melody," she said when she set eyes on me.

"I didn't."

"You should have come home with me. I worried about you all night. Anyway, here's the money," she said, handing me an envelope packed with bills.

"Thank you, Alice."

"Don't get robbed this time."

"I've learned my lesson, don't worry."

"Well, I better get to school."

"Don't tell anyone about me until I'm long gone," I asked.

"Okay."

We hugged.

"Don't forget to write as soon as you can," she reminded.

"I won't," I promised.

I watched her walk away and then I sat on the floor with my back against the wall, trying to get up the strength and the energy to begin this long and dangerous journey to California. I had no idea about the route or the cheapest, safest means of travel, or even how to go about finding Mommy once I got there.

Finally, I rose and left the trailer, pausing to take one last look at it as I left Mineral Acres and headed to town. On the way I paused at a stream and dipped my hands into the cold water, washing the sleep from my face. I was sure I looked a mess.

The bus depot was in the Mother Jones luncheonette. I ordered a cup of coffee and a buttered roll at the counter. The waitress asked me why I wasn't in school and I told her I wasn't living here anymore, just visiting. Still, I drew a lot of attention. I was afraid to go up to the information desk and ask about routes to California. In the end I decided to take the bus back to Richmond, thinking it would be much easier to plan a cross-country trip from a big city like that. I didn't wait long for the bus.

This time, when I got on, I sat up front near the driver. There weren't many passengers and the driver was talkative. I told him I was going to Richmond to stay with my grandparents for a few days. Lies, I found, were coming to me easier, now that I was on the run. I didn't like doing it, but I could see how much easier it was than telling people the truth.

At the depot in Richmond, the ticket seller gave me a map that outlined a few different routes. I sat on a bench, trying to figure which route would be the cheapest and fastest. I was concentrating so intently on the bus map, I didn't see or sense that someone was standing right beside me. When my gaze moved off the page and I looked at the feet, I recognized the shoes.

"Cary!" I screamed.

"Talk about luck," he said smiling. I was shocked, but very happy to see his face. "I got off the bus and was just on my way to buy my ticket to Sewell when I saw you sitting here."

"What are you doing here? How—"

"Grandma Olivia was furious when she found out what I did and you did. She gave me the money to buy my bus ticket here and our bus tickets back," he said.

"I'm not going back, Cary," I said. "I'm going to Los Angeles to find my mother and get her to tell me the truth."

"You don't have to go to Los Angeles, Melody. I think I know the truth," Cary said. "Grandma Olivia and I had some down-to-earth talk, and I got her to tell me all she knows.

"I think I know who your father is," he said.

330

18
❧

Not Alone

I told you her bark was worse than her bite," Cary said, escorting me to the first bus back to Boston. "The moment she found out what you had done, she summoned me. Boy, did she ever bawl me out! How could I be so stupid as to give you the money to travel alone? Why didn't I bring you right back to her instead of driving you to Boston? How could I let you go back to West Virginia? She made it sound as if I had sent you to work in the coal mines. I thought she would take me out to sea and make me walk the plank."

"What did you do?" I asked him.

"I let her chop up the water until she was exhausted and red in the face and then I calmly stood up and said, "'Grandma, it was all your fault.'"

"You did?"

We boarded the bus and took our seats.

"Aye, I did."

"What did she do?"

"She flopped back in her seat, so shocked by my accusation and courage, she could only move her mouth. Nothing came out. Then it was my turn.

331

" 'How dare you just lay all that misery on Melody like that,' I told her. 'What did you expect would happen if you made someone feel less than nothing, if you took away years and years of belief, of the only life she's ever known? She loved Uncle Chester like a father,' I said.

" 'Well . . . well,' she stuttered, 'the girl wanted to hear the truth and so I gave it to her.'

" 'How would you like someone to give it to you right between the eyes like that, Grandma?' I demanded. Then she just stared at me for a moment."

"What did she say?" I asked.

"She said that was exactly what had happened to her. First, with her sister and then, nineteen years later, with your mother, Haille. I told her she should have known better, then. She should have known how it would feel. Then I sat across from her and watched her. She stared at the floor for the longest time without speaking. Finally, she said, 'You're right, Cary. You're a lot older and wiser than I thought. In some ways you're the smartest of all of us.' She straightened up in her chair the way she does, you know, and in that regal voice of hers demanded I go find you and bring you back. She told me she would give me the money and she wanted me on the road immediately. She said she would take care of my father, not to worry.

"So," he said smiling, "here I am."

The bus started away.

"But I thought you told me you knew who my father was. I thought you said she told you more."

"I was getting to that. I didn't just jump up to do her bidding, you know," he said proudly. It amused me to see how proud he was that he had stood up to his grandmother. "I just sat there and stared at her until she said, 'Are you going after her or not?'

"I thought a moment and said, 'I can't bring her back unless you tell me the truth, Grandma. Otherwise, why would she want to come back?' Well, Grandma Olivia deflated like a punctured blowfish and nodded.

" 'It was your father,' she began, 'who came to me one day after Haille and Chester had left. Even though he had had this terrible fight with Chester—and gotten the worst of it, I might add—he felt very low, very bad that he had lost his brother. The three of them had been inseparable. But not always, Jacob hinted, indicating he knew something more. I pursued this, and he told me that many of the nights Haille was supposed to be spending with a girlfriend, she had been spending at the Childs'.' "

"The Childs'? You mean she was with the judge's family?" I asked.

"Yes, specifically Kenneth. During that last year, Kenneth was in Provincetown a lot," Cary said. "He was going to Boston University undergraduate school. He was supposed to go on to become a lawyer, but he was also heavily into his sculpture and the judge had a studio built for him at their home. Your mother was there almost every weekend Kenneth was there."

"Kenneth Childs is my real father?" I asked.

"It's very likely, from what Grandma said. I didn't get the opportunity to talk about it with my father. I took the money and went off to fetch you, leaving Grandma Olivia to explain it to him."

"But why didn't my mother just tell the truth? Why would she blame Grandpa Samuel?"

"That's something you're going to have to ask her, Melody. She was either protecting Kenneth or herself or—"

"Or what?"

He shrugged.

I sat back, digesting the story. If what he told me was true, then my real father was back in Truro and I was going to the right place.

"Have you ever spoken to Kenneth Childs?" I asked.

"I've said hello when I've seen him, but it's not easy to see him. He lives like a hermit on the Point. It's like the judge said the other night: all he does is work."

"He doesn't have a wife or other children?"

"No. Everyone thinks he's strange, but as I told you, they accept it because he's an artist."

"Some artistic hermit living in a beach house away from people—that's my father?" I muttered, stunned with each and every revelation Cary uttered.

"Anyway, at least you'll get a chance to find out the truth now," he said.

I shook my head. Maybe I shouldn't, I thought. Maybe I should live with the lies.

"What am I going to do?" I asked, the reality dropping all around me and over me. "Walk up to him and ask, 'Are you my real father?'"

"I'm not sure. We'll have to talk to my father about it, perhaps," he said.

"Your father?" I started to laugh. "You think he would talk to me about this?"

"Yes," Cary said, his eyes small. "He will or I'll tell my grandmother and she'll wring his neck."

I laughed, just thinking about Grandma Olivia chewing into Uncle Jacob.

Cary smiled. "I'm glad I found you so quickly, Melody."

I nodded and then sighed deeply, the sadness in my heart sprouting its dark flowers again.

"Papa George died," I told him. "There was no one there when I arrived yesterday. Mama Arlene had already moved away to live with her sister. The trailer home was closed, and my old home had nothing in it."

"I know. Alice told me. I'm sorry."

"Alice helped me a lot, but I spent last night in the trailer, sleeping on the floor. I have no idea where my things are. I didn't even think about them. I went to the cemetery, too. It felt so strange. I was angry and sad and . . . confused. Mommy didn't call while I was away, did she?"

"Not when I was home," he said. "How did you ever hope to find her just by going to Los Angeles? It's huge. I hear that even people who live there get lost."

334

"I didn't know what else to do. I was alone," I said mournfully.

"You're not alone. You'll never be alone. Remember that," he declared, his eyes firm and determined and full of sincerity.

"Thank you, Cary."

He smiled warmly, his eyes soft, loving. Then, he changed expression and took a breath. "Now I'll tell you the truth," he said. "I was shaking in my boots when I snapped at Grandma. I was afraid she would throw me out and call my father and that would be that."

"I thought you said her bark was worse than her bite."

"I did, but that doesn't mean her bite doesn't hurt, too."

The bus rolled on to Boston. I was like a ball in a pinball machine, rolling back and forth, but it wasn't for nothing, I thought. After all, I was unraveling those lies that had been spun so tightly around me, and soon, soon, I would reach the truth. It should have made me happy to realize that, but all it did was make my heart thump and make me tremble inside.

Since I hadn't slept much in the trailer, I dozed for most of the trip, my head on Cary's shoulder. When we arrived in Boston, we had something to eat and then we got into his truck and started for Provincetown. It was nearly morning by the time we saw the town with Pilgrim's Monument ahead of us. The rim of the sun was just peeking over the eastern horizon, turning the sky violet and orange, its bright gold edged with all those heavenly colors. The darkness retreated from the ocean, rising away like a blanket being peeled from a silver sheet. A tanker was silhouetted against the orange sky. It was breathtaking.

The beauty of the Cape, the promise of revelation and truth, the return after my desperate flight—it all made me dizzy with emotion. I was nervous, afraid, elated, and excited, happy and sad. I didn't know whether to cry or sigh with pleasure, to feel relief or more tension.

335

"Lucky I was suspended, huh?" Cary said, smiling, as we entered the city limits.

"Lucky?"

"Sure. I wouldn't have been free to go find you. Actually, I would have left anyway and then I might have been suspended because of that."

"Let this be the end of all that, Cary. You've got to graduate."

"Aye, aye, Captain," he said, saluting. We cruised through town and made the turn toward his house. How would we be greeted? Would anyone be awake?

"Maybe I should just sleep on the beach," I said.

He looked at me with a wry smile. "It's time you got a good rest," he said. "You've got a lot to do during the next few weeks. For one thing, you've got to get me through my finals and take finals of your own."

How right he was, I thought. Maybe he was the smartest and wisest of all of us after all.

It was deadly quiet when we entered the house. A small hall light had been left on. We looked at each other and then, as silently as we could, started up the stairs, but the steps creaked like tattletales. By the time we reached the landing, Uncle Jacob, standing in his long nightshirt, was at his bedroom door. We paused. He stared at us a moment and then nodded.

"Get some sleep. We'll talk tomorrow." He retreated to his bedroom, softly closing the door.

"That's his way of saying he's glad we're back safely," Cary explained.

"Well, why can't he just say so? Doesn't he ever show any emotion beside anger? I've never seen him laugh or cry."

"The only time I ever saw my father cry was when he heard Laura was missing. He went off toward the cranberry bog and stood on the hill, sobbing. Then, and at the memorial service. He's not a man to show emotion."

"Except his anger," I reminded him.

"That's just—"

336

"I know," I said smiling, "his bark not his bite."

Cary smiled.

I had to admit the sight of the soft mattress and comforter was a wonderful sight. I didn't even bother to get undressed. I just plopped onto the bed, hugged the fluffy pillow, embraced my stuffed cat, and fell asleep. I didn't waken until late in the afternoon. Vaguely, I recalled, as if it were a dream, Aunt Sara coming into the room and standing by the bed, gazing down at me, even stroking my hair. I may have groaned and turned over, but I didn't speak, and after a moment, she left.

My bones creaked when I sat up. I felt so scuzzy it was as if I had cobwebs under my arms. A hot shower had never been so marvelous. I washed my hair and brushed my teeth and then got dressed in a pair of jeans and a clean blouse. I smelled the aroma of something delicious even before I came down the stairs.

"You're up! How are you feeling, dear?" Aunt Sara asked.

"I'm fine, Aunt Sara. I'm so sorry," I said quickly.

"Nothing to be sorry about my dear, now that you're home safe again. I have a fish stew cooking and ready for you. I bet you're hungry."

"Starving," I admitted. My stomach churned in anticipation of the good food, the Portuguese bread.

"Just sit at the table and I'll bring it. It's not supper time, but you've got to get something warm in your stomach."

"Where's Cary?" I asked. "Is he still asleep?"

"Cary? Oh no. He was up to take May to school and then return to school himself."

"He must be exhausted," I said.

"It isn't the first time he was up most of the night and I'm sure it won't be the last. That's a fisherman's life, dear. Cary's used to it."

"Do you know why I left like that, Aunt Sara?"

"No dear." She quickly walked away to demonstrate that she didn't care to know, either. Aunt Sara was definitely the clam in the family, ready to slam shut her shell and ignore anything unpleasant. It seemed almost cruel to make her listen or see what she didn't want to see.

I said nothing. I ate and waited for Cary, May, and Uncle Jacob to return. But before they did, Aunt Sara and I had a surprise visitor. My aunt came running into the dining room as I was finishing my stew.

"She's here!" she cried. "Oh dear, dear, the house is a mess, too," she said, wringing her hands with an invisible dish towel of worry.

"Who's here, Aunt Sara?"

"Olivia," she announced. "She hasn't been here since—since . . . I can't remember." She went rushing about, picking up anything and everything that looked out of place.

Moments later Grandma Olivia came to the front door. Aunt Sara shouted for me to let Grandma Olivia in and I rose, trembling a bit myself. When I opened the door, she stormed past me and walked into the living room.

"Hello Olivia," Aunt Sara said. "It's so nice to see you."

"I want to talk with Melody alone," she snapped.

"Oh, of course." Aunt Sara smiled at me and retreated. Grandma Olivia peeled off her black velvet gloves and sat in Uncle Jacob's chair. She gazed at me with her eyes dark and small. "Sit," she ordered, and I went to the settee. "What did you think you would accomplish with this dramatic gesture—running off like that?"

"It wasn't a dramatic gesture. I wanted to go home."

"Home." She spit the word out as if it filled her mouth with an ugly, bitter taste. She looked away. "Home is here," she said, pointing to her temple, "and here," she added, pointing to her heart.

"I was going to go live with people who don't lie," I said.

"Everyone lies. It's a matter of survival," she declared.

338

"Then why hate my mother for lying?" I retorted. She widened her eyes.

"I'm not here to talk about your mother. I'm here to talk about you," she said. "As I told you, you are my sister's granddaughter and I made promises to my father."

"I know," I said. "Thank you for being so honest." I wanted to add: and for using the truth like darts.

"I didn't tell you everything," she confessed.

I sat back as she paused.

"My father left both my sister and me a considerable fortune. Most of what you see, what we have, does not come from my husband's brilliant business acumen. Samuel was never a good businessman. To this day I don't think he understands what a profit-and-loss statement is," she said disdainfully. "But that's a different matter. As I told you, Belinda is under a doctor's care. That is eating away at her inheritance, but even if she lives to be a hundred, it won't eat but a small portion of it. The money was well invested and earns good interest. To come directly to the point, your mother would have inherited what was left of Belinda's fortune if I hadn't helped Belinda to see more clearly. Instead, a trust has been formed and you are the heir."

"I?"

"That's correct. It's specifically set up to provide you with your educational needs, your basic needs, until you are twenty-one. After that, you can waste it as you see fit. I'm the administrator of the trust."

"Why didn't you tell me before?" I asked.

"Why? I didn't feel you needed to know all this until you were sufficiently retrained."

"Retrained?"

"Until you had lived with a family in a moral setting and lost whatever bad habits Haille might have instilled in you."

"She didn't instill any bad habits in me," I replied firmly.

339

"I wish that were true, but frankly, I don't see how it's possible for you to have grown up as her daughter and not be somehow affected. Anyway, I'm glad Cary got you to come to your senses and return."

"Why?" I challenged. "You obviously hate my mother and hate the sight of me."

"I don't hate the sight of you. I told you why I have the feelings I have toward your mother, but I'm . . . sufficiently impressed with you to believe you have the capability to overcome your unfortunate upbringing. If you will behave and listen to wiser minds, you have a lot to gain, as you now know. It will be a considerable fortune, more than most people make in two lifetimes of hard work. There, now I've given you your incentive and I've welcomed you back," she said, as if that were the prescription to treat her bout of conscience.

"Welcomed me back?" I shook my head and snorted.

"I came here, didn't I?" she protested.

I stared at her a moment. This was the closest she would come to an apology, I thought. Whether it was because of the promise she had made to her father or came from genuine and sincere remorse for telling me things bluntly and causing me to run off, I didn't know.

"I would just ask you for one thing," she continued.

"What's that?" I asked.

"Let the past be the past. Concern yourself with your future. Nothing can be gained by digging up the ugly days and ugly memories," she said.

"I don't know if I can do that," I said. "There are still things I need to know."

Her eyes grew small again and her face firm. She leaned toward me. "I would not like to hear that you were going around Provincetown asking questions and stirring up gossip about the Logan family."

"I wouldn't do that."

"Make sure," she warned. Then she rose. "Stop by the house from time to time to tell me how you are getting along," she said. "Have Cary bring you," she added before leaving the room.

340

Aunt Sara was in the hallway. "Would you like to stay for dinner, Olivia?"

"Certainly not," Grandma said. She looked at me for a moment and then turned and walked out of the house. It was as if a wind had blown through and shut the door.

"Wasn't that nice?" Aunt Sara said, as if some member of royalty had lowered herself to visit. "Dear, come help me set the table."

I stood there for a moment in a daze. I was to inherit a fortune? Had Mommy or Daddy ever known? If they had, they couldn't tell me about it without telling me everything else. The more I learned, the more I was amazed by what they had sacrificed to run off together the way they had.

May and Cary arrived only minutes before Uncle Jacob. Cary looked tired but did his best to hide it. May was very excited to see me and was filled with so many things to tell me, her hands never stopped moving. Aunt Sara went on and on about Grandma Olivia. Cary looked at me with surprise and expectation and I whispered that I would tell him everything later. In the meantime, I helped serve dinner. Since I had just eaten, I ate only dessert: a piece of Aunt Sara's blueberry pie.

After I helped clean up, I went upstairs and joined Cary in his attic room. I told him everything Grandma Olivia had told me. He had not known about any fortune.

"I'm not even sure my father knows about that," he said. "That's wonderful, Melody."

"Money isn't very important to me right now, Cary. The truth is, I think Grandma Olivia was hoping I would willingly forget all the lies just so I could get my inheritance. It was as if she were trying to buy me off with the promise of it."

He nodded, thinking.

"Can we talk to your father now? Would he talk to us?" I asked. I was afraid to approach him myself.

"Let's try," Cary said.

We descended the stairs together and found Uncle

341

Jacob reading his paper and listening to the news on the radio. He looked up, surprised.

"What is it?" he asked.

"Melody has some questions to ask you, Dad," he said. "Because of the things Grandma told her and me about her mother."

"You know how I feel about talking about that." He started to raise his paper.

"Grandma feels we're old enough to know things, why can't you?" Cary challenged. I think he was braver with me standing beside him, only now I felt responsible for any bad feeling between him and his father.

Uncle Jacob thought a moment and then lowered the paper to his lap. He turned off the radio. "You want to hear about your mother? You want to hear the ugly truth?" he said with a note of threat.

"I want to know the truth," I replied undaunted, "ugly or otherwise."

"All right. Sit," he said, nodding at the settee. We both went to it. Uncle Jacob lit his pipe and puffed for a few moments.

"Haille was always getting in trouble with boys. Either Chester or I had to come to her aid all the time, trying to save her from herself. On more than one occasion, I found her down on the beach with someone doing things I'd rather not describe. I got into fights and so did Chester. We were teased a lot. The family was disgraced a lot, but nothing seemed to change her. She was fascinated with herself.

"Your mother was always a source of misery for my parents," he said, pointing with his pipe. "She was caught smoking, drinking, and doing all sorts of immoral stuff in school dozens of times. If my mother hadn't had influence in this town, they would have thrown Haille out of the public school. She was actually arrested twice for lewd behavior on the beach when she was in high school." He paused. "You still want to hear this?"

I swallowed back a throat lump and nodded.

"About when she was fifteen, sixteen, she got caught

342

with a truck driver out on the dunes. They were going to throw the book at the guy. He was about twenty-eight or so and she was obviously under age. Only, my mother was worried about the scandal, so it was kept quiet and the truck driver was let go. Mother tried to get a doctor to help Haille, the same doctor who was treating Belinda at the time, I recall, but nothing seemed to help. She was a wild creature. She'd do whatever she wanted, whatever she fancied. Chester and I did our best to cover up for her, to protect her."

He paused and sat back, thinking. The lines in his face grew deeper, his eyes colder. Then he took a breath and continued. "The year she was supposed to graduate from high school, Kenneth Childs began coming up and spending time with us more and more. We liked Kenneth and our families were close. In those days Chester and I thought of him as another brother. Kenneth was going to college in Boston. He would come up weekends. Sometimes Chester and I didn't know he was in town, but Haille always did. She was over at the Childs' lots of times, and sometimes, there was no one else there but Kenneth.

"That was the year she got pregnant. She made up that story about my father. Chester always favored her more than I did, overlooked her sins. He made excuses for her all the time. He refused to believe Kenneth would make her pregnant and not own up to it. Haille filled him with lies about Dad and he swallowed them, because he was so hypnotized with her himself.

"I told him she was a liar and a whore. I told him she once tried to seduce me, and he got into a fight with me. He took her side and they ran off together. That's the story," he concluded, like a slap of thunder at the end of a rain storm.

There was a heavy silence in the room. Cary looked at me.

"Have you ever spoken with Kenneth Childs since?" I asked.

"We've had some words, mainly because of the judge.

343

I went to his mother's funeral, of course, but it's hard for me to look him in the face and not think about what happened."

"Did you ever ask him outright about it?"

"No," he said, "and I don't intend ever to talk about it. You're my mother's sister's grandchild. Your Aunt Sara is fond of you, and from what I hear, you're doing well in school. You're welcome to stay here as long as you need to or until your mother decides to be a mother instead of a tramp. That might never happen, of course, and soon you'll be on your own anyway. But I won't have any more talk about those days in my house," he said firmly. "And I don't want any scandals." He looked at Cary. "Satisfied?"

Cary turned to me. "You want to ask him anything else, Melody."

"No," I said. I was crying inside, the tears falling behind my eyes and over my heart.

Uncle Jacob went back to his paper and put the radio on again. I left the room, pounding up the stairs. I threw myself on the bed and lay there embracing my stuffed cat.

There was a soft knock on my door.

"Yes?"

Cary poked his head in.

"Are you okay?"

"No, but it's all right," I said. "I guess in my heart I knew everything your father said. It's just hard hearing it like that."

Cary nodded. "It'll be all right. Things will be just fine," he promised.

I smiled at him. "Sure."

"I'd better go up and start studying," he said. "I gotta pass those finals."

"Yes, you better. Cary," I said, as he started to close the door. He raised his eyebrows. "One day this week, will you take me to see Kenneth Childs?"

"Sure," he said. "I don't know what he'll do. He

344

doesn't like people coming around much, I know. I hear that when he works, he won't even come to the door."

"Still, I'd like to try to meet him," I said.

"Okay. Nose to the grindstone," he said and left.

I lay there for a long time, just thinking, remembering silly things Mommy had done, recalling her whining and crying and Daddy's soothing her all the time. Then I thought about her with Archie Marlin.

Children inherit so much from their parents, I thought. Would I become like her one day? It frightened and intrigued me. I had to know who my real father was. Then I could learn what part of him I had inherited and whether that part was strong enough to overcome the bad I had inherited from Mommy. To be without a past is almost like being without a future, I thought.

I would know my past. No temptation of a fortune, no threat, nothing would keep me from pursuing the truth.

No one at school knew anything about my trip back to West Virginia. They didn't question why I had been absent. Some of the girls thought it was in sympathy with Cary and his unfair suspension. I didn't say it was, but I didn't deny it. There was a lot of excitement because of the school year's approaching end.

The week before finals was a week mainly for review. At the end of the week of finals, the school would have its variety show, the proceeds of which went toward college scholarships. The principal, Mr. Webster, hadn't forgotten that I played the fiddle. He had Mrs. Topper, the school music teacher who was in charge of the show, ask me to perform.

I tried to get out of it, claiming the truth: I hadn't been playing much these past months.

But Mrs. Topper was desperate. "I barely have enough performers to fill a half hour, much less an hour. I need you. You have to do two numbers," she pleaded. "It's all in good fun and for a good cause. Won't you help us?"

How could I refuse? But this, along with my anticipated visit with Kenneth Childs and my final exams made me more nervous than a flock of hens with a fox at the gate. I couldn't eat. I couldn't sleep. Cary was more excited about my performing than I was. He insisted on watching and listening to me practice. Aunt Sara thought it was wonderful, too, and even Uncle Jacob looked and listened with interest.

I decided I would play one of Papa George's favorites, "Katy Cline," and a traditional Woody Guthrie folk favorite, "This Land is Your Land." I sang when I played, of course. Uncle Jacob looked amazed and Aunt Sara had the widest, happiest smile yet on her face. Cary beamed. I felt sorry for May, but she seemed content just feeling the vibrations when I let her or just watching my face and actions. I didn't think I was good enough to actually perform, but even Uncle Jacob said I was. He hinted that he would attend the show, which Cary said would be a first.

"The only community event I've ever seen him attend is the Blessing of the Fleet."

Cary suggested that on Thursday, after we had brought May home from school, he and I would go to the Point to see if I could speak to Kenneth Childs.

"What are you going to say?" he asked.

I thought a moment. "I'll introduce myself first and then see what he says."

"What if he says nothing? What if he just nods and walks away?"

"I'll find a way to get him to talk to me," I said. Actually, I was excited with the idea of just seeing him, seeing if there was anything about him that reminded me of myself. I couldn't really tell much from the few photos I'd seen.

"The last time I saw him, he had a beard," Cary said. "Laura and I used to go to the beach up there, but I've never been in his house or studio. What excuse are we going to use for driving over to see him?" he asked.

"We'll tell him my mother asked me to stop by to say hello," I replied. Cary nodded and smiled.

"You've been scheming, haven't you?"

"That's all I've been doing lately," I admitted.

"Okay, Thursday," he promised.

My heart was pounding in anticipation.

The night before, I sat at the desk and, after stuffing the envelope with the money Alice had given me, wrapping it carefully so no one would know what it was, I wrote her a letter.

Dear Alice,

You'll be surprised to learn that I didn't go to Los Angeles after all. My cousin Cary was sent by Grandma Olivia to bring me back to Provincetown and he found me at the bus station in Richmond. I agreed to return when he told me he thought he knew who my real father is. He's an artist who lives in Provincetown. Tomorrow, Cary is taking me to his house and studio and for the first time in my life, I will set eyes on the man who could be my father. I have seen pictures of him when he was younger, but seeing pictures is one thing. Standing before him in the flesh will be another.

I am rehearsing what I will say and how I will say it. You'd laugh if you saw how I pose before the mirror in my room and pretend I'm seeing him. Everything I can think to say sounds silly. I'm afraid he will just look at me and shake his head and maybe shut the door in my face. I don't know how I would feel if that happened.

Apparently, he is a man who keeps to himself, so that just might happen. I'll write to tell you all about it afterward.

Speaking of rehearsals, you won't believe this, but I've been talked into performing at the school's annual scholarship variety show. I'll be playing my fiddle—two tunes. I practice and have played for the family. They all seemed impressed, but I'm terrified.

I'm returning all the money you lent me. It was

347

nice of you to do it and I know now that you are my one true friend. I hope we will always remain friends, no matter how many miles apart we might be.

I still haven't heard from Mommy. When I asked her why she lied to me the last time she called, she sounded frantic and very distant and I have this fear she won't call again. There is a lot she and I have to discuss now, now that I'm old enough to understand. I have heard unpleasant things about her when she was younger—my age and a little older. It saddens and sickens me, but I try not to think about it.

My grandmother has told me that I'm an heiress and that someday I'll have a lot of money. How's that for a surprise? Me, someday rich? Right now, I don't even think about it. It really doesn't seem important.

What's important is that I might be on the verge of learning the whole truth about myself and my family. It frightens me and yet, I know how much I want to know everything.

As I write this letter, I am looking at the watch Papa George gave me. Inside, I placed a blade of grass from Daddy's grave. Even though I was just there, I feel so far away, not only in miles but in time. It makes me feel that I'm about to become someone else, as if I lived a different life, a life that will soon end. After all, this and a few of the things I was able to bring with me are all that I have from my former life. Of course, I have memories, but they're burning down like candles. I'm afraid of being left in the dark.

As soon as I finish this letter, I'm going to practice my fiddle and then I'm going to go to sleep and dream of a new tomorrow, where lies crumble like fallen autumn leaves beneath my feet and where promises of happiness and hope sprout rich and green like our mountains and hills in spring.

Say a prayer for me. And thanks for being my truest friend in all the world.

Love,
Melody

I put the letter in the envelope. I played my fiddle and then I crawled into bed and had the dream I told Alice I would have.

Tomorrow would be a new day.

19
ℬ

Lost and Found

The way to Race Point was along a road so narrow and hidden between two hills of sand, it could easily be overlooked. Cary explained that at Kenneth Childs's request, no sign was posted to designate the road. He was the only one who lived on it and it had become known as Childs Road. After its entrance, protected by the two hills, the road was covered with sand that was six to eight inches deep in spots.

"The best way to navigate this is to let air out of my tires," Cary explained and stopped the truck to do just that.

It was late afternoon and the powder blue sky was streaked with flat, soft clouds that looked like vanilla icing smeared across it in odd shapes. Cary said it meant it was very windy in the upper atmosphere. We went in about three quarters of a mile before we reached the peak of the incline and were able to see the ocean. It looked a darker metallic blue, making its whitecaps whiter. The beach here was cluttered with twisted seaweed that lay in clumps combed by the fingers of the waves. Terns walked gingerly around and through the seaweed as if they were part of some bird ballet entitled Searching for Food.

"This is one of the best places to find driftwood," Cary said. "Laura and I spent hours gathering strangely shaped pieces. Local artists will buy them from you. Seashells too," he added.

"Where's Kenneth's home?"

"Just to the right here," he explained and we made a turn. Ahead was a smoke-gray cedar saltbox house. The sea air, sun, and rain had faded its black shutters to a light charcoal. Behind the house was another small structure that looked like a barn.

"That's his studio," Cary explained.

I saw no one. The front of the house was spotted with pink wild beach grass, no flowers, no trees. On the side of the house facing us was an upside-down row boat, its hull sun-bleached. There was a dark blue jeep in what served as a driveway. An inky black Labrador was lying on the rear seat and lifted his head with curiosity as we approached.

"That's his dog, Ulysses. He's fifteen years old, half blind and deaf," Cary said. "At least that's what the judge says. His jeep's here, so Kenneth must be home," Cary muttered with some anxiety.

From the moment we had left the house, a small, but persistent trembling vibrated through every bone and muscle in my body. My heart was in a continual drum beat. Cary tried to keep up some conversation, but I could only smile or nod.

"You sure you want to do this?" he asked one final time before turning into the driveway. I nodded and took a deep breath.

Ulysses rose on his legs as if he had to lift three times his weight, but once he was on his feet, he hopped out of the jeep and began barking. It was a friendly bark, not a growl.

"Whenever Laura and I stopped by here, we had the feeling we were being watched, but Kenneth didn't come

351

out but one or two times and then it was just a quick hello and some comment about the weather."

"I'm going to do this," I said firmly. I opened the truck door and stepped out. Ulysses came to me first, his tail wagging. "Hello," I said and patted him. The sight of company excited him and he was licking my hand and rushing back and forth between Cary and me for our strokes and words.

"Some watchdog, huh?" Cary said with a laugh.

I looked at the front door. It was gray and weather-beaten, with no knocker, no buzzer, no indication the inhabitant of this house wanted anyone coming to it.

"You wouldn't think he had any money the way he lives," Cary muttered. "That jeep's about ten, twelve years old, and the furniture in the house looks as if he got it all at a thrift shop. We were never inside," he quickly added, "but Laura and I once peeked through the window. There aren't even any pictures on the walls. All his art is in his studio, I guess. We never got close enough to look in there."

"Kenneth has eyes that can scare you."

"What do you mean?"

"You'll see," he said. "I think. He might not answer the door."

We stared at it. I could see Cary wasn't going to be the one to knock, so I stepped forward slowly over the walkway, which consisted of small rocks. Ulysses stayed at my side, Cary remained a foot or so behind. I knocked and waited.

The roar of the ocean, the waves breaking on the beach, the cry of the terns, and the whistle the sea breeze made was all we heard. I knocked again, louder.

"What'dya want?" Both of us nearly jumped out of our sneakers. We turned to see Kenneth Childs standing at the corner of the house. He wore a pair of jeans, no shoes or socks, and a faded brown T-shirt. He was long-legged and slim. His hair, a little darker than mine, was, as Cary had described, tied in a pony tail, the end of which reached the base of his neck. His full-face beard was even a little darker. He had a wide forehead with deep-set dark eyes and a long, straight nose, under which his strong, firm lips stretched to dip at the corners. I couldn't help staring at his face, looking for more evidence of my own, but it was hard because of that thick beard. To me it was like a mask.

"She wanted to come see you," Cary said quickly, embarrassed and made more nervous by the long silence.

"What for?" Kenneth asked, his eyes on me.

"My mother told me to say hello," I said.

"Who's your mother?" he asked, without softening his face. He was miles from smiling.

"Haille," I said. "Haille Logan."

He stared for a moment longer and then he drew closer. Ulysses went to his side immediately.

"You're Haille's daughter?"

"Yes."

"Haille sent you?" he asked with skepticism. I nodded, positive he could see through my fabrication. "Why didn't she come herself?" he asked me.

"She's not here. I'm here, living with my uncle and aunt," I explained and tried to swallow so my words wouldn't sound so tiny. I couldn't take my eyes off him. His eyes were so hard, as if made of stone. This was what Cary meant, I thought.

"What's your name?" he asked.

"Melody."

His lips softened just a bit. He looked at Cary and then he looked at me.

"I'm going to school here now," I said, too nervous to permit any long silences. "For a while."

"Where's your mother then?"

"She's in California," I said. "She's auditioning to be an actress or a model."

353

His face finally relaxed.

"That figures," he said. He looked as if he was going to turn and walk away.

"I met your father at my grandmother and grandfather's house," I said quickly. He raised his eyebrows.

"And what did he say when he found out who you were?" he asked.

"He was . . . nice," I replied, not sure what he meant.

"Dad's the most charming man on the Cape," Kenneth said as if it were a basic fact everyone knew. He looked at Cary. "You're Jacob's boy?"

"Yes sir."

"Sorry about your sister. I don't get to hear much news out here, but I heard about that."

Cary nodded, biting down on his lower lip, his eyes glassy.

Kenneth turned back to me. "Are you a good student?"

"Yes, sir."

"Your father here too?" he asked, his face firm again.

"No sir. My father died in a coal mining accident a few months ago."

"Really?" He looked at Cary and then at me. "Coal mine? Where were you living?"

"West Virginia, a town called Sewell."

He nodded.

"Yeah, I knew they had gone south." His eyes were full of thoughts for a moment and then he blinked and looked at me more sharply. "You look a lot like her," he said. "I guess she's still as pretty as she was if she's looking to become a model or an actress."

"She is," I said.

"Well," he said, starting to turn. "Thanks for stopping by."

"Can I see some of your work?" I blurted. Cary's eyes widened. He looked at me and then at Kenneth, who stopped turning and considered.

354

"Why?" he asked, his eyes small, suspicious.

"I've heard a lot about it," I said.

"You know anything about art?"

"A little, what I learned in school."

"An artist's work is very personal until the day he puts it up for sale in some gallery," he said.

"I know."

"You know?" He widened his smile. "Are you an artist?"

"I play the fiddle and sing," I said. "I don't like doing it in front of people until I'm sure I'm ready. I guess an artist doesn't like showing his work until he is confident it's ready."

His eyebrows lifted again. "That's right." He thought a moment. "Okay, I'll show you something I've nearly completed," he said. "Maybe I need a completely fresh pair of eyes looking at it. I'll let you look at it if you promise to be honest about what you think."

"I don't like to lie about my feelings," I said, my eyes now as firm and as hard as his.

"I bet you don't. Follow me." He started around the house. Cary looked as if he had seen a ghost—shocked, surprised, still afraid. "You can bring him along," Kenneth added without turning back to us.

Between the house and the studio was a patch of beach grass, a bench, and a small, man-made pond in which minnows burst into frenzied swimming when our shadows touched the water. Kenneth opened his studio door and paused.

"Don't touch any of my tools," he warned. I nodded and so did Cary.

The studio was just a large room. On one side were tables and a kiln, and on the tables were his tools and materials. There was a beaten-up tweed settee to our immediate left with a driftwood table in front of it, on which were a large coffee mug and a plate, with a half-eaten muffin on it.

Kenneth's work in progress was to our right. It was a

355

figure about five feet high of a woman whose arms were changing into wings just above the elbow. The face was interesting, her eyes turned upward and her mouth was open as if to express a great sigh. She was naked and it looked as if feathers were growing along her back, sides, and stomach.

"Well?" Kenneth said. "What do you think I'm trying to show?"

"Someone turning into an angel," I said.

He smiled warmly. "Exactly. I'm calling it *Angel in Progress*. I have a lot of detail work left to do yet."

"It's very exciting, especially the look in her face," I said. "It's as if she's . . ."

"What?" He drew closer to me.

"Seeing heaven for the first time."

"Yes," he said, gazing at her. "She is."

"Do you always work in clay?" I asked.

"No. I've done stone, metal, and wood, but here I'm trying to capture and record a fleeting impression, much the way a painter does in a quick sketch. After I'm finished, I'll cast this in bronze."

"How do you do that?" I asked. He checked my expression to see if I really wanted to know. Satisfied, he gestured toward his tools and his kiln.

"In two stages. First, a negative mold is formed, and then a positive cast is made from the negative impression. Plaster is used for the negative mold and bronze for the positive. I call that the slave work, since all the artistic work is completed."

"You do all that by yourself?"

"Yes," he said with a short laugh. "So," he said, his eyes small again, "what do you know about sculpture?"

"Just what I learned in history about the Greeks. Gods and athletes were their favorite subjects," I recited. "I remember our teacher passed around a picture of the *Three Goddesses*."

He raised his eyebrows. "That's right."

"My best friend's parents have a small replica of

Michelangelo's *David* in their house," I said. "But I've never been to a museum and the only galleries I've ever seen are the ones on the street here."

"Take her to Gordon's on Commercial," Kenneth told Cary. "You know where it is?" Cary nodded quickly. "I have some pieces there."

"I'd like to see them."

He nodded. "Well, you've restored my faith in the educational system. Have you ever tried to do anything with art—draw, paint?"

"No."

"Maybe you should," he said. Was he telling me I had inherited some of his talent? I glanced at Cary, who still looked timid and nervous. His eyes shifted from side to side, as if looking for escape routes.

"School's almost over for you, isn't it?" Kenneth asked.

"Yes, just a little more review, finals, and that's it for this year. I graduate next year. Cary graduates this year,"

Kenneth looked at him. "What are you going to do with yourself?" he asked him.

"What I do now, fishing, cranberry harvest."

Kenneth nodded. "And you, what do you want to become?" he asked me.

"I think a teacher," I said.

"Not an actress or a model like your mother?"

"I don't think so," I said. He looked pleased. "You were very friendly with my mother once, weren't you?"

"Yes," he said. He gazed at his work in progress. "And with your father and with Cary's father. We all grew up together."

Cary and I looked at each other. In his eyes I could see the tension. Was I just going to come out and ask him if he could be my father?

"Well, I got to get back to work," he said. He walked toward the door to indicate he wanted us to leave. I gazed again at Cary and then I followed Kenneth. Cary followed me. Ulysses waited at the door.

"I like your dog."

"He's old, but faithful. I'm afraid he doesn't get enough exercise either."

"Maybe I can walk him for you sometime," I offered. "I'd like to hunt for seashells on the beach here."

He nodded.

"What are you going to do this summer?" he asked.

"I don't know. I'm waiting for my mother to come back or call for me."

"Well, tell her hello when she calls you." He stepped back into the studio and closed the door.

I looked at Cary.

"I didn't know how to say anything or ask anything," I explained.

"It's all right. Let's go. I don't think he would have admitted anything anyway. Maybe he doesn't even know himself." We started back to the truck, Ulysses following us.

"I should have said something more, asked something specific," I moaned.

"Next time. Did you get any sort of feeling about him?" Cary asked as he backed out of the driveway and started us toward the road.

"I think so," I said. "It's hard and it's not fair," I cried. "Mommy has to tell me the truth. She must!" I said firmly. "There's no reason for her not to now."

We bumped along the sandy road. When I looked back, I saw Ulysses turn and trot back toward the jeep. He looked disappointed.

After Cary stopped at a garage to refill his truck tires with air, we headed home. We had just made the turn toward the house when we both saw the police car parked right behind Uncle Jacob's.

"What's this all about?" Cary wondered aloud. We pulled up beside the police car and got out slowly. Both of us noticed that the front door was still open. We glanced at each other and then hurried inside.

There were two policemen standing in the hallway, the

taller one with his hat in his hands. Uncle Jacob was
talking to them softly. They all turned as we stepped in,
Uncle Jacob's face darker and firmer than I had ever seen
it. We heard soft sobbing coming from the living room
and looked in to see Aunt Sara seated on the settee, May
at her side stroking her arm.

"What happened?" Cary asked.

"There's been an accident," Uncle Jacob said.

"Who?" Cary asked. Uncle Jacob looked at the two
policemen and when he turned back, his eyes were on
me. My heart stopped and started.

"Mommy?" I cried. He nodded. "What happened?"

"Officer Baker here came to tell us they received a call
from police in . . . where was it?"

"Pomona, sir," the taller policeman said. "It's near
Los Angeles," he explained.

"What happened? Is she all right?" My heart stopped.

"Tell her what you know," Uncle Jacob said to the
policeman.

The officer turned to me. "There was an accident on
the freeway out there, single car, car caught fire. The
gentleman driving the car was thrown from the vehicle,
but—"

"My mother?"

"Apparently she was trapped in the car. The man
survived and is in the hospital. His name's—" He
checked a note pad, "Marlin, Richard Marlin. He claims
the woman who died in the car fire was Haille Ann
Logan and told the police to call here. The car exploded
and there wasn't much anyone could do."

"Mommy's . . . dead?"

The policeman looked at Uncle Jacob. Aunt Sara
started to cry louder. Cary reached for my hand, but I
pulled away. "Tell me!" I screamed. I had to have them
say it.

"That's what they're saying," Uncle Jacob stated.

I shook my head. "She was having auditions. She was
calling me."

The policeman turned to Uncle Jacob. "They want to know if you want the remains shipped here," he said.

"Call Olivia," Aunt Sara cried.

"Aye, we'll want that," Uncle Jacob replied.

"Stop it!" I screamed. "Stop all these lies!"

I put my hands over my ears and shook my head.

"Easy now," Uncle Jacob said holding out his hand. "You—"

"You're lying! Everyone just spins one lie after another!"

I looked at Cary.

He shook his head. "Melody," he said softly.

"It's not true," I begged him. I turned and ran out of the house.

"Jacob!" Aunt Sara screamed.

I nearly tripped on the steps, but I recovered my balance and went around the corner of the house. I ran as hard and as fast as I could. I needed to get away from them, away from the story, away from the policeman's eyes. When I reached the sand, I slipped and fell, catching myself with my hands and then shooting up and running harder, tears flying off my cheeks. My lungs were screaming, but I wouldn't stop. I ran up the hill and fell again, this time just lying there, sobbing.

Mommy wasn't going to call me. She wasn't going to send for me or return. I cried until my ribs ached and then I just stared out at the cranberry bog. I never heard Cary coming, but he was suddenly at my side.

"Mom's worried about you," he said and squatted. He put a blade of beach grass in his mouth. I gazed ahead, not hearing, not seeing, not feeling. "The police said they were going very fast and probably lost control. They rammed into a pole and the car turned over, spilling your mother's friend onto the road. Her door didn't open and the car rolled over and over and then just went up in flames. Nobody's lying."

I turned from him. Mommy had done a selfish thing by leaving me here and by keeping secrets, but I could

360

never harden my heart against her enough to stop loving her. There were good times to remember, lots of soft moments. Sometimes, I would catch her looking at me with a gentle smile on her lips and I could almost hear her thinking how pleased she was with me. She had come to depend on me so much. If only I had been with them, I thought. I would have made them slow down.

"They're going to bring her back and put her in the Logan section of the cemetery," Cary said.

I spun on him, my eyes on fire. "When she was alive, they didn't want her within ten feet of them, but now that she's dead, they'll put her in the ground near them?"

He had no answer. He looked down.

"She should be sent back to Sewell and buried beside my father," I said. "It's where she belongs."

Cary shrugged. "Tell Grandma."

I thought a moment. "I will. Take me there right now."

"Right now?"

I stood up and so did he.

"Right now," I said and started down the hill. I was running on anger and disappointment. He caught up.

"I'll just go tell Dad," he said when we reached the house.

"Just drive us there, Cary. Don't go asking for permission for every breath you take."

He looked at me, then nodded. "Okay, let's go."

We got into the truck and he backed out of the driveway. As we pulled away from the house, I saw Uncle Jacob step out and look after us. The moment we drove up Grandma Olivia and Grandpa Samuel's driveway, I opened the door. Cary hadn't even brought the truck to a stop. He hit the brakes and I was out, rushing toward the front door.

Cary slammed his door and followed. I pushed the buzzer, waited a second, and pushed it again. Grandpa opened the door, his face somber.

"Melody," he said, surprise overcoming sadness quickly.

361

"Where's Grandma Olivia?" I demanded. There was no sense talking to him, I thought quickly. She makes all the decisions in this family. I rushed in past him.

"Just what's going on here?" she demanded. She was standing in the sitting room doorway.

"You heard about my mother, your niece?" I fired. She stiffened.

"Jacob just called."

"What a terrible thing," Grandpa said, coming up beside me.

"I don't want her buried here. I want her buried back in Sewell beside my daddy," I said. "It's where she belongs."

"Sewell?" Grandma looked at Grandpa and then at Cary. "She's my sister's daughter. She doesn't belong there. She belongs here."

"Where she hasn't been welcomed for years and years," I spit back at her. "How can you be such a hypocrite!"

Grandma Olivia's face lost whatever color it had and became a pale, mean moon, bent on destruction.

"I'm no hypocrite. I have never said one thing and done another. I have never lied and I have always been a woman who keeps her word and her promises. Your mother was my sister's child and belongs in our ground near my father's and my mother's graves. She doesn't belong in some strange place beside a man who married her for all the wrong reasons."

"That man is your son," I reminded her.

"*Was* my son," she reminded me. "I will not lay out money to send her remains there. She should be with her family."

"Why couldn't you feel that way when she was alive?"

"You know the answer to that question," she said. "You're overwrought, emotionally disturbed. All of us have been taken by surprise. None of us wanted to see such a tragedy, but it's happened. It began some time ago and has finally been brought to this horrible end. The

362

least we could do for Haille's poor soul is put her remains where she has some familial company. You're too overwhelmed to discuss the matter." She turned away.

"I'll dig her up and bring her back to Sewell. Someday I will. I swear."

"When I'm dead and gone, you can do whatever you want, but I would hope that by then you would have grown up," she replied. "I'm sorry for your sorrow. Losing a mother is never easy, no matter how your mother has treated you, but we must go on and do what is right, the things that are good. Cary, see that she gets home." She left us.

I stood there for a few moments.

"She's right, my dear." Grandpa put his arm around me. "She usually is. She's a remarkable woman."

"She's an ogre," I said. "The only thing that's remarkable is how you all let her get away with bullying you." I pulled away from him and marched out of the house.

Cary followed and we got back into the truck. "There's nothing we can do," he said. "We have no money, no authority—"

"I know. Let's go home." I lowered my head.

The house was deadly quiet upon our return. I went directly to my room and lay there, thinking, remembering, crying when I had built up some tears again. May came to my door to sign her regrets. I thanked her, but I didn't want to be consoled, even by her. I was still quite bitter and angry. Later, Aunt Sara sent May up with a tray of food. I couldn't eat anything, but I let her stay with me and tried to explain and describe Mommy to her when she asked me to tell her about her.

Signing the thoughts, checking the book to be sure I was making the right gestures, made me think more about the incidents and the descriptions. For the moment it occupied my mind and my sorrow lifted a bit. I was exhausted and fell asleep early, curled up on the bed, still in my clothes. Aunt Sara stopped by to put a blanket over me. Late in the night, I heard my door open softly and looked through my cloudy eyes to see Cary tiptoe in. He stood by the bed, gazing down at me for a few moments. Then he knelt down to kiss my cheek. I pretended to be in a dead sleep.

Morning light brought a moment of disbelief, a moment of hope. Perhaps it had all been a horrible nightmare after all. But here I was waking in my clothes. Reality would not be held back. I got undressed, showered, and changed. By the time I went downstairs, Cary and May had gone to school. The house was quiet. Even Aunt Sara was gone. I made myself some coffee and toast and then I sat on the porch. About a half hour later, I saw Aunt Sara coming down the street. She was nicely dressed.

"Good morning, dear. Have you had anything to eat?"

"Yes, Aunt Sara."

"I was just at church, praying for Haille."

"Thank you," I said. I felt guilty not getting up and going with her.

"You can go with me tomorrow, if you like. It's a horrible tragedy," she continued, "but I want you to know you have a home here forever, dear. We love you."

"Thank you, Aunt Sara."

"I stopped at Laura's grave on the way home," she said with a sigh, "and told her the sad news. She was such a crutch for me whenever there was bad news. Laura had a way of filling me with hope, her smile, her loving, gentle smile. You should go to her grave and pray. You'll be comforted."

"Maybe I will," I said. That pleased her.

"Come in whenever you want, talk whenever you want," she said. I nodded and she went into the house.

I was on the porch when Cary and May returned from school. May started running the moment she spotted me. We hugged and she signed stories about her day, showing me a paper with stars all over it.

When she went in to change, Cary sat on the steps and

364

told me about school, how everyone had heard the news. "All your teachers send regards and told me to tell you not to worry about your exams. They'll provide make-ups."

"I'll take my exams on time," I said. "I don't need to make extra work for them."

"Are you sure?"

"Yes."

He thought a moment and then smiled. "I was really surprised by how many kids came over to me to ask about you this afternoon, once the news had spread. You're more popular than you think. I bet you could have run for senior class president and gotten elected, instead of that blowfish, Betty Hargate."

"Somehow, that doesn't seem too important right now."

"Yeah, I know." After a moment he said, "My father says the funeral will be Saturday. Your mother's—your mother will be back here by then."

I turned away and then I got up.

"Where are you going?" he asked, concerned.

"Just for a walk on the beach."

"Want company?"

"Not right now," I said. I threw him a smile and walked away.

It seemed as if the terns were following me, circling overhead. Against the horizon, I saw a cargo ship heading south. The ocean was calming, the tide more gentle than I had ever seen it. I walked close enough so my bare feet would be washed by the tip of the waves. The cool water felt wonderful, like some magic balm.

One of my science teachers told me that scientists believe all life came from the ocean and that was why we were all fascinated by it, drawn to it. Somehow, the sound of the surf, the feel of the spray on my face, the sharp smell of the salt air in my nostrils, and the freshness of it filling my lungs was comforting. A thousand sympathy cards, a thousand mourners in church, dozens of sermons, and hours of organ music couldn't bring any more consolation than the cry of the terns and the sight of the seemingly endless blue water. It revived me and gave me the strength to do battle with my own sadness.

The funeral was two days later. The church service for Mommy's funeral was long and very impersonal. Of course the casket was closed. The minister barely mentioned her name. Because she was a member of the Logan family, the church was filled to capacity. Grandma Olivia, regal as ever, ran the service with a nod of her head, a turn of her eyes, the lifting of her hand. Cars were drawn up instantly and the procession moved on to the cemetery. There, beside Grandma Olivia's father and mother, my mother's remains were laid. The minister said his words and pressed my hands. I was in a fog most of the time, but when I turned away from the grave, I saw Kenneth Childs off to the side watching. He wore a dark blue sports jacket and a pair of slacks. He actually looked rather handsome. His father, the judge, had been at Grandma Olivia's side throughout the funeral.

Cary was as surprised as I was to see Kenneth attending, even if he stood apart from the party of mourners. He left before I could say anything to him.

I went back to school the following Monday to take my finals. All of my teachers were sympathetic, but I asked for no special treatment. Studying helped take my mind off the tragedy. Cary worked hard to prepare for his exams as well. The day after they ended, Cary, Aunt Sara, May, and even Uncle Jacob surprised me at breakfast.

It was my birthday. I had vaguely thought about it but between studying and taking exams and all the tragedy, the event didn't have any meaning or joy for me. Somehow, they remembered and there were presents waiting for me at the breakfast table. I opened May's first. It was a tape recorder. She explained how she picked it out by herself and paid for it with her own money. She said she wanted me to tape myself practicing on the fiddle and singing. I thought it was amazing that someone so young would think so selflessly of those around her. She was truly like a little angel. I kissed and hugged her.

Aunt Sara and Uncle Jacob had bought me two gifts. One was a gold dress watch and the other was a pretty white cotton sundress with pastel embroidery trim. The hem was at least five inches above the knee. I was quite surprised, but Aunt Sara explained she had asked the shop owner for something fashionable and then had convinced Uncle Jacob it was proper and nice and something Laura would have loved.

Cary whispered that he had my gift on the sailboat.

"Taking you sailing today is my first gift," he explained. After breakfast, that was exactly where we went. He made it all look easy, and in minutes we were riding the waves, both of us screaming at the spray and laughing at the fish we saw jumping out of the water. When we settled into a calm for a few moments, he handed me a small, gift-wrapped box. I opened it to find an I.D. bracelet. On each side of the inscription, Melody, was a musical note.

"Look on the back," he said and I turned it over.

May there always be wind in your sails. Love, Cary

"This is beautiful, Cary. Thank you," I said and leaned over to give him a kiss on his cheek, but just as I did, he turned his head and my kiss fell on his lips. He smiled.

"Happy birthday, Melody," he said.

I sat back, stunned. I put on my I.D. bracelet and we continued our wonderful sail.

As we walked up from the beach later in the afternoon, I saw Cary squint and then I heard him say, "I'll be damned."

I gazed toward the house.

"What?"

367

"Kenneth Childs's jeep is in our driveway," he said. We glanced at each other and quickened our pace. When we reached the house, we hurried inside to find Kenneth sitting in the living room with Uncle Jacob and Aunt Sara.

"Well now, how was the sailing?" Uncle Jacob asked quickly.

"It was good, Dad," Cary said. We both looked at Kenneth, who sat with his legs crossed. He wore a light brown safari jacket and khaki pants with sneakers, no socks. "Well, you two know Kenneth Childs, apparently. You've visited him, I discover."

"Aye," Cary said. He nodded at Kenneth, who was concentrating on me. My heart was thumping.

"Hello," I said.

"I didn't know today was your birthday," he said. "Happy birthday."

"Thank you."

"Kenneth has come with a proposal. Seems you told him you weren't doing much this summer, Melody."

"I had plans, but they have changed."

Kenneth didn't smile. Instead, his eyes darkened.

"I've decided I need an assistant," he said, "to help with the slave work, do odd jobs around the house and the studio, take Ulysses for walks," he added with a smile. "Naturally, I would like someone who has an appreciation for art and understands a little about my needs."

"Oh," I said. I glanced at Uncle Jacob, who looked very satisfied with himself.

"It's a trip to get out to my place, I know. But I get up early every morning to do my shopping. Beat the tourists," he added looking at Uncle Jacob, who nodded. "I could swing by and pick you up. Of course, I would see to it that you were brought home."

"Well?" Uncle Jacob said.

"I guess . . ." I looked at Cary, who looked even more amazed than I felt. "Sure," I said. "I'd like that."

368

"Okay. Jacob and I have settled on a salary we both feel is fair," Kenneth said.

"I think you should discuss that with me," I blurted.

Uncle Jacob lost his self-satisfied expression and Kenneth smiled.

"Absolutely. I was thinking of a hundred a week. And food of course," he said. "Is that fair?"

"Yes, it is," I said not really knowing if it was or not, but happy I had taken control of my life.

"Then, it's settled. You can start right after the last day of school. Oh," he said standing, "you can bring your fiddle along. Ulysses likes music."

He started out, Uncle Jacob following. Cary and I gazed at each other with surprise again and then I looked at Aunt Sara who seemed confused as she stared at me. It was as if she had discovered I wasn't the person she had thought I was. It gave me a chill. I tried smiling at her. She smiled back, and then I offered to help with dinner. But it was to be a special dinner because of my birthday: she wanted to do it all herself.

We had lobster and shrimp, wonderful home fries and mixed vegetables, Portuguese bread and a chocolate birthday cake. May helped blow out the candles and sang along with everyone else. I thanked them all. Even Uncle Jacob looked calmer, softer. How complex and confused all the people in my life now had become, I thought.

Cary pleaded with me to play the fiddle and finally I gave in. I brought it down and played for them. Afterwards I went outside for a walk with Cary. The stars blazed above, barely a wisp of a cloud to block their majestic beauty.

"Why do you think Kenneth's done this?" I asked him.

"It's probably the easiest way he knows to get to know you and to eventually tell you the truth," Cary said. "I'll come by as much as I can to see if everything's all right."

"You don't have to worry so much about me."

"Of course I do," he said. He smiled. "I see you wore Laura's scarf tonight. That's nice."

369

"Somehow, because of all that's happened, I feel closer to her than ever," I said.

He smiled softly and reached for my hand. Then he turned me toward the ocean. We stood there, listening to the surf. In the roar both of us heard voices, his different from mine, of course. And then we walked back to the house under a downpour of starlight.

Epilogue
&

Who I Am

*T*he auditorium was filled to capacity. People even stood in the rear. Mrs. Topper said it was the biggest variety show they had ever had. I knew that many people had come to see and hear me play. The principal, Mr. Webster, revealed that when he came around to wish us all good luck.

"I knew a fiddle would attract interest," he said, but I understood many people hadn't come to hear the music so much as to see Olivia Logan's new granddaughter.

Everyone in the family attended, even Uncle Jacob. None of the students, except for the ones who had been at our rehearsal, had ever heard me play. Some of the girls came to laugh. I know the three witches from *Macbeth* had. They found themselves front-row seats. Behind them sat Adam Jackson with his friends and girl friends surrounding him, all woven together with giggles of ridicule.

Most of the other students in the show sang or played guitar. One student played "Carnival of Venice" on the trumpet. It was a performance that brought the house down. Two girls performed part of a scene from *The Taming of the Shrew,* and a boy juggled eggs. When one

371

splattered at his feet, the audience roared and cheered. He was embarrassed, but he continued to do his act until they stopped laughing and applauded.

After so much talent, I felt even more nervous. When it came to my performance, I waited in the wings while Mrs. Topper introduced me as the newest student. There was polite applause when I walked out onto the stage. I could feel all eyes fixed on my every movement. I was wearing the new dress Aunt Sara and Uncle Jacob had bought me. I also wore my identification bracelet, as well as what had once been Laura's charm bracelet.

I don't know what made me want to do this after so much sadness. I could easily have been excused, but I felt Papa George especially have been proud to see me on the stage. My fingers trembled so badly when I started, however, that I hit a sour note. Those waiting for me to fail roared and clapped. I stopped, took a deep breath, and looked beyond the audience. I looked back through time and saw Papa George on his patio, his pipe in his mouth. I saw Mama Arlene sitting on the lounge and then I heard Daddy shout, "Wait for me!"

I turned on the stage as if he were running from our trailer to Papa George and Mama Arlene's, and when he sat down, I lifted the bow.

The audience grew quiet. I began to play "Beautiful Dreamer" and closed my eyes to sing. When I did, I saw my Daddy's smiling face. He had loved me so much. Perhaps he never told me the truth because he had come to believe I really was his daughter, or perhaps he didn't want me to ever love him less.

I could never love him less.

The music and my singing continued. Papa George was smiling, Mama Arlene beamed.

Somewhere behind me, Mommy was chattering, complaining that, as usual, we hadn't waited for her.

Daddy told her to stop chewing on her lip and hurry over. I was about to begin another one. She joined him, and for a moment we were a family again, untouched by lies and deceits, without jealousies and fears. Our smiles

372

glowed, love was in our eyes, and I wished only that this moment could go on forever.

I played harder to keep it so.

I was singing too—my voice had never been as strong, never so filled with hope. I was so into my own performance, I had nearly finished before I realized the entire audience had joined with me, even the students who had come to mock me.

Cary was beaming. Aunt Sara was smiling broadly and Uncle Jacob was nodding as if he had seen something special. Even May, who had experienced so much less, clapped and shouted my name. Grandma Olivia looked pensive and Grandpa Samuel was shaking his head and laughing.

Way in the rear, I thought I saw Kenneth Childs standing by the door. Before the deafening applause ended, he had disappeared.

But he would be there that first morning as he had promised.

I waited for him on the porch. The morning sun wasn't very old or high and the air was still quite cool. Cary had already gone to the boat with Uncle Jacob. May was still asleep and Aunt Sara was cleaning up after breakfast, humming to herself, pausing occasionally as if she heard Laura's voice, and then nodding and smiling and going on as usual.

His jeep made the turn toward the house. A long time ago, perhaps, my mother waited like this for him. That was before the great lies began and, like some monster, took over all our lives for a long time.

This was the beginning of the end of that, I thought. This was the beginning of truth. Lies had brought me here, but I would stomp them out. There was a reason for all this then.

Kenneth Childs knew it too. He was coming to get me because in his heart, he had seen and heard a similar voice. The voice that had said, "Tell her. Let her know who she is."

HEART SONG

Prologue
❧

As a little girl, I'd spend hours looking out our trailer window, dreaming of the life I'd have when I grew older. I dreamed of all the friends I'd make, the parties I'd attend, the special boyfriends I'd bring home to meet Mommy and Daddy. Oh, if I'd only known that the coming years would bring more sadness and pain than I could ever imagine. If only I'd wished harder, dreamed longer, maybe my life would be different, maybe I wouldn't be sitting on this beach so lonely and confused.

Instead of parties and friends to occupy my time, I spend many of my days here, staring out at the ocean, thinking about Mommy and my step-daddy, about how they're gone now, dead and buried, leaving me all alone, an orphan. Of course, I'm not completely alone. I have my new family, the Logans: Grandma Olivia, Grandpa Samuel, Grandma Belinda, Uncle Jacob, Aunt Sara, and Cary, too, but they all have their own reasons for making me feel unwelcome, unwanted. After all, they hadn't asked me to come

377

live with them. In fact, in all my sixteen years they hadn't asked for me at all.

When Mommy first brought me to Provincetown after my step-daddy died, I couldn't believe she was going to leave me with strangers. I didn't know them, and, family or not, they made it clear they didn't want to know me. They couldn't get past the fact that I was Haille's child and the Logans had nothing but hate and contempt for my mother. I begged Mommy to take me with her, not to leave me grieving all alone. I had just lost the only daddy I had ever known, and now she was leaving too! But nothing I did or said would make her stay; she was determined to become a famous actress or model and she said I would just stand in her way.

At first I believed Mommy would come back for me. Surely she would miss me as much as I missed her. Didn't she cry herself to sleep each night as I did, missing Daddy, missing our old life back in Sewell, West Virginia? But no, Mommy was too self-absorbed to miss me or think of me or even to remember to call when she said she would. I finally realized that I was stuck in Provincetown for good. Oh how I hated Mommy for being so selfish, for running off with her lover Archie Marlin and leaving me with this family who hated me, hated her, and wanted me to be someone I wasn't. It seemed the only way I fit into the Logans' life was if I replaced my cousin Laura, Cary's twin who had died in a boating accident.

But I didn't want to be Laura, I wanted to be me! But who am I? When Daddy died and I learned he was really my step-daddy, I was left with a million questions. Who was my real Daddy? Did he think of me? Did he even know I existed? I thought I could find some answers with the Logans, but they refused to discuss my search for my father and became more secretive with each question I asked. Cary was the only one who would help me, and together we learned that Kenneth Childs, a local artist and friend of the family, was once in love with Mommy and could possibly be my father.

I hadn't had long to rejoice in my news when word came that Mommy had been killed in a car accident in California. Was I never to be happy again? It seemed that whenever anything good happened to me it was always followed by some horrible tragedy. What could be worse than losing Mommy? I thought a part of me died with Daddy, but it wasn't until Mommy was gone too that I realized how truly alone I was. If only I could find my real father I knew he would make things different. Better. I would have a whole new life with him, a life where I was loved and cared for, a life like the one I remembered in West Virginia. Kenneth Childs just had to be my real daddy. He had to be.

1
&

Curiosity Killed the Cat

"*I*'m leaving, Aunt Sara!" I shouted toward the kitchen as I hurried to the front door after hearing Kenneth Childs blow the horn of his jeep. Cary had introduced me to Kenneth at the beginning of the summer, and it wasn't long after that Kenneth hired me to be his assistant. Kenneth was mostly a loner and a bit of a slob, so I helped him around the house, cooking, cleaning, generally keeping him organized, as well as helping him around his art studio. As I cleaned and swept and dusted I waited, waited for him to open up to me, to tell me if I was his daughter.

When Grandma Olivia revealed that my true grandmother was really her sister Belinda, I realized that Uncle Jacob and Aunt Sara were not actually my uncle and aunt; they were my cousins, as were Cary and May. But because Jacob was my step-father's brother, I continued to call him Uncle and call Sara, Aunt Sara. Cary was happier knowing we weren't as closely blood related as we both originally thought. Ironically, this made him behave more shyly toward me, as though now that a true relationship was not forbidden as some unforgivable sin, he wasn't sure how to proceed.

I put these thoughts of Cary and our blossoming friendship behind me as I grabbed my gear and headed outside to meet Kenneth.

As usual, Kenneth's dog, Ulysses, was sitting in the rear of the jeep. His pink tongue was out, and he was panting, looking as if he were smiling in anticipation of my arrival. His ebony coat had streaks of gray running through it, especially around his snout. During one of Kenneth's rare warm moments, he told me Ulysses had become sprier since I had begun to look after him. "Despite his age," Kenneth added, for Ulysses was nearly a hundred in human years.

So far, that remark about Ulysses was the closest Kenneth had come to giving me a compliment. He had merely grunted his approval when he saw how well I had cleaned and organized his home, and he simply nodded when I did the same in the studio. Most of the time, he was so absorbed in his work, we barely spoke. He made it clear from the beginning that he wouldn't tolerate any interruptions to his concentration, so once he stepped into that studio and began something, I had to move like a ghost.

"An artist has to step out of the real world and dwell in the world of his own creation if he is to succeed," he explained. "It takes a while to get there, and when he's jarred out of it, for whatever reason, it's like starting all over again each time he goes back to what he was doing. Understand?"

I nodded and he seemed satisfied.

"Morning," he said as I stepped up and into the jeep.

"Good morning."

I had my hair brushed back and tied with one of Laura's mauve silk ribbons and I was wearing what was to become my summer uniform: a sweatshirt and dungarees and a pair of sneakers without socks. The

382

sweatshirt was navy blue with Provincetown printed on it in faded white lettering and it, too, had been Laura's.

When I had first arrived in Provincetown to live with Uncle Jacob and Aunt Sara, I felt funny wearing Laura's things. I saw how much it bothered Cary, but if I refused to wear anything Aunt Sara suggested I wear, she became very hurt. Now, Cary accepted it and I . . . I had the feeling Laura would want me to wear her clothes, even though I had never met her and knew her only from what I heard and the pictures of her I had seen.

Ulysses leaned forward for my hug and licked my face.

"Good morning, Ulysses." I laughed. "Don't eat me for breakfast."

"I think it's going to be overcast all day today. Might even rain," Kenneth said as he turned the jeep around and we bounced over the road.

For New Englanders, especially Cape Codders, I thought, the weather was the safest topic to discuss. Everyone had something to say about it, and it usually had nothing to do with politics or religion, although I had heard Judge Childs at one of Grandma Olivia's formal luncheons recently blame the Democrats for too much rain last year.

"I don't mind the thunderstorms. We had them in West Virginia, but I wouldn't want to be in a hurricane," I said.

"No. I've been in a few and they're not pleasant."

We turned onto the highway and headed out toward the Point, where Kenneth lived and had his studio. Although the jeep rode well enough, it looked as weathered and worn as an old pair of shoes, the sort you hated to give up because they were so comfortable. Despite his success as an artist, Kenneth had few of the trappings of wealth. He just didn't look as if he belonged in a shiny new luxury automobile. It would be impractical for him to drive it over the beach road to his home anyway.

I had been working for him only a little more than a week, but I already knew that he didn't spend much time relaxing by the ocean. Occasionally, he went for a walk to think through something artistic that confused him, and it was mainly from those walks and the driving he did in the open jeep that he got his bronze color. His darkened complexion brought out the hazel specks in his otherwise often dark brown eyes, especially during the morning hours, when he looked so bright and alert.

As usual, he wore a pair of leather sandals, ragged jeans, and one of his faded blue T-shirts. This one had some small holes down the right side. With his full beard looking a bit more straggly than usual, he could easily pass for a homeless man, I thought. However, he did keep his dark brown hair neatly tied in a pony tail. Most of the time, he simply had it tied with a short piece of string. Today he had it bound with a thick rubber band. He had a small gold dot of an earring in his right lobe, and wore a shiny piece of black driftwood shaped in a half moon tied around his neck with a string of tiny sea shells.

He drove quietly, his eyes fixed on the road, his face so still, it reminded me of the faces on his statues. There was just the slightest twitch in the muscles of his jaw. I thought he had the type of face that would make any woman's heart flutter when he looked her way, or even when he didn't.

Despite the cloudy sky, the air was warm. Provincetown was crowded with summer tourists. There was much more automobile traffic than usual, and even at this early hour, there were people walking along the streets. Kenneth didn't rage about the invasion of outsiders as did so many other Cape Codders I had met. He spent so little of his time in town, he didn't seem to notice or care. And then, of course, there was the prospect of his works being sold faster when the tourists arrived. Their dollars were just as good as local dollars he told me when I mentioned Uncle Jacob's attitude.

"Did you see anything in the marble block yet?" I asked as we approached the beach road that wound around and over the dunes to his home and studio.

He glanced at me quickly, looked forward, and then shook his head.

"Nope," he said. "Nothing."

"How can you be sure it will come?" I asked. It took him so long to respond, I thought he wasn't going to answer.

"It always has before," he finally said.

The first day he brought me to the studio to work for him, I saw he had a six-foot-tall by nearly four-foot-wide block of marble. He told me it had been delivered the week before.

"It's just like a blank canvas," he explained. When I said I didn't understand, he approached it, put his hand on the stone, and lowered his head as if in prayer. Then, he walked around the piece as he began his lecture.

"The ancient Greeks believed the artistic work was already in the stone. The artist's job is to free it, to bring it out."

"It's in the stone?"

"Yes," he said, almost smiling at my incredulity. "This is what is meant by the artist's vision. In time it will appear to me."

I stared at the marble, looking for some hint, some small indication of a shape within, but I saw nothing. At the time I wondered how long it would be before he saw something. According to him it had been over two weeks and he still hadn't, but he didn't seem upset or nervous about it. He had a patience, a calmness, I had already come to admire.

Although I had been trying to ask him casually

about himself all week, I still knew very little about him. He never volunteered any information and getting him to answer my questions was like pulling porcupine quills out of a hound dog.

The house and studio came into view.

"Were you always artistic?" I asked. "Even as a child?"

"Yes," he said. We pulled up to the house and he turned off the engine. Then he reached back for a bag of groceries he had bought before picking me up.

"Did my mother ever see anything you created?" I asked quickly. He didn't pause. He opened the door, the groceries under his arm.

"Everyone I know has seen something I did one time or another," he said and headed for the house. I watched him in frustration as he walked away from my questions. I keep giving him opportunities to open up a conversation about the past, I thought, and every time, he shuts the door in my face. No matter how hard I struggled to find a common ground, a topic of conversation that would lead us to talk about the past and maybe produce the revelations I expected, Kenneth either ignored me or changed the subject. So far, he had succeeded in keeping himself shut up in his work and his private thoughts.

I got out of the jeep, Ulysses following behind me. Kenneth paused at the door.

"Just put all this away and then come to the studio. I want you to prepare some clay. I've decided to do those vases for the Bakerfields to kill time while I wait for my vision. They've been after me for months and they have so much money, it's obscene. Might as well help them lessen the burden of their wealth," he added dryly and entered the house.

Were all artists as disdainful of their customers? I wondered. He acted as if he were doing everyone who liked his art work a favor, instead of being grateful for all the attention he was receiving. Hundreds, probably thousands of artists would die to be in his shoes, I thought.

I was beginning to wonder if I even liked the man who could be my father, much less ever come to love him. Was it possible for me to love him anyway? Is blood enough to bind two people? Surely love had to come from other things, the most important of which was trust. Trust was coming hard to me these days, as one by one everyone and everything I'd come to believe in had let me down.

When I decided to take the job and work for Kenneth, I hoped that just being around him, seeing how and where he lived, would make it possible for me to understand him, but Kenneth's house, furniture, clothing, and possessions were as inscrutable as everything else in his life. The day Cary first brought me to the house, I ventured up to the front windows and peered in. Cary had described Kenneth's furniture as something from a thrift store. When I looked in, I realized he hadn't been exaggerating.

I did the best I could with the thinned and frayed rugs and the worn easy chair, settee, and scratched wooden tables, however polishing and cleaning only seemed to bring out their age and damage. But the house did need a good once-over. I found cobwebs in almost all the corners and sand tracked in everywhere. The windows were clouded with salt and dust and the kitchen was a disaster. The stove was caked with grime, the stove top stained. It took me most of my first week just to get the kitchen clean enough to use. Again, I wondered if all artists were like Kenneth Childs, and if they were, why would anyone really want to be one?

His bedroom wasn't any different from the rest of the house. I could have planted flowers in the dirt under the bed and behind the dresser. I swept and washed the wooden floors. I took all of his clothes out of the closet and organized them, after I had washed

387

and ironed most of them. I emptied the dresser drawers and arranged everything in an orderly fashion and then I washed the windows and polished everything I could.

At first I really thought he was absentminded. He didn't seem to notice any difference, or if he did, he behaved as if he expected it. I had to fish for approval.

"Is the housework all right?" I finally asked. That was when he gave me his grunt.

Kenneth's lack of appreciation for my work made me furious, and I left to walk Ulysses on the beach and blow off some steam. In many ways Kenneth was as selfish and self-absorbed as my mother. He was so oblivious to others around him that I thought I could probably up and quit and it would take him three or four days to notice that I wasn't coming around anymore. But I couldn't just give up and go home. Kenneth could hold all the answers I'd been searching for. If only he'd just notice something other than his damn art. He wasn't like my step-daddy, who took the time to praise the little things I'd done around our little trailer, even things I thought were too insignificant to notice. It seemed as if nothing mattered to Kenneth but his art, and if I didn't fit neatly into the world he'd created around his talent, then I would surely be left out of his life, no matter whether I was his daughter or not.

In my short time with Kenneth I'd found that walking along the beach had a soothing effect on me. The rhythm of the waves, the sheen on the surface, the vastness of the horizon put everything in perspective and made me realize I needed to be patient, to wait calmly for answers. If Kenneth were truly my father, he would let me know in his own time, in his own way. No matter how long it took, I would wait for him to tell me the truth; it was coming as surely as the next wave would wash upon the shore.

So I swallowed my pride and returned to keep

Kenneth's house in order, prepare his meals, and help with his artistic materials. Occasionally, he left me alone in his studio, and when he did, I wandered about gazing at some of his drawings and sculptures, always looking for some clue, something that would tell me more about him. And maybe, just maybe, about myself.

The studio itself was mainly just a large room. On one side were tables and a kiln, and on the tables were his tools and materials, which I had recently reorganized. There was a beat-up tweed settee in the far corner with a driftwood table in front of it. When someone sat on the settee, a cloud of dust rose from the cushions, so I spent a lot of time vacuuming it.

The only truly curious thing in the studio was a door set into the back wall that Kenneth kept locked with a combination lock. I assumed it was where he kept his hazardous chemicals and asked him if he wanted me to do any cleaning in there. He virtually barked at my question. "No. Leave that room alone."

But I couldn't help thinking about it. Why was it necessary for him to keep that door locked? He didn't even lock his house, nor did he bother to lock the door to the studio. One afternoon, when I was alone in the studio, I tried to peek through the locked door, but it was too dark behind it to see anything. I told Cary about it and he was intrigued, too.

Today, I spent most of the morning working with Kenneth in his studio, watching him shape and mold the vases. The first few times I had been in the studio while he worked, he simply acted as if I weren't even there. Of course, after hearing his warning about it, I didn't make a sound, but twice, and now a third time, he talked while he worked, but it was always about art.

"Yes, I've been artistic for as long as I can remember," he said, returning to the conversation we'd started that morning, "but I'm primarily a sculptor now. Sculpture is probably the oldest art form and has undergone only minor variations. Real sculpting, that is," he added glancing at me. I sat on a wooden stool and watched and listened. "I don't go for this new, radical stuff, welding, using neon tubes. A gimmick is not art. An artist has to be authentic. That's the most important thing. An artist must always be true and as pure and simple in his impulse as he or she can be," he lectured.

He stepped back and looked at the vase he was shaping. It was different from any I had ever seen. It was almost shaped like an S.

"I don't recall seeing any of your works in Grandma Olivia's house," I said. "How come she doesn't have anything? She's such good friends with your father and he's so proud of you."

Kenneth paused and stiffened as if I had lashed him with a whip. He never talked about his father, nor, as far as I could tell, did they ever spend time with each other. Without answering my question, he turned back to his work.

"By using soft, yielding materials like this," he explained, "a sculptor can capture and record fleeting impressions much the way a painter does in a quick sketch."

"It's very interesting," I said.

"Everything I do is different. I don't believe true art can be mass produced. It's a contradiction to reproduce it. If it's art, it is by definition one of a kind."

"But then how would people who can't afford them ever have nice things? Not everyone can afford an original."

"Let them go to museums," he replied. Then he paused and glanced at me. "I've given things away to people who can't afford to buy them if I believed they really appreciated the art. Lawyers do pro bono work; so can artists," he added. "This town is full of business people disguised as artists. If you're in it for the money, you're a hypocrite," he added bitterly.

"But everyone needs money to eat, to live," I protested.

"That just follows," he said. "You don't make it a priority. The art, that's the priority." He paused and really looked at me. "Don't you feel that way about your music?"

"I'm not really that good," I said.

He turned away with a shrug.

"If you say you're not, you're not," he muttered. "You have to believe in yourself if you want anyone else to believe in you," he added. The hardness of his words brought tears to my eyes. I felt a lump grow in my throat and had to look away for a moment, but he didn't notice, or if he did, he chose not to pay attention.

"I'm actually working up an appetite," he said. "Why don't you go think about lunch."

I nodded and slipped off the stool. I looked back once before leaving the studio. He was working on his vase, seemingly oblivious to the questions his words brought to my mind. Would I ever find something to believe in so strongly? Kenneth had his art, Momma'd had her acting, even Uncle Jacob had his fishing business. But does believing in yourself mean you become so distanced from others that no one can believe in you?

It was the first, but far from the last time the thought occurred to me that Kenneth Childs hid behind his art, used it like a shield or a fortress to keep anyone and everyone away from touching him. Why? I wondered, and understood that when I found the answer to that, I would find the answer to everything there was between us.

Sometimes Kenneth chose to eat his lunch in his studio, staring at his work in progress and thinking as

391

he ate. If he did that, I ate my lunch on the beach with Ulysses at my side. But it was when Kenneth and I ate lunch together in the kitchen that he was the friendliest and the warmest. At these times I had the feeling he was trying to relax with me, ease himself into more personal conversations, almost the way someone might lower himself into a hot bath.

This particular afternoon, we ate together in the kitchen. I made us cheese and turkey sandwiches on Portuguese bread and some fresh lemonade.

"How do you like going to school here?" he asked.

"It's all right. I've had good teachers. Mama Arlene used to tell me school was like anything else—it's as good as you make it, as you want it to be."

"Who are this Mama Arlene and Papa George you've mentioned? I don't recall any Logan relatives by those names," he said. When he grimaced, the lines at the corners of his eyes deepened and cut through his temples, almost as if someone had taken a pencil and drawn them.

As I explained who they were, he ate, listened, and nodded.

"Despite what I have learned about my family, I still think of them as my grandparents," I concluded.

"But Papa George died and Mama Arlene moved away from Sewell?"

"Yes. I visited his grave when I visited my stepdaddy's."

He stared at me intently and then looked out the window. I thought he would grow interested in something else, the glide of a tern, the shape of a cloud, and drift off in his own thoughts as he so often did. But instead he turned back to me.

"What exactly have you learned about your own family?" he asked. My heart began to thump. Was this it? Was this the moment I had been waiting for?

"First, I was surprised to discover Mommy had

been brought up with my step-daddy, the two of them living as brother and sister. Neither of them had ever told me that."

He nodded.

"Yes," he said, "they were like brother and sister. Brothers and sister I should say, for Jacob was there, too. When I was little and I used to play with them, I didn't realize Haille had been adopted by the Logans. As far as I knew, she had always been there, part of that family. And then one day, I think I was about nine or ten, something like that, Jacob told me. He just blurted it out like kids do. He said something like. . . . Haille's not really our sister. She's a waif."

Kenneth laughed to himself and I didn't move or utter a sound for fear he would stop and I'd never learn anything about my past. He continued, "At the time I thought he said 'wave.' But he said it again, and finally I asked my father what that meant and he explained that the Logans adopted her, but I didn't learn who her mother was until much, much later. No one has a better lock on the door to their closet of skeletons than the Logans, especially Olivia Logan."

"How did my mother feel about being an orphan?"

"I think it bothered her only because Olivia made a point of reminding her," he said.

"Maybe that's why . . ."

"Why what?"

"She was so wild," I said reluctantly. I hated saying anything bad about her, especially since she was no longer here to defend herself. "She was just rebelling."

Kenneth didn't agree or disagree. He just glanced out the window again then said, "I like Olivia. She and I have a healthy respect for one another when we see each other, but she is like the dowager queen of Provincetown. There's no one with bluer blood. Haille was never impressed with all that. In a sense

393

you're right. The truth is I think she hated not knowing where she came from, hated who Olivia wanted her to be."

"No one likes not knowing who their parents are," I said. "No one wants to be an orphan."

He turned to me again, and again I held my breath.

"Sometimes, you're better off not knowing," he finally replied.

"How can you be better off not knowing?"

"It's like you have a clean slate, no one's sins to overcome or forget. You can be yourself, and anyone who can be an individual these days is lucky, especially if he can make a living at the same time. Speaking of which, I've got to go into town to get some supplies," he added and stood. "Got to earn money. I'll be back in a few hours."

I sat there fuming, feeling as if I had hit another wall of silence about my past. How could he be so cold about it? If he was my father, why didn't he just admit it? Was he afraid I would ask to move in with him? Was he afraid he would have to provide for me?

Maybe, just as he said, I was better off not knowing. I could create my father out of my own imagination and make him perfect. He would have no skeletons in his closet and no sins to weigh on both of us. He would be like some mythical god, who sailed in on a cloud of sea mist and strolled confidently into Provincetown and when he saw Mommy and she saw him they fell in love instantly and spent warm nights on the beach. One day, he was just gone and then I was born.

Now that I was here, one day or one night I would be on the beach and my mythical father would appear and tell me everything was all right. I wasn't an orphan and I had a destiny.

Dreams, I thought. They're the riches of a poor person, stashed in treasure chests buried deeply in the imagination. But are dreams enough?

I cleaned up and took Ulysses for his afternoon walk. The clouds had broken up and the sky had become a quilt with deep, large patches of blue. The breeze was still strong, making my hair dance around my face. The breakers were high and sparkling, and once again I turned to the sea for answers.

I was so lost in my own thoughts and the surf was so loud, I didn't hear the horn or the shouts until I turned to look back at the house and saw that Cary had driven up in his truck and was waving wildly from the top of a dune. I waved back and started toward him.

"What are you doing here?"

"The water is too rough today. My father decided to come in early, so I thought I'd take a ride over to see how you were doing. Where's Kenneth?"

"He went on an errand he said would take him a few hours," I replied.

Cary knelt and patted Ulysses, but kept his eyes on me.

"Has he said anything?"

"Very little. I thought he was going to say something at lunch today, but—"

"But?"

"He said some people are better off not knowing who their parents are."

"He said that?"

I nodded.

"Strange."

"Something's making him very bitter. I wish I could get him to tell me more."

"I guess he will, in time."

"I'm afraid I might be old and gray by then," I wailed.

Cary laughed and stood up, reaching out to help me climb up the knoll.

"Somehow I can't imagine you old and gray." He continued to hold my hand even though I was beside

395

him. His eyes washed over my face. "The sun's bringing out your freckles," he said. When I started to moan, he quickly added, "but that's cute."

"Cute? I'm too old to be cute," I snapped, pulling my hand from his as I started for the house.

"Hey," he called, but I just kept walking. Suddenly I felt like screaming at everyone and everything. "I'm sorry," he said catching up. "I didn't mean—"

"It's all right," I said. "It's just that I'm so sick of everyone treating me like a child."

"Huh?"

I walked slower, my arms crossed under my breasts. The blood that had rushed into my cheeks warmed my face. I couldn't explain why I was suddenly so angry. Maybe I wasn't angry; maybe I was just afraid, afraid that no one would ever take me and my questions seriously. Cary seized my arm at the elbow and I spun around.

"If you want," he said, "I'll just confront him. I'll just come right out and ask him. I'm not afraid of him," he bragged.

"If he won't tell me anything, what makes you think he would tell you?"

"Then maybe you shouldn't work here anymore," he said.

"Maybe I shouldn't. Maybe I shouldn't have let you talk me into coming back to the Cape in the first place."

I had run away when Grandma Olivia told me about Mommy being raised a Logan. I had gone back to Sewell, but that was when I found out Papa George had died and Mama Arlene had gone to live with her sister in North Carolina. I had no one in Sewell, either, except my best friend Alice Morgan. But I couldn't live with her. Her mother couldn't understand how a daughter of hers would befriend someone raised in a trailer park.

"Of course you should have come back. This is where you belong," Cary insisted. "People care about you here."

"People care about me? I've got a grandmother who wishes I would wash out to sea so I don't embarrass her; an uncle, your father, who thinks I'm the daughter of Satan; a man who could be my father but is unwilling to tell me—"

"I care about you," he said. "A lot."

I tried to hold on to my anger but instead I took a deep breath and let my shoulders sag. I believed Cary, but somehow it wasn't the same. I needed someone to love me the way my daddy did. Of course this thought made me feel guilty, as if I were trying to replace him in my heart. But wasn't that exactly what I was doing?

"It's all just confusing," I said. "Confusing and frustrating."

He nodded.

"Well, you've been here a while. You clean his house, see his things. Are there any hints, clues? Pictures, letters?"

"Nothing I've seen." And then I remembered. "There's only one place I haven't looked."

"Where's that?"

"Remember I told you about that door he has locked in the studio?"

"Oh, yeah. Let me look at it," he said. My heart began to pound.

"Kenneth doesn't like anyone going into his studio when he's away."

"He keeps it unlocked, doesn't he?"

"Yes, but—"

"We won't touch anything. Let me just look," he said.

I looked toward the dune road and thought about Cary's plan. Kenneth had said he would be away for hours.

"Okay," I said, "but don't touch any of his things in the studio. Even though it's usually a mess, he would know if something had been moved an inch."

"Fine," Cary said.

We walked to the studio, pausing momentarily to look into the fish pond.

"When did he add the turtle?" Cary asked.

"I don't know. Maybe last weekend. He calls him Shell."

Cary laughed and we went into the studio. He saw the block of marble and asked about it immediately. I explained the artistic vision just the way Kenneth had explained it to me, but Cary squeezed his eyebrows toward each other, smirked, and asked, "How can you see anything in a block of marble?"

"You can if you have an artist's eyes," I said. He shrugged again and then went to the closet door. For a few minutes, he studied the lock and the hasp.

"Just a combination lock, but it would take forever to figure out the combination. However . . ."

"However what?" I asked coming up beside him.

"This hasp is attached with only these four screws. It would be easy to unscrew them, take off the hasp, leave the lock in place, and open the door. I could do it in five minutes," he claimed. I started to shake my head. "And I can put it back just the way it is so no one would notice. It's easier than finding seaweed on the beach."

"No," I said, turning away. He seized my wrist.

"You haven't gotten him to say anything important and you haven't found anything that would give you any clues."

"He wouldn't have put a lock on it if it wasn't very private," I said.

"You have a right to know about yourself. No one has a right to keep that under lock and key, do they? Well?" he pursued.

I thought a moment.

398

"You can put it back just the way it is?"

"Easily." He reached into his pocket and produced his Swiss Army pocket knife to show me the small screwdriver. "Okay?" he asked.

I looked at the lock again. Maybe there was nothing behind this door. Maybe it was just filled with some of his vases or statues, but Cary was right. I would always wonder.

"Okay," I said. He smiled and put the screwdriver to work. In minutes, just as he had predicted, the hasp came free of the wall and with it, the lock. He folded his knife and turned the handle.

"Ready?"

I took a deep breath and nodded. He opened the door. It was a deeper closet than I had anticipated. Apparently, no one had been in it for a long time. There were cobwebs across the doorway. Cary cleared them out of our way and we stepped into the closet. We saw an easel on the right, a carton filled with brushes, and another carton filled with carving tools beside it. There was an artist's smock hanging from a hook on the wall above the cartons.

"Nothing unusual," I said, my voice tinged with disappointment.

"Isn't there a light in here?" Cary asked as he groped through the air for a pull chain. He found a string and pulled it to turn on a single, naked bulb dangling from the ceiling. The illumination washed away the shadows and revealed a pile of canvases under a white sheet. The sheet was caked with dust. Cary curiously lifted one edge and gazed under it, but I had been hoping we would find a box of letters from Mommy or a diary, something I could read to discover information.

"It just looks like some pictures of someone, but I can't tell anything. I'll hold this up. You pull one out," he instructed.

"We shouldn't, Cary. He's going to know."

"We'll just put it back the way we found it," he said. "Go on," he urged. "Aren't you curious?"

I was, but I was also afraid. Ulysses stood in the doorway behind us, watching, and to me it was as if he were wondering why I had betrayed his master.

"Let's just back out of here and put the hasp back in place, Cary."

"We're in here already; we might as well look at everything," he insisted and held the sheet up with one hand while he worked the first canvas off the top of the pile. As it came out, I stepped closer.

First, we saw a pair of legs and then, as more and more of the canvas was revealed, we saw it was a naked woman sprawled on a beach blanket. The picture was done in a most realistic style; it was practically a photograph. Cary got so excited, he dropped the sheet entirely and used both hands to lift the canvas and place it on the floor.

We both stared down, neither of us able to speak, for we both recognized the woman. She couldn't be mistaken. It was Mommy, and the picture was done when she was much younger, perhaps in her late teens.

"Wow," Cary said.

"Put it back, Cary," I urged, my throat quickly closing. Instead, he reached in and pulled out the next canvas. This, too, was of Mommy, only in this one, she was standing, completely naked, gazing at the ocean. It had been drawn and painted very precisely. I recalled the small birthmark just below her left hip.

Cary said nothing as he continued to look at the other paintings.

"They're all of her," he said. "Different poses, different places. Here's one on a boat. She could have been a Playboy centerfold."

"Put it all back!" I cried, tears burning my eyes. I turned away. Suddenly, the small room had become stifling and I couldn't breathe. I rushed out and threw

400

myself onto the settee. Cary put everything back the way it was and shut off the closet light.

"Are you all right?" he asked.

"No," I wailed. My tears were freely carving wet lines down my cheeks.

Cary hurried to replace the hasp on the door, and after he had tightened the last screw, he came to me. I raised my eyes and wiped the tears away, a pit of bitterness growing inside me.

"You were right. Those paintings are so explicit they belong in one of those magazines. No wonder he's keeping them behind a locked door."

"Well, no one ever said your mother was shy," Cary offered with a smile.

"Thanks for reminding me," I spit back. I got up and charged out of the studio, my arms folded, my head down. Cary hurried behind, but I kept walking. Ulysses trotted alongside.

"I'm sorry. I just don't know what to say. I was just as surprised as you were."

I stopped by his truck and stared out at the sea.

"Obviously, they were very close when they were younger, for her to have done that. That must mean something," Cary continued.

"Maybe," I said. "Maybe she was just being his model. She never told me anything so I can only guess."

"Just come out and ask Kenneth," Cary suggested.

"And tell him what? That I went spying in his closet?"

"Well . . ."

"I don't want him to hate me," I said. "He'd never tell me anything then." I spun on Cary. "I don't want anyone to know about this."

"Sure," he said quickly. "Who would I tell, anyway?"

"It's not that you would tell anyone. It just might slip out one day."

401

"It won't," he promised.

"It would be better if you weren't here when he returns," I said nervously, checking the road into town for signs of Kenneth's jeep.

"Okay. We can talk about it all later, if you want."

I nodded. Quickly, before I realized what he was going to do, Cary reached out and put his arms around me to draw me closer and hug me.

"Everything will be all right," he promised. Then he got into his truck and started the engine. He smiled and waved as he backed it up and drove away. Ulysses and I stood watching the truck bounce over the dune road until it disappeared from sight.

I returned to the house to do some cleaning, and nearly an hour and a half later, I heard the sound of Kenneth's jeep and the quick honking of its horn. Curious, I came out of the house, dust rag still in hand, and watched as Kenneth drove his jeep faster than usual down the dune toward the house. He shut off the engine and leaped over the driver's-side door without even bothering to open it. From where I stood I could see that he had a small package under his arm. I had never seen him so excited.

"I've got it!" he cried, his face beaming.

"What is it?" I asked nodding at the package.

"Not this," he said. "This is just a new tool I needed," he added quickly and took my hand. "Come, quickly!"

"Where?" I asked, starting to laugh at his newfound enthusiasm.

He pulled me along, around the corner of the house and back toward the studio. He thrust open the door but stopped after we entered. We were facing the block of marble. He stood in the doorway, still holding my hand and staring at the marble block. Then he nodded and said, "Yes, yes, yes." He looked at me, nodded again, and looked at the marble.

"What is it?" I asked, now holding my breath.

"The vision. It finally came to me. It happened as I was on my way back home. I was thinking about you."

"Me?"

"And then I looked toward the ocean and it just burst before me, the whole finished work."

"But why me?"

"Because you're the center of this work," he said, nodding at the marble.

"I am?"

"Sit," he ordered, and pulled me toward the settee. I did as he instructed and watched him pace around the block, as I'd seen him do a hundred times before. Except this time there was a peculiar light shining in his eyes.

"Out of a wave emerges this beautiful young woman. I want to catch that transition, that birth from the water, which I will call, The Birth of Neptune's Daughter!" he exclaimed, whirling about to face me.

I had never seen Kenneth's face filled with more excitement. His eyes were positively luminous. He seemed so full of energy, I thought he might just burst before my eyes. The veins strained in his neck and around his temples.

"It's almost as if the muses, the gods and goddesses of art, sent you here," he declared.

I smiled. At last he was looking at me, talking to me, not at me, not through me, or above me. He stepped forward and took my hands into his, pulling me to my feet again.

"Kenneth are you sure?"

"Just stand there," he said bringing me to the marble block. He placed me where he wanted me and then stepped back and stared so intently at me, I couldn't help blushing. He nodded. "Yes, yes," he said. "This is it."

"I don't think I completely understand," I said.

"You will. First, I'll draw the picture and then I'll

403

figure out a method, materials I want to use to make a mockup. You'll be more than just the model. You'll be my assistant. I'll show you how to start on the block and you'll do some of the preliminary work. Artistic assistants often help with the rough cutting and chiseling."

"Model?" I said.

"Of course. It's you I see emerging. Think about it. You came back here to start a whole new life. It is as if you were emerging from the sea. You've been reborn."

He was so excited he could hardly contain his words.

"I'll explain more to you as we go along, but this work is more than just a classical piece about the god of the sea; it's about the birth of femininity, of a woman, the depiction of a young girl's transition into maturity, blossoming, blooming, exploding in her sexuality. Just the way you are right now," he added.

I didn't think it was possible for me to turn any more crimson than I had, but my skin felt as if it were on fire.

"Me?" I said again, horrified at the thought that Kenneth could see all those emotions brewing inside me.

"Of course you. This might very well be the most important work of my whole life, the pinnacle of my career," he said. He grew serious as he stepped closer. "You'll do this with me, won't you? You're not too shy or afraid?"

"I—"

"I'll take my time with you and I'll show you everything you need to know every step of the way." He took my hands into his again. "We're going to do this together. You'll be part of something very significant, Melody."

I nodded, slowly, still in a daze, bowled over by his exhilaration.

"We'll start tomorrow," he said. "First, I want to

spend some time thinking, envisioning. I want to go down to the sea and stare at the waves until I get the shape and the movement I need. In the morning, I'll show you how to use the tools for the rough cut. You can practice on another piece first, okay?"

"I guess," I said. He laughed and slapped his hands together. Then he went back to the marble block and put his hands on it as if he drew some sort of energy and power from it. He stood there with his eyes closed and whispered loudly.

"Yes, yes. I can feel it. This is the vision I've been waiting for."

I guess I was wide eyed, for when he looked at me again, he laughed.

"I'm scaring you, huh?"

"No, I'm just surprised," I said. "Is this what happens to all artists when they get an idea?"

He laughed.

"I don't know about other artists; I know only about myself." He approached me and again took my hands into his as he fixed his intense eyes on me. "Are you afraid you can't be a model?"

"I've never done anything like that."

"We'll go about it slowly. I won't rush you into anything until you're comfortable because if you're not comfortable, you'll be sending out the wrong emotions and I won't be able to create what's in my mind and what's in the marble," he said. "But once we start," he added, smiling, "you'll see it's nothing to be afraid of or ashamed of. You'll feel the power of your own intrinsic beauty and you'll flourish."

His words exhilarated me and I wondered if this was what he had said to my mother? Was this the way he had gotten her to model? Or was there something else between them, the love I suspected? Perhaps what Kenneth really had discovered was his way, his path to follow to tell me about himself and about me and all that had occurred.

405

I couldn't deny that the idea made me tremble. He must have felt my hands shaking. He squeezed a bit tighter and held his gaze on me firmly as he continued.

"Few people really understand the artistic vision," he said. "Or appreciate it. Somehow, I think you do."

"Why?" I asked, curious to know what he had seen in me.

"It's just a feeling I have, an instinct, and my instincts have always been accurate, especially when it comes to people," he added, his eyes darkening to tell me some of those accurate instinctive readings were unpleasant.

But what was he really telling me with these words and those eyes? Was he saying I would appreciate the artist's instinct because I had inherited it from him?

"For now," he continued, "I think it would be best if you didn't mention this to anyone else, especially your uncle Jacob and the rest of the Logans. Their thinking, like too many others', I'm afraid, is quite narrow. They just wouldn't understand. Can you do that? Can you keep a secret for a while?"

"I'm used to secrets," I said pointedly, but he just smiled and nodded.

"Good." He turned back to the marble. "I know I haven't been this excited in years," he said. And then he looked at me again, "And I know now it's because of you."

I looked at the block of marble and just like him, I suddenly saw that it was more than stone.

It was possibly the way to my father and to the truth, and to the happiness I hoped lay just behind it.

I couldn't wait to begin.

2

A Model's Life

All the way back to Uncle Jacob's house, Kenneth talked continuously about his new art project, barely pausing to take a breath between sentences. He described the mythological background, the idea of creating Neptune's daughter, how art helps us to understand problems in the modern world and why he believed the artist was the only true prophet. Sitting in his jeep as we drove along, I felt as if I were sitting in a college classroom. He made it all sound so interesting. I noticed when he spoke about the things that were close to his heart, his whole face brightened; he seemed to rise out of his visions and ideas and become more vibrant. I was too shy to say it, but often, when I played my fiddle and closed my eyes, I felt just the way he felt now. Maybe that was the link that would bind us together, I thought, our mutual artistic loves.

"I'll see you bright and early in the morning," he declared when we stopped at the house. "Tomorrow, we'll begin."

"Okay."

407

He grabbed my elbow as I started to open the door.

"And remember what I said. Let this just be something between us for now, okay?" His eyes were full of warning.

I nodded and stepped out of the jeep, feeling his eerie gaze on my back.

"Don't do anything different with your hair. It's perfect as it is," he said. I started to smile. "It's the way I saw her in my vision. Bye," he said and drove off.

What did he mean? It's the way he saw *her* in his vision? Was he looking at me, as I had thought, or was he seeing some mythical creature, some figment of his imagination, or even a young girl from his past, created out of memories? Wasn't I the most important thing in his life right now? Or was it Mommy taking away my happiness from beyond the grave? I was more confused than ever when I turned and walked into the house.

Uncle Jacob was coming down the stairs as I entered. He looked as if he had been taking a nap. His hair was disheveled, his face was full of crinkles, and his eyes were glassy. The shadows on his unshaven chin resembled bruises. The sleeves of his shirt were rolled to his elbows and he wore his fur-lined slippers over his bare feet. He paused on the steps and stiffened when I gazed up at him.

"He ought to bring you home a little earlier so you can help Sara with dinner," he said.

"I'm sorry. I'll tell him."

Uncle Jacob grunted.

"So, what's he been up to?" he asked. "Did he come forth and confess his sins yet?"

"I don't know about any sins."

He smirked with skepticism.

"When's he supposed to pay you?"

"Every two weeks is what he told us when he first came to the house," I reminded him.

"Remember to put half in the kitchen pot," he countered and continued down the steps toward the living room.

"Is that you, dear?" I heard Aunt Sara call from the kitchen doorway, where she stood wiping her hands on her apron. She came forward, looking very excited.

"Hi, Aunt Sara."

"I have some news for you." She stepped forward and in a loud whisper asked, "Did Jacob tell you?"

I shook my head.

"Olivia called this afternoon to invite you to lunch on Saturday. Just you!" she exclaimed girlishly.

"Just me? Why?"

"I don't know dear, but isn't that nice? She's sending Raymond with the car to pick you up at twelve sharp. You'll wear something nice, one of those sun dresses. Maybe the one with the yellow tear drops and the white collar?"

I really hadn't gone through Laura's entire wardrobe and didn't recall the dress, but I nodded anyway because Aunt Sara acted as though I had worn it.

"I'll just go wash up and then come down to help you, Aunt Sara."

"Everything's done," she said. "Don't hurry. Rest. You're a working girl now." Her smile froze. "Laura always wanted to be working, but Jacob didn't want her to do anything involving tourists. She liked Kenneth, especially his paintings and statues. She would have wanted to work for him, too," she added, sighing deeply as she returned to the kitchen.

I gazed into the living room and saw Uncle Jacob sitting in his chair, staring out at me. He had the strangest look on his face, a dreamy, far-off expression, softer than I had ever seen. He realized he was staring and quickly dropped his gaze to the newspaper in his lap. I hurried up the steps to my room and saw that the ladder to Cary's attic hideaway was down. That meant he was up there working on his models. I was only in my room for a few moments when May appeared at my door. Most evenings she would come to my bedroom to excitedly relay the events of her day.

May continued attending her special school during the summer and had only a short ten-day break before the start of the regular school year. Her summer day was abbreviated, but she would rather have had the summers off just like the kids who attended the regular public school. Ever since I started working for Kenneth she had been begging me to take her to see his studio. Uncle Jacob had forbidden it up until now, telling her she couldn't miss a day of her school just to waste time watching me clean someone else's house and make someone else his lunch. But with Cary on the fishing boat and me away most of the day, she had to spend more time alone than ever. She was starved for conversation and attention by the time Cary and I returned from work each day.

As usual, May's hands went a mile a minute, signing questions, telling me about things she had done, and expressing her desire to accompany me to Kenneth's studio.

I promised I would ask Uncle Jacob again, but she didn't look hopeful. In fact she looked downright sad. May was smaller than most girls her age, and it seemed to me that she was even paler and thinner these days. I thought she resembled a flower without enough rain and sunshine, withering under dark, oppressive clouds. In her large, shadowed hazel eyes lingered more dark sufferings than a child her age should know, I thought. She lived in a silent world, hearing only her own thoughts, craving smiles, wondering about the sound of laughter.

It occurred to me that May didn't even know what

it was like to hear someone cry. Of course, from the looks on people's faces, she knew happiness from sadness, anger from approval, but for me, someone who loved to make music and listen to it, the idea of being deaf seemed overwhelming. The eternal silence would drive me mad, I thought, and wondered what made May so strong. Sometimes her strength worked against her, and people forgot that she still needed little joys in her life. How could Uncle Jacob refuse her anything? He must have beach sand in his veins instead of blood, and a heart made from an old barnacle.

I told May about the things I had done all day, though I didn't reveal that Cary had visited. I was sure she would be upset that he hadn't offered to take her along. As I described my walks along the beach with Ulysses and even the cleaning I did in Kenneth's house, May stood looking at my hands as though I were drawing the most wonderful pictures of fun. Her eyes were wide and she nodded and smiled to keep me going. She laughed aloud when I described how Ulysses hid under Kenneth's jeep whenever the sky filled with thunder and lightning. When she asked me about Kenneth's paintings and statues, I looked away in shame, thinking about Mommy in Kenneth's secret paintings.

For the first time I realized that Mommy had lived a whole other life here. She had made friends she had never mentioned, especially boyfriends. How could she keep secret growing up at that big, wonderful house, living on the beach with the sailing and the swimming and all the parties? How could she drive those memories down so deeply that she never even slipped and mentioned something nice to me? Didn't she have any happiness here? Wasn't there anything that she had longed to see again, to hear again? The smell of the ocean was so strong, it soaked into your very being. I was sure of that because it already

411

seemed to be part of me. How hateful and traumatic her flight from Provincetown must have been for her to keep so many secrets, I thought.

May tapped me on the shoulder. I had become so absorbed with my musings, I forgot that she was standing there. I smiled at her and then began to describe the vase Kenneth was creating. She nodded, thought about something for a minute, and then asked me to wait right there in the room until she returned. She hurried out and I went to the closet to search for the dress Aunt Sara had described. I found it hanging all the way in the back of the closet. She was right: it was a happy, bright dress, perfect for an afternoon. Moments later, May returned with a drawing pad in her hands. She hesitated, her eyes filled with trepidation, and then handed it to me.

Curious, I sat on the bed and lifted the cover. What I found amazed me. In the pad were excellent India-ink drawings, many of which were of me. There were pictures of me standing on the beach, pictures of me in the kitchen, and pictures of me holding May's hand and walking with her down the street toward town.

I quickly signed how wonderful I thought her pictures were, and then she shook her head.

"What?" I asked, even more curious. She took the pad from me and flipped the pages to the end to show me the inside of the back cover. I gazed down at it and felt my blood freeze in my veins.

"I don't understand," I signed. "Aren't these your drawings?"

She shook her head and I looked at the words scribbled on the inside back pages again.

"But—"

I flipped through the pad, gazing more closely at the drawings I thought were drawings of me. I guess it was just that I assumed it was I who had been depicted. How strange . . . eerie. This pad had belonged to

412

Laura. She had been the artist and she had drawn pictures of herself and pictures of herself with May.

Somehow, maybe because of the way Aunt Sara treated me and spoke to me, or because I was living in her room and wearing her things, I had mistaken Laura for myself in these drawings. At this moment I could appreciate and understand what Aunt Sara was experiencing when she looked at me with sad eyes that told me I reminded her of Laura.

"Do you draw, too?" I asked May. She shook her head and asked me if I wanted to show the pictures to Kenneth.

"Yes, maybe I will," I signed, which pleased her. I perused the rest of the pad and found a picture of Cary that intrigued me. In it he was standing on the beach, holding his hands out while sand was falling through his fingers. It was as if he were saying that something he thought was important really had no meaning.

Just then, as if on cue, I heard Cary coming down the ladder. May saw the direction my eyes had taken and turned in anticipation, too.

"Hi," he said. "How did the rest of the day go?"

"Fine."

"But nothing . . ."

"No."

"What do you have there?" he asked stepping through the doorway.

"May brought me these pictures Laura drew and gave her. She wants me to show them to Kenneth."

He saw that I had turned to the page containing the picture of him.

"I gave May that pad the week Laura died," he said, his dark eyes gone bleak, "so she would have something to cherish, but it's not the sort of thing I wanted to show everyone. I don't mind your seeing it, but Laura was very choosy about whom she would show

413

those drawings. Nobody in school saw them, not even her art teacher, and if she wanted Kenneth to see them, I'm sure she would have shown them to him herself."

"Okay," I said, trying to hide my nervous laughter.

"What's funny?"

"I thought May had done them and was bringing them to me to show her own work." I answered, though I didn't add that I thought they were pictures of me.

He signed to May, telling her she should keep the pad in her own room where it belonged. She looked disappointed, but took the pad back when I handed it to her.

"Did you deliberately pose for any of them?" I asked. It was more than just curiosity. I wanted to know what he felt like modeling for someone, but he wasn't willing to talk about it.

"For a few," he admitted. "I'm starving," he quickly added to change the subject. "Is dinner ready?"

"I think so. Did you hear about my invitation to Grandma Olivia's?"

"As soon as I walked in the door. It was the first thing Ma told me," he said.

"Why just me?"

He shrugged.

"She wants to get to know you better?"

I smiled skeptically.

"Maybe Grandma's easing up. Old age," he added with a grin.

We all went down to dinner, where I helped serve. I noticed throughout the meal that Uncle Jacob was staring at me from time to time. Finally, before we were finished, he stopped chewing, drank some water, and leaned back.

"You mean to tell me," he said as if we were still in the middle of our earlier conversation, "you've been

414

there over a week and he hasn't mentioned nothin' about Haille?"

Cary shifted his eyes to me quickly.

"He spoke of her," I said, "but he didn't say they had been romantically involved."

"Romantically involved?" Uncle Jacob said with a laugh. He shook his head. "Romantically involved for Haille meant sneaking behind some boat house."

"Jacob!" Aunt Sara said. "Shame on you speaking of the dead that way, and especially in front of young people."

"I'm sure they've heard a lot worse," he said, glancing at me and then at Aunt Sara. "I'm just sayin' how it was."

"There's a time and place for such talk and you know it's not at the dinner table, Jacob Logan," she insisted.

He turned a little crimson at the reprimand. The tension was so thick, it felt as if we were sitting in a roomful of cobwebs. Yet I thought I knew the underlying purpose to all these questions about Kenneth and me.

"I'm sorry I'm a burden to you, Uncle Jacob," I said. "I know you would like Kenneth Childs or someone to admit to being my father so he would have to look after me," I said firmly.

"Well that isn't my whole reason, but it would be the right thing to do, wouldn't it?" He looked across the table at Aunt Sara. "The Bible tells us to suffer the children. It means our own, Sara."

"She is our own," Aunt Sara said. "God brought her for a purpose, Jacob," she retorted with more grit than I had seen or heard in her voice since first coming to their home. She looked as if she would heave a plate at him if he uttered one syllable of disagreement.

Uncle Jacob just grunted and mumbled about being finished. He left the table.

415

I helped clean up and while I washed the silverware and dishes, Aunt Sara told me not to mind anything Uncle Jacob said.

"What he says today, he regrets tomorrow," she told me. "He's always been like that. That man has swallowed more of his own sour words than anyone I know. It's a wonder he doesn't walk around all day with a bellyache."

"He's not completely wrong, Aunt Sara. People shouldn't have children and then leave them for someone else to look after. Even though you've been more of a mother to me than my own mother, she shouldn't have just dumped me here," I added. Aunt Sara's eyes filled with tears. She turned to hug me.

"You poor child. You never think of yourself as being dumped here, understand? And don't you ever think of yourself as being an orphan, Melody. Not while I have a breath left in my body, hear? We've both got holes in our hearts and we're plugging them up for each other," she said and kissed my forehead. I hugged her back and thanked her before going upstairs. Cary poked his head through the attic trapdoor as soon as I reached the landing.

"Want to see the model I just finished?" he asked.

"I promised May I'd play Monopoly with her."

"So, you will," he said. I looked toward May's doorway and then hurried up the ladder into the attic.

The attic hideaway wasn't much bigger than my room. The biggest piece of furniture up there was the table on which Cary worked meticulously on his model ships. Above the table were shelves filled with the models he had completed over the years. There were also a small sofa and some boxes and sea chests sharing the space.

Cary knew a great deal about ship building from studying the historical models he had completed. There were Egyptian, Greek, and Roman models, even Chinese junks. He had clipper ships and battle ships, steamships, tankers, and luxury liners, including a replica of the *Titanic*. His newest model was a nuclear submarine.

"Look," he said drawing me closer. Carefully, like a surgeon operating on a human heart, he snapped off one side of the submarine and showed me the interior. I couldn't believe the details, even down to tiny lights.

"It's beautiful, Cary. All of your work is tremendous. I wish you would let more people see it."

"I don't do it for people. I do it for myself," he said sharply. "It's almost like . . . like why Kenneth painted those portraits of your mother."

The smile left my face and I thought again about Kenneth's proposal for me to become his model. I wondered if I could confide in Cary, or if he would get so upset about it, he would do something to stop me. In my mind I still saw the whole thing as Kenneth's way to reveal his deep secrets and perhaps bring me truly home. I wasn't willing to risk losing that just yet. The other thoughts, of me being like my mother and posing just like a model in a sleazy magazine, I pushed to the back of my mind.

"A real artist like Kenneth doesn't look at someone the same way," I offered, but turned as I spoke so I could gaze out the small window toward the ocean in the distance. The moonlight cut a pathway over the silvery surface. "He sees something else."

"What?" Cary pursued.

"He sees beauty; he sees deep meaning."

"That's hogwash. A man sees one thing when he looks at a naked woman."

"Cary Logan, that's not true!" I snapped, turning sharply on him. "Does a doctor see one thing when he looks at a woman patient?"

"Well no, I guess not," he admitted.

417

"Then it all depends on his purpose for looking, doesn't it?" I asked sharply, not knowing whom I needed to convince more, Cary or myself.

Cary shook his head.

"I'm sorry, Melody. I can't imagine looking at you with your clothes off and thinking about anything else but you. My hand would shake so much, the paintbrush would go all over the page," he added smiling. The way he looked at me made me blush all over. It was as if I were really naked and standing in front of him.

"That's because you're not an artist," I insisted. "They have more control of themselves."

"I guess so," he said. Then he laughed. "I don't think I'd want to be an artist if that's what happens to them."

I stamped my foot in frustration.

"You're just like any other boy, Cary Logan." I started toward the door, but he reached out and grabbed my wrist.

"Whoa. Set anchor for a minute, will ya. I'm just teasing you a little. I thought you believed we were all too serious in this house. Didn't you tell me that once?"

I hesitated, the smoke I imagined coming out of my ears, disappearing.

"Yes, I did, and I still say it."

"So?"

"That doesn't mean you should tease me like that," I said. "Don't joke about anything when it comes to Kenneth. You of all people know how sensitive I am about it all."

"Okay." He let go of my wrist and raised his hand. "I promise."

I relaxed.

"I better get down to May."

"Okay. But you didn't tell me anything. What happened when he returned?"

418

"He was all excited," I said. "He had an idea for his block of marble."

"You mean he saw the shape in the stone finally?"

"Yes."

"What's the shape?"

"He calls it Neptune's daughter. I'll know more tomorrow and the day after. He's going to draw it first."

"Artists really are strange," Cary said shaking his head.

"You better stop saying things like that, Cary Logan. You're an artist, too. All this is creative," I said sweeping my hand toward the shelves of models.

"It's just something I do to take up time, but it's really what I'd like to do someday—build ships. I want to build custom sailboats for people. You know I'd rather do that than anything," he admitted.

"Did you do what I said? Did you tell your father?"

"Yeah." He dropped his gaze and turned away.

"He disapproves, of course," I concluded, "but did he see how much you wanted to do it?"

"We've been fishermen forever in this family. He has this religious belief in tradition."

"What you want to do still has to do with the sea, doesn't it?"

"It's not the same thing to him," he said.

"Well, it's not fair. It's not his life, it's yours. You've got to do what you want to do," I asserted.

Cary nodded, but smiled.

"Sure. Only one small thing. It takes money."

"Well, I'm getting a lot of money someday. You remember what Grandma Olivia told me about my inheritance. And when I get it, I'm giving you what you need to start your business."

"You are?"

"Yes," I said firmly. "Uncle Jacob will probably hate me a little more, if that's possible, but I don't care," I said. Cary beamed.

"For someone who has had such a hard time of it, you're the most generous, sweetest person, I know," he said as he stood up from his desk. Because of the size of the room, we were only inches apart. He took my hand in his.

"I'm glad you're not my uncle Chester's daughter, Melody. I'm glad you're only a distant cousin, at most. No one can condemn me for feeling more for you," he confessed. I saw that it took all his courage, but these were words that had been hanging between us for months now. I knew that having feelings for your cousin, even a distant one, was supposed to be wrong, but neither Cary nor I could hold back our hearts.

I didn't speak. Our eyes seemed incapable of moving away from each other's faces. Slowly, almost as slowly as the turning of the earth, our mouths moved toward each other until our lips grazed and then gently pressed together. His left hand moved to my shoulder and his right to my waist. My hands remained at my sides.

I was both surprised and a little frightened by the small bursts of heat I felt coursing through my body. It was as if warm massaging fingers moved under my clothing, tracing down between my breasts, over my stomach. He slipped his lips off mine and kissed my cheek as his right hand began to move up my side, over my ribs. I raised my hand quickly and caught his just as it touched my breast. We stood there, gazing into each other's eyes, neither moving, neither speaking, each feeling as if we had opened some door to a forbidden room. It was the moment when we would decide to go further or softly close the door again between us.

"I can't help myself," he simply admitted. Was I to say the same thing or was I to bear the responsibility of stopping something that we both knew would bring more problems into this already unstable family? If I

420

lifted my hand from his, I would be pulling him into that room. I wanted to, but I also wanted to be confident that it was right. My heart was thumping so hard, I thought I would lose my breath. His lips had tasted sweet and the warmth that trickled down my spine and through my body was a delightful feeling. Nothing about our kiss was unpleasant to me.

The moonlight reflecting off the ocean lit the world outside the small window. It was as if a giant candle had been lit on a birthday cake to celebrate this birth of love, if it truly was love. What was that special *yes* that followed the surge of excitement in your body? How did you know when the kiss that tingled was a greater kiss than any other? Where were the bells, the trumpets, the voices of angels that were supposed to sound when true love appeared?

These thoughts zipped through my mind with lightning speed. Meanwhile, Cary's courage grew. His kisses became more intense, firmer, and his other hand moved up to caress my shoulders. I felt my resistance soften as I kissed him back and let him turn my body neatly into his. He started to move me with him toward the sofa. What would happen? What would we do? I wanted to go along almost out of a curiosity about myself, to see what I was capable of wanting, of doing.

But just as we reached the side of the sofa and were about to lower ourselves to it, we heard May's cry at the bottom of the ladder.

Cary moaned his great disappointment and his body tightened with frustration.

May called again for me. She had gone into my room looking for me and then realized I was upstairs. We heard her start up the ladder. Quickly, we parted and I straightened my hair. There was no way I could quickly diminish the flush in my face, but I was sure May wouldn't understand. She poked her head through the attic doorway.

Cary quickly signed his anger. She looked confused, hurt.

"Don't Cary. I promised her I would play with her."

He turned away and took a deep breath. I put my hand on his shoulder and he looked at me.

"She's all alone much of the day, shut up in a soundless world. We're all she really has right now," I said.

He nodded, looking ashamed. Then he shook his head and lifted his eyes to me.

"You're just like Laura. You bring out the good in all of us," he said.

I know he meant it to be a big compliment, but it left me cold. When would he stop comparing me to his dead twin sister? Did he have these feelings for her as well? Did everyone see me as someone else? Was that to be my fate? Kenneth saw me as some mythical goddess, Aunt Sara saw me as her lost daughter, and even May must have seen some of Laura in me to have brought me those drawings earlier. Perhaps I wouldn't be able to be my own person until I found out who my real father was and everyone knew where I had come from and to whom I really belonged.

All the threads of lies I had started to unravel had to lead me to the threads of truth.

Instead of shouting out that I did not *want* to be like Laura, I kept my anguish inside and signed to May that I would follow her down the ladder. When I looked up as I reached the bottom, I saw Cary gazing down at me. The disappointment that lingered in his eyes made him look as distant and as forbidden as love itself is for one still searching for her own name.

Kenneth's excitement over his new artistic vision hadn't diminished one bit by the time he arrived to pick me up the next morning. Even Ulysses seemed to be affected by the change in Kenneth's mood and demeanor. He was more energetic; his tail wagged like a windshield wiper in a rain storm and he barked as soon as I appeared in the doorway. I laughed and hurried to the jeep. Almost before I closed the door, Kenneth put the vehicle in gear and whipped it around to accelerate and head back to the studio.

"I couldn't sleep last night," he said. He didn't look fatigued or drowsy to me, however. "I got up twice and went into the studio to look at the block. That statue wants to burst out of there. An artist literally frees the art, releases it into the world. It's chained to darkness by the ignorance and blindness of people. The artist comes like someone carrying a candle in the night and peels away the shadows."

He paused and looked at me.

"You think I'm babbling away, don't you?"

"No," I said quickly. Actually, I was afraid he would stop. The exhilaration in his voice was contagious.

He was quiet a moment as he drove. Then he nodded.

"Maybe you can understand."

"My mother wasn't artistic," I said. "Was she?"

He smiled at me.

"Well, in her own way, maybe. Haille always liked beautiful things. I used to tease her and say beauty's only skin deep, and she would reply, so who wants to go deeper?" He laughed. "Maybe she was right." He turned onto the dune road.

"Did you spend a lot of time with her?"

"Not a lot. Some," he replied. Then, as if he realized he was telling me things that might lead to more questions, he stiffened. "What would you say to working on Saturday, too?"

"I can't this Saturday. I've been invited to Grandma Olivia's for lunch."

"Oh?" He shook his head. "And no one refuses an invitation from Olivia Logan," he added.

423

"Why should I refuse?"

"You shouldn't if you want to go. Well, maybe the following Saturday. Just like any other employee anywhere, you'll get time and a half for coming," he said as we came to a stop by his house.

"If I come it's not for the money," I said firmly. I felt my eyelids narrow into slits of anger and he saw it, too. It brought a smile to his face.

"You're more like your mother than you know," he said.

"How come you know so much about her if you only spent *some* time with her?" I countered.

"It's not how long you're with someone, it's the quality of the time," he replied. "Come on, let's get started."

He reached back for the daily groceries he had purchased before picking me up and I followed him to the house. The kitchen was a mess from breakfast, but he wanted to get started on our project right away. After he put away the groceries we went directly to the studio, where he had an easel set up across from the block of marble and a large artist's pad open on it.

"I want to play around with some lines for a while this morning, sort of experiment with shapes, sizes, relationships. All you have to do is stand there as quietly and as still as you can," he added, pointing to the marble.

"Just stand?"

"Stand. I'll give you instructions as we go along."

Ulysses folded his body at Kenneth's feet as I positioned myself in front of the marble. I felt a little silly just staring back at him as he stared at me. My stomach was nervous, too. It made me self-conscious to have him look at me so intently, and for so long, and we'd only just begun. I shifted my weight from one leg to the other and waited.

"Look off to the left. Good. Now lift your chin just a little. A little more. Good. No, don't fold your arms.

424

Just try to stand with them down at your sides for a while. Okay," he said and worked his pencil quickly over the page. In no time at all my neck began to feel stiff.

"You're not relaxing," Kenneth said. "If you don't relax, you'll get tired faster and need more breaks. But don't worry," he added quickly. "In time you'll get used to it and you'll ease up."

"Do you work with models often?" I asked. He didn't reply for a while.

"Very rarely," he finally said. "Usually, if I need a face or a figure, I take a mental picture and commit it to memory."

"Then why can't you do the same now?"

"This is different. This is very special, and I told you," he said, not without a note of impatience, "the work requires a sense of transition, movement, change. I'm trying to capture a metamorphosis."

"Have you ever done anything like this before?"

"You'll have to stop asking me questions," he said. "You're breaking my concentration."

I pressed my lips together and closed my eyes.

"Don't close your eyes," he said immediately. I opened them a bit wider than usual and he groaned with impatience. "Relax. Please. Try to relax."

"It's not easy," I complained. "Now I know why people are paid a lot of money to do this."

He laughed. "Who said they are?"

"Aren't they?"

"You're tricking me into talking, Melody. Every time I answer one of your questions or you force me to respond, I stop thinking artistically. An artist has to lose himself in the work, not really see the person as a person anymore, but as the object of his art, and that takes very intense concentration."

I thought about Mommy in his paintings and wondered if that was precisely what had happened with her or if was Cary right. Did Kenneth look at her

425

not as his subject but as a woman he desired? If Cary was right, what did that mean about the way Kenneth was looking at me?

Kenneth told me to turn toward him and he studied me for a while. Then he asked me to look more to my right. He flipped his pages and worked and flipped some more pages. Finally, he slapped his pencil on the easel and stepped back.

"Something's not right," he said.

"Am I doing something wrong?"

"No, it's not you. It's me." He thought a moment. "I'm going down to the sea. You can work in the house until I return," he said and marched out of the studio.

I went into the house and cleaned up the kitchen. Kenneth still hadn't returned by the time I finished, so I went to his bedroom. It looked as if he had been wrestling with someone in his bed. The blanket was twisted, the sheet was pulled up and nearly half off, and one of his pillows was on the floor. Clothes were scattered about as if he had thrown them against the walls. I scooped everything up, deciding what needed to be washed and ironed and what needed to be just folded and put in the closet or the dresser. When I couldn't find a second sock, I got on my hands and knees and looked under the bed. Something else attracted my attention. It looked like a photograph. I knew it hadn't been there the week before when I cleaned, so Kenneth must have dropped it recently.

I strained and reached under until my fingers found it and I could bring it out. Then I turned, sat with my back against the bed frame, and looked at the picture. It was a picture of Mommy and me when I was no more than two or three. It had been taken in front of our trailer home in Sewell and it was badly faded, the black and white had turned brown. I turned it over and saw the writing was nearly faded, too, but I could make out most of the words and figure out the rest.

426

I thought you'd like this picture. Her name is
Melody. I'm sorry.

Sorry? Why was she sorry? Surely, she wasn't sorry
simply because she had named me Melody. Should I
just confront Kenneth with the picture and ask him
about it right now? I wondered.

I stood up, holding the picture close to my heart. I
went to the window and looked out at the beach. I
could barely see Kenneth, sitting a little below a sand
hill, gazing at the waves.

I've waited long enough for answers, I thought. I
want to know the truth. Armed with the photograph
and my own resolve, I marched out of the house and
over the sand toward Kenneth. Ulysses was at his
side, and his tail began wagging as soon as I appeared.
Kenneth didn't turn, didn't move. He looked as if he
had turned to stone himself.

"Can I talk to you?" I asked.

"Can't it wait?" he replied.

"No," I said adamantly. His shoulders sagged a bit
with his annoyance and he turned.

"What's so important?" he moaned. "I can't keep
having my concentration broken. This entire thing is
an ongoing process. It develops in small stages, but
the creative period has to remain smooth, fluid. I
thought you understood."

"I don't understand a lot of things," I said sharply.
He raised his eyebrows. I extended my arm toward
him, the picture in my hand. "I found this when I was
cleaning up your room. It was under the bed. It wasn't
there the other day."

He looked at the picture and then took it from my
hand.

"I wondered where this went," he said. "I was
looking at it last night."

"Why do you have it and what does it mean?" I
demanded.

427

"What do you mean what does it mean? It is what it is. A picture of you with Haille. She sent it to me years ago."

"Why?"

"Why? I told you. We were friends once."

"Just friends?"

"Good friends," he said.

"Why does she say 'I'm sorry'?"

He shook his head.

"You know most of this. She got pregnant and ran off with Chester. I guess she thought I was disappointed in her so she wrote, I'm sorry. What's the mystery?"

"Were you disappointed in her?"

"Yes," he said looking at the picture. "I had higher hopes for her. I wasn't surprised that she eventually had problems with Olivia and Samuel, but I had higher hopes. Okay?"

Tears burned under my eyelids, but I pressed my lips together and held my breath. He put the picture in his pocket and turned back to the sea.

"Why drag up the ugly past now?" he muttered.

"That's what Grandma Olivia says," I retorted harshly.

"This time she's right. Nothing can be changed and all it does is make people unhappy."

"Except I'm the one who doesn't know what she has to know. I don't know who my real father is," I said. He was quiet. "Do you know?"

"Look," he said, "this can't be a pleasant subject for you. I don't think I should be the one to say anything. If you want answers to those questions, ask your relatives. Once, I knew your mother. She was a beautiful young woman. We had a good relationship for a while and then her lifestyle got between us and she went her way and I went mine. I don't condemn her, blame her, look down on her. I don't judge people."

428

"You're not answering my questions," I pursued. He shook his head.

"I don't know the answer," he snapped. "There were a lot of rumors, nasty rumors, and the next thing I heard was she and Chester had run off."

The tears were streaming down my cheeks now. I turned away from him.

"You're not telling me what you really know," I fired back and stomped down the sand hill to the beach. I folded my arms and walked along, just out of reach of the waves. Moments later I felt his hand on my shoulder.

"Why do you want me to tell you unpleasant things?" he asked when I turned.

"I'm old enough to hear the bad with the good, Kenneth," I said, full of fire and determination. He nodded.

"Okay. You want the bad with the good? The bad is that your mother was very promiscuous. She slept around a lot; she was very wild. Some guy would come riding through here on a motorcycle and minutes later, your mother was sitting behind him speeding down the Cape highway for some rendezvous on a beach blanket. Then the guy was gone. She dirtied her reputation just to put a blot on the perfect Logan name, I think. She was angry at everyone in the family for one reason or another.

"She would come to see me often and confide in me and I would give her the best advice I could. Sometimes, I thought she had followed my advice, and then she would disappoint me. It happened more times than I care to remember. I got angry with her and I told her to stay away from me. She was driving me mad. Then she got into trouble, had that awful argument with Olivia and Samuel, and ran off with Chester, who was always head over heels in love with her anyway.

"She had him wrapped around her finger and she

429

could get him to do anything she wanted anytime she wanted. I can't even begin to imagine how many times he rescued her from a bad scene, picked her up when she was dead drunk or stoned or just worn out from a night of wildness. He would forgive her anything if she would just talk to him or let him help her. So, she ran off with him. You told me you knew what happened afterward. You know how your uncle Jacob feels about it all, and you know Olivia's views."

"You let her go, too?" I asked softly. "You gave up on her?"

"I tried my best at first. You can't even begin to imagine the frustration I experienced. Haille could make a promise that sounded as if it were chipped in cement—or marble, I should say." He smiled. "She could make the worst agnostic a believer, melt a hard heart in seconds, charm a fish out of water. And then she would break that promise and laugh and just promise again, and you know what, everyone, especially men, wanted to believe her so much, they refused to see her for what she was. Only, finally I saw the truth. What else do you want me to tell you?"

"I want to know who my father is," I said.

"I can't tell you that."

"Because you don't know?"

"Let's just leave it, Melody. Have this conversation with someone else. Go back to Olivia," he pleaded. "I like you," he said. "You're a very intelligent, sensitive young woman, and as you were probably told, I don't have many acquaintances, so I don't throw those compliments around lightly. I would really like for us to be friends. I hope you'll stay with me and help me create the Birth of Neptune's Daughter," he added, turning to walk away. Ulysses trotted at his heels.

The rhythmic chant of the waves sounded behind me and sea spray hit my cheeks. Terns circled and swooped over the waves. The breeze tickled my neck.

Some of what he had told me was the truth, but I

knew in my heart that there was more. The secret he kept was burning at him. It was as if he had been branded with the knowledge and knew that every time he was forced to talk about the past, he suffered the agony of remembering.

How strange, I thought as he walked away with his head down. He had a lean, tall figure. His face was bearded, browned by the sea, sun, and wind, and his eyes were full of wisdom and insight beyond his years. I should have felt angrier at him, disappointed, and yet, at this moment, for reasons I was yet to understand, I felt more sorry for him than I did for myself.

And I was the one left standing in the darkness. I was the one who still felt incomplete, lost, drifting in the ocean breeze. I felt like a lone leaf that had fallen from the branch and longed to return if only someone, something showed it the way.

I followed behind Kenneth. He sat again by the sand hill and stared at the waves. I sat beside him and looked out at the turbulent sea.

"I'm looking for just the right one," he said. "Just the right shape, the right image. If I look long enough, the sea will unveil it. Truth requires patience," he said.

I wondered if he were giving me advice. I wondered if he were asking me to be patient.

Just like the sea, he had something more to offer. It was only a matter of time, time to strengthen me so I could handle the truth.

I finally decided.

I liked him. And I would trust Kenneth Childs whether he was my father or not.

3

Don't Look Back

I couldn't help feeling nervous before I went to Grandma Olivia's for lunch on Saturday. I was always jittery whenever I was around her, but it seemed to me she made everyone stand or sit on pins and needles. The only one who appeared at all at ease in her presence was Judge Childs. Even Grandpa Samuel looked uncomfortable most of the time. I winced at the way she dished out biting criticism of him and the things he did. She talked down to him as if he were an insignificant or unintelligent person. I wondered why he tolerated it, and I couldn't imagine the two of them, younger, falling in love.

Nowadays, Grandpa Samuel wore his marriage as if it were a shoe two sizes too small. From what Cary told me and from what I had observed on other occasions, Grandpa Samuel spent as much time as he could away from home, even though he was retired. He played cards with his old friends a few nights a week, never turning down an opportunity to go somewhere in the evening if and when he was invited. Cary said Grandpa regretted retirement and had only stopped working because Grandma Olivia thought it looked as if they needed money if he continued to go to work year after year. During the day he was often down at the docks talking with fishermen and boatmen.

But Grandma Olivia would never permit him to miss one of her formal luncheons on Saturday. Usually, from what I understood, she invited someone of importance from Provincetown or the surrounding area. Political candidates, wealthy business people, even from as far away as Boston, were honored by her invitations and attended.

Grandma Olivia's driver Raymond was a man in his mid sixties, and what people in Provincetown called a Brava, half Negro, half Portuguese. He was one of Roy Patterson's uncles. Roy worked for Uncle Jacob and Roy's daughter Theresa was in my class at school. Everyone knew everyone else here, whether they socialized with each other or not.

Raymond came for me in Grandma and Grandpa Logan's vintage Rolls Royce. It was a partly cloudy day with just enough of a breeze to lift the sand and send it across the road in waves to salt the pavement. The sea air was crisp and fresh like the morning after the first snow in West Virginia. The clouds were the soft, marshmallow type, puffy, large, lazily drifting across the blue. It was a perfect day for an afternoon social affair.

I should have felt like some little princess in the back of the Rolls, sitting on the spotless leather, having a driver open and close doors for me and drive me up to the Logan compound, as it was known. Cary had long since left to work with Uncle Jacob by the time the limousine arrived. I was glad, because I knew he would tease me about it. Uncle Jacob only took Sundays off, and sometimes, not even the entire day. I felt sorry for May, who stood in the doorway watching me get into the limousine. She looked like a sad little rag doll gently waving good-bye. Why couldn't Grandma Olivia have invited her? I wondered. I asked Aunt Sara before I left.

"I don't know, dear," she replied. "Maybe she just wants to spend more time with you or introduce you to important people. But don't worry about May. She'll be fine with me. I'm going to take her in to town for lunch and some shopping."

Still, I thought it was a bitter pill for a little girl to have to swallow. How could a grandmother be so insensitive, especially to a grandchild like May who needed extra care and affection? It put tears in my eyes and washed away any joy or excitement I could have felt going to the luncheon in this plush automobile.

When I arrived, I found only Grandma Olivia, Grandpa Samuel, and Judge Childs sitting on the rear patio. As usual, whenever Grandma Olivia had company, she had servants. A maid was offering them hors d'oeuvres and glasses of champagne. They all turned as I stepped through the doorway.

Even seated, Grandma Olivia had a way of rising beyond her actual height. She stood only a little more than five foot four in her stocking feet, but because of the manner in which she carried herself and the way she sat regally in chairs and somehow managed to gaze down at people (even those who stood a foot taller), she presented a firmer, stronger appearance. As usual, her snow white hair was pulled back in a bun as severely as Aunt Sara's, with a pearl studded comb at the crown. Sometime after I had first met Grandma Olivia, I realized the reason Aunt Sara wore her hair that way was because it was the way Grandma Olivia wore hers. Whether she did it simply to please Uncle Jacob or because she believed everything Grandma Olivia did was, as Mama Arlene would say, "The cat's meow," I don't know, but she did it.

The tiny age spots clustered at Grandma Olivia's

hair line and on her cheeks looked more like freckles in the sunlight. Today, she wore a little blush on her cheeks. It was about the only makeup I ever saw on her. She had small features, her mouth just the width of her chin. Under her jaw, her skin hung loosely like a hen's, but her collarbone stood out prominently beneath her nearly transparent complexion. Tiny veins crisscrossed her temples. I was sure that when she gazed at herself in the mirror and saw the illusory azure fluid running through her, she was further convinced she was a true blue-blood.

Today she wore an ivory cotton dress with frilled sleeves and a frilled hem. It had tiny pearls sewn onto the collar and down between her breasts. She had an elegant gold bracelet spotted with diamonds on her right wrist and a small gold watch she must have worn just for show. The hands and numbers were so tiny I couldn't imagine how she could read the time.

Despite her temperament, Grandma Olivia's skin was smoother than the skin of most women her age, her perpetual frowns had not put any wrinkles in her face. Her hands were graceful, the knuckles a bit bony with some age spots across them, but the skin wasn't crinkled. I was willing to bet she had never washed a dish or ironed an article of clothing in her life.

Grandpa Samuel looked dapper in his light blue sports jacket and matching slacks. He wore a pair of polished white loafers and bright blue socks. Grandpa Samuel's hair was mostly gray, but he still had a remarkably full and healthy looking head of it. It was trimmed neatly at the ears and sides with the top brushed back. There was a trace of a wave running through it. His green eyes brightened at the sight of me and he relaxed his lips into a soft smile.

Judge Childs held a cigar in his right hand, a glass of champagne in his left, his big diamond pinky ring glittering in the sunlight. Ever since I had begun thinking that Kenneth Childs might be my real father,

435

I looked at the judge with a great deal more interest each time I saw him. After all, I thought, this man could be my grandfather.

The judge was a distinguished looking, elderly man with gray hair still showing some of its original light brown color. He wore it neatly trimmed and parted on the right side. He dressed more conservatively than Grandpa Samuel, wearing a charcoal jacket and pants, a bow tie, and black shoes and socks. I had seen pictures of Kenneth's mother in Kenneth's home. She was a very attractive woman with dark brown hair, but there was no question in my mind that Kenneth took after his father and had the same shape nose and chin. Kenneth's eyes were a darker brown, but the judge's eyes always seemed to darken when he gazed at me.

"Well, the guest of honor has arrived," the judge said. Both he and Grandpa Samuel rose, each bowing slightly. It brought a smile to my lips. I felt as if I had walked into a scene from *Gone with the Wind*.

I looked at Grandma Olivia and then at the rear of the house. There were no other guests, no elaborate setup of tables, tents, and chairs. Was I really the guest of honor?

"Good afternoon, Grandma Olivia," I said.

"I always liked that dress on Laura," she replied instead of greeting me. The way she said it made me feel as if I was a poor relation dressed in a hand-me-down.

"You look very nice, Melody," Grandpa Samuel said, nodding. "Come sit here," he said, patting the cushioned lawn chair beside him.

"Just like Samuel to want to sit next to the pretty lady," the judge said.

"You're just jealous because I invited her first," Grandpa said.

"Don't the two of you start acting like idiotic school boys," Grandma Olivia warned. "Sit where

436

you want," she told me. I sat next to Grandpa Samuel, who beamed a smile back at the judge.

"Now here's a young woman with some taste," he said, making the judge laugh.

The maid brought the tray of hors d'oeuvres to me and I choose one and took a napkin. It was shrimp in a pastry shell and it was absolutely delicious.

"Please get her some lemonade," Grandma Olivia told the maid. She nodded and hurried out.

"What's going on at Jacob's house?" Grandpa Samuel asked.

"Cary and Uncle Jacob are working. May and Aunt Sara are going to town."

"I hate going to town during the season," Grandma Olivia remarked. "It's too crowded on those narrow streets with all those tourists gawking into store windows. I don't know why she drags that disabled child all about like that," she added looking at me as if I had the answer. I did.

"Aunt Sara is just trying to keep May occupied," I said pointedly. "She was all alone when I left."

"Yes," Grandpa said nodding. "I guess you could have invited Sara and the child, Olivia," he told her.

"Don't tell me who to invite and who not to, Samuel Logan," she snapped. He stared at her a moment, his eyes cold and sharp but quickly warming as he folded his face into a smile again.

"Did you hear that whip snap, Judge?"

When the judge didn't respond immediately, I gazed at him and saw he was staring intently at me.

"What's that? A whip? Oh, yes, yes," he said laughing. "Well, I warned you, Samuel. Years and years ago, I warned you about the Gordons."

"You have that backwards," Grandma Olivia said. "Everyone in Provincetown warned me about the Logans."

The judge roared and sipped some champagne. He and Grandma Olivia exchanged furtive glances.

437

"I understand you are working for Kenneth," Grandma Olivia said, turning back to me. "How has that been going?"

"It's been fine, thank you."

"My son hasn't been too hard a boss then?" the judge asked quickly. "You're not bored out there in no-man's-land?"

"No. Actually, I'm learning a great deal about art."

"You're artistic too?" he followed.

"No, sir."

"She's musically inclined. Didn't you hear her play at the variety show?" Grandpa Samuel asked.

"Oh, I know she's musically inclined, but some people have a variety of talents."

"And some have none," Grandma Olivia inserted, her eyes fixed on Grandpa Samuel. "Except when it comes to putting their foot in their mouth." Grandpa Samuel looked uncomfortable and shifted his weight in his chair. Then he cleared his throat.

I didn't like the nasty tone of voice Grandma Olivia used, but I couldn't help being in awe of her strength and power. From what well did she draw it? I wondered. Where did she get such confidence, such self-assurance? I didn't like her, but I couldn't help wanting to learn something from her. She was living proof that women could be tough and strong when need be, and someday, someday soon, I too would need to find that strength.

"What's Kenneth have you doing there?" the judge asked.

"I help straighten up his home, make lunch, prepare his supplies, keep his studio in order, do odd jobs, take care of Ulysses. He showed me how to prepare the clay he uses for vases and small statues."

"Whatever he pays you to straighten up that home of his it can't be enough. He barely makes enough on that art work of his to feed the dog," the judge quipped.

"He doesn't believe an artist should be obsessed with making money," I offered and immediately regretted it, because they all looked at me as if I had said something blasphemous.

"Apparently, you've gotten to know him well already," the judge said after a moment of deep silence.

"No, not really," I replied. "We're just getting to know each other."

"Did he tell you he used to practically live here?" Grandpa Samuel asked with a wide smile. "I had to wash him off the welcome mat most of the time."

"Samuel, please," Grandma Olivia said. "He didn't live here."

"Well, he was here enough, wasn't he, Nelson?" Grandpa Samuel asked the judge.

"When Kenneth was younger, I had less of a fix on him than I have now," the judge said mournfully. Everyone sipped their champagne, but the judge and Grandma Olivia gave each other that sideways glance again. I took the lemonade from the maid, thanked her, and took a sip. I still wasn't sure why I had been invited to this luncheon, but I knew from everything I had been told and everything I had observed that Grandma Olivia didn't do anything unless it had a purpose.

"I hope you're hungry," Grandpa Samuel said. "We've got a small feast. Cold lobster, some of those wonderful fried potatoes I shouldn't eat, hickory-smoked ham."

"From the way he talks, you'd think that's all he cares about these days is food," Grandma Olivia said with a sigh. "I guess we had better get to it before he chews the arm off the chair." She started to rise.

"That is all he cares about," the judge quipped, and stood. Grandpa Samuel held out his arm for me to take and we followed the judge and Grandma Olivia into the house to the dining room, where the luncheon had been set out in smorgasbord style. The maid stood beside the table, waiting to hand us each a plate. Grandma Olivia went first and the judge stepped back for me to follow. The lobster meat had been shelled and dressed on a platter. Beside the potatoes Grandpa Samuel favored, there was a variety of vegetables, cranberry sauce and apple sauce. The hickory-smoked ham looked delicious.

Aunt Sara had warned me not to fill up my plate at Grandma Olivia's luncheons. That was something Grandma Olivia believed real ladies didn't do. It was proper to have something else afterward, a second helping of ham or vegetables, but not to fill the plate again. I saw how she watched out of the corner of her eye as I moved behind her, and I took a lot less than I wanted. The judge and Grandpa Samuel loaded their plates to the brim. We sat at the dining room table.

"As usual, wonderful, Olivia," the judge said. She nodded slightly, as one who expected compliments would nod.

"You seem to have adjusted well to your new home," Grandpa Samuel said to me.

"What choice did she have?" Grandma Olivia snapped. "What you have to do, you do."

"Well, sometimes you can be lucky and you can like the things you have to do, too," he offered, without any hint of contradiction in his voice. He winked at me and we ate in silence until the judge and Grandma Olivia exchanged another one of those quiet looks filled with question marks.

"What do you do while Kenneth works in his studio?" Grandma Olivia asked.

"Sometimes I use the time to clean the house or walk Ulysses and sometimes I watch Kenneth work. He doesn't mind as long as I don't break his concentration," I added. "Once, he asked me to play my fiddle while he worked."

"He's not very talkative then?" she asked.

"When he talks about his art, he is," I said. I tilted

my head, wondering why, if Kenneth had practically grown up here and this was his father who was sitting across from me, they were asking all these questions about him? They all acted as if they barely knew him and they should have known him far better than I did.

"Is that all he talks about?" the judge asked me insistently. He seemed impatient.

"Let the girl eat," Grandpa Samuel said. Grandma Olivia shot darts at him from her eyes, causing him to shake his head and return his concentration to his food.

I swallowed what I was chewing and replied.

"No. Sometimes he talks about the past," I said. The judge's eyes widened and Grandma Olivia held her fork frozen between the plate and her mouth.

"Oh? And exactly what has he told you about the past?" the judge followed.

"Just a little bit about what it was like to grow up here in Provincetown," I said.

Grandma Olivia put her fork down and looked at the judge, shaking her head in the slightest, but just discernable way. The judge returned to his food and the topic of conversation changed to what would happen to the country's economy if the Republicans didn't win control of the Senate.

After we had eaten, Grandma Olivia proposed something that made my eyes bulge with surprise.

"While you two idiots go have your cigars, Melody and I will walk out to the gazebo and have a private talk," she said. "Come along," she told me as she rose from the table.

"We'll be there shortly," Grandpa Samuel said.

"Don't rush your filthy habit on my account," she replied. The judge laughed and Grandpa shrugged. I followed Grandma Olivia out of the house and down the back steps. She paused and waited for me to walk alongside her.

"Did you enjoy the lunch?"

441

"Oh yes. Thank you. Everything was wonderful."

"Later, we'll have some tea and some petit fours. Tell me more about this summer job of yours," she said and continued down the pathway toward the gazebo.

Why was my working for Kenneth such an important topic? What did they expect me to tell them?

"There's not much more to say about it, Grandma Olivia. I enjoy watching Kenneth work. He lives in an interesting place, so close to the sea, to nature. I enjoy my walks along—"

"When he talked to you about the past," she interrupted, not satisfied with my response, "he didn't mention anything about his father?" When I didn't respond immediately, she stopped and looked at me. "Well?"

"He doesn't like talking about his father very much," I offered, but I saw that wasn't enough. She grimaced as if she had bitten into a sour apple, and then turned to step into the gazebo. I followed her inside and sat across from her on a pristine white garden bench.

"What did you want to talk about?" I finally asked. Surely my summer job wasn't the topic; it was obvious by now that I had been brought here for some sort of cross-examination.

"I think you're a lot smarter than your mother was at your age," she began. "Your mother's interests were quite simple to begin with, and her curiosity about anything more than boys was limited."

"I don't think it's fair to talk about her this way. She's not alive. She can't dispute anything," I countered. Standing up to her brought tears to sting my eyes. I took a deep breath and then looked away.

"Nonsense. If we couldn't talk about anyone who was dead, a great many mistakes would be made. It would also be a mistake for you not to tell me what, if anything, Kenneth Childs said about his father."

442

I turned back to her.

"Why is that so important to you?" I asked.

"Don't you dare ask me questions in response to questions I ask you," she admonished.

"All I know is that they don't talk much to each other, but I don't know why."

She raised her eyebrows.

"He didn't say?" she asked cautiously.

"No, not really."

"What's that mean, not really? Either he did or he didn't," she said, leaning impatiently forward in her seat.

"He didn't," I replied, the tears welling again in my eyes.

"I see," she said, continuing to scrutinize me. I felt as if I were sitting under a bright light in a police station.

"Is this why you invited me to luncheon, to interrogate me about what Kenneth said about his own father?" I demanded to know, despite her strict warning about questioning her.

"Don't be impudent," she snapped.

"I think it's pretty sad if the only way the judge can find out about his own son is through someone spying on him," I added.

"Don't you dare say anything like that to the judge," she chastised. "No one said anything about you spying on anyone," she added, but I glared back at her.

"You could have invited Kenneth to this luncheon," I suggested, "and asked him the same questions."

She glared at me and shook her head.

"Obviously, my son did not impart any of the good manners to you that I taught him, or if he did, your mother ruined them," she said.

"How can you still hate her even though she's dead?" I asked. Finally, I had said something that

443

made her turn away. She gazed toward the ocean, a blank look coming over her face.

"I don't hate her. I disapproved of her and I actually ended up feeling sorry for her, pitying her and Chester. To permit himself to believe such a terrible thing about his own father, just to have her as his wife. To think that my husband would seduce a young girl and embarrass me." She shook her head. "Well, that's all over now. Terrible words and ideas are like the tide. Once they go out, you can never pull them back. You can't unring a bell." She sighed. "So there's no point in discussing it now."

"Yes there is," I said boldly.

She turned to me. If her eyes were daggers, I'd have a hundred holes in me, I thought.

"What did you say?"

"I want to know the truth," I said. "Is Kenneth Childs my father? Is that why you have been questioning me about him?"

She started to smile.

"Is that what he told you?"

"He hasn't told me anything."

Her smile faded.

"I'm sure if there is one thing I don't know and don't care to know it's which of Haille's many men friends sired you. It would be easier to find the father of some shark in the ocean," she added with a wave of her hand toward the sea.

"Perhaps my real grandmother would know," I said, and Grandma Olivia burst out laughing.

"Belinda? Know anything that goes on around her? Please."

"I'd like to meet her. I would," I insisted.

She stopped laughing.

"Don't be silly. She wouldn't have the slightest idea who you were or be able to make sense out of anything you said or asked her," Grandma Olivia said. "It would be a pointless visit."

444

"Still, I'd like to do it. Isn't she permitted to have any visitors?"

"She can have visitors, but I can't think of anything that would be more of a waste of time than visiting Belinda Gordon."

"I have the time to waste," I said. "Did my mother ever visit her?"

"Not once," Grandma Olivia replied and smirked. "And let me tell you, it wasn't because I forbade her either."

"Then that's all the more reason for me to go," I said firmly. She raised her eyebrows again and widened her eyes as she nodded.

"Maybe I'm wrong," she said. "Maybe I should have taken an interest in who your father was. Whoever he was, he must have had some backbone."

If ever I was to receive a backhanded compliment, I thought, this was it.

"Okay," she said after another moment. "You're so determined to meet your real grandmother," she added, pronouncing real as if it were a dirty word, "I'll even have Raymond drive you up there."

"Thank you," I said quickly. "When?"

"Tomorrow. Sunday is visitors' day. He'll pick you up at ten A.M. They like the patients to have visitors in the morning," she said.

"Haven't you ever visited her?" I asked.

"Of course not."

"But she's your sister," I said. She looked as if she had a rod of steel down her back.

"I did more for her than she would have ever done for me," she retorted, "especially under the circumstances."

"What circumstances?"

"Please. I don't want to have to till that soil again. Just make your dutiful visit and get it over with," she added with another wave of her hand. Ideas or words she disapproved of or disliked were like flies for her to

445

swat away from sight. No one could ever be more infuriating, I thought.

"It's not a dutiful visit. I really would like to meet her."

"You're going to be quite disappointed," she warned, almost gleefully.

"I've been disappointed many times before," I said. She sent fire from her eyes again and then calmed down when we heard the judge and Grandpa Samuel as they emerged from the house and started toward us. Grandma Olivia sat forward.

"Don't mention this conversation to anyone else," she ordered. "And especially say nothing to Kenneth. I don't expect your loyalty, but I do expect your obedience," she said. "And I'm sure you know," she added, leaning closer toward me, her eyes filled with warning, "what is at stake should you disappoint me."

The threat hovered over me like a storm cloud and then the judge and Grandpa Samuel stepped into the gazebo.

"Well now, did you two have a good womanly chat?" Grandpa Samuel kidded.

"I assure you, Samuel, our conversation was miles above the one you two jabbered through cigar smoke," she replied.

"Now, now, Olivia, no sexism," the judge chided. He and Grandma Olivia exchanged a quick look and I saw the question in his face. She shook her head slightly and I thought he looked relieved. Then he smiled at me.

"Well now," he said, sitting on the bench adjacent to me, "let's hear some more about my son's new art project."

"I think it would be easier if you came out and spoke to him about it yourself, Judge Childs," I said. "I don't mean to seem secretive about it," I quickly

446

added. "It's just that I don't want to describe it incorrectly."

He held his smile a moment and then nodded.

"Of course," he said. "That's just what I intend to do. One of these days," he said. "One of these days."

Grandma Olivia had the maid serve us our tea and small cakes in the gazebo. The conversation drifted to political subjects again and I was practically ignored until the judge announced he had to leave. When he rose, he turned to me.

"It's been delightful spending the afternoon with you, Melody. Perhaps one day you'll visit me at my beach house. Do you play chess?"

"No, sir."

"Fine. I'll teach you. In no time you'll be able to beat your grandfather Samuel."

"I'm sure she has better things to do than waste her time with senile old men," Grandma Olivia said scowling.

"Maybe," the judge said and winked. "Say hello to my son for me. Olivia." He bowed.

"I'll walk you out," she said and rose.

I suddenly realized it was the first time Grandpa Samuel and I had ever been alone. He quietly watched Grandma Olivia and the judge and then he turned to me.

"You mustn't be too quick to pass judgment on Olivia," he said, obviously noticing the disapproving look on my face. "She appears to be a very hard woman, but she has had more than her share of burdens to bear."

His sympathy for her took me completely by surprise.

"What burdens?"

"You know a little about the difficulties we had with her sister."

"My grandmother," I said.

"Yes, your grandmother." He shook his head sadly.

"Their father was a difficult man, according to what Olivia tells me. He made many demands on Olivia and tried to set a strict atmosphere. Belinda rebelled and became promiscuous; Olivia stood up to him and I suppose that was how she developed such a strong backbone."

"She's always snapping at you," I said. He shrugged.

"It's her manner. We get along better than many couples married as long as we've been married. Don't worry," he added with a smile. "I'm not as browbeaten as most people think. But that will be our little secret, okay? Now, I want you to come to me if ever you have any problems, especially with my son Jacob. I know he can be sterner than a constipated minister at times. You're a good girl, a talented and smart young woman. You'll be fine. I'm sure.

"We all have to find ways to rise above our bad luck from time to time," he added with a deep sigh.

"I'm going to visit my grandmother Belinda tomorrow," I said.

"Oh?" He looked toward the house. "Does Olivia know?"

"She's arranging for Raymond to take me."

"Really? Well, that's very nice. You know of course that Belinda is not quite all there these days."

"I don't know anything about her. That's why I'm going."

He nodded and then leaned toward me to whisper.

"She has a tendency to fantasize about people she knew. Don't believe most of it. Just come and ask me if you want to know if anything she says is true. Okay?" I nodded. "Don't tell Olivia. Just come to me," he added and sat back quickly when Grandma Olivia emerged from the house again. He smiled and winked.

All these people living side by side and keeping

secrets from each other, I thought. It had to mean something terrible. How much of it, I wondered, had to do with me?

Cary was home by the time the limousine brought me back. From the way he emerged from the house the minute I stepped out of the Rolls, it was obvious he had been waiting and watching at the window.

"How was lunch?" he asked as I drew closer.

"At least the food was good," I said and he rolled his eyes.

"Uh-oh. I don't like the sound of that."

"I'm going to change out of this hand-me-down, as Grandma Olivia characterized it," I said.

"Then let's go for a walk to the cranberry bog."

"Okay. Where's May?"

"She and mother aren't back from wherever they went," he said.

I hurried upstairs and changed into a pair of jeans and a comfortable sweatshirt. Uncle Jacob was apparently taking a nap. The bedroom door was closed. I walked softly down the stairs and out into the front yard, where I found Cary tossing rocks across the road. The late afternoon sun had fallen behind a long stream of clouds, turning the ocean a metallic blue, making the breakers glitter like mirrors.

"Ready?" he asked.

"Ready."

We started across the beach. As we walked, I told Cary about the afternoon and how I had been cross-examined about Kenneth.

"It made me feel like Grandma Olivia's little spy. Do you know why Kenneth and his father don't get along?"

"Probably because he failed to follow in his father's footsteps and become a lawyer. Look at all the money they wasted sending him to law school," Cary surmised.

"It's something more than that," I said. Then I told him I was going to visit Grandma Belinda.

"Grandma Olivia's sending the car?"

I nodded. I told him what Grandpa Samuel had said to me about coming to him with any stories Grandma Belinda might babble. Cary thought about this for a few minutes.

"I don't know. I don't think any of it means anything," he concluded. "Grandpa Samuel is probably just trying to let you know he's not hard and bitter like his wife."

We sat at the top of the hill and gazed at the bog.

"It's gonna be a good crop. We need it," he said. "The lobster-fishing business stinks these days." He played a blade of crabgrass over his lips and stole a quick glance at me. "About last night, before May came," he said.

"Yes?" My heart began to thud in my chest, as if we'd just finished jogging the entire way to the bog.

"I hope you're not mad."

"Why should I be mad?"

He smiled.

"I thought you might think I had invited you up just so something like that would happen."

"Didn't you?" I asked, and he blushed.

"No."

"Really?" I teased. His face went from red to cherry-blossom white, especially around his lips.

"No! I'm not like Adam Jackson. I don't trick girls into believing one thing and then trap them or something," he said, his voice cracking with indignation.

"Okay. Then, it just happened."

"Yes," he said firmly.

"Think it will happen again?" I asked hesitantly, not sure myself how I felt about our new relationship.

He turned, surprised.

"I don't know."

"Do you want it to?" I pursued.

"Do you?" he countered.

"Maybe," I said, thinking that at least with Cary I could be myself, that he wouldn't take my confusion as a sign of weakness.

He stared at me and then he began to lean toward me, his lips slightly parted and wet. I inched toward him and we kissed, softly, quickly. I immediately turned onto my stomach and lowered my chin to my arms as I gazed at the bog. He turned on his back beside me and neither of us spoke for quite a while.

"I came right out and asked Kenneth if he knew who my father was," I said finally, breaking the uncomfortable silence.

"You did? What did he say?"

"First, he said he didn't know. Then he said he couldn't tell me." I turned on my back. Cary braced himself on his arm and gazed down into my face.

"What's that supposed to mean?"

"I don't know. I think it means he knows but he doesn't want me to be hurt, or maybe it means he can't face the truth himself. Oh Cary," I said, nearly in tears. "I just know there's something terrible left to discover, even more terrible than the things I've already learned."

"Then maybe you should stop asking questions," he suggested. "It's like when you didn't want me to open the door to that closet in the studio. You were probably right. Some doors are better left locked."

"I didn't want it unlocked, but once it was, I wanted to go in and look, and I didn't want you to pull out those pictures, but once you had, I looked too."

He nodded and then swallowed hard and looked away.

"What?"

"You're like Lot's wife in the Bible."

451

"I forget who she was."

"Lot told her not to turn around and look because if she did, she would turn into a pillar of salt."

"And?"

"She looked," he said, and it was as if thunder had clapped across the sky. The heat that moment before had been flooding my body disappeared instantly, leaving a cold, hard ball of fear in the pit of my stomach.

Maybe he was right.

Maybe I should stop asking questions.

4

∞

To Grandmother's House I Go

Raymond arrived at the house promptly at ten A.M. I was very nervous and babbled a bit, asking him a million questions, but, just as he was when he picked me up to go to the luncheon, Raymond was not talkative. He actually seemed frightened of questions. I assumed he was afraid of Grandma Olivia and of losing his job, but most of the New Englanders I had met had their lips glued most of the time, especially around people they considered outsiders. Sometimes, the way some of them talked about people who didn't come from here made me think I was walking around with a third eye in my forehead.

Cary tried to explain it by telling me that people who lived off the sea tended to distrust landlubbers, thinking of them as softer, spoiled, unappreciative, taking the fish on the plate for granted.

"How far is the rest home, Raymond?" I asked when we started off.

"Not far."

"Have you been there before?" I asked, and he

turned and looked at me as if to see if I were asking a serious question.

"Aye," he replied.

"To take my grandmother to see Belinda?" I asked. Maybe Grandma Olivia had lied to me.

"No."

"Do you have a relative there?" I persisted.

"No," he said, but he didn't continue.

No wonder they all loved clams so much here on the Cape, I thought. This family and all the people associated with them couldn't be within a tighter shell.

It had rained earlier and I thought it was going to be a dark, dreary day, one of those days when the sea breeze was so chilly you wanted to wear a sweater, even in the summer. But just before Raymond arrived, the blanket of charcoal gray clouds developed a seam of blue that widened and widened until the clouds began to melt away like snow in spring sunshine. The warm rays made me squint when I gazed at the scenery, but at least I felt a little better.

I had woken this particular morning with a stomach so tight I could barely swallow water. I floundered about the bedroom, sifting through the clothes in my closet, trying to decide what would be appropriate to wear, not only to a rest home, but to meet my real grandmother for the first time ever. I didn't want to get too dressed up and look formal, but I didn't want to look underdressed, as if I didn't place great importance on this visit.

Because of the gloomy looking day I found when I first looked out the window in the morning, I chose a light blue cotton cardigan with a matching tank top and a silky rayon posy print skirt. The hem rested a little less than an inch above my knees. It was another one of Laura's outfits I had tried on but not worn. I brushed out my hair and put on some lipstick, even though Uncle Jacob had told me on more than one

454

occasion that a young woman shouldn't be wearing lipstick during the day. I didn't know from what well of information he drew these rules, but I began to feel more pity for my dead cousin Laura, imagining what she had gone through, although Uncle Jacob never missed an opportunity to tell me how obedient and respectful she was. Intimidated and terrified was more like it, I thought.

He gave me a disapproving look when I went down to breakfast.

"How do you eat with lipstick painted on your mouth?" he asked.

"It's not a problem," I said softly. Aunt Sara looked away and busied herself with something to avoid the discussion.

"Disgusting habits some young women have these days," Uncle Jacob muttered. I felt the blood rush into my face.

"Men are more disgusting when they puff on pipes, cigars, and cigarettes, filling their mouths with nicotine and tar and turning their teeth yellow and giving themselves breath like a dragon," I countered. Cary laughed. Uncle Jacob turned purple with anger, but swallowed his words and went back to his food instead.

Naturally, May was full of questions about why I was dressed up and where I was going. I did my best to explain, but she couldn't understand why I kept referring to Belinda as Grandma Belinda. Cary promised her he would spend the morning with her and help her understand.

I expected to be back before lunch and Cary had proposed that he, May, and I go to town. I agreed, even though it was hard to think past my meeting with my grandmother. I hoped it would go well and I would return feeling I had someone I could really call family, but the trepidation that had seeped into my body all night was now making my legs tremble and

455

my heart kept thumping harder and faster than normal all the way to the rest home.

We rode for nearly a half an hour before Raymond turned up a side road into more wooded country. It was heavy with pine, wild apple, and scrub oak. At a clearing on our right, I saw a flock of song sparrows circle and then soar to the right over the tops of the trees before they parted. It was another ten minutes before the rest home came into view. Whoever had planned its location obviously wanted it away from the more populated areas. I wondered if the owners were thinking how much people like to keep their sick and elderly out of sight and out of mind.

As we drove on in silence, I couldn't keep from wondering who came to visit Grandma Belinda if Grandma Olivia didn't? There was no one else in her family that I knew. What was it like to be housed, institutionalized, in a world without friends and relatives, dependent entirely on the kindness of strangers? Did she feel helpless, forgotten and discarded? Did this keep her from ever trying to get well?

Knowing this family, I thought, she might be better off where she is.

The rest home wasn't in an unpleasant setting. The ocean was behind it with the sun now glimmering on its silvery-gray surface. The front of the building faced a long, rolling lawn with benches, a rock garden, and some fountains. It looked peaceful, clean, and well maintained. It was obviously a rest home for the wealthier sick and elderly.

The building itself had three stories, with a steeply pitched gabled roof. It had a front porch the width of the building with a short set of cement steps. The wooden wall cladding was done in a Wedgwood blue and the shutters on the windows were bone white. As we pulled up the drive, I saw there were two elderly gentlemen sitting on the porch, rocking and gazing at us with some interest. The driveway pitched to the right and the parking area was just adjacent to the building. I could see that behind the large house there was a more elaborate garden, more benches and seating areas, and a gazebo twice the size of Grandma Olivia's. There were some full red maple trees, more scrub oak and pine, and the pathways were lined with trimmed bushes.

After he shut off the engine, Raymond stepped out and came around to open my door. I got out slowly.

"The front entrance is right there," he said nodding. "I'll wait in the car."

"The whole time?"

"I don't mind," he said and returned to his seat, pulled his cap down over his eyes, and settled in for a nap. I walked over the flagstone walkway and started up the stairs. One of the elderly men smiled at me; the other continued to look in the direction from which we had come, as if he expected to see more cars. The man who smiled, nodded.

"Hello," I said.

"You bring the paper?" he asked.

"Pardon?"

"Today's paper. You bring the paper?"

"No. I'm sorry. I'm here visiting Belinda Gordon."

"Where's the paper?" the other elderly man asked him, holding his hand behind his right ear.

"She ain't got it," he said.

"What?"

"She ain't got it," he shouted.

"What's today, a holiday?" the second man asked. I smiled at them nervously and entered the home.

The lobby was bright and homey with light blue curtains and a blond oak floor. The walls had large paintings depicting rustic country scenes and ocean scenes in rainbow colors, some with fishermen, some simply with sailboats painted against the twilight sky. The cushioned chairs and settees were all done in a light blue floral pattern. There were small wooden tables, book and magazine racks, with rocking chairs in front of the large, brick fireplace. Light, classical music was being piped in through two small wall-mounted speakers.

A little more than a dozen residents were seated in the lobby, a few reading magazines, some talking, two playing checkers, and some just sitting and staring at nothing. Two women in nurses' uniforms circulated around the lobby, seeing to the needs of the residents. Everyone was well dressed and appeared well looked after. Those who seemed aware of what was happening around them gazed up at me with anticipation as I entered. Almost all looked as if they hoped I was there to visit them. I could practically feel the loneliness.

A tall, thin woman with dark hair and a narrow face that held her dark eyes close to each other came strutting out of the corridor to the right. She wore a dark gray cotton suit that looked tailored to her lean figure. Her high heels clicked sharply on the wooden floor. It reminded me of the tap, tap, tap of a woodpecker. She wore her chestnut brown hair cut short, barely below her ears, where she wore tiny opal earrings. Her nose was long and a bit pointed and her mouth turned down at the corners. She didn't smile when she approached.

"Can I help you?" she asked.

"I'm Melody Logan, here to see Belinda Gordon."

"Oh yes. Mrs. Logan called to say you would be coming. I'm Mrs. Greene. Miss Gordon is in recreation. You haven't brought her any candy, have you? We try to limit the sugar intake. Many of our residents are diabetic, but they don't watch themselves and they offer each other candy."

"No ma'am," I said. "I've brought nothing but myself."

"Fine," she said nodding. "Right this way, please."

I looked back at the people lounging in the lobby.

458

Everyone looked frozen. One of the men playing checkers was holding his hand in midair, a checker piece between his fingers, and one thin lady in a rocker had stopped it in its forward motion and sat with her mouth wide open, leaning and staring at me. She looked as if she might break into tears any moment.

"This way," Mrs. Greene said, pausing in the doorway to the corridor. I hurried to catch up.

"How is Miss Gordon?" I asked.

"Actually, she's doing very well. Being on a healthy diet with proper exercise has given her a new lease on life and has added years. She happens to be one of the residents of whom I am very proud. Are you a friend of the family?" she inquired as we turned down another corridor toward a double door.

"I happen to be her granddaughter," I said as matter-of-factly as I could. She stopped walking.

"Granddaughter?" Her smile was like a stretching of her thin lips to the point where they looked like rubber bands about to snap. "But my understanding is Belinda Gordon had no children."

I shrugged. "That's who I am," I said. She squeezed her eyebrows toward each other and then shook her head, clicking her tongue as she continued toward the double doors.

"I would have thought Mrs. Logan would have mentioned that," she muttered.

"She must have just forgotten," I said. She looked at me sideways as she opened the double doors to a room filled with game tables, a television set, and imitation leather settees and easy chairs. There were at least another dozen residents here. They looked younger, more alert and healthier than the elderly people in the lobby.

I paused as the realization hit me: I didn't know what my own grandmother looked like! The only pictures I had seen of her in Grandma Olivia's basement were pictures of her when she was much, much younger.

Mrs. Greene turned to me and waited.

"I'm afraid I've never met her," I said.

"You've never met her? Well," she said. "Well." She shook her head and turned and nodded toward a tiny woman sitting by the window reading what looked like a child's picture book. She wore a white knit shawl over a pale green dress. Even from across the room, I could see the resemblances between her and Grandma Olivia. They were both small featured, however, as I drew closer, I thought Grandma Belinda's features were more dainty, more doll like. Her eyes were bluer and brighter and when something she read brought a smile to her face, her smile was warmer, happier.

With Mrs. Greene not far behind, I started across the room, my entrance drawing as much interest from these residents as it had with the residents in the lobby. Only Belinda didn't break her concentration. She turned the pages of the picture book and widened her smile.

"Hello," I said. She looked up slowly and I could see she had very young looking crystal blue eyes that highlighted her gentle, soft smile. Her skin didn't look as translucent as Grandma Olivia's. In fact, Grandma Belinda appeared healthier and more robust, with a richer complexion, despite being locked away in a rest home.

"Where have you been?" she asked quickly.

"Where have I been?" I looked at Mrs. Greene.

"This is a visitor, Belinda. She doesn't work here and she's not a volunteer."

She squinted at me.

"Oh," she said with great disappointment. "I thought you came here to read to me."

"I could do that," I replied and sat in the chair just across from her. Mrs. Greene turned to speak to

460

another resident, but she didn't move too far away from us. "My name is Melody," I told Grandma Belinda and waited to see if there would be any note of recognition. She simply widened her smile a bit.

"That's a very nice name." She paused and tilted her head a bit. "I think I once knew someone named Melody."

Had she heard of me?

"My mother's name was Haille," I said. I glanced again at Mrs. Greene, who was obviously leaning closer to hear our conversation.

"Oh." Grandma Belinda's lips remained in the shape of an O, as if she had just realized something significant.

"You know who I am then?" I pursued. She shook her head, more like someone who wanted to deny what she knew than someone saying she didn't know.

"Haille lived with your sister Olivia," I said, "and her husband Samuel."

"I haven't seen my sister today," she said. She turned and looked toward the door. "She's probably in her room, sulking as usual, just because, just because Nelson asked me to go for a walk with him and didn't ask her."

She gave a slight laugh that sounded like the tinkle of wind chimes. Her eyes brightened mischievously.

"I showed her the bracelet he bought me and she just sucked in her cheeks and turned her face into a big old sour puss. She said I asked him to buy it for me. Can you imagine? I wouldn't ask a man to buy me anything, especially Nelson Childs. I've never had to ask." She leaned forward to whisper. "But she does," she said and laughed again. "She asked Paul Enfield to take her to the Fleet dance Saturday night because no one had asked her. But he said he wasn't going. I knew he was going," she assured me with a knowing nod. "So . . ." She leaned back. "She had to go with Samuel Logan. Rather, he had to go with her. He

461

didn't want to go. He wanted to ask me, but someone else had already.

"I don't ask men for things," she emphasized with another small nod. "I don't have to." She paused to drink me in and then nodded. "I bet you don't have to ask them, either."

I laughed. Mrs. Greene left the side of the other resident and moved directly behind us.

"What are you going to read me? Are you going to read me Sleeping Beauty? I like Sleeping Beauty," Grandma Belinda said emphatically.

"If you'd like," I said. "Where is it?"

"Don't you have it? Didn't you bring it?" she asked a little frantically.

"No. I'm sorry."

She pouted. I gazed at the pile of children's books on the small table between us and chose one.

"Would you like me to read this?"

She glanced at the cover and then nodded slightly. I looked about the room. The other residents were back to doing their own things for the most part. Only one or two continued to gaze our way. I started to read, putting as much drama into it as I would if I were reading to a five- or six-year-old child. She relaxed and turned back to me to listen. I noticed Mrs. Greene move around the room, in front of us, to the side, and then behind us again, circling, spending some time with others, but always keeping within earshot. It didn't take long to read the children's story, and when I finished Grandma Belinda clapped.

"Isn't that a nice story?" she said. "I love stories with happy endings. Olivia says there are no happy endings, only endings."

"Has she been to see you?"

"She's too busy to see me. She's in high society now. She has rich people to entertain. Her nose is up here," she said tilting her head back like someone who had a nosebleed and pointing to her forehead. "I'm an embarrassment to her. That's what she says. She sounds like the big bad wolf when she says it," Grandma Belinda said, lowering her voice to make it gruff. "You're an embarrassment. Stay in your room."

She stared at me a long moment and then she smiled impishly again.

"But even if I'm in my room, they come to see me. They knock on the window. And . . . sometimes, I open the window and let him in."

"Who?"

"Wouldn't you like to know," she sang and laughed. I had to laugh, too. She was obviously confusing time, mixing in events that had occurred years and years ago with events that had occurred more recently.

"Don't you know anything about me?" I asked hopefully. "I'm Haille's daughter, Melody. You know who Haille is, don't you?"

She stopped smiling.

"Can't talk about her or she'll have them heave me out on the street," she muttered.

"Is that what Olivia said?" I asked.

"Can't talk about her," she said and pretended she was zipping her lips shut.

"You can talk to me," I said. "I'm Haille's daughter. I'm your granddaughter."

She stared, her eyes blinking rapidly. Then she turned away and gazed out the window.

"Look how blue the sky is," she said. "I wish I could reach up and touch it. I bet it's soft."

Mrs. Greene was practically on top of us.

"Would you like to go for a walk? It's beautiful today," I said. Mrs. Greene's eyes widened. I looked up at her. "Can I take her for a walk?"

"Well, does she want to go out?"

"Would you like to go out, Grandma?"

"Yes," she said firmly, not even noticing I had

463

called her Grandma. I got up to help her, but she didn't really need any assistance. She rose quickly, turned her head as if everyone were watching her every move, and started out.

"Just stay in the garden and walk on the pathway," Mrs. Greene said. "There are attendants if you need any help."

"She seems fine," I said. "You were right. She's being well taken care of," I added, but Mrs. Greene didn't smile at the compliment. She watched us with the eyes of a hawk as we left the room.

I took Grandma Belinda's arm into mine and started down the corridor to the door that led out to the gardens. She was spry, energetic. She wore a flowery scent that smelled refreshing.

"I like your perfume," I said.

"Do you? Nelson gave it to me."

"Nelson? He was here recently?"

"Just the day before yesterday or the day before that. He brings me a bottle of perfume whenever he comes and we sit and talk about old times. Nelson is still quite a handsome man, don't you think?"

"You mean Judge Childs?" I asked.

"Yes," she said, laughing. "Imagine, Nelson's a judge."

When we stepped out, she paused to squint at the sunlight.

"Oh, it's warmer than I thought," she said. "It should be my birthday," she added and laughed. "I always say that on nice days. Olivia thinks it's very silly. What a silly thing to say, I wish it was my birthday. Like you could pick your birthday, she says. Your head is full of cranberries, she says."

I had to laugh at Grandma Belinda's imitation of her sister.

"Shall we go into the garden?" I asked.

"Oh yes. I love to smell the flowers."

We walked silently for a while and then she paused

464

and looked back to see if anyone were near us. One of the attendants had come out and was watching us.

"You know why she says all those things and calls me all those names, don't you?" Grandma Belinda asked in a deep whisper, snapping her head around to face me again. I shook my head. "Because she knows Daddy loves me more. Daddy buys me nice clothes. Daddy takes me places. Daddy is proud to introduce me to his friends. Daddy wants her to stay in her room." She smiled coyly. "Daddy told her to get married or else."

She leaned toward me again.

"I put my ear to the door and I heard him yelling at her. She was crying and he was yelling. But I felt more sorry for Samuel Logan than I did for her. He has to wake up every morning and see that grouchy face. I told him to sleep with his back to her so when he opened his eyes, he could see the sunshine and not Olivia with her puffed up eyes and her puffed up lips and her sour breath."

She started to walk again.

"You know he was here," she said softly.

"He was here? You mean, Samuel?"

She nodded. And then she stopped suddenly.

"But don't you tell. Promise?"

"I promise. When was here?"

"Last night. He came to my window and knocked and I opened it and I said, Samuel Logan, what are you doing here at my window the night before your wedding?"

"Wedding?" I shook my head. "I don't—"

"'If you don't let me in,' he said, 'I'll kill myself.'"

"Last night?"

"Shh," she said looking around. She continued to walk, moving a little faster. The attendant followed. "People here tell Olivia things. She has her spies everywhere. Let's sit on this bench," she said.

It was under a spreading maple tree with a row of

465

multicolored impatiens behind it. I sat next to her. She leaned back and waited as the attendant walked slowly by us, pausing only a half-dozen feet away.

Whispering again, Grandma Belinda continued. "I said, 'you won't kill yourself' and he said, 'I will. I will. I swear.' So I let him in."

"Let him in?"

"He crawled through the window and fell to the floor. It was quite a sight. 'Shh,' I told him. 'Someone will hear and how will that look? You here the night before you marry my sister?' He lay there on the floor so I sat on the floor and he told me how sad he was and how terrible it was to be sad on the night before your wedding. He wanted me to make him feel better. So I did. If Olivia knew, she would have them put poison in my food."

"She wouldn't do that, Grandma."

"Oh yes, she would. She poisoned my song bird. I know she did, even though she says she didn't. Daddy bought it for me on my sixteenth birthday and she was jealous. Nelson bought me something nice too," she added, "and that made her more jealous. He bought me a gold locket with a red ruby at the center. It had his picture inside." She smiled and then she grimaced. "Do you know where the locket is?"

"No. Where is it?"

"Ask Olivia. She took it and buried it somewhere. I'm sure. One day, it wasn't in my jewelry cabinet and that was that. You can kill my birds, you can steal my jewelry, but you can't keep them from liking me more, I told her. She said she didn't care, they were all ugly philanderers. But that's like the story about the fox and the grapes, right?"

"The fox and the grapes?"

"The fox couldn't reach the grapes so he said they were sour. Yep, sour grapes. That's Olivia all right." She laughed and then took a deep breath.

"Look at the bluebird," she said pointing.

"It's beautiful."

"Yes. I wouldn't mind being turned into a bird. When people get old, they should be turned into birds," she concluded. "I read a story like that once." She turned back to me. "Are you going to read another story?" she asked.

"If you want me to, I will when we go back inside."

"Of course I want you to. I want to hear happy endings, only happy endings, more happy endings," she chanted.

She wanted to walk some more and then she decided it was time to go back. When we stepped back into the building, she said she was tired, already forgetting that she had asked me to read another story.

"I'm not as young as I was. I get so tired so fast now. Thank you," she told me. I knew she thought I was just someone else who worked there.

"Grandma," I said pressing my hand into hers, "I'm your daughter Haille's daughter, Melody. I'm your granddaughter and I'm going to come back and visit you often. Would you like that?"

"Haille?" she said. She shook her head slightly. "I know someone named Haille. Nelson told me about her. She's very pretty, isn't she?"

"Yes," I said. There was no point in telling her all that had happened. She had taken in too much already, I thought. She was physically strong for her age, but mentally, she was very fragile, as fragile as a little girl, and I knew, from personal experience, how easy it was to shatter a little girl's heart.

"She should go for her nap before lunch," Mrs. Greene said, suddenly appearing in the corridor.

"Yes, I was taking her to her room."

"I'll see to it she gets there," she said and nodded to the attendant who had been outside, hovering around us. He moved quickly to Grandma Belinda's side.

467

"I'll see you soon, Grandma. Have a good nap and then a good lunch," I said. I kissed her cheek and she touched it as if I had planted something very precious on her face. Then she turned and looked at me, blinking rapidly for a moment.

"You look like someone I know," she said. Then she smiled. "I remember. You look like me when I was your age." She leaned closer to whisper. "Don't give your heart away too quickly. They like to break hearts. That's what they like to do the most. Just ask Olivia," she said and laughed. "Ask her and tell her I told you to ask. What?" She looked at the attendant as if she had heard him say something. There was some mild chastisement in his expression and she straightened up. "Oh."

I stood watching them as the attendant led her down the hall.

"I'll show you the way out," Mrs. Greene said.

"I remember the way," I told her. "Thank you." I hurried down the corridor, through the lobby, and out the door, my heart thumping. Raymond sat up quickly the moment I appeared and then got out to open the door for me.

"Everything go all right?" he asked.

"Yes," I said. "Just fine."

I sat back, locked within my own thoughts, feeling rather sad and vulnerable. I wasn't looking out the window, so I didn't realize he wasn't taking me directly home until I noticed the driveway of Grandma Olivia's house.

"Why are you taking me here?" I demanded.

"It's what Mrs. Logan told me to do," he said and drove up the driveway.

"What am I supposed to do now?" I asked. He shrugged.

"I guess Mrs. Logan expects you."

"Be nice if she told me her plans for me," I snapped and got out.

She came to the door herself when I rang.

"Raymond said you told him to bring me directly here after my visit," I said.

"Yes. Come into the living room." She led the way and took her high-backed seat, which, as usual, made her look like some sort of dowager queen. "Sit," she ordered as if I were Ulysses the dog.

"Why did you tell him to bring me here?"

"I'm not accustomed to people standing over me when we talk," she replied and sat back, waiting for me to obey her and sit on the settee. I did so quickly.

"Well?" I demanded.

"I thought it best you speak to me about your visit before you spoke to anyone else. Tell me how it went and don't leave out any details."

"I'm surprised you don't know everything already," I said.

"What's that supposed to mean?"

"The way they were hovering around us, listening."

"Ridiculous."

Maybe it was, I thought, but it was easy to become paranoid where this family was concerned. I took a deep breath and wondered what I should tell her. I didn't want Grandma Belinda to appear foolish just because she loved children's books and confused time and places now, and I remembered Grandpa Samuel telling me to come to him with any stories first.

"She's very sweet and I thought she looked very healthy. She's only a year or so younger than you?" I asked deliberately. Grandma Olivia stiffened.

"Never mind that. What nonsense did she tell you? I'm sure she rambled on and on about something silly."

I shrugged.

"She told me about her youth, how many boyfriends she had, one of them being the judge."

Grandma Olivia's eyes narrowed into hateful slits.

"He wasn't her boyfriend when she was younger.

That is just one of her fantasies. This is exactly the sort of nonsense I'm talking about," she said, her words biting and sharp. I suddenly saw how vulnerable and helpless Grandma Belinda must have been, growing up with Olivia.

"She said you were often jealous of her and you poisoned her song bird and stole a locket the judge gave her," I said in an accusatory tone.

"Oh." She shook her head and smiled as though I had uttered the most ridiculous things. "She tells that story to everyone. That bird died of natural causes and I don't know why she carries on and on about it. When it was alive, I was the one who had to take care of it. She never fed it or cleaned its cage, and as for a locket, it was a present I received from someone and she fantasized it was for her. Men never bought her things. They didn't have to," she added dryly. "All they had to do was turn a flirtatious face in her direction and she was theirs. What else did she say?"

"She said your marriage was forced on you," I blurted, unable to hide my anger at the way she diminished and criticized my real grandmother at every turn. Is this why she brought me here? Did she get some sadistic pleasure from it?

"It wasn't forced on me, but parents had a great deal more to say about whom their children married then. It was better that wiser minds prevail. Far fewer of those marriages ended in divorce, and if she had listened to my father, she wouldn't be in this predicament today."

"She said you forbade her to mention my mother. Is that true?"

"That," Grandma Olivia said, "is the first true thing she told you. Yes, of course I forbade her to mention Haille. What sort of a situation would we have had with her babbling about this embarrassing event? You think I wanted the gossip mongers clicking their tongues? It was bad enough that some servants

470

knew and the doctor knew, but somehow, I managed to keep everyone from suffering. You sit here now with your eyes full of condemnation and accusation, but do you pause to think what I provided for your mother? No, you don't," she said, answering herself quickly. "Well, I'll tell you.

"Your mother was a child born out of wedlock, normally a disgrace, but I gave her a home and my name and the best of everything. She could have had a fine education, met the most distinguished men, had a real future, but she was contaminated by Belinda's bad blood."

"And now you think I am too, is that it?"

"That remains to be seen," she snapped.

"Not by you. I'm not auditioning for your approval," I fired back at her, the tears burning under my eyelids, tears I would die before releasing in her presence.

"Nevertheless," she said, her smile sharp and her eyes bright and fiery, "you'll do nothing to risk my disapproval or—"

"Or you'll see to it I never get my inheritance. I know," I said.

"That's right," she replied and sat back.

There was a moment of silence, a truce between us.

"I wouldn't recommend that you return to the home to see Belinda," she said slowly. "She'll only fill you with more ridiculous fantasies and it might cause problems for everyone."

"She needs visitors, family. You can't leave her there like that, alone, lost."

Grandma Olivia laughed.

"She's far from alone and far from lost. She has the best care money can buy. If anything, she's spoiled, but she was spoiled all her life. That's why she ended up as she did," she concluded. "Don't go back there," she said standing.

"I will. She's my real grandmother," I said.

471

Grandma Olivia's eyes looked as if they could burn through my skull and sear my brain.

"She's a mental invalid, totally dependent upon my charity. I could have her put in a county poorhouse in minutes," she threatened. "What do you expect she can give you?"

"Love," I said not backing down or looking away.

Grandma Olivia sucked in her breath as if I had punched her in the stomach. She started to speak, but stopped, her eyes strangely softening, her look turning from anger and condemnation to an unexplainable look of pleasure, respect.

"Don't push me too far, Melody. I would like to see you have a good life, despite what you think of me, but you have to rise above yourself, your own contaminated blood."

"Am I dismissed?" I asked. I was trembling inside, but I wouldn't show it.

"Dismissed? Yes, but keep my advice hanging up front in your closet," she said. "Raymond will see to it you get home."

"Thank you," I said. I turned and marched out of the house, never welcoming the fresh sea air as much.

5
∞

Someone's Watching Over Me

Cary and May were already gone by the time Raymond brought me home. Aunt Sara said they had just left.

"Cary waited as long as he could, dear, but he felt sorry for May. He told me to tell you he was taking her to the Sea and Shell on Commerce Street and, if you came home early enough, to join them. How was your visit with Belinda?" she asked, but looked away quickly as if she didn't want to hear my answer.

"It was nice. She's very sweet," I said, "even if she is confused about events and time."

"Jacob asked me to make my meat loaf for dinner tonight," Aunt Sara continued, as if I hadn't said a word. "It's one of his favorites." She laughed, her laugh sounding as fragile as thin china. "He says I proved the old adage that the shortest distance to a man's heart is through his stomach. He says he fell in love with my cooking first and then looked up and saw there was an angel in the kitchen."

"Uncle Jacob said that?" I asked skeptically. Aunt Sara heard the note of doubt in my voice.

"Oh yes," she declared. "When he wants to, Jacob can say very sweet things."

"I guess he hasn't wanted to for a while," I muttered. "Aunt Sara, did you know my grandmother before she was sent to the rest home?"

Aunt Sara's smile faded quickly and she turned away.

"Not really, no," she said. "I mean, Belinda was always different. Jacob thought it best we didn't have much to do with her."

"Why? Because Grandma Olivia wanted it that way?" I asked pointedly.

"It's better not to say anything if you can't say anything nice about someone," Aunt Sara lectured. "Oh, I forgot. Could you pick up some garlic for me on the way home? Here, let me give you some money," she said, hurrying to her cookie jar. It looked more as if she were fleeing from my questions.

I went upstairs to change into a pair of jeans and a faded gray sweatshirt with our high school letters on the front. I put on a pair of sneakers, too, and then went running down the stairs, hurrying to catch up with Cary and May. Aunt Sara was waiting at the front door to hand me the money for the garlic.

"Thank you," she said, but she didn't move out of the way. After a moment she lifted her eyes and said, "Laura liked Belinda." It was as if guilt had been buzzing around in her head like a bee in a jar, threatening to sting her if she didn't open the lid.

"She did?"

"She even went to visit her at the home once." She lowered her voice to a whisper even though there was no one else around. "Olivia never knew, but Jacob found out and he was very upset with her for doing it. It was one of the few times he got angry at Laura. She promised never to go again and that was that."

"Why was everyone so mean to my grandmother?"

474

"It wasn't that we were mean to her, dear. She was . . ."

"What?"

"Telling horrible lies, and lies are . . . lies are what Jacob says they are, like termites. They get into your moral foundation and tear you down. Only sinners have reason to lie."

"Then Grandma Olivia might be the biggest sinner of all," I blurted and Aunt Sara's face nearly collapsed with shock. She turned white.

"If Jacob ever heard you say such a terrible thing—"

"Don't worry, Aunt Sara. I won't say it again. If you can't say something nice about someone, don't say anything," I reminded her.

"Yes." She nodded. "Oh dear, oh dear," she chanted as she returned to the kitchen.

I felt bad about shocking her with my outburst, but I was so frustrated and angry about the way this family treated Grandma Belinda that I felt like lashing out at all of them, all of them with their holier-than-thou attitudes, gazing down their noses at the rest of us as if they stood on Mount Olympus. Even if something was wrong with Grandma Belinda and she babbled silly things, confusing time and place, that wasn't a reason to ostracize her and forbid everyone from seeing her. Maybe there was another reason why destiny brought me here, I thought. Maybe it was for Grandma Belinda, who otherwise had no one to come to her defense but the shadowy figures of her flustered memory.

When I got to town, I found the streets jammed with people and traffic. There were many families, mothers and fathers walking with their children, everyone holding hands, their faces full of smiles, their eyes bright with excitement as they gazed at the pretty things in store windows or at other people

475

rushing by on the way to restaurants, the dock, and the shops. I couldn't help standing wistfully and watch them walk by. Why couldn't that teenage girl be me and that man and woman be my real father and mother? Why couldn't I lead a normal life and be on vacation with my parents? What had turned fate in my direction and chosen me to be the one who had to flounder about searching for her identity?

A chorus of horns and then loud laughter shook me out of my self-pity. When I looked around, a smile returned to my face. Provincetown on weekends was filled with excitement. Yes, these people were tourists and some of them littered and some of them drove badly or complained vehemently about prices, but most enjoyed themselves and were appreciative of the ocean, and respected and admired the fishermen and boatmen. Shop owners, restaurant owners, hotel and bed-and-breakfast owners needed the business. To me, those who were securely planted in their wealth and property here and who looked down on all this were selfish and arrogant. They lived in their own world and Grandma Olivia was queen of it, I thought.

Well, as long as I lived here, I would never be like that. I wouldn't become one of them no matter how much money I inherited, I vowed.

I hurried on toward the Sea and Shell, a small, inexpensive eatery near the dock. When I turned a corner, looking back when I should have been looking forward, I rammed into someone who shouted, "Whoa, there!" I gazed up and into the eyes of the very handsome and distinguished looking man I knew to be Adam Jackson's father, T. J. Jackson, one of the most prominent attorneys in Provincetown. Before this, I had seen him only from a distance at school functions or on the street. Whenever he saw me, he looked at me with a very pensive look on his face. I thought that was because of something Adam might have told him about me, something nasty of course.

Adam, his sister Michelle, and his mother, Ann, a very attractive brunette who was just as tall as her husband, stood directly behind Mr. Jackson. Adam gave me his usual smirk of self-confidence, but Michelle grimaced with disgust. Her shiny braces glittered on her teeth, making her mouth as mechanical and cold looking as her dull brown eyes. She was thirteen, going into the eighth grade, and from what I had heard, just as snobby as a skunk.

"Well, hello," Mr. Jackson said, widening his smile when he recognized me.

"I'm sorry," I said.

"That's all right. No harm done. Where are you heading in such a hurry?"

"I'm late. I have to meet my cousins for lunch," I said, avoiding Adam's gaze. Ever since the time on the beach and the subsequent fight Cary had with Adam in the cafeteria, we had had little to say to each other. He had graduated and was going off to college in late August. He had told me he would become a lawyer like his father, although he didn't seem to have any great passion to be an attorney. He was doing just what was expected of him.

I had never really been this close to his mother before. She was a very pretty woman with big green eyes and a nose and mouth so perfectly shaped she could have been a model. She reminded me a lot of Mommy, because she had the same high cheekbones and elegant neck. I wondered if she had ever wanted to be a model, too. She didn't smile, so much as keep a soft and friendly look in her eyes and mouth.

"Well, if you're too late, you're welcome to join us for lunch," Adam's father offered. Michelle shifted her weight to her other foot and swung her eyes toward the sky with a grunt of annoyance.

"Thank you, but I'm sure they're waiting for me."

"We're going right in here," he continued, pointing to one of the more expensive Provincetown restaurants. "Come right back and join us if you've missed them," he insisted.

"Thank you."

"I never had the opportunity to tell you how much I enjoyed your fiddle playing at the variety show," he said. "Wasn't she something, Ann?"

"Yes, she was," Adam's mother said with a small smile. "A very nice surprise."

"How's your grandmother these days? I haven't seen her in quite a while," Adam's father continued as if we had all the time in the world to waste away. In truth, only Michelle seemed impatient and bothered. Adam continued his self-satisfied smirk, enjoying my discomfort. His mother looked patient and very friendly.

"She's very well, thank you," I said.

"Well, perhaps we can treat you to lunch another time," Adam's father said. I gazed at his soft blue eyes and gentle smile. I didn't know whether lawyers could turn the charm on and off at will because of the work they did in court before juries, but he seemed so sincere and warm, I almost wished I could have lunch with him. "It's the least we can do to show our appreciation for the fine performance you gave," he added. "Don't stop playing that fiddle."

"I won't. Thank you," I said and hurried away confused as to why he seemed so interested in me. It was hard to believe that someone as nasty as Adam came from such nice parents.

Cary and May were just finishing their sandwiches when I arrived at the Sea and Shell.

"Sorry I was late," I said sliding across from them in the booth. "I didn't know Grandma Olivia was having Raymond bring me to her after the visit for an interrogation."

"Interrogation?"

"An inquisition is more like it."

"Oh? I just thought you had decided to stay and have lunch with Belinda."

"I didn't eat lunch anywhere. Grandma Olivia didn't even offer me a glass of water."

Cary shrugged.

"That's Grandma. Go on and order. We'll wait and watch you eat," Cary said with a smile.

"Don't let me forget to bring home garlic for your mother," I said as I chose a sandwich from the menu. Then I told him about my literally bumping into Adam Jackson's father and family and how Mr. Jackson practically insisted I join them for lunch. Cary's eyes grew dark with anger just at the mention of Adam's name.

"Figures he'd want to show off. He was always like that," Cary said. "Like father like son."

"How do you know what Mr. Jackson was like when he was younger, Cary?" I asked, wondering at the venom behind his words.

"He went to school with my father and your stepfather. Dad's told me about him. He was always spoiled, arrogant. That's just the way the Jacksons are and always will be."

"He didn't seem to be just now."

"Well, he is," Cary insisted. "They ought to be known as the Snobsons and not the Jacksons," he added. Whenever he got very angry, his ears would turn red at the edges. They were that way now, so I dropped the subject and began talking about Grandma Belinda instead. I had to remember to sign as I talked so May wouldn't feel left out. I didn't sign everything, of course. Cary shook his head with disbelief when I described what Grandma Belinda had said happened between her and Grandpa Samuel.

"I never knew any details, but I knew she was saying outrageous things."

479

"Now I understand why Grandpa Samuel wanted me to come to him with any questions," I said. "Grandma Olivia has little love for her sister and I think some of what Grandma Belinda told me may be true."

"I don't know," Cary said, shaking his head uncertainly. "I could probably count on my fingers how often her name's been mentioned in our house or at Grandma's."

"That's just it, Cary. There's got to be more of a reason why she is persona non grata in this family."

"What? Persona?"

"Not wanted," I explained impatiently. "You don't disown someone because she's mentally ill, do you?" He started to shrug. "Your mother told me Laura went to see her once."

His smile froze.

"She told you that?"

"Yes."

"My father was very upset with her."

"She told me that, too. Don't you think that was wrong, to treat a sick old lady like the plague? Well, don't you?" I pursued when he didn't respond. May was signing question after question, but I didn't turn from Cary.

"All I know is my father said Belinda was very immoral when she was younger and he didn't want Laura around that sort of woman," Cary said, a bit sheepishly. "I'm sorry."

"Your father . . . infuriates me," I wailed. Cary laughed. "He does! What makes him so high and mighty? Isn't there something in the Bible about judging others?"

"Judge not that ye be not judged," Cary said softly, nodding.

"Well?"

He shrugged.

"Tell him that," he said.

"I will," I declared, amazed at my newfound conviction to stand up for my poor, defenseless grandmother.

Cary smiled, doubting that I had the courage. It added fuel to the fire of wrath building in my chest. He glanced at May and then he leaned toward me.

"When you're angry, you're about twice as pretty as you are normally and that's a lot," he said.

His words brought a different shade of crimson to my cheeks. My thoughts became jumbled and confused, and when I realized that those words could have such an effect over me, I looked away quickly, not knowing whether I should cry or laugh at the turmoil that raged in my heart and in my head.

After we had gone to the supermarket and bought Aunt Sara her garlic, we headed home. There wasn't a cloud in the afternoon sky and the breeze had warmed up. The ocean looked soft and inviting with the sunlight glittering on the waves. The anger inside me was forgotten once I glimpsed the beauty of the sea, and our conversation returned to more pleasant subjects than family. Cary talked again about his desire to build real boats. He was full of ideas for customizing them and improving on their mobility. When Cary talked about his dreams he became a different person, more confident and intense, and I worried that Uncle Jacob's tyranny would slowly crush the hope and life from him.

"If your father really cared, he would want to see you turn your dreams into reality," I said, but he continued to make excuses for Uncle Jacob on the basis of family and tradition.

As we drew closer to the house, May said she wanted to go hunting sea shells, but Cary was determined to return to the model boat on which he was

481

currently working. I sensed that this one was very important to him, so I offered to take May to the beach and keep her out of his hair.

"Come on up when you get back," Cary whispered. "I have something special to show you," he added. I felt a flutter in my breast and nodded.

May didn't seem unhappy that Cary wasn't accompanying us. She looked as if she wanted to be alone with me, and as soon as we reached the seashore, I saw why. She began to ask me questions about my life in West Virginia and boyfriends I had had. When I asked her why she wanted to know, she blushingly told me she had a boyfriend.

"What?"

I laughed, and we sat on a mound of sand as she explained how she had been partnered with this boy at school for different tasks and how they had grown to like each other. On Friday, when no one was looking, he had leaned over and kissed her on the cheek. She was so excited by it, she confessed, that she hadn't washed her face since.

I started to laugh, but saw how serious and intense she was about the experience and instead turned my thoughts to the first time a boy had kissed me. First times for some things were so special they stayed with you all your life, I thought, especially a girl's first kiss.

"Did Cary ever kiss you?" she asked. Apparently May, although deaf, was not blind to the attraction between Cary and me, how we looked at each other, how we spoke and touched each other, in ways that she knew were significant. Now it was my turn to blush. And worry that others in the family had noticed as well.

"We're just good friends," I said quickly, without really answering her questions. "What's your boyfriend's name?" I asked, desperate to change the subject.

"Laaaa . . . ry," she pronounced proudly. "Were you ever in love?" she signed quickly.

"I've had crushes on boys," I told her, "but I don't think I was really in love."

"How do you know when you're in love?" she asked.

"It's not an easy question to answer," I told her. "When you have a crush on a boy, you can't think of anything else. You write his name on everything and you walk about in a daydream and act so silly, people say you're lovesick."

"Sick?" She lost her smile. "Do you have to take medicine?" she asked.

"No," I said laughing. Then I realized she had been brought up with doctors and nurses and medicine most of her life. The word sick had only one meaning to her. "You're not actually sick. You're just . . . doing silly things all the time."

That made her thoughtful for a while. Then, she looked around to be sure no one was near before telling me that something was happening to her and that was why she was so worried when I mentioned sick.

"What do you mean?" I asked, concerned. She was still for a minute and then unbuttoned her blouse to show me the rise around her nipple. "Oh, you're just developing breasts," I said and told her as much as I could about a woman's body. When I mentioned the monthly period, she was astounded.

"Bleeding?" she made me repeat, grimacing as she signed.

"Hasn't your mother ever told you any of this?" I asked. She shook her head. "What about Laura?"

She reminded me that none of this was happening to her when Laura was alive and Laura probably thought she wasn't ready.

I told her more. Of course she knew that babies come from mothers, but the details of the process

483

were still a mystery. She was shocked to learn that women carry eggs and men carry the sperm. When she asked me how the sperm got to the egg, I hesitated, wondering if I should be the one to tell her. Why hadn't Aunt Sara had a mother-daughter talk yet? How long did she think May would remain a child? Did she and Uncle Jacob assume that May's deafness made her immune to a young girl's thoughts and desires?

Had Mommy and Daddy thought I was immune to these desires? Mama Arlene took pity on me and all my questions and I told May about the birds and the bees the way I remembered Mama Arlene telling it to me. I described sex as Nature's trick to bring two people who loved each other together so they could create the greatest expression of their love: a baby. I didn't go into vivid detail, but I let her understand that a man and a woman had to join to make it all happen.

She was still, almost stunned, and then she signed a question that nearly brought me to tears: Would her baby be born deaf because she was deaf?

Of course, I didn't know for sure, but I told her I didn't think so. I told her her baby would be a separate person. She liked that and smiled again. I told her to come to me with any questions any time she wanted.

She looked up at me seriously and made the signs to indicate I had become her older sister. That did bring tears to my eyes and I hugged her. Then we got up and resumed our search for precious sea shells.

As May walked ahead of me along the beach, I now saw her as more than just a little girl. Sooner than Aunt Sara expected, May would become a young woman, a very pretty and sensitive young woman whose deafness made her even softer and more gentle than most. She would search for someone to trust, someone who loved her deeply. He would have to be someone special, I thought, because she was so special.

When we returned to the house, May went to her room to put away her new sea shells and I climbed the ladder to Cary's attic. As soon as I stepped through the trapdoor, I saw him hovering over his new model boat. He was working with such intensity, he hadn't heard me come up. Feeling like a spy, I stood there very quietly watching him concentrate. His mouth was slightly open, his eyes fixed on the tiny paint brush. He seemed to be holding his breath. After a few more minutes, he sat back and sighed with pleasure at his accomplishment. Then he realized I was there and turned quickly, blushing.

"How long have you been here?"

"Just a few seconds. I'm sorry. I didn't want to interrupt," I said.

"It's okay. Perfect timing. I just finished," he said, rising. "Come, take a look."

I stepped closer and gazed at the beautiful, sleek sailboat he'd been working on. He had just painted Melody on the hull. Surprised, I looked up at him.

"It's for you," he said.

"Really? Oh, it's beautiful, Cary."

"The engineering of its shape is my creation. If you look closely," he said, "you'll see two people inside the cabin. That's us."

I leaned over and peered through the cabin window. There were a tiny man and a woman standing beside each other, gazing into each other's eyes.

"It's so precious," I said softly, my breath catching in my throat.

"After it dries I'll bring it to your room," he said. "You can keep it on the shelf by your bed."

"Thank you, Cary. I'll always cherish it. Did you ever give anyone else a boat you made?" I asked.

485

Curiosity had gotten the best of me. I should have smothered the question, for I saw it brought back unpleasant memories.

"I gave one to Laura once, but she didn't think it was that special," he said turning away. "She was seeing Robert Royce then," he added, as if that explained everything.

"I didn't see it in the room," I said.

"That's because it's not there."

"Where is it?"

"Floating some place in the ocean," he said dryly. "Where's May?"

"Organizing her new sea shells," I said.

"Good."

"She told me she has a boyfriend," I told him.

"What?" He smiled. "A boyfriend? Our May?"

"Yes, really. There's a boy at school who likes her. She was full of questions about boys and love."

"Did you have the answers?"

"Some. She wanted to know how you know you're in love," I told him.

A small smile crossed his lips and a twinkle came into his eyes.

"What did you say?"

"I told her I didn't know for sure. It was different for everyone," I said, trying not to meet his eyes. "Then she wanted to know how babies are made. Apparently, your mother hasn't told her anything."

"What did you tell her?" he asked with some trepidation.

"The truth," I said. "Not in great detail, of course, but the basics at least. She's becoming a young woman, Cary. It's time she understood what was happening to her body and what *could* happen, don't you think?"

"I can't think of anyone I'd rather have tell her about it," he said after a moment's thought.

486

"Your mother, that's who," I countered, but he shook his head.

He continued to stare at me, and as his glimmering eyes met mine, my pulse quickened. He stepped closer, and as he leaned toward me, I lifted my mouth in anticipation of his kiss. We kissed and then we kissed again only harder and longer. He took my hand and gently brought me to the small sofa. When he sat, he pulled me onto his lap and brought his lips to mine once again. This kiss was more intense.

"Oh Melody," he said, moving his lips down my cheek to my neck. I lay back, enjoying the feelings rushing through my body. "I've gotten so I don't think of anything but you. Even on the boat, I'm dreaming of you, forgetting to do things. Yesterday, I wandered about for twenty minutes, forgetting why I had a wrench in my hand. Dad thought I was sick."

"Lovesick," I laughed and he pulled back as if I had shot him.

"Yes, lovesick," he said with a sneer. "I guess I'm not as sophisticated about it as, say, Adam Jackson." He stood up, pulling his hand out of mine as if he'd been burned.

"Cary, I was just kidding. I just told May all about that and—"

"What do you think, I'm acting like an eleven-year-old?" he asked astounded.

"No, I . . ."

He shook his head and turned away.

"Cary, I'm sorry. Really. I didn't mean to insult you. I don't want to drive you away from me," I added. He sat in his chair and sulked. I got up quickly and went to him. "I'm sorry," I said and kissed him on the cheek. He took a deep breath.

"I guess I'm just nervous," he admitted. "I don't have all that much experience with women."

"Neither do I with men," I said. "So we've got to be

487

kind to each other, gentle, loving, and most of all forgiving," I added.

He liked that and his smile was warm again.

"I forgive you. Now, where were we?" he asked and put his arms around my waist.

"I think right here," I said and leaned over to kiss him.

"Maybe I should have you tell me how babies are made, too," he kidded. "I'm not sure I've got it right."

"I doubt that, Cary Logan."

He laughed and then stood up, tightening his embrace around me. As we kissed, his hands slid under my sweatshirt. His fingers moved up my side and up my back until he found the clip on my bra.

I didn't move. He fumbled a while with the clip and then suddenly, it unfastened. The thrill that shot through my body made my legs weak. I moaned under his kiss and he brought me back to the sofa. When his fingers moved over my nipple, I thought my heart would shatter from pounding.

"Oh Melody, I am lovesick, but I don't care," he whispered. "I don't care if I die of it."

He started to pull my sweatshirt up but I stopped him. No one but Mommy and Mama Arlene had ever seen me undressed before, I thought. It was exciting, but it was scary, too.

"Don't you want to?" he asked.

"Yes, but slowly," I said. He kissed me again, and again he started to pull up my sweatshirt. He brought his lips to my breast and I slipped farther down under him. His right hand moved to my hip and over to the button that fastened my jeans. The suddenness with which he did it surprised me. For a moment, I couldn't catch my breath.

"No," I said. "Not yet."

He pulled his hand back, kissed my breasts, and pressed himself to me. I felt the small explosion building inside me and then I felt his hardness, even through his pants, and I grew more frightened. It was happening, and if we let it go one second more, I thought, it would be like trying to hold back the tide.

"We'd better stop," I whispered. He held me tightly, his breathing coming hard and fast.

"Are you sure?"

"Yes, for now. Please, Cary."

"Okay," he said. After another long moment, he stood up and turned away, embarrassed by his obvious sexual excitement. I sat up quickly and reached back to fasten my bra. "I should be going down to help Aunt Sara with dinner."

"Right," he said. He returned to his desk and started shuffling model parts back and forth noisily.

"Are you okay?"

"Yes," he said, nodding but not looking at me. After a minute, he added, "I think it's easier for girls to stop once you start, especially when you've gone that far."

"I don't really know," I said, wondering if what he said was true.

"I do," he said harshly. "I don't need to practice too much to learn that lesson." He was trying not to be angry and frustrated, but I could see the battle within him had filled his eyes with fire and turned his skin cherry red.

I fumbled with my hair and realized my hair clip had fallen out. It wasn't on the sofa, so I looked beside it and then behind it.

"I lost my hair clip some place," I said. "It must have fallen behind the sofa."

"I'll find it for you," he said and started to get up.

"It's okay. I can do it."

I pulled the sofa back just a little and saw the clip. When I reached down for it, however, I saw something else, something that put a cold, shocking chill in my heart. It looked like the floor boards were parted. Light was coming up and through the floor. I leaned closer and realized I was looking down into my room, looking right over the bed.

"What is this?" I asked. When I raised my head, Cary was staring at me, a look of terror on his face.

"It's . . . nothing."

"Nothing? It's an opening in the floor. Right over my bed."

"It was just there, just the way the boards settled or something. That's why I put the sofa over it," he said quickly.

When you're close enough to someone to see the love in his eyes, I thought, you can also see the deceit. Cary was lying.

"How long as it been there, Cary?"

"Since the house was built, I guess." He gave an exaggerated shrug of his shoulders. "I don't know."

I gazed at the hole in the floor again. I didn't know a lot about the structure of houses, but I knew that hole hadn't just formed there. He had obviously used one of his tools for constructing models to punch out the opening.

"Why did you do this, Cary?"

He shifted his eyes guiltily away and just sat there with his hands in his lap.

"I know you did this, Cary. Stop lying to me," I demanded, confusion again coming to take the place of my happiness.

He nodded.

"I did it when Laura started bringing him home and they spent time together in her room," he confessed angrily.

"Robert Royce?"

"Yes," he said, turning to me. He had his eyes squinted shut as he spoke. It was as if he were trying to block out some scene scorched on his brain. "I didn't trust him. I told her, but she wouldn't listen, so I thought I had to look in on her and be there if she needed me, if he . . . tried something."

490

"Don't you think she would have been able to stop him?"

He opened his eyes and shook his head.

"No. I don't know. What if she couldn't? I did it for her," he insisted. "I couldn't help it," he admitted. "But, I haven't looked down that hole at you, if that's what you think. I swear. I'm not a peeping Tom. Really," he pleaded, his face contrite with his effort to convince me and his need to have me forgive him.

"I believe you," I said, and he relaxed. "You should repair it though."

"I will. I just forgot about it," he said. "The sofa was over it, so I just forgot about it."

I nodded and put my hair clip back in. Then I started for the trapdoor. He reached out to take my hand.

"Melody, you don't think less of me because of that, do you?"

"No," I said. I smiled at him, but in my heart I was confused. I didn't know exactly what to think or feel at the moment. I needed time. "I better go down before everyone starts wondering where I am," I said.

"Maybe we'll take a walk after dinner or something."

"Maybe," I said. I nodded at the work table. "Thank you for the sailboat."

He smiled and watched me descend. When I entered my room, however, I gazed up at the ceiling. Now that I knew it was there, I could see the small hole. A second later, it was darkened. Cary had covered it.

But had he closed his heart on all that had made him drill the hole? Only time would tell, I thought.

What had he seen down here and what had it done to him? I wondered. How confusing and wonderful, exciting and yet frightening sex was, I thought. I didn't tell May, of course, but I could see it was the greatest mystery about ourselves. It inspired us, made

491

us do creative things and yet strange things, weird things.

May had turned to me for answers on the beach, answers I had no idea myself where I would find. In a real sense both she and I were orphans. She had a mother who refused to acknowledge her needs and I had no mother to help me with mine. Whatever discoveries I made through my awkward stumbling, I would bring to May so she would benefit. Perhaps this was another reason why I was brought here, I thought.

But all these good plans and good intentions were soon to be shattered.

Uncle Jacob apparently had walked in on May and Aunt Sara just as May was signing a question that made Aunt Sara turn blue in the face. And what followed was about as furious as a hurricane. I had just gone down to see what I could do to help with dinner, but when I reached the bottom of the stairway, I heard Uncle Jacob call my name. He spit it out the way he spat out hateful Biblical names like Jezebel and Satan, Delilah and Cain.

I stepped into the living room. He was standing near the fireplace and when he turned, it looked as if embers from the fire had jumped into his eyes. There was no doubt that if he could have set me afire and turned me to ash, he would have done it in a heartbeat. I held my breath. No one had ever looked at me with such disdain. It chilled me to the bone.

"How dare you?" he said. "How dare you come into my home and pollute my child? I warned you about this. I told you it was in your blood."

I shook my head, tears of confusion clouding my vision.

"What have I done?"

"You have filled her mind with unclean thoughts, with pornography."

"I have not. All I did was tell her how babies are

492

made. What's wrong with that? She's old enough to know these things now and you and Aunt Sara should be telling her more."

His eyes widened.

"Your mother was a whore," he said through clenched teeth. "It's no surprise she bore a daughter like you." He nodded, satisfied with his thoughts. "The old sayings are full of truth. The apple doesn't fall far from the tree. I forbid you to talk to May on this subject, do you understand?"

I shook my head defiantly at him and recalled the Biblical quotation Cary had given me at lunch.

"Judge not that ye be not judged," I fired back at him.

He recoiled as if I had been big enough and strong enough to slap his face. His mouth moved, but nothing came out. He backed up a bit and then waved his finger at me, but not as firmly or with as much confidence as before.

"Just . . . mark my words," he said and turned his back on me.

I spun around just as Cary came down the stairs. I was crying now, the tears streaming down my cheeks.

"What's wrong?"

"The high and the mighty Logans have spoken again!" I spit through my teeth and charged up the stairs.

"Where are you going? It's dinner time."

"I'm not hungry. I'd rather starve than sit at the same table with him anyway," I cried and went into my room, slamming the door behind me. My body shuddered with my sobs. When I stopped to take a breath, I saw that Cary had put the beautiful sailboat on the shelf.

I went to it and wiped my cheeks as I stared at the tiny parts and the two people inside the cabin, looking happy and in love.

493

"No wonder Laura got into a sailboat with Robert," I muttered. "She just wanted to get away from here, get away from all this."

They did, but they died to do it, I thought. I looked at Laura's picture on the dresser.

Did you know what would happen to you that day, Laura? Did you deliberately sail into a storm? Maybe you were running away from a lot more than they all knew, or maybe you had seen something beyond the darkness, something more attractive and full of more hope. I wish I had known you; then maybe together we could have confronted the Logan misery.

I went to the window and gazed out at the ocean. The horizon seemed to mark the edge of the world. No wonder people believed you could fall off if you sailed too far. Tonight I wished I could do that. I'd rather take my chances in another world and escape the misery, the sadness, the deceit, and the loneliness I found in this one.

Almost two years before, Laura had stood at this window and looked out at that dark horizon. Did she see an answer? Did she see hope?

I wear your clothes and I sleep in your bed, and maybe, just maybe, I dream your dreams, Laura. Do I?

Answers, like the wispy clouds that drifted past the stars, lay beyond my reach. I gazed up, tantalized, tormented, feeling more and more lonely and afraid of what tomorrow would bring.

6
❧
Revelations

The knock on my door was so gentle that at first I thought I had imagined it. I was lying on my bed, staring up at the ceiling, drifting with my own childhood memories, memories that floated by like an old-time silent movie, the characters and events passing in silence: silent laughter, silent tears, Mommy and my step-daddy being playful, Papa George gazing up from his paper, Mama Arlene standing nearby, a soft, loving look on her face, everyone waving, applauding, arms held out, my step-daddy lifting me into the air, Papa George standing over me as I practiced on my fiddle. The memories became more liquid, rushed by faster, scenes merged, faces were swept away, the silent music stopped and there was my step-daddy's gravestone before me, growing larger, taller until there was nothing else in my vision.

The knocking grew louder.

"Yes?"

The door opened and Cary entered sheepishly, carrying a tray with my dinner.

"Hi," he ventured.

495

"Hi."

"Ma wanted me to bring this up to you."

"I'm not eating anything in this house again," I said. "I'm just resting a while and then I'm leaving."

"Don't be silly, Melody," Cary replied and put the tray on the desk. "Where will you go?"

"I don't care. Anywhere but here. I'll find work as a waitress or a scrub woman some place."

Cary laughed.

"I mean it. You know I left before and I can leave again, Cary."

"Okay, but in the meantime, if you don't eat, you'll only get sick and spite yourself. Go on. I'll keep you company. It's good meat loaf. Ma does a great job on that."

"I know she does. She told me. It's your father's favorite," I said, spitting the words at him. Cary shrugged.

"Doesn't make it taste any better or any worse. I like it a lot too, and so does May. And so will you," he added. "Come on, eat so I can brag how successful I was."

I gazed at the food. I was hungry and it was stupid to permit Uncle Jacob to make me suffer. I rose from the bed and went to the desk. The aroma of the meat loaf was enticing and I had to admit, it tasted wonderful and succulent, all the flavors just perfectly mixed. Cary sat watching me.

"I think your mother became a wonderful cook just so she would have some place in the house where she could be away from your father much of the time," I said.

"They were different before Laura died," Cary revealed. "We were all different. We did more things as a family. Dad wasn't as uptight about everything. We went for rides, went to restaurants, took walks on Sunday. During the cranberry harvest, we were all out

496

there working, and then there would be a big feast and celebration. Dad even danced with Ma."

"I don't believe it. Dancing is surely sinful," I said between mouthfuls.

"Everything became sinful after Laura's drowning. I told you. He blamed himself."

"Why was that, Cary? You've told me that, yes, but I don't understand. If your father lived such a moral life, read the Bible every night, made sure you were all so prim and proper, why would he feel responsible for an accident?"

Cary shook his head.

"That's between him and his own conscience, I suppose. I never asked him," he admitted.

"Maybe you should. If he's going to make everyone else suffer, he should at least explain why," I insisted.

"If we suffer, we suffer because of our own sins," Cary claimed. Then he looked away. I knew why.

"Maybe what you think is a sin isn't," I said softly. "It's not a sin to love someone too much."

"Yes, it is," he said quickly. "Remember Adam? Remember Original Sin?"

"Should I? Did I commit that, too?"

I started to smile. "All right, tell me."

"After Eve ate of the fruit and was doomed to be cast from Paradise, Adam ate so he would not be without her. That's loving too much," he explained.

"Just like a man to find another way to blame a woman for his own mistakes," I said. Cary's eyes widened.

"What?"

"That's just a Bible story, Cary. Do you really believe it?"

He turned away again.

"The Bible is full of lessons that prove true in our own lives," he recited mechanically.

I tried to see through his rehearsed words to the

497

true heartfelt feelings that lay behind them. There was something more he wasn't telling me. I could feel it in the silence and see it in the tight way he held his jaw.

"Everyone seems to want to bury his head in the sand in this family, Cary. It seems to be in the blood," I said dryly.

"What do you mean?"

"What do I mean? Right from the start, Grandma Olivia and Grandpa Samuel created a lie about who my mother was. My mother continued the lies and so did my step-daddy Chester. They put Grandma Belinda away so no one would learn the truth, whatever that is, and everyone went along with it, including your parents. Your mother told me lies are like termites eating at the moral foundation. If that were true, you'd all be living in rubble," I said.

Cary didn't argue. He nodded, looked horribly sad and tired. He stared at the floor for a while and when he finally lifted his head, his eyes were glassy, tearful.

"I lied too," he said. "I didn't make that hole in the floor just to watch over Laura when she was seeing Robert Royce. I made it before. I didn't know many girls and Laura was the softest, prettiest person in my life. Until she started seeing Robert, we did everything together. We never hid anything from each other.

"One day," he continued, "she started to lock her door. Everything in her life became so private and secret. She grew up faster, I suppose, even though we were twins. I felt left out, alone. I never had many friends at school. Laura was starting to make more friends, be invited to things without me. We were drifting apart. I don't know why I did it," he said. "She locked me out and I wanted to spy on her, I suppose, and see what it was that she would do by herself, why she wanted to be alone."

He raised his eyes to me again, this time tears emerging and trickling down his cheeks.

"I never told anyone this before."

"And you think that was your sin?" I asked softly.

"It was," he said. He took a deep breath. "I watched her without her knowing and at her most private times," he confessed.

My heart was pounding. The silence between the words was loud and revealing, as was the look in his eyes. I thought about the times I would have hated anyone spying on me. He was right: it was a serious violation.

"I'm sorry for it," he concluded. "The morning she left with Robert to go sailing, I was angry at her and she was angry at me and we never had a chance to make up. She had found out I had been watching her with Robert," he said. The pain in his voice made my heart ache.

"How?"

"I said something that only someone who had been spying on her would know. Maybe I wanted her to know; maybe I couldn't keep it inside anymore, the guilt. She never came back, so I could never tell her how sorry I was.

"That's why I went looking for her as long as I did. There were times during that search I stood up in my boat and shouted over the water, 'Laura, I'm sorry,' shouted until my throat ached. But she was gone. It was too late. She died hating me."

"I'm sure she didn't really hate you for it, Cary. She was angry, but you two were too close for hate to have a chance to set in any roots," I said trying to soothe his fears.

He shrugged, a small smile of gratitude on his lips.

"I was telling you the truth about the hole upstairs. I put the sofa over it and wiped it from my memory."

"I believe you, Cary."

499

"I didn't want you to think I was invading your privacy, too."

I smiled at him and he wiped the tears from his cheek.

"I believe you, Cary. I really do."

"Well, you ate. I guess I can brag," he said. He stood up, his eyes fixed on me, strong, loving, and very caring. "Don't run away, Melody. Ma's angry at Dad for what he said to you and he's feeling low. If you just pretend he never said anything—"

"More burying of the truth?"

"Sometimes, that's easier, I suppose."

"Easier, Cary, but there's always a price to pay when we hold a funeral for honesty, isn't there?"

"Maybe. All I know is I don't want you to leave."

"I won't leave," I said finally. "I still have some unfinished business, like finding out who my real father is," I added dryly.

Cary took the tray.

"I'll take it down myself," I said. "I don't need your father complaining about me being waited on, too."

"I don't mind waiting on you," Cary said.

Our eyes met again and the memory of our kisses and caresses upstairs in his attic workshop rushed back over me. I felt a flush come into my face, a tingling up and down my body. It was almost an ache, a craving, and it was so strong, it actually frightened me. Yet for all the warmth that flooded through me, I still felt an eerie chill as I thought of Cary's odd behavior and feelings for his sister. Thoughts and feelings that were definitely wrong, even sinful, Uncle Jacob would call them. I couldn't help wondering if the feelings Cary claimed to have for me were really leftover desires he'd had for Laura. Would I ever be loved or wanted for who I really was? But even as these thoughts flew through my mind I felt my body respond to Cary, felt the undeniable pull in my most

500

secret places. What was wrong with me that I could feel both repulsed and attracted at the same time?

Perhaps Uncle Jacob was right, perhaps I was truly a sinful wanton. Maybe there was something flowing through our veins, something lustful, sinful, evil. After all, I thought, I am Haille Logan's daughter. Maybe I would hurt Cary just the way Mommy had hurt young men, men like Kenneth Childs. Cary took a step toward me and I moved quickly to seize the tray and step around him.

"I'll take it down now," I said, avoiding his eyes. I knew if I looked, I would find two dark pools of disappointment.

When I reached the bottom of the stairway and turned, I saw Uncle Jacob in his chair listening to the news on the radio. May was sprawled on the rug by his feet, reading. Of course, she didn't hear me. Uncle Jacob's eyes fixed on me a moment and then shifted away, guiltily, I thought. I continued to the kitchen.

Aunt Sara wasn't there and the dishes were still piled in the sink. I rinsed mine off and put them in, too. I was going to clean up for her, but I was curious where she was. I saw that the back door was slightly open, so I went to it and peered out. There she was, sitting alone on the small bench, her arms folded across her chest, gazing into the darkness.

"Aunt Sara?"

"Oh," she said as if she had been caught doing something illegal or immoral. I stepped out quickly.

"I'm sorry," I said. "I didn't mean to ruin your dinner tonight."

She shook her head.

"Jacob doesn't mean half of what he says," she insisted. I tried to keep a look of disbelief from my face. It was something she had to believe to live in peace, I thought. "He always regrets his blustering," she continued. "I told him. I explained it. I was just taken by surprise. May is just curious. I know it's natural. You didn't do anything terrible. I should have been the one to start to explain. It's just that it's all so overwhelming, isn't it? You're going along, growing alongside boys, even playing the same games, and suddenly you find you're very different." Her laughter trickled off into the darkness.

I smiled at the simple but true statement. Then I sat beside her.

"Did you have a lot of boyfriends before Uncle Jacob, Aunt Sara?"

"Me? No. I never—no," she said. "Well, there was someone I had a crush on," she confessed, "but every girl had a crush on him."

"Who was that?"

"Teddy Jackson. He was always so handsome, even when he was only twelve."

"Oh," I said. It didn't surprise me that any woman would see Adam's father as a handsome dreamboat, it was just that my dislike of Adam was so strong, I wasn't happy to hear about it. Aunt Sara was into her own memories, however, and didn't notice my reaction.

"Of course, he never gave me a second look. He had all the prettiest girls. I was never much to look at."

"That's not true, Aunt Sara. You're a very pretty woman."

"Oh, I guess when I fix my hair and put on something nice, I don't embarrass Jacob, but I'm no movie star," she said, laughing. "Laura, Laura was the prettiest one."

"Yes."

"And so are you. Your mother was always pretty. She had the kind of beauty that caused everyone to stop and take notice."

"You better not mention her name anywhere near Uncle Jacob," I warned her bitterly.

502

She was silent as she looked into the darkness again.

"He didn't always feel that way about her," she said, but the way she said it sounded almost as if she were jealous. "He used to think the sun rose and fell on her smile. Just like all the young men, I guess."

"You'd never know it," I said. This revelation was making my head spin. It was the first time Aunt Sara had really talked about the past.

"Oh, I know it," she replied quickly. She shook her head. "I know it."

"What are you saying, Aunt Sara?" I asked, holding my breath.

"What? Oh." She laughed. "I'm not saying anything. Not anything important at least. Don't you think anything of anything Jacob bellows," she emphasized, patting me on the hand. "He's just uncomfortable around women and women talk, is all. He shouldn't have taken it out on you and I told him so." She looked away again.

"Someday, Aunt Sara," I said taking her hand and forcing her to turn back to me, "everyone in this family is going to have to start telling the truth."

"What do you mean, Melody?"

"I don't know what I mean yet, Aunt Sara, but I have a feeling you do, and so does Uncle Jacob, and especially Grandma Olivia."

She stared, fear in her eyes.

"Maybe you shouldn't have gone to see Belinda," she said, her voice in a whisper, "maybe she put bad thoughts in your head."

"Or maybe she pointed me toward the truth," I replied.

Aunt Sara shook her head sadly.

"Don't go out too far, Melody," she said in a voice suddenly full of wisdom and firmness, a voice unlike any other she had used before. "It's what happened to Laura."

503

She turned away to stare into the darkness as if she half expected her lost daughter to come walking up the beach, in from the sea and the storm.

I left her alone and cleaned up the dinner dishes before going up to bed to ponder her warning.

"I guess you didn't have such a great weekend," Kenneth said after glancing at me when I got into his jeep Monday morning. He put it in gear and drove away before I could respond. He glanced at me again as we turned down the street and headed out of town. I sat stroking Ulysses and gazing out at the ocean. A number of times during the night I had wakened from sleep, nudged by a troubling image or the memory of harsh words. I would lie there staring into the darkness, listening to the creaks in the old house as the wind blew in from the sea. Even on the brightest of days, there were too many shadows in this home, I thought, and the wind sounded more like whispers on the stairs or just outside my door.

I wasn't the only one struggling with the past. There was a silent war being conducted here, a war with no guns, but fierce battles nevertheless, with the casualties being truth, happiness, and contentment.

"Don't want to talk about it?" Kenneth finally asked.

"I visited Grandma Belinda," I said.

"How did it go?"

"She said many things, some silly, I suppose, but some that infuriated Grandma Olivia."

"I bet," he said with a smile.

"She said Grandpa Samuel liked her more and she said your father was one of her boyfriends and that made Grandma Olivia jealous," I blurted.

His smile froze first and then metamorphosed into a hard, deep expression of pain.

"That's why she's in a rest home," he mumbled.

504

"She looks healthy and she's sweet, gentle, child-like," I continued. He drove, his face sullen.

"I'm sorry about what she said about your father."

"It doesn't surprise me," he replied. He turned to me with a smirk on his face. "I've heard such talk about him before. Dad was always what is euphemistically referred to as a ladies' man," he said, sarcastically.

"He can be very charming," I admitted.

Kenneth looked at me askance.

"You too?" He shook his head. "As long as it's in a skirt, he can't resist, no matter what the age."

"Is that why you don't get along?" I asked quickly, trying not to be offended by his callous remark.

"How he conducts himself is his business, not mine," Kenneth replied. "Let's not talk about him. It puts me into a bad mood," he said and then turned to me. "Just as you've been told, digging up the past is only going to revive unhappiness and we have enough to contend with in the present.

"Besides," he added, "you're my special model now. I don't want you coming around with a long, sad look on your face. I want you fresh, lovely, and curious about yourself, not others. Concentrate on our concept when you're with me," he added as we drew closer to his house and studio.

"You're the one who asked me about the weekend," I shot back.

He thought on that and then nodded.

"You're right." He held up his hand. "I'm guilty, which shows you, even I can be tempted into the wrong frame of mind. I'll make a pact with you," he said as he pulled into the driveway. "I won't ask you any questions about your private life and you won't ask me any about mine. We'll just be in the world of art, okay?"

"Art isn't a world separate from the real world," I

said, my eyes narrow, my gaze fixed and determined. "Ideas, images, colors all come from your experiences, don't they?"

He stared silently at me, a friendly, almost loving glint coming into his eyes before he smiled.

"You're quite a kid," he said. He said it with such admiration and pride, I had to blush. "Okay, you're right. But we'll do our best. Deal?" He extended his hand. I stared at it a moment. He wanted me to swear to be silent, to lock up my thoughts and questions, to put aside my quest for truth. I shook my head.

"I can't promise something I'm not sure I have the strength or even the willingness to do," I said.

He sighed with frustration and then smiled again.

"All right, but at least promise you'll try. It's important to my work." He waited.

"I'll try," I offered, weakly.

It was enough for now. He hopped out of the jeep and I followed, Ulysses at our heels.

"I've been working all weekend," he said as we went around the house to the studio. "Even without my star," he added, throwing a smile back at me.

When he opened the studio door, I saw what he meant. Near the marble block, there was a large papier-mâché mass shaped like a wave about to crash on shore.

"It's not exactly right yet, but that's something like the wave I've envisioned," he said. "Do you see the opening in the center?"

"Yes."

"I want you to go behind the wave, crawl under, and come up through that hole."

"Really?"

"That's the idea. I can picture you emerging from a wave, as part of the wave, this way. Understand?"

"Yes," I said, thinking it was a very clever idea.

"Just crawl in first and then I'll tell you how I want you to stand and so on." He went to his drawing table.

506

Then he nodded at me and I walked around the papier-mâché wave. I found where he had left room for me to go under and come up through the opening. At first, I felt a bit silly, but I did it.

"Okay," he said and stepped away from his table. "Okay." He nodded, stared, thought, walked about and then nodded again. "Okay, this is going to be a bit tricky, but don't worry. We'll get it right. Go back down and come up very, very slowly. I just want to see the top of your head at first."

I did as he asked.

"Stop," he said when my head was visible. "Very slowly now, keep coming up, yes, slower, stop. Perfect. Is that very uncomfortable for you?"

"Yes," I admitted.

He thought a moment and then moved quickly to the settee. He gathered up the big cushions and brought them behind the paper wave.

"Hold that position until I stuff these pillows under you," he said. "Okay, you can sit there."

He ran around to the front again.

"That'll work for a while," he said. "Come on out and I'll explain it to you in more detail," he said.

I wriggled out of the wave and took my place beside him. He had already drawn a sketch of the wave, but had left the middle undone, waiting for me.

"It's hard to think of a picture, a painting, a sculpture as having movement, but this is what I have to capture here because the movement is your development, your emergence from the sea into this beautiful young woman. Your body will first appear liquid, flowing, but it will start to emerge separate from the wave."

I nodded, although I wasn't sure I really understood.

"Now," he said, pausing and turning to me, "you wouldn't emerge dressed in a sweatshirt and a pair of jeans. Do you understand what I'm trying to say?"

My pulse began to throb, my heart racing at the thought of what he was alluding to. The idea of standing naked before Kenneth, whether he was my father or not, made me queasy.

"Yes," I said almost too softly to be heard.

"I have to have you comfortable, at ease. You've got to get past yourself and me and become part of this work, the essence of this work. Think of yourself as the sculpture and not as Melody Logan undressed in some barn, okay?"

I nodded, weakly.

"My shoulders are too bony and my collarbone sticks out too far," I complained. "I also have a patch of freckles all over here," I said, pointing to my chest just below my collarbone.

Kenneth smiled.

"I don't think that's going to be a problem for us, Melody, and you're far from bony. Look," he said more patiently, "I know it's unfair to ask you to achieve a professional attitude the first time you model for someone, and I won't expect perfection right away, but in time, you'll see," he said with a warm smile. "As hard as it is to believe, it will become very ordinary after a while."

He paused and looked at the door.

"You didn't tell anyone about this, did you?" he asked quickly.

I shook my head.

"Good."

The realization of what he feared made me laugh, especially when I considered how Uncle Jacob had reacted to the little I had told May about a woman's body. Suddenly, all the fear and nervousness left me, as I realized that modeling for Kenneth was just the thing to get Uncle Jacob's goat.

"What's so funny?" he asked, smiling.

I told him about May's revelation of her first kiss

508

and then her questions, and how I had described the changes a girl experiences as she matures. I explained that I had even given her some information about making a baby. And then I told him what had happened between me and Uncle Jacob when May, brought up something I had said in front of him and Aunt Sara.

"I can't wait to see Uncle Jacob's face when he sees Neptune's Daughter," I said, still unable to keep the laughter from my voice.

"Jacob's a horse's ass," Kenneth said. "He always was. He never had many friends and he was always the object of jokes and ridicule because of this high-and-mighty moral attitude of his, as if he were some sort of Old Testament prophet. Haille teased him a lot, too," he added with a small laugh.

"She did? Will you tell me about it?"

He sighed.

"All right. Here's the deal. I'll tell you about the old days when we break for lunch or rests, if you promise not to ask any questions, not to talk while I work. Deal?" he offered.

This time I seized his hand so fast, it brought a real laugh to his lips. Then he grew serious.

"We'll do this slowly," he said, "as slowly as I envision it in the work itself. Just take off that sweatshirt for now. I want to see you up to here this morning," he said indicating just above my breasts. "Your face, neck, and shoulders. Model, take your position," he ordered with a smile and wave of his hand.

I went behind the papier-mâché wave and pulled off my sweatshirt. Then I crawled through the opening and sat on the pillows, just my head emerging. He began to work, and as he did, I saw his face become so intense, his eyes so riveting, I couldn't keep mine off him.

509

After a while he said, "Another pillow."

I understood he meant for me to put another sofa pillow under myself so I would come up a bit more. When my head was as high as he had indicated he wanted he continued to work on and on.

"This is just the shape, the outline," he explained. "We're going to spend a lot of time discussing the expression on your face, how I want you to look, your eyes, your mouth. The best way to do that is to get you to think of something in your own past that will fit this, some event, some moment, some thoughts and experiences."

"Just as I told you: art isn't in a world by itself," I quipped smugly. He paused and smiled.

"All right. Don't be a smartass," he said and we both laughed.

Maybe I would be able to do this. Maybe I would be able to relax and help him create his greatest work, I thought.

"Break," he called after nearly another hour. He brought me a large bath towel to drape over my shoulders, and put on some water for tea. The towel covered my shoulders and bra. I used it to wipe the perspiration from my face and neck.

"It really is work just standing still," I said. He nodded.

"I'd rather be on this side of the brush," he admitted. "You take sugar, right?"

"Just one teaspoon, thank you."

"You know, what you were telling me about May and her questions is exactly the sort of thing I'm after here," he said. He sat at the small table and I sat on a stool beside him. "She's emerging out of childhood into the first stages of womanhood. Can you recall when this first happened to you?"

"Yes, I guess so."

"What was it like?"

"Scary and wonderful," I said. He nodded, obviously encouraging me to continue. I thought about it. "There were new feelings in old places." He smiled.

"Yes," he said. "Exactly."

"When May told me about her first kiss, I thought about mine and how I had run all the way home and gone into my room to be alone with my excitement. I wrote the boy's name about two million times and dreamed about more kisses, longer kisses."

"Did you tell your mother about it?"

"After a while."

"And?" he asked, very interested in what she had said.

"She laughed and told me not to believe in kisses or any promises made while kissing. She said to make them pay, that they're never too young to pay. I didn't understand at the time," I said, waiting to see what he would offer as an explanation for Mommy's bitter attitude about men.

"She ruined the moment with that kind of talk. You have to believe in the magic first. Haille didn't stop for magic. That was her problem," he said. "I don't think she enjoyed growing up, or gave herself enough time for innocence, understand?"

"Sort of. You mean she grew up too fast?"

"Worse. She gave herself away too young," he said. My breath caught.

"How do you know that?"

"She told me," he said, and I understood it hadn't been with him. "But let's get back to you. When you're coming up out of the wave, you're just feeling these new sensations and you're full of the same sort of questions May had about herself, questions you had, too. Understand? Think of that, concentrate on it." He paused and glanced at me. "Your body is developing. There are tingles, feelings, sensations in places there never were before. You're standing in

511

front of the mirror, naked, and you're seeing things that, as you said, surprise, frighten, and thrill you at the same time. Okay?"

I nodded. The air was so warm around me. I did feel as if I had slipped back in time. His words worked magic. My body remembered itself, the first tingles returned, the images—

The teakettle whistled, breaking my reverie. He poured us each a cup and offered me a cracker.

"How do you know so much about women?" I asked, and he laughed.

"Me? I'm far from the expert on women. You're confusing me with dear old Dad."

"Is that réally why you and he don't get along so well?"

"That's part of it," he said, taking a sip of tea. "Parents shouldn't try to force their children to follow in their footsteps, especially if their feet are made of clay," he said.

He talked a little about how his father had pressured him to go to law school and then how he had rebelled. I told him about Cary and his dream to leave fishing and become a ship builder of custom boats.

"I told him to tell his father."

"Did he do it?" he asked, his eyebrows raised in anticipation.

"Yes."

"And?"

"His father threw a fit, telling him it was family tradition to be a fisherman and a cranberry farmer and he had to continue."

"Horse's ass," Kenneth said.

"Cary will do it. Some day," I said firmly. Kenneth stared at me, a softness in his eyes.

"You like him a lot, don't you?"

"Yes," I admitted.

"Romantically?"

512

not the neatest, most organized individual you've met.

"Anyway," he added, "you can do what you can here for twenty minutes or so. We're finished for the day. I'm just going down to the beach for a while to think. Then I'll come back and take you home," he said.

He left with Ulysses at his heels and I went to work cleaning and organizing the studio. I swept up the dust and chips from the marble block, cleaned and arranged the tools, and fixed the sofa again. As I was moving about, I paused at the drawing desk. I hadn't looked at the pictures yet. Kenneth hadn't offered and I was afraid to ask. Now, they were covered with a white sheet, and I wondered if Kenneth was the type who hated anyone looking at a work in progress. I hesitated.

I couldn't help feeling we had grown closer because of this project and I hated to do anything that might threaten our relationship. Little betrayals, indiscretions, and lies eventually tore down a foundation of love and friendship, I thought. I had enough evidence of that, and now, because of how things were going between us, I regretted permitting Cary to take off the lock on Kenneth's storage room so that we could invade his private and secret cache of paintings, even if they were paintings of my mother and stirred more mystery.

I continued to clean and organize the studio, but my attention kept returning to the drawing table. What harm would one peek do? I thought. Surely, if Kenneth really wanted me not to look, he would have said something. I listened for him, heard nothing, and returned to the drawing table. Slowly, I lifted the sheet and gazed at the first drawing.

There was far more detail in my face than I had anticipated. This was more than a sketch, but the face I saw on the paper looked more like my mother's face

513

I nodded, sensing Kenneth wouldn't judge me for my relationship with Cary.

"Not your first boyfriend, is he?" he asked. He was sounding more like my father now, a father who hadn't seen his daughter growing up.

"No, but he's the most . . ."

"Serious?"

I nodded again and sipped my tea.

"Don't give your heart away too quickly, Melody. It's the most precious gift you can give any man," he advised.

"I won't be like my mother, if that's what you mean," I said sharply.

He smiled.

"Good," he said. "That's good."

We returned to work. Kenneth put more detail into his drawing. He explained that he intended to do at least a half dozen of these pictures, each taking the metamorphosis to another stage so that it would be like doing an animation. When he flipped the pictures quickly, he would get the illusion of movement and that illusion would be embedded in his mind as he hoped it would be in the marble block.

After lunch he showed me how to use some of the carving tools to do the preliminary work on the block. Even though it was hard work, I enjoyed it, enjoyed knowing I really was contributing to this artistic masterpiece. The day flew by and I didn't have much time to tend to my usual chores, but when Kenneth announced it was time to stop, I was actually disappointed.

"It's all right," he told me when I complained about not being able to clean and organize his house, especially after a weekend. Mondays were always the hardest because he seemed to get even sloppier on Saturdays and Sundays. "This is what an artist's life is like. Now you can understand and appreciate why I'm

than it did mine. At least, I thought it did, and that caused me to drop the sheet quickly when I heard Kenneth's footsteps. He entered just as I moved away. His eyes shifted from the table to me and then back to the table.

"Well," he said, crossing the studio, "you've got this place looking proper again. Makes me feel guilty every time I mess it up," he said with a smile. He paused at the table and lifted the sheet. "What do you think?" he asked gazing at the picture.

"What?"

"I'm sure you snuck a peek, Melody. I would have."

"Oh. I . . . yes. I did. I was surprised at how much detail you got into it already," I said, trying to keep the disappointment out of my voice.

"Uh-huh. That sounds diplomatic."

"I'm not an art critic. Not yet, at least," I said. "But it looks like the beginning of something special." If only it was my face that would grace his masterpiece, I thought.

"Yes. It's only a figment of my imagination right now, but soon, it will grow. You know, this is going to take us all summer," he said.

"I'm not going anywhere," I replied. "I was going to run away yesterday, but then I thought, where would I run to?"

He stared at me and I held my breath, hoping he would offer his home as a sanctuary should I need it. But he remained silent. If the words were on his tongue, he swallowed them.

"I guess the bottom line is none of us can really run away. We can escape but we can't run away," he said.

"How can we escape if we don't run away?" I asked.

"You find another place to go inside yourself," he said, staring at the block of marble.

"As you found with your art?"

He nodded.

"What were you escaping from?" I asked and

515

waited as he hesitated, his eyes still on the block of marble.

"Myself," he said.

"Yourself?"

"Who I found out I was," he said. He shook his head. "Give me time, Melody. Give me time to find a way to tell you what you want to know."

My heart skipped a beat.

The rebirth Kenneth was creating out of this block of marble might truly be my own.

7

∞

Sing for Your Supper

Cary was in the driveway washing Uncle Jacob's truck when Kenneth brought me home. He was in cut-off shorts, shirtless and barefoot. May was helping, soaping up the fenders, getting almost as much suds dripping down her arms and legs as she was putting on the truck. Unhindered by clouds, the late afternoon sun was still strong enough to make things gleam, especially Cary's bare shoulders and back, emphasizing his muscularity. He turned toward us as we slowed to a stop.

"Good-looking boy," Kenneth muttered. "He has the best of the Logan features, softened by his mother's side fortunately. I see why you're drawing hearts in the sand," he added with a wink. I blushed so crimson, I was sure I looked sunburnt.

Cary's face lit up with a smile as soon as he saw us, and May came rushing over to play with Ulysses.

"Hi, Mr. Childs," Cary said, approaching. "I'd shake your hand, but . . ." He held up his soapy fingers.

"It's all right. I'm not allergic to soap and water,

517

even though Melody might have told you otherwise," he said.

My jaw dropped.

"I wouldn't—"

"How's the catch these days?" Kenneth asked Cary after laughing at me.

"We had a very good day. Dad's quite pleased," he said, glancing at me. "It's put him in a good mood. For once."

"That's good. And the cranberries?"

"Looks as if it's going to be a heavy harvest," Cary replied. "Heavier than last year."

"Melody tells me you're into boat building."

Cary shot me a look of surprise.

"Well, yes, I am but—"

"I have a boat plan I'd like to show you one day. Maybe I'll have Melody bring it home and you can take a quick look at it and make some suggestions," Kenneth said. Cary's face changed from surprise to genuine awe.

"Really?"

"I've always had it on the back burner, but perhaps it's time to get the construction under way," Kenneth said. "See you bright and early, Melody."

"I'll be early, but I don't know how bright I'll be," I said.

He laughed, checked to be sure May was not standing too close to the jeep, then shifted the gears and pulled away. Cary, May, and I watched him and Ulysses disappear around the turn, Ulysses facing us all the way, looking like a small child who wished he could stay with his friends.

"Was he kidding about the boat?" Cary asked.

"It's the first time I've heard him mention it, Cary. But he's full of surprises and secrets, no different from anyone else around here."

Cary nodded, the soap suds dripping off his forearm.

518

"Need some help?" I asked.

"No, we're just about finished. May and I will just dry her off." He signed instructions and May returned to the pail and sponge.

"I have to shower," I said. "I'm full of marble dust." I started toward the house.

"How about a quick dip instead?" Cary suggested. "Just throw on your suit and we'll go down to the beach."

"Then I'll have to wash the salt out of my hair before I sit down at the dinner table," I complained.

"Women," he said, groaning.

"Why don't we go after dinner—a night swim," I suggested. His eyes brightened.

"Really? Great." He looked at May. "Ma doesn't like her swimming at night so—"

"We'll bring her tomorrow." I said, hoping that May wouldn't mind.

"Okay. I'll find something for her to do while we're gone, so she won't feel left out," he said and returned to the truck.

Cary was right about Uncle Jacob. He was in a rare happy mood, actually buoyant. He didn't apologize for the way he had yelled at me the night before, but his tone of voice was softer when he asked me to pass him things at the dinner table and when he thanked me. Also, whenever he spoke, he actually spoke to me, rather than around me. Apparently, today's catch was as good as they used to be. It was like striking gold.

The happiness in Aunt Sara's face made her eyes younger as well as brighter. It was nice to hear her laugh, and even to hear Uncle Jacob laugh. As I gazed at them, all full of smiles, everyone treating everyone politely, considerately, the food as wonderful as ever, the cranberry wine sparkling in the glasses, I was able to envision this family before Laura's tragedy and I

519

was able to see what Cary had described. Even if it were destined to be short lived, the joviality warmed my heart and made me feel I was part of a real family again. There was no better music to drive away the shadows than the sound of laughter.

Suddenly, as the meal was coming to an end, Uncle Jacob leaned on his elbows toward me, his eyes dark and fixed, his smile gone.

"What say you earn your supper tonight, Missy?" he said. I glanced at Cary, who shrugged, and then at Aunt Sara, whose mouth hung open.

"How?" I asked.

"You know, like people did in olden times. Found a way to pay for their dinner."

"What do you want me to do?" I asked, my throat tightening, my voice hardening.

He slapped his hands together.

"We'll all adjourn to the living room and have a private concert. What do you say, Sara? Can you let these dishes wait?"

"You mean, you want me to play my fiddle?" I asked, astounded.

"It's somethin' you do real good," he replied. Cary was beaming like the cat that had gotten to the fish on the counter in the kitchen.

"I—" I gazed at Aunt Sara. She'd never looked happier. For a moment I felt as if I had sat at the dinner table in the wrong house.

"Well?" Uncle Jacob pursued.

"Okay," I said, still amazed at his request.

"Then it's settled," he said slapping his hands together and standing. "Mrs. Logan?" He held out his arm and Aunt Sara giggled and joined him. "We'll adjourn to the sitting room for a private concert," he said and held his other arm out for May. Cary had signed a quick summary of what was happening. She leaped to her feet and took her father's arm.

"What's going on?" I asked Cary as we watched them leave the room.

"I don't know. But as Dad often says, don't look a gift horse in the mouth. Shall we?" Cary held out his arm and I took it, still quite shocked and confused. When we got to the stairway, I went upstairs to get my fiddle.

They were all sitting in the living room waiting for me with great expectation on their faces when I appeared in the doorway. Uncle Jacob was settling back in his chair, puffing his pipe. Aunt Sara sat on the couch with Cary on one side and May on the other.

"May has a way of hearing this," I explained and gestured for her to come to me. She understood. When I put the fiddle up, she placed her hand on the case so she could feel the vibrations while I played. I did seven tunes, singing along with three of them. Aunt Sara looked very pleased and Uncle Jacob nodded and tapped his fingers along with the rhythms. Cary never took his eyes from me.

"Well, that's real nice," Uncle Jacob said. "You earned yourself a few dinners."

"I'll see to the dishes," Aunt Sara said, rising. "That was wonderful, Melody. Thank you."

"I'll put away my fiddle and come help you clean up, Aunt Sara."

"Oh no, you don't," she said. "You heard Jacob. You earned your keep. Just go enjoy yourself," she insisted.

I went back upstairs to put away my fiddle. While I was busy returning it to its case, Cary poked his head in the door.

"How about that dip in the ocean?" he asked.

"What about May?"

"I gave her something to do on one of my models. She's painting."

"You mean you bribed her?" I said, laughing.

521

"Whatever works," he said.

"Okay. I'll put on my bathing suit."

"Put it under your clothes," he said. "I'd rather it be our secret."

I nodded and did as he said. We met down by the front door and left quickly, letting Uncle Jacob and Aunt Sara think we were just taking a walk.

"I don't like doing things behind their backs like this, Cary," I complained.

"Why make Ma nervous, which is what would happen," he said. "It's not really a lie when you're doing it to help someone else, Melody. It's only a lie when you hurt someone or you can't live with it," he added.

Maybe he was right, I thought. Maybe I was holding up too high a standard because I had been lied to so much and for so long. He took my hand and we first went to the lobster boat where he said there were towels. After we got them, we crossed the sand toward one of his favorite places on the beach. It was a small cove, hidden by two small dunes.

I didn't really notice the stars until Cary spread out the biggest towel and we sat for a few moments, gazing out at the ocean and then up at the sky. Cary pointed out the Big Dipper, the North Star, and what he said was Venus.

"A sailor has to be able to read the stars," he explained. "They're his map."

"I've never been on a boat at night, but I can imagine how lost and alone you could feel if you didn't know how to steer your boat," I said.

"Without the stars, the darkness is so thick, you feel as if the ocean has risen all around you and you're sailing into it," Cary said. "Of course, we have our compasses. I think I was on the water before I could walk on land. Dad wanted me to have my sea legs first."

I laughed and he pulled off his shirt and stood up.

"It will be cold at first," he warned, "but after you're in it a few seconds, it will feel great."

It was a warm night, wonderful for a dip in the ocean. I stood up and unbuttoned my blouse. He stepped out of his pants and then kicked off his shoes. I took off my dungarees, placed my shoes and socks on the towel and then reached out to take his hand when he offered it. We walked down to the water slowly. When the white foam ran over my toes, I jumped.

"Easy," Cary said putting his arm around my waist.

"It's colder than I thought," I said and tried to retreat, but he tightened his grip on my waist.

"You'll love it."

"Cary, I don't think so," I said shaking my head. He laughed and tugged until I stepped farther down the beach. The water reached my ankles.

"You've just got to go for it," he advised. He let go of me and turned to dive right into the waves. When he popped up, he was laughing. "It's great," he claimed. "Makes you feel alive all over."

"Sure," I said, hesitating.

"Come on. Be brave."

My heart was pounding. Suddenly, the stars looked more like drops of ice above me. Cary splashed about to demonstrate how comfortable he was. He called again, urged and pleaded. I took a deep breath and ran forward, falling into the water. The shock made me scream. Cary was at my side, laughing. He embraced me and we stood with the sand washing out from under our feet as the tide rushed in around us. I grew a little afraid, even with his arms around me, and started for shore.

"I'm freezing!" I screamed, "and I'm going to be washed out to sea."

He laughed but followed. We splashed through the

water, and ran up the sand to the beach towel. Cary unfolded another towel quickly and put it around my shoulders, hugging me and rubbing me at the same time.

"Aren't you cold?" I asked, my teeth chattering.

"Not when I'm with you," he said and kept rubbing me dry. "How's that?"

"A little better," I said, still shivering. The chill on my skin tingled. I sat on the beach towel and Cary wrapped a towel around his own shoulders and then began to massage my feet, my ankles, and my calves.

"Weren't you really cold in the water, Cary Logan?"

"I guess I'm just used to it," he said.

"It looked so warm all day, I thought it would still be." My body shook with a spasm and he laughed.

"Nature can be deceiving," he warned and sprawled beside me.

"I don't know if I can stay out here much longer, Cary," I said. It was as if the chill had gone deep into me and turned my stomach to ice. "It's the wet bathing suit."

"Why don't you take it off then?" he said.

"What?"

"Slip out of it, dry yourself, and put on your pants and shirt," he suggested. "There's no one around," he added. I gazed back. The dunes were empty, not a soul in sight. All we heard was the sound of the surf. He moved closer to me and then he kissed me.

"Your lips are warm," I said, "even though your face feels cold."

He laughed, rubbed my shoulders, and then kissed my neck. The mixture of the chill and the warm tingle that shot down my spine made me shudder and then moan. Cary's fingers slid beneath the straps of my suit, lifting them off my shoulders. As he shifted me into a sitting position, holding me closer to him, the straps slid further down my arms. Then he ran my

524

towel under the suit, drying me as the suit fell away. He reached around the side of my breasts.

"Cary," I whispered, "don't."

"Shh. I'll warm you up again," he promised. My heart was pounding, the blood rushing through my body, making me feel lightheaded and dizzy. I felt as if I would spin into unconsciousness if I lifted my eyes toward the sky of blazing stars. Cary gently lifted my arms, one by one, until they were both free from the straps. Then he peeled the front of the suit away and my breasts were uncovered, my nipples tingling in the cool night air. They were so erect, they arched. Cary lowered me slowly to the blanket and continued to peel away my suit. I started to resist until he lowered his head and kissed my breasts, moving his tongue quickly over one nipple and then the other. I closed my eyes and lay back, lifting myself gently to help him take the wet suit from my body. When it fell beneath my hips and I realized I would soon be totally naked, I gasped.

"Cary."

"It's all right," he said. "It's only me. We're alone."

I lifted my hand to touch his face and then he pulled the bathing suit down and over my knees. Immediately, he wrapped me in my towel and held me close, so close I could feel his heart thumping. Then he rubbed the towel all over me, wiping me dry, warming my body until I felt absolutely comfortable and content.

Cary then lay down beside me, kissing my cheeks, my nose, my eyes, nibbling softly on my chin and then kissing my neck and shoulders as his hands continued to rub my body in circles, finding my breasts, moving his palms in circles over them and then coming down the sides of my body until he held my hips. He leaned over me, gazing down at me. His face was in darkness, but just enough light came from the stars to allow me to see his gentle lips in a small smile.

525

"Melody, you were meant to be here. Ma's right. You were brought here to make us all well again, especially me," he said.

He kissed me long and hard on the lips and then he slipped beside me, moving about until I realized he was taking off his own bathing suit.

"Cary, wait—"

"Just touch," he said. "We'll just touch."

Then he was naked too, and I felt him throbbing, moving in between my legs as he threw his towel over us like a blanket.

"Cary, don't," I said. "We could make a baby like this."

"I know. I'll be careful," he said, but he didn't stop. The sensation that flew through my body when he touched me where no boy had ever touched me before made me tremble so, I thought I would be unable to stop him if things started to go too far. He nudged me again and again. I began to cry softly, but his lips drank my tears before they could go far down my cheeks. He kept reciting my name, chanting it like a prayer.

"I love you, Melody," he said. "I couldn't love anyone as much as I love you."

I didn't know if I could speak. My heart was racing. Cary was out of control. In a few more moments, I was sure I would be too.

This is what happened to your mother, I heard a voice inside me say. Remember what Kenneth said? Remember him telling you how she would jump on the back of a motorcycle and end up on a beach blanket? Well you're on a beach blanket now, Melody Logan, and you're naked and about to do what she did.

I shook my head at the words resounding inside me.

"No," I cried and pushed at Cary's chest.

"Melody, I love you."

"Please, stop Cary," I said.

"I can't," he said. "I can't."

But he pulled back, his sex exploding on the blanket, his head against my chest, his whole body shuddering and then coming to rest.

Neither of us moved. It was as though the world revolved around us as we stayed perfectly still. Caught in a moment of time. My heartbeat started to slow and my breathing came easier. Still, neither of us moved, neither said anything. We lay there, holding each other, both equally amazed at our discoveries about ourselves and each other.

"I'm sorry," he finally said. "I'm so clumsy and inexperienced. You were right. I shouldn't have started to do this without the proper protection. You probably think I'm an idiot." He sat up quickly.

"No, I don't, Cary. I'm not very experienced at this either, no matter what you might think." I sat up, too, holding the towel around me.

"You're not?" he said skeptically.

"No, I'm not. Why?" I asked, turning on him. "Do you think I'm like my mother when she was my age? Is that it?" I asked hotly.

"No," he said.

"Maybe I am. Maybe it is in my blood," I said bitterly. "I shouldn't have let you go as far as you did, but . . ."

"But what? It's not a sin if you love me as much as I love you," he said. "You wouldn't do this with any other boy, would you?"

I shook my head.

"So? Don't you see? That means we love each other." He leaned toward me again to kiss me, but I pulled back.

"No more, Cary. I just want to get dressed and go back to the house."

"You're not mad at me, are you?"

"No. I'm just a little confused about everything. Please try to be understanding," I insisted.

527

"Okay," he said. He stood up and we both dressed silently in the darkness.

"I probably look as if I've been rolling around on the beach," I moaned.

"We'll stop at the boat and you can straighten up," he said, but his voice was different, strained. I knew he was displeased with my reaction, but I really was confused. I had wanted this and yet, when it started to happen, I was too afraid to continue. Was I just like my mother or was I really as in love with Cary as I imagined? Was it the fact that so many people would frown on our relationship that worried me?

He gathered the towels and we started away, carrying our wet suits. Cary walked a little faster, remaining a foot or so in front of me.

"Don't be angry at me, Cary," I said. "I have too many confusing things going on inside me right now to think clearly about anything. Do you really, truly believe that it is right for there to be love between us, when there is also blood? I want to believe that it is right Cary, but aren't you afraid of what everyone will think?"

He plodded along, not answering me.

"Cary?"

"It will be all right," he said. "I'm not angry at you. The truth is I'm just as confused. Nothing is as simple as we think, I suppose, even love."

I went into the bathroom on the boat, where there was a small wall mirror, and repaired myself the best I could. When I came out, Cary was sitting and gazing out at the ocean. I came up beside him and put my hand gently on his shoulder. He put his hand over mine and continued to look out at the water.

"The water keeps moving," he said. "It looks the same, but it never is. Everything's in a constant state of change. Trees grow new leaves. They look the same as last year's leaves, but they're different. Even the sand on the beach moves. The wind shifts it. Maybe

528

we're changing all the time, too," he said. "Maybe I was different yesterday, even though I look the same today."

"That's what they say in science class. We're always breaking down and rebuilding cells."

"So," he said, turning quickly, "what about our feelings? Do they break down and change, too? If I love you today, will that love be different tomorrow?"

"I don't know."

"I don't think love changes. I think that it stays the same even though everything around it becomes different. I'll love you the same way when you're old and gray and I'm old and gray. No matter what anyone thinks Melody, I know it is right between us. Our love is special."

I smiled.

"You believe me, don't you?" he asked with worried eyes.

"Yes, Cary."

"Then, don't be afraid to love me too," he said. "No matter what your mother was or did. You're not your mother."

"I know," I said. "I just need a little more time to figure everything out. I want to be ready, Cary. I need to be sure."

He nodded and then turned back to the ocean. I stood by him and we both watched the waves dance with the stars until we grew tired and walked home, holding hands, silent, full of wonder.

I noticed something different about Kenneth immediately the next morning. Even Ulysses appeared changed, more subdued, as if he had been chastised just before they arrived to pick me up. Kenneth mumbled a quick good morning and pulled away with an awkward jerk that sent me back against the seat. He drove fast, the wheels squealing as he made the turn and accelerated, pulling around a slower car and going even faster. He never took his eyes off the road. I was afraid to say anything. Artists were so moody. One minute they were ecstatic, the next, they were melancholy. We bounced hard on the dune road because he took that faster than usual also. I was relieved when we finally came to a stop in his driveway.

He got out, slammed the door behind him, and then, to my surprise, instead of heading for the studio, turned and walked toward the beach. Even Ulysses looked confused, turning from Kenneth to me and then back to Kenneth.

"Aren't we going right to the studio?" I asked, running to catch up with him.

"No. I have to calm down first," he said over his shoulder, not even bothering to turn around.

"Calm down? Why? What happened?"

Instead of replying, he sped up and walked on. I followed, slowly this time, until we reached the top of the rise on the beach and he stood there gazing out at the ocean, his hands on his hips.

"What's this all about, Kenneth?" I asked, my heart thumping now. "Did I do something wrong?"

"Did you?" he snapped, spinning on me. His eyes were just as full of pain as they were of anger.

"No," I said softly, feeling shame flush my cheeks.

He smiled with disdain.

"Lying is just in the blood, is that it? It comes so quickly, so naturally to you people." He turned away again.

I couldn't keep the tears from climbing over my eyelids and sizzling down my cheeks.

"I'm not lying," I said.

"Really?" He reached down to take a handful of sand and watched it fall through his fingers. "Then you didn't go into my private storage room?" he said without looking at me.

I stopped breathing, the breath that was already

caught in my throat choking me. After a moment, I found the strength to reply.

"Yes, I did," I admitted. The shame that had made me hot with embarrassment turning to cold fear.

He turned slowly, nodding.

"I noticed the hasp had been removed. Whoever broke in did a fine job, but in haste one bottom screw was left a little too far out. I wouldn't have thought anything of it, however, if, when I opened the door myself last night and entered the room, I didn't notice that the cobwebs were all broken and the canvases had been moved and not put back as neatly as they were. Got a good look at everything, did you?"

"No," I said.

"Did you take the hasp off yourself?" When I didn't answer immediately, Kenneth made the right conclusion. "No, you didn't. Who went in there with you, Cary?"

I nodded and looked down.

"I took you into my home, trusted you with my privacy, my possessions, my work. Now you can understand why I don't have many people out here," he said. "People." He spit the word as if it burned his tongue to utter it. "They always let you down."

"I'm sorry, Kenneth," I said. "I—"

"Yes? Tell me. How do you justify breaking and entering my private place? Go on," he taunted and challenged. "Let me hear your excuse."

"I was looking for the truth," I cried through my tears.

"The truth?"

"About you and me and my mother," I said. "Everyone thinks you're my father, and you told me that you couldn't tell me what you knew, so I thought . . . I thought you were ashamed of it or just didn't want to have a daughter," I wailed back at him.

He shook his head, speechless for a moment. I couldn't stop my crying. My shoulders heaved and fell

531

and my stomach felt so weak and twisted, I had to wrap my arms around myself.

"Everyone thinks I'm your father? Who's everyone?"

"Uncle Jacob, for one. He says that's why you offered me the job. It was your way of trying to amend for your sin of never acknowledging me."

"Jacob would say something like that." He laughed. "It's nice to know how his parents treat him," he said.

"I don't understand," I said, shaking my head in confusion.

"Never mind. Look, Melody, if you were my daughter, I would tell you immediately. I thought by now you would have realized that I admire you and certainly wouldn't be ashamed to acknowledge you were mine, but it's not true. I wish it were true. You have no idea how much I wish it or how long I've wished it.

"That," he continued, "is the real reason why your mother sent me the picture of you and her and wrote 'I'm sorry' on the back of it." He took a deep breath and sat on the sand. "She wasn't just apologizing for not living up to my hopes for her; she was apologizing for not being able to be the woman I loved. It wasn't all her fault either," he added, sighing as he closed his eyes and leaned forward, his knees up, his arms around them.

I stopped crying, sucked in my breath, and sat beside him.

"Then you loved my mother?" I asked softly.

"Yes, very much."

"And those pictures of her in the room?"

"She enjoyed posing for me. She was so beautiful I wanted to capture her forever and art was a way to do it. Eventually, it became the only way to do it, and that made it both wonderful and painful for me. I got so I couldn't look at those pictures and had to keep

532

them under lock and key, almost as if I were locking them away from myself as much as anyone else.

"As you and your boyfriend saw when you went in there," he continued, bitterly, "there were cobwebs over the door. That's how infrequently I enter to gaze upon those pictures. After you arrived, I thought about Haille constantly and I couldn't resist going in there again. That's when I made the discovery."

"I'm sorry, Kenneth," I said. He was silent, so I reached out and touched his hand. He nodded.

"Well, I can understand what you're going through, I guess. Living with Jacob, hearing his moralistic trash. He never really knew or understood your mother. He was always jealous of her affection for me, too. And when Chester came to her defense—" He shook his head. "Did anyone tell you they actually had a fist fight on the beach?"

"Yes, Grandma Olivia mentioned it."

"Chester whipped him, of course, which helped widen the chasm between them and the whole family. Haille enjoyed having men fight over her. All that I told you about her was true," he said. "She was bedazzling, tormenting, a tease with a capital T, but all of us let her get away with it."

He smiled, remembering. Then he looked at me.

"I should have made it perfectly clear to you that I wasn't your father, that Haille and I never . . . that I never had the opportunity to be your father."

This revelation came as a shock to me, but I knew now was the time to press on for more information. "Then who is my father? Is he someone here in Provincetown?"

"I really can't say, not because I don't want to, but because I don't know." He shook his head. "It all happened so fast. She and I weren't seeing each other much at the time."

"Why not?"

"That's something very personal to me, Melody. All of us have to hold on to something. It doesn't have anything to do with what you want to know. Just like everyone else close to your family at the time, I heard that Haille was pregnant, and the next thing I heard was she had accused Samuel. I knew that was untrue. I had been at their house often enough to see that Samuel treated her the way he would treat a daughter and not a lover. He was always charming and kind and probably spoiled her. It's sort of an example of biting the hand that feeds you. When it came time to blame someone, for some reason, a reason she wouldn't reveal to me, she turned on him. He seemed the most logical, I guess."

"Why?"

"Olivia was harder on her. Anything she got, she got because of Samuel. He bought her the clothes, the jewelry. He doted on her. Olivia was the ice queen who treated her the way the evil step-mother treated Cinderella. If Olivia demanded she do a chore, Samuel would find a way to get her out of it or pay someone else to do it. If Olivia punished her for misbehavior, Samuel got her a reprieve. I suppose she played him the way she played all the men around her at the time, even me," he said.

"She wasn't very nice then, was she?"

"Well, she was like a beautiful but dangerous creature," he replied with a smile. "I think some men like being manipulated. Samuel certainly had to know she was beguiling him, using him, but he enjoyed it. He had no daughters and one of his two sons took after his wife and treated him as poorly as she did. His other son . . . his other son became jealous of him, I think."

"Jealous? My step-father? Why would he be jealous of his own father?"

"He was jealous of how Haille treated him and how

534

he lavished gifts on her. Chester was always in love with Haille. So was Jacob, but Jacob thinks his own feelings were sinful. In his case it might be true. Jacob hated her because he loved her, if you can understand that. Chester, as I told you before, worshiped her and eventually paid a dear price for that worship: his family.

"That's really all I know about it, Melody. She named Samuel as the father of her baby. Chester either believed her or wanted to believe her and they ran off. So as I've told you, your father could be someone here or could have been someone just passing through. I'm afraid the truth died with her."

He turned to me again.

"This is why I advised you to stop the search. Stop trying to look back on the painful past and look to the future now. Take advantage of the situation, take anything you are given from that mad family, and go on to be your own person. You're bright, talented, and beautiful. You have far more than most girls your age, even the ones with parents."

I turned away. The ache around my heart felt like a hand closing on it, squeezing the very life from me.

"It's not easy to do that," I said.

"Yes, I know, but essentially, it's what I've done, Melody."

I turned back to him.

"Because of how you think of and treat your father?" He didn't reply. "That's the one private thing you want to keep to yourself, isn't it?"

"Yes," he admitted.

We were both quiet. The surf roared and the terns cried to each other above the water. In the distance we could see an oil barge creeping along, looking as if it slid against the sky. The breeze made strands of my hair dance about my forehead and cheeks. The lines in Kenneth's face deepened with his grimace. Ulysses, lying quietly at our feet, lifted his head with curiosity at the sudden silence. Kenneth reached out to pat him. I wiped away my lingering tears.

"Well," I said. "I guess we have to get back to work. That is, if you still want me to be the model."

"What do you say, Ulysses? Should we keep her?" Kenneth asked. As if he understood the question, Ulysses wagged his tail vigorously and we both laughed. "That's it," Kenneth said standing. "The boss has spoken."

I stood alongside him and then we started back to the house. He wasn't my father, I thought, but there was still something strong binding us. Perhaps it was the fact that we had both loved my mother.

"Kenneth," I said as we turned toward the studio, "please don't be mad at Cary. He only did it because of me."

"I bet," he said. "He won't be the last young man who does something to please you."

"I won't be like my mother was," I insisted, my eyes narrow but firm. He gazed at me.

"No, I don't think you will. The fact is, I think you're twice the woman she was," he said. "Now let's get all that into the sculpture."

I followed, buoyed by his words and yet saddened by them as well.

Cary was right, I thought. We're in a constant state of change. Nothing was permanent except real love, deep love, love that transcended time and place. It was the rope we cast to each other to keep each other from drowning in the sea of turmoil otherwise known as life.

I wondered if I should take hold or swim on, searching until I discovered there were no more answers waiting for me, at least in this world.

8
∞

Daydreams

*I*n the days that followed, Kenneth and I did grow closer. I felt something magical being born between us because of the artistic work he was creating, with me as his muse. The way he included me in his creative thinking made me feel I was so important to the vision that I gradually began to believe it, to feel as if I really were an essential part of his work. And then one day after I had finished chipping away on the block where Kenneth had told me to chip, I stepped back. As I gazed at the partially carved marble, I began to see it take form. It was just as he said: the sculpture was emerging. Kenneth was using his talent, his vision to bring it out, and because I had grown closer to him, I could share somewhat in that vision. It was as if I had been staring and staring at the same scene and suddenly I saw the colors, the shapes, the movement I had been told were always there, but until now had never been able to see.

He had warned me that once we got into this, he would eat, sleep, and drink it. He reminded me of a deeply religious person who had taken a vow and dedicated his life to a single prayer. I was always the first to become hungry and ask if we could break for lunch. Usually, he never heard me the first time I spoke. He would be looking at me, but it was as if he had already transcended this world and was living and breathing on another plane. He was in the world of his creation, traveling over the highway of his own imagination, and I was afraid he would leave me somewhere far behind.

"Kenneth, my stomach is growling," I moaned.

"What?"

"I've been pleading for the last half hour. Aren't you hungry?" I cried.

I was still basically in the same position he had originally placed me. It seemed that whatever he was doing was never good enough to please him. He would rip off pages and crumble them with frustration and then start anew, pacing, studying, coming up to me and adjusting my shoulders or my head, changing a strand of hair, finding something to do with the most minute detail of my being before making a new attempt to satisfy his artistic appetite. Meanwhile, my lowly, earthly appetite whined and groaned.

"Oh. Yes. Right. Is it lunch time already? It seems like we just started."

"We've been at it for nearly three hours, Kenneth. Even to a fanatic like you, that's more than just starting, isn't it?" I asked.

He laughed and threw up his hands.

"Sorry. Okay, go fix us some lunch. I'll be right there," he promised.

"I'm not going to call you, Kenneth. This time, I'm going to start eating without you if you don't come," I warned.

"A model is not supposed to nag the artist," he decreed. "She has to remain subtle and discreet, very

538

unobtrusive, or the artist will lose the vision and have to start all over again," he threatened.

"That's blackmail," I told him as I pulled on my sweatshirt.

"No, it's basic artistic survival," he replied.

I paused before leaving the studio and looked at him sharply. It caught his attention.

"What?" he asked.

"You're not above taking advantage of your art to escape from things," I accused. He started to grimace and then turned it into a smile.

"Looks like the model is beginning to develop some vision herself," he said nodding. "Go make lunch. I'll be right in. That's an artistic promise."

I laughed and hurried out. Whenever he smiled at me and spoke warmly to me, it changed the face of the world. Every day had become more interesting and a little more exciting for me since Kenneth and I had had our heart-to-heart discussion, confessing more to each other, finally being honest with each other. It was as if another barrier had crumbled between us. Realizing that Kenneth could not be my father changed everything. Something different, some new feeling was emerging from the deepest places in my secret, put-away heart. Even when I was away from him, home from work, helping Aunt Sara in the kitchen, playing with May, I couldn't stop thinking of Kenneth. I would go over the things he said to me that day, the way he'd looked at me; it all took on new meaning. I even imagined that the long, slow looks he'd given me while we were working were looks not of an artist in love with his art, but of a man in love with his model.

Cary lost patience with me a number of times because I wasn't listening or paying attention to him. I resembled someone going in and out of a coma, drifting, walking about with a soft grin on my face, nodding at sounds, but never really hearing anything but the whispering voices emerging from my own tingling heart. Through the fog of it all I knew that I was disappointing Cary, letting him down, but I just couldn't help wanting something more from Kenneth, something I was afraid Cary could never give me.

No matter how I tried, I couldn't stop fantasizing that Kenneth was falling in love with me.

In the library, I read stories about famous artists who had developed passionate affairs with their models, affairs of love that drove them mad with desire. Age didn't matter when it came to such strong emotion. It would be the same between Kenneth and me, I thought. After all, we had so much in common, and that came from his own lips. He had said we were both like orphans, rejecting and rejected by family. Most important, he had been in love with Mommy, and now, he surely saw something of her in me, enough of her to stir his suffering heart. It went deeper, I told myself, and he not only saw Mommy in me, but something more. He had said that, too. He had told me I was twice the woman. Could that mean he cared for me twice as much as he'd cared for Mommy?

Perhaps because of these new feelings, as well as my growing understanding of the artistic process, I was even more anxious to go to Kenneth's studio each day. I even offered to work overtime at no pay and come Sunday as well as Saturday if he wanted.

"We'll see," he said. "An artist can't rush things, can't overdo them either. I'm not complaining, you understand. I would never complain about it, but the work is very intense, exhausting. When you leave here, I usually crash."

"And don't even eat the supper I prepared for you, right?"

He shrugged.

"I know you don't because when I return the next day, I can see how much food is still there. I should stay longer, eat dinner with you," I suggested hopefully.

"Don't they expect you home to help?"

"If I don't eat there, I don't have to earn my keep," I told him.

"We'll see," he said, always the cautious one.

Twice during the week, however, I got him to permit me to serve him dinner and eat with him. I pretended that this was our house and Kenneth and I had long discussions over the meal I'd so lovingly prepared. One night our discussion turned to family, and, as always, our words became heated.

"I'm not looking for any confrontations with Jacob Logan," he said. "Not now."

"He wouldn't dare cause any trouble. I would just—leave. That's all." When Kenneth didn't say anything, I added. "I could just move in here, sleep in your other bedroom."

"Are you kidding? Jacob would set the authorities on me, get me arrested for corrupting the morals of a minor," he said.

"I'm not a minor," I snapped. He started to smile but stopped when he saw how lobster red with indignation my face had become.

"In the eyes of the law, you most certainly are a minor. You're miles above the average girl your age, I admit," he added to soften the tension between us. "But we have to be careful, Melody. Many people would not fully understand or appreciate what we're doing here."

"I haven't told anyone anything," I said.

"Not even Cary?" he asked, his eyes narrow with suspicion.

"Not even Cary. I realize he's not mature enough yet to understand what we are doing," I replied, throwing my hair back and gazing at him with a defiant air that brought a small, but intriguing smile to his face. I was a little sad, though, that what I'd said was true; Cary wouldn't understand. He was too much like Uncle Jacob.

Kenneth shook his head and laughed lightly, the specks in his brown eyes brightening.

"You've got spirit, Melody. I am really lucky to have found you," he said.

I thought my heart would explode with joy. Every night afterward, I went to sleep with his words on my lips: "I am really lucky to have found you."

"And I you, dearest Kenneth." I hugged my pillow and dreamed of the day he would come to me and say, "Forget society. Forget what those busybodies would say. You and I will make great art together and should be together forever. I can't sleep without saying your name over and over until it becomes a song in my heart. Melody . . . Melody."

Was I the lovesick schoolgirl I had warned May she had become? Or was I really mature enough in heart and spirit to attract the romantic interest of an older man, a handsome and interesting older man?

Cary misunderstood my daydreaming and deep thoughts and grew impatient with me often during our walks after dinner. It wasn't that I'd lost all feelings for him as he accused, just that being with Kenneth made me realize the limitations of my relationship with Cary. For as much as Cary was my confidant, my only true friend here on the Cape, he just would never understand the thoughts and yearnings I discovered growing within myself as I helped Kenneth create his most prized work of art. Nor would he understand the role I played in its creation. I feared that Uncle Jacob had been too much of an influence on Cary, that no matter how he fought it, Cary would always be his father's son.

"You're just being polite spending time with me, is

542

that it?" he accused one night as we walked along the surf.

"Pardon me?" I asked, startled by his tone and sudden outburst.

"I talk and talk and you nod but you hardly say anything to me unless I pull it out of you like pulling on a fish line that's gotten tangled on a sunken barge. And when you kiss me it's quick, with your eyes slammed closed, and then you rush off to bed just like—just like—You're just different," he finally stammered, unable to complete the thought. But I knew. I knew all right. Cary was accusing me of being just like Laura!

"I am not," I said defensively, though I knew in my heart he was partially right. I wasn't like Laura. Oh, no. I wasn't as saintly as his beloved sister. But I was different, changing before his very eyes.

"Yes you are. It's because of what happened that night on the beach, isn't it? You think I went too far too fast and you're punishing me."

"Cary, that's ridiculous," I insisted.

"No, it isn't. I know girls can be like that. They'll sulk or pretend you don't exist until you come pleading and begging for a kind word or some attention. I don't know why they call you the weaker sex," he said bitterly. "We're the ones who act like clowns or lose our self-respect just for a favor or a kiss. Men are the powerless ones," he concluded.

"That is so untrue, Cary Logan," I said, spinning on him, my hands on my hips. "Men break the hearts of women much more than women break the hearts of men. Men are usually the unfaithful ones. They make all sorts of promises that are supposed to last forever and ever, and they buy expensive presents to convince us of their love, and then, after a while, they go looking for love with someone else.

Cary's eyes widened.

"I wouldn't," he said. "And that's not just an empty

543

promise. I thought you knew me," he said sadly. "I thought I knew you, too. I guess we're both fooling ourselves." He marched off, leaving me standing alone on the beach.

"Cary!"

"I'm tired," he called back without turning. "I've got to get up early tomorrow."

I watched him march back to the house, his fists balled with rage. I shook my head in pity.

He's been through a lot, I told myself, but he's still a boy compared to Kenneth. In time he'll be a much stronger person, but it's not my destiny to wait. "Is it?" I asked the stars. They blinked but had no answers, yet I felt sure that even if Cary were right and I had changed, it wasn't wrong for me to change. It simply meant I was growing up.

Later that evening, Aunt Sara called me to the telephone. It was Alice Morgan, my best friend in Sewell. She was very excited because her mother had finally given in and said she could make the trip to Provincetown to visit me.

"I can leave the day after tomorrow!" she exclaimed. "Is that all right?"

"Oh Alice," I said and thought a moment. What would I do with her now? How could I bring her along with me to Kenneth's studio? What was happening there had to be kept private for a number of reasons, not least of which was the growing feelings we were developing for each other.

Alice was always the immature one, even though she was one of the brightest students in school. Her family was one of the richest in Sewell, but she had never had a boyfriend. She was much too interested in books and studying to be bothered with clothes and makeup, which seemed to be the only thing that boys our age noticed. Despite our differences, she was a faithful friend. I hated hurting her.

"What's wrong, Melody? I thought you would be

happy about it. We're finally going to see each other after all this time apart," she cried.

"I know. It's just that . . ."

"Just that what?"

"Just that I've taken a job and I won't have time to properly entertain you. You'd have to spend hours and hours alone, and I couldn't leave you alone at this house. My uncle Jacob would make you miserable and Aunt Sara would drive you crazy. It wouldn't be much of a holiday for you."

"What about Cary?" she asked timidly. Was that her real motive for wanting to come?

"Oh, he works long hours too, Alice. He's never around."

"I see," she said, her little voice drifting away. It brought tears to my eyes as I imagined her in her room, her bubble of excitement bursting. "What kind of a job do you have?"

"I work with a local artist," I said. "Sometimes, he uses me to model for his pictures."

"Really? A model?"

"Just simple things," I said quickly, "like a girl walking on the beach or walking with his dog on the dunes. But I have to do a lot more. I'm there from early morning to dinner and sometimes later, so you see why it wouldn't be a very fun vacation."

"Oh."

"Maybe before the summer's over, I'll have a break and you can come. I'll stay in touch and call you as soon as I know when I can get some time off, okay?"

"Okay," she said, but her disappointment was more than obvious.

After I cradled the receiver, I felt just awful. There wasn't anything Alice wouldn't have done for me if I had asked her, and when I was desperate, she was ready to give me money, have me move into her house, anything. Cary was right, I thought. I was becoming a different person, but perhaps when you became mature, you also left part of yourself behind with the little girl in you. Becoming an adult seemed to mean becoming a little more selfish in different ways.

I promised myself I would put aside a few days for Alice before the summer ended. Once the sculpture was almost finished Kenneth was sure to need me less and then I could call Alice and have her come for a visit, I thought. It eased my troubled conscience and helped me to put her voice and probable tears out of my mind for the time being. I couldn't dwell on it anyway. I was too busy.

Kenneth had me work a half a day on the following Saturday. When Cary heard, he was full of questions. He came to my door, knocked, and started asking.

"Why does Kenneth need you on Saturday? What does he want you to do?"

"Same things I do all week, Cary," I said. I still hadn't mentioned my modeling and now I probably never would.

"Doesn't he take time off?"

"It's only for half of the day and he takes off Sundays. When he gets into a project, he becomes totally involved, absorbed by it."

"Sounds like he has nothing else to do with his life," he muttered. "Did he mention that boat again?"

"No, not yet."

Cary smirked.

"Thought so. Everyone is so full of . . . seaweed," he remarked.

"Kenneth doesn't say something if he doesn't mean it, Cary Logan. He'll bring it up soon. I'm sure."

Cary raised his eyebrows.

"How come you're so sure of whatever he says all of a sudden?"

"I just am," I said. He nodded, smirked again, and went up to his workshop.

After breakfast on Saturday morning, Uncle Jacob had the nerve to ask me if my working on the weekend meant Kenneth was paying me time and a half.

"Yes, he is," I said.

"Good. Don't forget to put half of the overtime as well in the pot," he ordered.

"I'm sure if I did forget, you'd be the first to remind me," I said brazenly, knowing I was sure to get a lecture.

"You're old enough to know responsibility and obligations," he replied. "Your mother never had an inkling of what those words meant and that was because everyone spoiled her. Spare the rod and you spoil the child," he recited.

"I am not a child," I fired back, but he didn't retreat an inch.

"Kids today don't grow up as fast as we had to grow up. They're given too much and don't have to give back much in return. It's gettin' harder and harder for me to find anyone under forty who wants to do a day's work. They all think it's just going to come to them," he declared.

"Yes," I said dryly. "I'm the living proof of a spoiled person."

He blinked, twisted his lips, and then shoved his pipe into his mouth, grumbling to himself.

I recalled how Kenneth had called him a moral horse's ass. It brought a smile to my lips.

"What's so funny?" he demanded.

"What? Oh, nothing," I said as I hurried out, praying harder for the day Kenneth would suddenly turn to me and say, "Come live with me and be my love."

He was already waiting for me. I hadn't heard him drive up, but it cheered my heart to see him there early. He was just as anxious to be with me as I was with him, I thought, and got into the jeep. We sped off and I saw there was something different on Kenneth's mind, some new excitement painting itself on his beautiful face.

"What are we going to do today?"

"We're moving ahead," he said. "I've completed the first stage and now I want to get into the meat of it." He glanced at me. "Neptune's daughter is coming up higher and revealing more of herself as she emerges out of the sea. She's filling out the female form."

I knew what he meant and it filled me with so much excitement I could barely breathe. I sat back, my heart thumping, the wind blowing my hair. Was I ready? Yes, I thought, I was ready. Almost overnight, I had grown up. I was ready to shed my innocence and share myself with Kenneth.

Ulysses barked because I had been ignoring him. I laughed and gave him a quick hug as we drove onto the dune road and Kenneth's studio.

The studio looked different to me this morning, perhaps because of what I knew was about to occur. It seemed darker, the shades drawn lower on the windows. As soon as we stepped through the door, Kenneth did something he had never done before: he locked the door behind us. His eyes shifted guiltily away when he saw my surprise.

"I'm too far into this to bear even the smallest interruptions," he explained. Since we had never been interrupted before, I didn't think much of his reason, but I smiled and nodded anyway.

He went to the model of the wave and studied it intently, his hands on his hips and his right hand stroking his beard as he continued to think and envision.

"Okay," he finally declared. "Here's what I want. Undress to your waist, take your usual position, and then come up until you're exposed up to here," he said drawing an imaginary line just above his stomach. Got it?"

I nodded. He returned to his easel and waited as I went around the wave and pulled off my sweat shirt. I hesitated a moment, my fingers actually trembling so badly I couldn't get them to undo the fastener on my bra. Finally, it was unfastened and I slipped the bra down my arms.

I had studied myself often in the mirror in my room, anticipating this moment. Mommy used to say I was a late bloomer, but that when I bloomed, I would bloom fast. I imagined it had been that way with her and that was why she knew. When I was fourteen, I barely had the bumps on my chest May now had. I thought I would never develop the curves and figure Mommy had.

And then, suddenly, between the ages of fifteen and sixteen, I began to develop quickly, finding a change in my body each succeeding day. I once went to Mommy and cried, pleading with her to get me to a doctor, afraid that my breasts would never stop growing. She just laughed and told me not to worry; they would stop growing eventually, and in the meantime I should learn to enjoy all the attention they brought me. I tried to do as Mommy suggested, but it was hard to enjoy yourself when you felt as if an alien had taken over your body.

Soon though, I did gain self-confidence. The boys no longer teased me about being flat as a board and instead took long looks at me and began spending more time trying to win my attention.

But now, I couldn't help thinking of all the beautiful, mature women Kenneth had seen naked. I was terrified that he would gaze at me and think of me as just a teenager and not a young woman. Cary had been in awe of my body, but was I shapely enough for a man like Kenneth? Would he gaze at me naked before him and think he had made a big mistake in

549

asking me to model for him? What if I was not the budding beauty he envisioned?

All the while I was trying to gather up my courage, to calm my trembling limbs, Kenneth was preoccupied with his preparations and never noticed my shyness and fears.

"Ready," he called.

I took a deep breath, crawled through the opening, and started up and out of the wave. As I rose, my heart began to pound, my legs picked up the trembling that had begun in my fingers, and I held my breath.

"Keep your eyes open," he ordered.

I swallowed and moved another inch or two, still not revealing my breasts. He waited, his drawing pencil in his hand.

"Come up," he instructed. "That's it. Good, good."

And there I was before him. He stared a moment. I felt the crimson color in my neck and face. It was as if Kenneth had walked over and run his brush over my skin. After what seemed like an hour, Kenneth nodded. If he noticed, he didn't mention my blushing.

"Just turn a bit to your right and then, if you can, pull your shoulders back a little. Lift your chin and concentrate on the ceiling. Don't be too stiff. Relax."

"I'm trying," I said.

"I know. Easy. That's it. Good. All right. Let's start with this pose first," he said and began.

Whenever I shifted my eyes to glance at him and see what sort of expression he had on his face, I saw only the same intense scrutiny I had seen before. There was no look of appreciation and none of disapproval. The total neutrality of his eyes, his lips, his entire being surprised and then annoyed me. I jerked my shoulders back.

"Getting tired?" he asked without taking his eyes from his paper.

"A little."

"Just a few more minutes and we'll take a short break. I think I have the curve I want and the lift in your head. Yes, this will work. This is it," he said.

"What about the rest of me?" I asked sharply.

He just nodded and kept working. It amazed me that I had been right when I told Cary an artist was like a doctor when he looked at a woman. I had expected more than this—this impersonal artistic eye.

"You're perfect," he finally declared as he stepped back and looked at me. "You're just what I wanted, what I needed."

"Really?"

"There's this innocence about you, this freshness in your body that makes the statement," he said.

"Statement?"

"My statement. Beauty emerging, the birth."

"Oh."

"Okay, let's do some more." I groaned, but he didn't pay attention. After another twenty minutes or so, he put down his pencil.

"You can take a rest. I want to map out some of this on the marble. I'm getting this faster than I thought I might," he declared proudly.

"Then I'm doing well as your model?" I fished.

"Outstanding."

I stood there, still undressed, facing him, waiting for him to look at me differently, to smile differently, to step up to me and take me in his arms, to kiss me long and deeply, my naked breasts turned into him, waiting.

Instead he went straight to his cold marble block and left me dangling in my own imagination. I didn't bother putting my bra back on. I slipped into my sweatshirt without it. Then I came up beside him, hoping he might still turn and look at me as a woman instead of a model, an object of love instead of an object of art.

"If you'd like to get some fresh air, take Ulysses for a walk on the beach," he suggested. "I might be a while."

"Fine," I said sharply, sharper than I had intended, but he didn't appear to notice. I don't think he even heard me. I started for the door and Ulysses got up as quickly as he could to follow.

"Come along, Ulysses. I can always count on your wanting to be with me at least," I said loud enough for Kenneth to hear.

"What's that?" he said after a moment.

"Nothing. I'll be right back."

"Take your time," he said and returned his attention to his precious block of marble.

I slammed the door hard behind me and marched toward the beach, Ulysses at my side, trotting, his ears flapping.

"Men," I fumed and planted myself with a hard thump on a hill of sand. Ulysses looked disappointed that I wasn't walking any farther, but I wasn't in the mood.

"Now when he looks at me," I told Ulysses," he looks right through me. He's not seeing me, he's seeing that—that vision of his."

Ulysses panted, his tongue hanging over his mouth, his eyes wide as if he understood my indignation.

"I bet when you see a female you like, you see a female," I told him. He sniffed as if in response and plopped down beside me, convinced I wasn't going to move.

I stared at the ocean. Maybe I'm being too sensitive, I thought. Maybe I'm being too selfish. After all, Kenneth has made art his life and he has decided to include me in it. That's significant. He probably could have chosen any of a number of pretty girls in town, or maybe imported one. He was very successful; he could afford a very expensive model if he wanted. Yet he had chosen me. I was his special vision.

As I looked out over the ocean a lone cloud in the distance seemed to take the shape of a heart. A good omen, I thought. I lay back and Ulysses suddenly put his head on my stomach. It made me laugh. I closed my eyes and felt the sun on my face and the warm sand beneath me. It was all so soothing. In minutes I was asleep. I don't know how long I slept, but I woke to the sound of Ulysses barking. He was up and facing the road that lead to and from Kenneth's house. I sat up and turned to see a small purple car with what looked like astrological signs painted all over it in white come bouncing down the sandy ruts. The driver tapped out long, loud beeps on the horn as the car came to a stop in front of Kenneth's studio.

"Who's that?" I asked Ulysses. He gazed at me and then ran down the sand hill toward the driver as she emerged from the car. She was wearing a long, one-piece green and white dress, the hem actually touching the ground. Even from this distance, I could see long, silver earrings dangling from her lobes. Her dark brown hair was down to her shoulder blades.

"Ulysses!" she cried, kneeling to open her arms to hug him. Ulysses was all over her, licking her face, her neck, her hair. Her laughter was carried back to me in the wind. The woman stood up, shaded her eyes with her hand, and gazed toward me. Without knowing who I was, she waved and then turned as Kenneth came strolling around the house. I watched as she ran to him with the same enthusiasm Ulysses had run to her. He opened his arms in welcome and she was in his embrace an instant later. They kissed on the lips. I felt my heart do flip flops.

When she pulled back, her musical laughter trailed up to me. She was looking my way and he was obviously explaining who I was. She waved again and I got up and started toward them, my heart thumping

553

with anticipation, a small fist of fear growing tighter and tighter in my stomach until I felt as if it would burn right through my skin.

"Melody," Kenneth said as I approached, "I'd like you to meet Holly Brooks."

"Hi, Melody," she exclaimed, her eyes wide with excitement. She wore a purple tinted lipstick that matched the color of the car. When she extended her hand to shake mine, the half dozen silver and copper bracelets on her arm all bunched up at her wrist. On each of her fingers she wore a ring, some simply silver embossed with a shape, two looking like some sort of polished stone.

She was a small woman made to look smaller in her oversized broomstick dress. She looked as if she were swimming in it, yet when the material shifted, I could see that she was braless, her breasts pressing up against the thin cotton. She wore a thin leather collar around her neck with tiny multicolored stones embedded in the material.

There was something very bright and airy about her smile, and her eyes were filled with a happy light, making them look more hazel than dark brown. She had a small nose and soft cheeks that dipped just slightly to diminish the roundness in her face and make her mouth small enough too, so that her iridescent lipstick looked pretty, not garish. There were the tiniest freckles on her forehead and down the sides of her temples.

"Hi," I said offering my hand. She seized it and shook firmly.

"When's your birthday?" she asked quickly.

"June twelfth," I said, looking at Kenneth. He wore a deep smile and nodded slightly.

"A Gemini," she declared. "I knew it."

"Holly is an astrologer," Kenneth explained. "As well as an artist."

"Oh. Aunt Sara believes in that."

"Really? Well, your aunt's a smart lady."

"Please," Kenneth said. "Spare us the hoo-doo voo-doo for a while."

"Oh Kenny," she said. "You know I come to see you only when it's the right astrological time and you know we're always good together, right?"

He shot a quick glance at me, his eyes full of embarrassment.

"Right. Melody," he continued, anxious to change the subject, "is my model for the new project."

"Oh yes. I can see why," she said, turning back to me. "She's so pretty. She must make a wonderful model, Kenneth."

"She's doing a terrific job," he said looking at me. I smiled, enjoying my moment in his sunshine.

"Good," Holly said. "It's so beautiful here, so conducive to art, to inner expression. There's a positive energy here. I feel it," she said, closing her eyes and embracing herself. She took deep breaths.

I looked at Kenneth and he smiled as we both waited. She popped her eyes open and gazed into my face with such intensity, I nearly laughed.

"The first time I drove up here, I knew Kenneth had felt the energy and that had brought him here. Remember, Kenneth? Remember how we just sat for hours and hours holding hands, soaking up the twilight and feeling the vibrations?"

"Yes, Holly," he said in a tired voice. "Why don't I help you with your things?"

"Oh, yes. It's *so* wonderful to be here again. You don't know how something like this can recharge your batteries, Melody, until you're away in the world of chaos, drowning in tension."

"I think she has some idea," Kenneth said with that inscrutable smile of his.

Holly turned back to me.

"Oh? I can't wait to get to know you, Melody. Kenneth hasn't told me very much. You're like his little secret," she said.

I glanced at him, wondering what that meant, delighted that he'd mentioned me to Holly. That meant I was important to him. But then, why had he invited her here? Who was she?

"He hasn't told me anything about you," I said. "You must be his other little secret."

Holly laughed and for the first time, I saw Kenneth Childs blush deeply.

"Your things?" Kenneth reminded her firmly.

"Oh, yes, my things." She uttered another little musical laugh and went to the trunk of her car. It was stuffed with small, battered suitcases. "Let's just take in these for now," she said pulling out the two largest. Kenneth took them from her and started toward the house. She opened the rear door of the car and something rolled out. It looked like a large, clear stone. The back seat was filled with clothes, books, and art supplies, and a lamp lay on the floor.

"Can you take this for me, Melody," she said, lifting the stone object. "I'll get the other things."

"What is it?"

"My crystal," she said. "The energy is drawn into it and then I draw it into myself. I never go anywhere without putting it alongside my bed. Kenneth doesn't mind," she said.

"Excuse me?"

"Oh, you'll see. We have so much to tell each other," she declared.

"How long are you staying here?" I asked.

She paused, gazed around a moment, took a deep breath, and then nodded, before closing and opening her eyes.

"Until I stop hearing it," she said.

"Hearing it? Hearing what?"

"The voice that called me here." She smiled.

"You'll understand. I promise," she said and reached down to pick up a packet of incense off the floor in the back of the car.

She closed the door and we started toward the house.

"I only know a little about Kenneth's new work, but from the way he talks, I can see it's the most exciting thing he's done in years. I'm glad he found it. He was beginning to worry me," she said with a serious face, her eyes darker, her lips tighter. "I was beginning to think the shadows of the past were overtaking his bright light and dimming his spirit. I'm so happy for him, and if you had anything to do with it, I'm grateful to you," she added.

I just looked at her, failing to find the words to respond to all this. I turned to carry her crystal to the guest room and she stopped me.

"Not that way, dear. I told you," she said, "that has to be beside the bed." She nodded toward Kenneth's bedroom and smiled.

I hesitated, my chest feeling hollow, no heartbeat, no blood, no lungs, just an echo chamber full of surprise and disappointment.

Kenneth appeared at the bedroom door.

"I put your suitcases by the closet. Anything else you want brought in right now?"

"No, Ken. Thanks."

"Okay. I'm going back to the studio." He turned to me. "Are you sure you don't mind staying the whole day?"

"I think I'm getting a little stomachache. But I'll be fine. I can stay," I said.

"Oh?"

"Stomach ache? Don't you worry, Ken. I'll help her. I have just the herbal medicine for stomach aches. Come along, Melody," she sang.

Reluctantly, my legs feeling like twin sticks of lead, I followed her into Kenneth's bedroom. She took the

557

crystal and placed it beside the bed on a night stand and then she turned to me and smiled.

"Time of the month?" she asked.

"What? Oh. No," I said.

"Did you eat something nasty this morning?"

"No."

"Just stress then," she concluded. "I have just what you need."

"I doubt it," I said harshly. She stared at me curiously.

"You have a lot of negative energy coming out of you, Melody. If you let me, I'll help you."

"No thank you," I said. "I'll just walk it off. That usually works." I turned and fled the bedroom.

Outside, I hesitated, not sure if I wanted to walk home or walk on the beach.

Why hadn't he told me she was coming? Why hadn't he told me anything about her?

"Is every man a liar?" I shouted at the sea and the sea roared back what sounded like a resounding yes to me.

Just when I had gotten to the point where I thought I knew Kenneth, I discovered he was more of a stranger than ever. Perhaps we never get to know anyone, I thought, not even people we love and people who claim to love us.

I took a deep breath and walked toward the sea, hoping that the roar of the waves I heard would grow louder and louder and drown the angry voices chattering away inside me.

9
❧

It's in the Stars

I took a long walk down the beach toward where I could see the Point's end and the vast North Atlantic. As I let the sea spray wash over me, I wished I could just drift away with the tide, away from Kenneth, away from the Logans, away. How could I have been stupid enough to think that Kenneth could love me? Holly and all her eccentric, exotic ways were what an artistic man like Kenneth wanted. I was just a silly teenager who bored him. But I hadn't bored Cary, Cary who truly loved me, Cary whom I rejected to follow my childish dreams of Kenneth and his love for me.

I felt awash in self-pity as I continued down the beach, noticing that the seaweed was thicker on this part of the Point. It looked like the ocean had been in a rage here, tearing up the underwater vegetation like a madwoman might rip out her hair. There was driftwood everywhere, made shiny from the constant scrubbing of the salt water. I spotted something that had washed ashore. As I drew closer, I realized that it was a doll, her hair matted, her face bleached by the

559

sun so that even the black button eyes were a dull gray. The lower half of her body was embedded in the sand where the tide had deposited her and would no doubt return to carry her back out to sea.

I plucked the doll from her temporary grave and brushed her off, imagining how this had once been a little girl's prize possession. In my mind's eye, I envisioned the little girl as sweet and as innocent as May perhaps, preparing a fantasy tea party with the doll seated at a toy table, the teacups and teapot set out. Surely the little girl had told her doll all her wishes and secrets. In the beginning, when she first had been given this doll, she probably slept with it beside her and carried it everywhere. It had become her precious little companion in which she had trusted her love and her dreams.

For whatever reason—maybe the girl had just grown up and left it at the bottom of a toy chest—the doll drifted from her private world and was forgotten, discarded, to take her place among all the other forgotten toys. Later, there might have been a house cleaning and toys were thrown away to make room for other things. Her mother might have held it up and asked, "Do you want this anymore?"

The little girl thought for a moment and remembered her childhood best friend fondly, but she was older now and her eyes had turned to boys; dolls were as embarrassing as an annoying little sister giving away intimate family secrets. Who wanted her new boyfriend to know she used to whisper I love yous to a doll instead of to him.

"No," she said, and sentenced her precious friend to the dump. How it came to be in the ocean was another story, but it had, and it had found its way to this beach. Even with her eyes bleak, her face lackluster, I thought I could hear the tiny doll's plea. She looked up at me, begging not to be left alone, condemned to this horrible fate.

I brushed her off and carried her back with me, really not sure what I would do with her. I wished someone would find me on the beach like this and brush off my grains of sadness and salty tears before carrying me off to a new and better home. Like this doll, I felt discarded and perhaps with even less fanfare. But hadn't I done the same to Cary? Was Holly's arrival my punishment for treating Cary so selfishly?

As I rounded a bend and approached the beach in front of Kenneth's house, I saw Holly seated on a blanket, her legs curled in a lotus position, her arms folded under her breasts, her head back so her face was awash in the afternoon sunshine. She was barefoot and wore a light green and white tie-dyed tank dress that came barely to her knees. She also wore different earrings. These looked like jade and glittered along with whatever she was wearing around her neck.

Ulysses hadn't come out with her. I imagined him pouting in the studio with Kenneth because I had rushed away without so much as glancing at him and beckoning for him to join me.

I was going to ignore Holly and go into the house, when I heard the exotic, Far Eastern–sounding music, and drew closer. Somehow, she sensed me and turned.

"Hi," she called.

I stepped closer and saw the small stream of smoke rising from a tiny bronze pot.

"What are you doing?" I asked.

"Greeting the zodiac. I've got to get in tune with the vibrations, the energy here, as soon as possible. Come," she said, shifting on her blanket to make room for me, "join me."

"To do what?" I asked with a smirk.

"Plug into the universe," she replied as if it were the

most obvious thing. "All the answers to your questions and your problems are in here," she said, pointing to her heart, "but you have to find the way to reach them, unlock the doors, and to do that, you have to strip away the worldly confusions, the tensions and the turmoil. You've got to lift your spirit from this bondage and free your inner self. I'll show you how if you want," she said.

I started to shake my head and laugh at her. Did she really expect me to believe these things?

"It won't cost you anything but a little of your time and energy," she said quickly. "And it might be just what you need, Melody."

"How do you know what I need?" I snapped back at her.

She smiled softly.

"I know you need some peace, some strength, some light. I know you have to rid yourself of your burdensome anger, and I know you're looking for meaning and love," she added.

I couldn't deny it. My face must be a window through which anyone could see my troubled heart, I thought, if someone who had just met me already knew all this.

"How can sitting on a blanket and staring at the sky and the ocean help?" I asked disdainfully.

"I'll show you if you give me a chance," she promised with friendly eyes.

"Why should you care about me?" I challenged.

"Why shouldn't I?" she responded quickly. "Come on. I don't bite." She patted the blanket beside her. I drew closer.

"What's burning?"

"Incense," she said.

"It smells funny. What is it?" I asked, grimacing.

"My own recipe of frankincense, styrax, and cascarilla bark. You've never smelled incense before?"

562

"No."

"It's really very pleasant. What do you have in your hand there?" she asked, leaning to see what I was carrying at my side.

"Someone's old doll. I found it on the beach," I said unashamedly and more possessively than I had expected.

"All my dolls were handmade for me when I was a little girl," she said. "My mother was a tailor and very talented. She made all my clothes and all my brother's and my father's clothes, too. She learned it from her mother. I don't know how far back the skill went, but it was something they brought over from Europe. Of course, all my friends made fun of my clothes because they knew practically everything I owned was home-made."

"Where did you live?" I asked, unable to prevent myself from being interested in her, especially when she talked about her mother. She seemed so open and free, revealing intimacies about herself without any fear. After living on the Cape for a while, I thought she was a breath of fresh air.

"Yonkers. It's just outside of New York City. My mother worked for a manufacturer in the Bronx. Ever been there?"

"No," I said.

"I haven't been back in ages, even though I live only a train ride away in Greenwich Village," she explained.

"I don't know where that is exactly," I said. "I know it's in New York City."

"Yes. It's where a lot of artists and writers, folk singers and musicians live. I have a shop there on Christopher Street. I do readings, sell candles and crystals."

"Readings?"

"Astrology," she said. "Personal horoscopes."

"Oh. My uncle Jacob thinks it's mumbo jumbo, even heathen. He's always bawling out my aunt Sara for reading her horoscope in the paper, but she does it anyway."

"It's not mumbo jumbo," she said softly. "Astrology was studied among the ancient Egyptians, Hindus, Chinese, Etruscans, and the Chaldeans of Babylonia. It all started with the Chaldeans about three thousand BC. It was very logical to them. When they noticed how the sun and the heavenly bodies affected seasons, crops, they just assumed it all affected human life as well."

"I don't really know all that much about it," I said. "Just that it's like fortune telling."

"Yes, in a way. Your destiny is dependent upon the sign of the zodiac under which you were born and the relationship of the planets at the time and throughout your life, but more depends upon the position and power of the sun and the moon at birth than upon all the planets of our solar system combined. The sun and the moon are the transmitters of the stellar forces. I make charts on a horoscope, working out the location of the sun, the moon, and the planets within the twelve segments of the zodiac known as houses," she continued. "Each house is named for a constellation and each takes up thirty degrees of space, the whole making the three hundred sixty degrees of a circle. That's why the number three hundred sixty is the symbol of completion," she lectured.

"It all sounds silly," I said. Why would Kenneth like someone who believed in these things? I wondered.

"Oh, but it's not. It's all logical. Listen," she insisted. "We all have five positive points of projection and four positive centers of energy. Four plus five makes up the mystical nine, the symbol of deity. The head, hands, and feet are the five points of projection

564

from which streams and streams of vital force are constantly radiating. We symbolize that with the five-pointed star," she added and showed me her wrist where she had a five-pointed star tattooed.

"The positive centers of energy are the brain, the spleen, the heart, and the generative organs, while the great center of reception is the solar plexus." She held her hand against her stomach. "Just think about it. When trouble or anxiety crosses our path, the first place we feel it is here, right? Usually we have no appetite. We have butterflies."

I nodded. That did make sense.

"Mental and psychic goodness depend upon the perfect freedom of the body. Anything that cramps, binds, or twists us out of natural proportion is fatal to real spiritual progress. That's why people in India, Chaldea, and Egypt wore loose-flowing robes and why the high priests did the same. It's why I dress like this, too," she explained. "Does that help you understand it a little better?"

I nodded.

"I can do a chart for you while I'm here, if you want."

I didn't reply. In a real sense I was afraid of knowing what was in store for me. The future seemed far more terrifying than the present, and I was also afraid that if she told me good things, it would only give me false hopes. I had had enough of that.

"Aunt Sara is impressed with the fact that my twin cousins were born under the sign of Gemini," I revealed.

"Yes. Castor and Pollux represent the twin souls. See?"

"No," I said sharply.

"I can explain it," she said.

"I'm not interested."

She just smiled.

"Well, if you change your mind, I'll be here."

"Who's watching your store while you're here?" I asked.

"A friend of mine, Billy Maxwell. He's paralyzed from the waist down, the result of a bullet wound he got when he was fleeing from a mugger. The mugger shot him in the back," she said without sadness or tragic overtones. "Billy's a poet so it didn't stop him from doing what he loves to do."

"Isn't he still bitter and unhappy?" I asked.

"He was in the beginning, but I helped him find a new wavelength, a new highway to travel spiritually, and he's become a happier, more beautiful person."

"Was he your boyfriend?"

"We loved each other, but it wasn't boyfriend-girlfriend in the way you mean."

I nodded and looked away.

"You're Kenneth's girlfriend though, aren't you?" I asked, my voice shaking.

She laughed.

"As much as anyone could be Kenneth's girlfriend. Kenneth is like a comet. He can't be chained to anything or anyone, except his art, of course."

"But you're here, living with him, aren't you?" I practically spit back at her.

"We touch like two meteors passing in the universe when the stars are lined up correctly, but he knows and I know it's not permanent in the sense you mean. It's permanent in our universe though. He and I will be this way for eternity, our two spirits touching," she said.

She saw the look of confusion on my face.

"You'll understand if you let me open a door for you."

"What door?"

"The door to yourself," she said. "First, you have to free your mind of turmoil, rid yourself of negative energy."

566

"How do you do that?"

"I'll show you how. First, close your eyes and concentrate on your own breathing. Don't breathe fast or slow. Just tune into yourself. Go on, try it," she urged. She patted the blanket again. "Come on."

I lowered myself slowly to the blanket, still looking at her skeptically.

"Concentrate on my breathing?"

"Every time a thought tries to enter your mind, drive it away, and the easiest way to do that is to concentrate only on your breathing. Go on."

"This seems very silly," I said.

"Everything new seems silly at first. It can't hurt you to try, can it? Just stare at the water and concentrate on your breathing. Go on," she urged.

I sighed and did what she said.

"It's not working," I declared after just a few minutes. All the sounds of the ocean invaded, the terns, the surf, even the wind whistling around my ears.

"You're not concentrating. Push the noise away, chase out the thoughts. Your breathing is all you want to know at the moment. Keep trying."

I did, and soon I didn't hear those other things. I felt and heard only my own breathing and a wave of relaxation and contentment washed over me. After a few more minutes, I felt her hand on mine.

"Did you do it?" she asked.

"I think so," I said, a bit impressed with myself.

"It takes practice. It's called meditation and it will allow you to travel to your inner self," she said. Then she lifted off her necklace and handed it to me. There was a deep cloudy green crystal in gold suspended from it. "Here, wear this."

"What is it?"

"Moldavite. It's from a meteorite that fell to the earth about fifteen million years ago."

"Really?"

567

"Yes, really," she laughed, amused by my amazement.

"What's it supposed to do?" I asked turning it in my fingers.

"It aids alignment with your higher self, channeling extraterrestrial and interdimensional sources. It's good for balancing and healing the body and the mind," she explained.

It was my turn to laugh. "No thanks," I said, trying to hand the necklace back to her.

"Why don't you give it a chance?" she said and pushed my hand away.

I thought for a moment and then shrugged and put it on. She smiled.

"There, you see. You've taken the first step: a little faith, a little hope."

"Every time I have a little faith or a little hope, I get disappointed," I said.

"Maybe you've been putting your energy into the wrong things, the wrong places."

"How do you know which is right and which is wrong?"

"That's why you have to develop a clearer vision," she said. She looked out at the sea and held that gentle, angelic smile on her lips. "You're very fond of Kenneth, aren't you?" she asked, not turning back to me.

"Yes," I said.

"It's not unusual to imagine things—wonderful things—with such a person. When I was your age, I did a lot of that, too." She looked at me, her eyes still warm, but smaller, more intense. "You're angry with me, aren't you? Angry that I showed up?"

I shifted my own eyes away quickly.

"Well," I said, "Kenneth and I are doing something very special. It takes a lot of concentration and—we can't be interrupted," I declared firmly.

"I'm sure you won't be, especially not by me. I've

known Kenneth a long time. I know when to be in his face and when to be out of it," she said, laughing. Then she looked at me very intently, her eyes soft but determined. "I know I'm good for him, Melody. I know I give him something he needs, something that helps him be the artist and the man he wants to be."

Tears came to my eyes. I was hoping that was what I would give him and who I would be.

"You'll do that for someone special someday, I'm sure. It's not something that happens overnight. It takes time."

I twirled the coarse, faded doll's hair in my fingers and stared at it.

"Do you have a boyfriend?" she asked.

"Sort of," I said thinking of Cary. The boy who loved me and who I had put aside to chase a silly dream.

"You'll have to tell me all about him," she said, "and I'll make up a chart for him too and tell you if you're destined to spend a long time together."

I had to laugh at that, thinking of Cary hearing Holly's ideas.

"He's like his father. He wouldn't listen or believe in anything you said."

"Oh. Well, let's wait and see," she said as if she knew something about Cary that I didn't. "What I like about coming here," she said, gazing out at the vast ocean again, "is the great privacy. I really feel as if I'm on the edge of the world and I can do whatever I want. Don't you feel that too? That sense of freedom?"

"Yes," I admitted.

"Well then, while you and Kenneth work, I think I'll just get some sun."

She started to unbutton her dress. I watched with surprise as she peeled it off to her waist. She wasn't wearing a bra. Topless, she turned on the blanket to expose her back.

569

"It feels like a warm bath," she said and moaned with pleasure. Then her eyes popped open. "Don't you ever sunbathe nude out here?"

I shook my head.

"I love the sense of abandon, the freedom. It's like getting back to basics. You oughta try it."

She closed her eyes again. Her Far Eastern music continued playing on her tape recorder and her incense continued to send tiny spirals of smoke into the wind. I sat with her a few minutes more and then I got up.

"I'm going back to work," I said.

"I hope I don't fall asleep out here," she muttered. "One year I got a bad burn. Kenneth got involved in what he was doing, of course, and completely forgot about me. Scream if I'm still out here when you finish."

"Okay," I said.

She lifted herself to continue talking to me before I walked away.

"Why don't you come back tomorrow and we'll have a picnic on the beach?"

"I have to go to my grandma Olivia's for a Sunday brunch," I said with a grimace.

"You don't look too anxious to go."

"I'm not. I hate going to her house. We have to tiptoe around and remember not to speak unless we're spoken to. My aunt is constantly on pins and needles, afraid one of us will do something to irritate my grandma Olivia."

"Oh. Sounds dreadful," she said, "but I guess we have to put up with family sometimes."

"She's not really my grandma. My real grandma is in a rest home," I said.

"Really? You'll have to tell me about it all," she said. "Maybe at our picnic. Couldn't you skip the brunch?"

570

"They'll have heart attacks," I said. "Especially my uncle Jacob." She laughed. Then she shrugged.

"So, wake up under the weather."

"What?"

"You know, use the old reliable," she suggested.

"What's that?"

"Female problems," she said. "Your uncle Jacob's not going to challenge that, is he?" I shook my head, laughing at the thought of it and amazed that she would join me in a conspiracy so quickly.

"Hardly," I said.

"So there. I'll come pick you up around eleven."

"But what will I say when they come home and find me gone?"

She shrugged.

"You felt better, thought you should get some air, and went to town or something and met me. What would you rather do, be out here with Kenneth and me or go to your stuffy brunch?"

"Be out here, definitely," I replied without hesitation.

"So? Do what makes you feel good. You have to be honest with yourself and then and only then, can you be honest with others," she said, smiling as she gave me another drop of her wisdom. "If you come, I'll do your chart," she threatened with a laugh.

I had to smile. Despite the conflicts raging within me, I couldn't help liking her. I started away, still undecided about her suggestion.

"Eleven o'clock?" she called. I walked a little farther and then I turned impulsively and yelled back into the wind.

"Okay. Come get me."

I ran down the small hill to the studio, clutching the discarded doll in my arms, feeling more confused and more excited than ever, but, strangely, more hopeful, too. It was as if I had finally found an adult who could be completely honest with me. An adult I could truly trust as my friend.

"I see Holly's begun to convert you," Kenneth said when I entered the studio. I had gone through the house, leaving the battered doll in the kitchen until I was ready to leave for home.

"What? What do you mean?"

"She gave you one of her crystals," he said, nodding at the necklace. Even Ulysses looked up with new interest.

"Oh. Yes. It's fifteen million years old and from a meteorite."

"Is that so? Did she show you the warranty?"

"What?"

He laughed.

"Nothing," he said with a wave of his hand.

"She wants to have a picnic tomorrow. She's coming to pick me up at eleven," I said quickly to see if he would disapprove. He just looked surprised.

"Really? What are you going to tell Jacob?"

"I'll take care of it," I said firmly. He widened his smile and lifted his eyebrows.

"I see. Holly wouldn't have given you any ideas on what to say to Jacob now, would she?"

"Maybe."

He shook his head.

"I thought so. It doesn't take Holly long to get right into the heat of battle when she sees an emotional conflict," he said.

"She's interesting," I offered cautiously. He laughed.

"Interesting? She's like a rain storm in Technicolor, psychedelic clouds, neon lightning with the wind playing tunes from the Zen Buddhists. Wait until she reads you some of her poetry," he continued.

"Don't you like her?" I asked, confused. It sounded as if he were making fun of her.

"Of course. She's fresh air. There's not a phony bone in her solar and lunar body. Come on, let's finish this," he said and nodded at the papier-mâché wave. I pulled off my sweatshirt and then took my position quickly. Maybe it was because I had done it before and the shock and excitement were over, or maybe it was because of some of the things Holly Brooks had said, but whatever the reason, my nervousness and inhibition were gone. I felt as if I had done this often.

"How long have you known her?" I asked after I'd gotten myself comfortable.

"A long time."

"Did you meet her here in Provincetown or in Greenwich Village?"

He paused.

"Melody, you know I can't talk and work at the same time," he said.

"Sorry."

"Just lift your chin a little and turn slightly to the right. Good."

"Could you just answer one question?" I begged.

"Okay. I can see if I don't, I won't have any peace anyway. What is it?"

"Do you believe in all this—the power of the crystals, the energies in the universe?"

He stared at me a moment.

"I don't believe in anything but my art," he said, but he didn't sound proud of that. He said it with an underlying tone of sadness and defeat. "Let's work."

I could tell by his tone that he was in no mood to continue the conversation, so I resigned myself to silence so Kenneth could begin.

When we were finished, I hurried out to see if Holly had fallen asleep on the beach. She was in the house, however, and greeted me as I passed through to pick up the doll and wait for Kenneth at the jeep.

"I have something else for you," she said, holding a large paper bag. She dipped into it and brought out

573

some sticks of incense. "Burn these in your room while you're meditating. It will help relax you," she said. Then she reached in again and pulled out a roll of yellow material. "You can wear it tomorrow when I come for you."

"Wear it? I don't understand. How do you wear it? What is it?"

"It's called a sari. It's traditionally worn by Hindu women. Here, let me show you how to put it on," she said. She wrapped it around me and even draped it over my head. Then she stepped back and bowed with her hands together.

"How do I look?" I asked, turning.

"Wonderful. It fills your face with a spiritual light," she said.

I took it off and practiced wrapping it around myself.

"Perfect," Holly said.

"Thank you," I said. She looked back to be sure Kenneth wasn't in earshot. "Don't wear anything else underneath. Remember what I said about confining the natural form."

I nodded, blushing, and put the sari back into my bag as Kenneth appeared.

"What are you two plotting?" he asked.

"Nothing more than a trip on a star," Holly replied.

"That's what I thought," he said. "Hop in, Melody, for an ordinary trip in a jeep." Ulysses got in with us.

"Bye," I said.

"See you in the morning."

"Be right back, Holly," Kenneth told her. "Are you going to make us one of those spiritual dinners tonight, all grain, vegetarian, organic?" he asked. She nodded.

"I'll be losing a few pounds before she leaves," he told me. Holly laughed and we drove away. "Where did you get the doll?" he said gazing at it in my hand.

"I found it on the beach."

574

"A bit beat up, isn't it?"

"I just didn't want to leave it there," I said. He looked at me askance for a moment and then smiled. "And what's in the bag?"

"A sari," I said. "And some incense."

He laughed.

"What's so funny?"

"I wish I could see Jacob's face when he sees you burning incense, walking around in sandals and one of Holly's dresses with crystals around your neck," he said, his brown eyes sparkling with mischief.

"It's not any of his business what I wear," I said firmly. He turned and stared at me. I tilted my head, questioning those intense eyes.

"What?"

"Just for a minute there you sounded so much like Haille it threw me back in time," he said in a wistful tone, his eyes darker.

He drove on, pensive, while my heart pounded as I wondered what it all meant.

Aunt Sara didn't pop her head out of the kitchen to greet me when I came through the front door. The house was deadly quiet, so quiet it made me uncomfortable. I glanced into the living room, saw there was no one in there, and then hurried down to the kitchen. It too was empty. Where was everyone? I started up the stairs.

Cary heard me and stepped out of May's room with May beside him.

"I thought you were only working a half-day today," he said, his eyes cold and accusing.

"Kenneth asked me to stay longer. He had a friend arrive today. Holly Brooks," I said. "Do you know her?"

"No. What's that around your neck?" he asked, like an attorney cross-examining a witness.

575

"It's a crystal with special healing qualities," I said and he smirked.

"That's pagan."

"It's not pagan if it makes you feel good. It happens to have a lot to do with spirituality, too, Cary Logan. You don't know anything about this."

May was signing and pointing to the doll in my hand. I signed back, describing how I had found it on the beach. She wanted to look at it. Even though it was so faded and ragged, May looked at me with that ecstatic rapture only the very young could express. She understood my rescue mission immediately and turned to Cary, signing. He shook his head.

"What is she asking?" I inquired, because she had her back to me.

"She wants me to fix that mess of a doll. What are you doing with it?"

"I found it on the beach and it's not a mess," I insisted and marched into my room. Cary came to the doorway with May.

"Well, what are you going to do with it?"

"I don't know, but I know it's not a mess. It was once a very pretty little doll." I spun on him, my eyes burning with swallowed back tears. "People cast each other aside just as easily as they cast aside their possessions these days," I complained.

A deep silence fell between us.

"Maybe I could do something with it," he finally said. "Can I look at it?" he asked in a softer tone. I handed it to him and he turned it over in his hands. "Body's still okay. Needs some paint and a new head of hair, as well as a new little dress. It's not so much, I suppose."

He saw the warm appreciation in my eyes.

"Could you do that?"

"I have all that paint upstairs and the tools. I'll just get something for the hair and May will make the new

576

dress." He signed that to her and she nodded emphatically. "What color do you want her hair?"

"My own," I said quickly. He nodded and explained all to May, who looked almost as happy as I was about it.

"What else do you have?" he asked, nodding at the bag in my hand.

"A dress Holly gave me and some incense."

"Incense?"

"Yes. You light it and it helps when you meditate."

"Huh? Meditate? You mean like a Buddhist monk or something?" he asked with a smirk.

"Where's Aunt Sara?" I asked instead of replying. He was getting me angry. "I thought I'd find her in the kitchen and help her with dinner," I said.

"She's not here. She and Dad went to dinner at the Wilson's," he said. I stepped back, surprised.

"Your father and mother went out to dinner?"

"Well, you know Ma. She prepared our dinner first," he said. "All we have to do is serve ourselves and clean up afterward. Dad and Jimmy Wilson are talking about buying a cranberry bog together. Ma put up quite a fuss when she heard she had to leave us, but I promised her we'd take care of everything."

"Oh. Well then, I'll clean up and go down and get our dinner set out," I said.

"I'll just put this up in my work room," Cary said, indicating the doll.

I signed to May, describing what we would do, and she told me she would set the table while I showered. After I finished towel-drying my hair I took out the dress Holly had given me and wrapped it around myself. When I stood before the mirror, I laughed at how I looked and then thought I would wear it to dinner to see Cary's reaction. He was downstairs in the kitchen and when he saw me, he stopped what he was doing and dropped his jaw.

577

"What is that?"

"It's called a sari."

"I'll say it's sorry," he remarked and laughed.

"Cary Logan, all you're doing is showing your ignorance," I accused. His smiled faded.

"Well, what's it supposed to be?"

I explained that it was the natural dress for Hindu women and a very special gift given to me. Cary started to smile after I finished, but when he saw the serious expression on my face, he tightened his own, swallowed back his ridicule, and sat at the dinning room table, tonight taking his father's seat.

It was as if the chair had powers, for Cary's face took on Uncle Jacob's serious demeanor. May and I took our usual seats. There was that same moment of quiet that preceded all of our dinners. May looked expectantly at Cary and he reached for the Bible.

"Dad left a marker where he thought I should read tonight," he explained and began. " 'Love not the world, neither the things that are in the world.' " He paused as if the words were choking him.

"Why don't you choose your own selection tonight, Cary?" I suggested. I could see the indecision in his eyes as he thought about my suggestion. It was like challenging the king, doing something deliciously forbidden. His eyes brightened with mischief.

"Okay," he said. "I will." He turned the pages, paused, and gazed at me as he read. "From the Song of Solomon. 'How fair is Thy love, my sister, my spouse! How much better is thy love than wine, and the smell of thine ointments than all spices! Thy lips, O my spouse, drop as the honeycomb: honey and milk are under thy tongue.' " He paused and gazed at May and then at me with his face bronzed in pride and defiance.

"Not one your father would have chosen," I said, impressed with the intensity of his reading. He had

578

never sounded more grown-up to me. For a second, he had actually taken my breath away.

"You wanted me to make my own choice and I did," he said with firm defiance.

He and I gazed at each other.

"I'm glad you did," I said.

He smiled.

"Actually, you look pretty in that dress," he said. "Sort of special."

I smiled.

"Thank you."

May began to sign, wondering why it was taking us so long to begin eating. Daddy never made us wait this long, she emphasized.

We laughed, grateful for the light moment, and started to pass the dishes to each other.

Afterward, Cary helped May and me clean up and put everything away. We left the kitchen as spotless as Aunt Sara did.

"What's this meditating all about?" Cary asked, and I told him some of the things Holly had told me. Of course, he was skeptical, raising his right eyebrow higher than his left as I spoke. I described what I had felt when I did what she instructed and concentrated on my breathing.

"You got like that just by listening to yourself breathe?" he asked with doubting eyes.

"By tuning into myself," I corrected. "Would you like to try?" I asked. "Or are you afraid of what you'll find?"

His eyes sharpened and then narrowed at my challenge.

"Okay. Show me."

"Wait in the living room," I said and ran upstairs to get the incense. I brought it down quickly and set it in a sugar bowl. Then I lit it and placed it in front of us on the floor. May sat by, watching with fascination as

I got Cary to assume the lotus position—or as close as he could get to folding his legs over one another without toppling over.

"I wish I had her music, but we'll try without it for now," I said.

"I can hum something. How about 'The Battle Hymn of the Republic.'"

"Cary Logan, if you're not going to be serious . . ."

"All right. I'm sorry," he said, holding up his hands and laughing. "That stuff sure smells."

"It's supposed to. Okay, concentrate, drive away all thoughts and just listen to yourself take breaths, but don't hurry or slow your breathing, understand?"

"Gotcha," he said and we began.

"Melody?" he said after only a few seconds.

"Shh. Concentrate," I said.

We were both quiet. I felt him gaze at me and then he stared ahead. I think he was really beginning to get into it, too, when suddenly, the front door opened and Uncle Jacob and Aunt Sara appeared.

"What burned?" Aunt Sara cried, worrying about the dinner she had prepared.

"What in the name of God is going on in here?" Uncle Jacob demanded from the living room doorway before we could get up. He looked from me to Cary and then back at me. Then he rushed past us and pulled the incense sticks from the bowl. He thrust them at Aunt Sara. "Get rid of this. Run water on it first."

"What are they doing?" she asked.

"Something pagan," Uncle Jacob said. He turned his fiery eyes on Cary. "I warned you, boy. I told you to watch for the devil and now you've gone and let him into our home."

"Dad, listen—"

"I don't understand," Aunt Sara said meekly. "Where did you get that dress, Melody?"

"From the devil himself, I'll wager," Uncle Jacob

580

said. "Satisfied now, Sara? Satisfied she ain't your dead and gone Laura? She's about as different from Laura as night is from day," he said.

"Stop it, Dad!" Cary cried.

Jacob moved forward quickly and slapped Cary across the cheek so hard it turned his head. Aunt Sara cried out, and Cary looked at me, his eyes burning with hot tears.

"Cary," I began, but before I could say another word, he shot from the room and out the door.

"Cary!" Aunt Sara cried after him.

Uncle Jacob turned to me.

"Now you've done what you came to do, what Haille brought you here to do. It's her revenge," he said.

"You're ignorant! You're ignorant and narrow-minded and cruel!" I fired back. I charged out of the house and after Cary, while poor May struggled with her hands to express the pain and confusion that had burst upon her like a hurricane.

10
&

Shelter from the Storm

I ran from the house out into the darkness. Heavy, ominous clouds had come sweeping down from the northwest, rolling and rumbling over the night sky, burying the stars and the quarter moon, shutting out any brightness and light. I had hoped to find Cary either right in front of the house or on the road, but he was nowhere in sight. When I walked around the house and toward the beach and the dunes, I couldn't see very far. He could have gone in any direction, I realized and groaned my disappointment. I walked over the sand and put my hands to my mouth to cup them in the shape of a megaphone.

"Cary!" I cried, but the wind tossed my desperate call back in my face. Perhaps he had walked toward the ocean, I thought, and continued on. My eyes grew used to the darkness, but the wind was so strong, I actually had to struggle to walk forward, my feet slipping and sliding in the soft sand that easily gave way beneath them. I took off my shoes because it felt easier to walk in bare feet. Every once in a while, I screamed Cary's name, but with the ocean roaring

louder, the surf riled up by the approaching storm, waves slamming onto the beach, and the wind now howling around me, I realized he would have to be only a few feet away to hear.

My sari flapped against my legs. Sand flew into my face so often I had to keep my eyes closed, my hands up for protection. My hair whipped around my forehead and temples, and then I felt the first drops of rain, cold, sharp, heavy. Nevertheless, I charged forward over the dune and looked toward the dock. Then, just as I was going to turn back, I saw a small light on the lobster boat. Lowering my head to keep my face protected, I ran as hard and as fast as I could toward the dock. The rain grew heavier, stronger, each drops feeling like a glassful. My hair was soaked to the scalp in seconds and my dress was drenched, the material now clinging to my wet skin.

I reached the dock and hurried onto the boat. It rocked hard in the water, but I managed to get to the cabin door and open it. A gust of wind blew behind me so fiercely, I was practically driven into the room. I struggled to close the door and then I turned and saw Cary sitting on the bench, his head down. There was a small lantern lit. I leaned against the closed door and caught my breath.

"Cary, are you all right?" I asked. How could he be so lost in his thoughts and not hear the commotion I made arriving? He lifted his head slowly, his eyes catching the glow of the lantern.

"Why did you follow me?" he replied.

"It was all my fault," I said. "I'm sorry. I didn't mean to get you into trouble."

"It's not your fault," he said bitterly. "I don't do anything I don't want to do. You're right about him. He's narrow-minded and stupid and cruel."

"You're just very angry right now, Cary. You don't mean those things. He's still your father," I said, although I was pretty sure I meant those things.

"How can you ask me to forgive him? He practically called you the devil's own daughter!"

"It doesn't matter what he calls me or what he thinks about me," I said. "He's not my father. He's yours."

Cary shook his head in confusion. He looked like a little boy, overwhelmed by the events that raged around him.

"I'm not going to live in his home forever, Cary. I don't need his blessing or approval. Don't worry about me," I said.

"Well, he's got no right. He can't call someone else evil. He's not special just because he reads the Bible at dinner and talks about sin and redemption all the time. I'm not going to forgive him and I'm not going to work with him. I don't care. I'll leave and get a job on my own working for some other fisherman, if I want. Or maybe, I'll just find a boat-building company and take a job there," he vowed.

"You're just upset, Cary. You can't leave your family. They need you more than ever now, especially your mother and May."

He shook his head and looked down. I went to him and sat beside him on the bench. When I put my hand on his shoulder, he raised his head slowly and turned to me, his eyes full of pain and sadness.

"What about you? You don't need me any longer, now that you have your work with Kenneth and your new friend, is that it?"

"Of course not," I said. "I need you very much."

"Really?"

"Yes. I'm just helping Kenneth with his most important art project. It's not anything more," I said. "And as for friends, you're the best friend I have right now."

His eyes warmed and his lips softened.

"You mean that?"

"Yes, I do. I mean it," I said firmly. His smile

widened. He stared at me a moment and then he looked very concerned.

"You're soaked to the skin. Look at you."

As soon as he mentioned it, I felt the cold and shuddered. Then I laughed at how I looked: the strands of my hair pasted together, the sari full of sand.

"I guess I'm not really dressed for the weather," I said. The rain was pounding the roof of the cabin now and the boat continued to rock. "Is it supposed to be a bad storm?"

"No, but it will be like this for a while," he said and hurried to light the kerosene heater. Then he opened the closet and pulled out some towels. "It might even be an all-nighter. There's not much here in the way of clothing," he said. "But I do have this raincoat."

"I remember putting it on right after you rescued me from Adam Jackson's clutches," I said smiling.

"Yes."

"And here you are, rescuing me again," I said.

"You should have turned back when it started to pour."

"I was worried about you," I said. We stared at each other for a moment.

"Your sari is pretty sorry right now," he said smiling. I laughed and rose to unwind it, pausing when I realized I had taken Holly's advice and worn nothing underneath. Cary gazed at me. His eyes were so full of love and desire, he made my heart pound. I kept my gaze fixed on his and continued to unwrap the garment until I was naked, the lantern flickering the shadows over me. Cary lost his breath for a minute and then he thrust a towel at me.

"Dry yourself off before you get pneumonia," he advised.

I took the towel and scrubbed my stomach and legs and then the rest of me while Cary turned up the heater. He gathered up the sari.

"This isn't going to dry so fast," he said. "It's really soaked through and covered with streaks of grime." He draped it beside the heater and turned back to me.

I had the towel wrapped around myself, but I still shivered. Cary hurried to get the raincoat over me and then he pulled out a rolled up thin mattress and untied it, spreading it out on the floor near the heater. The rain continued to beat a drum roll over the sides of the cabin and the roof, drops zigzagging down the windows. Just the sound made me shiver. Cary stripped off his shirt.

"Here," he said. "Put this on too."

"But aren't you going to get cold?" I asked.

"Don't you remember? I don't get cold," he said smiling. I took the shirt from him and slipped it on. Then I lowered myself to the mattress and rubbed my hands together in front of the heater. Now that I was dry, I began to feel a bit cozy and my shivering stopped. Cary stood, staring down at me, the light from the lantern glittering on his chest and shoulders.

"I was just getting into that meditating, too," he said, going to his knees beside me. His polished smile shone again.

I laughed and he reached past me to take some empty sacks out of a cabinet near the bench. He crunched them together to form something of a pillow for both of us. He patted it and lay back, his hands behind his head, gazing up at the ceiling. The rain thumped, but the wind seemed to die down a bit so that the boat rocked less.

"Maybe you and I can just get a boat like this and live in it," he said.

"Oh sure. I'll break into my piggy bank tomorrow," I said and sprawled out beside him.

"No, really," he said turning. "Why can't we do something like that? I could find a job and make enough to do payments on an old boat. It doesn't have to be seaworthy, just liveable."

"Cary, I'm not exactly legally on my own yet," I pointed out. "Do you think Grandma Olivia would permit us to live like that within her precious world? Or your father?"

"I don't care. We'll defy them all. We'll just run off and get married."

"What?" I started to laugh, but saw he was serious. "I'm not going to start life the way my mother did," I said. "I'm not going to be impulsive and then regret it every day and make everyone else's life miserable."

"Is that what she did?"

"Yes. She made my step-father hate himself, hate what he was doing, hate his family. The more unhappy she was, the more unhappy he became. And then we all suffered."

"I'd work myself to the bone to make you happy, Melody," he said. His green eyes were soft and luminous in the dim light of the small lantern.

"Sometimes, you can't help what happens around you, and then you only feel guilty and hate yourself, Cary. Let's not be foolish. Let's be smarter than our parents, okay?"

He nodded.

"As long as you promise not to run off and marry the first rich man who proposes to you," he said.

"I would never do that," I said. "I want much more than a hefty bank account."

He laughed, and then looked serious again, his eyes burning with such love that the stretch of silence between us began to palpitate with sensuality. He kissed my right cheek and then my left before he cupped my head so he could tip it at an angle that made his next kiss a kiss on my lips, intense enough to take my breath away.

He leaned over me and then pressed his lips to my wet hair.

"Melody," he whispered as if my name were a prayer. His lips were at my ear. "Melody."

He was doing exactly what I dreamed Kenneth would do. But this wasn't Kenneth. It was Cary who loved me, Cary who made my body respond quickly.

The tingling in my body became long, overwhelming waves of deep passion that filled my thighs and made me moan through my slightly opened mouth. He caught my breath between his own lips and kissed me again, his hands finding my breasts, the thumbs rolling over my nipples.

Above us the thunder crashed, and through the window I could see lightning crackle. The towel I had wrapped around my waist came apart. I closed my eyes and lay back as he moved his mouth down over my lips, over my chin, to my neck and then my breasts. I heard him fumbling with his pants.

"Cary—"

"I'm ready this time," he whispered. "You don't have to worry about getting pregnant."

My eyes snapped open.

"Cary, no."

"I love you, Melody, completely, fully."

Was this going to happen? Would I let it happen?

The dark voice of my heavy conscience began to warn me, but all I could see was Uncle Jacob's face of displeasure smeared into one giant blob with huge, hostile eyes. It was as if he were the voice of my conscience now and that was a voice I wanted to defy, to despise.

I am not evil. I am not the devil's own daughter. There is nothing bad in my blood and my mother's sins are not my sins, I fired back in my thoughts.

Cary and I were doing exactly what Uncle Jacob had forbidden, but who was he to forbid anything? What Cary and I felt for each other at this moment was pure and good, I cried. I will not feel guilty for loving him.

I felt him against me, throbbing, lifting me gently, kissing me with lips so hot they drove away even the thought of a chill. And then he was there, pressing forward. The sharp, short pain I felt frightened me for an instant and then that passed and was replaced with a sensation so thrilling it vibrated throughout my body. Soon we were both clinging to each other with a passionate desperation that pressed me back to the border between consciousness and unconsciousness. I rose and fell with the waves that lifted the boat beneath us. The storm that raged died away and was replaced by a blazing sun inside me. We quivered against each other, both of us exploding, our sex sweetening our lips.

"I want to be one with you forever and ever," he pledged as we reached the end and eased our bodies, folding softly into each other's arms, our breaths still heavy, our hearts still pounding. We lay there, waiting for it to all to subside. I kept my eyes closed and after another few minutes, I heard him move away and start to dress himself.

When I opened my eyes, I felt as if I had just wakened from a dream. Cary had his back to me. I watched him a while before wrapping the towel around myself again and curling up on the mattress. He took the raincoat and put it over me for a blanket, kissing me softly on the cheek. Then he went to the door and looked out.

"It's still coming down pretty hard out there," he said.

"We should go back. They'll wonder where we are."

"I don't care. Let them. Let him," he corrected. He closed the door and returned to my side, brushing my hair back and gazing down at me. "I love you, Melody. I feel I am truly free when I am with you. I am not afraid of saying anything, telling you anything, revealing anything to you."

"I'm glad, Cary. Trust is the most important part of loving someone."

"Then you do love me, too?" he fished.

589

"I do," I said, convinced it was so. "Yes."

He smiled.

"Then nothing that happens matters. Nothing he can say, nothing anyone can say matters. I can say good-bye to nightmares, to dreary days and dreary, lonely nights. We'll be together forever now, won't we?" he asked.

I started to nod, but stopped. After all I had been through, I was afraid to let too much sunshine come into the shadows of my heart.

"Let's take it a day at a time, Cary. When promises get too big, they have a way of turning into great disappointments."

"I'm not afraid to make a big promise," he said, smiling. He lay beside me and put his arm under my head so I could lie in the softness. He stroked my hair and we were both silent for a long while. The movement of the boat became softer, undulating, hypnotizing. I felt as if I were in a big cradle being rocked.

"Love me half as much as I love you and we'll be all right," I heard Cary say.

It was the last thing I heard before I fell asleep.

We were lucky it was Sunday, for neither Cary nor I woke with the light of morning until the sunshine blazed through the window and wiped over our faces to wash away dreams and sleep. If it had been a weekday, Uncle Jacob would have come through the door before our eyelids had opened and he would have discovered us wrapped in each other's arms, asleep, me still half naked, with only a towel and Cary's shirt to cover me.

I stirred first and then Cary blinked, closed his eyes, ground the sleep from them, and sat up, a look of confusion on his face. We gazed at each other.

"It's morning," he said as if he had made a most wondrous discovery. The look of fear on my face wiped the stunned expression from his. He shot up, gazed around a moment, and then scooped up my dress. "It's not completely dry."

"It's all right. I have to put something on," I said.

He handed it to me and I began to wrap it around my body quickly while he put on his shirt and straightened up the cabin. I put on my shoes and he put his on, too. When he opened the door, the glitter of the morning light on the sand made us both squint.

"What are we going to tell them, Cary?" I asked.

"The truth. We got trapped by the storm and slept in the boat," he replied. "And if he says one nasty thing about it, I swear I will leave for good," he vowed.

My heart thumped like the slow drumbeat of a military funeral march as we made our way over the dunes to the house. I just hoped Uncle Jacob wasn't waiting by the door. When we arrived, we paused, looked at each other, and then Cary turned the knob. To our surprise, it was locked.

"Why did he do that?" I asked.

"He just wanted us to ring the bell so he would know exactly when we came back," Cary said. "That way Ma would wake up too." He shook his head and then smiled. "Follow me," he said and we walked around the house, where there was a ladder lying beside the wall. Cary lifted it carefully and gently laid it against the house just under my bedroom window.

"What if he locked the windows, too, Cary?"

"The window in Laura's room doesn't lock," he said. "It broke a long time ago and we never fixed it. I'll go up first and get it open," he added and started up the ladder. When he reached the window, he opened it gently, smiled down at me, and then came back down the ladder.

"Why didn't you go in?"

"You go first. I want to be sure you climb up all right," he said, stepping back.

I gazed around. It was very early, so there were no

591

other people or cars about. Surely, they might suspect burglars if they saw us, I thought. I looked up the ladder at the open window and shook my head in amazement.

"I can't believe we have to do this," I said, but I started up the ladder slowly. I trembled a few times, but I made it up to the window sill and climbed in, Cary right behind me. He closed the window softly, indicating we should be quiet. Then he went to the door and peered out.

"They're still asleep," he whispered. Then he leaned forward to kiss me and slipped out of my room.

After I got out of the damp sari and into a night-gown, I crawled into bed and fell asleep again, not waking until I heard Uncle Jacob shouting in the hall, complaining about our getting into the house through a window. Obviously he had gone out and seen the ladder still leaning against the house.

"Like common thieves, Sara. They used the ladder and broke into the house. Like thieves in the night!"

"Shh, Jacob. Let them sleep," I heard her say.

"Let them sleep? Where were they? How dare they climb up a ladder to get into the house?"

"You locked them out, Jacob," she reminded him. "Now hush up," she said sharply.

I heard him mumble loudly and then stomp noisily down the stairs. Not ten minutes later, there was a gentle knock on my door and Aunt Sara entered.

"Melody?" she said. "Are you asleep?"

I turned to face her.

"No, Aunt Sara. I'm sorry about climbing up a ladder and through a window, but we couldn't get into the house without waking everyone otherwise," I said.

She nodded, but looked dreadfully sad.

"Where were you?"

"We got caught in the storm and spent the night in

the lobster boat," I said. It was the truth, albeit not all of it.

"What were you doing last night when we came back from the Wilson's?" she asked.

I explained meditation the best I could and apologized if I had caused any trouble. I emphasized that it wasn't Cary's fault.

"Laura never did anything like that," she said, shaking her head woefully.

"She might have if she had lived to learn more about it," I said and Aunt Sara nodded, pleased with that thought.

"Yes, that's true. She might have," she said. "She might even have worn that dress, just for fun once. Yes," she said. Her face brightened. "Well, do you think you'll be up and about soon? We do have the brunch at Olivia's today."

"I don't feel up to it this morning, Aunt Sara. Please give Grandma Olivia my apologies," I said.

"Oh dear. I just hate when we have to do that. Olivia gets so upset. What will I tell Jacob? He'll just get even more riled," she moaned.

"If he has to know, tell him I'm having cramps," I said.

"Cramps?"

"Time of the month," I said but shifted my eyes quickly so she couldn't see I was lying.

"Oh." She brought her hand to her mouth. "I see. Well, will you be all right by yourself?"

"I'll be fine as long as I can rest a while, Aunt Sara."

"Yes, yes. It can be debilitating," she said. "I'll tell him. I'll look in on you before we go," she added and left.

I just hated lying, especially to Aunt Sara, but I could see that this time it was the better thing to do. It got her off the hook as well.

I was still in bed when Cary came by, knocked softly, and peeked through the opened door.

593

"Hi," he said smiling.

"Hi. What's happening?"

"Nothing. I told Dad we got caught in the storm. I guess you had already told Ma. He didn't say anything about it, but he was fit to be tied. I've never seen his face so red or his eyes bulge with so much frustration. Glad you missed it," he added. "You're not going to the brunch?"

I shook my head.

"I heard Ma tell Dad it was woman trouble. First time I ever wished I was a girl too," he said and I laughed. "I'll see you later. If I'm still alive," he added and pretended he was in a noose and being hanged.

"Stop it!" I said laughing. He threw me a kiss and backed out.

Aunt Sara stopped by as she had promised and I pretended to be asleep. She stood by the bed a long moment. I felt her hand on my forehead and then I heard her sigh before she turned to leave.

When the house was deadly quiet, I rose, showered and dressed, and went down to make myself some hot chocolate. A little before eleven, I heard the muffled beep of Holly Brooks's car horn. The beep that funny little car made sounded more like a groan.

Holly was wearing a pink, blue, green, and white tie-dyed one piece with a matching headband, and she was driving barefoot. She wore a rope of crystals around her neck. I was wearing the Moldavite, but I couldn't put on the sari because it was still a little damp and needed a good washing. I was dressed in jeans and a sweatshirt with a pair of light pink sneakers and no socks.

"How did it go this morning?" she asked as I got in.

"It worked," I said and she laughed.

"It always does," she said, driving away. "You should have worn the sari this morning."

I explained how I had gotten caught in a storm and it was still wet and full of sand and grime. I didn't want to tell her why I was out in the storm, but she asked and I had to describe the events that led up to Cary's flight and my searching for him.

"Pagan? Devil? Is that what your uncle thinks? I thought I was in Provincetown, not Salem," she added. "You have a rough road to travel here. How did you come to live with these relatives?" she asked. Apparently, Kenneth hadn't told her much about my past, which I found curious.

I described it as quickly as I could and when I finished, she shook her head.

"I'm almost afraid to do your horoscope," she said and then laughed. "I'm sure it's all going to change for you now. You'll see."

When we arrived at Kenneth's, I saw his car was gone. Ulysses came running at the sound of the engine. I couldn't imagine Kenneth leaving him. He never did unless I was there, I thought.

"Where is he?"

"He had to go to Boston," she said, "so it's just the two of us. Do you mind?"

"No," I said, even though I was a little disappointed. I hadn't spent much time just relaxing with Kenneth and I wondered how different he would be away from his studio and his work.

"Besides, it's good to just be around feminine energy from time to time. Masculine energy throws us off. Too much of the other sort of static. Let me lend you something more comfortable to wear on the beach."

I followed her into the house and the bedroom where she had her things unpacked and hanging in Kenneth's closet. She pulled out a frilly, one-piece tie-dyed dress similar to her own.

"Why don't you just throw this on for now? I've almost got our picnic all packed, just need to throw in a few last-minute things," she said. She went out to finishing packing while I changed.

595

I noticed that the bed was still unmade, the blanket twisted, the pillows practically on top of each other. Holly's bowl for incense was on the nightstand, full of ashes. Like Kenneth, Holly was obviously not much of a housekeeper, I thought.

"Now that's much better," she said when I came out wearing her dress. I was barefoot, too. "Wait," she said and ran into the bedroom. When she returned, she had a pink, blue, and white headband. "Here, wear this."

I put it on and she clapped.

"Now you're a true guru."

She gave me one of the baskets to carry and we headed out to the beach.

"I have a favorite spot," she said and pointed to a place not far from where I had found the discarded doll. Once there, we spread out a blanket. Holly turned on her tape recorder to play her music and then she assumed the lotus position, instructing me to do the same.

"It takes practice to get good at meditation," she explained. "Someday, you'll be at the point where turmoil can be raging around you, and you'll just close your eyes and tune it all out. Everyone will be amazed and then jealous of your power," she promised. "People who bother you and get under your skin will become meaningless."

After what had occurred the night before, what she was promising sounded wonderful. I listened to her instructions and did what she said. The two of us sitting in the lotus position on the beach and facing the ocean must have made quite a sight. We were so far away from the tourists however, there was little chance of anyone discovering us. I understood why she cherished coming here.

"There are places in the world that have more spiritual energy than others," she said, "and Kenneth's beach is one of them."

596

After we practiced our meditation, Holly took out her charts and books and asked me questions, beginning with all I knew about my date of birth. It happened that I had been told the actual time of day I was born, which meant she could give me an even more detailed reading. She plotted out the location, the sun and the moon at the time, and began to work on my horoscope.

"Gemini is in the constellation of the planet Mercury which absorbs an energy that appears to be a compound of all other planets. It's why he is known as the messenger of the Gods," she said. She reached into her basket. "Now that I've gotten to know you better, I want you to have this."

She handed me a ring with an emerald set in silver.

"What is it?"

"Emerald, the mystical gem of Gemini, which is the talisman stone."

"Oh, I can't take another thing from you."

"Of course you can. It's good karma for me to give something spiritual to you. The emerald," she continued, "is a variety of beryl. It strengthens the heart, liver, kidneys, immune system, and nervous system. It's a tonic for the body, mind, and spirit. It enhances dreams and deeper spiritual insight as well as meditative powers."

"It does all that?" I asked staring at the ring on my finger.

"It does," she said firmly. She returned to her charts and then looked up at me and began my horoscope.

"You have a sensitive, active mind. Emotionally you are quite affectionate, generous, and impulsive. You have great powers of observation and are able to grasp facts quicker than the average individual.

"You are somewhat of a dreamer and when those dreams are shattered you are deeply disillusioned and hurt. You can be too romantic. You are sensitive and

597

affectionate as a lover. Your imagination plays an important role in your love life." She paused and looked up. "Does that sound accurate?"

I shrugged.

"I suppose," I said. I guess I was something of a dreamer. She looked at her chart again.

"You have a mind of your own and want independence, so be careful whom you choose as a lover and especially whom you choose to marry."

"What if I choose another Gemini?" I asked. She smiled and nodded.

"I thought you would ask that." She studied her charts, made some notes, and looked up. I held my breath. "You'd be compatible because you would understand each other. The sexual demands and needs would be mutual. I have to know his date of birth, time, and so on, because the one exception to all this would occur if one or the other has Scorpio rising at the time of birth. You didn't."

"What would happen?" I asked, breathless.

"The demands of Scorpio would prove to be too much for the mercurial Gemini nature. Your approach to sex is more spiritual. The Scorpio influence is more physical. Just wouldn't work," she concluded.

"I don't think that's true for us then," I said quickly, too quickly. Her eyes widened.

"Oh?"

I blushed and turned away.

"Somehow, I have the feeling you already know you could be compatible, is that it?"

I nodded.

"The first time you made love?" she asked and I nodded again.

"I remember my first time, although it seems like one of my previous lives by now," she added with a laugh. I looked up with interest. "It's all so new and surprising, you expect it will be that way all the time, but often it's not," she warned. "Even with the same man."

"How many men have you—"

She laughed.

"Let's not talk about me. You think you're head over heels in love, is that it?"

"Yes."

"Maybe you are; maybe you're just discovering love itself," she said. "Compassion for each other is so important," she continued. "That's why I made the point about Scorpio. When one lover is more self-centered than the other, when all he or she wants is to satisfy himself or herself, it becomes something different and soon leads to unhappiness. Find a man who cares for you more than he cares for himself and you've found love.

"But, alas," she said, gazing at the ocean again, "that can be as hard to find as a drop of water after it's been spilled in the ocean."

"You never did?" I asked.

"Once, but unfortunately he died young. That was how Kenneth and I met. He and Brad, my lover, were roommates in college."

"Oh. Kenneth never told me. Actually, he hasn't told me all that much about his past."

She smiled.

"Don't be put off by that. Kenneth lives in the moment, in his art. I've done his horoscope. He'll never change, Melody. Events in his past mirrored the movement of the sun and the moon and produced the dramatic disappointments. They're sewn forever into his being and into his future.

"That's why he and I get along so well. He knows I won't make any demands, won't stay long. I come and go like . . . a cloud," she said, looking at the sky.

"Can't he live like a normal person ever?" I asked, still unable to let go of the dream that Kenneth just

599

might have feelings for me. Though in my heart of hearts, I knew whatever feelings he had would never be able to compare to Cary's love for me.

"Kenneth? Kenneth Childs is one man who is terrified of becoming normal in the sense you mean. Responsibilities, obligations, and the guilt that follows on their heels is very frightening to a true, pure artist. God forbid he had to do something for the house or family just when he was about to begin his work. In the end he would only hate his own wife and children. He doesn't want to be involved in anything or with anyone that will lead to something permanent, something demanding his time and energy. His only commitment is to his art, because it's safe. If he fails, he only fails himself," she concluded.

Then maybe Kenneth is my father after all, I thought, and what Holly was telling me about him was the reason why he would lie or avoid the truth. Would I ever really know the truth?

"What did you mean by Kenneth's dramatic disappointments?" I asked.

"I really don't have a right to talk about it, Melody," Holly said. "Kenneth's memories of happiness and sadness are his possessions. He has to be the one to share them with others."

"It has to do with my mother," I said. "I know it does."

She just held her soft smile.

"Sometimes, I gaze into the stars and I see things I know I must not touch, must not disturb, must not reveal. Sometimes, Melody, it takes more strength to leave a discovery where you found it."

"Is that what Kenneth did?" I shot back at her.

Her smile faded a bit.

"It's something we all do, Melody, sometime, at some place in our lives. Hungry?" she asked, changing the topic.

"Yes," I said. After all, I had skipped breakfast.

As we ate, Holly told me more about her own past, about Kenneth's college roommate, Brad, and how much they had been in love. She read me some of her favorite poetry and she talked more about the power of her crystals. We took a walk on the beach, searching for sea shells, and then sunbathed in the afternoon sun. For one day, at least, I felt as if I had an older sister who would listen to my deeper thoughts and fears and who wasn't afraid to tell me about some of her own.

The sun began to show its descent toward the horizon and I thought I should probably head home soon. The family had surely returned from Grandma Olivia's by now. I changed back into my own clothes and Holly drove me home. I didn't see the car and the truck was still in front. The house looked dark, too.

"It doesn't look as if they've come back yet," Holly said.

"They would have had to by now."

"Maybe they went some place else. Your uncle might have taken his family for a Sunday drive," Holly suggested.

"Not likely," I said. "Not in the mood he was in." I got out. "Thanks for a wonderful day. I guess I'll see you tomorrow when Kenneth brings me to work."

"Okay. Watch that sunset. You'll feel a lot of good energy," she said and drove off. When I entered the house, I found it empty, dark. In the kitchen, my empty mug was right where I had left it.

Upstairs I found everything quiet and just as deserted. Why weren't they back yet? I went into my room, showered, put lotion on my browned face and shoulders, and then dressed again. Still, I heard no one in the house. I descended the stairs, thought for a moment, and then stepped outside and decided I would sit and wait facing the road. Nearly another hour passed.

Finally, I saw the Logans' car come around the turn

and head toward the house. I stood up in anticipation, but was surprised to see Cary driving, Aunt Sara in the front seat, and May in the rear. Where was Uncle Jacob?

They drove in and parked. I walked toward the car as Cary got out, his face drenched in worry and sadness. Aunt Sara had apparently been crying.

"What's going on? Where's your father?" I asked.

"He . . . had chest pains at Grandma Olivia's," Cary said, "so we had to rush him to the hospital. The doctors said he had a heart attack."

"Oh no! Is he—"

"He's still alive, but he's critical," Cary said. "We were there most of the day."

I bit down on my lower lip and then rushed to help Aunt Sara go to the house.

"I'm all right," she said. "We've got to stay strong. No one's really eaten all day. See to May," she said. "I'll fix us some dinner."

"Oh no, Aunt Sara. Let me do it."

"No, no. I have to do it. I always do it. See to May," she said.

May looked like a small flower, wilted, her little face pale, her eyes wide and full of fear. I embraced her and we all went into the house. At the stairway, Cary turned to me, his eyes wet with tears.

"He's going to die," he said. "I know he is."

"No, Cary. Don't say that."

"I did it to him, you know."

I shook my head.

"Yes, it was my fault. I drove him away just the way I drove Laura and they both left angry at me."

"No," I insisted, but he turned and started up the stairs to his attic hideaway, his shoulders slumped, his head down, drowning in his own guilt.

May clung to me harder. Her little hands moved like small sparrows seeking answers and all I could do was keep telling her it would be all right. Everything would be all right.

My hands trembled like lips caught in lies as I signed.

If there was any place on earth where everything wouldn't be all right, it was in this house, I thought, and took her back with me to the kitchen to help Aunt Sara face another night of agony and loneliness.

11
❦
Last Confession

Aunt Sara had prepared a meat loaf for us before she left for the brunch at Grandma Olivia's. She moved about the kitchen like a robot, not really looking at things. Her eyes resembled two glass orbs, lifeless on the outside with no light of their own, merely reflecting what was in front of her. I imagined that inside, her thoughts were lightning bugs zigzagging from one end of her head to the other, tracing her fears, anxieties, and sorrow across the black wall of her despair.

May set the table and I worked on the mashed potatoes while Aunt Sara checked her meat loaf and prepared some steamed vegetables. We all kept busy, avoiding each other, and taking solace in our labors.

"We were just sitting around talking," she suddenly began as if she had heard me ask what had happened.

"Everyone was having a good time. The food was as delicious as ever and Samuel was very jolly, I thought. Olivia had invited Congressman Dunlap and his wife Joan. We were all having such a good time."

She paused to look at me.

"Olivia was very concerned about you. She asked me dozens of questions, wanting to know how you were, what you had been doing, how well you were getting along at your job. She was very disappointed about your not coming. I think Samuel was even more disappointed. The judge kept asking about you, too. Finally, Congressman Dunlap burst out with, 'Who is this young lady everyone is so interested in? I have to meet her.'

"Everyone laughed. Even Jacob."

"What about Cary?" I asked.

"Oh, he had taken May down to the beach. They weren't far off."

She sighed deeply and continued to prepare dinner, talking as she went to the stove.

"They got into a political discussion and the judge had an argument with Congressman Dunlap about taxes. They were getting pretty riled up. No one noticed Jacob rubbing his chest and taking deep breaths until suddenly—" She paused and looked at the wall as if the scene were being projected onto it. "Suddenly, he struggled to his feet, made a strange guttural sound, and fell forward on the grass. The congressman was the first at his side. He had been in the army and had some training in CPR. Jacob complained about pressure on his chest and pain up his arm to his shoulder. The congressman said it looked like a heart attack and we should get an ambulance quickly.

"I was no good to anyone. I couldn't move. My legs turned right to butter. All I could do was hold onto the chair and cry.

"But Olivia. You should have seen her, Melody," she said with a wide smile of appreciation and admiration on her lips. "She stood up and like a general, coolly dictated commands," Aunt Sara said and then demonstrated, pointing this way and that.

"Samuel, go make the phone call. Nelson, go get a

605

pillow and a few blankets from the maid. She even told the congressman's wife to pour some water for Jacob. In minutes, everyone was moving about, doing something. Then she turned to me," Aunt Sara said, imitating Grandma Olivia's expression.

" 'Sara, get a grip on yourself. Go get the children immediately,' she ordered, and I tell you when she turned her eyes on me, I felt my buttery legs harden into stone and my spinal cord turn to steel. I nodded and went down to the beach.

"Cary was devastated. He couldn't believe his father was—had collapsed. Jacob's been such a tower of strength. He's never been sick, never missed a day's work, and he never complains about muscle aches and pains, no matter how hard he works and how miserable the weather. I've seen him come home with his face blue from cold, but he never so much as moaned.

"When the ambulance arrived, Olivia hovered over the paramedics making sure they did everything as quickly and efficiently as possible. Then she organized us into two cars and we followed the ambulance to the hospital. Cary drove our car. When we arrived, she went to the emergency room doctor immediately and got him to go see to Jacob. He reported to her before he reported to anyone else. It seemed like only minutes before they had a heart specialist beside Jacob and Jacob in the CCU. I never saw Olivia any stronger. She inspired me and I kept myself together.

"After a few hours, she came to us and said we should go home and get some rest. There was nothing more to do but wait to see how his condition developed. All the while I kept thinking, if Olivia, who is Jacob's mother, can be so strong, I have to be strong, too. So I kept my tears back and did what she said.

"Cary worries me now," she continued. "He didn't say a word until he spoke to you."

"He'll be fine, Aunt Sara," I promised, even though

I didn't know if I had any right to make such assurances. I certainly had no track record of success when it came to predictions about people.

She sighed again and returned to the meat loaf.

"Everything's ready," she declared. "Can you get Cary, Melody?"

"Of course, Aunt Sara."

I went to the stairway and called him, but he didn't respond, so I went upstairs to get him. I called him again from the bottom of the attic ladder and still he didn't answer me. When I looked in the attic room, I found him sitting and staring at a model of a lobster boat.

"Cary, dinner's ready," I said. "Your mother wants you to come down. She needs you, Cary."

"I made this when I was only seven years old," he said, staring down at the model. "Dad was really surprised at how well it came out. For a while we kept it downstairs on the mantle so Dad could show it to his friends. He wasn't always the way he is now. When I first started to go out on the boat with him, we were more like brothers than father and son. He taught me everything about the boat and the business and said I was his good luck charm. We had much better catches in those days.

"After Laura's death everything changed. Sometimes I think we all died with her," he said, "in different ways, I guess. Dad kept too much of it inside him, eating away. Then . . . I became a disappointment to him."

"You're not a disappointment to anyone, Cary. Anyone who says that just doesn't know. You've been a better son than any boy I ever met, but you are your own person and it's not a sin for you to want things that are different from your father's desires. Deep inside himself, your father knows that. You had nothing to do with this. I'm sure," I said.

He raised his shoulders slowly and turned.

"But after last night . . . He hasn't struck me for years," he said.

"And he shouldn't have last night. I'm sorry, Cary. I don't mean to say anything bad about him, now, of all times, but he was wrong and I think he realized that right away and that's what bothered him the most. You have to be strong for your mother, Cary, and for May. She's so dependent upon us and especially you. She's like someone who's fallen overboard and is barely floating on a tiny raft of hope. You know how much harder it is for her."

He nodded.

"Yes. You're right, of course."

"You've got to be as strong as your father has been for this family," I said and he straightened up even more. "Now come on down and eat something," I ordered.

He smiled.

"Aye, aye, Captain," he said, saluting. He rose and followed me down the ladder and into the dining room. When Aunt Sara saw him, she brightened a bit. Serving the meal helped her keep herself together.

"We'll need a special reading tonight," she told him when we all sat at the table. He nodded and opened the Bible.

" 'The Lord is my shepherd,' " he began, and read the psalm so beautifully, it brought tears to my eyes.

None of us had much of an appetite, but even May saw how important it was to eat as much as she could to please Aunt Sara. After dinner, we all helped with the cleanup and then Cary announced he would drive us all to the hospital.

"Oh dear," Aunt Sara said. "Maybe I should change into something fresh, and maybe May should put on—"

"None of that matters, Ma," Cary said with authority. "We're only there to be at Dad's bedside and give him comfort."

608

She nodded. Cary had already taken the reins. He was at the helm and in control of our actions and direction. We got into the car and he drove us to the hospital, no one saying much until we arrived.

The cardiac-care unit permitted only immediate family visits, for five minutes every hour on the hour. Cary decided May should wait in the lounge with me while he and Aunt Sara went in to see how Uncle Jacob was doing.

Grandma Olivia and Grandpa Samuel had gone home for the night and left orders for the doctor to call them if there were any dramatic changes. I kept May amused and answered her questions about the hospital, people we saw working, and as much as I knew about heart attacks. One of Papa George's friends had died of a heart attack two years before and I recalled some of the details about blocked arteries, destroyed muscle, water in his lungs.

I didn't tell May any gruesome details, but her eyes were dark with worry and fear when I explained how the heart worked. She was closed up so tightly in her silent world, and now all this tightened the doors and windows, bringing her more darkness. A touch, a smile, constant signing and embraces helped bring back some light to her face, but in the pauses, the silence grew more deafening and drove her down deeper and deeper into her own loneliness.

We feel like strangers to each other so often in our lives, I thought. It's hard enough as it is for most people to explain, express, and communicate their feelings, fears, and dreams to each other. May was born with a disadvantage and given another obstacle to overcome. It was at times like these when that handicap would announce itself most loudly and make the rest of us feel even more frustrated trying to help her and, therefore, help ourselves.

When Cary and Aunt Sara came out, they both looked glum. Aunt Sara was dabbing her eyes with a

609

handkerchief. Cary looked pale. Even his lips had lost most of their color. He guided his mother to the settee and then he turned to me.

"It's hard seeing him hooked up to oxygen and all those heart monitors clicking away. He looks so small in that bed—he looks like a corpse," he blurted and his tears broke free to burn down his cheeks. May started to cry and move her hands about desperately for news.

Cary signed to her that Uncle Jacob was still sick but getting better and told her to go sit with their mother. She did so and Aunt Sara embraced her. The two rocked gently on the settee. Cary turned back to me.

"He can talk," he said. "Just barely whisper, but he can talk. Just before we left, he asked me about you and I told him you were out here."

"He asked about me?"

"Yes. Then he said—" Cary paused, looked back at his mother and then back at me. "Then he said he wanted you to go in to see him alone."

"What?"

"That's what he said, Melody. I told the head nurse and she said to wait fifteen minutes and then send you in to see him. She said it would be all right. I told her you were my sister," he said.

"Why does he want to see me?" It felt like a hand of ice was stroking the back of my neck and then moving down my spine.

"He thinks he's going to die tonight," he said, "and he wants to tell you something before he does," Cary replied, taking a deep breath before going to sit with his mother and sister.

I felt as if I had swallowed a dozen goldfish and they were all flopping about in my stomach. Cary checked his watch and looked at me across the small lobby. It seemed he was looking at me across a chasm so wide and deep we could never reach each other again.

I sat back. Of all people for Uncle Jacob to want to see. Me! Maybe he wanted to lay some curse on me or blame me for his condition. Maybe he wanted me to promise to leave his house for good. Or maybe, maybe one of those deeply buried secrets was about to rear its ugly head.

I took deep breaths. May gazed at me with her eyes big, the expression on her face mixed fear and hope. Aunt Sara bit down on her lower lip and nodded to unheard voices. Cary stared ahead. I vaguely heard the voices of other people around us and heard the footsteps of nurses and technicians. My heart pounded harder with every passing minute.

And then Cary gazed at his watch again and looked up at me.

"It's time," he said. "Go on. They'll show you where he is," he added.

I didn't think I could stand, but I did. I gazed at Aunt Sara, who looked up at me with curiosity and confusion, and yet with a prayer on her lips and in her eyes. I smiled at her and at May and then I started toward the door to the cardiac-care unit, my legs and feet floating over the hard tiled floor. I opened the door and entered the large room with the circular nurses' station in the center, a bank of monitors reporting the heartbeats of the patients around them. Everyone looked efficient and serious, emphasizing the critical care and the possibility of life-and-death choices that were made there each and every day.

I sucked in my breath and started across the room, passing elderly patients, until the head nurse greeted me.

"Melody Logan?" she asked with a brief smile.

"Yes, ma'am."

"Right this way," she said and nodded toward the last bed on the right where Uncle Jacob, hooked to his life-saving machinery and his monitors lay waiting, inches from death's grasp. Cary was right about him, he did resemble a corpse, pallid, small, withered.

I looked at the nurse.

"You can stay here a few minutes and see if he wakes. Otherwise, come back later, on the hour," she suggested. She checked the drip in his I.V. bag and then walked back to the nurse's station. Timidly, I drew closer to Uncle Jacob's bed and gazed down at him. The beep, beep, beep of the monitors seemed to mirror my own drumming heart.

Half of me wanted him to remain asleep, while the other half couldn't contain my curiosity. I was tempted to flee and also tempted to touch his hand to see if he would waken. His eyelids trembled and I saw his lips writhe and then stiffen.

"Uncle Jacob," I said, or at least, I thought I did. Maybe I had just thought it. He didn't acknowledge me. "Uncle Jacob?" I said a little louder.

His eyelids fluttered and then opened. He turned slowly and looked at me. There were oxygen tubes in his nostrils and tiny beads of sweat had broken out on his brow. I took a cloth from the table beside the bed and wiped his forehead. As I did so, he mouthed my name.

I leaned in because he was barely whispering.

"Melody . . . come closer," he said. I looked back at the nurses' station and then brought my face as close to his as I could.

"What is it, Uncle Jacob? You should just rest, get better."

He shook his head.

"Won't get better," he said. He swallowed, the effort causing him to close his eyes. His Adam's apple strained against his skin and bobbed. Then he opened his eyes again. "My fault," he said. "It was my fault."

"What was your fault, Uncle Jacob?"

"Haille."

612

"My mother? I don't understand, Uncle Jacob. What are you saying?"

"Haille . . . When I was a young boy . . . she was barely thirteen but I . . . did a terrible thing . . . made her do it. She never told, but it was my fault . . . my fault she became what she became and we had all the family trouble."

I stared at him. His eyes were watery, dark, the pupils smaller.

Suddenly, he found my hand and squeezed my fingers as hard as he could, which wasn't very hard.

"I didn't mean to be so hard on you, but I feel more responsible," he said after a big breath. He closed his eyes and then opened them quickly. "A sin can last forever, be passed on from mother to daughter, from father to son . . . forever. Be a good woman and end the devil's hold on us all." He swallowed hard and closed his eyes. Then he whispered, "My poor Laura. Poor, poor Laura . . ."

His head fell to the right and the monitor began a long, shrill humming sound. I released his hand and stepped back.

"Stat!" I heard behind me. Two nurses rushed past me and the doctor on duty came across the CCU. I backed away slowly as they all gathered around Uncle Jacob's bed. Electric pads were being placed on his chest.

Someone shouted, *"Clear!"*

I saw Uncle Jacob's body jump and heard the doctor say, "Again, clear!"

I fled the CCU. Cary was waiting in the hallway and I ran into his arms.

"What?" he cried.

"Something's happening to him. I—"

"Dad!" he groaned and charged through the door-way into CCU. I waited a moment and then turned to see Aunt Sara and May standing in the lounge, Aunt

613

Sara's hand on May's shoulder, both of them gazing at me with the same horrified look in their eyes.

I started to cry. My stomach felt hollow, just the way it had felt when I learned Daddy had been killed in the mining accident. Aunt Sara started to shudder with her own sobs. May's face wrinkled with pain, her moans distorted by her great fear and sadness. I went to both of them and the three of us embraced, held each other, and waited, all of one heart, small and trembling, alone and helpless against the dark cloud encroaching, moving with the wind raging around us.

"He's back!" Cary cried from the doorway. He was laughing through his tears. "It's a resurrection."

We turned and gazed at him. He wiped his cheeks with the back of his hand and took a deep breath.

"Back?" Aunt Sara said.

"What does that mean, Cary?" I asked.

"His heart stopped but they got it started again," he said, "and he's doing okay for now."

"Oh, praise God," Aunt Sara cried. "Praise God." She held on to May and rocked with her on the settee.

I took a deep breath, closed my eyes, and said my own prayer of thanks. When I fled the CCU, I believed I had caused him to have the heart failure for sure. It was the great effort he had made to speak to me.

Cary regained his calm demeanor and strength.

"How about a cup of hot tea, Ma? I can get it from the machine downstairs," he said.

"Yes, thank you, Cary."

"I'll get May a soda. Melody, you want something?"

"I'll come with you," I said and got up. We walked to the elevator. When the door opened, he took my hand and we stepped in and he pressed the button.

"I really thought he was a goner," Cary muttered. "I watched them struggling, but that doctor hung in

614

there and suddenly, the monitor began clicking away again. Everyone cheered. They waited and his pulse built up. It's a miracle," he added. "Don't you think?"

"Yes, Cary."

He nodded, so filled with joy he was beside himself. Then, he remembered I had been in there. As the door of the elevator opened, he turned to me.

"What did he want?"

"I think it was something he wanted only me to know right now, Cary. I don't feel right talking about it. I hope you understand."

"Oh. Sure," he said, although his eyes betrayed his hurt. It wasn't a time for a father to keep secrets from his son. "I understand. It must have been pretty important to him, though. He was willing to chance dying to do it, huh?"

I nodded and we went to the vending machine. We brought Aunt Sara her tea and May her soda and then Cary went to check on Uncle Jacob one final time. He returned to say Aunt Sara could go in with him now and Aunt Sara decided they should take May so she would see Uncle Jacob was still alive.

I waited for them in the lounge, thinking about the things Uncle Jacob had said. He sensed death at his door and felt he had to confess to me. I realized how much blame he had carried in his heart all these years, but I doubted if he was the main cause of any sins Mommy had committed afterward.

"He's stabilized," Cary told me after they emerged from CCU. "Let's go home and get some sleep. We're all exhausted."

I couldn't argue with that. May actually fell asleep in my arms on the way home and Aunt Sara looked as if she would topple herself any moment. Cary helped her out of the car and into the house. She wanted to go to the kitchen to do some final cleanup, but he insisted she go right upstairs and get to bed.

"Dad's going to need you stronger than ever, Ma. You can't run yourself down now," he said with authority. She nodded.

"Yes, yes, you're right, Cary. Thank God we have you. You're my strength now," she said and squeezed his arm. He kissed her and watched her go upstairs, taking May along with her. Then he turned to me.

"What a day, huh?"

I smiled.

"I can think of better ways to spend our time, if that's what you mean," I said. He laughed. It was good to see his face brighten. "But I confess I am tired, too."

"I'll make sure everything's off and put away," he said. "Then I'll stop by to say good night." He leaned over to kiss me on the cheek and walked off.

I hurried upstairs, washed, and dressed for bed, putting on a light blue cotton nightgown. If there was ever a time to practice Holly's meditation, it was now, I thought, and sat in the lotus position on the bed and concentrated. I was so deeply involved, I didn't even hear Cary come up to my door. I felt his hand on my shoulder and opened my eyes.

"Did it work?" he asked. "Your meditating?"

"Yes. I felt the tension drain from my body, just as Holly said."

"I guess I'll have to learn how to do it then," he said.

I unfolded my legs and sat back against the pillows.

"Mind if I stay here with you for a while?" he asked.

"Of course not."

He took off his shoes and sprawled out beside me on the bed, putting his head on my lap. I stroked his hair and he closed his eyes.

"When Laura and I were very little and one of us got scared, we would lie together like this for a while. I

616

think we did it until we were about fourteen or fifteen," he admitted. "It's nice having a safe haven in a storm, whether the storm's in your heart or out there."

"You were lucky to have each other," I said.

He opened his eyes and looked up at me, thinking.

"It must have been difficult for you, growing up alone, away from family."

I smiled.

"I had Papa George and Mama Arlene, as well as Daddy. Sometimes, Mommy was there for me, too."

He nodded, still thoughtful. Then he smiled.

"Sing me one of those fiddle songs, a soft one," he asked. I laughed and then I began, singing one Papa George had taught me. It was really the prayer of a miner's wife, praying her husband would always be safe in the bowels of the earth, and it ended on a happy note because he always came up, smiling through the coal dust.

Singing it reminded me of Daddy and I couldn't help the tears that burned under my eyelids. But Cary didn't notice the crack in my voice. When I looked down at him, I saw he was fast asleep, his chest rising and falling gently. I didn't have the heart to wake him, so I crawled under the blanket and fixed the pillow under his head, too. Then I reached over and turned off the light.

Darkness fell like a heavy blanket. The moon peeked out from between two passing clouds and sent a ray of white light through the window, washing over us both. Then the clouds closed and shut out the illumination. I closed my eyes and in minutes, I was as deeply asleep as Cary.

Hours later, I awoke with a start. For a moment I forgot what had happened. It all came rushing back and I sat up, realizing Cary was no longer beside me. He was at the window, gazing out.

617

"Cary?"

"Oh," he said turning. "I should have just gone to my room. I didn't mean to wake you."

"You didn't. Are you all right?"

"Yeah. I just woke up and felt a little nervous. I like looking out at the ocean whenever I'm nervous or afraid. I guess that's where I find my meditation. Laura's room always had a better view of the coast than mine. I would either come here or go up to the attic. I'll leave and let you sleep," he said, turning from the window and starting toward the door.

"No, don't leave," I said. He paused.

"I can't stay here all night. Ma wouldn't understand," he said.

"Just stay a little while longer."

"I'll fall asleep again," he threatened.

"I won't let you do that," I said. Something in my voice brought a smile to his face that was so bright, I could see it even in the darkness. He returned to my bed and sprawled out beside me. Then he leaned forward and kissed me gently on the lips. We embraced and kissed again. His hands moved over my shoulders and down my arms. He brought my fingers to his lips and then he put his head against my bosom and moaned. I closed my eyes and drank in the warm feeling that comforted me as much as it must have comforted him.

"I feel guilty thinking about you, wanting you at a time like this," he whispered.

"You mustn't feel that way. If we care for each other, we can't be ashamed of needing each other," I told him, though I was worried that Aunt Sara or May might hear us.

"Oh Melody," he said. "I do care for you, love you, need you more than I will ever need and love anyone."

"Then throw your guilt overboard," I said and he

laughed. He rose, pulled off his shirt, unbuttoned his trousers, and crawled under the cover beside me. We kissed, held each other tightly, and then his hands went under my nightgown until they found my breasts. Our lovemaking was different, more like a dream. We weren't driven by sexual appetite as much as we were by the need to reassure each other. We moved gently, slowly, and when it was over, he slipped away so quietly and smoothly, I wondered if it had actually happened. But his place beside me in my bed was still warm from his body. I ran my hand over it and moaned softly to my pillow.

Then I closed my eyes and didn't open them again until the first light of morning kissed my face.

I was almost afraid to rise, yet I couldn't escape the vivid memory of Uncle Jacob's heart stopping right before my eyes. As I showered and dressed I tried to think of something else, anything else, but still the memory returned. With trembling legs, I started down the stairs. Apparently, everyone else had risen before me. Aunt Sara was already in the kitchen making pancakes and Cary and May were at the table.

"Why didn't anyone wake me?" I asked.

"Oh you wouldn't be sleeping if you didn't need it," Aunt Sara said. I looked at Cary. His face had the shine of polished stone, his eyes luminous with joy.

"I called the hospital. Dad spent a good night and the doctor was already there."

"That's wonderful, Cary."

"He told the nurse to tell me not to bother coming to the hospital and waste my time standing around. He'd rather I take the boat out and check our traps," he said laughing. "I'll do both. Grandma Olivia and Grandpa Samuel are coming by to take Mama over to the hospital. May's going to go to school."

I nodded. Cary apparently had things organized.

"You can go to work as well," he said.

"Oh, I should stay and help Aunt Sara."

"Nonsense, dear. I'm fine," she said. "Cary's right."

"Cary is becoming a bit bossy, isn't he?" I asked, fixing my eyes on him.

"He's the man of the house until Jacob's back on his feet," Aunt Sara said. Cary beamed.

"As long as he doesn't get too big for his britches," I remarked and then signed the idea to May, who thought it was very funny.

"Now just a minute," Cary protested. "Let's have a little more respect for the captain of this ship."

"We'll give the captain the respect he deserves, but if he's an ogre, there's always the chance of a mutiny," I countered, and Cary laughed.

It was good to wake up to sunshine and hope and happiness again. I prayed it wouldn't be short lived.

Kenneth had already heard about Uncle Jacob, as had most of the local residents in Provincetown. Like any small town, news traveled fast, but bad news traveled even faster. When Kenneth came to pick me up, I brought him up to date.

"It doesn't surprise me, this heart attack," Kenneth said. "The man was always brooding, grinding away at his insides, even as a teenager. You all right?" he inquired.

"Yes."

"Sara must be a mess."

"She's doing okay," I said. "Cary's been a source of strength."

"Really? Good for him. Are you going to be able to work?" he asked cautiously.

"Yes. It's the best thing, the best way to deal with worry, work it under the sand."

Kenneth laughed.

"That sounds like some beachcomber's wisdom," he remarked and drove on.

620

We did work hard that week and Kenneth made a great deal of progress, deciding by week's end that he was ready to begin the actual sculpture. Holly did some painting of her own while we worked. By her own description, her work was ethereal, spiritual, abstract, full of bright colors and ghostly shapes. In one painting, the woman she'd painted had stars looking down instead of eyes. Kenneth said she usually sold all of her works in New York at her shop.

Holly was always upbeat and pleasant and fun to be with, which proved refreshing during these troubled times. During my breaks, or if Kenneth finished with me early, Holly and I usually walked along the beach, practiced meditating, talked about crystals and astrology, sunbathed, and dressed in her headbands and saris. One day she decided to repaint her car and I helped her create new images over a pea-greenish yellow exterior. Kenneth thought our work was so far out, Holly might be pulled over on the highway for violating sanity. Everyone laughed. I felt very comfortable being with the two of them, especially with Holly.

During this week Cary had taken over his father's role and actually had some very good days at sea, which he said buoyed Uncle Jacob and helped his recovery. I didn't go back into the CCU with them, but two days after they moved Uncle Jacob to what they called Step Down care, I accompanied the family on a visit. I noticed that Uncle Jacob avoided looking at me the whole time and then, just before we were about to go home, he whispered something to Cary. As we were all leaving the room, Cary asked me to remain.

"My father wants to talk to you privately again," he said. "We'll wait for you in the lobby."

I looked at Uncle Jacob, but he kept his eyes closed and lay back on his pillow. It wasn't until the others

621

left that he opened his eyes. Actually, they snapped open, and he gazed at me with that all-too-familiar look of accusation.

"Cary said you wanted me to stay for a few minutes?" I said, approaching his bed.

"Yes." He looked away, sipped some water, and then turned back to me. "He tells me I asked to see you while I was in the CCU."

"Yes," I said, surprised that he had to be told. "It was only for a few minutes, but—"

"I have no memory of this, but my doctors tell me I could easily have hallucinated and said ridiculous things. You are to disregard anything I might have said under the condition I was in," he ordered. "I hope you haven't gone blabbering any of it to anyone."

"No. I wouldn't do that," I said.

"Not even to Kenneth Childs?" he asked, his eyes shifting to me.

"No."

"Good. Then forget it all. It was gibberish, the babbling of a confused, sick man. Do you understand?" he asked. "Do you?" he insisted.

"Yes, Uncle Jacob."

"Good," he said again. "I hope you're helping Sara during this hardship."

"Of course I am."

"And you're not taking advantage of my incapacity," he added.

"I never took advantage, even when you were well, Uncle Jacob."

He widened his eyes and I looked away. I didn't want to get into any arguments with him now. If something should happen, I would surely be to blame. Maybe that was what he hoped.

"Just remember this discussion."

"Okay," I said. "I hope you feel better," I added and turned to leave.

"Oh, I will," he said. It sounded like a threat. I didn't look back. I couldn't wait to get away from him, and I marched out quickly.

Cary looked up expectantly when I stepped out of the elevator. Aunt Sara had been talking to a hospital aide, but stopped and looked my way, too.

"Everything all right?" Cary asked quickly.

"All right?" I thought a moment. "Everything's . . . back to normal," I said dryly. Cary raised his eyebrows.

Aunt Sara heard my words and misunderstood.

"Yes," she said. "Isn't it wonderful? The doctors think Jacob will be home sooner than we thought. Of course, it will be hard for us to make sure he doesn't try to do anything he shouldn't. He'll have to rest and avoid stress of any kind," she added.

"Sounds as if I should move out then," I muttered under my breath. I thought Cary might have heard anyway because he looked very troubled.

I took May's hand and we left the hospital. As we walked to the car, my mind went to how important family could be at times like this. I thought about Grandma Belinda and how long it had been since I had visited. I decided I would return this weekend. Even though she wandered about in a state of semi-confusion, I felt there was a possibility of love between us. Or at least I hoped there was.

I knew I would need it. The days that lay ahead were full of bleak promises and even more obstacles to my happiness. But I had no idea just how much more, no idea at all. Not even Holly's horoscopes could reveal that.

12
&

Showdown

After work on Saturday, I told Kenneth and Holly of my plans to visit Grandma Belinda again.

"How will you get there?" Kenneth asked.

"I guess I'll take a taxi. Olivia practically forbade me to visit, so I won't get Raymond to take me, and Cary has his hands full with Uncle Jacob in the hospital as well as having to do all the work. He's very worried about this year's cranberry harvest, too."

"I can take you," Holly offered. When I started to shake my head, she insisted. "Really, I don't mind."

I thought about it and started to laugh, thinking what it would be like for us to drive up in Holly's psychedelic car. It would certainly catch everyone's attention. Kenneth saw the wide grin on my face.

"Melody is imagining what sort of an entrance you two will make dressed in your saris, headbands, crystal earrings, and sandals, Holly," he said, staring at me with laughter in his eyes.

"Why?" Holly asked.

"Why? This is a rest home for New England blue-

624

bloods. They haven't seen anything like you, even in their senile hallucinations," he replied.

Holly thought a moment and then smiled.

"Well, then we'll be a special treat for them, won't we?"

"I don't think I can dress that way," I said softly, not wanting to hurt Holly's feelings. "I've only just met my grandmother. She might not even recall the meeting, so I had better not do anything to confuse her. I was thinking I would wear what I wore the first time."

"Oh, dress any way you want, Melody. So will I. This might be fun," she squealed. "I like talking to elderly people. Often they have a better understanding of the cosmic center."

"That's because they're closer to becoming pure energy," Kenneth quipped and then winked at me.

Once Kenneth had determined he was ready to begin sculpting the marble block, he became more relaxed and more confident about focusing his creative energy. He declared that the work was already completed.

"Completed?" I looked at the block and then shook my head in confusion.

"In here," he said pointing to his head. "It's done. All I have to do is bring it out, follow the blueprint. I become a mere tool of my artistic consciousness. Do you understand?"

"Oh. Yes, I think I do," I told him. A month ago I might have thought him weird, even mad, but after having him lecture to me daily about the creative eye, and after hearing Holly talk about the power of focused energy, I really did appreciate what he was saying. He was pleased I understood.

At the end of our work days now, Kenneth would pour the three of us a glass of cranberry wine, my glass being only a third or so full. It was really Holly's idea.

"People who work as hard as you two do have to

625

step back and permit their spirits and their bodies to join hands again," she said.

We usually sat on the small patio between the house and the studio and watched Shell, the turtle, navigate around the rocks and the fish in the small pond. The sun was still high enough in the sky to provide warm rays, but it wasn't unbearably hot and there usually was a late-afternoon breeze coming off the sea. The conversation was mostly between Holly and Kenneth, the two of them talking about people they had known and things Holly did in New York City. I never felt like a mere observer, however, because one or the other would often turn to me to explain something or someone. It was from these conversations that I gleaned an idea of what Kenneth had been like when he was only a few years older than I. There appeared to have been a bright period to his life, a period when he was as bohemian as Holly, carefree and far more sociable.

And then, from what they said, I understood that he had lost contact with all their mutual friends and had done little or nothing with anyone, even here in Provincetown. Holly constantly complained about his failure to visit her and her shop in New York. Kenneth merely smiled and promised he would some day.

"When the stars are correctly aligned for it," he added, shifting his eyes impishly to me.

"The stars have been aligned for it many times, Ken. You've got to be aligned," Holly replied and we all laughed.

Holly was right about our quiet time. Although I was tired, our half hour or so of relaxation always put me in a good mood and I was able to bring some of that joviality home to help cheer up Aunt Sara during this troubled time.

When I arrived at the house after work this particular Saturday however, I found Aunt Sara was more upset than usual. Cary was still out on the lobster boat and she was worried about visiting Uncle Jacob.

"He's called three times asking for Cary," she moaned. "I can't imagine what's keeping him. He knows how his father worries up there and he knows we can't let him worry," she said, her face full of a thousand anxieties.

"Uncle Jacob surely understands that things can keep Cary busy and working late. It's happened many times before, hasn't it, Aunt Sara?" I asked.

I knew that since Uncle Jacob had been given phone privileges, he called a number of times during the day, giving Aunt Sara orders, making demands, and questioning her to death. I assumed many of those questions had to do with me.

"It's hard for him," she said. "He feels like a prisoner chained to his bed by doctors and nurses, fed medicines, and prohibited from doing the simplest things. They had to give him bathroom privileges faster than they wanted because Jacob refused to sit on a bed pan," she added. "He's been hounding the doctor to let him go home."

I wanted to say it was very hard for Cary, too, and especially hard for her and May, but I put a zipper on my lips and helped her get dinner ready instead. However, when Cary wasn't home an hour later, even I became worried. Uncle Jacob called to speak to him, complaining that Cary had neglected to report the day's catch. Aunt Sara had to tell him Cary wasn't there.

"I don't know," I heard her say. "I'm getting very worried. Should I send Melody down to the dock?" she asked him. I saw her eyes shift from me as she listened to him speak. She nodded and promised to call him as soon as she had news. Then she cradled the phone and wrung her hands.

"What did Uncle Jacob say? Should I go to the dock?" I asked her. May sat staring at us, her eyes full of worry, too.

"He said you wouldn't know what to look for or what to ask anyone," she replied, shaking her head as she did so.

"I can see if the boat's there, can't I?"

"Yes," she said. I saw that it took great courage for her to disagree with anything Jacob uttered.

"Then I'll go," I declared and started out of the kitchen. May called to me and then signed her desire to go too.

I nodded and she leaped to her feet and took my hand. The two of us marched out of the house and over the dunes, both straining to see the activity at the dock. We had only to go a few thousand yards down the beach to discover there wasn't anyone there. The lobster boat was nowhere in sight either.

"Where is he?" I asked myself aloud. May tugged on my hand and signed the same question. I shook my head and continued toward the dock. When we got there, we stood looking out at the sea, searching in every direction for a sign of the boat. I saw an oil barge going south and larger cargo ship, but no sign of the lobster boat. I just hated returning to the house with no news, but I knew the longer we remained here, the more Aunt Sara would worry, and Uncle Jacob was sure to call again.

Maybe there was a reason to worry, I thought. This wasn't like Cary. Even though the weather was picture perfect, accidents do happen at sea. It would be just horrible if something bad had happened now, with Uncle Jacob still in the hospital, I thought. Since I had been practicing tuning into the cosmic energies with Holly, I paid more attention to my feelings and instincts, and I didn't like the heavy little ball of worry that was growing in my chest. There was nothing to do but go home and wait with Aunt Sara.

I started to turn away when May tugged hard on my hand and then pointed north. I looked, but saw nothing.

"What?"

She pointed more emphatically. Her eyes were more seaworthy than mine, for she had grown up here and she knew how to read the twilight glitter on the surface of the ocean. I strained to see as two almost indistinguishable dots grew into shapes that were slowly moving closer to the shore.

"What is it?"

We walked to the edge of the dock and waited as the shapes became two boats, one looking like a tugboat. Finally, I could make out the lobster boat clearly. It was being towed toward the dock.

"Oh, thank goodness," I declared. May smiled and started to sign an explanation. She recalled something like this happening before. The boat had broken down at sea and Uncle Jacob had to radio for help.

When Cary drew close enough to see us, he waved from the starboard bow. The sun had almost completely dipped behind the horizon as the lobster boat was delivered to the dock. Cary and Roy Patterson got it tied up and Cary hurried off to tell us the story.

"The catch was good, but suddenly our engine died and we weren't able to fix it. How's Ma?" he asked quickly, knowing she would be concerned.

"She's very worried, Cary. Uncle Jacob keeps calling from the hospital."

"Let's get up to the house," he said.

Roy said he would take care of everything and we hurried back. Cary looked exhausted. His hands were full of grease, and there were streaks of it across his face, which was darker, even red at the crests of his cheeks.

"I'll wash up and go right to the hospital," he said, taking such long, deep strides over the sand May and I had trouble keeping up with him.

"You have to have some supper first, Cary. Just call him."

He nodded, but he looked more concerned about his father than he was about the problems with the boat.

"He's going to blame it on me," he muttered, "but I didn't do anything different. We had oil pressure problems."

"I'm sure he'll understand. May said something like this happened before anyway, right?"

"Right," he said, but he didn't sound confident.

Aunt Sara was at sixes and sevens by the time we arrived. She had practically worn the skin off her fingers wringing her hands with worry. Cary quickly explained what had happened, and she told him to call Uncle Jacob.

"You guys just eat," he said after he had the conversation with his father and hung up. "I've got to wash up and run up to the hospital."

"But Cary—"

"It's okay," he said. "He wants to know the details. I'll eat something later. Go on. Don't wait."

"But—"

He charged up the stairs before I could protest any more. I looked at Aunt Sara. She shook her head and went about serving our dinner.

"Be back as soon as I can," Cary called from the front door less than ten minutes later.

"I don't know why you can't get something to eat first," I called back, but he was already out the door. I looked at Aunt Sara. She was troubled, but silent. "Uncle Jacob's being pretty selfish, Aunt Sara. Cary's had a miserable day. He's tired and hungry. You should have made him eat."

"I can't worry Jacob now," she cried in defense. "He's still recuperating."

I choked back my angry words and drank them down with water. If Uncle Jacob had been an ogre

630

before, I thought, he would be a bigger monster now, for he was sure to take advantage of his own illness at every opportunity.

It was nearly three hours later before Cary returned. Aunt Sara had been trying to do needlepoint, but her eyes lifted every time she heard a creak in the house or the sound of an automobile outside.

"I should have gone too," she muttered.

When Cary entered, she threw down her needlepoint and jumped up to greet him at the living room door.

"He's fine," Cary said quickly. He looked more exhausted than I had ever seen him, and I saw that the fatigue didn't come from his day's labor so much as from the emotional tension he had just experienced. "I think he might even be released in a day or so."

"Really? Oh, that would be wonderful," Aunt Sara cried, clapping her hands together. She quickly signed the news to May, whose face lit up with a smile.

It occurred to me that no matter how I saw Uncle Jacob or what I thought of him, he was still Aunt Sara's husband and May's father. They loved him, and in his own way, he surely loved them. I had no right to be critical of him, I thought, especially now when he was recuperating from one of the worst illness anyone could have.

"But one of his doctors stopped me in the hallway," Cary continued, "and made it perfectly clear that Dad can't go back to the way he was, not for some time. If he doesn't rest, eat right, and exercise, he could have a relapse."

"Oh dear. Did they make that clear to Jacob?" Aunt Sara asked, her hands flitting about, nervously tugging on her dress and brushing at her hair.

"Too clear," Cary said, shifting his gaze to me. I understood this was a major reason why his visit was so long and difficult. "He's furious about it. Says they don't know what they're talking about, that it's work that makes a man strong, emotionally, physically, and spiritually. He vowed he won't be anyone's cripple and the doctors threatened to keep him in the hospital. You'll have to tell him, Ma. You'll have to put your foot down too," Cary said.

Aunt Sara nodded, her eyes wide with fear and worry.

"Of course, I will, Cary," she said. "Yes. All of us will do what we can to help him understand, won't we?" she asked, turning to me. I smiled.

"Yes, Aunt Sara. Did you eat anything, Cary?"

"I had a candy bar. Got it from the machine in the hospital."

"Oh. Well I kept everything warm for you, Cary," Aunt Sara said. "Just sit and I'll get you a plate."

"I'm not hungry, Ma."

"Of course you are, especially after the day you've had," she insisted. "Now," she added when he opened his mouth, "if you expect me to tell your father what to do, at least listen when I speak to you," she said.

Cary laughed.

"Okay. Let me just call Roy and see about the repairs on the boat. I have to give Dad a report before he goes to sleep, too," he said and went to the phone.

Afterward, May and I joined him at the dining room table and watched him eat. When Aunt Sara went back into the kitchen, he leaned over to whisper to me.

"He's bad, Melody, cranky and meaner than ever. He swears he's going to sneak back on the boat first chance he gets. I told him I wouldn't go out then and he fumed at me for a good half hour until I calmed him down. When I first got there, he accused me of not checking the oil before I took out the boat. I always check the engine, Melody," he assured me. "I know what can happen out there," he said.

"I believe you and I don't know why he wouldn't."

"It's just his condition, I guess. It makes him ornery."

"Well, he should be just the opposite. He should be pleased and proud he has a son who can step in during this emergency and keep the business going. I'll tell him, too," I threatened.

"No, please. That's all I need, him thinking we were conspiring against him while he was ill."

"He thinks it of me anyway, Cary."

"No, he doesn't," Cary said, but I saw the way he dropped his eyes quickly.

"What did he ask you about me? Come on," I urged. He started to look up and reply but Aunt Sara returned. When she left again, I repeated my question. Reluctantly, he answered.

"His brain is all jumbled from the heart attack, I'm sure."

"Come on, Cary."

"He wanted to know if you were spreading stories about him and your mother. I told him he had to be hallucinating to think of something like that and he got so mad at me, I had to leave the room for a while. That's when I met his doctor and heard what was going to happen. Can you think of any reason why he would ask me that question?" Cary asked, his gazed fixed on my face.

"No," I said quickly. What Uncle Jacob had said to me in the CCU was never meant to be repeated. It was as sacred as a dying person's confession to a priest. I had no intention of uttering a word of it, ever.

Cary shrugged and returned to his dinner.

"That's why I said he was hallucinating," he muttered. He eyed me scrupulously as he chewed his food and I turned to May and asked her if she wanted to play Chinese checkers.

Before we rose to go into the living room, I told everyone I was going to visit my grandmother tomorrow. Aunt Sara stopped clearing the dishes.

633

"Oh dear, is that wise, Melody?" she asked.

"Very wise," I said. "I like her and she likes me. We have to get to know each other before it's too late."

"Yes, I suppose you do," Aunt Sara said, "but I'm sure Olivia—"

"Has nothing to say about it," I chimed in quickly.

"Oh dear," Aunt Sara said. "All this commotion at once. Oh, dear." She hurried back to the sanctuary of her kitchen.

Cary gazed up at me with eyes of appreciation and glee.

"Grandma Olivia has met her match in you, Melody Logan," he said, struggling to contain his amusement.

"Yes, she has. Whether she likes it or not," I fired back, and Cary gave in to a fit of laughter.

Confused at all the commotion, May tugged on my hand for explanations. Instead, I took her into the living room for our game of Chinese checkers. Cary came in to watch us play and fell asleep in his father's chair. No one had the heart to wake him.

"Jacob does that often now," Aunt Sara said gazing at Cary with her eyes twin pools of sadness. She sighed. "Let him sleep."

May and I went up to bed. Aunt Sara tinkered around the house until she had gotten herself tired enough and came up, too. Hours later, I heard Cary's footsteps on the stairway. He paused at my door and then went on to his own room. The boy in him was being shoved further and further back into his memory as he was forced to become a man of responsibility and duty. How lucky were those who could have a full and happy youth.

Holly was there in the morning as she had promised. It was the first time Cary had seen her car, or her, for that matter. She wore one of her long, flowing dresses, a matching headband, opal earrings in a

634

silver setting, a jade necklace, and her pink and green sandals. She had even painted a small pink and green dot on each of her cheeks.

At first Cary was amazed and then he thought it was all very amusing. Aunt Sara merely dropped her jaw and retreated into the house with May. I introduced Cary to Holly and she immediately asked him his date of birth.

"Why?" he asked.

"I know you're a Gemini," she said, "but I need more details about your birthday."

"Huh?" Cary turned to me.

"We have to go," I said quickly. "I want to make visiting hours."

"Oh yes," Holly said. "Perhaps I'll see you soon and we can talk again," Holly told Cary.

He nodded and I got into Holly's car.

"I made something for your grandmother," she told me as we drove away. "It's right on the back seat."

I turned and found a crystal embedded in a blob of silvery-gray stone that looked like petrified scrambled eggs.

"What is it?" I had to ask.

"It's a paperweight," Holly explained, "but that's lepidolite in the center. It aids muscles, strengthens the heart, and is very beneficial to the blood. What is most important, it aids sleep, which I know is a problem for the elderly. Try to get her to keep it close to her bed," she advised.

"Thank you, Holly," I said, wondering not only what Grandma Belinda would think, but what Mrs. Greene and her assistants would do.

Holly thought the rest home was in a truly beautiful and tranquil place.

"Whoever chose the location was sensitive to positive energy," she declared. "I can feel it. It's ideal for meditation."

There were a half dozen or so other vehicles in the

635

visitors' parking lot when we pulled up. I saw a man and a woman helping an elderly lady walk along a garden pathway. The two elderly gentlemen I had met when I came the first time were on the porch again, sitting in the same seats. Only today, both were wearing suits and ties and had their hair neatly combed.

"Well now," the one who had first spoken to me last time said, "you come to entertain us, have you?" He was looking at Holly.

"No sir," she said. "We're just visiting someone."

"That them?" the other man shouted.

"No, they're just visiting someone."

"Who'd you say they were?"

"Just visiting," he repeated. Holly laughed and followed me through the front entrance.

Mrs. Greene was in the lobby, talking with some of the residents, who were apparently waiting to be entertained. One of the attendants, a tall, dark haired man with a pock-marked face and thin, very red lips, stepped out from behind the desk on our right, where he had been talking to a young girl. Mrs. Greene straightened up quickly and hurried toward us, the attendant moving to join her.

"Yes?" she said.

"I'm Melody Logan. Remember? I visited my grandmother, Belinda Gordon, recently."

"Yes, I recall." She pulled her shoulders back and stiffened her jaw. "I remember I specifically asked you not to give her any candy," she said sharply.

"What?"

"I explained how important it was that she not be given any candy. They share what they are given and they don't know who is diabetic and who isn't. I thought you understood that. It's a simple enough request," she added, drawing her lips thin.

"I didn't give her any candy," I said.

636

"No? Well she had it in her room right after you left," Mrs. Greene said with a twisted smirk.

"I don't think Melody would lie, ma'am," Holly said softly. She had a way of disagreeing with someone that made it sound pleasant, but Mrs. Greene stepped back and drank her in with a look of disgust.

"And who might you be?"

"Just a friend," Holly said.

"Yes, well, I'm afraid I can't permit anyone but immediate family to visit," Mrs. Greene said, "and we do ask that our visitors dress decently. We value our reputation here. Our clients are highly respectable people and there are a number of them visiting their loved ones at the moment."

"Decency comes from the heart, not from our outer garb," Holly said, still speaking softly.

Mrs. Greene ignored her and turned back to me.

"I have spoken with Mrs. Logan," she said, "and she has left instructions that for the time being, no one is to visit her sister. I assumed she would have told you."

"What do you mean, no one? I'm her granddaughter!" I raised my voice. "I'm not just anyone!"

The attendant moved closer. Some of the residents stopped talking and turned our way.

"Please, lower your voice," Mrs. Greene said shooting a glance at some people who were visiting a relative.

"Why can't I see my grandmother?" I demanded.

"Her condition is very delicate. We're just trying to do what's best for her," Mrs. Greene replied with a smile so phony it dripped.

"Surely, having a loved one visit can't be anything but good," Holly said. Mrs. Greene shot her a look that, if it had been a dart, would have pierced Holly's pleasant smile and gone right through her head.

"I'm not leaving here without seeing my grandmother," I fired at her and planted my feet so firmly, it was as if they were nailed to the floor.

Mrs. Greene studied us a moment. I saw a look of retreat in her eyes, which quickly fell to the gift in my hand.

"And what is that you're bringing her?"

"It's a crystal paperweight and it has healing powers," I said.

Mrs. Greene smiled coldly.

"I can't permit it. We have to have control over what is brought into the rooms."

"What harm can this do her?"

"I can't permit it," she repeated. "It's against my better judgment, but I will permit you, and you alone, to visit with your grandmother for half an hour."

"Why am I limited in time? No one else is," I protested.

"That's my final decision. I have a major responsibility here. The welfare of my guests, all my guests, must be taken into consideration. And I repeat, only immediate family," she said, sending another look of disgust Holly's way.

Holly put her hand on mine and smiled.

"I'll just wait for you out on the porch," she said with a wink. I knew she would enjoy speaking with the two elderly gentlemen. She took the paperweight from my hands and turned to Mrs. Greene. "Perhaps I can make this a present to you," she said. "One of the qualities of lepidolite is that it enhances one's expression of inner light and joy."

"Ridiculous," Mrs. Greene said and pivoted. "Gerson, show Miss Logan to Miss Gordon's room."

"She's in her room?" I asked. It was such a beautiful day, and most of the residents had been brought to the lobby for their entertainment. Why was Grandma Belinda shut up in her room?

"Yes," she said, lifting the corner of her mouth until it cut into her cheek. "She's not feeling well today.

That's why I want to limit your visit. Your cooperation will be appreciated," she added and returned to the people with whom she had been talking when we arrived.

"This way," the attendant said. He wore a sharp, sarcastic smile on his lips. Holly pressed my hand and nodded.

"Go on. I'll be fine," she said.

I followed the attendant through the lobby and down the corridor toward the residents' rooms, my heart thumping with every furious thought that bounced from one side of my brain to the other.

I was even angrier when I saw Grandma Belinda. Her door was shut and she was sitting in her rocking chair near the window, gazing out like a child who had been punished and sentenced to stand in a corner. The lights were off, so the room was full of shadows. She was wrapped in a shawl and appeared smaller than I remembered her. Her eyes were red, her face pale, and it looked as if she had been crying. I waited for a moment, but she didn't even notice I had entered her room.

"You got a half hour," the attendant reminded me firmly and stepped out, closing the door behind me. I went to Grandma Belinda and touched her hand. She turned slowly and looked up at me, expressionless, indifferent, a lost lamb.

"Hi Grandma. It's Melody. I came to see you again. How are you?" I asked quickly. "Why are you sitting in the shadows?"

She stared at me blankly, her eyelids blinking rapidly.

"I told her I was pregnant," she began, "and I told her it was Nelson's baby. She got very angry and swore at me and called me a liar. She called me terrible names and said she wouldn't help me if I told my lie to anyone else, ever, but I wasn't lying. I wouldn't lie."

"Nelson? You mean Judge Childs?" I asked and sat on the bed, facing her. She rocked and nodded.

"Yes. There were other young men. I've always been very popular," she said with a flirtatious smile. Then, in a heartbeat her face changed expression until she looked older, serious. "But I should know who is the father of my child, don't you think?" Her face turned angry. "How can you doubt me, Olivia? You want to doubt me; you don't want it to be true because you've always loved Nelson. Well, don't blame me because he loves me more than he loves you."

"Grandma," I said softly. She seemed to be looking through me and not at me, her gaze distant.

"Stop that laughing. I'm not lying. I'm not!" she said, straining her throat until the veins in her neck were well outlined.

"It's all right, Grandma. It's all right. I believe you," I said and took her hand.

She stopped rocking and looked at me. She began to blink rapidly again. And then, like magic, her face brightened with a childlike smile.

"It's a nice day," she said, glancing through the window. "It should be my birthday."

She laughed and rocked. Then she stopped again and her face grew darker, her eyes small, her lips taut. She shook her head.

"I was screaming upstairs, screaming at the top of my voice. It's time. It's time! The door was locked. She wanted me to lose the baby, you know. Oh, don't look at me that way," she said, turning to me. "You're always taking her side."

"Grandma," I said softly. "It's Melody."

She shook her head. Was she telling me the truth or was everything so jumbled in her mind that her words were like one crossword puzzle confused with another, the answers all to the wrong questions?

"She left me, no doctor, no midwife, no one. I guess you never knew that part, huh?" A crazed twist shaped her lips and she smiled so coldly it put ice in my veins. "I delivered my own baby and when she came up and found the baby was all right, she nearly died herself with disappointment. You never knew. I can see it on your face, Nelson. You never knew."

She turned and rocked. I held my breath until I saw her chin begin to quiver and the first tear emerge.

"Grandma," I said. "Please, try to look at me and see me. Please."

What had they done to her? Why was she so much more confused, lost. How long had she been kept in this room? Her rocking stopped again. She took a deep breath and lowered her face until her chin rested on her chest. Then she closed her eyes and in moments was asleep.

I sat, waiting to see if she would wake and go into another exclamation, drawing thoughts, memories, words from some secret place in her mind. The minutes ticked and she slept.

If Nelson Childs was the father of her baby . . . then he was my real grandfather, after all, and that made Kenneth my uncle. Did he know? What if none of this were true? What if it were?

Oh please wake up, Grandma, I thought. I want to know more; I want to be sure.

There was a gentle knock on the door. When I turned, a short, plump nurse entered carrying a cup and some water.

"She's dozed off again, has she?" she remarked.

"What's wrong with her? She's so different from the way she was the last time I was here, and it wasn't that long ago," I questioned.

"When they reach this age and they've been sick or lived a hard life, changes can occur from hour to hour," she said. "She's falling into Alzheimer's," she added. "In some cases that's merciful."

"Well not in hers. She has a lot of years left and she can get better," I cried.

The nurse raised her eyebrows and looked at me as if I were the one who was suffering mental aberrations. She shook Grandma Belinda's shoulder.

"Come on, Belinda. Time for your medicine," she said.

Grandma's eyes fluttered open and she turned slowly.

"Come on, dear. Take your pills. Remember?"

"Pills? Again? Why so many pills, Olivia? Did the doctor really say I should take these, too?"

"Yes, he did."

The nurse looked at me.

"Who's Olivia?" she whispered.

"Her sister."

"Oh. Yes, Belinda, he did. Come on, honey. That's it," she said. "Now wash them down. Good girl."

"What are those pills?" I asked.

"They're just a form of a tranquillizer to keep her calm," she said.

"Maybe they're doing her more damage."

"Are you a doctor?" the plump nurse asked with a face full of ridicule.

"No, but—"

"Well, her doctor has prescribed them. If you have a problem with that, speak to Mrs. Greene," she added and left the room.

"I'd rather speak to the wall," I mumbled.

Grandma Belinda was staring out the window again. I touched her hand and she turned slowly, very slowly, toward me, her eyes so sad, they put tears in my heart.

"Grandma, it's me, Melody. Remember?"

She smiled.

"Yes. He told me about you. He said you look just like your mother." Her smile evaporated. "Only, I can't remember what she looked like."

"She looked like you," I said.

"Did she?" She smiled again and then gazed out the

642

window while she spoke. "It's my birthday you know. We're having guests and a cake."

"Happy birthday, Grandma," I said, tears now building under my eyelids.

"Everyone's going to sing Happy Birthday to me." She turned. "Even Olivia, because I'll look right at her and she'll have to sing. Right?"

"Yes," I said and smiled.

"Happy birthday to me, happy birthday to me, happy birthday, dear Belinda, happy birthday to me."

She closed her eyes.

There was a harder knock on the door and the attendant appeared.

"It's time," he said.

"It can't be a half hour."

"It is," he insisted. "Don't make it hard for me, will ya," he muttered with threatening eyes.

"No," I said standing. "I'll leave that to Mrs. Greene."

I leaned over and kissed my grandmother on her cheek. She didn't open her eyes. Then I turned and marched past him and down the corridor.

The residents were being entertained by a singer in the lobby. She played the accordion as well. Mrs. Greene was standing in the rear with some attendants, a receptionist, and some visitors. She glared my way and I glared back as I left the lobby and stepped out of the building, my heart thumping so hard I thought it would drown out the singing.

There was no one on the porch, but I saw Holly on a bench talking softly to some song birds who stared up at her as if they really understood. Even though I was still shaking, the sight brought laughter to my lips. She saw me and hurried up the walkway.

"How was your visit?" she asked.

"Very bad," I said. "They're medicating her into oblivion and I have the feeling it's Grandma Olivia's fault. I've got to pay her a visit."

"Oh, that's so sad. If we just taught them how to meditate, there would be no need for chemical therapy."

"There's no need for it now," I said. "Unless keeping the truth buried is a good reason."

Holly's eyebrows lifted into question marks, but I didn't want to say anything until I was certain what I had heard was really the truth. At least now I understood why Grandma Olivia had been so interested in learning what her sister had told me the first time. I felt as if I were opening the door to a vault, a vault covered in dust and cobwebs, its hinges rusted. This was no time to walk away.

"Could you do me a favor," I asked, "and take me to my Grandmother Olivia's house? It's just a little out of the way."

"No problem," Holly said. "If that's what you want."

"Oh, it's what I want," I said nodding. "I never wanted it more."

13

Accusations

When we turned into Grandma Olivia's driveway and came to a stop, I sat quietly while I tried to catch my breath. Confronting Grandma Olivia was always difficult, but this was going to be twice as hard and the anticipation made my heart race.

"Are you all right?" Holly asked.

"Yes. You don't have to wait for me," I said. "I might be here a while."

"But how will you get home?"

"Grandma Olivia's driver will take me, I'm sure."

I gazed at the house. Despite the bright sunshine glittering on the windows, the beautiful rainbow colored flowers and perfectly trimmed hedges, the house looked dark and full of foreboding to me. Holly sensed my tension.

"Maybe she's not home. Maybe nobody's home," Holly said.

"I'll wait for her," I said in a tone of voice that indicated I would wait forever, if need be.

Holly gazed at me and then at the house. She

squinted, closed her eyes, and then opened them and nodded as if she had reached a conclusion.

"There's a lot of static here, a bed of negative energy. Remember what I told you about my friend who went to India and walked on a bed of hot coals?"

"Yes." I smiled, recalling the story and how animated Holly had been when she told it.

"You've got to build a wall between yourself and that which can hurt you, Melody. You have the power in your own mind. Rely on your concentration, focus."

"I'm doing just that," I said. "Thank you." I got out. She remained in the driveway, watching me walk up to the front door. I pushed the buzzer and waited and then pushed it again. Holly was still in the driveway, unwilling to leave me here. Finally, Loretta, the maid, came to the door. I looked back and waved to Holly to indicate it was all right. Reluctantly, she backed out. I didn't want to send her away, but I knew that if she came into the house with me, Grandma Olivia might use her as an excuse to refuse to talk to me. I was determined she wasn't going to find any avenue of escape from the truth this time.

"Hello, Loretta," I said. "I want to see my grandmother. Is she here?"

"Mrs. Logan is upstairs in her bedroom. She wasn't feeling well today. I just brought her a little lunch, but she didn't eat much."

"I have to speak to her," I insisted.

"She's in her bedroom," Loretta said, intending that I take that as a reason why I couldn't. She was a tall, thin woman with a face that looked as if it were made from porcelain and would crack and shatter if she smiled or laughed.

"People talk in their bedrooms," I said and marched past her.

"Oh, but Mrs. Logan doesn't want to be disturbed," she cried.

"No one wants to be disturbed, Loretta," I replied and started up the stairway.

I had been upstairs only once before, when Cary had given me my first quick tour of the house, but I had seen Grandma Logan's bedroom. I remembered she had a bed next to a wide, dark cherry wood, three-drawer nightstand on which sat a large Tiffany lamp. Behind the bed were two big windows over which hung sheer wine-colored drapes. The bed was on a matching oval area rug. On the right was a cherry wood desk and on the left, adjacent to the door, were the closets, dressers, a very uncomfortable looking spindle chair, and a side table. The walls were covered with a light brown wallpaper that had what looked like tiny flowers stenciled around the borders. I saw no paintings on the walls and thought the room was rather cold for a bedroom.

At the moment the door was closed. I knocked and waited and then knocked again.

"What is it?" I heard Grandma Olivia cry with sharp annoyance. Rather than answer and announce myself, I just opened the door.

My appearance was almost as shocking to her as hers was to me. She was sitting up, her face covered with some sort of milk-white facial cream. Her watery red eyes peered out of the mask of lotion and her bland lips looked like a line drawn with a broken crayon. Her blanket was folded back at her waist. Surrounded by her oversized pillows, her thin hair down, her egg-shell white silk nightgown loosely clinging to her bony shoulders, she appeared smaller than she did when dressed and moving about the large rooms. The portion of her chest that usually remained covered now revealed age spots and tiny moles. Minus her jewelry and her hair combs, and wearing this skin lotion, she looked naked, vulnerable, caught unprotected by her wealth and power, a queen without her crown. My seeing her like this filled her face with

647

immediate rage. She stuttered and gasped before she could get out her angry reprimands.

"How—how dare you come up here without being announced? Who do you think you are barging into my bedroom? Where do you get the audacity— Haven't you learned anything about manners?"

She reached over the bed to fetch a towel and wipe the cream from her face, whipping her eyes back at me as she did so. There was so much fire coming from them that if I had been made of ice, I'd have been a pool of water in seconds.

"I just came from visiting with Grandma Belinda," I said in response.

She threw the towel to the floor and pulled her blanket up until it covered her to the neck.

"Where's Loretta? Did she permit you to enter the house?"

"Don't blame Loretta. She told me you were up here and I insisted on coming up to see you."

"Well, you just turn yourself around and march back down those stairs and out of the house. I am not entertaining guests today. I have a splitting headache, a sinus problem and—"

"I'm not here to be entertained, Grandma Olivia. I'm here to confirm the truth, once and for all," I fired back. Her eyes widened as her anger peaked.

"How dare you speak to me like that? And with all the family trouble now, too. Poor Jacob and Sara having to contend with Jacob's heart attack and now your insolence. I warned you about your behavior. I told you—"

"I said I have just come from seeing Grandma Belinda," I interrupted, raising my voice just enough to grab her attention. She stared a moment, her lips pursed.

"What of it?" she demanded.

"First, I was told you left orders for no one to see her," I began in a smaller, quieter voice.

648

"That's correct."

"Why?" I asked, my eyes narrowed as I took a step toward her.

"I don't think I have to explain myself to you and I will not be cross-examined in my own home. Get out," she said, pointing to the door.

"I'm not leaving until I hear the truth from your lips. It may burn your tongue, but I want to hear it," I said.

My calmness fanned the flames of her rage even more. Her mouth opened and closed without a sound emerging as she choked on her own fury.

"Grandma Belinda was not in good health," I said. "She was under some medication that's turning her into a zombie."

"Oh, so you've become a doctor, too, is that it? You want to go up there and tell them how to treat their patients. Is that why you've come bursting into my home?" she added with a cold smile spreading from her twisted lips to her steely eyes. "This is exactly why I left orders for no visitors. She's not well. She's not up to visitors anymore, and I'm disappointed that you were permitted to see her. I will have a stern talk with Mrs. Greene."

"Mrs. Greene knew if she didn't permit me to see my grandmother, she would have a bigger fight on her hands with me than she would have with you," I said.

"Oh, so you pushed your way in there just as you've done now, is that it? You think I'm going to tolerate this sort of behavior? You think just because my son is in the hospital that I won't call Sara and tell her to throw you out on the street? Don't you know that it's only because of my generosity that I permit you to live here? By all rights you should be in some foster home until they find a family strong enough to stomach you," she spit back at me.

"I'm not going to be intimidated by your threats this time, Grandma Olivia. If you threw me out on

649

the streets, I would just go down to the Provincetown newspapers and tell them about this family and its dark secrets."

She laughed.

"Do you think anyone in Provincetown would do anything to upset me?" she challenged. "You don't know how ridiculous you sound. Now do as I say and—"

"Grandma Belinda told me the truth about my mother's birth," I blurted. I didn't add that she had babbled it in what sounded like insane rambling. "She told me she was kept shut up in the house, not even provided with proper medical care, in the hope that she would lose the baby. She told me how you made her deliver her own baby."

"What? That is such a preposterous story, I don't think it requires a response."

"And then she told me who the father was, my mother's father, my grandfather," I added.

Grandma Olivia seemed to sink a little in her bed. She leaned back against the pillows, her ashen face almost transparent now. Then she brought the corners of her mouth up and into her cheeks, thinning her lips so they looked like strings of pale pink wool strained to the point of tearing.

"Which one of her many, many lovers did she call the father of her baby? This time," she added.

"She said it was Judge Childs."

Grandma Olivia's lips trembled and then broke into another, very forced, hard smile.

"Oh she's gone back to that story, has she? Last year it was Samuel, you know. And before that, it was Martin Donnally, a policeman who died two years ago. Once it was Sanford Jackson, Teddy Jackson's father. I told you not to go up to see her anymore. I knew she was going to tell you with one ludicrous story after another. She was always a liar, always fantasizing about this or that man. Belinda never had

650

more than one foot in reality and most of the time, not even a toe. She was always doing terrible things and then making up stories. In her deranged mind, she thought the wealthiest, most handsome men in Provincetown were going to rush off and marry her. Nothing was further from the truth.

"She was crazy even before she began drinking and sleeping around. All that just put her over the top, and after she gave birth, she went completely mad. Why, if I hadn't had the judge's help at the time—"

"The judge's help?"

"Yes. That's why she's making up this story now. It was Judge Childs who came to my aid and helped me place her in the home where she was treated well and where she has lived comfortably in her madness up until now. I needed his political influence. You can imagine the waiting list for that place. That's why she accuses him of such a thing."

She wagged her head and then nodded.

"Belinda's getting worse. I didn't know how bad things were until very recently and that's why I left orders for her not to have visitors. Satisfied? Now that you know all the nitty gritty dirt I've been trying to keep swept out of sight?"

She leaned forward, strengthened by the venom of her lies. For I could tell, she *was* lying.

"We are one of the most respected and well known of the original families here," she continued. "Reputation is as important as money in the bank. Despite the unfortunate circumstances surrounding Belinda and your mother, I was able to protect my family. Now, after we've been overly generous and permitted you to live amongst us, given you opportunities, you continue to threaten our peace and well being. How dare you come here with your accusations? I shut my sister up pregnant? I didn't give her medical assistance? What do you think I'm doing now?"

"But, that's what she told me," I said, weakening.

651

She laughed again and shook her head.

"So you will go around and tell people what a deranged, mentally ill woman who has been institutionalized for years and years said? This is why you come running here? This is how you threaten me?

"Please," she said, wagging her head and waving her hand as if she were chasing away flies, "go home and try to be of some assistance to my son's wife during this trying time. If you can't, well, we'll see about making some other arrangements for you," she said, but not as a threat, more like a logical conclusion.

I stepped back. Was I wrong? Was Grandma Belinda just fantasizing? Oh, why couldn't the truth be as plain as day? Why was everything to do with this family so cloudy and confused? Was it like that in all families?

Grandma Olivia leaned back and moaned.

"You've made my head pound again. Please, send Loretta up immediately. I need her to get me more of my medicine," she said in a thin, breathless voice.

"Where is it? I'll get it," I offered.

"I'd rather do without it and suffer," she retorted. "Just send Loretta up on your way out." She thought a moment and sat forward again. "How did you get here?"

"A friend brought me."

"A friend? Is your friend downstairs, too? Is my house full of strangers?"

"No, I sent her away."

"And how do you intend to get home then? Go walking on the highways so I hear about it?"

"I thought maybe if Raymond were here—"

"He's not. He's running errands. And of course Samuel is down at the docks wasting time with fishermen. Damn your insolence," she muttered. "Hand me my pocketbook and I'll give you taxi fare," she said.

"I don't need your money. I've been working and have my own," I said.

"Suit yourself. Actually, that's good. I'm glad you have some independence. I have a feeling you're going to need it. Go downstairs and call your taxi and take yourself and Belinda's idiocy home," she ordered.

She fell back against her pillow and put her hand over her forehead.

"Loretta!" she cried.

I turned and went out the door. Loretta must have been waiting at the bottom of the steps, for she heard Grandma Olivia's cry and was already coming up quickly.

"I told you not to go up," she said. "I told you. Now she'll be furious at me." She glared angrily at me as we passed each other on the stairs.

I hurried down and went to the phone in the kitchen where the telephone numbers for various services were posted on the wall. I found the number for the taxicab company and called for a car. Then I went out front and sat on a stone bench and waited. As I sat there, I thought about Grandma Belinda. She didn't seem mean enough to make up a story about Judge Childs just to get back at him. How I wished there was someone else to talk to, someone who had been around at the time. Grandpa Samuel was there, but he wouldn't contradict Grandma Olivia. That was certain. There was no point in asking him anything.

I longed to be with people like Papa George and Mama Arlene again, people who had no affectations, who didn't connive and plot against people they supposedly loved. I longed for people who meant what they said, people who didn't hide behind innuendo and double meanings, whose pasts weren't cloaked in shadows, simpler people who wore their hearts on their sleeves and whose smiles had nothing behind them but love and affection. They weren't rich and they didn't live in big, luxurious homes. They had no political power and influence. No one feared them, but they were more content and they could sleep with crystal-clear consciences.

Everyone had some regrets, some choices they wished they hadn't made. Everyone's life was stained with mistakes and blotched with sadness, but simple, honest people had more smiles and more laughter in their hearts. Their wealth wasn't as easily counted, but it was there, and I longed to be with them again. Maybe I really should leave, I thought. Maybe I should welcome being thrown out on the street. Grandma Olivia's threats could be rewards in my way of thinking.

The taxi arrived and I got in quickly. The driver was an older man with curly, gray hair and a round, red face.

"Where to, Miss?" he asked as we moved down the driveway.

I thought a moment.

"Do you know Judge Childs?" I asked.

"Nelson Childs? Sure do. Everyone who's lived here most of his life knows the judge, Miss."

"Good. You know where he lives then?"

"Sure. Post Hill Road, about a mile from here. You can't miss his house. It's one of the biggest on the Cape. Is that where you want me to take you?" he asked.

I hesitated.

"Yes," I said firmly. "That's where I want to go."

"Then we'll pull up anchor and set sail," he said and turned left instead of right, which was the way back home.

The jovial taxi driver was full of questions, but if he had hoped to make a meal of my answers, he was going to starve. I answered everything with a yes or a no or a maybe. When it came to being closed-

654

mouthed, I had many models to learn from in this New England community.

Post Hill Road was a paved street that turned for a quarter of a mile or so up a rise and then toward the beach. There were only two other homes on the street, both small Cape Cod houses. But the judge's home was a true New England mansion, even more impressive than Grandma Olivia and Grandpa Samuel's home.

"You know this is a historical house, don't you?" the taxi driver asked.

"No."

"The judge bought it for a song and then he and his wife restored it. It's even been featured in a few magazines. My wife knows all about that stuff," he added. "It's a three-story colonial," he said as we drew closer. The house had been restored in a weathered grey cladding and had a semicircular entry porch. What made it even more unusual was its large octagonal cupola.

The driveway was circular. Like Grandma Olivia and Grandpa Samuel's grounds, the lawn was pampered and designed with fountains, walkways, and small rock gardens, but there was almost twice as much acreage here. When we entered the circular drive, I looked off to the right and saw the dock, the moored sailboat and motor boat, and some small dinghies. Just behind the house was a large gazebo and another area for flowers, where I saw a swing seat under a large maple tree.

The judge's car was in front of the garage so I felt confident he was home.

"How much would it cost to have you wait for me?" I asked the taxi driver.

"How long?"

"About twenty minutes," I said. He shrugged.

"I have to charge you another fifteen dollars for half hour or part of," he replied.

"That's fine," I said and got out. I think he would have waited for nothing just to satisfy his curiosity. He didn't take his eyes off me as I stepped up to the front door and rang the bell. I heard a deep ding-dong sound on the inside and waited. Moments later, a short, balding man who looked to be in his early sixties opened the door. He wasn't dressed like a butler or a servant. He wore a white shirt opened at the collar and a pair of dark slacks. The small ridges of gray hair resembled steel wool over the sides of his head and down the back where it was a great deal thicker. He had a caramel complexion with dark brown eyes and his nose was thick at the bridge and his lower lip was fuller than his upper.

He took a pair of wire-rimmed glasses from his top pocket and placed them slowly over his eyes to gaze out at me. They magnified his eyes and made them look even rounder. Without speaking, he looked over at the taxicab and then he turned back to me.

"Didn't hear you drive up," he said. "How can I help you?"

"My name is Melody Logan. I'd like to see Judge Childs," I said.

"Judge expecting you?" he asked. He seemed astounded by my visit. Didn't the judge ever have people calling on him?

"No, but he asked me to drop by when I had an opportunity," I replied.

"That so?" he said and stood there chewing on the idea for a moment. Then he shook his head. "He don't usually see people unless they have an appointment with him," he added.

"Can you please tell him I'm here?" I asked, not hiding my impatience.

He didn't move.

"He might be nappin' in the den. That's where he usually is if he don't go someplace on Sunday. He falls asleep after he reads the papers."

"I have a taxicab waiting for me," I pointed out so he would appreciate the time he was wasting. He nodded.

"Yeah. Okay. I'll go check." He started to close the door on me. "I suppose you could wait inside," he decided and stepped back to let me enter. He closed the door. "Be right back," he promised and started down the short corridor.

The only illumination in the entry way and the living room on my right came from the sunlight that penetrated the windows with their curtains drawn back, but I could see some decorative wood ornaments applied to the walls in the corridor. There were paintings on these walls as well, but I didn't think any of them were Kenneth's. They weren't his style. They were original oils depicting colonial scenes, realistic with subdued colors, all set in thick, ornate frames.

All the furniture I saw looked antique. It was as if it had come with the house and it, too, had been restored. I felt as if I had stepped into a museum or one of those reconstructed homes open to tours. It didn't feel lived in, warm. Yet from somewhere deep in the house came music I recognized. I listened hard until I recalled it from music class. It was Debussy's *La Mer*.

Moments later, the balding man appeared, followed by Judge Childs dressed in a maroon satin robe with matching slippers. His hair was a little disheveled, and as he drew closer, I saw he hadn't shaved. His eyes were somewhat bloodshot and he looked flushed, as if he had been jolted out of a deep sleep.

"Melody, my dear. What a wonderful surprise," he said, holding out his hands. "When Morton told me I had a beautiful young lady visiting, I thought he was joking. You did right to wake me, Morton," the judge told his butler.

"I didn't mean to disturb you," I said.

"Oh nonsense. Old men like myself need to be

657

disturbed. Otherwise, they would just waste away musing about their glorious lost youth. How about something to drink? A lemonade perhaps?"

"That would be fine," I said.

"Morton, we'll be in the sitting room," the judge said. "Two lemonades if you please."

"Very good, Judge."

"My maid, Toby, is off today," he explained. "This way, my dear," he said, moving toward the room to our right. When we entered, he rushed over to turn on the lamps. "Please have a seat," he said, indicating the strange looking bench to his right. I hesitated. "Oh, you can sit on it," he said with a smile. "It's actually comfortable."

"I've never seen anything like it," I said.

"Neither had I until my wife bought it at an auction in Boston. It's called an empire hall bench and it was made around 1810. Most everything in this house is an antique of one sort or another. Our furnishings are quite eclectic, as is the artwork. My wife made the house her life. She would rush off for hours, go miles and miles if she heard there was an auction or a sale of antiques, and New England has an antique shop or an auction every ten feet," the judge remarked. "I swear—"

He sat in a high-backed, ornate gold chair with a red cushion backing and red seat. He looked uncomfortable because the chair was small, but he didn't complain.

"But I'll say this for her, she never bought something and didn't put it to use. No showcase furnishing for her. We had to use it all. Wait until I show you the dining room. The table is from the early eighteenth century, Baroque style, I think. I can't remember it all. Anyway," he rattled on, "you can see where Kenneth got his first education in art, architecture, and the like. I blamed his mother for that," he said.

"He's a wonderful artist though, isn't he?"

"Yes, I guess he is. People do pay large sums of money for his work. Ah, here's our lemonade," he said as Morton returned with two tumblers on a silver tray. "The glasses are contemporary, but that tray—what about that tray, Morton?"

"French, 1857," Morton recited.

"There, you see. Morton knows it all. He drove my wife everywhere in those days, didn't you, Morton?"

"Yes sir."

"Morton's been with me, what, forty years now, Morton?"

"Forty-two years and four months, Judge."

Judge Childs laughed.

"What a memory. I depend on Morton for all my dates and responsibilities now, don't I, Morton?"

"I do my best, Judge."

"That he does, that he does. Well, drink up. Thank you, Morton."

"Yes sir," Morton said and left.

"Don't know where I'd be without him. When I lost my wife, I was lost myself. I didn't know where my own medicine was kept. So," he said, his eyes shifting to me, "you came to visit, did you? How did you get here, by the way?"

"Taxicab," I said. "I have him waiting."

"Oh, that's terrible. Unheard of. Let me take care of that," he said. He started to get up.

"It's all right, Judge Childs."

"No, no. Morton will drive you home. I don't want any taxicab driver hanging about. It will only be a moment," he insisted and left. I heard him whispering to Morton in the hallway and then I heard Morton go out.

"I have to pay him," I said as soon as the judge appeared again.

"That's taken care of, my dear. I'm honored you've come to visit. The least I can do is take care of the cab driver. Now then—oh, how's Jacob? I should have asked you that first thing," he said returning to his seat.

"He's doing well and might come home very soon. Maybe even tomorrow."

"That's wonderful." He sipped his lemonade. "Yes, I have antiques that would make a museum curator's mouth water," he continued. He seemed driven to talk, nervous. It suddenly occurred to me that Grandma Olivia might have called him and told him the gist of my conversation with her.

"You know I've been visiting my grandmother Belinda," I began.

"Oh?" He said, nodding. "I do think Olivia mentioned that. Yes. How is Belinda doing?"

"Haven't you visited her yourself, Judge Childs?" I asked.

"Me? Oh, not for some time," he said. "Why, did she say I was there?"

"Yes."

He laughed.

"Poor Belinda. Even before she was, well, disturbed, she had a problem with reality," he said. It sounded like a line he and Grandma Olivia had rehearsed.

"But you have visited her?"

"Oh sure. You see that painting there," he said nodding to a large portrait on the wall behind me. "My wife found that in a sale just outside of Hyannis Port. Bought it for two hundred and fifty dollars. Turns out it's an original and probably worth ten thousand if it's worth a penny. She was good at making finds like that.

"So," he said without taking a breath, "how's your fiddle playing?"

I put the lemonade down slowly on the small marble table beside me. Morton had left a wooden coaster that looked as if it, too, was some sort of antique. Then I turned to the judge. My silence made

660

him swallow hard. He stared a moment and then he nodded softly.

"This isn't just a casual visit, is it? You came here to ask me something specific, didn't you?"

"Yes sir," I said. "I think you know what it is, too," I said. He nodded again, put his own glass down, and took a deep breath, closing his eyes and then opening them.

"You sure you want to ask me these questions?" he said.

"Yes. I know everyone tells me there's no point in stirring up the past, that it just brings a lot of pain to a lot of people. But I grew up believing I was one person and then I found out, in a hard and shocking way, that I was someone else, that the people I had loved and trusted all my life were lying to me about the most basic thing of all, me, my identity," I said.

The judge nodded.

"When you get to be as old as I am, you look back on your life and it seems as if you've led at least two different lives. I wasn't a wild young man. I never did much that would make my parents ashamed, and I did do a lot that made them proud. Funny thing is, if you've had good parents and you've loved them and known they loved you, even after they're dead, you worry about doing things that would make them ashamed. I guess that's what people mean when they say you can live on in your children."

"I don't know both my parents," I said. "I may never know who my real father is, but I know my mother and now I know my grandmother. Are you my grandfather?" I asked bluntly. He stared at me. "Grandma Olivia doesn't want me to know the truth, but I think she has her own private reasons for that."

He smiled.

"You're a bright young woman. Any man would be proud to call you his granddaughter."

"Are you that man?" I pursued.

He brought his head back and gazed up at the ceiling. When he lowered his head, his eyes were glassy with tears. I held my breath.

"My Louise knew, but she was too much the lady to ever bring it up," he said. "And you should have seen her around Haille. She never made that girl feel unwanted. Hers was a heart so full of charity and love, it could forgive Judas.

"Oh, I could say I drank too much in those days. I could blame it on bourbon, or I could say Belinda was beautiful and enticing, which she was, but in the end, I have to bear the burden of my own sins."

"Then you are my mother's father and, therefore, my grandfather?"

"Yes," he said. He shook his head and smiled. "Look how simple it is to say it now. Maybe because I'm looking at you and I see the pain. I can't lie in the face of that. At least, I can't now," he said. "I never had to lie to Louise. She never came right out and asked me," he said. "Isn't that wonderful? I didn't deserve her."

"Did my mother ever know?"

"Yes, but not until she was much older. Actually, not long before she got herself into trouble and she and Chester left Provincetown."

"You mean pregnant with me?"

He nodded.

"I think I suddenly need something stronger than this," he said, holding up the lemonade. "If you'll excuse me a moment." He rose and went to a cabinet to take out a bottle of Tennessee whiskey. He poured himself a half a glass and drank most of it in a gulp. "Fortifies the courage," he explained, poured himself another, and stood by the window.

"How did she find out?" I asked.

"I had to tell her eventually. When I discovered she and Kenneth were getting too serious about each other. It broke my heart to do it, but under the circumstances, I had no choice." He turned, looking as if he had aged years in minutes. "They both resented me for it."

"Especially Kenneth?"

"Yes," he said, bowing his head in sorrow. "It's terrible enough when a son learns his father was unfaithful to his mother, but when that infidelity steals away the woman he loves, the pain is far more and the chasm it creates between father and son . . . well, it would be easier to step across the Grand Canyon than bridge the gap that's grown between my son and me. I'm afraid, I'll take that to my grave."

"Why was my grandmother locked away in that place?" I asked, my eyes narrow with suspicion. Judge Childs shifted his eyes away guiltily and gazed out the window as he spoke.

"I never approved of how Belinda was treated during her pregnancy. Olivia was embarrassed about it, of course, and kept her out of sight, literally a prisoner in her home. I wasn't the one to complain, for obvious reasons, although I did express as much disapproval as I could.

"In short, the pregnancy, the imprisonment, her history of promiscuity, drinking, they all took their toll and she became a rather disturbed woman after Haille's birth. We consulted with a doctor, a psychiatrist friend of mine, who recommended an institutionalized setting. In the beginning we—I hoped it would be temporary, but it went on and on."

"Because that was what Grandma Olivia wanted— her embarrassment shut away."

He looked at me and then lowered his eyes with shame.

"You have to understand my predicament at the time. I was married. I had children. Kenneth had recently been born. I was in politics."

"She threatened you. If you didn't cooperate, she threatened you," I concluded. He didn't deny it.

"Ironically, it might have been the best thing for Belinda anyway. I did visit her whenever it was possible."

"To ease your conscience," I accused, my eyes fixed unflinchingly on him. He returned my gaze and shook his head.

"When you look at me like that, you resemble Olivia more than Belinda. I could never hide my weaknesses from her, nor my shame. I know Olivia holds you in higher regard than you think," he added.

"It's like being complimented by the devil."

"Oh, she's not all that bad. She's had a difficult life and she's done well. She's actually been Samuel's strength. He owes his success to her."

"I know. She lets everyone know how indebted they are to her, especially me," I muttered. I looked up at him again sharply. "Since I first visited Grandma Belinda, Grandma Olivia has had them give Belinda medicine that keeps her in a daze, and she tried to keep me from visiting."

"Oh? I didn't know that."

"Well now you do."

He nodded.

"I'll see that it stops," he promised.

"Somehow, someone should make it possible for her to come home," I said, tears in the corners of my eyes.

"Yes," he said in a tired, defeated voice, "only where is her home now? Where she is, I'm afraid," he replied to his own question.

"Maybe someday I'll be able to make a home for her."

"Maybe you will," he agreed.

"First, I have to find my own home," I said. "I want to know who my real father is."

"If I knew, I would tell you, but Haille never confided anything intimate to me. I just know it's not Kenneth, thank God. What a mess that would have

664

been. Sins of the father," he muttered and shook his head.

"For what it's worth to you," he added, as I started to turn away, "my home is always open to you."

I thought about this and then just nodded without reply.

"I wish there was some way I could earn your forgiveness, Melody," he said.

"It's not my forgiveness you need."

Unable to look at me, he finished the whiskey in his glass.

"I've got to go home," I said.

"Of course. I'll fetch Morton."

We walked out into the hallway.

"Do you think," he began, "there will ever be a time when you can look at me as your grandfather?"

"For as long as I've known you, you've pretended it wasn't true."

"I know, and I regret it," he said.

"So do I," I replied. "I suppose it comes down to who regrets it more."

He smiled.

"When it comes to regrets, I have the edge."

I softened my eyes. He did look like a broken, remorseful old man and for the moment, I felt pity more than I felt anger. Anger was a sword, sharp and hot, but it also burned and cut the person who held it in their vengeful grasp.

"What's Grandma Olivia going to do when she learns you've told me the truth?" I asked.

He thought on this and then smiled.

"Pretend I didn't," he said, which brought a smile to my face, too.

Then he leaned forward and kissed me on the cheek.

"I'm glad you came here today, Melody," he said. "Morton will be right with you."

I stepped out and took a deep breath. My lungs felt

665

full of hot air, enough to make me explode. From practically every point around this house, there was a good view of the ocean. The front steps were no different.

I saw a sailboat bucking the waves, the ocean spray shooting up around it, its sails full of wind. It was too beautiful here to plant a garden of lies. Eventually, the ocean, like time itself, would wash them away and leave us with the naked truth on the beach.

I wasn't as afraid of tomorrow as I had been yesterday. In fact, I looked forward to it.

14

Jealousy

*F*rom the way Morton spoke about Judge Childs when Morton drove me home, it was apparent to me that he loved him as he would love his own father. Apparently, my grandfather had helped Morton when he had gotten himself into trouble with the law. He was about twenty at the time. My grandfather offered him a job driving for him, helping around the house, being his all-around assistant, and Morton had remained with Judge Childs ever since. I wondered just how much Morton really knew about the family secrets. However, I could see he wasn't one to tell tales out of school, especially if it involved my grandfather. He'd rather cut out his own tongue than speak a word against him.

I wondered about my grandfather, a man who could earn so much respect and such devoted loyalty from a complete stranger. I wanted to believe that meant he had some very fine qualities, but what the judge had done to Grandma Belinda was wrong, very wrong. He compounded the sin by cooperating with Grandma Olivia, who wanted her sister kept out of sight. He succumbed to Olivia's jealous rage and paid a high price to protect his own name and reputation. It cost him his peace of mind at a time in his life when he most needed it, and most important, it cost him his son's love. Despite his wealth, his big house full of valuable antiques, his beautiful property, his position in the community, he really was someone to be pitied. That much Morton did reveal.

"You made the judge happy," he said with admiration. "I could see it in his face. He hasn't worn a smile like that for years. At least, not since his wife died."

"Did you like her as much as you like Judge Childs?" I asked.

"Oh surely yes. Mrs. Childs was a real lady. She never let down her hair in public, and she always treated everyone with the utmost respect, no matter what color he or she was, or what their family did for a living. She was a pretty woman, too, and she wrote poems. She published some in those small magazines, and once in a big magazine from New York City. I don't recall exactly which one, but I know it was an important magazine. Mr. Kenneth was right proud of her at the time."

"I work for Kenneth, you know," I told him as we drove into town.

"Oh, that's right. You're Mrs. Logan's granddaughter. The judge told me you were helping Kenneth around his house and such." He shook his head. "The next time you see him, you tell him he should come visit more."

"Do you know why he doesn't?" I asked softly.

"That isn't my business. I just know a son should visit his father when his father is along in age. That's where you're living, right there?" he said, nodding at Uncle Jacob and Aunt Sara's house.

"Yes."

I saw the car in the driveway beside the truck and

knew Cary was home. Why wasn't he visiting Uncle Jacob at the hospital? I wondered.

"Here we are," Morton said, pulling into the driveway. "You come visit again. I know the judge would like that," he said.

"Thank you."

I got out and hurried to the front door. As I entered, Aunt Sara was climbing the stairs with a tray in her hands. There was a bowl of clam chowder, crackers, and a piece of filleted bass with some vegetables on a plate. She swung her head around to see me come in and flashed a smile at me, her eyes full of sparkling light.

"He's home!" she announced. "Jacob's home. He insisted they release him today instead of waiting until tomorrow. I'm just bringing him some home cooking. He said he didn't miss anything as much as my cooking. You can come up to see him in a little while," she added and continued up the stairs.

"Where are Cary and May?" I called.

"In the kitchen having a late lunch," she shouted back. "Go on in there if you're hungry."

I walked down the hallway and paused in the kitchen doorway. Cary was signing to May as she ate her sandwich, explaining more to her about their father's illness. Her eyes widened and he turned to see me standing there.

"Hi. How was your visit?"

"There's a lot to tell," I said. "You brought your father home already, I see."

"He threatened to get up and walk out anyway. The doctors had no choice. They weren't happy about it. We've got to keep him quiet, resting, taking his medicine. I hope he doesn't wear out my mother. She's been up and down those stairs a half dozen times for one thing or another already and she insists on doing everything herself."

"I'll help her anyway," I said.

669

"You'll be away working with Kenneth," he reminded me.

"Well, I'll help her every chance I get, and so will May." I smiled and signed the same to her. She nodded eagerly and told me Aunt Sara had already agreed to let her stay home tomorrow to do just that. "See? It will be all right," I said.

"Sure," Cary said without enthusiasm. "You hungry?"

"Actually, now that I see you eating, I realize I am. I've been going ever since I left this morning."

"Going where?" he asked.

"From Grandma Belinda to Grandma Olivia and then to Judge Childs's home," I replied. His face brightened with curiosity.

"Oh, so that's what you mean by having a lot to tell?"

"I'll make myself a sandwich and tell you everything from start to finish," I promised and I did just that.

Cary shook his head, amazed at the revelations when I completed a summary of my travels and experiences.

"If Dad knew, he never let on to me," he said. "I guess this family does have its closets full of skeletons. Didn't the judge have an idea who your father might be?" Cary asked.

"No," I said. "He just told me that it wasn't long after Kenneth and Haille found out about him that she got herself into trouble and she and my stepdaddy left Provincetown."

I gazed at May, who had been watching us with curiosity as I told Cary everything. Somehow she sensed she shouldn't interrupt, but my intensity and Cary's firm attention piqued her curiosity. I quickly told her I was describing my visit with Grandma Belinda and then, to get away from going into it any

670

further, I suggested that we take a walk on the beach after I said hello to Uncle Jacob.

"We'll all go for a walk," Cary decided.

The three of us went upstairs. The bedroom door was open. Uncle Jacob was sitting up, his back against two large, fluffy pillows. He wore a nightshirt, and although he didn't look as small as he had in the hospital bed, he still looked pale and quite a bit thinner to me. Aunt Sara was sitting at his bedside trimming his fingernails. It looked as if she had just brushed his hair, too. If Uncle Jacob was happy about being home, you couldn't tell by looking at him. He didn't smile when we appeared.

"You're sure that engine's working fine now, eh Cary?" he asked.

"Yes, Dad. She's purring better than she was."

"Doubt that," he muttered. "I always took good care of my boat."

Cary glanced at me to see if I read a reprimand in Uncle Jacob's remark.

"Hello, Uncle Jacob," I said, refusing to be ignored. "I'm happy you're home."

He grunted what sounded like a thank you, but avoided looking at me.

"You send Roy around after work tomorrow," he told Cary. "I want a word with him."

"Sure. You need anything? We're just going to take a walk on the beach."

"I have a list of groceries, Cary," Aunt Sara said.

"Oh."

"Let's do that first, Cary," I suggested.

"Sure. Where's the list, Ma?"

"Right beside the tea kettle. Add a five-pound bag of sugar, please," she said. Cary nodded and we started out.

"You have money?" Uncle Jacob called.

"Yes," Cary said.

"Stay close to home afterward. Your mother can't do everything herself," Uncle Jacob warned.

"I'll help as much as I can," I said. He finally focused his gaze on me, his eyes searching my face to see if I were looking at him any differently since our conversations in the hospital. I forced a smile and he turned back to Aunt Sara to tell her to open the window a little more.

At the supermarket, we split up the list, giving May a half dozen items to fetch herself. As Cary and I walked down the aisle pushing our cart, he grinned at me, his eyes glittering impishly.

"What's with that look you have on your face, Cary Logan?" I asked him.

"I was just pretending you and I were married and shopping together, pretending May was our little girl."

"We're kind of young to have a daughter as old as May, aren't we?"

"I just pretended she was much younger," he said with a shrug. If everything was as easy as pretending, we would all be forever happy, I thought.

"Suppose she was that young? Do you think I would let her go off by herself like this, Cary Logan? What sort of a mother do you think I would be?"

"A perfect one," he responded. "Don't you think I'll be a good father?"

"Maybe," I teased.

"Maybe? Why—" He stopped when the man in front of us turned around. It was Adam Jackson's father.

"Well, we meet again," he said, fixing his soft blue eyes on me. He wore a pair of jeans, a heather grey sweater, and sneakers and looked rather young and athletic. There was a warmth in his smile that went beyond mere cordiality, I thought. Despite Cary's discomfort, I didn't mind Adam's father.

"It's nice to run into you again," I said.

"At least you're not knocking me over this time," he kidded. I couldn't help blushing. "Hello, Cary."

"Hello," Cary answered, rather sulkily I thought.

"How's your father doing? I was sorry to hear about his illness," Mr. Jackson said.

"He's home," Cary replied and leaned over to get some cans of soup.

"That's good. Give him my regards." Mr. Jackson looked at me again. "Cary's father and I used to go fishing together once in a while. He ever tell you about that marlin we caught, Cary?"

"No sir, he didn't," Cary said. "We have to move along. My mother needs these things," Cary added gruffly.

"Oh sure. Well, don't forget to give him my best, and if he needs help with anything . . ."

"Okay," Cary said.

Mr. Jackson winked at me.

"I bet if you play the fiddle for him, he'll feel a lot better a lot faster," he said.

"Thank you."

I smiled and we walked past him. When I turned back, he was still looking our way.

"Don't look back at him. He's just flirting with you," Cary muttered.

"What?"

"Everyone knows T. J. Jackson's reputation here. Like father like son," he said. "And he doesn't care about age either. That's why he can't hold onto a secretary long."

"Really? But he has such a beautiful wife," I said, gazing back at him again despite Cary's admonition.

"Some men are never satisfied. It's an ego thing."

"Oh. Since when did you get so wise about these matters?" I asked, perhaps a bit too sharply.

He shot me a pained look.

673

"I'm just looking out for you, Melody," he said. He walked on in a sulk until I put my hand on his and he turned back to me.

"I'm glad you are, Cary," I said. It brought the lightness and gaiety back to his face.

May met us at the dairy counter and we finished our shopping. As we left the store, I saw Mr. Jackson putting his groceries into his car. He saw me, too, and paused to wave. I started to wave back when I saw Cary was watching out of the corner of his eye.

"Damn flirt," he said under his breath.

Was he right? I wondered. I didn't know whether to be flattered or frightened by the attention of an older man. After all, look where daydreaming about Kenneth got me. Nowhere but sad. It made sense, however. Even Mama Arlene used to use that expression as if it were gospel: Like father like son. Except, what about Kenneth? I thought. He wasn't like his father, and Cary wasn't like his.

I wondered. Was I anything like mine? Unfortunately, I doubted that I would ever know.

When we arrived home, we found Aunt Sara halfway up the stairs again, this time carrying a tray with a mug of hot tea and some biscuits.

"He wanted a cup," she explained. "I'll be right there to help put it all away," she added, nodding at the bags of groceries we carried.

"We'll take care of it, Ma," Cary said, his jaw taut with anger. "He's going to wear her out completely," he told me as we watched Aunt Sara continue up the stairs.

It wasn't a wild prediction. Uncle Jacob had a bell next to his bed that he would ring about every five minutes it seemed. He interrupted supper twice that night demanding things from Aunt Sara. She never uttered a word of complaint, she was so happy to have him home, but it was apparent to both Cary and me

674

that she couldn't run up and down the stairs all day and night. She wasn't even able to relax enough to eat!

"Maybe you could get them to hire a special duty nurse for a while, Cary," I suggested. "If your family needed the money, maybe Grandpa Samuel and Grandma Olivia would help."

"It's not the money. You know how my father is when it comes to strangers in his house," he replied.

"Then maybe we can get him to sleep in the living room until he's a lot better," I said. "At least your mother wouldn't have to go up and down the stairs so much."

Cary thought it was a good suggestion, but when he brought that idea to Uncle Jacob, he roared with anger.

"Turn my house into a hospital, would you? I'll be up and about soon. I don't need people walking in here and seeing me laid out on some sofa like a sick child," he declared. "Who came up with that idea?" I heard him shout.

"It was my idea," Cary said. "Sorry."

"Just keep your mind on your work. That's enough for now," Uncle Jacob told him.

Aunt Sara became flustered because Uncle Jacob lost his temper. I felt so bad because Cary was upset with himself. I told him it was my fault.

"It's not your fault," he snapped at me. "I thought it was a good idea and it is."

He climbed upstairs to his work room because he was just as embarrassed by his father's reprimands as he was angry. I entertained May, playing Chinese checkers until she couldn't keep her eyes open. I kept looking for Cary to come down to the living room, but he didn't leave his attic retreat until after I had gone to bed myself.

So much for Uncle Jacob's first night home from the hospital, I thought. In any other house, it would be a night of joy, but in this one, it was a night of tension.

675

During the night I heard Aunt Sara leave the bedroom and go downstairs to fetch something for him, and before morning, I heard her do it again. At breakfast, the fatigue was still planted well in her eyes. She got herself up early enough to give Cary his breakfast before he went down to the dock, and then she began bringing things up to Uncle Jacob. I tried to help, but she said it would be better for now if she did it herself.

"He's a little grouchy about being so confined," she explained.

I hated to leave for the day, but at least May was going to remain at home to be of some assistance. If Uncle Jacob would let her help, that is.

I wondered when Grandma Olivia and Grandpa Samuel would be by to visit. I asked Aunt Sara.

"Later today," she told me. "Olivia's mad at Jacob for forcing the doctors to release him from the hospital. She wasn't going to come at all, but I begged her and told her Jacob would only become more upset and it wasn't good for him."

"She wasn't going to come?" I asked, astounded.

"Oh, she was just blustering about," Aunt Sara explained. "I swear. This is the most stubborn family." She bit down on her lower lip as if she had uttered the worst profanity or heresy. "It will be all right. Please, God, everything will be all right," she said.

I heard the sound of a muffled car horn and hurried out, but instead of Kenneth, Holly was there to pick me up.

"He can't drag himself away from his block of marble," she explained. "I think I saw him for ten minutes yesterday. So, how was your visit with your other grandmother?"

"Interesting," I said in a neutral voice. She raised her eyebrows.

676

"Oh? Aren't you the cool one? Trying to teach the teacher a thing or two?" she added and I had to laugh.

"There are some things I have to work out yet. Myself," I added.

"Okay. Remember though, I'm here for you if you need me," she said.

"Thanks."

"I hope someone needs me soon," she declared. "I'm beginning to feel like a piece of furniture around Kenneth's house."

I laughed, but we arrived at Kenneth's I saw what she meant. He was so involved in his work, he barely acknowledged my arrival. I wanted to tell him about my visit with his father and all I had learned, but I was afraid of breaking his concentration. I didn't need someone else mad at me, especially Kenneth.

"I need to check something," he said. "Would you pose for me for just a few minutes?" I did so while he studied me, thought, studied and then nodded.

"Okay, I'm fine," he said and returned to the block. "You can return to work on the base," he said when I didn't move. I gathered my tools and began. We worked quietly for a while, only the sound of the chipping and the tapping of the hammer echoing in the studio.

Finally after what seemed like hours, he stepped back, wiped his face with a towel, nodded at the block and then turned to me. I was on my knees, staring up at him. He blinked and refocused his eyes as if he were returning to this world.

"So," he said, "Holly told me you had an unpleasant visit when you went to see Belinda yesterday. What was she, sick or something?"

"No, not exactly," I said. He stared at me. I'd never make a good Logan, I thought. I couldn't keep the truth from pressing its face right up against the window pane.

"You have something to tell me?"

677

"Yes."

He nodded and looked away. Then he wiped his hands and walked to the window that faced the ocean. He stood there for a while staring out. I wiped my hands and brushed down my clothes. He took a deep breath and then turned back to me.

"Grandma Belinda told me things," I said. "They were keeping her shut up and giving her some medicine that made her dopey, but she told me things."

"What sort of things?" he asked.

"Things about my mother, about how she was born."

"Uh-huh," he said staring at me so oddly, his face so still, it looked chiseled from marble itself.

"As Holly told you, I then went to see Grandma Olivia. She denied everything," I said with disgust. "She continued the lies, but I knew they were lies. I just knew it," I said.

"And so?"

"I went to see your father."

"I see." He looked out the window again. "Might get some rain later today," he said. "Looks like some boomers coming out of the northeast." He looked down and then crossed to the sink to get himself a glass of water. "Want some?"

"No thanks." I didn't move. He went to the sofa and sat down. After a moment he turned back to me.

"I didn't lie to you, Melody," he said. "I just didn't tell you everything I knew. It was more painful for me, believe me," he said.

"I think I understand," I said. His raised his eyebrows.

"Really? I don't," he muttered bitterly and sipped some more water.

"It was terrible for them to keep the secret so long and permit you to grow up thinking my mother was someone else, someone you could love," I said.

He nodded, a small, tight smile on his lips.

"Yes," he said. "Terrible is a good word, but I'm afraid I can think of many others not suitable for a young girl's ears."

"Your father's a very sad man, Kenneth. I think he's very sorry," I said. Kenneth widened his smile.

"You? You want to forgive him? He let you grow up without ever knowing he was your grandfather. He never sent you a dollar or inquired about your well-being. He let Haille and Chester run off without a penny to their names to live in the hills of West Virginia, and when you arrived here, he made no attempt to tell you who you were and who he was to you. If Belinda hadn't babbled to you in the rest home, you still wouldn't know the truth," Kenneth pointed out. "Forgive him?"

He shook his head.

"I don't want to hate him," I admitted.

"Just like him to win you over even after all that. The master charmer strikes again," he said bitterly.

"I just want everyone to tell me the truth. I just want to know who my father is," I said, my throat tightening as my tears built a reservoir beneath my eyelids.

"He didn't say?"

"He told me he didn't know. He said my mother wouldn't confide in him and that all he knows is that she got into trouble after she found out the truth."

"That's right. It was his fault," Kenneth spit out. "Especially the way he told her. What did he expect would happen?"

"How did he tell her?" I asked, breathless.

Kenneth turned away. I saw by the way he was working the muscles in his jaw that it was not just difficult but painful for him to resurrect these memories. This was just why everyone was warning me about raking up the painful past, but unspoken suffering just festers like sores in your heart and eventually bursts and eats you alive inside.

679

"One afternoon while I was away, my father invited your mother to go sailing with him. Haille and I had gone with him before, and on one other occasion, she and my mother joined him on the sailboat. I thought there was nothing unusual about this particular time, and she certainly didn't.

"Imagine her," he said, turning to me, his eyes bloodshot with tears, "young and beautiful and still very innocent, dressed in one of her newest sailing outfits, her face fresh and tender with the morning dew. She liked my father, actually loved him for his charm and sense of humor. None of us ever put any special importance on the attention he rained on Haille. He flirted and beguiled every female who was in reach of his smile."

Kenneth smiled to himself for a moment, lost in some memory.

"She used to say being with my father was second best to being with me."

His smile faded.

"We were all so happy-go-lucky, the rich kids enjoying our sailboats and our cars, our clothes and jewelry, able to go almost anywhere we wanted to go, almost any time we wanted. We could have parties on the beach and pay for everything without the slightest concern. Everyone else envied us. College was nothing more than an expected promise. If we worked, we worked only to fill time and amuse ourselves. We didn't work out of necessity.

"What could go wrong for us?" he asked, shaking his head. He wasn't looking at me so much as he was at his memories now. "If we got sick, we received the best medical attention; if we broke something, it was replaced, no matter the cost. Our entire futures seemed to be laid out on a primrose path. All of us knew how lucky we were and we had only a vague interest in those who weren't. Maybe that was be-

680

cause, deep inside, the smartest of us knew life can be a bubble that bursts at any moment and everything you thought was so important can vanish in an instant."

He sighed deeply, his shoulders rising and then falling as he lowered his head.

"She arrived early that afternoon. Surprise! My mother wasn't going along this time. It was to be just her and dad."

He raised his head.

"She described every little detail about that day to me afterward, alternating between crying and laughing, her laughter thin and on the verge of insanity.

"Dad looked dapper, handsome, younger than ever. She noticed he was more talkative than usual when she arrived, but his talk was about new things my mother had bought at auctions, plans he had to redo this and redo that around the house, small talk. Until they got out to sea, that is.

"He sailed into a cove and started to talk about his own youth. Pretty soon he was talking about Belinda. Haille began to feel a little uncomfortable as he described his own romantic interest in Olivia's sister. And then, he just lowered the boom on her and told her he was her father. He said it the way you might say: I have to confess, I broke that piece of china yesterday.

"Haille was stunned of course. This man sitting across from her in the sailboat, this man she had known all her life as my father, this charming friend of Olivia and Samuel Logan, one afternoon chose to tell her he was her father. He took her out to sea so she was more or less trapped on the boat and had to hear his side of the story, of course. She said she was tempted to jump into the water and swim to shore, but she was trembling so badly she couldn't trust her body to be strong enough to make it.

"The impact of hearing he was her father was great, but what was even greater was the realization that she and I—that we were half-brother and sister and the budding love between us was incestuous and forbidden. Imagine the feeling of betrayal she felt at that moment.

"My father defended himself by saying that if she and I had never shown any indications of becoming serious lovers, he would never have told her the truth. Isn't that incredible? He would have kept it secret forever, for as you know now, who would believe poor deranged Belinda, right? Oh, they made sure of that, my father and Olivia Logan.

"Of course, he insisted Belinda was really in need of psychiatric help and they were giving her the best, most expensive treatment possible. All men who have affairs and impregnate their lovers should have his opportunity and logic."

Kenneth laughed.

"Some force their lovers to have abortions, some pay them off and send them away, some deny having ever known them, if they can. The fortunate rich and powerful stuff their lovers into rest homes where they can be kept institutionalized, medicated, and humored. Everything Belinda said after that was just fantasy or lunacy.

"And you want me to forgive him," he said. He lay his head back again.

"That's because I see him now, Kenneth," I replied in a small, trembling voice. "I wasn't there from the beginning and I didn't know the details as you do. What did my mother do when he finally brought her back to shore?"

"She got away from him as quickly as she could. At first she called him a liar, thinking Olivia had put him up to it to keep her and me from being together."

"Why?"

682

"That's something only Olivia can answer. She and Haille never got along, and I think—" He hesitated and gazed up at me, deciding whether or not I was old enough to understand or whether he had a right to say it. He decided to continue. "I think Olivia always loved my father and was jealous of her own sister. That jealousy manifested itself in her relationship with Haille. Olivia treated her like Cinderella, the beautiful but inferior step-daughter.

"Anyway, Haille came home and shut herself in her room. No one knew why yet, I suppose. When I got home that night, Dad called me into the den and, fortified with a half dozen bourbon and waters, told me what he had told Haille.

"Now it was my turn to call him a liar. Who wanted it to be true? I, too, was hoping it was just a connivance to keep Haille and me from becoming boyfriend and girlfriend and eventually marrying, but he broke down and cried and confessed and blabbered like I had never seen.

"I was stunned. I rushed out of the house and over to see Haille. That was when she described the sailing and the way Dad broke the news. She was already different," Kenneth said, nodding to himself.

"How?"

"I sensed this abandon, this feeling that whatever had been keeping her in check was gone. She was like a kite whose string had broken and she was being tossed about, but not minding it. She was laughing a lot, acting like the daughter of a mentally disturbed woman. I got frightened, especially when she embraced me on the beach and said, 'Let's not care. Let's do what we want and let's do it right now, right here.'

"I panicked. It was as if a vampire had asked me to become a vampire with her. I broke her hold on me and ran from her, hearing her laughter trail after me. I still hear it sometimes.

"Anyway," he said, "the rest you know. Haille became the woman Olivia accused her of always being: promiscuous, uncaring, indifferent, reckless, and wild. The rest is as I told you. Oh, I tried to be friends anyway, tried to give her good advice, come to her aid whenever she needed me, but it was like holding back the tide, the inevitable disaster. Dad was right. It wasn't very long afterward that she became pregnant with you and then Chester came to her defense. Blindly in love with her, he stood by while she accused Samuel of unthinkable things. Maybe that was her way of getting back at my father, attacking his close friend. To her, they were all the same: Olivia, Samuel, my father, all part of the conspiracy. Anyway, shortly after that, they ran off to West Virginia.

"I don't know who your father is," he added before I could ask again. "I'm not holding back anything anymore, especially since you have spoken with my father. Haille never told me. When I asked her, she laughed and said, 'You are Kenneth. In my heart, you always will be.'

"That was why I was so taken aback when you told me you suspected I might be your father. It was eerie, as if Haille were speaking again through you. I know how much you want to know. I wish I could give you the information, give you that gift, but I can't. The truth is buried with your mother, Melody. I'm sorry."

I didn't realize I was crying until I felt the tears drip off my chin. Kenneth rose and handed me a handkerchief. I blew my nose, wiped my eyes, and took a deep breath. He smiled and nodded at me.

"You know this makes me your uncle, don't you?"

"Yes."

"Do you mind?"

"No," I said but I meant yes. I minded because for a while I had dreamed of him as a lover, too. Now, that looked even more ridiculous. I felt so ashamed, so lost. Will-o-wisp dreams never came true for me and never would. There were too many clouds in the skies over my family's past.

"Well, we'll have to give all this some serious thought now," he added and turned back to the sculpture.

"Serious thought? What can we do about any of it?" I wondered aloud.

"Depends," he said, picking up his chisel.

"On what?" I said, following him.

"On whether Dad is really ready to reveal the sins of the past, and on how Olivia and Samuel react. You're related to Olivia through Belinda, of course, but you're not a Logan." He smiled. "So," he said, bringing the hammer and the chisel to the block, "you might move in here with me, if you want." He turned. "Being as I'm a close relative now."

My jaw dropped and I gaped at him.

"Move in with you?"

"And not have to put up with that horse's ass," he added.

"You would want me to live with you?"

"Look at it from my point of view. I get a great cook and housekeeper for free," he joked. He started to tap the chisel and then stopped. "Of course, that means I would have to do something legal like file to be your guardian or something. I suppose that means I would have to attend a parent-teacher's conference, too, doesn't it? And sign your excuses for absence, parental permission slips, all that stuff?"

He looked at me but I just stared. Live with Kenneth?

"Do I have to go shopping with you and see to your dental appointments?"

"Are you serious?"

His eyes darkened a little as his face lost its touch of lightness and humor.

685

"One way or another I knew Haille would come back into my life," he said.

He turned and tapped the hammer harder. Chips began to fall. The echo resounded.

One way or another?

I hadn't found my father, but perhaps I had found the next best thing.

15
❧

The Damage Is Done

Kenneth and I spent the rest of the day so involved in our work, we lost track of time. Now I appreciated why Kenneth devoted his life to his art. It was truly an escape from the heavy burdens and the turmoil that often rained down around us. Working together, he and I developed a rhythm that overtook and absorbed us. We were aware of each other, but never spoke and rarely even looked at each other. It was almost a religious experience as Kenneth's hands began to mold shapes and bring his vision out of the block of marble.

So lost in the artistic effort, we were both surprised to hear Holly's knock on the door, followed by her plaintive cries beseeching us to come up for air.

"I ate lunch myself. I meditated, did two personal charts, walked Ulysses until he begged for mercy. Don't you people get tired?" she exclaimed.

Kenneth and I looked at each other.

"What time is it?" he asked.

"Five-twenty," she replied.

"Oh no," I said. "I promised I'd be home early to help take care of Uncle Jacob."

"Five-twenty?" Kenneth repeated. He looked at me, astounded. "Did we eat lunch?"

I shook my head, amazed my stomach hadn't reminded me or complained.

"Fanatics," Holly accused.

I looked at myself, full of dust, my hair almost gray, my face streaked. Kenneth, too, resembled a ghost, the chips and dust turning his beard practically white.

"Someone has to take me home right away," I wailed.

"I will, if only to have some human company for a while," Holly said, glaring at Kenneth, who shrugged off her look of reprimand with that boyish smile that could charm the heart of the most wicked witch.

I brushed myself off as quickly and as best I could and then hurried out to Holly's car.

"The man's dangerous, a bad influence," she said when we started away. "Hang around him long enough, and you'll start to look like him. You might even grow a beard!" she growled. "Do you realize how long you two were shut up in there?"

"Funny," I said. "I don't feel tired. I should, doing that so long, but it's . . ."

"Invigorating?" she suggested.

"Yes."

"Well, I suppose for Kenneth, and maybe now for you, it's so deep an involvement it's like meditating, moving to a higher plane of consciousness, leaving this burdensome world of woe," she said and smiled. "You do look a lot happier than you did this morning."

She gazed at me again, her eyes narrowing suspiciously.

"You're wearing a very coy smile, Melody Logan. Something is afoot."

"Maybe," I said and laughed. "Maybe."

"Whatever it is, I'm happy for you." We rode a little longer in silence and then she turned back to me with a face of concern. "When am I going to know, or is it something so secret I may never know?"

"You'll know soon," I said.

She nodded.

"I saw it in your chart, but I didn't say anything."

"What?"

"A big change, something very dramatic involving family."

I raised my eyebrows.

"Am I warm?" she wondered.

"Overheated," I said and we both laughed. I hadn't felt this cheerful for a long time. A ray of sunshine had sliced its way through the dark, brooding clouds. But my light and happy mood vanished as soon as we arrived at the house. There was something about the way it looked that put a hard and heavy feeling in my chest. Maybe it was all in me, in my trepidation and anticipation, or maybe some of Holly's powers had rubbed off and I could sense negative energy even before it reared its ugly head.

"You all right?" she asked when we pulled into the driveway. I hadn't realized I had sighed so deeply and loudly.

"Yes, I'll be fine. Thanks for the ride."

"It's okay." She thought a moment and then said, "If Kenny goes back into the studio again tonight after dinner and stays there all night, I think I'll start planning my return to New York."

"Oh, really?" I was genuinely disappointed.

"This is just not the right time for me to visit, but I'll be back," she promised with a smile.

"When will you go?"

"I'll see. Not tomorrow anyway," she added. "There is still some battery recharging I want to do for myself here. Bye."

"Bye and thanks," I said and got out.

I found the house ominously quiet when I entered. I closed the door softly and practically tiptoed. There were no lights on in the living room and no sounds coming from the kitchen. No one appeared to greet me. As I walked from room to room I wondered if there was anyone home.

Oh no, I thought. I hope Cary didn't break down in his boat again. Maybe Uncle Jacob had had a relapse.

Just as I turned to go upstairs, I heard someone sobbing. I went down the hallway to the dining room and peered through the door. There sat Aunt Sara, her head down on her folded arms, her shoulders shaking.

"Aunt Sara," I cried and rushed to her side. "What's wrong? Did something happen to Cary? Uncle Jacob?"

She lifted her head slowly and then smiled through her tears.

"Oh Melody, dear. You're home. Good."

"Why are you crying?"

"Oh, it's nothing," she said quickly and dabbed the tears away with the hem of her apron. "I'm just a little tired, I guess."

"I'm sorry I didn't get home earlier, but I just didn't realize the time."

"That's all right, dear." She smiled weakly and took a deep breath. It was as if she carried a lead weight on a chain around her neck.

"Where is everyone? Where are Cary and May?"

"May's upstairs in her room. Cary just left for the supermarket. I made a meat loaf, but I forgot to tell you kids to pick up the beer he likes. He likes it with my meat loaf."

"He had to have it tonight?"

She stared at me.

"That's why you're crying, isn't it? He was upset so you got upset? And Cary had to run out as soon as he got back from work, right?" I asked, the whole scenario flashing before my eyes.

"It's nothing. I should have remembered." She sighed. "I usually do."

"I bet he's not even supposed to be drinking it," I exclaimed. "And after all you've been doing for him, for him to make a scene and—"

"It's all right, dear. Cary will be back soon. I have the meat loaf on low and—"

"That's not the point, Aunt Sara. If he drives you until you get sick, too, where will everyone be?"

"I'll be fine," she insisted. "I wanted to have an earlier dinner tonight, though. Olivia and Samuel were here today. We had a nice lunch and their visit cheered Jacob, but before they left, Olivia told me to tell you she would be sending Raymond for you about seven."

"What?"

"She said she wanted to see you and—"

"Well, maybe I don't want to see her," I snapped.

Aunt Sara's face filled with shock. She shook her head as if to deny the words.

"Not want to see her?"

"Who is she, the queen? Demanding this and that? I'm tired and I was looking forward to relaxing tonight. I have a lot to think about," I added, but Aunt Sara heard nothing. Her huge scared eyes stared woefully back at me. "Oh, just forget it, Aunt Sara. Forget I said anything. I'm going up to wash off this marble dust and then I'll come down and help you with supper or anything else you need."

I turned and left her, a sailboat drifting in a windless sea. She was kind and loving, willing always to sacrifice her own happiness and comfort for someone else, especially for Uncle Jacob. Yet she was the saddest and most tragic person I knew right now. I wished I'd had Holly there. I'd ask her what went wrong with Aunt Sara's stars? Where were the sun and the moon when Aunt Sara was born?

May was waiting for me in my room. She was

691

sitting on the floor, her knees up, drawing on her pad, her back against the frame of the bed. She saw my feet and looked up quickly.

I asked her why she was waiting in my room and she quickly signed back that she was upset for Cary. He had come home exhausted, his head drooping, his shirt off and over his shoulder, looking forward to a shower and a good meal, but Aunt Sara greeted him at the door and told him what Uncle Jacob demanded. May said Cary didn't even set foot in the house. He turned and hopped into his truck. May claimed she had gone out after him, trying to get him to wait. She wanted to go along, but he shot off angrily and drove so fast, he nearly turned over making the turn! she exclaimed through her hands and eyes. May told me she had come into my room afterward because she was actually frightened by all this. She had been hoping I would soon come home and comfort her.

It filled me with rage, but rage that wasn't aimed at Uncle Jacob as much as it was at the whole situation. How could I go down there later and tell Aunt Sara that I was going to move in with Kenneth Childs? How could I desert her and May and Cary at this point? Aunt Sara still thought I had been sent to fill the gap made in her heart by Laura's death. Cary and May needed me more than ever. I felt frustrated, turned and twisted. Aunt Sara wasn't the sailboat in a windless sea, I was. I was the one who had little or no control of her destiny. Capricious fate blew at my sails or left me in a state of dreary calm whenever it had a whim to do so.

I assured May that everything would be all right. I promised her I would help Aunt Sara and we would make Uncle Jacob comfortable and happy again. Then I went into the bathroom and took a quick shower, feeling as if I had swallowed a lump of bread dough and it was stuck in my chest. As I was toweling my hair dry, I heard shouting in the hallway and hurried to my door.

What was going on now?

Cary was standing outside his father's bedroom, his head lowered until his chin rested on his chest, listening to Uncle Jacob rant and rave.

"We never had a catch that bad! What the hell was Roy doing? I bet he's been slacking off without me looking over his shoulder, is that it? The man works for you. You can't treat him like a friend. You treat him like an employee or else he'll take advantage."

"It wasn't his fault, Dad, or mine. We did everything we always do."

"Two lobsters! Two lobsters! And each barely a pound and a quarter?"

"I told you we have to get out of the lobster business, Dad," Cary said softly.

"Never mind that nonsense. I see I've got to get myself up and out of this bed faster. Tell your mother I'm ready to eat," he snapped.

Cary nodded and turned. He saw me wrapped in a bath towel standing in the doorway. His eyes brightened for a moment and then became dull again when he realized I had been there while Uncle Jacob verbally whipped him.

"Hi," I said.

"Hi. I thought you'd be home before me," he added as he walked with me down the hallway.

"We got so lost in the work, we didn't realize the time until Holly came knocking on the studio door."

Cary smirked at my excuse.

"I have to go down and tell Ma to bring up his food."

"He's becoming a real monster," I declared, glaring furiously at Uncle Jacob's doorway.

"He's just frustrated," Cary muttered and started for the stairs.

693

"Your mother was crying when I got home, Cary."
He paused and looked at me.

"She's near the breaking point herself," I warned strongly.

"I'm doing the best I can!" he cried, tears filling his eyes.

"I didn't mean—I'm not blaming you, Cary."

He spun around and stomped so hard down the stairs, I thought he would crack a step. The last thing I had intended was to upset him. The look on his face turned my heart to glass which was quickly shattered by my boiling blood.

It's Uncle Jacob's fault, I fumed. Damn him. Without hesitation, I marched across the hallway to his bedroom door. He was sitting back against his pillow, anticipating his tray of food, looking like some spoiled member of royalty who thought everyone else existed merely to please him.

"Uncle Jacob," I said, addressing him as sternly as a schoolteacher.

He opened his eyes slowly, but when he saw me, they widened quickly and drank me in from head to foot. For an instant I thought he looked pleased, but it was as if the realization of that heightened his anger.

"How dare you come here dressed like that?"

"Forget about how I am dressed. I don't care. You're being unreasonable, throwing tantrums like a baby when everyone is doing their best to make you comfortable and help you get well. But if you don't stop shouting and demanding, you'll make Aunt Sara sick, too!"

His mouth opened and closed without a word. Then he waved his fist at me.

"Get out! Get out of my sight you daughter of temptation."

The veins in his neck strained and he fell back against his pillow, his face red.

694

"I'm just telling you this for your own good as well as everyone else's," I concluded.

He slammed his eyelids shut as if he had to wipe out the sight of me. It's futile, I thought. The man's too selfish. I returned to my room and got dressed. Just as I finished, I heard Cary coming up the stairs. He was carrying the tray of food and Aunt Sara was trailing behind, her every footstep a monumental effort now. Cary and I exchanged glances as he continued down the hallway, but Aunt Sara paused.

"Everything's ready downstairs, dear. May's at the table. Just serve the dinner. I have to stay with Jacob and help him eat his meal."

"When will you eat, Aunt Sara?"

"I've already had more than I need. Please, just be sure May eats."

"Okay, Aunt Sara. Don't worry. I'll take care of her."

"Don't forget," she said. "Raymond's coming for you at seven."

Cary looked back, his eyebrows raised with curiosity.

"I'm sure Grandma Olivia wouldn't permit me to forget," I muttered and went downstairs.

"What does Grandma Olivia want?" Cary asked when he joined May and me at the dinner table.

"I don't know. All I know is I'm being summoned to the palace. But she might be in for a surprise," I added and went to the kitchen to get the meat loaf. May had already set the table and brought out the bread and the jug of ice water.

"What sort of surprise?" Cary asked when I sat at the table. He was in his father's seat again, the Bible opened and ready for his reading.

Instead of answering, I stared down at my plate and kept my head lowered.

"What surprise, Melody?" he asked.

695

"The meat loaf's getting cold, Cary."

Reluctantly, he picked up the Bible. I lifted my eyes toward May and saw her looking small and frightened. It amazed me how although she was deaf, she could still pick up on the tone of conversations. Years of silence had made her perceptive when it came to a turn of the head, a movement in the eyes, a twist of the lips. She could read people's moods better than most people who had no trouble hearing.

"Luke, Chapter 6," Cary began. There was a bookmark stuck at the pages his father wanted read. Cary opened to them and then, in his father's voice, he read, "'For a good tree bringeth not forth corrupt fruit; neither does a corrupt tree bring forth good fruit.

"'For every tree is known by his own fruit . . .'"

He read to the end of the chapter and then put the Bible down without another word. I began to serve the meat loaf, thinking that Uncle Jacob was always with us at this table as long as he chose the Bible selections to be read.

"You have some new secret?" Cary asked after he took his first forkful. When I didn't reply, he added, "I kind of thought we weren't keeping secrets from each other."

"It's not a secret, Cary." I glanced at May. She watched me with question marks in her eyes, too. I turned to Cary. "I already told you what Judge Childs told me."

"So?"

"So since Judge Childs is really my grandfather, Kenneth is my true uncle."

"What does that mean?"

"It means he could be my guardian," I blurted.

Cary stared at me, his fork frozen in the air. Then his eyes darkened with the realization.

"You mean, you're thinking about going to live with him?"

"Maybe," I said. "At the moment he's my closest true relative," I added.

He continued to stare at me instead of eating.

"Your food's getting cold, Cary."

"I'm not hungry."

"Look, this might even be better for now, considering the way your father is," I said.

"How could it be better?"

"He doesn't want me here. It's only irritating him and he has to recuperate."

"Do what you want," Cary snapped and pushed his plate away. "Everybody should just go and do what they want!" he cried and rose from the table.

"Cary!"

He marched out of the dining room and out of the house. I heard the front door slam.

May's hands were going like birds chasing each other.

"He's just upset about your father," I signed, "and your mother. He'll be all right. Could you clear the table when you're finished? I'll go after him."

She nodded and I hurried down the hall and out of the house. He hadn't gone far. He was leaning against the truck, his arms folded across his chest, his head down. The sky had changed to a dark plum color streaked with crimson that looked like freshly spilled blood and the ocean had an inky-gray sheen. I saw no boats, and with no traffic on our street and no other people about, I felt smaller, alone, like the two of us were the last people on earth.

I put my hand on his shoulder. He didn't look up.

"First Laura and then you," he said.

"If I move in with my uncle, I won't be leaving you for good, Cary. I'll still be in Provincetown. We'll still see each other whenever we want to see each other."

"Will we?"

He raised his head. His green eyes were darker and strangely haunted.

697

"Yes," I said emphatically. He smiled as if I had said the silliest thing. "I promise," I added.

"Promises," he muttered and gazed toward the ocean. "You of all people know they're like balloons. When you first get them, they're fresh and bright and full and then time passes and they lose air or simply explode. Laura and I used to make all sorts of promises to each other."

"I'm not Laura, Cary. I never intended to be. I'm not your sister. I'm—"

He looked at me, his eyes full of expectation.

"Yes?" he said.

"I'm your girlfriend, or at least, I hope I am."

"Do you?"

"I wouldn't say it if I didn't mean it, Cary. You know how I feel about lies."

He smiled.

"Yes, that I know," he said, nodding. He took a deep breath and looked up at the windows on the second floor of the house. "I'm never going to please him, you know."

"That's his fault, Cary, not yours," I said.

"It doesn't matter whose fault it is. I've been at his side all my life. Ever since I was old enough to walk out to the dock with him. He's a good sailor—the best. I never felt anything but safe being out there with him."

"That's good," I said. "That's the way a son should feel about his father."

He shook his head. And then he shut his eyes as if a vision so terrible it cut through his brain like a knife had appeared.

"What is it, Cary?"

"I didn't tell Ma everything," he said after a short pause and another deep sigh.

"What do you mean?"

"The doctor doesn't think he will ever be what he was. He wants him to go on disability and stop working altogether," he said. "Too much damage to his heart."

"Oh." I slumped back against the truck beside him, suddenly feeling guilty about yelling at Uncle Jacob. "He doesn't know?"

"He knows; he just won't accept it," Cary said. "When I brought him home, he said, 'I don't want to die on land. I'll die on my boat.'"

I thought about Aunt Sara and how she would fall apart like a figure of ice surprised by the spring sunshine.

"You've just got to make him understand, Cary."

"Understand? I might as well shout at the wind or stand on the beach and try to scare away the tide. The sea is in his blood. Almost every day of his life, he got up and went to sea." He smiled. "He always says he wobbles when he walks on dry land. He says he gets land sick the way most people get seasick.

"And, he'll worry about the family, making a living. He was planning on expanding the cranberry business, you know."

"You can do all that, Cary."

"It won't be the same for him. Dad's not a man who can spend the rest of his life sitting in a rocker, waiting for me to come home with a report."

"Well what's his solution?" I cried.

"There is no solution," he said. "We'll just do what we have to do when we have to do it, I guess." He took a deep breath and looked at the house. "Let's go back before Ma comes down and finds we ran away from her dinner."

I took his arm and he turned his troubled, dark green eyes to me.

"I'll be at your side to help you whenever I can, Cary."

His eyes brightened and he looked young again, young and strong and hopeful. Then he leaned closer and we kissed. It was just a soft kiss, a moment, but it

699

was like a promise, and not a promise that would burst like a balloon.

At least, that's what I believed in my heart.

Raymond was there promptly at seven. Aunt Sara came down from Uncle Jacob's room to be sure I was ready and that I would go. Why pleasing Grandma Olivia reigned so importantly in her mind, I would never understand. But it did. It was as if Grandma Olivia left her shadow on the walls here and Aunt Sara always felt that shadow hovering above or behind her, waiting to pounce and approve or disapprove of anything she said or did.

I hurried out and into the car. The moon was out now, big and bright, full and smiling, with long dark clouds streaking its face and making it seem sinister one minute and gay the next. It was as if a voice whispered in my ear, telling me to beware everything, for nothing was what it appeared to be.

"Probably get some showers tonight," Raymond said as we drove off.

The weather again, I thought. And then I thought, maybe it was a secret language; maybe it was another way of revealing what was in your heart.

"As long as it's not a storm," I replied.

"No, nothing like that. Just a refreshing downpour to drop us out of this unusually humid and warm air," he said.

"And tomorrow the sun will shine?"

"Expect so," he said.

I smiled to myself and we drove on.

The great house was surprisingly dark when we arrived. Raymond got out quickly and opened my door. I hurried up to the front and rang the bell. Loretta opened the door and glared out at me. She still hadn't forgiven me for bursting in the day before, I realized.

700

"Grandma Olivia wants to see me," I said sharply. She grimaced as if she had a bellyache.

"In the living room," she said, stepping back.

There was only a small light on in the hallway, and there wasn't much light coming from the living room either. When I entered, I saw a single lamp lit on the table beside the chair in which Grandma Olivia sat, perched like a buzzard, her eyes in half shadow, her face wearing the darkness like a veil. She was dressed in a very plain, dark blue dress, and less jewelry than usual. Her hands grasped the knobby ends of the arms of the chair as if she were afraid she might be shaken out of it.

"You sent for me?" I asked. Her deathly silence actually frightened me and I lost much of the confidence and anger that had helped me feel firm and secure. There was a long, ungodly pause that started my heart thumping.

"Sit down!" she said sharply.

I backed myself to the sofa, not taking my eyes from her. Anyone watching me would have thought I was afraid to turn my back on her. I folded my hands in my lap and waited. She moved forward just enough to bring her face fully out of the shadows and into the light. Even so, she looked ghostly, her face so pale that her dark eyes seemed to leap out at me. I actually gasped.

"So you went from here to Nelson's house and you heard his pathetic tale," she recited, as if telling the last line of a ghost story.

"I knew my grandmother was telling the truth," I said. "I didn't believe you."

"Men," she said so disdainfully it sounded as if she thought they were the lowest form of life. "They are so weak, so at the mercy of their lust. Every man I've known, my own father, his father, my child of a husband, even my sons, even Jacob, marrying that

701

dishrag who wallows in her own tears. I told him she wasn't strong enough to be a Logan's wife, but he didn't listen to me, not even Jacob," she moaned. The tone surprised me, and I actually thought she might start crying.

"Aunt Sara is a sweet woman who's had more than her share of terrible tragedy and—"

"Oh stop it," she snapped. "You don't have any more respect for her than I do. You're too much like me," she declared. "You're more a Gordon than a Childs, believe me," she added and with some sense of pride. It sounded like a compliment, and hearing her give me one so unexpectedly took the wind from my sails.

"I respect her," I said, but without as much firmness as I thought I would have.

"You don't respect her. You pity her. Would you like to be like her?" she asked with a wry smile on small, tight lips. "Is she the sort of woman you see yourself becoming after you marry?"

"Everyone's different," I said.

She laughed.

"You don't like to say unpleasant things, even if you believe them in your heart."

"How do you know what's in my heart?" I replied, regaining my self-assurance.

"I know," she said, nodding. "In many ways you remind me of me when I was your age, even younger."

That surprised me. She, admitting she was like me?

"You will find it a disadvantage, this need to always be pleasant and do what Sara idiotically preaches: 'don't say anything about anyone if you can't say something nice,'" she recited, wagging her head in mimicry. "Isn't that what she always parrots?"

"She's a very kindhearted, considerate person who thinks the sun rises and falls on your wishes," I said. "And if she knew how you felt about her, she would feel just terrible."

702

"She's merely afraid of me," Grandma Olivia said with a wave of her hand. "She has about as much love for me as you do, but I don't mind. If you spend your time worrying about who loves you and who doesn't, you'll end up—end up like Belinda," she concluded.

"Why didn't you tell me the truth?" I demanded.

"It wasn't my truth to tell," she said with a pained sigh. "And it's not something I care to remember." The sadness dropped from her face and was quickly replaced with that habitual take-charge look. "Besides, what good does that do now? Belinda is in a rest home. Your mother is dead. Your real father remains a mystery. You have only what I can give you. Nelson may have confessed to his youthful sins, but believe me, he has nothing more to give you than agony. He's wasting away in that house, living alone, his other children content to be far away, his son Kenneth unforgiving."

"Kenneth told me everything he knows. He's my uncle. I have that now," I retorted.

She snickered.

"Relatives. If you ask me, they're just additional burdens. You inherit their weaknesses and problems on top of your own. If you have a relative who committed a crime, people treat you as if you committed the crime. You're tainted. Overcoming the burden of my sister has been a lifelong endeavor for me," she said. "I've done well and I'm not about to countenance any setbacks," she added, leaning forward to focus her steely eyes on me.

"What's that supposed to mean?"

"It means that I called you here tonight after speaking with Nelson and hearing him slobber like a baby over the phone, because I wanted to be certain, absolutely certain that what he told you goes nowhere else. I'm too old to do battle with a new scandal. He was a fool to break down and tell you."

"I had a right to know. It's my life, too," I protested. "Now, I know that Kenneth Childs is my uncle," I continued. "He's asked me to move in with him and permit him to become my guardian."

She recoiled as if stung by a bee.

"What? Absolutely not. Why, that would be as good as standing on the street corner and announcing it all. Is he mad?"

"He was in love with my mother," I said. "You know when he learned about his father and my grandmother, that ended their hope of becoming man and wife. He wants to do this for me."

"I will not permit it," she insisted. She reached for a small bell on the side table and rang it. Loretta appeared as if she had been dangling above the doorway. "Call Kenneth Childs for me," she ordered.

"He doesn't have a telephone," I reminded her.

"Send Raymond to his house immediately and tell him I want to see him tonight."

"Stop!" I shouted. Her eyes widened into two small balls of fire as her shoulders lifted. "He's in the middle of something very important. He can't be disturbed."

The fierce anger that sprang to Grandma Olivia's face shocked me, and Loretta just stood in the doorway, afraid to move a muscle.

"That will be all for now, Loretta."

"Should I send Mr. Raymond for Mr. Kenneth?"

"No, not at the moment," Grandma Olivia said. She sat back after Loretta left, and we contemplated each other warily. She nodded slightly, as if reaching a conclusion.

"You don't like living with my son. I imagine he's going to be especially difficult now that he'll be home so much," she added as an afterthought.

"That's not the only reason I want to move out and live with my uncle," I said.

"Nevertheless." She stiffened in her chair like a

monarch. Then she leaned toward me again, stabbing me with her hard, penetrating glare.

"You will move in here," she declared, "and live with Samuel and me for your remaining year of public school. Then you will attend one of the finer colleges and pursue whatever interests you."

"What?" My jaw hung open.

"Naturally, I will expect the most exemplary sort of behavior. I will, in return, provide you with all of your needs, a fine wardrobe, one that reflects what a granddaughter of mine should wear, and Raymond and the car will be available to take you wherever you have to go. We will tell the world that you didn't want to be an added burden to Jacob and Sarah at this time, with Jacob so sick and all. Actually, that's not far from the truth. I imagine you and Jacob don't see eye to eye and your continued presence won't help his recovery."

"You expect me to move in here with you?" I asked, still astounded at the suggestion.

"It's a much better solution. Kenneth will approve of it as well, I assure you," she said with sickening confidence.

I stared, amazed. Once, I was almost homeless, without anyone, and now, three homes were available to me.

"You and I don't have to fall in love with each other," she continued, "but we can have respect for each other."

"You, respect me?" I almost laughed.

"You have shown some resourcefulness that, as I said, reminds me of myself at your age. I'm a good judge of character, and I think you are even more like me than you want to admit. It's not a sin to be strong, Melody. And Lord knows it's up to the women in this family to be strong, since the men are all weak."

"Cary's not weak," I blurted.

"What Cary is or isn't remains to be seen. He was too attached to his twin sister to show any independence from her. Even since her death I still haven't seen Cary show any sign of backbone. There is a large fortune here and much responsibility to be assumed."

"And you're saying that I will be the one to assume it?" I asked, even more amazed at her proposals.

"We'll see. Let me just say that I am running out of good candidates." She sat back. The grandfather clock bonged the hour.

"Aunt Sara will be heartbroken," I muttered, thinking aloud.

"What would she be if you moved in with Kenneth Childs? Ecstatic? Can you imagine the gossip, Jacob's ranting? Oh, I know what my son is like. I don't need you to tell me."

"I always thought he was trying to be like you," I said. She laughed.

"Do I behave like a woman enveloped in religion? I have no false modesty nor do I pretend to be the most moral person, looking condescendingly on all those who don't pray as much. I attend church on occasion, contribute heavily to its coffers. My son Jacob is a moral snob. Don't look so shocked. I've often told him as much to his face.

"So you see, my dear Melody, you and I might have more in common than you care to admit. You'll move in immediately," she concluded and started to rise.

"I'll have to talk about it with Kenneth first," I said.

"I will not permit Nelson Childs's maudlin confessions to paint profanities across this family's good name," she declared with regal authority. "No one should doubt the firmness of my determination, nor the intensity and impact of my wrath should I be crossed."

Her words resounded like church bells, vibrating through my bones.

"Make your arrangements as soon as possible," she ordered and left the room.

As soon as she was gone I was left to contemplate her words, which still echoed in the room. I gazed about this large house. Once, my mother had lived here, and now, Grandma Olivia was proposing I do the same, ordering, I should say.

I would much rather be with Kenneth, I thought. Despite Grandma Olivia's threats and dire predictions, I was determined to make that my first choice, but I trembled, wondering just what her threats could do. Right now, the last person I wanted to hurt was Kenneth.

Confused, frightened, feeling like a leaf prematurely torn from the branch, driven this way and that by capricious winds, I left the house. Raymond looked up from where he stood by the car as I started toward him. He barely moved. Everything seemed so still. It was as if the world had frozen and I was the only one left moving through the air on a crystal breeze.

And I had no idea where it would take me.

16
❧

A Glimmer of Hope

*M*ay saw that Cary had looked up sharply from their Monopoly game when I entered the house and paused by the living room door. She turned too, her eyes as wide and as filled with curiosity and worry as her brother's.

"You were gone a long time," Cary said.

"Where's Aunt Sara?" I asked.

"Upstairs with Dad," he replied. His eyes searched my face. "You all right?"

I started to nod and then stopped and said, "No."

Cary glanced at May and then back at me.

"Want to go for a walk?" he asked. "We can get some ice cream in town or—"

"I'd rather just walk on the beach, Cary, and then go to bed early tonight," I replied.

He nodded and signed to May to ask her to run up and tell Aunt Sara we were all going for a walk. She jumped to her feet and hurried upstairs. Cary took my hand and we went outside to wait for May. The sky had become overcast, not a star in sight. There was a strong breeze coming from the northeast. I laughed to myself, thinking that the people I knew back in West Virginia would be so impressed with my knowledge of weather systems, they would start calling me The Weather Girl of Sewell.

"Why are you smiling?" Cary asked.

"I was just thinking about people back home and how different I would seem to them now," I said.

"I wish you thought of this as your home," Cary said softly. "It's the only place you have any real family, the only place where someone who really cares about you lives."

I didn't reply, even though I felt his eyes on me and my heart had warmed with his soft words. Instead, I looked out over the dark blue-black ocean that seemed to flow into the sky. Terns, barely visible, looking more like ghost birds, called to each other. To me there was a note of desperation, fear in their cries. It was as if they were afraid they would lose each other forever in the darkness.

Off in the distance, I saw the lights of a tanker just emerging on the horizon. It looked so small and far away. The sea is a place for people who don't mind being alone, I thought, for people who actually crave being away from the din and clatter of society. Out there, the sky must be overwhelming at night and make one feel either tiny and insignificant or part of something much bigger than anything one could experience on the shore.

"I'd like to go for a real sea trip one day, Cary."

"You mean like overnight, days?"

"Yes."

"Okay," he said. "When?"

"Someday," I said with a smile.

"Something very, very serious is happening, isn't it, Melody?" he asked in shaky voice.

I nodded just as May came out to join us. I took her hand and the three of us began our familiar walk over the sand. Although it was harder to see it because of

709

the thickening darkness, the ocean was just as loud, if not louder, than ever.

"Looks like a storm, but it's not," Cary said. "These clouds will all be gone before morning."

"Nevertheless, it's a bad night for astrologers," I said.

"What?"

"People who read the stars to tell your future." I explained.

"Oh, you mean like your new friend Holly?"

"Yes."

"She read your future lately?" he asked in a timid voice.

"Yes."

"And?"

"She predicted a big change involving family and she was right."

As we continued along the beach, I told him about my discussion with Grandma Olivia and what she had suggested, or rather, what she had demanded, backing it all up with threats. Cary was astounded.

"She wants you to live with them?"

"I think she can make a lot of trouble for everyone if she doesn't get her way."

"I'll go talk to her tomorrow," he said firmly. "She can't run everyone's lives."

"No, Cary. I don't want to be the cause of any more family turmoil."

We plodded on in silence for a while and then Cary turned back to me.

"What's Kenneth going to say about it?"

"I don't know. I'll tell him in the morning."

"Then you've made up your mind?" Cary asked, stopping. I felt May's grip tighten. We had told her nothing, but she surely sensed the tension in my fingers.

"Maybe I can do more good this way, good for Grandma Belinda, too. I think Grandma Olivia and I

710

have reached an understanding. We're like two pit bulls who've faced each other, claimed our own territory, and backed away. Besides, she's not all wrong about men," I said with some bitterness. "Judge Childs, my grandfather, wasn't exactly thinking about how his actions would affect people he supposedly loved. I feel sorry for him now, but I don't approve of what he did. Every time I think of Kenneth's face when he described what happened with my mother, I get a little sick about it all. Kenneth blames him for my mother's bad behavior, for everything. It's terrible for a son and a father to be so estranged. I don't want anything like that to happen between you and Uncle Jacob, Cary."

"It won't. It doesn't have to happen if you stay here, either," he said.

"It might. And then in the end, you would only hate me for it."

"I would never—"

"Besides," I offered, "you and I will probably have an easier time seeing each other this way. We would actually go on dates."

He thought about it and I saw that pleased him. We walked on until we came to a small hill, spotted with scrub bushes. We all sat there a while, the wind making my and May's hair dance over our foreheads and faces. She laughed about it as we brushed the strands away from each other's eyes.

"May's not going to understand your moving out," Cary said.

"I'll explain it to her somehow so she doesn't feel terrible about it."

"She'll miss you almost as much as I will," he warned.

"You'll bring her to see me and she'll spend lots of time there."

"It won't be the same for her. She's never been

comfortable at Grandma Olivia's. She's always afraid of breaking something valuable or tracking in dirt."

"I'll see to it that she's more comfortable there," I assured him.

"You're not thinking you will change Grandma Olivia, are you, Melody?" Cary asked with a smile.

"You never know," I said and he laughed.

"I swear you have more blind faith than Laura had and that's saying a lot, too."

May stood up and went to fetch something in the sand. While she was away, Cary leaned over and kissed me softly on the lips.

"It's going to be hard for me not having you right across the hall, Melody," he whispered.

"I won't be far away," I promised and he kissed me again.

May returned with what looked like a girl's light brown shoe. The discovery excited her and she handed it to Cary and signed questions quickly. He shook his head.

"Someone could have lost it running on the beach," he explained. Turning to me, he added, "She thinks it comes from a boat that sank, but the ocean doesn't give up its treasures that easily," he remarked. May wanted to keep it. However, Cary didn't want her to have it, calling it garbage. "In the back of her mind," he muttered, "she thinks it's a gift from Laura. She's always expecting some sign to prove her sister hasn't forgotten her."

"It's not a bad thing to hope for, Cary," I told him, but he shook his head.

"It's useless and painful. It's better we don't give her any encouragement," he insisted.

Reluctantly, May left the shoe and we walked on, making a circle before returning to the house. Aunt Sara was downstairs preparing tea and some biscuits for Uncle Jacob. I told Cary I wanted to hold off telling her about my discussion with Grandma Olivia.

712

"Grandma Olivia will probably tell her herself," Cary said, and sure enough, Aunt Sara revealed that Grandma Olivia had called to say she was coming to visit again tomorrow.

"Two days in a row. Isn't that nice?" she added.

Neither Cary nor I said anything, suspecting the real reasons for the visit. May was tired, so we went upstairs and I helped her get ready for bed. I watched her sign and mouth her prayers and then kissed her cheek and fixed her blanket. As I started away, she seized my hand and told me she had a secret. I watched as she described how she was going back tomorrow to get that shoe and put it with the other things she had found on the beach. They were all in a box in her closet and she had shown them to no one but me. I promised I wouldn't tell Cary. All of us, especially little girls, needed someone to trust, someone with whom we could share our deepest secrets. She looked relieved, happy, and wished me a good night.

I lay awake for a long time, listening to the sounds in the house. The wind died down just as Cary had predicted it would. I could hear Aunt Sara's and Uncle Jacob's muffled voices. They sounded like ghosts in the walls. After a while, they were silent and there was nothing but the creaks in the floors and ceilings. One of those creaks grew louder and then I heard my door open and close. Cary's silhouette moved quickly to the side of my bed where he knelt. My heart was pounding.

"Cary, if your father knows you've come in here—."

"Shh," he said, putting his fingers on my lips. "I can't sleep. I keep thinking I'm going to lose you."

"You won't," I said. His fingers moved over my chin and down my neck. I could feel the thump, thump, thump of my heart chasing my blood through my veins. My body began to tingle in all my secret

713

places. Cary lifted the blanket away and brought his face closer, laying his cheek on my stomach and then bringing his lips up to kiss the small valley between my breasts.

"Cary," I whispered weakly. His left hand moved down over my shoulders and across my breasts to my stomach. He rose gently and slipped in under my blanket. The bed springs groaned and we both froze because it sounded so loud. "Cary, you better—"

"Let me just lie beside you for a while," he pleaded. I tried to back away, but it was as if there were two voices inside me: the voice of my body that wanted his touch and the voice of my conscience that clamored for me to be good. Soon, my body's voice grew louder, drowning out the warnings and the pleading. I felt my resistance crumble. His lips found mine. We kissed and held each other tightly. His hand was on my thigh, inching toward the hem of my nightgown.

Weakly, I urged him to stop, but it was as if I wanted to stifle my own voice; there was barely any force behind my words. It wasn't until I felt him between my legs that an electric chill of panic shot down my spine.

"Just let me get close to you, please," he begged. My resistance collapsed like a sand castle at high tide and he was pressing forward. The bed groaned again and then we heard a door open and close in the hallway.

Cary and I became paralyzed, both of us hardly breathing. There was a gentle knock. Cary slid quickly off the bed and to the floor. The door opened and Aunt Sara appeared.

"Melody, dear, are you still awake?" she called in a loud whisper.

I didn't speak, but she stood there, silhouetted in the hall light.

"I just—felt bad about not getting to speak to you after you returned from Olivia's," she muttered, more to herself than to me. I remained silent, actually

714

holding my breath. My heart drummed so loudly, I thought she would feel the vibrations if she didn't hear the beat.

But after another minute, she backed out and closed the door softly.

Neither Cary nor I moved for a long moment. Then he got back into bed with me and started to caress me again. I put my hand over his and stopped him.

"You better go back to your room, Cary."

He moaned.

"Please. I'm too frightened."

"All right," he said.

"Be careful she doesn't see you leave, or your father hear you in the hallway."

"I will," he said, his voice dripping with disappointment. He leaned over to kiss me goodnight. "I love you, Melody," he said. "I really do."

"I know," I said. It sounded almost sad. I hadn't meant it to sound that way, but it made him hesitate.

"You love me, too, don't you, Melody?"

"Yes," I said, truly believing I did. It felt more like love than anything I had ever felt for any other boy, and no one had become a part of me as quickly as Cary had.

"I don't trust my grandmother," he said before leaving. "She probably knows how we feel about each other and she wants to do something to stop it."

"She can't," I said. "Not even she is that powerful."

Through the darkness I could see him smile, his face was that bright with happiness at my response.

"Good night," he said again and quietly slipped out of my room.

I waited, holding my breath, hoping and praying neither Uncle Jacob nor Aunt Sara caught him leaving. The silence continued and I let out my trapped breath.

Maybe moving into Grandma Olivia's wasn't such a bad idea after all, I thought.

Something had to put the brakes on this roller coaster Cary and I were riding. I had just proved to myself that I certainly couldn't.

To calm my raging blood, I practiced the meditation techniques Holly had taught me and soon I found the doorway to sleep.

Once again it was Holly instead of Kenneth who came for me in the morning. Cary was already off to work and May to school. Aunt Sara was on her way upstairs to bring Uncle Jacob a second cup of coffee and the morning paper.

"I've got a lot to do today," she told me. "Olivia always looks at the house through a microscope and she'll be here before lunch."

"You have your hands full with Uncle Jacob, and besides, few people take as good care of their home as you do. She has no right to pass judgment anyway. She has a housekeeper and probably never lifted a broom in her life."

"Oh no. When she was younger, she had to do all the housework because her father wouldn't employ a maid, and Belinda—"

She stopped and bit down on her lower lip, realizing she was about to violate her own rule: if you can't say something nice about someone, don't say anything.

Holly beeped her horn and I knew it was she who had come for me because her horn sounded like a goose with laryngitis. This time I was more definite about my promise to be home early enough to help with dinner and then I left the house. Holly was wearing half moon silver earrings that dangled nearly to her shoulders and a shimmery tank top and a dark blue full-length skirt with sandals. Her toenails were neon pink.

"He slept in the studio if he slept at all," she muttered as I got into the car. "I didn't realize he

716

hadn't come to bed until I woke this morning. Either he's hypnotized himself or the sculpture has possessed him. Artists," she said raising her eyes. "When they get hooked on their own work, they're worse than those monks who take vows of silence. But," she added, turning to me, "I must admit I've never seen him so taken with anything else he's done."

She blinked and took another look at me.

"What's with you this morning? You look as serious as a truck driver with hemorrhoids."

"I've got to make some very important decisions," I said.

"Oh? Well, I told you that your day of birth indicates you possess an imaginative mind coupled with excellent powers of observation. Don't trust too much to luck. Depend more on your own intuitive vision."

"Luck," I said with a laugh. "Whatever I bet on is sure to lose."

"Don't be down on yourself. Remember what I said about negative energy," Holly warned. "Your personal planets are Saturn and Uranus," she continued. "Under favorable influences, it's good for seeking favors from elderly people, but use tact and diplomacy instead of force."

"And under unfavorable influences?" I asked.

She nodded.

"Postpone change and long journeys."

"Is it a favorable or unfavorable time?" I asked.

"I'll study my charts and let you know later," she promised.

Holly was so serious about her beliefs, I couldn't laugh. Who knew? Maybe there was some truth to it.

Kenneth was in the studio when we arrived, but I wasn't prepared for what he looked like when I entered. He was pale and drained, his beard scraggly and his cheeks and neck unshaven. His clothes were wrinkled and looked slept in. His eyes were distant, bloodshot, the eyes of someone who was looking beyond everything that stood before him. He barely muttered a good morning when I greeted him.

I saw he had made considerable progress on the sculpture, especially with the face. It was becoming the face in the drawings, the face of my mother, more than it was my face. There was that slight turn in the upper lip that Mommy had, especially when she was being coy.

Kenneth's hands did have miraculous artistic power, I thought. As I gazed at the work in progress, I felt the movement. It was almost as if the stone girl would become flesh and blood at any moment and pull herself up and out of the base. Under his surgical fingers, the marble looked malleable, easier to form than clay. The figure's shoulders and face already showed skin-like texture, down to the way it rippled over the embossed cheekbones and breastbone. Perhaps, I thought, an artist was a person born with more life in him than other people and he puts some of that life into the work itself, diminishing himself every time he creates something as great as this, until one day, he is just an ordinary man surrounded by his creations, but comforted by the thought that he could never die as long as his work lived.

How was I to compete with this for his attention and love? I wondered.

"Did you have any breakfast yet, Kenneth?" I asked. For a while I thought he either hadn't heard me or didn't care to reply. Then he paused and looked at me.

"I had some coffee and a piece of something," he said.

"Piece of something?"

"A doughnut, I think." He thought another moment. "Or was that yesterday?" He shrugged and looked at his sculpture.

"Grandma Olivia sent for me last night, Kenneth, because your father told her what he had told me."

"Oh?" He brushed off the left earlobe on the sculpture and stepped back to study the face of Neptune's Daughter. "Just a minute," he said. "I want to check something."

I thought he was going to look at me to compare, but instead, he went to his drawings. He nodded to himself and wiped his hands on a rag.

"What were you saying about Olivia?"

"She sent for me because Judge Childs told her about our conversation."

"What did she want?"

"She wanted to be sure I told no one. She's afraid of a new scandal and she is so concerned about it that she wants—she practically ordered, I should say— me to come live with her and Grandpa Samuel. She forbade me to live with you."

Kenneth stared at me and, just when I thought he was going to say something, turned back to his drawing.

"The way you just raised your right eyebrow," he said, "I never saw you do that. It's interesting. It sort of indicates some mature insight. I like it, but Haille never did that," he muttered more to himself than to me.

"Did you hear what I said, Kenneth? Grandma Olivia wants me to live with her. She says it would be better for Uncle Jacob's recovery if I was living there right now, too, and it would only fan the flames of scandal if I came to live with you."

"She's right about that," Kenneth said. "Olivia's always been the sensible one, the one with solutions in that family."

"You think my moving in with her and Grandpa Samuel is the right solution?" I asked and held my breath.

719

"Might be," he said and turned again to his sculpture.

I stood there, fighting down a throat lump and swallowing back my tears. I had hoped he would tell me not to go to live at Grandma Olivia's. I had hoped he would insist I move in with him, that there was no other real solution, no other place I belonged but at his side. Why should he care about scandals?

"One thing's for sure," he said as he approached the marble, "you'll get the best of everything living there."

"Except love," I muttered sharply. At first I thought he hadn't heard. He just stared at his work. Then he turned and looked at me with his eyes finally focusing on me.

"Don't put too much stock in that, Melody. Love is fragile at best and often a burden or something that blinds us. It's fodder for poets and song writers and they build it into something beyond human capacity. Falling in love means enrolling yourself in the school of disappointment. Being human means failing each other often, and no two people fail each other more than two people who pledge to do things for each other that they'll never do because they're just incapable of it."

He gestured toward his sculpture.

"That's why art is enduring. The look of love or hope, or the look of compassion, bravery, whatever, is captured forever. We spend our lives trying to get someone to be as enduring as a painting or a sculpture and we can't because feelings crumble as quickly as the flesh."

"That's not true, Kenneth," I insisted.

He turned back to me and sighed. Then he shook his head and smiled.

"You know what I miss the most about my youth? My gullibility. It's nice believing in everything and everyone. It makes you feel secure, but be strong and

720

depend more on yourself and you'll be ready for disappointments. That's the best advice I can offer you.

"Go live with Olivia. She's the real guru, not Holly with her stars and moon. Olivia can read the future better than anyone. She's the true captain of her soul and the master of her fate. She's endured and she's stronger than anyone. Disappointment withers in front of her. She can stare down disaster. My father cries in his beer, mourns his lost youth and his mistakes, while Olivia will rage on until the day she dies. And even death gets little satisfaction when it takes someone like her. For death, Olivia is a reminder that it, too, is a slave to something bigger. It's just an errand boy for Nature.

"So live with her and learn from her," Kenneth concluded. Then he took up his tools and returned to his marble creation, not seeing the tears brim in my eyes.

I sucked in my breath and left the studio. He didn't need me there, I thought. The vision is all in his head now anyway, just as he always claimed.

Holly was sitting in front of the house on a stone bench, Ulysses at her feet as she worked on a chart and thumbed through her books. When I appeared, she looked up with surprise.

"Why aren't you working?"

"There's nothing for me to do in there. You were right about him," I said.

She raised her eyebrows.

"Oh? Ignored you, too, huh?"

"Something like that."

"Were you crying?" she asked after she gazed at me closer.

"No." I turned away quickly and took a deep breath.

"Oh honey, don't let him get to you. Artists are so moody and—"

721

"It's okay," I said and smiled at her. "Could you take me home? I'd do more good helping Aunt Sara today."

"Sure. Oh," she said, "about your chart, the planets . . ."

"Yes?"

"It's a favorable time, a time for change," she said. She didn't have to tell me. I already knew.

Grandma Olivia's Rolls Royce was just leaving the house as Holly and I made the turn. The sight of the luxury limousine made my heart do flip-flops for I was afraid of how Aunt Sara would react to what Grandma Olivia was proposing. I was sure Uncle Jacob was ecstatic.

"I've made up my mind," Holly said as we pulled into the driveway. "I'll be leaving the day after tomorrow."

"Oh, no! I'll miss you," I said. She smiled and leaned forward to squeeze my hand and give me a kiss on the cheek.

"And I'll miss you too, sweetheart. You're a very nice girl, Melody, full of good energy, compassion, and love. Someday, you'll make a lucky man a wonderful companion."

I hurried into the house, worrying more about Aunt Sara than myself at the moment. May was in the kitchen washing out the pot in which Aunt Sara had made some hot oatmeal for Uncle Jacob. She was surprised to see me and obviously did not yet know what Grandma Olivia had wanted. She told me Aunt Sara was upstairs with Uncle Jacob. I waited for her to come down, but when nearly a half hour passed and she still hadn't, I went upstairs. The door to Uncle Jacob and Aunt Sara's room was closed. I hesitated and then knocked softly. They must have thought it was May and wondered why she was knocking.

722

Aunt Sara opened the door and looked out at me with bloodshot eyes. Uncle Jacob was dressed in a cotton flannel shirt and pants. Aunt Sara was helping him dress.

"Melody. You're home already?"

"Yes, I thought—" I looked past her at Uncle Jacob, who struggled to pull on one of his socks. He did look stronger, with more color in his face. I was sure the news Grandma Olivia had brought had cheered him. "I thought you might need me here more."

"She doesn't need you," Uncle Jacob snapped. "Everything's fine here."

"He insists on getting up and going downstairs," she said mournfully.

"Did you ask the doctor, Uncle Jacob?"

"I don't need the doctor to tell me what I can do and what I can't," he said and pulled on the other sock. Aunt Sara hurried to kneel at his feet and help him put on his shoes. He turned to me as she did so.

"Good you came home early though. You can start packing," he said. "Your grandmother can send the car over for you earlier than she thought," he added, and Aunt Sara uttered a cry and then pressed her hand against her mouth as he glared down at her. "Now Sara, you heard it all and you know that it's best for everyone all around. We're just lucky to have my mother and father alive and strong enough to handle the problem."

"Is that how everyone sees me now?" I asked. "The problem?"

"She's never been a problem for me," Aunt Sara said. "And the children—"

"Everyone will be better off," Uncle Jacob insisted. "Especially the children."

"I'm not full of contamination, Uncle Jacob."

"You're Haille's daughter," he said as if that ex-

723

plained everything. "We can't help what's been passed through the blood. It takes someone as strong as my mother to keep things right," he said.

"Yes, she's got a wonderful track record," I snapped.

"Now don't you be insolent and disrespectful. You ought to be grateful someone wants to take you into her home. You're the result of lust and sin and—"

"Jacob!" Aunt Sara exclaimed. She stood up and he turned his head away.

"I've got to get some exercise," he muttered, "so I can build myself up and get back to work."

He started to stand, wobbled, and sat down hard on the bed.

"Jacob!"

"I'm fine. Just a little bed weary," he said. When he started to stand again, Aunt Sara put her arm around his waist and he reluctantly leaned on her shoulder. "There," he said, standing. "That's a start."

Aunt Sara looked at me with eyes so full of sadness, I had to turn away.

"I'll go pack," I said.

"Good," Uncle Jacob muttered.

My throat tightened and my tongue felt glued to the bottom of my mouth, so all my words were swallowed back. There was nothing more to say to him anyway, I thought. After his confession in the hospital, I was a constant embarrassment to him. He couldn't look at me and not feel guilty. It brought him much needed relief to see me go. Grandma Olivia didn't know how right she was when she suggested my moving out would improve Uncle Jacob's chances for recuperation.

May was waiting for me in the hallway, her eyes full of questions and confusion. She wanted to know if we could go for a walk to town. I smiled at her and took her hand. I brought her into my room and sat her on the chair by the desk.

724

I began by reminding her why I had come, why I had been left there, and why I had been forced to stay.

She was sad about my mother, but she quickly told me she was happy I was there. I thanked her and then told her about Grandma Olivia's offer and why it would be good for everyone. I didn't tell her about my grandfather or his sinful history. I tried to make it seem as if I would be gone only for a short while. I would always be nearby, I told her, and she would come to visit me as much as she wanted, that Cary had promised to bring her often, but she was still confused.

How could it be good for everyone? Didn't I help her mother?

How could I explain it all to her? I wondered and then I did the one thing I had tried never to do: I told a lie to make things easier. I told her Grandma Olivia needed me.

The idea of Grandma Olivia needing anyone surprised but interested her. May was so forgiving and compassionate she couldn't deny anyone anything, even someone like Grandma Olivia, who seemed to have everything she could want.

In the end she accepted it. It brought tears to her eyes, but she didn't cry. She offered to help me pack. I explained I had very little to bring with me. Grandma Olivia was going to buy me many new things. When I heard Uncle Jacob and Aunt Sara in the hallway, I told her she had better see what she could do to help her mother and she left.

Uncle Jacob and Aunt Sara made a lot of commotion going down the stairs. Uncle Jacob got dizzy once, but when I came out to help, he made a miraculous recovery and completed the journey. Aunt Sara brought him outside to sit on the porch.

As I sifted through the things I would take with me, I recalled when I had first come to stay in this room. I looked at Laura's picture and thought about her

725

again. Cary insisted Laura and I were alike in so many ways. Holly would call it a kindred spirit. There were nights when I had lain here and felt another presence, felt encouragement and comfort, as if someone warm and loving had touched my cheek or stroked my hair or taken my hand during the night. It turned my nightmares into sweet dreams.

I had no idea what sort of a room Grandma Olivia would provide for me. Chances were it would be bigger, of course. I hadn't done very much to change this room. So much of what was in it still had significance and great importance for Aunt Sara. Laura's love letters were where they had always been. Her clothes remained in the closet and bureau. Her dolls and music box were undisturbed.

Aunt Sara was sure to return the room to its shrine status after I moved away, I thought. Now, she would mourn her daughter's death a second time. I had tried to be a daughter to her, but the truth was no one could replace Laura, and the hole in her heart Aunt Sara had hoped I would fill would always be there. Maybe it was more painful, even deceitful, for me to wear Laura's clothes and sleep in Laura's bed. Maybe as Kenneth had said, Grandma Olivia was the real guru for this family. She knew best.

I was tired of fighting anyway, tired of pursuing the elusive truth, tired of uncovering lies, tired of expecting love to simply blossom like a flower and beam under the sunlight of my smiles. People like Grandma Olivia always get what they want in the end, I thought, and those of us who think we can fight them find we are just living in a fantasy world.

I wished there was a way I could say goodbye to Laura's memory, a way that made sense or made me feel better about what I had done and what I would now do. But everything I looked at had seemed unmoved and unaffected by my arrival and stay here and it was unmoved now at my leaving. I had changed nothing.

I picked up my two small suitcases and the box that contained Cary's sailboat and started out of the room and down the stairs just as May was rushing back into the house. At first I thought something had happened to Uncle Jacob, but she was waving a big envelope at me. She signed it had come special delivery.

I put my suitcases down at the top of the stairs when she reached me, and with great curiosity I took the envelope from her. It was from Alice Morgan.

What is it? May signed. I shook my head and sat on the top step as I ripped the envelope open. How silly, I thought. She's sent me the latest *En Vogue* catalogue, a mail-order fashion company whose clothing was very expensive. I knew her mother subscribed to it and had ordered from it, but why send it to me? The top right corner of one page was folded in.

First, I read the letter she had sent with the catalogue.

Dear Melody,
I was sitting in the kitchen and eating a sandwich for lunch, when I decided to thumb through Mom's latest En Vogue. *Usually, the fashions bore me and nothing ever looks as good as it does in the catalogue. At least, that's what I always tell my mother.*
But, when I got to page 42, I noticed something I think might interest you, too. The model on the page looks so much like your mother, I couldn't resist mailing this to you as quickly as possible. Her hair is a different color, of course, but, well, look for yourself. Amazing, isn't it?
I still want to come visit, and I am waiting for you to tell me when is a good time. Let's not stop being friends just because we live far apart from each other.
What's new in your life? Boyfriends? Girlfriends? Are you doing anything fun?

727

*Please write back as soon as you can or call. Call
collect if you want.*
I miss you.

Love,
Alice

I folded the letter and then opened the catalogue
slowly. May watched with interest as I stared at the
model on the page. It triggered a chill that started up
my spine and then circled my body and froze my
heart. My breath caught. I didn't realize how long I
was holding it until I felt my chest constrict and May
shook my hand, demanding to know what was wrong.

This woman, I explained, stuttering through my
thoughts, looks so much like my mother it's scary.

May's eyes widened with interest and she peered
over my shoulder.

"I've got to show this to Kenneth," I muttered. I
stood up and gazed at my suitcases. "Before I go to
Grandma Olivia's."

I put the suitcases back in the room and hurried
down the stairs. I went to the kitchen and called the
taxi company, asking for a car immediately. Then I
went outside, hardly able to take my eyes from the
face of the model in the latest En Vogue catalogue.
She even had that little turn in her upper lip.

Uncle Jacob and Aunt Sara were sitting on the front
porch. Both looked up with surprise and interest as I
burst out of the house, the catalogue in my hand.

"What did you get, dear?" Aunt Sara asked. Uncle
Jacob didn't want to show any interest, but couldn't
help himself.

"My friend—Alice Morgan. Remember? From
Sewell?"

"Oh yes."

"She sent me this catalogue because there is a
model in it who looks so much like my mother," I

728

explained. Uncle Jacob's eyes widened with more interest.

"Oh. Really?" Aunt Sara said, leaning toward me as I opened the catalogue to the page Alice had marked. "Yes, there is some resemblance. Isn't there, Jacob?" she asked showing him the catalogue. He stared and then grunted.

"Some. What of it?" he muttered.

"There's more than some," I said taking the catalogue back.

"What about it?" he asked.

"I want to know more about her," I said.

"What for? When someone dies, we should let her rest in peace," he said, directing his gaze more at Aunt Sara than at me. The reference to Laura was clear. She pressed her lips together and looked away.

I saw my cab coming down our street.

"That's for me," I said as it drew closer.

"For you? What for? My mother's sending her car. No need to waste money," Uncle Jacob said, "just because you're going to be living with people that have some."

"I'm going to show this to Kenneth," I said. "I'm going back to his house."

"Now?" Uncle Jacob demanded.

"No one knows my mother's face better than Kenneth," I explained. "I'll feel better showing it to him."

"You're just wasting good time, your own and everyone else's," he said. "There's enough to do and—"

"I'm all packed. There wasn't that much to do. My bags are upstairs, ready to be brought down," I added to please him.

"Good," he said.

The cab pulled up front and I started for it.

"Melody," Aunt Sara called. I turned back. She

stared like someone who had forgotten why she had called me.

"Yes?"

"Don't you want any lunch, dear?"

"No, but thank you, Aunt Sara. I'll be back as soon as I can," I said.

"Just have Kenneth or the cab take you to Grandma Olivia's house," Uncle Jacob said. "I'll call for Raymond and he'll take your bags there while you're wasting everyone's time."

"Thank you, Uncle Jacob," I said. "I hope you get better soon and get back to the sea you love so much."

He looked surprised. I smiled as his thoughts stumbled over my words of kindness. Then I hurried into the cab, the magazine clutched tightly in my hand.

17
&

Out of the Ashes

Holly was just coming off the beach when the cab, the driver complaining about the beach road, pulled up in front of Kenneth's house. I paid him and he drove off swearing that if he had known where I wanted him to take me, he would never have accepted the assignment. Holly waved and hurried along, breaking into a fast walk, Ulysses barking and rushing past her to greet me.

"What's up? Why are you back?"

"I have to show Kenneth something that came special delivery to me," I replied.

"What is it?"

She followed as I walked toward the studio, explaining what it was. She looked at the pictures, even though she had never known Mommy nor seen any photographs of her.

"They say everyone has a twin someplace," Holly offered, handing the catalogue back.

Kenneth was seated on his small sofa staring at the sculpture when we entered the studio. He looked up

731

so casually I realized he hadn't even known I had left earlier.

"Lunch time, huh?" he said.

"No Kenneth. I brought you that sandwich you have wasting away on the table there," Holly said, nodding toward a plate on a tray. He gazed at it.

"Oh? You brought it to me? What about Melody?"

"I've been home and back, Kenneth," I said. "There didn't seem much for me to do here and I had to pack to move in with Grandma Olivia, remember?"

"Right, right," he said. "So. I forgot to eat lunch, huh?" He reached over and grasped the sandwich. "Looks good. What is it, Holly, sprouts, tomatoes, herbs?"

"Just eat it, Kenneth," she said. He took a bite, smiled, and chewed. Then he took his first real look at me.

"What's happening? If you went home to pack, why are you here?" He looked at Holly for some hint.

"She has something to show you, Ken."

"Oh?"

I handed him the catalogue, opened to the page Alice had folded. He gazed at it a moment, put the sandwich down, and sat up. Then he looked at me, his eyebrows dipping toward each other.

"What is this?" He turned the catalogue to the front. *"En Vogue."*

"My girlfriend in Sewell sent it to me. Her mother orders clothes from that company. She just happened to be browsing through this latest copy and saw those pictures of that model who resembles Mommy."

"Latest copy?" He narrowed his eyes suspiciously and turned to the fine print on the inside of the cover.

"Does it look like her, Ken?" Holly asked.

"It is a remarkable resemblance," he muttered. He got up and went to his tool table, shifting some things around to find his magnifying glass. Then he thumbed

732

through the pictures. He stared ahead for a moment and shook his head gently before looking again.

"I thought if anyone knew my mother's face and could decide about those pictures, it was you," I said. He nodded. I held my breath, waiting.

"It might be something she did before the accident," he offered. "But it's Haille. No doubt about it," he concluded.

A surge of heat moved up my neck and brought a crimson flush to my cheeks. I used to wonder what it was like for the families and loved ones of actors and actresses to turn on the television set and see them on the screen. I imagined it had to be wonderful and painful at the same time.

"But if it is Mommy, why is her hair black?" I asked. "Even her eyebrows."

"It might just have been what the company or the photographer wanted for this shoot," Holly suggested. Kenneth looked at the pages again.

"I don't see why. Actually, Haille's real hair color would have worked just as well with these shots and the color of these clothes."

"Maybe she had just done something else, Kenneth. There are a dozen reasons for it, I imagine," Holly said. He nodded.

"I'm sure," he said. He stared at the magazine as if he couldn't let go of it, couldn't stop looking at the picture. He flipped to the front again and reread the fine print. "Charlie Dunn could probably find out more about this for us," he said. He looked up at me. "Charlie's a friend of mine in Boston who is big in advertising."

"What do you expect him to find out, Ken?" Holly asked. I caught the way she moved her eyes toward me to suggest he was doing something wrong, but Kenneth was intrigued on his own and not just for me. I could see it in his face and in the way his eyes continued to look at the pictures.

"Just to settle our minds about it," he replied softly. "When the pictures were done. Was this Haille?"

"I thought you said it was," Holly said.

"Nothing's for sure, but it sure looks like her to me, especially that turn in her lips, the way her cheekbones stand out, the way she's holding her head just a little to the right."

He went quickly to a drawer in the table and riffled through some papers before coming up with a photograph. He placed it beside the pictures on the catalogue page and studied the two. I drew closer. The picture he took out of the drawer was a picture of Mommy taken on Judge Childs's dock.

"The face in this picture is about the same size," he muttered. He began to make some measurements with a thin ruler and then nodded again. Apparently, he knew Mommy's face so well, he remembered the inches between her nose and mouth or across her forehead. "If it's not her, there was a twin I never knew about," he concluded.

"When are you going to call this friend of yours in Boston?" I asked softly.

He thought a moment, looked at his sculpture and then shrugged.

"How about right now? It's time for a break," he said. "Let's go down to the Mermaid and have a brew while I call Charlie. You can have a root beer," he told me and smiled.

"What? You're actually going to set foot out of this studio during my lifetime?" Holly kidded.

"Is this still your lifetime? I thought we were already living another spiritual existence," he replied and went to change his shirt and wash his hands and face before we drove into town in his jeep.

I found myself holding my breath every time my thoughts went to the catalogue and the things Kenneth had said. Mommy had never written to tell me she had modeled for this catalogue, nor had she

734

mentioned it the few times we had spoken on the telephone. Wouldn't she have been proud of it? Perhaps it was as Holly thought: someone who just happened to have a close resemblance.

The Mermaid was a small pub on a side street. I had never actually been inside, although I knew Kenneth went there whenever he spent any time in town. There was a short bar on the right with thick, cherry wood tables and captain's chairs on the left. Everything looked worn and weathered, presenting the illusion that this tavern had been here to greet the first pilgrims. There were whale bones on the walls, pictures of fishermen and sailors, sailboats and trawlers. A net filled with fishing gear and accessories dangled from the ceiling, and there was a large ship's bell at the far corner of the bar. There were only a half dozen customers, all of whom knew Kenneth and gave him a warm, loud greeting. He ordered a mug of amber ale for himself and Holly and told the bartender, a short man with curly light brown hair, to give me a cold root beer.

"Sure she's old enough, Kenneth? Our root beer has a bite to it, you know?"

"Just give it to her with none of your jokes, Clancy," Kenneth said and winked at us. Holly and I sat at a table in the corner as Kenneth went to the rear to use the pay phone. All of the drinks had been delivered to our table when he returned.

"Charlie's doing the research for us and promises to call back within the hour. He knows this company well," Kenneth said. He spread the catalogue before him and stared down at the pictures. "Tell me about the man your mother went off with," he asked and I described Archie Marlin and how as soon as we left Sewell, I was instructed to start calling him Richard.

Kenneth sipped his beer and listened, his eyes taking on a deep, dark glint as I spoke.

"Changing his name sounds suspicious, doesn't it,

735

Ken?" Holly asked. Kenneth nodded and then shook his head.

"Haille was gullible, trusting, eager to believe in fairy tales," he said, "especially if the teller of the tale made her the princess. So," he said, sitting back, "Olivia told Sara and Jacob what she wanted you to do?"

"Yes." I described what it had been like when I returned to the house. "Uncle Jacob practically salivated at the prospect," I added and Kenneth laughed.

"It sounds as if you will be better off at your grandmother's, Melody," Holly said.

"She's not really my grandmother. My real grandmother is shut up in that home. I'm sure it won't be easy living with Grandma Olivia, no matter what she promises," I added.

Kenneth and Holly exchanged looks but Kenneth said nothing. I had no reason to blame him, I thought. A teenage girl is quite a responsibility to take on at this point in his life, and he would be the first to say he wasn't stable enough for it. He was a free soul. Right now if he had the artistic impulse to drive off and stay away for days, he would do so. He couldn't if he had me to watch over.

A little over a half hour later, we heard the phone ring and the bartender called Kenneth.

"It's for you," he said. As Kenneth got up and went to the rear of the tavern, my heart started thumping again. Holly smiled at me and put her hand over mine.

"I'm sure this is all going to be easily explainable," she said.

I nodded, but my heart felt as if it had doubled in size and would soon hammer itself through my chest. We watched Kenneth as he listened. He nodded, turned his back, spoke softly, and then he cradled the receiver and just stood there without turning around.

736

When he started toward us, I knew it wasn't going to be easily explainable.

"That layout was done a little more than two months ago," he said. "The model on the page is someone called Gina Simon."

"When did you mother pass away?" Holly asked.

"It's been a little more than two months. About the same time," Kenneth said.

"So, that could be her in the catalogue," Holly said.

"But if it's my mother, why did she change her name?" I asked.

"Someone might have suggested it, told her it sounded more professional," Holly suggested. "Right, Ken?" she asked. He didn't respond and so I looked up at him. His face was pale, his eyes troubled.

"What is it, Kenneth?" I demanded.

"Charlie said the guy he spoke to in L.A. told him Gina Simon was currently doing another shoot. She got the job because of this catalogue."

"Oh," Holly said.

My heart seemed to have stopped beating. It was as if all the world, all movement, all time, had frozen.

"What else did he say, Kenneth?" I asked, my voice barely above a whisper. I wasn't sure I had even spoken. Perhaps it had just been a thought. Kenneth shook his head.

"He said her manager—"

"What?" Holly asked quickly.

"Was someone named Richard Marlin."

I shuddered as if a wave had crashed against the tavern. Someone laughed loudly and then another man entered the tavern and everyone greeted him. Kenneth gulped his ale and took a deep breath. Holly sat back, dumbfounded.

"What does it all mean, Ken?"

"I don't know. Haille supposedly died in a car fire. The remains were sent back here for the funeral and burial. The police had identification, right, Melody?"

737

I nodded.

"Amnesia?" Holly suggested.

"I don't know."

"That woman in the catalogue is my mother, living under a different name," I said because I had to hear the words spoken.

"Ken?"

"I don't know what to tell you, Holly."

"Well, Melody can't just be left with that," Holly said.

"I'll make some more calls, find out where this Gina Simon lives and—"

"And I'll go there," I said quickly. They both stared at me.

"Go to L.A.?" Holly asked, sitting back.

"Yes. I have to go there. Don't you see? You understand, don't you, Kenneth?"

He ran his hand through his hair.

"Why would she do this? Even after her death, she does overwhelming things. I'm right in the middle of this work. I—"

"I'm not asking you to go with me, Kenneth."

He stared at me.

"I couldn't go anyway," he said. "I couldn't get myself to go chasing after her. Not anymore."

"You're not just going to put her on an airplane and send her to Los Angeles, Kenneth Childs, are you?" Holly said.

"No. It's not my decision anyway. You had better talk to Olivia about this first, Melody," he said.

It was as if I had swallowed a rock.

"Don't look at me like that. I can't be the one who sends you off looking for your mother. I'm not one hundred percent sure it's your mother."

"It's like ninety-nine percent," Holly quipped.

"I can't just forget about it, Kenneth. I won't," I insisted. "I don't care what you or Grandma Olivia say," I shouted, tears burning under my eyelids.

738

"Don't get yourself upset, sweetheart," Holly said putting her arm around my shoulders. "We'll figure out what to do. Won't we, Kenneth?" she asked sharply.

Kenneth nodded.

We were all silent a long moment and then Holly sighed.

"I'll call my sister and tell her to meet you in Los Angeles if you go. She'll do me a favor and look after you. I'd go, but I have to get back to the store."

"You have a sister in Los Angeles?"

"Dorothy Littlefield is her married name. She and I get along as well as oil and water, but she's very well off. Lives in Beverly Hills, drives a Mercedes, shops on Rodeo Drive, eats nouvelle cuisine, but probably knows a lot about models and fashions. Her husband is an accountant. She's an Aries, born March twenty-second. As an Aries," Holly recited, "she has a quick temper, is inclined to hold a grudge, which she has against me for about twenty years, is aggressive, self-willed, and determined. But she's very intelligent and was always an A-plus student with little effort. She is really a good businesswoman. They have no children," Holly added. "Thank God. But I know she would do this. She likes to be needed."

"Debbie Novell is out there, too," Kenneth said. "I think she just got divorced, didn't she?"

"That was five years ago, Kenneth. Debbie Novell is a ditz anyway. I wouldn't trust my cat with her. Remember when she left her car running all night in front of the dorm? What am I talking about? That's not the worst of it. She left her four-year-old at the pharmacy and didn't realize it until they called and told her hours later."

"Yeah," Kenneth said, smiling. "I remember now, but I thought she was a big deal in California real estate."

"So?"

739

Kenneth shook his head. Then he turned to me and nodded softly.

"Okay, I'll make the call and find out what I can about this so-called Gina Simon. What do you want to do now?" he asked.

"Go see Grandma Olivia," I said. "I'm going to ask her for the money I'll need to make the trip."

"Olivia? You expect her to fork over the money?" Kenneth asked. He was about to smile.

"When she finds out what it's for, I think she might double the amount," I muttered.

Kenneth thought about this and then laughed.

"I think Melody's capable of taking care of herself, Holly," he said. Holly raised her eyebrows.

"I'll take her to Grandma Olivia's, Ken. In fact," she said, turning to me, "I'll take you to New York and get you on the plane, if you'd like."

"Would you?"

"It's the least I can do. We'll leave tonight," she added.

"I could," I said thinking about it. "I'm already packed."

Loretta nearly smiled when she opened the door this time. I wondered if that meant she had accepted the fact that I was to live in this house.

"I had your suitcases taken to your room," she said. Then she saw Holly standing just behind me and her eyes widened. Holly was wearing one of her tie-dyed dresses, a pink and yellow headband, and John Lennon sunglasses. Her lipstick was tangerine.

"Where are Grandma Olivia and Grandpa Samuel?" I asked.

"Mrs. Logan is in her garden and Mr. Logan is out back reading his papers," Loretta said, unable to take her eyes from Holly. "Would you like me to show you to your room?"

"I have to speak to my grandmother first," I said.

740

"We'll just go around to the garden, Loretta. Thank you."

The sight of Grandma Olivia down on her knees with a gardening fork in hand and that wide-brimmed hat on her head took Holly by surprise.

"She doesn't look so tough," she muttered. "She looks like anyone's little old grandmother."

"You haven't met her yet," I replied dryly.

Grandpa Samuel saw us from his lounge chair before Grandma Olivia did. He put down his papers and waved, standing as he did so.

"Well, hello there, my dear. Welcome," he called.

"Hello, Grandpa Samuel. This is my friend Holly Brooks. Actually, she's Kenneth's friend and now mine," I added. He widened his smile and nodded.

"Pleased to meet you, Holly. Any friend of Kenneth's is a friend of mine, and that goes double for any friend of my granddaughter here. Visiting the Cape?"

"I was," Holly said. "I'm leaving tonight."

"Oh. That's too bad. I was looking forward to getting to know you," Grandpa Samuel said.

"Somehow, I expect you'll live through the disappointment, Samuel," Grandma Olivia said. She had risen and stood wiping her hands on her apron. "Your things are up in your room," she added.

"I know. Loretta told me. This is Holly—"

"I heard all that," she snapped. "This isn't exactly the best time to be entertaining people. I would advise you to first settle yourself in, learn our schedule, including when it's proper and not proper to invite guests, and—"

"I'm not staying long, Grandma Olivia," I said quickly.

"What's that?" Grandpa Samuel said, turning to her. "I thought—"

"What does that mean? You're moving in with Kenneth Childs?" she asked.

741

"No. I'd like to show you something and then explain," I said.

She glared at me and then walked around the border of the garden toward the lounge chairs and table. She peeled off her gardening gloves, poured herself some iced tea and watched as I approached, the catalogue in hand.

"A friend of mine from West Virginia mailed this to me," I said, holding it out to her. Grandma Olivia gazed at it as if I were about to hand her something dirty or smelly.

"What would I want with that?" she asked.

"Just look at the woman modeling the clothes on this page," I requested.

She put her glass down slowly, reached into her apron, and came up with a pair of glasses. Grandpa Samuel moved to her side and gazed over her shoulder. They stared at the catalogue and then they both looked at us, unsure what it meant.

"That's Haille, right? What happened to her hair?" Grandpa Samuel asked.

"She obviously dyed it black," Grandma Olivia said and handed the catalogue back to me. "Are you here to tell me this proves your mother was some sort of success?"

"No, Grandma. Kenneth phoned a friend and it turns out the woman in those pictures is still alive and living under the name Gina Simon."

"Gina Simon?" Grandpa Samuel said. "Let me see that again," he said. I handed him the catalogue. "Looks like Haille to me."

"To all of us," I said. "That's why I'm leaving. I'm going to Los Angeles to find out if it is Mommy."

"Going to Los Angeles? But I don't understand," Grandpa Samuel said, once again turning to Grandma Olivia for guidance. She sat on the bench and looked from Holly to me.

"Are you taking her?" she asked Holly.

"I offered to take her to New York. She can catch a flight to Los Angeles from there. I have a sister who lives in L.A. and I'll call and ask her to meet Melody and look after her," she replied. "It's a good time for her to take a trip."

"Pardon?"

"Her astrological chart," Holly replied, "indicates that."

"What nonsense. Astrological chart, rushing clear across the country. You can't go to Los Angeles. I absolutely forbid it," Grandma said.

"No, you don't, Grandma." I smiled. "This woman could be my mother, and if she is, I have someone to live with and someplace else to live," I said.

"But how do we know this is Haille and—"

"We don't for sure, but it looks as if it might be," Holly replied. "The man with whom Haille left for L.A. is that model's manager. Kenneth found out for us."

Grandma smirked.

"Amazing," Grandpa Samuel said. "But if that's Haille and she's still alive, who did we bury in our family plot?"

"What difference does it make?" Grandma Olivia snapped at him. She sat thinking a moment and then looked up at us.

"Such a trip costs a lot of money. Where would you get it?" she asked.

"From you," I said calmly. "Call it an advance on my inheritance."

Grandpa Samuel laughed and shook his head until Grandma Olivia shot him a withering look.

"Who else knows about this—this idiotic idea?"

"Just Kenneth and my friend in Sewell," I said. How this family appeared in public was her only real concern. "Unless of course, I have to go begging for the money. I could go see my grandfather, I suppose,"

I added. She pulled her shoulders back and turned her eyes to stone.

"How dare you try to blackmail me?"

"I'm not, but I'm going and I'm going tonight," I said firmly.

She ripped the catalogue from Grandpa Samuel's hands and gazed at the photographs again, shaking her head.

"This is insane," she mumbled. "Very well." She rose. "Come with me," she ordered.

"Don't we know someone who could look into this for us, Olivia?" Grandpa Samuel asked. "Rather than send the girl, I mean."

"You think I want more people to know about this?" she spit back at him.

"Well, I just thought—"

"Don't think," she ordered. "It's a waste of time. Come along," she told Holly and me, and we followed her into the house.

She took us to the office and went behind the large, dark oak desk. Holly's presence gave me courage and I was proud not to feel even a little bit intimidated, until she raised her head and focused those eyes on me.

"You will sign this," she said, scribbling on a plain sheet of paper. I gazed at Holly, who looked amazed. Grandma Olivia turned the paper to me and handed me the pen.

The paper described my taking two thousand dollars as an advance on my inheritance. It was dated and signed by her. I signed it quickly and she folded it and put it in a small wall safe, from which she drew out money.

"Count it," she ordered. I did so. It was two thousand dollars in fifty-dollar bills. I had never seen so much money at once, much less held it in my hands. She gave me an envelope.

"If you lose that, don't come running back here for

more. Make your way on your wits," she commanded. She sat again, folding her hands and leaning forward. "I expect to hear from you as soon as you confirm something and some decision is made on your future, especially if you are coming back here."

I nodded.

"Thank you," I said.

She leaned back.

"Did it ever occur to you that even if that is your mother, she might not be worth finding? If she wanted you to know she was alive, she would have called to tell you, wouldn't she?"

"I don't know," I said. "That's why I want to go."

She smirked and then looked up at me with an expression that bordered on concern and friendliness.

"I'll give you this advice: if someone's drowning and you can't save her, you'll only drown yourself as well if you don't let go," she said.

No one was more of an expert when it came to saving herself, I thought, but I didn't say it. I held her gaze for an instant and then turned to leave.

"May I ask you when you were born? The month, day, year?" Holly asked Grandma Olivia.

"You may not. That's impertinent."

"You were born between November twenty-second and December twenty-first," Holly replied, undaunted. Grandma Olivia's eyes widened and she looked at me. She must have thought I had given Holly the correct information.

"I don't know why I care, but what is that supposed to mean if it's so?"

"That you're a Sagittarius," Holly replied.

"Whatever that may mean to you, it means nothing to me," Grandma Olivia said.

Holly smiled as if she thought that was exactly what a Sagittarius like Grandma Olivia would say.

Grandma Olivia then saw to it that my two small suitcases were brought back down.

"I had had them placed in what was your mother's room," she told me at the door. "Somehow, I think you will be back."

Holly and I put my bags in her car and drove away.

"You were right," she said after a few minutes of deep silence, "she's definitely not like everyone's little old grandmother."

I started to smile and then thought about Cary.

"I have one more good-bye before we leave, Holly," I said.

"I know. I'll drop you off at the house and go get my things. Then we'll be off."

I sucked in my breath, closed my eyes, and prayed for the right words to help Cary understand the things that I didn't understand myself.

Aunt Sara and May were surprised, but happy to see me return. They were preparing dinner. Even though Cary had not come in from the sea yet, Uncle Jacob had apparently gone back upstairs to his room.

"I had a very difficult time of it," Aunt Sara said in a loud whisper, her eyes shifting toward the ceiling. "It took nearly fifteen minutes to get him up the stairs. He had to keep catching his breath. He's very upset about it. Do you have a nice room at Olivia's?" she asked with a sad smile.

"She's giving me my mother's old room," I said.

"Oh. That's very nice. I remember that room. It's airy and the windows face the sea."

"But first I have to take a trip, Aunt Sara."

"A trip? Where?"

I told her, but instead of surprising and exciting her, the news made her sad and withdrawn. She lowered her eyes and went back to her work.

"I'll come see you as soon as I return," I promised and threw my arms around her before giving her a good-bye kiss on the cheek.

"I don't understand the things some people do. It

746

seems they just want to make the people who love them unhappy. Like Laura, going out to sea that day. Cary said he warned her," she mumbled, her eyes on the potatoes she was mashing. "Why did she have to go?"

She wiped her eyes and turned to me.

"You don't have to go, do you, Melody?"

"Yes, Aunt Sara. I have to go or I'll never be able to sleep one single night," I said.

She nodded, wiped away her tears, smiled, and stroked my hair before returning to her work. That was how I left her.

Outside, I sat on a bench and explained my trip to May. She wished she could come along. I promised I would write her letters and post cards every chance I got and I asked her to look after Cary for me while I was away. She promised she would and we embraced and kissed. Then she ran back into the house so I wouldn't see her cry.

I sat there for a while, just enjoying the breeze on my face and watching the thin veil of clouds move in from the sea. I hadn't lived here that long, but my experiences went so deep, it seemed I had lived most of my life by the ocean. The cry of the terns was familiar now, and the colors in the water didn't surprise me as much. In my heart I was no longer an outsider. I welcomed the salty sea air, the roar of the surf, the sand between my toes. Maybe Cary was right, maybe this really was my home, and maybe Grandma Olivia's confidence about my returning came from her intuitive knowledge about me and what was true for me.

I rose and walked out on the beach. Looking toward the dock, I saw the lobster boat had arrived. I hurried over the sand and waved as soon as I drew close enough for Cary to see me. He waved back and then watched me approach. He had his hands on his hips and I knew his sharp sea eyes were fixed on my every move. He came off the boat quickly when I reached the dock.

"What's happening now?" he asked with that tight smile and those deeply penetrating eyes.

Practically without stopping for a breath, I related the day's events and then showed him the catalogue. He was speechless. All he could do was shake his head. He looked back at the boat and then shouted to Roy.

"I'll be there in a few minutes."

"No problem," Roy called back.

Cary handed the catalogue back to me and we walked up the beach. He had his hands in his pockets and walked looking down. I had my arms folded under my breasts, my head up, waiting, wondering what words would pass between us.

"You probably won't come back," he finally said. "You'll probably end up living in California."

"That's not true, Cary. Even if—if this is my mother and she has a sensible explanation for all this, I'll still come back to see you and someday—"

"Someday, what?" he said, turning. His eyes were so full of sadness and pain, I couldn't look directly at him. I gazed out at the ocean.

"Someday you and I will have our own home and you'll design boats and—"

"And May will hear and Laura will come in from the sea and my father won't die and my mother will stop crying herself to sleep. Why stop with one pipe dream when there are so many?" he said and turned away, walking quickly back toward the dock.

"Cary!"

He kept walking.

"Cary! I swear, I'll be back. Cary!"

He turned and looked at me. I ran to him and threw my arms around him. At first he let me dangle there. Then he put his arms around my waist and sighed.

"Please, just wish me luck," I said.

He nodded.

"Good luck. I'd come with you if Dad weren't so sick."

"I know you would. I'll call you and write you and—"

He put his finger on my lips

"No promises."

"No promises," I agreed, "except just this one." I kissed him hard and long and then I smiled at him and his eyes warmed. "You can believe in that, Cary Logan, and throw your skepticism overboard."

I left him standing there, smiling at me, his shoulders gleaming in the late-afternoon sun, the sea, roaring behind him, and my heart . . .

My heart crying with the terns.

Epilogue

I was outside the house waiting when Holly returned. Taking one last visual gulp of the house and the beach, I got into her car and we puttered away. I didn't look back.

"You all right?" she asked.

"Yes."

"This is for you," she said, reaching beneath her seat to come up with a small bag. "Kenneth sent it along."

"What is it?"

I opened the bag and dipped my fingers in to pull out a silver heart locket on a silver chain.

"He made it himself, years and years ago," she told me.

I found the tiny lever and flipped it open to look at a picture of Mommy when she couldn't have been much older than I was now. The picture on the other side had been removed. I imagined it had been a picture of Kenneth.

"He told me to tell you he gave that to your mother and before she left with your step-father, she gave it back. I think it meant a great deal to him and it wasn't easy for him to give it away."

"Yes," I said, nodding and staring at the picture of Mommy. She was, as they say, so photogenic.

"Maybe, if she's suffering from some form of amnesia, that," Holly said, nodding toward the locket, "will help revive memories."

"You don't think just looking at me would?" I asked.

"I don't know. I've heard of strange cases where people face people they've lived with all their lives and look at them as strangers: children, parents, husbands, and wives. When the mind wants to shut something out, it slams a door of steel and it takes fingers of steel to open it again."

She laughed.

"A friend of mine," she continued, "thinks amnesia proves we have other lives. She thinks it occurs when something puts us on the border between two existences, and we can't recall either one." She shrugged. "Who knows?"

"Yes," I said as the Cape Cod scenery rushed by, "who knows?"

I looked out the window at the ocean and the tourists on the beaches. In the distance I saw the lighthouse.

"How was Kenneth when you left him?" I asked.

"Back to work." She turned, a soft smile on her face. "Did you expect less? If ever he had to escape reality, he has to now," she added.

"Mommy was always trying to do that, especially when we lived in Sewell. Actually, I shouldn't be surprised by all this," I said and then I sighed. "I forgot to call Alice Morgan to thank her."

"You can call from the motel tonight."

"I want to share all the expenses, Holly. I insist."

"No problem. I saw your grandmother give you that pile of loot." She laughed.

Provincetown fell farther and farther behind us.

Mommy had brought me here under false pretenses. Supposedly, we were just visiting Daddy's relatives after his death. She made it seem like the right thing to do, and then she surprised me by telling me arrangements had been made for me to live here until she could send for me.

Well, she never did.

Or maybe she had. Maybe, ironically, she had sent for me through these pictures in the catalogue. Perhaps fate had taken control after all, and those stars and the moon Holly talked about so much had played a role in my destiny.

I had been on a mad and desperate search to discover the identity of my father. During the course of that pursuit, I entered Cary's private world, filled with his sorrows and dreams, and we discovered each other in ways I had not expected.

I would miss our walks on the beach, our talks, our laughter and tears. I knew he would spend all of his nights in his attic workshop while I was away. He would mold his dream ships and he would stop and remember me sitting quietly beside him, watching him work. We were like two people who had been cast overboard by cruel events in their lives, two people who had found each other adrift, and we had joined hands to take each other to our own private beach; our paradise.

On it we sat and watched the twilight sun kiss the horizon and leave us night after night with promises to help us face each morning. It made us stronger, gave us courage, filled our hearts with hope.

I don't want to say good-bye, Cary, I thought, but I'm afraid of where this road leads. You were right in saying we should make no promises to each other. Too often promises were made to us that could never be kept.

I came here to unravel lies, to dig away the sand

753

until I reached the hidden truths about ourselves, and often, like the tide, our family pushed the sand back. Here I was on a journey to unravel more, to push away more sand.

Why bother? Your eyes asked me, Cary. Why care anymore?

The answer is if I can't find the answer to who I am, then I can't be truthful to you, and Cary, my darling, my darling Cary, if there is one thing I will never do, it's lie to you.

Lies are what we have inherited, but it's not the legacy we'll leave our children.

That's why I go on.

And why I looked toward the road west and why, as we passed the sign that read Now Leaving Provincetown, Cape Cod, I smiled.

I knew I would be back, and when I returned, I would be armed with the truth.